More Praise for
PETER BENCHLEY
AND
JAWS

"A super-thriller! . . . If you have any imagination at all, the book will give you the shivers."　　　—*The New York Post*

"From the opening chapter when a young woman plunges into the surf . . . and meets the 20-foot shark . . . the reader is hooked."　　　—*Newsday*

"Benchley keeps it moving, fulfills all expectations . . . *Jaws* is lean, all sinew, everything directed toward a climax that is implanted on the retina from the very first sentence."
　　　—*New York* Magazine

BEAST

"Just when you thought it was safe to go back in the water, Peter Benchley has written another thriller about a set of jaws looming up out of the deep. . . . *Beast* is most satisfying to read."　　　—*The New York Times*

"Like *Jaws, Beast* will keep readers on the edge of their beach chairs."　　　—*USA Weekend*

"Benchley is in high gear. . . . He's a fine smooth writer, taut of technique, inventive of language." —*The Washington Post*

PETER BENCHLEY

THREE COMPLETE NOVELS

PETER BENCHLEY

THREE COMPLETE NOVELS

JAWS

BEAST

THE GIRL OF THE SEA OF CORTEZ

WINGS BOOKS
New York • Avenel, New Jersey

This omnibus was originally published in separate volumes under the titles:

Jaws, copyright © 1974 by Peter Benchley
Beast, copyright © 1991 by Peter Benchley
The Girl of the Sea of Cortez, copyright © 1982 by Peter Benchley

This 1994 edition is published by Wings Books,
distributed by Random House Value Publishing, Inc.,
40 Engelhard Avenue, Avenel, New Jersey 07001,
by arrangement with Random House, Inc., for *Beast* and with the author for *Jaws* and *The Girl of the Sea of Cortez.*

Random House
New York · Toronto · London · Sydney · Auckland

Printed and bound in the United States of America

Library of Congress Cataloging-in-Publication Data

Benchley, Peter.
   [Selections.   1994]
   Three complete novels / Peter Benchley.
      p.   cm.
   Contents: Jaws — Beast — The girl of the Sea of Cortez.
   ISBN 0-517-10021-5
   1. Sea stories, American. 2. Sharks—Fiction. I. Benchley, Peter.
Jaws. 1994. II. Benchley, Peter. Beast. 1994. III. Benchley,
Peter. Girl of the Sea of Cortez. 1994. IV. Title. V. Title: 3 complete novels.
PS3552.E537A6 1994
813'.54—dc20
                                            93-41486
                                           CIP

8 7 6 5 4 3 2 1

Contents

JAWS

For Wendy

Part One

1

THE GREAT FISH moved silently through the night water, propelled by short sweeps of its crescent tail. The mouth was
open just enough to permit a rush of water over the gills.
There was little other motion: an occasional correction of the
apparently aimless course by the slight raising or lowering of
a pectoral fin—as a bird changes direction by dipping one
wing and lifting the other. The eyes were sightless in the
black, and the other senses transmitted nothing extraordinary
to the small, primitive brain. The fish might have been asleep,
save for the movement dictated by countless millions of years
of instinctive continuity: lacking the flotation bladder common to other fish and the fluttering flaps to push oxygen-bear-
ing water through its gills, it survived only by moving. Once
stopped, it would sink to the bottom and die of anoxia.

The land seemed almost as dark as the water, for there was
no moon. All that separated sea from shore was a long,
straight stretch of beach—so white that it shone. From a
house behind the grass-splotched dunes, lights cast yellow
glimmers on the sand.

The front door to the house opened, and a man and a
woman stepped out onto the wooden porch. They stood for a
moment staring at the sea, embraced quickly, and scampered
down the few steps onto the sand. The man was drunk, and he
stumbled on the bottom step. The woman laughed and took
his hand, and together they ran to the beach.

"First a swim," said the woman, "to clear your head."

"Forget my head," said the man. Giggling, he fell backward

onto the sand, pulling the woman down with him. They fumbled with each other's clothing, twined limbs around limbs, and thrashed with urgent ardor on the cold sand.

Afterward, the man lay back and closed his eyes. The woman looked at him and smiled. "Now, how about that swim?" she said.

"You go ahead. I'll wait for you here."

The woman rose and walked to where the gentle surf washed over her ankles. The water was colder than the night air, for it was only mid-June. The woman called back, "You're sure you don't want to come?" But there was no answer from the sleeping man.

She backed up a few steps, then ran at the water. At first her strides were long and graceful, but then a small wave crashed into her knees. She faltered, regained her footing, and flung herself over the next waist-high wave. The water was only up to her hips, so she stood, pushed the hair out of her eyes, and continued walking until the water covered her shoulders. There she began to swim—with the jerky, head-above-water stroke of the untutored.

A hundred yards offshore, the fish sensed a change in the sea's rhythm. It did not see the woman, nor yet did it smell her. Running within the length of its body were a series of thin canals, filled with mucus and dotted with nerve endings, and these nerves detected vibrations and signaled the brain. The fish turned toward shore.

The woman continued to swim away from the beach, stopping now and then to check her position by the lights shining from the house. The tide was slack, so she had not moved up or down the beach. But she was tiring, so she rested for a moment, treading water, and then started for shore.

The vibrations were stronger now, and the fish recognized prey. The sweeps of its tail quickened, thrusting the giant body forward with a speed that agitated the tiny phosphorescent animals in the water and caused them to glow, casting a mantle of sparks over the fish.

The fish closed on the woman and hurtled past, a dozen feet to the side and six feet below the surface. The woman felt only a wave of pressure that seemed to lift her up in the water and ease her down again. She stopped swimming and held her breath. Feeling nothing further, she resumed her lurching stroke.

The fish smelled her now, and the vibrations—erratic and sharp—signaled distress. The fish began to circle close to the surface. Its dorsal fin broke water, and its tail, thrashing back and forth, cut the glassy surface with a hiss. A series of tremors shook its body.

For the first time, the woman felt fear, though she did not know why. Adrenaline shot through her trunk and her limbs, generating a tingling heat and urging her to swim faster. She guessed that she was fifty yards from shore. She could see the line of white foam where the waves broke on the beach. She saw the lights in the house, and for a comforting moment she thought she saw someone pass by one of the windows.

The fish was about forty feet from the woman, off to the side, when it turned suddenly to the left, dropped entirely below the surface, and, with two quick thrusts of its tail, was upon her.

At first, the woman thought she had snagged her leg on a rock or a piece of floating wood. There was no initial pain, only one violent tug on her right leg. She reached down to touch her foot, treading water with her left leg to keep her head up, feeling in the blackness with her left hand. She could not find her foot. She reached higher on her leg, and then she was overcome by a rush of nausea and dizziness. Her groping fingers had found a nub of bone and tattered flesh. She knew that the warm, pulsing flow over her fingers in the chill water was her own blood.

Pain and panic struck together. The woman threw her head back and screamed a guttural cry of terror.

The fish had moved away. It swallowed the woman's limb without chewing. Bones and meat passed down the massive gullet in a single spasm. Now the fish turned again, homing on the stream of blood flushing from the woman's femoral artery, a beacon as clear and true as a lighthouse on a cloudless night. This time the fish attacked from below. It hurtled up under the woman, jaws agape. The great conical head struck her like a locomotive, knocking her up out of the water. The jaws snapped shut around her torso, crushing bones and flesh and organs into a jelly. The fish, with the woman's body in its mouth, smashed down on the water with a thunderous splash, spewing foam and blood and phosphorescence in a gaudy shower.

Below the surface, the fish shook its head from side to side, its serrated triangular teeth sawing through what little sinew still resisted. The corpse fell apart. The fish swallowed, then turned to continue feeding. Its brain still registered the signals of nearby prey. The water was laced with blood and shreds of flesh, and the fish could not sort signal from substance. It cut back and forth through the dissipating cloud of blood, opening and closing its mouth, seining for a random morsel. But by now, most of the pieces of the corpse had dispersed. A few sank slowly, coming to rest on the sandy bottom, where they moved lazily in the current. A few drifted away just below the surface, floating in the surge that ended in the surf.

THE MAN AWOKE, shivering in the early morning cold. His mouth was sticky and dry, and his wakening belch tasted of Bourbon and corn. The sun had not yet risen, but a line of pink on the eastern horizon told him that daybreak was near. The stars still hung faintly in the lightening sky. The man stood and began to dress. He was annoyed that the woman had not woken him when she went back to the house, and he found it curious that she had left her clothes on the beach. He picked them up and walked to the house.

He tiptoed across the porch and gently opened the screen door, remembering that it screeched when yanked. The living room was dark and empty, littered with half-empty glasses, ashtrays, and dirty plates. He walked across the living room, turned right down a hall, past two closed doors. The door to the room he shared with the woman was open, and a bedside light was on. Both beds were made. He tossed the woman's clothes on one of the beds, then returned to the living room and switched on a light. Both couches were empty.

There were two more bedrooms in the house. The owners slept in one. Two other house guests occupied the other. As quietly as possible, the man opened the door to the first bedroom. There were two beds, each obviously containing only one person. He closed the door and moved to the next room. The host and hostess were asleep on each side of a king-size bed. The man closed the door and went back to his room to find his watch. It was nearly five.

He sat on one bed and stared at the bundle of clothes on the other. He was certain the woman wasn't in the house. There had been no other guests for dinner, so unless she had met someone on the beach while he slept, she couldn't have gone off with anyone. And even if she had, he thought, she probably would have taken at least some of her clothes.

Only then did he permit his mind to consider the possibility of an accident. Very quickly the possibility became a certainty. He returned to the host's bedroom, hesitated for a moment beside the bed, and then softly placed his hand on a shoulder.

"Jack," he said, patting the shoulder. "Hey, Jack."

The man sighed and opened his eyes. "What?"

"It's me. Tom. I hate like hell to wake you up, but I think we may have a problem."

"What problem?"

"Have you seen Chrissie?"

"What do you mean, have I seen Chrissie? She's with you."

"No, she isn't. I mean, I can't find her."

Jack sat up and turned on a light. His wife stirred and covered her head with a sheet. Jack looked at his watch. "Jesus Christ. It's five in the morning. And you can't find your date."

"I know," said Tom. "I'm sorry. Do you remember when you saw her last?"

"Sure I remember. She said you were going for a swim, and you both went out on the porch. When did *you* see her last?"

"On the beach. Then I fell asleep. You mean she didn't come back?"

"Not that I saw. At least not before we went to bed, and that was around one."

"I found her clothes."

"Where? On the beach?"

"Yes."

"You looked in the living room?"

Tom nodded. "And in the Henkels' room."

"The Henkels' room!"

Tom blushed. "I haven't known her that long. For all I know she could be a little weird. So could the Henkels. I mean, I'm not suggesting anything. I just wanted to check the whole house before I woke you up."

"So what do you think?"

"What I'm beginning to think," said Tom, "is that maybe she had an accident. Maybe she drowned."

Jack looked at him for a moment, then glanced again at his watch. "I don't know what time the police in this town go to work," he said, "but I guess this is as good a time as any to find out."

2

PATROLMAN LEN HENDRICKS sat at his desk in the Amity police station, reading a detective novel called *Deadly, I'm Yours.* At the moment the phone rang the heroine, a girl named Whistling Dixie, was about to be raped by a motorcycle club. Hendricks let the phone ring until Miss Dixie castrated the first of her attackers with a linoleum knife she had secreted in her hair.

He picked up the phone. "Amity Police, Patrolman Hendricks," he said. "Can I help you?"

"This is Jack Foote, over on Old Mill Road. I want to report a missing person. Or at least I think she's missing."

"Say again, sir?" Hendricks had served in Vietnam as a radio man, and he was fond of military terminology.

"One of my house guests went for a swim at about one this morning," said Foote. "She hasn't come back yet. Her date found her clothes on the beach."

Hendricks began to scribble on a pad. "What was the person's name?"

"Christine Watkins."

"Age?"

"I don't know. Just a second. Say around twenty-five. Her date says that's about right."

"Height and weight?"

"Wait a minute." There was a pause. "We think probably about five-seven, between one twenty and one thirty."

"Color of hair and eyes?"

"Listen, Officer, why do you need all this? If the woman's

drowned, she's probably going to be the only one you have—at least tonight, right? You don't average more than one drowning around here each night, do you?"

"Who said she drowned, Mr. Foote? Maybe she went for a walk."

"Stark naked at one in the morning? Have you had any reports about a woman walking around naked?"

Hendricks relished the chance to be insufferably cool. "No, Mr. Foote, not yet. But once the summer season starts, you never know what to expect. Last August, a bunch of faggots staged a dance out by the club—a nude dance. Color of hair and eyes?"

"Her hair is . . . oh, dirty blond, I guess. Sandy. I don't know what color her eyes are. I'll have to ask her date. No, he says he doesn't know either. Let's say hazel."

"Okay, Mr. Foote. We'll get on it. As soon as we find out anything, we'll contact you."

Hendricks hung up the phone and looked at his watch. It was 5:10. The chief wouldn't be up for an hour, and Hendricks wasn't anxious to wake him up for something as vague as a missing-person report. For all anybody knew, the broad was off humping in the bushes with some guy she met on the beach. On the other hand, if she was washed up somewhere, Chief Brody would want the whole thing taken care of before the body was found by some nanny with a couple of young kids and it became a public nuisance.

Judgment, that's what the chief kept telling him he needed; that's what makes a good cop. And the cerebral challenge of police work had played a part in Hendricks' decision to join the Amity force after he returned from Vietnam. The pay was fair: $9,000 to start, $15,000 after fifteen years, plus fringes. Police work offered security, regular hours, and the chance for some fun—not just thumping unruly kids or collaring drunks, but solving burglaries, trying to catch the occasional rapist (the summer before, a black gardener had raped seven rich white women, not one of whom would appear in court to testify against him), and—on a slightly more elevated plane— the opportunity to become a respected, contributing member of the community. And being an Amity cop was not very dangerous, certainly nothing like working for a metropolitan

force. The last duty-related fatality of an Amity policeman occurred in 1957 when an officer had tried to stop a drunk
speeding along the Montauk Highway and had been run off
the road into a stone wall.

Hendricks was convinced that as soon as he could get
sprung from this God-forsaken midnight-to-eight shift, he
would start to enjoy his work. For the time being, though, it
was a drag. He knew perfectly well why he had the late shift.
Chief Brody liked to break in his young men slowly, letting
them develop the fundamentals of police work—good sense,
sound judgment, tolerance, and politeness—at a time of day
when they wouldn't be overtaxed.

The business shift was 8:00 A.M. to 4:00 P.M., and it called
for experience and diplomacy. Six men worked that shift. One
handled the summertime traffic at the intersection of Main
and Water streets. Two patrolled in squad cars. One manned
the phones at the station house. One handled the clerical
work. And the chief handled the public—the ladies who complained that they were unable to sleep because of the din coming from the Randy Bear or Saxon's, the town's two gin mills;
the homeowners who complained that bums were littering
the beaches or disturbing the peace; and the vacationing
bankers and brokers and lawyers who stopped in to discuss
their various plans for keeping Amity a pristine and exclusive
summer colony.

Four to midnight was the trouble shift, when the young
studs from the Hamptons would flock to the Randy Bear and
get involved in a fight or simply get so drunk that they became
a menace on the roads; when, very rarely, a couple of
predators from Queens would lurk in the dark side streets and
mug passersby; and when, about twice a month in the summer, enough evidence having accumulated, the police would
feel obliged to stage a pot bust at one of the huge waterfront
homes. There were six men on four to midnight, the six largest men on the force, all between thirty and fifty years old.

Midnight to eight was usually quiet. For nine months of
the year, peace was virtually guaranteed. The biggest event of
the previous winter had been an electrical storm that had set
off all the alarms linking the police station to forty-eight of
Amity's biggest and most expensive homes. Normally during

the summer, the midnight-to-eight shift was manned by three officers. One, however, a young fellow named Dick Angelo, was now taking his two-week leave before the season began to swing. The other was a thirty-year veteran named Henry Kimble, who had chosen the midnight-to-eight shift because it permitted him to catch up on his sleep—he held a daytime job as a bartender at Saxon's. Hendricks tried to raise Kimble on the radio—to get him to take a walk along the beach by Old Mill Road—but he knew the attempt was hopeless. As usual, Kimble was sound asleep in a squad car parked behind the Amity Pharmacy. And so Hendricks picked up the phone and dialed Chief Brody's home number.

Brody was asleep, in that fitful state before waking when dreams rapidly change and there are moments of bleary semiconsciousness. The first ring of the phone was assimilated into his dream—a vision that he was back in high school groping a girl on a stairwell. The second ring snapped the vision. He rolled over and picked up the receiver.

"Yeah?"

"Chief, this is Hendricks. I hate to bother you this early, but—"

"What time is it?"

"Five-twenty."

"Leonard, this better be good."

"I think we've got a floater on our hands, Chief."

"A floater? What in Christ's name is a floater?"

It was a word Hendricks had picked up from his night reading. "A drowning," he said, embarrassed. He told Brody about the phone call from Foote. "I didn't know if you'd want to check it out before people start swimming. I mean, it looks like it's going to be a nice day."

Brody heaved an exaggerated sigh. "Where's Kimble?" he said and then added quickly, "Oh, never mind. It was a stupid question. One of these days I'm going to fix that radio of his so he can't turn it off."

Hendricks waited a moment, then said, "Like I said, Chief, I hate to bother . . ."

"Yeah, I know, Leonard. You were right to call. As long as I'm awake, I might as well get up. I'll shave and shower and grab some coffee, and on my way in I'll take a look along the beach in front of Old Mill and Scotch, just to make sure your 'floater' isn't cluttering up somebody's beach. Then when the day boys come on, I'll go out and talk to Foote and the girl's date. I'll see you later."

Brody hung up the phone and stretched. He looked at his wife, lying next to him in the double bed. She had stirred when the phone rang, but as soon as she determined that there was no emergency, she lapsed back into sleep.

Ellen Brody was thirty-six, five years younger than her husband, and the fact that she looked barely thirty was a source of both pride and annoyance to Brody: pride because, since she looked handsome and young and was married to him, she made him seem a man of excellent taste and substantial attraction; annoyance because she had been able to keep her good looks despite the strains of bearing three children, whereas Brody—though hardly fat at six-foot-one and two hundred pounds—was beginning to be concerned about his blood pressure and his thickening middle. Sometimes during the summer, Brody would catch himself gazing with idle lust at one of the young, long-legged girls who pranced around town—their untethered breasts bouncing beneath the thinnest of cotton jerseys. But he never enjoyed the sensation, for it always made him wonder whether Ellen felt the same stirring when she looked at the tanned, slim young men who so perfectly complemented the long-legged girls. And as soon as that thought occurred to him, he felt still worse, for he recognized it as a sign that he was on the unfortunate side of forty and had already lived more than half his life.

Summers were bad times for Ellen Brody, for in summer she was tortured by thoughts she didn't want to think— thoughts of chances missed and lives that could have been. She saw people she had grown up with: prep school classmates now married to bankers and brokers, summering in Amity and wintering in New York, graceful women who stroked tennis balls and enlivened conversations with equal ease, women who (Ellen was convinced) joked among themselves about Ellen Shepherd marrying that policeman because he got her pregnant in the back seat of his 1948 Ford, which had not been the case.

Ellen was twenty-one when she met Brody. She had just

finished her junior year at Wellesley and was spending the summer in Amity with her parents—as she had done for the previous eleven summers, ever since her father's advertising agency transferred him from Los Angeles to New York. Although, unlike several of her friends, Ellen Shepherd was hardly obsessed by marriage, she assumed that within a year or two after finishing college she would wed someone from approximately her own social and financial station. The thought neither distressed nor delighted her. She enjoyed the modest wealth her father had earned, and she knew her mother did too. But she was not eager to live a life that was a repetition of her parents'. She was familiar with the petty social problems, and they bored her. She considered herself a simple girl, proud of the fact that in the yearbook for the class of 1953 at Miss Porter's School she was voted Most Sincere.

Her first contact with Brody was professional. She was arrested—or, rather, her date was. It was late at night, and she was being driven home by an extremely drunk young man intent on driving very fast down very narrow streets. The car was intercepted and stopped by a policeman who impressed Ellen with his youth, his looks, and his civility. After issuing a summons, he confiscated the keys to Ellen's date's car and drove them both to their respective homes. The next morning, Ellen was shopping when she found herself next to the police station. As a lark, she walked in and asked the name of the young officer who had been working at about midnight the night before. Then she went home and wrote Brody a thank-you note for being so nice, and she also wrote a note to the chief of police commending young Martin Brody. Brody telephoned to thank her for her thank-you note.

When he asked her out to dinner and the movies on his night off, she accepted out of curiosity. She had scarcely ever talked to a policeman, let alone gone out with one. Brody was nervous, but Ellen seemed so genuinely interested in him and his work that he eventually calmed down enough to have a good time. Ellen found him delightful: strong, simple, kind—sincere. He had been a policeman for six years. He said his ambition was to be chief of the Amity force, to have sons to take duck-shooting in the fall, to save enough money to take a real vacation every second or third year.

They were married that November. Ellen's parents had wanted her to finish college, and Brody had been willing to wait until the following summer, but Ellen couldn't imagine that one more year of college could make any difference in the life she had chosen to lead.

There were some awkward moments during the first few years. Ellen's friends would ask them to dinner or lunch or for a swim, and they would go, but Brody would feel ill at ease and patronized. When they got together with Brody's friends, Ellen's past seemed to stifle fun. People behaved as if they were fearful of committing a faux pas. Gradually, as friendships developed, the awkwardness disappeared. But they never saw any of Ellen's old friends anymore. Although the shedding of the "summer people" stigma earned her the affection of the year-round residents of Amity, it cost her much that was pleasant and familiar from the first twenty-one years of her life. It was as if she had moved to another country.

Until about four years ago, the estrangement hadn't bothered her. She was too busy, and too happy, raising children to let her mind linger on alternatives long past. But when her last child started school, she found herself adrift, and she began to dwell on memories of how her mother had lived her life once her children had begun to detach from her: shopping excursions (fun because there was enough money to buy all but the most outrageously expensive items), long lunches with friends, tennis, cocktail parties, weekend trips. What had once seemed shallow and tedious now loomed in memory like paradise.

At first she tried to re-establish bonds with friends she hadn't seen in ten years, but all commonality of interest and experience had long since vanished. Ellen talked gaily about the community, about local politics, about her job as a volunteer at the Southampton Hospital—all subjects about which her old friends, many of whom had been coming to Amity every summer for more than thirty years, knew little and cared less. They talked about New York politics, about art galleries and painters and writers they knew. Most conversations ended with feeble reminiscences and speculations about where old friends were now. Always there were pledges about calling each other and getting together again.

Once in a while she would try to make new friends among the summer people she hadn't known, but the associations were forced and brief. They might have endured if Ellen had been less self-conscious about her house, about her husband's job and how poorly it paid. She made sure that everyone she met knew she had started her Amity life on an entirely different plane. She was aware of what she was doing, and she hated herself for it, because in fact she loved her husband deeply, adored her children, and—for most of the year—was quite content with her lot.

By now, she had largely given up active forays into the summer community, but the resentments and the longings lingered. She was unhappy, and she took out most of her unhappiness on her husband, a fact that both of them understood but only he could tolerate. She wished she could go into suspended animation for that quarter of every year.

Brody rolled over toward Ellen, raising himself up on one elbow and resting his head on his hand. With his other hand he flicked away a strand of hair that was tickling Ellen's nose and making it twitch. He still had an erection from the remnants of his last dream, and he debated rousing her for a quick bit of sex. He knew she was a slow waker and her early morning moods were more cantankerous than romantic. Still, it would be fun. There had not been much sex in the Brody household recently. There seldom was, when Ellen was in her summer moods.

Just then, Ellen's mouth fell open and she began to snore. Brody felt himself turn off as quickly as if someone had poured ice water on his loins. He got up and went into the bathroom.

It was nearly 6:30 when Brody turned onto Old Mill Road. The sun was well up. It had lost its daybreak red and was turning from orange to bright yellow. The sky was cloudless.

Theoretically, there was a statutory right-of-way between each house, to permit public access to the beach, which could be privately owned only to the mean-high-water mark. But the rights-of-way between most houses were filled with garages or privet hedges. From the road there was no view of the beach.

All Brody could see was the tops of the dunes. So every hundred yards or so he had to stop the squad car and walk up a
driveway to reach a point from which he could survey the
beach.

There was no sign of a body. All he saw on the broad, white
expanse was a few pieces of driftwood, a can or two, and a
yard-wide belt of seaweed and kelp pushed ashore by the
southerly breeze. There was practically no surf, so if a body
was floating on the surface it would have been visible. If there
is a floater out there, Brody thought, it's floating beneath the
surface and I'll never see it till it washes up.

By seven o'clock Brody had covered the whole beach along
Old Mill and Scotch roads. The only thing he had seen that
struck him as even remotely odd was a paper plate on which
sat three scalloped orange rinds—a sign that the summer's
beach picnics were going to be more elegant than ever.

He drove back along Scotch Road, turned north toward
town on Bayberry Lane, and arrived at the station house at
7:10.

Hendricks was finishing up his paperwork when Brody
walked in, and he looked disappointed that Brody wasn't
dragging a corpse behind him. "No luck, Chief?" he said.

"That depends on what you mean by luck, Leonard. If you
mean did I find a body and if I didn't isn't it too bad, the
answer to both questions is no. Is Kimble in yet?"

"No."

"Well, I hope he isn't asleep. That'd look just dandy, having
him snoring away in a cop car when people start to do their
shopping."

"He'll be here by eight," said Hendricks. "He always is."

Brody poured himself a cup of coffee, walked into his office, and began to flip through the morning papers—the early
edition of the New York *Daily News* and the local paper, the
Amity *Leader,* which came out weekly in the winter and daily
in the summer.

Kimble arrived a little before eight, looking, aptly enough,
as if he had been sleeping in his uniform, and he had a cup of
coffee with Hendricks while they waited for the day shift to
appear. Hendricks' replacement came in at eight sharp, and

Hendricks was putting on his leather flight jacket and getting ready to leave when Brody came out of his office.

"I'm going out to see Foote, Leonard," Brody said. "You want to come along? You don't have to, but I thought you might want to follow up on your . . . floater." Brody smiled.

"Sure, I guess so," said Hendricks. "I got nothing else going today, so I can sleep all afternoon."

They drove out in Brody's car. As they pulled into Foote's driveway, Hendricks said, "What do you bet they're all asleep? I remember last summer a woman called at one in the morning and asked if I could come out as early as possible the next morning because she thought some of her jewelry was missing. I offered to go right then, but she said no, she was going to bed. Anyway, I showed up at ten o'clock the next morning and she threw me out. 'I didn't mean *this* early,' she says."

"We'll see," said Brody. "If they're really worried about this dame, they'll be awake."

The door opened almost before Brody had finished knocking. "We've been waiting to hear from you," said a young man. "I'm Tom Cassidy. Did you find her?"

"I'm Chief Brody. This is Officer Hendricks. No, Mr. Cassidy, we didn't find her. Can we come in?"

"Oh sure, sure. I'm sorry. Go on in the living room. I'll get the Footes."

It took less than five minutes for Brody to learn everything he felt he needed to know. Then, as much to seem thorough as from any hope of learning anything useful, he asked to see the missing woman's clothes. He was shown into the bedroom, and he looked through the clothing on the bed.

"She didn't have a bathing suit with her?"

"No," said Cassidy. "It's in the top drawer over there. I looked."

Brody paused for a moment, taking care with his words, then said, "Mr. Cassidy, I don't mean to sound flip or anything, but has this Miss Watkins got a habit of doing strange things? I mean, like taking off in the middle of the night . . . or walking around naked?"

"Not that I know of," said Cassidy. "But I really don't know her too well."

"I see," said Brody. "Then I guess we'd better go down to

the beach again. You don't have to come. Hendricks and I can handle it."

"I'd like to come, if you don't mind."

"I don't mind. I just thought you might not want to."

The three men walked down to the beach. Cassidy showed the policemen where he had fallen asleep—the indentation his body had made in the sand had not been disturbed—and he pointed out where he had found the woman's clothes.

Brody looked up and down the beach. For as far as he could see, more than a mile in both directions, the beach was empty. Clumps of seaweed were the only dark spots on the white sand. "Let's take a walk," he said. "Leonard, you go east as far as the point. Mr. Cassidy, let's you and I go west. You got your whistle, Leonard? Just in case."

"I've got it," said Hendricks. "You care if I take my shoes off? It's easier walking on the hard sand, I don't want to get them wet."

"I don't care," said Brody. "Technically you're off duty. You can take your pants off if you want. Of course, then I'll arrest you for indecent exposure."

Hendricks started eastward. The wet sand felt crisp and cool on his feet. He walked with his head down and his hands in his pockets, looking at the tiny shells and tangles of seaweed. A few bugs—they looked like little black beetles—skittered out of his path, and when the wavewash receded, he saw minute bubbles pop above the holes made by sandworms. He enjoyed the walk. It was a funny thing, he thought, that when you live all your life in a place, you almost never do the things that tourists go there to do—like walk on the beach or go swimming in the ocean. He couldn't remember the last time he went swimming. He wasn't even sure he still owned a bathing suit. It was like something he had heard about New York —that half the people who live in the city never go to the top of the Empire State Building or visit the Statue of Liberty.

Every now and then, Hendricks looked up to see how much closer he was to the point. Once he turned back to see if Brody and Cassidy had found anything. He guessed that they were nearly half a mile away.

As he turned back and started walking again, Hendricks saw something ahead of him, a clump of weed and kelp that seemed unusually large. He was about thirty yards away from the clump when he began to think the weed might be clinging to something.

When he reached the clump, Hendricks bent down to pull some of the weed away. Suddenly he stopped. For a few seconds he stared, frozen rigid. He fumbled in his pants pocket for his whistle, put it to his lips, and tried to blow. Instead, he vomited, staggered back, and fell to his knees.

Snarled within the clump of weed was a woman's head, still attached to shoulders, part of an arm, and about a third of her trunk. The mass of tattered flesh was a mottled blue-gray, and as Hendricks spilled his guts into the sand, he thought—and the thought made him retch again—that the woman's remaining breast looked as flat as a flower pressed in a memory book.

"WAIT," SAID BRODY, stopping and touching Cassidy's arm. "I think that was a whistle." He listened, squinting into the morning sun. He saw a black spot on the sand, which he assumed was Hendricks, and then he heard the whistle more clearly. "Come on," he said, and the two men began to trot along the sand.

Hendricks was still on his knees when they got to him. He had stopped puking, but his head still hung, mouth open, and his breathing rattled with phlegm.

Brody was several steps ahead of Cassidy, and he said, "Mr. Cassidy, stay back there a second, will you?" He pulled apart some of the weeds, and when he saw what was inside, he felt bile rise in his throat. He swallowed and closed his eyes. After a moment he said, "You might as well look now, Mr. Cassidy, and tell me if it's her or not."

Cassidy was terrified. His eyes shifted between the exhausted Hendricks and the mass of weed. "That?" he said, pointing at the weed. Reflexively, he stepped backward. "That *thing?* What do you mean it's her?"

Brody was still fighting to control his stomach. "I think," he said, "that it may be part of her."

Reluctantly, Cassidy shuffled forward. Brody held back a piece of weed so Cassidy could get a clear look at the gray and gaping face. "Oh, my God!" said Cassidy, and he put a hand to his mouth.

"Is it her?"

Cassidy nodded, still staring at the face. Then he turned away and said, "What happened to her?"

"I can't be sure," said Brody. "Offhand, I'd say she was attacked by a shark."

Cassidy's knees buckled, and as he sank to the sand, he said, "I think I'm going to be sick." He put his head down and retched.

The stink of vomit reached Brody almost instantly, and he knew he had lost his struggle. "Join the crowd," he said, and he vomited too.

3

SEVERAL MINUTES PASSED before Brody felt well enough to stand, walk back to his car, and call for an ambulance from the Southampton Hospital, and it was almost an hour before the ambulance arrived and the truncated corpse was stuffed into a rubber bag and hauled away.

By eleven o'clock, Brody was back in his office, filling out forms about the accident. He had completed everything but "cause of death" when the phone rang.

"Carl Santos, Martin," said the voice of the coroner.

"Yeah, Carl. What have you got for me?"

"Unless you have any reason to suspect a murder, I'd have to say shark."

"Murder?" said Brody.

"I'm not suggesting anything. All I mean is that it's conceivable—just barely—that some nut could have done this job on the girl with an ax and a saw."

"I don't think it's a murder, Carl. I've got no motive, no murder weapons, and—unless I want to go off into left field—no suspect."

"Then it's a shark. And a big bastard, too. Even the screw on an ocean liner wouldn't have done this. It might have cut her in two, but . . ."

"Okay, Carl," said Brody. "Spare me the gore. My stomach's none too hot already."

"Sorry, Martin. Anyway, I'm going to put down shark attack. I'd say that makes the most sense for you, too, unless there are . . . you know . . . other considerations."

"No," said Brody. "Not this time. Thanks for calling, Carl." He hung up, typed "shark attack" in the "cause of death" space on the forms, and leaned back in his chair.

The possibility that "other considerations" might be involved in this case hadn't occurred to Brody. Those considerations were the touchiest part of Brody's job, forcing him constantly to assess the best means of protecting the commonweal without compromising either himself or the law.

It was the beginning of the summer season, and Brody knew that on the success or failure of those twelve brief weeks rested the fortunes of Amity for a whole year. A rich season meant prosperity enough to carry the town through the lean winter. The winter population of Amity was about 1,000; in a good summer the population jumped to nearly 10,000. And those 9,000 summer visitors kept the 1,000 permanent residents alive for the whole year.

Merchants—from the owners of the hardware store and the sporting goods store and the two gas stations to the local pharmacist—needed a boom summer to support them through the winter, during which they never broke even. The wives of carpenters, electricians, and plumbers worked during the summer as waitresses or real estate agents, to help keep their families going over the winter. There were only two year-round liquor licenses in Amity, so the twelve weeks of summer were critical to most of the restaurants and pubs. Charter fishermen needed every break they could get: good weather, good fishing, and, above all, crowds.

Even after the best of summers, Amity winters were rough. Three of every ten families went on relief. Dozens of men were forced to move for the winter to the north shore of Long Island, where they scratched for work shucking scallops for a few dollars a day.

Brody knew that one bad summer would nearly double the relief rolls. If every house was not rented, there wouldn't be enough work for Amity's blacks, most of whom were gardeners, butlers, bartenders, and maids. And two or three bad summers in a row—a circumstance that, fortunately, hadn't occurred in more than two decades—could create a cycle that could wreck the town. If people didn't have enough money to buy clothes or gas or ample food supplies, if they couldn't afford to have their houses or their appliances repaired, then the merchants and service firms would fail to make enough to tide them over until the next summer. They would close down, and Amity's citizens would start shopping elsewhere. The town would lose tax revenue. Municipal services would deteriorate, and people would begin to move away.

So there was a common, though tacit, understanding in Amity, born of the need to survive. Everyone was expected to do his bit to make sure that Amity remained a desirable summer community. A few years ago, Brody remembered, a young man and his brother had moved into town and set themselves up as carpenters. They came in the spring, when there was enough work preparing houses for summer residents to keep everyone busy, so they were welcomed. They seemed competent enough, and several established carpenters began to refer work to them.

But by midsummer, there were disquieting reports about the Felix Brothers. Albert Morris, the owner of Amity Hardware, let it be known that they were buying cheap steel nails instead of galvanized nails and were charging their customers for galvanized. In a seaside climate, steel nails begin to rust in a few months. Dick Spitzer, who ran the lumberyard, told somebody that the Felixes had ordered a load of low-grade, green wood to use in some cabinets in a house on Scotch Road. The cabinet doors began to warp soon after they were installed. In a bar one night, the elder Felix, Armando, boasted to a drinking buddy that on his current job he was being paid to set supporting studs every sixteen inches but was actually placing them twenty-four inches apart. And the younger Felix, a twenty-one-year-old named Danny with a stubborn case of acne, liked to show his friends erotic books which he bragged he had stolen from the houses he worked in.

Other carpenters stopped referring work to the Felixes, but by then they had built enough of a business to keep them going through the winter. Very quietly, the Amity understanding began to work. At first, there were just a few hints to the Felixes that they had outworn their welcome. Armando reacted arrogantly. Soon, annoying little mishaps began to bother him. All the tires on his truck would mysteriously empty themselves of air, and when he called for help from the Amity Gulf station, he was told that the air pump was broken. When he ran out of propane gas in his kitchen, the local gas company took eight days to deliver a new tank. His orders for lumber and other supplies were inexplicably mislaid or delayed. In stores where once he had been able to obtain credit he was now forced to pay cash. By the end of October, the Felix Brothers were unable to function as a business, and they moved away.

Generally, Brody's contribution to the Amity understanding—in addition to maintaining the rule of law and sound judgment in the town—consisted of suppressing rumors and, in consultation with Harry Meadows, the editor of the Amity *Leader*, keeping a certain perspective on the rare unfortunate occurrences that qualified as news.

The previous summer's rapes had been reported in the *Leader*, but just barely (as molestations), because Brody and Meadows agreed that the specter of a black rapist stalking every female in Amity wouldn't do much for the tourist trade. In that case, there was the added problem that none of the women who had told the police they had been raped would repeat their stories to anyone else.

If one of the wealthier summer residents of Amity was arrested for drunken driving, Brody was willing, on a first offense, to book him for driving without a license, and that charge would be duly reported in the *Leader*. But Brody made sure to warn the driver that the second time he was caught driving under the influence he would be charged, booked, and prosecuted for drunk driving.

Brody's relationship with Meadows was based on a delicate balance. When groups of youngsters came to town from the Hamptons and caused trouble, Meadows was handed every fact—names, ages, and charges lodged. When Amity's own youth made too much noise at a party, the *Leader* usually ran a one-paragraph story without names or addresses, informing the public that the police had been called to quell a minor disturbance on, say, Old Mill Road.

Because several summer residents found it fun to subscribe to the *Leader* year-round, the matter of wintertime vandalism of summer houses was particularly sensitive. For years, Meadows had ignored it—leaving it to Brody to make sure that the homeowner was notified, the offenders punished, and the appropriate repairmen dispatched to the house. But in the winter of 1968 sixteen houses were vandalized within a few weeks. Brody and Meadows agreed that the time had come for a full campaign in the *Leader* against wintertime vandals. The result was the wiring of forty-eight homes to the police station, which—since the public didn't know which houses were wired and which weren't—all but eliminated vandalism, made Brody's job much easier, and gave Meadows the image of a crusading editor.

Once in a while, Brody and Meadows collided. Meadows was a zealot against the use of narcotics. He was also a man with unusually keen reportorial antennae, and when he sensed a story—one not susceptible to "other considerations" —he would go after it like a pig after truffles. In the summer of 1971 the daughter of one of Amity's richest families had died off the Scotch Road beach. To Brody, there was no evidence of foul play, and since the family opposed an autopsy, the death was officially listed as drowning.

But Meadows had reason to believe that the girl was on drugs and that she was being supplied by the son of a Polish potato farmer. It took Meadows almost two months to get the story, but in the end he forced an autopsy which proved that at the time she drowned the girl had been unconscious from an overdose of heroin. He also tracked down the pusher and exposed a fairly large drug ring operating in the Amity area. The story reflected badly on Amity and worse on Brody, who, because several federal violations were involved in the case, wasn't even able to redeem his earlier insouciance by making an arrest or two. And it won Meadows two regional journalism prizes.

Now it was Brody's turn to press for full disclosure. He intended to close the beaches for a couple of days, to give the shark time to travel far from the Amity shoreline. He didn't know whether or not sharks could acquire a taste for human flesh (as he had heard tigers do), but he was determined to deprive the fish of any more people. This time he wanted publicity, to make people fear the water and stay away from it.

Brody knew there would be a strong argument against publicizing the attack. Like the rest of the country, Amity was still feeling the effects of the recession. So far, the summer was shaping up as a mediocre one. Rentals were up from last year, but they were not "good" rentals. Many were "groupers," bands of ten or fifteen young people who came from the city and split the rent on a big house. At least a dozen of the $7,000–$10,000-a-season shorefront houses had not yet been rented, and many more in the $5,000 class were still without leases. Sensational reports of a shark attack might turn mediocrity into disaster.

Still, Brody thought, one death in mid-June, before the crowds come, would probably be quickly forgotten. Certainly it would have less effect than two or three more deaths would. The fish might well have disappeared already, but Brody wasn't willing to gamble lives on the possibility: the odds might be good, but the stakes were prohibitively high.

He dialed Meadows' number. "Hey, Harry," he said. "Free for lunch?"

"I've been wondering when you'd call," said Meadows. "Sure. My place or yours?"

Suddenly Brody wished he hadn't called at mealtime. His stomach was still groaning, and the thought of food nauseated him. He glanced up at the wall calendar. It was a Thursday. Like all their friends on fixed, tight incomes, the Brodys shopped according to the supermarket specials. Monday's special was chicken, Tuesday's lamb, and so forth through the week. As each item was consumed, Ellen would note it on her list and replace it the next week. The only variables were bluefish and bass, which were inserted in the menu when a friendly fisherman dropped his overage by the house. Thursday's special was hamburger, and Brody had seen enough chopped meat for one day.

"Yours," he said. "Why don't we order out from Cy's? We can eat in your office."

"Fine with me," said Meadows. "What do you want? I'll order now."

"Egg salad, I guess, and a glass of milk. I'll be right there."
Brody called Ellen to tell her he wouldn't be home for lunch.

HARRY MEADOWS WAS an immense man, for whom the act of
drawing breath was exertion enough to cause perspiration to
dot his forehead. He was in his late forties, ate too much,
chain-smoked cheap cigars, drank bonded Bourbon, and was,
in the words of his doctor, the Western world's leading candidate for a huge coronary infarction.

When Brody arrived, Meadows was standing beside his
desk, waving a towel at the open window. "In deference to
what your lunch order tells me is a tender stomach," he said,
"I am trying to clear the air of essence of White Owl."

"I appreciate that," said Brody. He glanced around the
small, cluttered room, searching for a place to sit.

"Just throw that crap off the chair there," Meadows said.
"They're just government reports. Reports from the county,
reports from the state, reports from the highway commission
and the water commission. They probably cost about a million dollars, and from an informational point of view they
don't amount to a cup of spit."

Brody picked up the heap of papers and piled them atop a
radiator. He pulled the chair next to Meadows' desk and sat
down.

Meadows rooted around in a large brown paper bag,
pulled out a plastic cup and a cellophane-wrapped sandwich,
and slid them across the desk to Brody. Then he began to
unwrap his own lunch, four separate packages which he
opened and spread before himself with the loving care of a
jeweler showing off rare gems: a meatball hero, oozing to-
mato sauce; a plastic carton filled with oily fried potatoes; a
dill pickle the size of a small squash; and a quarter of a lemon
meringue pie. He reached behind his chair and from a small
refrigerator withdrew a sixteen-ounce can of beer. "Delightful," he said with a smile as he surveyed the feast before him.

"Amazing," said Brody, stifling an acid belch. "Absofuck-
inlutely amazing. I must have had about a thousand meals
with you, Harry, but I still can't get used to it."

"Everyone has his little quirks, my friend," Meadows said

as he lifted his sandwich. "Some people chase other people's wives. Some lose themselves in whiskey. I find my solace in nature's own nourishment."

"That'll be some solace to Dorothy when your heart says, 'That's enough, buster, adiós.' "

"We've discussed that, Dorothy and I," said Meadows, filtering the words through a mouthful of bread and meat, "and we agree that one of the few advantages man has over other animals is the ability to choose the way to bring on his own death. Food may well kill me, but it's also what has made life such a pleasure. Besides, I'd rather go my way than end up in the belly of a shark. After this morning, I'm sure you'll agree."

Brody was in the midst of swallowing a bite of egg salad sandwich, and he had to force it past a rising gag. "Don't do that to me," he said.

They ate in silence for a few moments. Brody finished his sandwich and milk, wadded the sandwich wrapper and stuffed it into the plastic cup. He leaned back and lit a cigarette. Meadows was still eating, but Brody knew his appetite wouldn't be diminished by any discussion. He recalled a time when Meadows had visited the scene of a bloody automobile accident and proceeded to interview police and survivors while sucking on a coconut Popsicle.

"About the Watkins thing," Brody said. "I have a couple of thoughts, if you want to hear them." Meadows nodded. "First, it seems to me that the cause of death is cut-and-dried. I've already talked to Santos, and—"

"I did, too."

"So you know what he thinks. It was a shark attack, clear and simple. And if you'd seen the body, you'd agree. There's just no—"

"I did see it."

Brody was astonished, mostly because he couldn't imagine how anyone who had seen that mess could be sitting there now, licking lemon-pie filling off his fingers. "So you agree?"

"Yes. I agree that's what killed her. But there are a few things I'm not so sure of."

"Like what?"

"Like why she was swimming at that time of night. Do you know what the temperature was at around midnight? Sixty.

Do you know what the water temperature was? About fifty. You'd have to be out of your mind to go swimming under those conditions."

"Or drunk," said Brody, "which she probably was."

"Maybe. No, you're right—probably. I've checked around a little, and the Footes don't mess with grass or mescaline or any of that stuff. There's one other thing that bothers me, though."

Brody was annoyed. "For Christ's sake, Harry, stop chasing shadows. Once in a while, people do die by accident."

"It's not that. It's just that it's damn funny that we've got a shark around here when the water's still this cold."

"Is it? Maybe there are sharks who like cold water. Who knows about sharks?"

"There are some. There's the Greenland shark, but they never come down this far, and even if they did, they don't usually bother people. Who knows about sharks? I'll tell you this: At the moment I know a hell of a lot more about them than I did this morning. After I saw what was left of Miss Watkins, I called a young guy I know up at the Woods Hole Oceanographic Institute. I described the body to him, and he said it's likely that only one kind of shark would do a job like that."

"What kind?"

"A great white. There are others that attack people, like tigers and hammerheads and maybe even makos and blues, but this fellow Hooper—Matt Hooper—told me that to cut a woman in half like that you'd have to have a fish with a mouth like this"—he spread his hands about three feet apart—"and the only shark that grows that big *and* attacks people is the great white. There's another name for them."

"Oh?" Brody was beginning to lose interest. "What's that?"

"Man-eater. Other sharks kill people once in a while, for all sorts of reasons—hunger, maybe, or confusion or because they smell blood in the water. By the way, did the Watkins girl have her period last night?"

"How the hell would I know?"

"Just curious. Hooper said that's one way to guarantee yourself an attack if there's a shark around."

"What did he say about the cold water?"

"That it's quite common for a great white to come into water this cold. Some years ago, a boy was killed by one near San Francisco. The water temperature was fifty-seven."

Brody sucked a long drag from his cigarette and said, "You've really done a lot of checking into this, Harry."

"It seemed to me a matter of—shall we say—common sense and public interest to determine exactly what happened and the chances of it happening again."

"And did you determine those chances?"

"I did. They're almost nonexistent. From what I can gather, this was a real freak accident. According to Hooper, the only thing good about great whites is that they're scarce. There's every reason to believe that the shark that attacked the Watkins girl is long gone. There are no reefs around here. There's no fish-processing plant or slaughterhouse that dumps blood or guts into the water. So there's nothing at all to keep the shark interested." Meadows paused and looked at Brody, who returned his gaze silently. "So it seems to me, Martin, that there's no reason to get the public all upset over something that's almost sure not to happen again."

"That's one way to look at it, Harry. Another is that since it's not likely to happen again, there's no harm in telling people that it did happen this once."

Meadows sighed. "Journalistically, you may be right. But I think this is one of those times, Martin, when we have to forget the book and think of what's best for the people. I don't think it would be in the public interest to spread this around. I'm not thinking about the townspeople. They'll know about it soon enough, the ones that don't know already. But what about the people who read the *Leader* in New York or Philadelphia or Cleveland?"

"You flatter yourself."

"Balls. You know what I mean. And you know what the real estate situation is like around here this summer. We're right on the edge, and other places are, too, like Nantucket and the Vineyard and East Hampton. There are people who still haven't made their summer plans. They know they've got their pick of places this year. There's no shortage of houses for rent . . . anywhere. If I run a story saying that a young woman was bitten in two by a monster shark off Amity, there won't be another house rented in this town. Sharks are like ax-murderers, Martin. People react to them with their guts. There's something crazy and evil and uncontrollable about them. If we tell people there's a killer shark around here, we can kiss the summer good-bye."

Brody nodded. "I can't argue with that, Harry, and I don't want to tell the people that there *is* a killer shark around here. Look at it from my point of view, just for a second. I won't dispute your odds or anything. You're probably right. That shark has probably gone a hundred miles from here and won't ever show up again. The most dangerous thing out there in the water is probably the undertow. But, Harry, there's a chance you're wrong, and I don't think we can take that chance. Suppose—just suppose—we don't say a word, and somebody else gets hit by that fish. What then? My ass is in a sling. I'm supposed to protect people around here, and if I can't protect them from something, the least I can do is warn them that there is a danger. Your ass is in a sling, too. You're supposed to report the news, and there's just no question but that someone killed by a shark is news. I want you to run the story, Harry. I want to close the beaches, just for a couple of days, and just for insurance's sake. It won't be a great inconvenience to anybody. There aren't that many people here yet, and the water's cold. If we tell it straight, tell people what happened and why we're doing what we're doing, I think we'll be way ahead."

Meadows sat back in his chair and thought for a moment. "I can't speak for your job, Martin, but as far as mine is concerned, the decision has already been made."

"What does that mean?"

"There won't be any story about the attack in the *Leader.*"

"Just like that."

"Well, not exactly. It wasn't entirely my decision, though I think that generally I agree with it. I'm the editor of this paper, Martin, and I own a piece of it, but not a big enough piece to buck certain pressures."

"Such as?"

"I've gotten six phone calls already this morning. Five were from advertisers—one restaurant, one hotel, two real estate firms, and an ice cream shop. They were most anxious to know whether or not I planned to run a story on the Watkins thing, and most anxious to let me know they felt Amity would best be served by letting the whole thing fade quietly away. The sixth call was from Mr. Coleman in New York. Mr. Coleman who owns fifty-five per cent of the *Leader*. It seems Mr. Coleman had received a few phone calls himself. He told me there would be no story in the *Leader*."

"I don't suppose he said whether the fact that his wife is a real estate broker had anything to do with his decision."

"No," said Meadows. "The subject never came up."

"Figures. Well, Harry, where does that leave us? You're not going to run a story, so as far as the good readers of the *Leader* are concerned, nothing ever happened. I'm going to close the beaches and put up a few signs saying why."

"Okay, Martin. That's your decision. But let me remind you of something. You're an elected official, right?"

"Just like the President. For four thrill-filled years."

"Elected officials can be impeached."

"Is that a threat, Harry?"

Meadows smiled. "You know better than that. Besides, who am I to be making threats? I just want you to be aware of what you're doing before you tinker with the lifeblood of all those sage and discriminating souls who elected you."

Brody rose to go. "Thanks, Harry. I've always heard it's lonely here at the top. What do I owe you for lunch?"

"Forget it. I couldn't take money from a man whose family will soon be begging for food stamps."

Brody laughed. "No way. Haven't you heard? The great thing about police work is the security."

TEN MINUTES after Brody returned to his office, the intercom buzzer sounded and a voice announced, "The mayor's here to see you, Chief."

Brody smiled. The mayor. Not Larry Vaughan, just calling to check in. Not Lawrence Vaughan of Vaughan & Penrose Real Estate, stopping by to complain about some noisy tenants. But Mayor Lawrence P. Vaughan, the people's choice— by seventy-one votes in the last election. "Send his honor in," Brody said.

Larry Vaughan was a handsome man, in his early fifties, with a full head of salt-and-pepper hair and a body kept trim by exercise. Though he was a native of Amity, over the years he had developed an air of understated chic. He had made a great deal of money in postwar real estate speculation in Amity, and he was the senior partner (some thought the *only* partner, since no one had ever met or spoken to anyone named Penrose in Vaughan's office) in the most successful agency in town. He dressed with elegant simplicity, in timeless British jackets, button-down shirts, and Weejun loafers. Unlike Ellen Brody, who had descended from summer folk to winter folk and was unable to make the adjustment, Vaughan had ascended smoothly from winter folk to summer folk, adjusting each step of the way with grace. He was not one of them, for he was technically a local merchant, so he was never asked to visit them in New York or Palm Beach. But in Amity he moved freely among all but the most aloof members of the summer community, which, of course, did an immense amount of good for his business. He was asked to most of the important summer parties, and he always arrived alone. Very few of his friends knew that he had a wife at home, a simple, adoring woman who spent much of her time doing needlepoint in front of her television set.

Brody liked Vaughan. He didn't see much of him during the summer, but after Labor Day, when things calmed down, Vaughan felt free to shed some of his social scales, and every few weeks he and his wife would ask Brody and Ellen out to dinner at one of the better restaurants in the Hamptons. The evenings were special treats for Ellen, and that in itself was enough to make Brody happy. Vaughan seemed to understand Ellen. He always acted most graciously, treating Ellen as a clubmate and comrade.

Vaughan walked into Brody's office and sat down. "I just talked to Harry Meadows," he said.

Vaughan was obviously upset, which interested Brody. He hadn't expected this reaction. "I see," he said. "Harry doesn't waste any time."

"Where are you going to get the authority to close the beaches?"

"Are you asking me as the mayor or as a real estate broker or out of friendly interest or what, Larry?"

Vaughan pressed, and Brody could see he was having trouble controlling his temper. "I want to know where you're going to get the authority. I want to know now."

"Officially, I'm not sure I have it," Brody said. "There's something in the code that says I can take whatever actions I deem necessary in the event of an emergency, but I think the selectmen have to declare a state of emergency. I don't imagine you want to go through all that rigmarole."

"Not a chance."

"Well, then, unofficially I figure it's my responsibility to keep the people who live here as safe as I can, and at the moment it's my judgment that that means closing the beaches for a couple of days. If it ever came down to cases, I'm not sure I could arrest anyone for going swimming. Unless," Brody smiled, "I could make a case of criminal stupidity."

Vaughan ignored the remark. "I don't want you to close the beaches," he said.

"So I see."

"You know why. The Fourth of July isn't far off, and that's the make-or-break weekend. We'd be cutting our own throats."

"I know the argument, and I'm sure you know my reasons for wanting to close the beaches. It's not as if I have anything to gain."

"No. I'd say quite the opposite is true. Look, Martin, this town doesn't need that kind of publicity."

"It doesn't need any more people killed, either."

"Nobody else is going to get killed, for God's sake. All you'd be doing by closing the beaches is inviting a lot of reporters to come snooping around where they don't have any business."

"So? They'd come out here, and when they didn't find anything worth reporting, they'd go home again. I don't imagine the *New York Times* has much interest in covering a lodge picnic or a garden-club supper."

"We just don't need it. Suppose they did find something. There'd be a big to-do that couldn't do anybody any good."

"Like what, Larry? What could they find out? I don't have anything to hide. Do you?"

"No, of course not. I was just thinking about . . . maybe the rapes. Something unsavory."

"Crap," said Brody. "That's all past history."

"Dammit, Martin!" Vaughan paused for a moment, struggling to calm himself. "Look, if you won't listen to reason, will you listen to me as a friend? I'm under a lot of pressure from my partners. Something like this could be very bad for us."

Brody laughed. "That's the first time I've heard you admit you *had* partners, Larry. I thought you ran that shop like an emperor."

Vaughan was embarrassed, as if he felt he had said too much. "My business is very complicated," he said. "There are times I'm not sure *I* understand what's going on. Do me this favor. This once."

Brody looked at Vaughan, trying to fathom his motives. "I'm sorry, Larry, I can't. I wouldn't be doing my job."

"If you don't listen to me," said Vaughan, "you may not have your job much longer."

"You haven't got any control over me. You can't fire any cop in this town."

"Not off the force, no. But believe it or not, I do have discretion over the job of chief of police."

"I don't believe it."

From his jacket pocket Vaughan took a copy of the corporate charter of the town of Amity. "You can read it yourself," he said, flipping through until he found the page he sought. "It's right here." He handed the pamphlet across the desk to Brody. "What it says, in effect, is that even though you were elected to the chief's job by the people, the selectmen have the power to remove you."

Brody read the paragraph Vaughan had indicated. "I guess you're right," he said. "But I'd love to see what you put down for 'good and sufficient cause.' "

"I dearly hope it doesn't come to that, Martin. I had hoped this conversation wouldn't even get this far. I had hoped that you would go along, once you knew how I and the selectmen felt."

"All the selectmen?"

"A majority."

"Like who?"

"I'm not going to sit here and name names for you. I don't have to. All you have to know is that I have the board behind me, and if you won't do what's right, we'll put someone in your job who will."

Brody had never seen Vaughan in a mood so aggressively ugly. He was fascinated, but he was also slightly shaken. "You really want this, don't you, Larry?"

"I do." Sensing victory, Vaughan said evenly, "Trust me, Martin. You won't be sorry."

Brody sighed. "Shit," he said. "I don't like it. It doesn't smell good. But okay, if it's that important."

"It's that important." For the first time since he had arrived, Vaughan smiled. "Thanks, Martin," he said, and he stood up. "Now I have the rather unpleasant task of visiting the Footes."

"How are you going to keep them from shooting off their mouths to the *Times* or the *News*?"

"I hope to be able to appeal to their public-spiritedness," Vaughan said, "just as I appealed to yours."

"Bull."

"We do have one thing going for us. Miss Watkins was a nobody. She was a drifter. No family, no close friends. She said she had hitchhiked East from Idaho. So she won't be missed."

BRODY ARRIVED HOME a little before five. His stomach had settled down enough to permit him a beer or two before dinner. Ellen was in the kitchen, still dressed in the pink uniform of a hospital volunteer. Her hands were immersed in chopped meat, kneading it into a meat loaf.

"Hello," she said, turning her head so Brody could plant a kiss on her cheek. "What was the crisis?"

"You were at the hospital. You didn't hear?"

"No. Today was bathe-the-old-ladies day. I never got off the Ferguson wing."

"A girl got killed off Old Mill."

"By what?"

"A shark." Brody reached into the refrigerator and found a beer.

Ellen stopped kneading meat and looked at him. "A shark! I've never heard of that around here. You see one once in a while, but they never do anything."

"Yeah, I know. It's a first for me, too."

"So what are you going to do?"

"Nothing."

"Really? Is that sensible? I mean, isn't there anything you can do?"

"Sure, there are some things I could do. Technically. But there's nothing I can actually do. What you and I think doesn't carry much weight around here. The powers-that-be are worried that it won't look nice if we get all excited just because one stranger got killed by a fish. They're willing to take the chance that it was just a freak accident that won't happen again. Or, rather, they're willing to let me take the chance, since it's my responsibility."

"What do you mean, the powers-that-be?"

"Larry Vaughan, for one."

"Oh. I didn't realize you had talked to Larry."

"He came to see me as soon as he heard I planned to close the beaches. He wasn't what you'd call subtle about telling me he didn't want the beaches closed. He said he'd have my job if I did close them."

"I can't believe that, Martin. Larry isn't like that."

"I didn't think so, either. Hey, by the way, what do you know about his partners?"

"In the business? I didn't think there were any. I thought Penrose was his middle name, or something like that. Anyway, I thought he owned the whole thing."

"So did I. But apparently not."

"Well, it makes me feel better to know you talked to Larry before you made any decision. He tends to take a wider, more over-all view of things than most people. He probably does know what's best."

Brody felt the blood rise in his neck. He said simply, "Crap." Then he tore the metal tab off his beer can, flipped it into the garbage can, and walked into the living room to turn on the evening news.

From the kitchen Ellen called, "I forgot to tell you: you had a call a little while ago."

"Who from?"

"He didn't say. He just said to tell you you're doing a terrific job. It was nice of him to call, don't you think?"

4

FOR THE NEXT few days the weather remained clear and unusually calm. The wind came softly, steadily from the southwest, a gentle breeze that rippled the surface of the sea but made no whitecaps. There was a crispness to the air only at night, and after days of constant sun, the earth and sand had warmed.

Sunday was the twentieth of June. Public schools still had a week or more to run before breaking for the summer, but the private schools in New York had already released their charges. Families who owned summer homes in Amity had been coming out for weekends since the beginning of May. Summer tenants whose leases ran from June 15 to September 15 had unpacked and, familiar now with where linen closets were, which cabinets contained good china and which the everyday stuff, and which beds were softer than others, were already beginning to feel at home.

By noon, the beach in front of Scotch and Old Mill roads was speckled with people. Husbands lay semi-comatose on beach towels, trying to gain strength from the sun before an afternoon of tennis and the trip back to New York on the Long Island Rail Road's Cannonball. Wives leaned against aluminum backrests, reading Helen MacInnes and John Cheever and Taylor Caldwell, interrupting themselves now and then to pour a cup of dry vermouth from the Scotch cooler.

Teen-agers lay serried in tight, symmetrical rows, the boys enjoying the sensation of grinding their pelvises into the sand, thinking of pudenda and occasionally stretching their necks to catch a brief glimpse of some, exposed, wittingly or not, by girls who lay on their backs with their legs spread.

These were not Aquarians. They uttered none of the platitudes of peace or pollution, or justice or revolt. Privilege had been bred into them with genetic certainty. As their eyes were blue or brown, so their tastes and consciences were determined by other generations. They had no vitamin deficiencies, no sickle-cell anemia. Their teeth—thanks either to breeding or to orthodontia—were straight and white and even. Their bodies were lean, their muscles toned by boxing lessons at age nine, riding lessons at twelve, and tennis lessons ever since. They had no body odor. When they sweated, the girls smelled faintly of perfume; the boys smelled simply clean.

None of which is to say that they were either stupid or evil. If their IQs could have been tested en masse, they would have shown native ability well within the top 10 per cent of all mankind. And they had been, were being, educated at schools that provided every discipline, including exposure to minority-group sensibilities, revolutionary philosophies, ecological hypotheses, political power tactics, drugs, and sex. Intellectually, they knew a great deal. Practically, they chose to know almost nothing. They had been conditioned to believe (or, if not to believe, to sense) that the world was really quite irrelevant to them. And they were right. Nothing touched them— not race riots in places like Trenton, New Jersey, or Gary, Indiana; not the fact that parts of the Missouri River were so foul that the water sometimes caught fire spontaneously; not police corruption in New York or the rising number of murders in San Francisco or revelations that hot dogs contained insect filth and hexachlorophine caused brain damage. They were inured even to the economic spasms that wracked the rest of America. Undulations in the stock markets were nuisances noticed, if at all, as occasions for fathers to bemoan real or fancied extravagances.

Those were the ones who returned to Amity every summer. The others—and there were some, mavericks—marched and bleated and joined and signed and spent their summers working for acronymic social-action groups. But because they had rejected Amity and, at most, showed up for an occasional Labor Day weekend, they, too, were irrelevant.

The little children played in the sand at the water's edge, digging holes and flinging muck at each other, unconscious and uncaring of what they were and what they would become.

A boy of six stopped skimming flat stones out into the water. He walked up the beach to where his mother lay dozing, and he flopped down next to her towel. "Hey, Mom," he said, limning aimless doodles with his finger in the sand.

His mother turned to look at him, shielding her eyes from the sun. "What?"

"I'm bored."

"How can you be bored? It isn't even July."

"I don't care. I'm bored. I don't have anything to do."

"You've got a whole beach to play on."

"I know. But there's nothing to *do* on it. Boy, am I bored."

"Why don't you go throw a ball?"

"With who? There's nobody here."

"I see a lot of people. Have you looked for the Harrises? What about Tommy Converse?"

"They're not here. Nobody's here. I sure am bored."

"Oh, for God's sake, Alex."

"Can I go swimming?"

"No. It's too cold."

"How do you know?"

"I know, that's all. Besides, you know you can't go alone."

"Will you come with me?"

"Into the water? Certainly not."

"No, I mean just to watch me."

"Alex, Mom is pooped, absolutely exhausted. Can't you find anything else to do?"

"Can I go out on my raft?"

"Out where?"

"Just out there a little ways. I won't go swimming. I'll just lie on my raft."

His mother sat up and put on her sunglasses. She looked up and down the beach. A few dozen yards away, a man stood in waist-deep water with a child on his shoulders. The woman looked at him, indulging herself in a quick moment of regret and self-pity that she could no longer shift to her husband the responsibility of amusing their child.

Before she could turn her head, the boy guessed what she was feeling. "I bet Dad would let me," he said.

"Alex, you should know by now that that's the wrong way to get me to do anything." She looked down the beach in the other direction. Except for a few couples in the dim distance, it was empty. "Oh, all right," she said. "Go ahead. But don't go too far out. And don't go swimming." She looked at the boy and, to show she was serious, lowered her glasses so he could see her eyes.

"Okay," he said. He stood up, grabbed his rubber raft, and dragged it down to the water. He picked up the raft, held it in front of him, and walked seaward. When the water reached his waist, he leaned forward. A swell caught the raft and lifted it, with the boy aboard. He centered himself so the raft lay flat. He paddled with both arms, stroking smoothly. His feet and ankles hung over the rear of the raft. He moved out a few yards, then turned and began to paddle up and down the beach. Though he didn't notice it, a gentle current carried him slowly offshore.

Fifty yards farther out, the ocean floor dropped precipitously—not with the sheerness of a canyon wall, but from a slope of perhaps ten degrees to more than forty-five degrees. The water was fifteen feet deep where the slope began to change. Soon it was twenty-five, then forty, then fifty feet deep. It leveled off at a hundred feet for about half a mile, then rose in a shoal that neared the surface a mile from shore. Seaward of the shoal, the floor dropped quickly to two hundred feet and then, still farther out, the true ocean depths began.

In thirty-five feet of water, the great fish swam slowly, its tail waving just enough to maintain motion. It saw nothing, for the water was murky with motes of vegetation. The fish had been moving parallel to the shoreline. Now it turned, banking slightly, and followed the bottom gradually upward. The fish perceived more light in the water, but still it saw nothing.

The boy was resting, his arms dangling down, his feet and ankles dipping in and out of the water with each small swell. His head was turned toward shore, and he noticed that he had been carried out beyond what his mother would consider safe.

He could see her lying on her towel, and the man and child playing in the wavewash. He was not afraid, for the water was calm and he wasn't really very far from shore—only forty yards or so. But he wanted to get closer; otherwise his mother might sit up, spy him, and order him out of the water. He eased himself back a little bit so he could use his feet to help propel himself. He began to kick and paddle toward shore. His arms displaced water almost silently, but his kicking feet made erratic splashes and left swirls of bubbles in his wake.

The fish did not hear the sound, but rather registered the sharp and jerky impulses emitted by the kicks. They were signals, faint but true, and the fish locked on them, homing. It rose, slowly at first, then gaining speed as the signals grew stronger.

The boy stopped for a moment to rest. The signals ceased. The fish slowed, turning its head from side to side, trying to recover them. The boy lay perfectly still, and the fish passed beneath him, skimming the sandy bottom. Again it turned.

The boy resumed paddling. He kicked only every third or fourth stroke; kicking was more exertion than steady paddling. But the occasional kicks sent new signals to the fish. This time it needed to lock on them only an instant, for it was almost directly below the boy. The fish rose. Nearly vertical, it now saw the commotion on the surface. There was no conviction that what thrashed above was food, but food was not a concept of significance. The fish was impelled to attack: if what it swallowed was digestible, that was food; if not, it would later be regurgitated. The mouth opened, and with a final sweep of the sickle tail the fish struck.

The boy's last—only—thought was that he had been punched in the stomach. The breath was driven from him in a sudden rush. He had no time to cry out, nor, had he had the time, would he have known what to cry, for he could not see the fish. The fish's head drove the raft out of the water. The jaws smashed together, engulfing head, arms, shoulders, trunk, pelvis, and most of the raft. Nearly half the fish had come clear of the water, and it slid forward and down in a belly-flopping motion, grinding the mass of flesh and bone and rubber. The boy's legs were severed at the hips, and they sank, spinning slowly, to the bottom.

On the beach the man with the child shouted, "Hey!" He was not sure what he had seen. He had been looking toward the sea, then started to turn his head when an uproar caught his eye. He jerked his head back seaward again, but by then there was nothing to see but the waves made by the splash, spreading outward in a circle. "Did you see that?" he cried. "Did you see that?"

"What, Daddy, what?" His child stared up at him, excited.

"Out there! A shark or a whale or something! Something huge!"

The boy's mother, half asleep on her towel, opened her eyes and squinted at the man. She saw him point toward the water and heard him say something to the child, who ran up the beach and stood by a pile of clothing. The man began to run toward the boy's mother, and she sat up. She didn't understand what he was saying, but he was pointing at the water, so she shaded her eyes and looked out at sea. At first, the fact that she saw nothing didn't strike her as odd. Then she remembered, and she said, "Alex."

BRODY WAS HAVING lunch: baked chicken, mashed potatoes, and peas. "Mashed potatoes," he said as Ellen served him. "What are you trying to do to me?"

"I don't want you to waste away. Besides, you look good chunky."

The phone rang. Ellen said, "I'll get it," but Brody stood up. That was the way it usually happened. She would say, "I'll get it," but he was the one who got it. It was the same when she had forgotten something in the kitchen. She would say, "I forgot the napkins. I'll get them." But they both knew he would get up and fetch the napkins.

"No, that's okay," he said. "It's probably for me anyway." He knew the call was probably for her, but the words came reflexively.

"Bixby, Chief," said the voice from the station house.

"What is it, Bixby?"

"I think you'd better come down here."

"Why's that?"

"Well, it's like this, Chief. . . ." Bixby obviously didn't

want to go into details. Brody heard him say something to someone else, then return to the phone. "I've got this hysterical woman on my hands, Chief."

"What's she hysterical about?"

"Her kid. Out by the beach."

A twinge of unease shot through Brody's stomach. "What happened?"

"It's . . ." Bixby faltered, then said quickly. "Thursday."

"Listen, asshole . . ." Brody stopped, for now he understood. "I'll be right there." He hung up the phone.

He felt flushed, almost feverish. Fear and guilt and fury blended in a thrust of gut-wrenching pain. He felt at once betrayed and betrayer, deceived and deceiver. He was a criminal forced into crime, an unwilling whore. He had to take the blame, but it was not rightly his. It belonged to Larry Vaughan and his partners, whoever they might be. He had wanted to do the right thing; they had forced him not to. But who were they to force him? If he couldn't stand up to Vaughan, what kind of cop was he? He should have closed the beaches.

Suppose he had. The fish would have gone down the beach —say, to East Hampton—and killed someone there. But that wasn't how it had worked. The beaches had stayed open, and a child had been killed because of it. It was as simple as that. Cause and effect. Brody suddenly loathed himself. And just as suddenly, he felt great pity for himself.

"What is it?" asked Ellen.

"A kid just got killed."

"How?"

"By a goddamn sonofabitch of a shark."

"Oh no! If you had closed the beaches . . ." She stopped, embarrassed.

"Yeah, I know."

HARRY MEADOWS WAS waiting in the parking lot at the rear of the station house when Brody drove up. He opened the passenger-side door of Brody's car and eased his bulk down onto the seat. "So much for the odds," he said.

"Yeah. Who's in there, Harry?"

"A man from the *Times,* two from *Newsday,* and one of my

people. And the woman. And the man who says he saw it happen."

"How did the *Times* get hold of it?"

"Bad luck. He was on the beach. So was one of the *Newsday* guys. They're both staying with people for the weekend. They were onto it within two minutes."

"What time did it happen?"

Meadows looked at his watch. "Fifteen, twenty minutes ago. No more."

"Do they know about the Watkins thing?"

"I don't know. My man does, but he knows enough not to talk. As for the others, it depends on who they've been talking to. I doubt they're onto it. They haven't had any digging time."

"They'll get onto it, sooner or later."

"I know," said Meadows. "It puts me in a rather difficult position."

"*You!* Don't make me laugh."

"Seriously, Martin. If somebody from the *Times* gets that story and files it, it'll appear in tomorrow's paper, along with today's attack, and the *Leader* will look like hell. I'm going to have to use it, to cover myself, even if the others don't."

"Use it how, Harry? What are you going to say?"

"I don't know, yet. As I said, I'm in a rather difficult position."

"Who are you going to say ordered it hushed up? Larry Vaughan?"

"Hardly."

"Me?"

"No, no. I'm not going to say anybody ordered it hushed up. There was no conspiracy. I'm going to talk to Carl Santos. If I can put the right words in his mouth, we may all be spared a lot of grief."

"What about the truth?"

"What about it?"

"What about telling it the way it happened? Say that I wanted to close the beaches and warn people, but the selectmen disagreed. And say that because I was too much of a chicken to fight and put my job on the line, I went along with them. Say that all the honchos in Amity agreed there was no point in alarming people just because there was a shark around that liked to eat children."

"Come on, Martin. It wasn't your fault. It wasn't anybody's. We came to a decision, took a gamble, and lost. That's all there is to it."

"Terrific. Now I'll just go tell the kid's mother that we're terribly sorry we had to use her son for chips." Brody got out of the car and started for the back door of the station house. Meadows, slower to extract himself, followed a few paces behind.

Brody stopped. "You know what I'd like to know, Harry? Who really made the decision? You went along with it. I went along with it. I don't think Larry Vaughan was even the actual guy who made the decision. I think he went along with it, too."

"What makes you think so?"

"I'm not sure. Do you know anything about his partners in the business?"

"He doesn't have any real partners, does he?"

"I'm beginning to wonder. Anyway, fuck it . . . for now." Brody took another step, and when Meadows still followed him, he said, "You better go around front, Harry . . . for appearances' sake."

Brody entered his office through a side door. The boy's mother was sitting in front of the desk, clutching a handkerchief. She was wearing a short robe over her bathing suit. Her feet were bare. Brody looked at her nervously, once again feeling the rush of guilt. He couldn't tell if she was crying, for her eyes were masked by large, round sunglasses.

A man was standing by the back wall. Brody assumed he was the one who claimed to have witnessed the accident. He was gazing absently at Brody's collection of memorabilia: citations from community-service groups, pictures of Brody with visiting dignitaries. Not exactly the stuff to command much attention from an adult, but staring at it was preferable to risking conversation with the woman.

Brody had never been adept at consoling people, so he simply introduced himself and started asking questions. The woman said she had seen nothing: one moment the boy was there, the next he was gone, "and all I saw were pieces of his raft." Her voice was weak but steady. The man described what he had seen, or what he thought he had seen.

"So no one actually saw this shark," Brody said, courting a faint hope in the back of his mind.

"No," said the man. "I guess not. But what else could it have been?"

"Any number of things." Brody was lying to himself as well as to them, testing to see if he could believe his own lies, wondering if any alternative to reality could be made credible. "The raft could have gone flat and the boy could have drowned."

"Alex is a good swimmer," the woman protested. "Or . . . was . . ."

"And what about the splash?" said the man.

"The boy could have been thrashing around."

"He never cried out. Not a word."

Brody realized that the exercise was futile. "Okay," he said. "We'll probably know soon enough, anyway."

"What do you mean?" said the man.

"One way or another, people who die in the water usually wash up somewhere. If it was a shark, there'll be no mistaking it." The woman's shoulders hunched forward, and Brody cursed himself for being a clumsy fool. "I'm sorry," he said. The woman shook her head and wept.

Brody told the woman and the man to wait in his office, and he walked out into the front of the station house. Meadows was standing by the outer door, leaning against the wall. A young man—the reporter from the *Times*, Brody guessed— was gesturing at Meadows and seemed to be asking questions. The young man was tall and slim. He wore sandals and a bathing suit and a short-sleeved shirt with an alligator emblem stitched to the left breast, which caused Brody to take an instant, instinctive dislike to the man. In his adolescence Brody had thought of those shirts as badges of wealth and position. All the summer people wore them. Brody badgered his mother until she bought him one—"a two-dollar shirt with a six-dollar lizard on it," she said—and when he didn't find himself suddenly wooed by gaggles of summer people, he was humiliated. He tore the alligator off the pocket and used the shirt as a rag to clean the lawn mower with which he earned

his summer income. More recently, Ellen had insisted on buying several shifts made by the same manufacturer—paying a
premium they could ill afford for the alligator emblem—to
help her regain her entrée to her old milieu. To Brody's dis-
may, one evening he found himself nagging Ellen for buying
"a ten-dollar dress with a twenty-dollar lizard on it."

Two men were sitting on a bench—the *Newsday* reporters.
One wore a bathing suit, the other a blazer and slacks. Meadows' reporter—Brody knew him as Nat something or other—
was leaning against the desk, chatting with Bixby. They
stopped talking as soon as they saw Brody enter.

"What can I do for you?" Brody said.

The young man next to Meadows took a step forward and
said, "I'm Bill Whitman, from the *New York Times.*"

"And?" What am I supposed to do? Brody thought. Fall on
my ass?

"I was on the beach."

"What did you see?"

One of the *Newsday* reporters interrupted: "Nothing. I was
there, too. Nobody saw anything. Except maybe the guy in
your office. He says he saw something."

"I know," said Brody, "but he's not sure just what it was he
saw."

The *Times* man said, "Are you prepared to list this as a
shark attack?"

"I'm not prepared to list this as anything, and I'd suggest
you don't go listing it as anything, either, until you know a
hell of a lot more about it than you do now."

The *Times* man smiled. "Come on, Chief, what do you want
us to do? Call it a mysterious disappearance? Boy lost at sea?"

It was difficult for Brody to resist the temptation to trade
angry ironies with the *Times* reporter. He said, "Listen, Mr.—
Whitman, is it?—Whitman. We have no witnesses who saw
anything but a splash. The man inside thinks he saw a big
silver-colored thing that he thinks may have been a shark. He
says he has never seen a live shark in his life, so that's not
what you'd call expert testimony. We have no body, no real
evidence that anything violent happened to the boy . . . I
mean, except that he's missing. It is conceivable that he

drowned. It is conceivable that he had a fit or a seizure of some kind and then drowned. And it is conceivable that he was attacked by some kind of fish or animal—or even person, for that matter. All of those things are possible, and until we get . . ."

The sound of tires grinding over gravel in the public parking lot out front stopped Brody. A car door slammed, and Len Hendricks charged into the station house, wearing nothing but a bathing suit. His body had the mottled gray-whiteness of a Styrofoam coffee cup. He stopped in the middle of the floor. "Chief . . ."

Brody was startled by the unlikely sight of Hendricks in a bathing suit—thighs flecked with pimples, genitals bulging in the tight fabric. "You've been *swimming,* Leonard?"

"There's been another attack!" said Hendricks.

The *Times* man quickly asked, "When was the first one?"

Before Hendricks could answer, Brody said, "We were just discussing it, Leonard. I don't want you or anyone else jumping to conclusions until you know what you're talking about. For God's sake, the boy could have drowned."

"Boy?" said Hendricks. "What boy? This was a man, an old man. Five minutes ago. He was just beyond the surf, and suddenly he screamed bloody murder and his head went under water and it came up again and he screamed something else and then he went down again. There was all this splashing around, and blood was flying all over the place. The fish kept coming back and hitting him again and again and again. That's the biggest fuckin' fish I ever saw in my whole life, big as a fuckin' station wagon. I went in up to my waist and tried to get to the guy, but the fish kept hitting him." Hendricks paused, staring at the floor. His breath squeezed out of his chest in short bursts. "Then the fish quit. Maybe he went away, I don't know. I waded out to where the guy was floating. His face was in the water. I took hold of one of his arms and pulled."

Brody said, "And?"

"It came off in my hand. The fish must have chewed right through it, all but a little bit of skin." Hendricks looked up, his eyes red and filling with tears of exhaustion and fright.

"Are you going to be sick?" said Brody.

"I don't think so."

"Did you call the ambulance?"

Hendricks shook his head no.

"Ambulance?" said the *Times* reporter. "Isn't that rather like shutting the barn door after the horse has left?"

"Shut your mouth, smart ass," said Brody. "Bixby, call the hospital. Leonard, are you up to doing some work?" Hendricks nodded. "Then go put on some clothes and find some notices that close the beaches."

"Do we have any?"

"I don't know. We must. Maybe back in the stock room with those signs that say 'This Property Protected by Police.' If we don't, we'll have to make some that'll do until we can have some made up. I don't care. One way or another, let's get the goddam beaches closed."

MONDAY MORNING, BRODY arrived at the office a little after seven. "Did you get it?" he said to Hendricks.

"It's on your desk."

"Good or bad? Never mind. I'll go see for myself."

"You won't have to look too hard."

The city edition of the *New York Times* lay in the center of Brody's desk. About three quarters of the way down the right-hand column on page one, he saw the headline:

SHARK KILLS TWO
ON LONG ISLAND

Brody said, "Shit," and began to read.

By William F. Whitman
Special to The New York Times

AMITY, L.I. June 20—A six-year-old boy and a 65-year-old man were killed today in separate shark attacks that occurred within an hour of each other near the beaches of this resort community.

Although the body of the boy, Alexander Kintner,

was not found, officials said there was no question that he was killed by a shark. A witness, Thomas Daguerre, of New York, said he saw a large silver-colored object rise out of the water and seize the boy and his rubber raft and disappear into the water with a splash.

Amity coroner Carl Santos reported that traces of blood found on shreds of rubber recovered later left no doubt that the boy had died a violent death.

At least fifteen persons witnessed the attack on Morris Cater, 65, which took place at approximately 2 P.M. a quarter of a mile down the beach from where young Kintner was attacked.

Apparently, Mr. Cater was swimming just beyond the surf line when he was suddenly struck from behind. He called out for help, but all attempts to rescue him were in vain.

"I went in up to my waist and tried to get to him," said Amity police officer Leonard Hendricks, who was on the beach at the time, "but the fish kept hitting him."

Mr. Cater, a jewelry wholesaler with offices at 1224 Avenue of the Americas, was pronounced dead on arrival at Southampton Hospital.

These incidents are the first documented cases of shark attacks on bathers on the Eastern Seaboard in more than two decades.

According to Dr. David Dieter, an icthyologist at the New York Aquarium at Coney Island, it is logical to assume—but by no means a certainty—that both attacks were the work of one shark.

"At this time of year in these waters," said Dr. Dieter, "there are very few sharks. It's rare at any time of year for sharks to come so close to the beach. So the chances that two sharks would be off the same beach at virtually the same time—and would each attack someone—are infinitesimal."

When informed that one witness described the shark that attacked Mr. Cater as being "as large as a station wagon," Dr. Dieter said the shark was probably a "great white" (*Carcharodon carcharias*), a species known throughout the world for its voraciousness and aggressiveness.

In 1916, he said, a great white killed four bathers in New Jersey on one day—the only other recorded instance of multiple shark-attack fatalities in the United States in this century. Dr. Dieter attributed the attacks to "bad luck, like a flash of lightning that hits a house. The shark was probably just passing by. It happened to be a nice day, and there happened to be people swimming, and he happened to come along. It was pure chance."

Amity is a summer community on the south shore of Long Island, approximately midway between Bridgehampton and East Hampton, with a wintertime population of 1,000. In the summer, the population increases to 10,000.

Brody finished reading the article and set the paper on the desk. Chance, that doctor said, pure chance. What would he say if he knew about the first attack? Still pure chance? Or would it be negligence, gross and unforgivable? There were three people dead now, and two of them could still be alive, if only Brody had . . .

"You've seen the *Times*," said Meadows. He was standing in the doorway.

"Yeah, I've seen it. They didn't pick up the Watkins thing."

"I know. Kind of curious, especially after Len's little slip of the tongue."

"But you did use it."

"I did. I had to. Here." Meadows handed Brody a copy of the Amity *Leader*. The banner headline ran across all six columns of page one: TWO KILLED BY MONSTER SHARK OFF AMITY BEACH. Below that, in smaller type, a subhead: Number of Victims of Killer Fish Rises to Three.

"You sure get your news up high, Harry."

"Read on."

Brody read:

Two summer visitors to Amity were brutally slain yesterday by a man-eating shark that attacked them as they frolicked in the chill waters off the Scotch Road beach.

Alexander Kintner, age 6, who lived with his mother in the Goose Neck Lane house owned by Mr. and Mrs. Richard Packer, was the first to die—attacked from below as he lay on a rubber raft. His body has not been found.

Less than half an hour later, Morris Cater, 65, who was spending the weekend at the Abelard Arms Inn, was attacked from behind as he swam in the gentle surf off the public beach.

The giant fish struck again and again, savaging Mr. Cater as he cried for help. Patrolman Len Hendricks, who by sheer coincidence was taking his first swim in five years, made a valiant attempt to rescue the struggling victim, but the fish gave no quarter. Mr. Cater was dead by the time he was pulled clear of the water.

The deaths were the second and third to be caused by shark attack off Amity in the past five days.

Last Wednesday night, Miss Christine Watkins, a guest of Mr. and Mrs. John Foote of Old Mill Road, went for a swim and vanished.

Thursday morning, Police Chief Martin Brody and Officer Hendricks recovered her body. According to coroner Carl Santos, the cause of death was "definitely and incontrovertibly shark attack."

Asked why the cause of death was not made public, Mr. Santos declined to comment.

Brody looked up from the paper and said, "Did Santos really decline to comment?"

"No. He said nobody but you and I had asked him about the cause of death, so he didn't feel compelled to tell anybody. As you can see, I couldn't print that response. It would have pinned everything on you and me. I had hoped I could get him to say something like, 'Her family requested that the cause of death be kept private, and since there was obviously no crime involved, I agreed,' but he wouldn't. I can't say I blame him."

"So what did you do?"

"I tried to get hold of Larry Vaughan, but he was away for the weekend. I thought he'd be the best official spokesman."

"And when you couldn't reach him?"

"Read."

It was understood, however, that Amity police and government officials had decided to withhold the information in the public interest. "People tend to overreact when they hear about a shark attack," said one member of the Board of Selectmen. "We didn't want to start a panic. And we had an expert's opinion that the odds against another attack were astronomical."

"Who was your talkative selectman?" asked Brody.

"All of them and none of them," said Meadows. "It's basically what they all said, but none of them would be quoted."

"What about the beaches not being closed? Did you go into that?"

"*You* did."

"I did?"

Asked why he had not ordered the beaches closed until the marauding shark was apprehended, Chief Brody said, "The Atlantic Ocean is huge. Fish swim in it and move from place to place. They don't always stay in one area, especially an area like this where there is no food source. What were we going to do? Close the Amity beaches, and people would just drive up to East Hampton and go swimming there. And there's just as good a chance that they'd get killed in East Hampton as in Amity."

After yesterday's attacks, however, Chief Brody did order the beaches closed until further notice.

"Jesus, Harry," said Brody, "you really put it to me. You've got me arguing a case I don't believe, then being proved wrong and *forced* to do what I wanted to do all along. That's a pretty shitty trick."

"It wasn't a trick. I had to have someone give the official line, and with Vaughan away, you were the logical one. You admit that you agreed to go along with the decision, so—reluctantly or not—you supported it. I didn't see any point in airing all the dirty laundry of private disputes."

"I suppose. Anyway, it's done. Is there anything else I should read in this?"

"No. I just quote Matt Hooper, that fellow from Woods Hole. He says it would be remarkable if we ever have another attack. But he's a little less sure than he was last time."

"Does he think one fish is doing all this?"

"He doesn't know, of course, but offhand, yes. He thinks it's a big white."

"I do, too. I mean, I don't know from whites or greens or blues, but I think it's one shark."

"Why?"

"I'm not sure, exactly. Yesterday afternoon I called the Coast Guard out on Montauk. I asked them if they'd noticed a lot of sharks around here recently, and they said they hadn't seen a one. Not one so far this spring. It's still early, so that isn't *too* strange. They said they'd send a boat down this way later on and give me a call if they saw anything. I finally called them back. They said they had cruised up and down this area for two hours and hadn't seen a thing. So there sure aren't many sharks around. They also said that when there are sharks around, they're mostly medium-sized blue sharks—about five to ten feet—and sand sharks that don't generally bother people. From what Leonard said he saw yesterday, this is no medium-sized blue."

"Hooper said there was one thing we could do," Meadows said. "Now that you've got the beaches closed down, we could chum. You know, spread fish guts and goodies like that around in the water. If there's a shark around, he said, that will bring him running."

"Oh, great. That's what we need, to attract sharks. And what if he shows up? What do we do then?"

"Catch him."

"With what? My trusty spinning rod?"

"No, a harpoon."

"A harpoon. Harry, I don't even have a police boat, let alone a boat with harpoons on it."

"There are fishermen around. They have boats."

"Yeah, for a hundred and a half a day, or whatever it is."

"True. But still it seems to me . . ." A commotion out in the hall stopped Meadows in mid-sentence.

He and Brody heard Bixby say, "I told you, ma'am, he's in conference." Then a woman's voice said, "Bullshit! I don't care what he's doing. I'm going in there."

The sound of running feet—first one pair, then two. The door to Brody's office flew open, and standing in the doorway, clutching a newspaper, tears streaming down her face, was Alexander Kintner's mother.

Bixby came up behind her and said, "I'm sorry, Chief. I tried to stop her."

"That's okay, Bixby," said Brody. "Come in, Mrs. Kintner."

Meadows stood and offered her his chair, which was the closest one to Brody's desk. She ignored him and walked up to Brody, who was standing behind his desk.

"What can I do . . ."

The woman slapped the newspaper across his face. It didn't hurt Brody so much as startle him—especially the noise, a sharp report that rang deep into his left ear. The paper fell to the floor.

"What about this?" Mrs. Kintner screamed. "What about it?"

"What about what?" said Brody.

"What they say here. That you knew it was dangerous to swim. That somebody had already been killed by that shark. That you kept it a secret."

Brody didn't know what to say. Of course it was true, all of it, at least technically. He couldn't deny it. And yet he couldn't admit it, either, because it wasn't the whole truth.

"Sort of," he said. "I mean yes, it's true, but it's—look, Mrs. Kintner . . ." He was pleading with her to control herself until he could explain.

"You killed Alex!" She shrieked the words, and Brody was sure they were heard in the parking lot, on the street, in the center of town, on the beaches, all over Amity. He was sure his wife heard them, and his children.

He thought to himself: Stop her before she says anything else. But all he could say was, "Ssshhh!"

"You did! You killed him!" Her fists were clenched at her

sides, and her head snapped forward as she screamed, as if she were trying to inject the words into Brody. "You won't get away with it!"

"Please, Mrs. Kintner," said Brody. "Calm down. Just for a minute. Let me explain." He reached to touch her shoulder and help her to a chair, but she jerked away.

"Keep your fucking hands off me!" she cried. "You knew. You knew all along, but you wouldn't say. And now a six-year-old boy, a beautiful six-year-old boy, my boy . . ." Tears seemed to pulse from her eyes, and as she quivered in her rage, droplets were cast from her face. "You knew! Why didn't you tell? Why?" She clutched herself, wrapping her arms around her body as they would be wrapped in a straitjacket, and she looked into Brody's eyes. "Why?"

"It's . . ." Brody fumbled for words. "It's a long story." He felt wounded, incapacitated as surely as if he had been shot. He didn't know if he could explain now. He wasn't even sure he could speak.

"I bet it is," said the woman. "Oh, you evil man. You evil, evil man. You . . ."

"Stop it!" Brody's shout was both plea and command. It stopped her. "Now look, Mrs. Kintner, you've got it wrong, all wrong. Ask Mr. Meadows."

Meadows, transfixed by the scene, nodded dumbly.

"Of course he'd say that. Why shouldn't he? He's your pal, isn't he? He probably told you you were doing the right thing." Her rage was mounting again, flooding, resuscitated by a new burst of emotional amperage. "You probably decided together. That makes it easier, doesn't it? Did you make money?"

"What?"

"Did you make money from my son's blood? Did someone pay you not to tell what you knew?"

Brody was horrified. "No! Christ, of course not."

"Then *why?* Tell me. Tell me why. *I'll* pay you. Just tell me why!"

"Because we didn't think it could happen again." Brody was surprised by his brevity. That was it, really, wasn't it?

The woman was silent for a moment, letting the words register in her muddled mind. She seemed to repeat them to herself. She said, "Oh," then, a second later, "Jesus." All of a sudden, as if a switch had been turned somewhere inside her, shutting off power, she had no more self-control. She slumped into the chair next to Meadows and began to weep in gasping, choking sobs.

Meadows tried to calm her, but she didn't hear him. She didn't hear Brody when he told Bixby to call a doctor. And she saw, heard, and felt nothing when the doctor came into the office, listened to Brody's description of what had happened, tried to talk to her, gave her a shot of Librium, led her—with the help of one of Brody's men—to his car, and drove her to the hospital.

When she had left, Brody looked at his watch and said, "It's not even nine o'clock yet. If ever I felt like I could use a drink . . . wow."

"If you're serious," said Meadows, "I have some Bourbon back in my office."

"No. If this was any indication of how the rest of the day's going to go, I better not fuck up my head."

"It's hard, but you've got to try not to take what she said too seriously. I mean, the woman was in shock, for one thing."

"I know, Harry. Any doctor would say she didn't know what she was saying. The trouble is, I'd already thought a lot of the things she was saying. Not in those words, maybe, but the thoughts were the same."

"Come on, Martin, you know you can't blame yourself."

"I know. I could blame Larry Vaughan. Or maybe even you. But the point is, the two deaths yesterday could have been prevented. I could have prevented them, and I didn't. Period."

The phone rang. It was answered in the other room, and a voice on the intercom said, "It's Mr. Vaughan."

Brody pushed the lighted button, picked up the receiver, and said, "Hi, Larry. Did you have a nice weekend?"

"Until about eleven o'clock last night," said Vaughan, "when I turned on my car radio driving home. I was tempted to call you last night, but I figured you had had a rough enough day without being bothered at that hour."

"That's one decision I agree with."

"Don't rub it in, Martin. I feel bad enough."

Brody wanted to say, "Do you, Larry?" He wanted to scrape the wound raw, to unload some of the anguish onto someone else. But he knew it was both unfair to attempt and impossible to accomplish, so all he said was, "Sure."

"I had two cancellations already this morning. Big leases. Good people. They had already signed, and I told them I could take them to court. They said, Go ahead: we're going somewhere else. I'm scared to answer the phone. I still have twenty houses that aren't rented for August."

"I wish I could tell you different, Larry, but it's going to get worse."

"What do you mean?"

"With the beaches closed."

"How long do you think you'll have to keep them closed?"

"I don't know. As long as it takes. A few days. Maybe more."

"You know that the end of next week is the Fourth of July weekend."

"Sure, I know."

"It's already too late to hope for a good summer, but we may be able to salvage something—for August, at least—if the Fourth is good."

Brody couldn't read the tone in Vaughan's voice. "Are you arguing with me, Larry?"

"No. I guess I was thinking out loud. Or praying out loud. Anyway, you plan to keep the beaches closed until what? Indefinitely? How will you know when that thing's gone away?"

"I haven't had time to think that far ahead. I don't even know why it's here. Let me ask you something, Larry. Just out of curiosity."

"What?"

"Who are your partners?"

It was a long moment before Vaughan said, "Why do you want to know? What does that have to do with anything?"

"Like I said, just curiosity."

"You keep your curiosity for your job, Martin. Let me worry about my business."

"Sure, Larry. No offense."

"So what are you going to do? We can't just sit around and

hope it will go away. We could starve to death while we waited."

"I know. Meadows and I were just talking about our options. A fish-expert friend of Harry's says we could try to catch the fish. What would you think about getting up a couple of hundred dollars to charter Ben Gardner's boat for a day or two? I don't know that he's ever caught any sharks, but it might be worth a try."

"Anything's worth a try, just so we get rid of that thing and go back to making a living. Go ahead. Tell him I'll get the money from somewhere."

Brody hung up the phone and said to Meadows, "I don't know why I care, but I'd give my ass to know more about Mr. Vaughan's business affairs."

"Why?"

"He's a very rich man. No matter how long this shark thing goes on, he won't be badly hurt. Sure, he'll lose a little dough, but he's taking all this as if it was life and death—and I don't mean just the town's. His."

"Maybe he's just a conscientious fellow."

"That wasn't conscience talking on the phone just then. Believe me, Harry. I know what conscience is."

TEN MILES SOUTH of the eastern tip of Long Island, a chartered fishing boat drifted slowly in the tide. Two wire lines trailed limply aft in an oily slick. The captain of the boat, a tall, spare man, sat on a bench on the flying bridge, staring at the water. Below, in the cockpit, the two men who had chartered the boat sat reading. One was reading a novel, the other the *New York Times*.

"Hey, Quint," said the man with the newspaper, "did you see this about the shark that killed those people?"

"I seen it," said the captain.

"You think we'll run into that shark?"

"Nope."

"How do you know?"

"I know."

"Suppose we went looking for him."

"We won't."

"Why not?"

"We got a slick goin'. We'll stay put."

The man shook his head and smiled. "Boy, wouldn't that be some sport"

"Fish like that ain't sport," said the captain.

"How far is Amity from here?"

"Down the coast a ways."

"Well, if he's around here somewhere, you might run into him one of these days."

"We'll find one another, all right. But not today."

5

THURSDAY MORNING WAS foggy—a wet ground fog so thick that it had a taste: sharp and salty. People drove under the speed limit, with their lights on. Around midday, the fog lifted, and puffy cumulus clouds meandered across the sky beneath a high blanket of cirrus. By five in the afternoon, the cloud cover had begun to disintegrate, like pieces fallen from a jigsaw puzzle. Sunlight streaked through the gaps, stabbing shining patches of blue onto the gray-green surface of the sea.

Brody sat on the public beach, his elbow resting on his knees to steady the binoculars in his hands. When he lowered the glasses, he could barely see the boat—a white speck that disappeared and reappeared in the ocean swells. The strong lenses drew it into plain, though jiggly, view. Brody had been sitting there for nearly an hour. He tried to push his eyes, to extend his vision from within to delineate more clearly the outline of what he saw. He cursed and let the glasses drop and hang by the strap around his neck.

"Hey, Chief," Hendricks said, walking up to Brody.

"Hey, Leonard. What are you doing here?"

"I was just passing by and I saw your car. What are you doing?"

"Trying to figure out what the hell Ben Gardner's doing."

"Fishing, don't you think?"

"That's what he's being paid to do, but it's the damnedest fishing I ever saw. I've been here an hour, and I haven't seen anything move on that boat."

"Can I take a look?" Brody handed him the glasses. Hendricks raised them and looked out at sea. "Nope, you're right. How long has he been out there?"

"All day, I think. I talked to him last night, and he said he'd be taking off at six this morning."

"Did he go alone?"

"I don't know. He said he was going to try to get hold of his mate—Danny what's-his-name—but there was something about a dentist appointment. I *hope* to hell he didn't go alone."

"You want to go see? We've got at least two more hours of daylight."

"How do you plan to get out there?"

"I'll borrow Chickering's boat. He's got an AquaSport with an eighty-horse Evinrude on it. That'll get us out there."

Brody felt a shimmy of fear skitter up his back. He was a very poor swimmer, and the prospect of being on top of—let alone in—water above his head gave him what his mother used to call the wimwams: sweaty palms, a persistent need to swallow, and an ache in his stomach—essentially the sensation some people feel about flying. In Brody's dreams, deep water was populated by slimy, savage things that rose from below and shredded his flesh, by demons that cackled and moaned. "Okay," he said. "I don't guess we've got much choice. Maybe by the time we get to the dock he'll already have started in. You go get the boat ready. I'll stop off at headquarters and give his wife a call . . . see if he's called in on the radio."

Amity's town dock was small, with only twenty slips, a fuel dock, and a wooden shack where hot dogs and fried clams were sold in cardboard sleeves. The slips were in a little inlet protected from the open sea by a stone jetty that ran across half the width of the inlet's mouth. Hendricks was standing in the AquaSport, the engine running, and he was chatting with a man in a twenty-five-foot cabin cruiser tied up in the neighboring slip. Brody walked along the wooden pier and climbed down the short ladder into the boat.

"What did she say?" asked Hendricks.

"Not a word. She's been trying to raise him for half an hour, but she figures he must have turned off the radio."

"Is he alone?"

"As far as she knows. His mate had an impacted wisdom tooth that had to be taken out today."

The man in the cabin cruiser said, "If you don't mind my saying so, that's pretty strange."

"What is?" said Brody.

"To turn off your radio when you're out alone. People don't do that."

"I don't know. Ben always bitches about all the chatter that goes on between boats when he's out fishing. Maybe he got bored and turned it off."

"Maybe."

"Let's go, Leonard," said Brody. "Do you know how to drive this thing?"

Hendricks cast off the bow line, walked to the stern, uncleated the stern line, and tossed it onto the deck. He moved to the control console and pushed a knobbed handle forward. The boat lurched ahead, chugging. Hendricks pushed the handle farther forward, and the engine fired more regularly. The stern settled back, the bow rose. As they made the turn around the jetty, Hendricks pushed the lever all the way forward, and the bow dropped down.

"Planing," said Hendricks.

Brody grabbed a steel handle on the side of the console. "Are there any life jackets?" he asked.

"Just the cushions," said Hendricks. "They'd hold you up all right, if you were an eight-year-old boy."

"Thanks."

What breeze there had been had died, and there was little chop to the sea. But there were small swells, and the boat took them roughly, smacking its prow into each one, recovering with a shudder that unnerved Brody. "This thing's gonna break apart if you don't slow down," he said.

Hendricks smiled, relishing his moment of command. "No worry, Chief. If I slow down, we'll wallow. It'll take us a week to get out there, and your stomach will feel like it's full of squirrels."

Gardner's boat was about three quarters of a mile from shore. As they drew nearer, Brody could see it bobbing gently in the swells. He could even make out the black letters on the transom: FLICKA.

"He's anchored," said Hendricks. "Boy, that's some lot of water to anchor a boat in. We must have more than a hundred feet out here."

"Swell," Brody said. "That's just what I wanted to hear."

When they were about fifty yards from the *Flicka*, Hendricks throttled down, and the boat settled into a slow side-to-side roll. They closed quickly. Brody walked forward and mounted a platform in the bow. He saw no signs of life. There were no rods in the rod-holders. "Hey, Ben!" he called. There was no reply.

"Maybe he's below," said Hendricks.

Brody called again, "Hey, Ben!" The bow of the AquaSport was only a few feet from the port quarter of the *Flicka*. Hendricks pushed the handle into neutral, then gave it a quick burst of reverse. The AquaSport stopped and, on the next swell, nestled up against the *Flicka*'s gunwale. Brody grabbed the gunwale. "Hey, Ben!"

Hendricks took a line from the lazaret, walked forward, and made it fast to a cleat on the bow of the AquaSport. He looped the line over the railing of the other boat and tied a crude knot. "You want to go on board?" he said.

"Yeah." Brody climbed aboard the *Flicka*. Hendricks followed, and they stood in the cockpit. Hendricks poked his head through the forward hatch. "You in there, Ben?" He looked around, withdrew his head, and said, "Not there."

"He's not on board," said Brody. "No two ways about it."

"What's that stuff?" said Hendricks, pointing to a bucket in the corner of the stern.

Brody walked to the bucket and bent down. A stench of fish and oil filled his nose. The bucket was full of guts and blood. "Must be chum," he said. "Fish guts and other shit. You spread it around in the water and it's supposed to attract sharks. He didn't use much of it. The bucket's almost full."

A sudden noise made Brody jump. "Whiskey, zebra, echo, two, five, niner," said a voice crackling over the radio. "This is the *Pretty Belle*. You there, Jake?"

"So much for that theory," said Brody. "He never turned off his radio."

"I don't get it, Chief. There are no rods. He didn't carry a dinghy, so he couldn't have rowed away. He swam like a fish, so if he fell overboard he would've just climbed back on."

"You see a harpoon anywhere?"

"What's it look like?"

"I don't know. Like a harpoon. And barrels. Supposedly, you use them as floats."

"I don't see anything like that."

Brody stood at the starboard gunwale, gazing into the middle distance. The boat moved slightly, and he steadied himself with his right hand. He felt something strange and looked down. There were four ragged screw holes where a cleat had been. The screws had obviously not been removed by a screwdriver; the wood around the holes was torn. "Look at this, Leonard."

Hendricks ran his hand over the holes. He looked to the port side, where a ten-inch steel cleat still sat securely on the wood. "You imagine that what was here was as big as the one over there?" he said. "Jesus, what would it take to pull that mother out?"

"Look here, Leonard." Brody ran his index finger over the outer edge of the gunwale. There was a scar about eight inches long, where the paint had been scraped away and the wood abraded. "It looks like someone took a file to this wood."

"Or else rubbed the hell out of it with an awful tight piece of heavy rope."

Brody walked over to the port side of the cockpit and, aimlessly, began to feel his way along the outer edge of the gunwale. "That's the only place," he said. When he reached the stern, he leaned on the gunwale and gazed down into the water.

For a moment, he stared dumbly at the transom, unseeing. Then a pattern began to take shape, a pattern of holes, deep gouges in the wooden transom, forming a rough semicircle more than three feet across. Next to it was another, similar pattern. And at the bottom of the transom, just at the water line, three short smears of blood. Please, God, thought Brody, not another one. "Come here, Leonard," he said.

Hendricks walked to the stern and looked over. "What?"

"If I hold your legs, you think you can lean over and take a look at those holes down there and try to figure out what made them?"

"What do you think made them?"

"I don't know. But *something*. I want to find out what. Come on. If you can't dope it out in a minute or two, we'll forget about it and go home. Okay?"

"I guess so." Hendricks lay on the top of the transom. "Hold me tight, Chief . . . please."

Brody leaned down and grabbed Hendricks' feet. "Don't worry," he said. He took one of Hendricks' legs under each arm and lifted. Hendricks rose, then bent over the transom. "Okay?" said Brody.

"A little more. Not too much! Jesus, you just dipped my head in the water."

"Sorry. How's that?"

"Okay, that's it." Hendricks began to examine the holes. "What if some shark came along right now?" he grunted. "He could grab me right out of your hands."

"Don't think about it. Just look."

"I'm looking." In a few moments he said, "Sonofabitch. Look at that thing. Hey, pull me up. I need my knife."

"What is it?" Brody asked when Hendricks was back aboard.

Hendricks unfolded the main blade from the body of his pocket knife. "I don't know," he replied. "Some kind of white chip or something, stuck into one of the holes." Knife in hand, he allowed Brody to lower him over the rail again. He worked briefly, his body twisting from the effort. Then he called: "Okay. I've got it. Pull."

Brody stepped backward, hoisting Hendricks over the transom, then lowered Hendricks' feet to the deck. "Let's see," he said, holding out his hand. Into Brody's palm Hendricks dropped a triangle of glistening white denticle. It was nearly two inches long. The sides were tiny saws. Brody scraped the tooth against the gunwale, and it cut the wood. He looked out over the water and shook his head. "My God," he said.

"It's a tooth, isn't it?" said Hendricks. "Jesus Christ Almighty. You think the shark got Ben?"

"I don't know what else to think," said Brody. He looked at

the tooth again, then dropped it into his pocket. "We might as well go. There's nothing we can do here."

"What do you want to do with Ben's boat?"

"We'll leave it here till tomorrow. Then we'll have someone come get it."

"I'll drive it back if you want."

"And leave me to drive the other one? Forget it."

"We could tow one of them in."

"No. It's getting dark, and I don't want to have to fool around trying to dock two boats in the dark. This boat'll be all right overnight. Just go check the anchor up front and make sure it's secure. Then let's go. No one's going to need this boat before tomorrow . . . especially not Ben Gardner."

They arrived at the dock in late twilight. Harry Meadows and another man, unknown to Brody, were waiting for them. "You sure have good antenna, Harry," Brody said as he climbed the ladder onto the dock.

Meadows smiled, flattered. "That's my trade, Martin." He gestured toward the man beside him. "This is Matt Hooper, Chief Brody."

The two men shook hands. "You're the fellow from Woods Hole," Brody said, trying to get a good look at him in the fading light. He was young—mid-twenties, Brody thought—and handsome: tanned, hair bleached by the sun. He was about as tall as Brody, an inch over six feet, but leaner: Brody guessed 170 pounds, compared to his own 200. A mental reflex scanned Hooper for possible threat. Then, with what Brody recognized as juvenile pride, he determined that if it ever came to a face-off, he could take Hooper. Experience would make the difference.

"That's right," said Hooper.

"Harry's been tapping your brain long-distance," Brody said. "How come you're here?"

Meadows said, "I called him. I thought he might be able to figure out what's going on."

"Shit, Harry, all you had to do was ask me," said Brody. "I could have told you. You see, there's this fish out there, and . . ."

"You know what I mean."

Brody sensed his own resentment at the intrusion, the

complication that Hooper's expertise was bound to add, the implicit division of authority that Hooper's arrival had created. And he recognized the resentment as stupid. "Sure, Harry," he said. "No problem. It's just been a long day."

"What did you find out there?" Meadows asked.

Brody started to reach in his pocket for the tooth, but he stopped. He didn't want to go through it all, standing on a dock in near darkness. "I'm not sure," he said. "Come on back to the station and I'll fill you in."

"Is Ben going to stay out there all night?"

"It looks that way, Harry." Brody turned to Hendricks, who had finished tying up the boat. "You going home, Leonard?"

"Yeah. I want to clean up before I go to work."

Brody arrived at police headquarters before Meadows and Hooper. It was almost eight o'clock. He had two phone calls to make—to Ellen, to see if the dinner leftovers could be reheated or if he should pick up something on the way home, and, the call he dreaded, to Sally Gardner. He called Ellen first: pot roast. It could be reheated. It might taste like a sneaker, but it would be warm. He hung up, checked the phone book for the Gardner number, and dialed it.

"Sally? This is Martin Brody." Suddenly he regretted having called without thinking the call through. How much should he tell her? Not much, he decided, at least not until he had had a chance to check with Hooper to see if his theory was plausible or absurd.

"Where's Ben, Martin?" The voice was calm, but pitched slightly higher than Brody remembered as normal.

"I don't know, Sally."

"What do you mean, you don't know? You went out there, didn't you?"

"Yes. He wasn't on the boat."

"But the boat was there."

"The boat was there."

"You went on board? You looked all over it? Even below?"

"Yes." Then a tiny hope. "Ben didn't carry a dinghy, did he?"

"No. How could he not be there?" The voice was shriller now.

"I . . ."

"Where *is* he?"

Brody caught the tone of incipient hysteria. He wished he had gone to the house in person. "Are you alone, Sally?"

"No. The kids are here."

She seemed calmer, but Brody was sure the calm was a lull before the burst of grief that would come when she realized that the fears with which she had lived every day for the sixteen years Ben had been fishing professionally—closet fears shoved into mental recesses and never uttered because they would seem ridiculous—had come true.

Brody dug at his memory for the ages of the Gardner children. Twelve, maybe; then nine, then about six. What kind of kid was the twelve-year-old? He didn't know. Who was the nearest neighbor? Shit. Why didn't he think of this before? The Finleys. "Just a second, Sally." He called to the officer at the front desk. "Clements, call Grace Finley and tell her to get her ass over to Sally Gardner's house right now."

"Suppose she asks why."

"Just tell her I said to go. Tell her I'll explain later." He turned back to the phone. "I'm sorry, Sally. All I can tell you for sure is that we went out to where Ben's boat is anchored. We went on board and Ben wasn't there. We looked around, downstairs and everything."

Meadows and Hooper walked into Brody's office. He motioned them to chairs.

"But where could he be?" said Sally Gardner. "You don't just get off a boat in the middle of the ocean."

"No."

"And he couldn't have fallen overboard. I mean, he could have, but he'd get right back in again."

"Yes."

"Maybe someone came and took him off in another boat. Maybe the engine wouldn't start and he had to ride with someone else. Did you check the engine?"

"No," Brody said, embarrassed.

"That's probably it, then." The voice was subtly lighter, almost girlish, coated with a veneer of hope that, when it broke, would shatter like iced crystal. "And if the battery was dead, that would explain why he couldn't call on the radio."

"The radio was working, Sally."

"Wait a minute. Who's there? Oh, it's you." There was a pause. Brody heard Sally talking to Grace Finley. Then Sally came back on the line. "Grace says you told her to come over here. Why?"

"I thought—"

"You think he's dead, don't you? You think he drowned." The veneer shattered, and she began to sob.

"I'm afraid so, Sally. That's all we can think at the moment. Let me talk to Grace for a minute, will you please?"

A couple of seconds later, the voice of Grace Finley said, "Yes, Martin?"

"I'm sorry to do this to you, but I couldn't think of anything else. Can you stay with her for a while?"

"All night. I will."

"That might be a good idea. I'll try to get over later on. Thanks."

"What happened, Martin?"

"We don't know for sure."

"Is it that . . . *thing* again?"

"Maybe. That's what we're trying to figure out. But do me a favor, Grace. Don't say anything about a shark to Sally. It's bad enough as it is."

"All right, Martin. Wait. Wait a minute." She covered the mouthpiece of the phone with her hand, and Brody heard some muffled conversation. Then Sally Gardner came on the line.

"Why did you do it, Martin?"

"Do what?"

Apparently, Grace Finley tried to take the phone from her hand, for Brody heard Sally say, "Let me speak, damn you!" Then she said to him, "Why did you send him? Why Ben?" Her voice wasn't particularly loud, but she spoke with an intensity that struck Brody as hard as if she were yelling.

"Sally, you're—"

"This didn't have to happen!" she said. "You could have stopped it."

Brody wanted to hang up. He didn't want a repetition of the scene with the Kintner boy's mother. But he had to defend himself. She had to know that it wasn't his fault. How could she blame him? He said, "Crap! Ben was a fisherman, a good one. He knew the risks."

"If you hadn't—"

"Stop it, Sally!" Brody let himself stamp on her words. "Try to get some rest." He hung up the phone. He was furious, but his fury was confused. He was angry at Sally Gardner for accusing him, and angry at himself for being angry at her. If, she had said. If what? If he had not sent Ben. Sure. And if pigs had wings they'd be eagles. If he had gone himself. But that wasn't his trade. He had sent the expert. He looked up at Meadows. "You heard."

"Not all of it. But enough to gather that Ben Gardner has become victim number four."

Brody nodded. "I think so." He told Meadows and Hooper about his trip with Hendricks. Once or twice, Meadows interrupted with a question. Hooper listened, his angular face placid and his eyes—a light, powder blue—fixed on Brody. At the end of his tale, Brody reached into his pants pocket. "We found this," he said. "Leonard dug it out of the wood." He flipped the tooth to Hooper, who turned it over in his hand.

"What do you think, Matt?" said Meadows.

"It's a white."

"How big?"

"I can't be sure, but big. Fifteen, twenty feet. That's some fantastic fish." He looked at Meadows. "Thanks for calling me," he said. "I could spend a whole lifetime around sharks and never see a fish like that."

Brody asked, "How much would a fish like that weigh?"

"Five or six thousand pounds."

Brody whistled. "Three tons."

"Do you have any thoughts about what happened?" Meadows asked.

"From what the chief says, it sounds like the fish killed Mr. Gardner."

"How?" said Brody.

"Any number of ways. Gardner might have fallen overboard. More likely, he was pulled over. His leg may have gotten tangled in a harpoon line. He could even have been taken while he was leaning over the stern."

"How do you account for the teeth in the stern?"

"The fish attacked the boat."

"What the hell for?"

"Sharks aren't very bright, Chief. They exist on instinct and impulse. The impulse to feed is powerful."

"But a thirty-foot boat . . ."

"A shark doesn't think. To him it wasn't a boat. It was just something large."

"And inedible."

"Not till he'd tried it. You have to understand. There's nothing in the sea this fish would fear. Other fish run from bigger things. That's their instinct. But this fish doesn't run from anything. He doesn't know fear. He might be cautious— say around an even bigger white. But fear—no way."

"What else do they attack?"

"Anything."

"Just like that. Anything."

"Pretty much, yes."

"Do you have any idea why he's hung around here so long?" said Brody. "I don't know how much you know about the water here, but . . ."

"I grew up here."

"You did? In Amity?"

"No, Southampton. I spent every summer there, from grade school through grad school."

"Every *summer*. So you didn't really grow up there." Brody was groping for something with which to re-establish his parity with, if not superiority to, the younger man, and what he settled for was reverse snobbism, an attitude not uncommon to year-round residents of resort communities. It gave them armor against the contempt they sensed radiating from the rich summer folk. It was an "I'm all right, Jack" attitude, a social *machismo* that equated wealth with effeteness, simplicity with goodness, and poverty (up to a point) with honesty. And it was an attitude that, in general, Brody found both repugnant and silly. But he had felt threatened by the younger man—he wasn't really sure why—and the sensation was so alien that he had reached for the most convenient carapace, the one Hooper had handed him.

"You're picking nits," Hooper said testily. "Okay, so I wasn't born here. But I've spent a lot of time in these waters, and I wrote a paper on this coastline. Anyway, I know what you're getting at, and you're right. This shoreline isn't an environment that would normally support a long stay by a shark."

"So why is this one staying?"

"It's impossible to say. It's definitely uncharacteristic, but sharks do so many uncharacteristic things that the erratic becomes the normal. Anyone who'd risk money—not to mention his life—on a prediction about what one big shark will do in a given situation is a fool. This shark could be sick. The patterns of his life are so beyond his control that damage to one small mechanism could cause him to disorient and behave strangely."

"If this is how he acts when he's sick," said Brody, "I'd hate to see what he does when he's feeling fine."

"No. Personally, I don't think he's sick. There are other things that could cause him to stay here—many of them things we'll never understand, natural factors, caprices."

"Like what?"

"Changes in water temperature or current flow or feeding patterns. As food supplies move, so do the predators. A few summers ago, for example, a completely inexplicable phenomenon took place off the shore of parts of Connecticut and Rhode Island. The whole coastline was suddenly inundated with menhaden—fishermen call them bunker. Huge schools. Millions of fish. They coated the water like an oil slick. There were so many that you could throw a bare hook in the water and reel it in, and more often than not you'd catch a menhaden by foul-hooking it. Bluefish and bass feed on menhaden, so all of a sudden there were masses of bluefish feeding in schools right off the beaches. In Watch Hill, Rhode Island, people were wading into the surf and catching bluefish with rakes. Garden rakes! Just shoveling the fish out of the water. Then the big predators came—big tuna, four, five, six hundred pounds. Deep-sea fishing boats were catching bluefin tuna within a hundred yards of the shore. In harbors sometimes. Then suddenly it stopped. The menhaden went away, and so did the other fish. I spent three weeks down there trying to figure out what was going on. I still don't know. It's all part of the ecological balance. When something tips too far one way or the other, peculiar things happen."

"But this is even weirder," said Brody. "This fish has stayed in one place, in one chunk of water only a mile or two square, for over a week. He hasn't moved up or down the beach. He hasn't touched anybody in East Hampton or Southampton. What is it about Amity?"

"I don't know. I doubt that anyone could give you a good answer."

Meadows said, "Minnie Eldridge has the answer."

"Balls," said Brody.

"Who's Minnie Eldridge?" asked Hooper.

"The postmistress," said Brody. "She says it's God's will, or something like that. We're being punished for our sins."

Hooper smiled. "Right now, anyway, that's as good an answer as I've got."

"That's encouraging," said Brody. "Is there anything you plan to do to *get* an answer?"

"There are a few things. I'll take water samples here and in East Hampton. I'll try to find out how other fish are behaving —if anything extraordinary is around, or if anything that should be here isn't. And I'll try to find that shark. Which reminds me, is there a boat available?"

"Yes, I'm sorry to say," said Brody. "Ben Gardner's. We'll get you out to it tomorrow, and you can use it at least until we work something out with his wife. Do you really think you can catch that fish, after what happened to Ben Gardner?"

"I didn't say I was going to try to catch it. I don't think I'd want to try that. Not alone, anyway."

"Then what the hell are you going to do?"

"I don't know. I'll have to play it by ear."

Brody looked into Hooper's eyes and said, "I want that fish killed. If you can't do it, we'll find someone who can."

Hooper laughed. "You sound like a mobster. 'I want that fish killed.' So go get a contract out on him. Who are you going to get to do the job?"

"I don't know. What about it, Harry? You're supposed to know everything that goes on around here. Isn't there any fisherman on this whole damn island equipped to catch big sharks?"

Meadows thought for a moment before he spoke. "There may be one. I don't know much about him, but I think his name is Quint, and I think he operates out of a private pier somewhere around Promised Land. I can find out a little more about him if you like."

"Why not?" said Brody. "He sounds like a possible."

Hooper said, "Look, Chief, you can't go off half-cocked looking for vengeance against a fish. That shark isn't evil. It's not a murderer. It's just obeying its own instincts. Trying to get retribution against a fish is crazy."

"Listen you . . ." Brody was growing angry—an anger born of frustration and humiliation. He knew Hooper was right, but he felt that right and wrong were irrelevant to the situation. The fish was an enemy. It had come upon the community and killed two men, a woman, and a child. The people of Amity would demand the death of the fish. They would need to see it dead before they could feel secure enough to resume their normal lives. Most of all, Brody needed it dead, for the death of the fish would be a catharsis for him. Hooper had touched that nerve, and that infuriated Brody further. But he swallowed his rage and said, "Forget it."

The phone rang. "It's for you, Chief," said Clements. "Mr. Vaughan."

"Oh swell. That's just what I need." He punched the flashing button on the phone and picked up the receiver. "Yeah, Larry."

"Hello, Martin. How are you?" Vaughan's voice was friendly, almost effusively so. Brody thought, he's probably had a couple of belts.

"As well as could be expected, Larry."

"You're working pretty late. I tried to get you at home."

"Yeah. Well, when you're the chief of police and your constituents are getting themselves killed every twenty minutes, that kind of keeps you busy."

"I heard about Ben Gardner."

"What did you hear?"

"That he was missing."

"News travels pretty fast."

"Are you sure it was the shark again?"

"Sure? Yeah, I guess so. Nothing else seems to make any sense."

"Martin, what are you going to *do*?" There was a pathetic urgency in Vaughan's voice.

"That's a good question, Larry. We're doing everything we can right now. We've got the beaches closed down. We've—"

"I'm aware of that, to say the very least."

"What's that supposed to mean?"

"Have you ever tried to sell healthy people real estate in a leper colony?"

"No, Larry," Brody said wearily.

"I'm getting cancellations every day. People are walking out on leases. I haven't had a new customer in here since Sunday."

"So what do you want *me* to do?"

"Well, I thought . . . I mean, what I'm wondering is, maybe we're overreacting to this whole thing."

"You're kidding. Tell me you're kidding."

"Hardly, Martin. Now calm down. Let's discuss this rationally."

"I'm rational. I'm not sure about you, though."

There was a moment of silence, and then Vaughan said, "What would you say to opening the beaches, just for the Fourth of July weekend?"

"Not a chance. Not a fucking chance."

"Now listen . . ."

"No, you listen, Larry. The last time I listened to you, we had two people killed. If we catch that fish, if we kill the son-ofabitch, then we'll open the beaches. Until then, forget it."

"What about nets?"

"What about them?"

"Why couldn't we put steel nets out to protect the beaches? Someone told me that's what they do in Australia."

He *must* be drunk, Brody thought. "Larry, this is a straight coastline. Are you going to put nets out along two and a half miles of beaches? Fine. You get the money. I'd say about a million dollars, for openers."

"What about patrols? We could hire people to patrol up and down the beaches in boats."

"That's not good enough, Larry. What is it with you, anyway? Are your partners on your ass again?"

"That's none of your damn business, Martin. For God's sake, man, this town is dying!"

"I know it, Larry," Brody said softly. "And as far as I know, there's not a damn thing we can do about it. Good night." He hung up the phone.

Meadows and Hooper rose to leave. Brody walked them to the front door of the station house. As they started out the door, Brody said to Meadows, "Hey, Harry, you left your lighter inside." Meadows started to say something, but Brody stepped on his words. "Come on back inside and I'll give it to you. If you leave it around here overnight, it's likely to disappear." He waved to Hooper. "See you."

When they were back in Brody's office, Meadows took his lighter from his pocket and said, "I trust you had something to say to me."

Brody shut the door to his office. "You think you can find out something about Larry's partners?"

"I guess so. Why?"

"Ever since this thing began, Larry has been on my ass to keep the beaches open. And now, after all that's just happened, he says he wants them open for the Fourth. The other day he said he was under pressure from his partners. I told you about it."

"And?"

"I think we should know who it is who has enough clout to drive Larry bullshit. I wouldn't care if he wasn't the mayor of this town. But if there are people telling him what to do, I think we ought to know who they are."

Meadows sighed. "Okay, Martin. I'll do what I can. But digging around in Larry Vaughan's affairs isn't my idea of fun."

"There's not a whole hell of a lot that is fun these days, is there?"

Brody walked Meadows to the door, then went back to his desk and sat down. Vaughan had been right about one thing, he thought: Amity was showing all the signs of imminent death. It wasn't just the real estate market, though its sickness was as contagious as smallpox. Evelyn Bixby, the wife of one of Brody's officers, had lost her job as a real estate agent and was working as a waitress in a hash house on Route 27.

Two new boutiques that were scheduled to open the next day had put off their debuts until July 3, and the proprietors of both made a point of calling on Brody to tell him that if the beaches weren't open by then, they wouldn't open their stores at all. One of them was already looking at a site for rent in East Hampton. The sporting goods store had posted signs announcing a clearance sale—a sale that normally took place over the Labor Day weekend. The only good thing about the Amity economy, as far as Brody was concerned, was that Saxon's was doing so badly that it laid off Henry Kimble. Now that he didn't have his bartending job, he slept during the day and could occasionally survive through a shift of police work without a nap.

Beginning on Monday morning—the first day the beaches were closed—Brody had posted two officers on the beaches. Together, they had had seventeen confrontations with people who insisted on swimming. One was with a man named Robert Dexter, who claimed a constitutional right to swim off his own beach and who allowed his dog to terrorize the officer on duty, until the cop pulled his pistol and threatened to shoot the dog. Another dustup took place on the public beach, when a New York lawyer started reading the United States Constitution to a policeman and a multitude of cheering youths.

Still, Brody was convinced that—so far, at least—no one had gone swimming.

On Wednesday, two kids had rented a skiff and rowed about three hundred yards offshore, where they spent an hour ladling blood, chicken guts, and duck heads overboard. A passing fishing boat spotted them and called Brody via the marine operator. Brody called Hooper, and together they went in *Flicka* and towed the boys to shore. In the skiff the boys had a flying gaff attached to two hundred yards of clothesline, secured to the prow by a square knot. They said they planned to hook the shark with the gaff and go for a "Nantucket sleigh ride." Brody told them that if they ever tried the stunt again, he'd arrest them for attempted suicide.

There had been four reports of shark sightings. One had turned out to be a floating log. Two, according to the fisherman who followed up the reports, were schools of jumping bait fish. And one, as far as anyone could tell, was a flat nothing.

On Tuesday evening, just at dusk, Brody had received an anonymous phone call telling him that a man was dumping shark bait into the water off the public beach. It turned out to be not a man, but a woman dressed in a man's raincoat—Jessie Parker, one of the clerks at Walden's Stationery Store. At first she denied throwing anything into the water, but then she admitted that she had tossed a paper bag into the surf. It contained three empty vermouth bottles.

"Why didn't you throw them in the garbage?" Brody had asked.

"I didn't want the garbage man to think I'm a heavy drinker."

"Then why didn't you throw them in someone else's garbage?"

"That wouldn't be nice," she said. "Garbage is . . . sort of private, don't you think?"

Brody told her that from now on, she should take her empty bottles, put them in a plastic bag, put that bag in a brown paper bag, then smash the bottles with a hammer until they were ground up. Nobody would ever know they had been bottles.

Brody looked at his watch. It was after nine, too late to pay a visit to Sally Gardner. He hoped she was asleep. Maybe Grace Finley had given her a pill or a glass of whiskey to help her rest. Before he left the office, he called the Coast Guard station at Montauk and told the duty officer about Ben Gardner. The officer said he would dispatch a patrol boat at first light to search for the body.

"Thanks," said Brody. "I hope you find it before it washes up." Brody was suddenly appalled at himself. "It" was Ben Gardner, a friend. What would Sally say if she heard Brody refer to her husband as "it"? Fifteen years of friendship wiped out, forgotten. There was no more Ben Gardner. There was only an "it" that should be found before it became a gory nuisance.

"We'll try," said the officer. "Boy, I feel for you guys. You must be having a hell of a summer."

"I only hope it isn't our last," said Brody. He hung up, turned out the light in his office, and walked out to his car.

As he turned into his driveway, Brody saw the familiar blue-gray light shining from the living room windows. The boys were watching television. He walked through the front door, flipped off the outside light, and poked his head into the dark living room. The oldest boy, Billy, lay on the couch, leaning on an elbow. Martin, the middle son, age twelve, lounged in an easy chair, his shoeless feet propped up on the coffee table. Eight-year-old Sean sat on the floor, his back against the couch, stroking a cat in his lap. "How goes it?" said Brody.

"Good, Dad," said Bill, without shifting his gaze from the television.

"Where's your mom?"

"Upstairs. She said to tell you your dinner's in the kitchen."

"Okay. Not too late, Sean, huh? It's almost nine-thirty."

"Okay, Dad," said Sean.

Brody went into the kitchen, opened the refrigerator, and took out a beer. The remains of the pot roast sat on the kitchen table in a roasting pan, surrounded by a scum of congealed gravy. The meat was brownish-gray and stringy. "Dinner?" said Brody to himself. He checked the icebox for sandwich makings. There was some hamburger, a package of chicken legs, a dozen eggs, a jar of pickles, and twelve cans of soda pop. He found a piece of American cheese, dried and curled with age, and he folded it and popped it into his mouth. He debated heating up the pot roast, then said aloud, "The hell with it." He found two pieces of bread, spread mustard on them, took a carving knife from a magnetic board on the wall, and sliced a thick slab of roast. He dropped the meat on one of the pieces of bread, scattered a few pickles on top of it, covered it with the other piece of bread, and mashed the sandwich down with the heel of his hand. He put it on a plate, picked up his beer, and climbed the stairs to his bedroom.

Ellen was sitting up in bed, reading *Cosmopolitan*. "Hello," she said. "A tough day? You didn't say anything on the phone."

"A tough day. That's about all we're having these days. You heard about Ben Gardner? I wasn't really positive when I

talked to you." He put the plate and the beer on the dresser
and sat on the edge of the bed to remove his shoes.

"Yes. I got a call from Grace Finley asking if I knew where
Dr. Craig was. His service wouldn't say, and Grace wanted to
give Sally a sedative."

"Did you find him?"

"No. But I had one of the boys take some Seconal over to
her."

"What's Seconal?"

"Sleeping pills."

"I didn't know you were taking sleeping pills."

"I don't, often. Just every now and then."

"Where did you get them?"

"From Dr. Craig, when I went to him last time about my
nerves. I told you."

"Oh." Brody tossed his shoes into a corner, stood up, and
took off his trousers, which he folded neatly over the back of a
chair. He took off his shirt, put it on a hanger, and hung it in
the closet. In T-shirt and undershorts he sat down on the bed
and began to eat his sandwich. The meat was dry and flaky.
All he could taste was mustard.

"Didn't you find the roast?" said Ellen.

Brody's mouth was full, so he nodded.

"What's that you're eating, then?"

He swallowed. "The roast."

"Did you heat it up?"

"No. I don't mind it like this."

Ellen made a face and said, "Yech."

Brody ate in silence, as Ellen aimlessly turned the pages of
her magazine. After a few moments, she closed the magazine,
put it in her lap, and said, "Oh, dear."

"What's the matter?"

"I was just thinking about Ben Gardner. It's so horrible.
What do you think Sally will do?"

"I don't know," said Brody. "I worry about her. Have you
ever talked money with her?"

"Never. But there can't be much. I don't think her children
have had new clothes in a year, and she's always saying that
she'd give anything to be able to afford meat more than once a

week, instead of having to eat the fish Ben catches. Will she get social security?"

"I'd think so, but it won't amount to much. There's welfare."

"Oh, she couldn't," said Ellen.

"You wait. Pride is something she won't be able to afford. Now there won't even be fish anymore."

"Is there anything we can do?"

"Personally? I don't see how. We're not exactly in fat city ourselves. But there may be something the town can do. I'll talk to Vaughan about it."

"Have you made any progress?"

"You mean about catching that damn thing? No. Meadows called the oceanographer friend of his down from Woods Hole, so he's here. Not that I see what good he's going to do."

"What's he like?"

"He's all right, I guess. He's young, a decent-looking guy. He's a bit of a know-it-all, but that's not surprising. He seems to know the area pretty well."

"Oh? How so?"

"He said he was a summer kid in Southampton. Spent all his summers there."

"Working?"

"I don't know, living with the parents probably. He looks to be the type."

"What type?"

"Rich. Good family. The Southampton summer type. You ought to know it, for God's sake."

"Don't get angry. I was just asking."

"I'm not angry. I just said you ought to know the type, that's all. I mean, you're the type yourself."

Ellen smiled. "I used to be. But now I'm just an old lady."

"That's a crock," Brody said. "Nine out of ten of the summer broads in this town can't do what you can for a bathing suit." He was happy to see her fishing for compliments, and happy to give them to her. This was one of their ritual preludes to sex, and the sight of Ellen in bed made Brody yearn for sex. Her hair hung down to her shoulders on both sides of her head, then tucked inward in a curl. Her nightgown was cut so deeply in front that both her breasts were visible, all but the nipples, and was so diaphanous that Brody was sure he could actually see the dark flesh of the nipples. "I'm going to brush my teeth," he said. "I'll be right back."

When he returned from the bathroom, he was tumescent. He walked to the dresser to turn out the light.

"You know," Ellen said, "I think we should give the boys tennis lessons."

"What for? Have they said they want to play tennis?"

"No. Not in so many words. But it's a good sport for them to know. It will help them when they're grown up. It's an entrée."

"To what?"

"To the people they should know. If you play tennis well, you can walk into a club anywhere and get to know people. Now's the time they should be learning."

"Where are they going to get lessons?"

"I was thinking of the Field Club."

"As far as I know, we're not members of the Field Club."

"I think we could get in. I still know a few people who are members. If I asked them, I'll bet they'd propose us."

"Forget it."

"Why?"

"Number one, we can't afford it. I bet it costs a thousand bucks to join, and then it's at least a few hundred a year. We haven't got that kind of money."

"We have savings."

"Not for tennis lessons, for Christ's sake! Come on, let's drop it." He reached for the light.

"It would be good for the boys."

Brody let his hand fall to the top of the dresser. "Look, we're not tennis people. We wouldn't feel right there. *I* wouldn't feel right there. They don't want us there."

"How do you know? We've never tried."

"Just forget it." He switched off the light, walked over to the bed, pulled back the covers, and slid in beside Ellen. "Besides," he said, nuzzling her neck, "there's another sport I'm better at."

"The boys are awake."

"They're watching television. They wouldn't know it if a bomb went off up here." He kissed her neck and began to rub his hand in circles on her stomach, moving higher with each rotation.

Ellen yawned. "I'm so sleepy," she said. "I took a pill before you came home."

Brody stopped rubbing. "What the hell for?"

"I didn't sleep well last night, and I didn't want to wake up if you came home late. So I took a pill."

"I'm going to throw those goddam pills away." He kissed her cheek, then tried to kiss her mouth but caught her in mid-yawn.

"I'm sorry," she said. "I'm afraid it won't work."

"It'll work. All you have to do is help a little."

"I'm so tired. But you go ahead if you want. I'll try to stay awake."

"Shit," said Brody. He rolled back to his side of the bed. "I'm not very big on screwing corpses."

"That was uncalled for."

Brody didn't reply. He lay on his back, staring at the ceiling and feeling his erection dwindle. But the pressure inside him was still there, a dull ache in his groin.

A moment later, Ellen said, "What's Harry Meadows' friend's name?"

"Hooper."

"Not David Hooper."

"No, I think his name is Matt."

"Oh. I went out with a David Hooper a long, long time ago. I remember . . ." Before she could finish the sentence, her eyes shut, and soon she slipped into the deep breathing of sleep.

A FEW BLOCKS away, in a small clapboard house, a black man sat at the foot of his son's bed. "What story do you want to read?" he said.

"I don't want to read a story," said the boy, who was seven. "I want to *tell* a story."

"Okay. What'll we tell one about?"

"A shark. Let's tell one about a shark."

The man winced. "No. Let's tell one about . . . a bear."

"No, a shark. I want to know about sharks."

"You mean a once-upon-a-time story?"

"Sure. Like, you know, once upon a time there was a shark that ate people."

"That's not a very nice story."

"Why do sharks eat people?"

"I guess they get hungry. I don't know."

"Do you bleed if a shark eats you?"

"Yes," said the man. "Come on. Let's tell a story about another kind of animal. You'll have nightmares if we tell about a shark."

"No, I won't. If a shark tried to eat me, I'd punch him in the nose."

"No shark is going to try to eat you."

"Why not? If I go swimming I bet one would. Don't sharks eat black people?"

"Now stop it! I don't want to hear any more about sharks." The man lifted a pile of books from the bedside table. "Here. Let's read *Peter Pan.*"

Part Two

6

ON HER WAY home Friday noon, after a morning of volunteer
work at the Southampton Hospital, Ellen stopped at the post
office to buy a roll of stamps and get the mail. There was no
home mail delivery in Amity. In theory, only special delivery
mail was brought to the door—any door within a mile radius
of the post office; in fact, even special delivery mail (except
that clearly labeled as sent by the Federal Government) was
kept at the post office until someone called for it.

The post office was a small, square building on Teal Street,
just off Main. It had 500 mailboxes, 340 of which were rented
to Amity's permanent residents. The other 160 were allotted
to summer people, according to the whims of the postmistress, Minnie Eldridge. Those people she liked were permitted
to rent boxes for the summer. Those she didn't like had to
wait in line at the counter. Since she refused to rent a box to
any summer person on a year-round basis, summer people
never knew from one year to the next whether or not they
would have a mailbox when they arrived in June.

It was generally assumed that Minnie Eldridge was in her
early seventies, and that she had somehow convinced the authorities in Washington that she was well under compulsory
retirement age. She was small and frail-looking, but decep-
tively strong, able to hustle packages and cartons nearly as
quickly as the two young men who worked in the post office
with her. She never spoke about her past or her private life.
The only common knowledge about her was that she had been
born on Nantucket Island and had left sometime soon after

World War I. She had been in Amity for as long as anyone living could remember, and she considered herself not only a native, but also the resident expert on the history of the town. She needed no prodding at all to embark on a discourse about Amity's eponym, a seventeenth-century woman named Amity Hopewell who had been convicted of witchcraft, and she took pleasure in reciting the list of major events in the town's past: the landing of some British troops during the Revolution in an ill-fated attempt to outflank a Colonial force (the Britons lost their way and wandered aimlessly back and forth across Long Island); the fire in 1823 that destroyed every building except the town's only church; the wreck of a rum-running ship in 1921 (the ship was eventually refloated, but by then all the cargo off-loaded to make the ship lighter had vanished); the hurricane of 1938, and the widely reported (though never fully ascertained) landing of three German spies on the Scotch Road beach in 1942.

Ellen and Minnie made each other nervous. Ellen sensed that Minnie didn't like her, and she was right. Minnie felt uneasy with Ellen because she couldn't catalogue her. Ellen was neither summer folk nor winter folk. She hadn't earned her year-round mailbox, she had married it.

Minnie was alone in the post office, sorting mail, when Ellen arrived.

"Morning, Minnie," Ellen said.

Minnie looked up at the clock over the counter and said, "Afternoon."

"Could I have a roll of eights, please?" Ellen put a five-dollar bill and three ones on the counter.

Minnie pushed a few more letters into boxes, set down her bundle, and walked to the counter. She gave Ellen a roll of stamps and dropped the bills into a drawer. "What's Martin think he's going to do about that shark?" she said.

"I don't know. I guess they'll try to catch it."

"Canst thou draw out leviathan with a hook?"

"I beg your pardon?"

"Book of Job," said Minnie. "No mortal man's going to catch that fish."

"Why do you say that?"

"We're not meant to catch it, that's why. We're being readied."

"For what?"

"We'll know when the time comes."

"I see." Ellen put the stamps in her purse. "Well, maybe you're right. Thanks, Minnie." She turned and walked toward the door.

"There'll be no mistaking it," Minnie said to Ellen's back.

Ellen walked to Main Street and turned right, past a boutique and an antique shop. She stopped at Amity Hardware and went inside. There was no immediate response to the tinkle of the bell that the door struck as she opened it. She waited for a few seconds, then called, "Albert?"

She walked to the back of the store, to an open door that led to the basement. She heard two men talking below.

"I'll be right up," called the voice of Albert Morris. "Here's a whole box of them," Morris said to the other man. "Look through and see if you find what you want."

Morris came to the bottom of the stairs and started up—slowly and deliberately, one step at a time, holding on to the banister. He was in his early sixties, and he had had a heart attack two years earlier.

"Cleats," he said when he reached the top of the stairs.

"What?" said Ellen.

"Cleats. Fella wants cleats for a boat. Size he's looking for, he must be the captain of a battleship. Anyway, what can I do for you?"

"The rubber nozzle in my kitchen sink is all cracked. You know, the kind with the switch for spraying. I want to get a new one."

"No problem. They're up this way." Morris led Ellen to a cabinet in the middle of the store. "This what you had in mind?" He held up a rubber nozzle.

"Perfect."

"Eighty cents. Charge or cash?"

"I'll pay you for it. I don't want you to have to write up a slip just for eighty cents."

"Written 'em a lot smaller 'n that," said Morris. "I could tell you stories that'd set your ears to ringing."

They walked across the narrow store to the cash register,

and as he rang up the sale on the register, Morris said, "Lots of people upset about this shark thing."

"I know. You can't blame them."

"They think the beaches oughta be opened up again."

"Well, I . . ."

"You ask me, I think they're full of—pardon the expression —bull. I think Martin's doing right."

"I'm glad to know that, Albert."

"Maybe this new fella can help us out."

"Who's that?"

"This fish expert from up Massachusetts."

"Oh yes. I heard he was in town."

"He's right here."

Ellen looked around and saw no one. "What do you mean?"

"Down cellar. He's the one wants the cleats."

Just then, Ellen heard footsteps on the stairs. She turned and saw Hooper coming the through the door, and she suddenly felt a surge of girlish nervousness, as if she were seeing a beau she hadn't seen in years. The man was a stranger, yet there was something familiar about him.

"I found them," said Hooper, holding up two large stainless-steel cleats. He walked over to the counter, smiled politely at Ellen, and said to Morris, "These'll do fine." He put the cleats on the counter and handed Morris a twenty-dollar bill.

Ellen looked at Hooper, trying to define her reminiscence. She hoped Albert Morris would introduce them, but he seemed to have no intention of doing so. "Excuse me," she said to Hooper, "but I have to ask you something."

Hooper looked at her and smiled again—a pleasant, friendly smile that softened the sharpness of his features and made his light blue eyes shine. "Sure," he said. "Ask away."

"You aren't by any chance related to David Hooper, are you?"

"He's my older brother. Do you know David?"

"Yes," said Ellen. "Or rather, I used to. I went out with him a long time ago. I'm Ellen Brody. I used to be Ellen Shepherd. Back then, I mean."

"Oh sure. I remember you."

"You don't."

"I do. No kidding. I'll prove it to you. Let me see. . . . You wore your hair shorter then, sort of a pageboy. You always wore a charm bracelet. I remember that because it had a big charm that looked like the Eiffel Tower. And you always used to sing that song—what was it called?—'Sh-Boom,' or something like that. Right?"

Ellen laughed. "My heavens, you have quite a memory. I'd forgotten that song."

"It's screwy the things that impress kids. You went out with David for what—two years?"

"Two summers," Ellen said. "They were fun. I hadn't thought about them much in the past few years."

"Do you remember me?"

"Vaguely. I'm not sure. I remember David had a younger brother. You must have been about nine or ten then."

"About that; David's ten years older than I am. Another thing I remember: Everybody called me Matt. I thought it sounded grown up. But you called me Matthew. You said it sounded more dignified. I was probably in love with you."

"Oh?" Ellen reddened, and Albert Morris laughed.

"At one time or another," said Hooper, "I fell in love with all the girls David went out with."

"Oh."

Morris handed Hooper his change, and Hooper said to Ellen, "I'm going down to the dock. Can I drop you anywhere?"

"Thank you. I have a car." She thanked Morris, and, with Hooper behind her, walked out of the store. "So now you're a scientist," she said when they were outside.

"Kind of by accident. I started out as an English major. But then I took a course in marine biology to satisfy my science requirement, and—bingo!—I was hooked."

"On what? The ocean?"

"No. I mean, yes and no. I was always crazy about the ocean. When I was twelve or thirteen, my idea of a big time was to take a sleeping bag down to the beach and spend the night lying in the sand listening to the waves, wondering where they had come from and what fantastic things they had passed on the way. What I got hooked on in college was fish, or, to be really specific, sharks."

Ellen laughed. "What an awful thing to fall in love with. It's like having a passion for rats."

"That's what most people think," said Hooper. "But they're wrong. Sharks have everything a scientist dreams of. They're beautiful—God, how beautiful they are! They're like an impossibly perfect piece of machinery. They're as graceful as any bird. They're as mysterious as any animal on earth. No one knows for sure how long they live or what impulses—except for hunger—they respond to. There are more than two hundred and fifty species of shark, and every one is different from every other one. Scientists spend their lives trying to find answers about sharks, and as soon as they come up with a nice, pat generalization, something shoots it down. People have been trying to find an effective shark repellent for over two thousand years. They've never found one that really works." He stopped, looked at Ellen, and smiled. "I'm sorry. I don't mean to lecture. As you can see, I'm an addict."

"And as *you* can see," said Ellen, "I don't know what I'm talking about. I imagine you went to Yale."

"Of course. Where else? For four generations, the only male in our family who didn't go to Yale was an uncle of mine who got thrown out of Andover and ended up at Miami of Ohio. After Yale, I went to graduate school at the University of Florida. And after that, I spent a couple of years chasing sharks around the world."

"That must have been interesting."

"For me it was paradise. It was like giving an alcoholic the keys to a distillery. I tagged sharks in the Red Sea and dove with them off Australia. The more I learned about them, the more I knew I didn't know."

"You dove with them?"

Hooper nodded. "In a cage mostly, but sometimes not. I know what you must think. A lot of people think I've got a death wish—my mother in particular. But if you know what you're doing, you can reduce the danger to almost nil."

"You must be the world's greatest living shark expert."

"Hardly," Hooper said with a laugh. "But I'm trying. The one trip I missed out on, the one I would have given anything to go on, was Peter Gimbel's trip. It was made into a movie. I dream about that trip. They were in the water with two great whites, the same kind of shark that's here now."

"I'm just as glad you didn't go on that trip," said Ellen. "You probably would have tried to see what the view was like from inside one of the sharks. But tell me about David. How is he?"

"He's okay, all things considered. He's a broker in San Francisco."

"What do you mean, 'all things considered'?"

"Well, he's on his second wife. His first wife was—maybe you know this—Patty Fremont."

"Sure. I used to play tennis with her. She sort of inherited David from me. That's a nice way of putting it."

"That lasted three years, until she latched on to someone with a family business and a house in Antibes. So David went and found himself a girl whose father is the majority stockholder in an oil company. She's nice enough, but she's got the IQ of an artichoke. If David had any sense, he would have known when he had it good and he would have held on to you."

Ellen blushed and said softly, "You're nice to say it."

"I'm serious. That's what I'd have done if I'd been him."

"What did you do? What lucky girl finally got you?"

"None, so far. I guess there are girls around who just don't know how lucky they could be." Hooper laughed. "Tell me about yourself. No, don't. Let me guess. Three children. Right?"

"Right. I didn't realize it showed that much."

"No no. I don't mean that. It doesn't show at all. Not at all. Your husband is—let's see—a lawyer. You have an apartment in town and a house on the beach in Amity. You couldn't be happier. And that's exactly what I'd wish for you."

Ellen shook her head, smiling. "Not quite. I don't mean the happiness part, the rest. My husband is the police chief in Amity."

Hooper let the surprise show in his eyes for only an instant. Then he smacked himself on the forehead and said, "What a dummy I am! Of course. Brody. I never made the connection. That's great. I met your husband last night. He seems like quite a guy."

Ellen thought she detected a flicker of irony in Hooper's voice, but then she told herself, Don't be stupid—you're making things up. "How long will you be here?" she said.

"I don't know. That depends on what happens with this fish. As soon as he leaves, I'll leave."

"Do you live in Woods Hole?"

"No, but not far away. In Hyannisport. I have a little house on the water. I have a thing about being near the water. If I get more than ten miles inland, I begin to feel claustrophobic."

"You live all alone?"

"All alone. It's just me and about a hundred million dollars' worth of stereo equipment and a million books. Hey, do you still dance?"

"Dance?"

"Yeah. I just remembered. One of the things David used to say was that you were the best dancer he ever went out with. You won a contest, didn't you?"

The past—like a bird long locked in a cage and suddenly released—was flying at her, swirling around her head, showering her with longing. "A samba contest," she said. "At the Beach Club. I'd forgotten. No, I don't dance anymore. Martin doesn't dance, and even if he did, I don't think anyone plays that kind of music anymore."

"That's too bad. David said you were terrific."

"That was a wonderful night," Ellen said, letting her mind float back, picking out the tiny memories. "It was a Lester Lanin band. The Beach Club was covered with crepe paper and balloons. David wore his favorite jacket—red silk."

"I have it now," said Hooper. "I inherited *that* from *him.*"

"They played all those wonderful songs. 'Mountain Greenery' was one. He could two-step so well. I could barely keep up with him. The only thing he wouldn't do was waltz. He said waltzes made him dizzy. Everybody was so tan. I don't think there was any rain all summer long. I remember I chose a yellow dress for that night because it went with my tan. There were two contests, a charleston that Susie Kendall and Chip Fogarty won. And the samba contest. They played 'Brazil' in the finals, and we danced as if our lives depended on it. Bending sideways and backward like crazy people. I thought I was going to collapse when it was over. You know what we won for first prize? A canned chicken. I kept it in my room until it got so old it began to swell and Daddy made me throw it away." Ellen smiled. "Those were fun times. I try not to think about them too much."

"Why?"

"The past always seems better when you look back on it than it did at the time. And the present never looks as good as it will in the future. It's depressing if you spend too much time reliving the old joys. You think you'll never have anything as good again."

"It's easy for me to keep my mind off the past."

"Really? Why?"

"It just wasn't too great, that's all. David was the first-born. I was pretty much of an afterthought. I think my purpose in life was to keep the parents' marriage together. And I failed. That's pretty crummy when you fail at the first thing you're supposed to accomplish. David was twenty when the parents got divorced. I wasn't even eleven. And the divorce wasn't ex- actly amiable. The few years before it weren't too amiable, either. It's the old story—nothing special—but it wasn't a lot of fun. I probably make too much of it. Anyway, I look for- ward to a lot of things. I don't look back a lot."

"I suppose that's healthier."

"I don't know. Maybe if I had a terrific past, I'd spend all my time living in it. But . . . enough of that. I should get down to the dock. You're sure I can't drop you anywhere."

"Positive, thank you. My car's just across the street."

"Okay. Well . . ." Hooper held out his hand. "It's been really great to see you again, and I hope I'll see you before I go."

"I'd like that," said Ellen, shaking his hand.

"I don't suppose I could get you out on a tennis court late some afternoon."

Ellen laughed. "Oh my. I haven't held a tennis racket in my hand since I can't remember when. But thanks for asking."

"Okay. Well, see you." Hooper turned and trotted the few yards down the block to his car, a green Ford Pinto.

Ellen stood and watched as Hooper started the car, ma- neuvered out of the parking space, and pulled out into the street. As he drove past her, she raised her hand to her shoulder and waved, tentatively, shyly. Hooper stuck his left hand out of the car window and waved. Then he turned the corner and was gone.

A terrible, painful sadness clutched at Ellen. More than ever before, she felt that her life—the best part of it, at least, the part that was fresh and fun—was behind her. Recognizing the sensation made her feel guilty, for she read it as proof that she was an unsatisfactory mother, an unsatisfied wife. She hated her life, and hated herself for hating it. She thought of a line from a song Billy played on the stereo: "I'd trade all my tomorrows for a single yesterday." Would she make a deal like that? She wondered. But what good was there in wondering? Yesterdays were gone, spinning ever farther away down a shaft that had no bottom. None of the richness, none of the delight, could ever be retrieved.

A vision of Hooper's smiling face flashed across her mind. Forget it, she told herself. That's stupid. Worse. It's self-defeating.

She walked across the street and climbed into her car. As she pulled out into the traffic, she saw Larry Vaughan standing on the corner. God, she thought, he looks as sad as I feel.

7

THE WEEKEND WAS as quiet as the weekends in the late fall. With the beaches closed, and with the police patrolling them during the daylight hours, Amity was practically deserted. Hooper cruised up and down the shore in Ben Gardner's boat, but the only signs of life he saw in the water were a few schools of baitfish and one small school of bluefish. By Sunday night, after spending the day off East Hampton—the beaches there were crowded, and he thought there might be a chance the shark would appear where people were swimming —he told Brody he was ready to conclude that the fish had gone back to the deep.

"What makes you think so?" Brody had asked.

"There's not a sign of him," said Hooper. "And there are other fish around. If there was a big white in the neighborhood, everything else would vanish. That's one of the things divers say about whites. When they're around, there's an awful stillness in the water."

"I'm not convinced," said Brody. "At least not enough to open the beaches. Not yet." He knew that after an uneventful weekend there would be pressure—from Vaughan, from other real estate agents, from merchants—to open the beaches. He almost wished Hooper had seen the fish. That would have been a certainty. Now there was nothing but negative evidence, and to his policeman's mind that was not enough.

On Monday afternoon, Brody was sitting in his office when Bixby announced a phone call from Ellen.

"I'm sorry to bother you," she said, "but I wanted to check

something with you. What would you think about giving a dinner party?"

"What for?"

"Just to have a dinner party. We haven't had one in years. I can't even remember when our last one was."

"No," said Brody. "Neither can I." But it was a lie. He remembered all too well their last dinner party: three years ago, when Ellen was in the midst of her crusade to re-establish her ties with the summer community. She had asked three summer couples. They were nice enough people, Brody recalled, but the conversations had been stiff, forced, and uncomfortable. Brody and his guests had searched each other for any common interest or experience, and they had failed. So after a while, the guests had fallen back on talking among themselves, self-consciously polite about including Ellen whenever she said something like, "Oh, I remember him!" She had been nervous and flighty, and after the guests had left, after she had done the dishes and said twice to Brody, *"Wasn't* that a nice evening!" she had shut herself in the bathroom and wept.

"Well, what do you think?" said Ellen.

"I don't know. I guess it's all right, if you want to do it. Who are you going to invite?"

"First of all, I think we should have Matt Hooper."

"What for? He eats over at the Abelard, doesn't he? It's all included in the price of the room."

"That's not the point, Martin. You know that. He's alone in town, and besides, he's very nice."

"How do you know? I didn't think you knew him."

"Didn't I tell you? I ran into him in Albert Morris' on Friday. I'm *sure* I mentioned it to you."

"No, but never mind. It doesn't make any difference."

"It turns out he's the brother of the Hooper I used to know. He remembered a lot more about me than I did about him. But he *is* a lot younger."

"Uh-huh. When are you planning this shindig for?"

"I was thinking about tomorrow night. And it's not going to be a shindig. I simply thought we could have a nice, small party with a few couples. Maybe six or eight people altogether."

"Do you think you can get people to come on that short notice?"

"Oh yes. Nobody does anything during the week. There are a few bridge parties, but that's about all."

"Oh," said Brody. "You mean summer people."

"That's what I had in mind. Matt would certainly feel at ease with them. What about the Baxters? Would they be fun?"

"I don't think I know them."

"Yes, you do, silly. Clem and Cici Baxter. She was Cici Davenport. They live out on Scotch. He's taking some vacation now. I know because I saw him on the street this morning."

"Okay. Try them if you want."

"Who else?"

"Somebody I can talk to. How about the Meadows?"

"But he already knows Harry."

"He doesn't know Dorothy. She's chatty enough."

"All right," said Ellen. "I guess a little local color won't hurt. And Harry does know everything that goes on around here."

"I wasn't thinking about local color," Brody said sharply. "They're our friends."

"I know. I didn't mean anything."

"If you want local color, all you have to do is look in the other side of your bed."

"I *know*. I said I was sorry."

"What about a girl?" said Brody. "I think you should try to find some nice young thing for Hooper."

There was a pause before Ellen said, "If you think so."

"I don't really care. I just thought he might enjoy himself more if he had someone his own age to talk to."

"He's not *that* young, Martin. And we're not *that* old. But all right. I'll see if I can think of somebody who'd be fun for him."

"I'll see you later," Brody said, and he hung up the phone. He was depressed, for he saw something ominous in this dinner party. He couldn't be sure, but he believed—and the more he thought about it, the stronger the belief became—that Ellen was launching another campaign to re-enter the world he had taken her from, and this time she had a lever with which to jimmy her way in: Hooper.

The next evening, Brody arrived home a little after five. Ellen was setting the dinner table in the dining room. Brody kissed her on the cheek and said, "Boy, it's been a long time since I've seen that silver." It was Ellen's wedding silver, a gift from her parents.

"I know. It took me hours to polish it."

"And will you look at this?" Brody picked up a tulip wine glass. "Where did you get these?"

"I bought them at the Lure."

"How much?" Brody set the glass down on the table.

"Not much," she said, folding a napkin and placing it neatly beneath a dinner fork and salad fork.

"How much?"

"Twenty dollars. But that was for a whole dozen."

"You don't kid around when you throw a party."

"We didn't have any decent wine glasses," she said defensively. "The last of our old ones broke months ago, when Sean tipped over the sideboard."

Brody counted the places set around the table. "Only six?" he said. "What happened?"

"The Baxters couldn't make it. Cici called. Clem had to go into town on some business, and she thought she'd go with him. They're spending the night." There was a fragile lift to her voice, a false insouciance.

"Oh," said Brody. "Too bad." He dared not show that he was pleased. "Who'd you get for Hooper, some nice young chick?"

"Daisy Wicker. She works for Gibby at the Bibelot. She's a nice girl."

"What time are people coming?"

"The Meadows and Daisy at seven-thirty. I asked Matthew for seven."

"I thought his name was Matt."

"Oh, that's just an old joke he reminded me of. Apparently, I used to call him Matthew when he was young. The reason I wanted him to come early was so the kids would have a chance to get to know him. I think they'll be fascinated."

Brody looked at his watch. "If people aren't coming till seven-thirty, that means we won't be eating till eight-thirty or nine. I'll probably starve to death before then. I think I'll grab a sandwich." He started for the kitchen.

"Don't stuff yourself," said Ellen. "I've got a delicious dinner coming."

Brody sniffed the kitchen aromas, eyed the clutter of pots and packages, and said, "What are you cooking?"

"It's called butterfly lamb," she said. "I hope I don't do something stupid and botch it."

"Smells good," said Brody. "What's this stuff by the sink? Should I throw it out and wash the pot?"

From the living room Ellen said, "What stuff?"

"This stuff in the pot."

"What—omigod!" she said, and she hurried into the kitchen. "Don't you dare throw it out." She saw the smile on Brody's face. "Oh, you rat." She slapped him on the rear. "That's gazpacho. Soup."

"Are you sure it's still okay?" he teased. "It looks all slimy."

"That's what it's supposed to look like, you clot."

Brody shook his head. "Old Hooper's going to wish he ate at the Abelard."

"You're a beast," she said. "Wait till you taste it. You'll change your tune."

"Maybe. If I live long enough." He laughed and went to the refrigerator. He rummaged around and found some bologna and cheese for a sandwich. He opened a beer and started for the living room. "I think I'll watch the news for a while and then go shower and change," he said.

"I put clean clothes out for you on the bed. You might shave, too. You have a hideous five o'clock shadow."

"Good God, who's coming to dinner—Prince Philip and Jackie Onassis?"

"I just want you to look nice, that's all."

At 7:05, the doorbell rang, and Brody answered it. He was wearing a blue madras shirt, blue uniform slacks, and black cordovans. He felt crisp and clean. Spiffy, Ellen had said. But when he opened the door for Hooper, he felt, if not rumpled, at least outclassed. Hooper wore bell-bottom bluejeans, Weejun loafers with no socks, and a red Lacoste shirt with an alligator on the breast. It was the uniform of the young and rich in Amity.

"Hi," said Brody. "Come in."

"Hi," said Hooper. He extended his hand, and Brody shook it.

Ellen came out of the kitchen. She was wearing a long batik skirt, slippers, and a blue silk blouse. She wore the string of cultured pearls Brody had given her as a wedding present. "Matthew," she said. "I'm glad you could come."

"I'm glad you asked me," Hooper said, shaking Ellen's hand. "I'm sorry I don't look more respectable, but I didn't bring anything down with me but working clothes. All I can say for them is that they're clean."

"Don't be silly," said Ellen. "You look wonderful. The red goes beautifully with your tan and your hair."

Hooper laughed. He turned and said to Brody, "Do you mind if I give Ellen something?"

"What do you mean?" Brody said. He thought to himself, Give her what? A kiss? A box of chocolates? A punch in the nose?

"A present. It's nothing, really. Just something I picked up."

"No, I don't mind," said Brody, still perplexed that the question should have been asked.

Hooper dug into the pocket of his jeans and pulled out a small package wrapped in tissue. He handed it to Ellen. "For the hostess," he said, "to make up for my grubby clothes."

Ellen tittered and carefully unwrapped the paper. Inside was what seemed to be a charm, or perhaps a necklace pendant, an inch or so across. "It's lovely," she said. "What is it?"

"It's a shark tooth," said Hooper. "A tiger-shark tooth, to be more specific. The casing's silver."

"Where did you get it?"

"In Macao. I passed through there a couple of years ago on a project. There was a little back-street store, where an even littler Chinese man spent his whole life polishing shark teeth and molding the silver caps to hold the rings. I couldn't resist them."

"Macao," said Ellen. "I don't think I could place Macao on a map if I had to. It must have been fascinating."

Brody said, "It's near Hong Kong."

"Right," said Hooper. "In any event, there's supposed to be

a superstition about these things, that if you keep it with you you'll be safe from shark bite. Under the present circumstances, I thought it would be appropriate."

"Completely," said Ellen. "Do you have one?"

"I have one," said Hooper, "but I don't know how to carry it. I don't like to wear things around my neck, and if you carry a shark tooth in your pants pocket, I've found you run two real risks. One is that you'll get stabbed in the leg, and the other is that you'll end up with a gash in your pants. It's like carrying an open-blade knife around in your pocket. So in my case, practicality takes precedence over superstition, at least while I'm on dry land."

Ellen laughed and said to Brody, "Martin, could I ask a huge favor? Would you run upstairs and get that thin silver chain out of my jewelry box? I'll put Matthew's shark tooth on right now." She turned to Hooper and said, "You never know when you might meet a shark at dinner."

Brody started up the stairs, and Ellen said, "Oh, and Martin, tell the boys to come down."

As he rounded the corner at the top of the stairs, Brody heard Ellen say, "It *is* such fun to see you again."

Brody walked into the bedroom and sat down on the edge of the bed. He took a deep breath and clenched and unclenched his right fist. He was fighting anger and confusion, and he was losing. He felt threatened, as if an intruder had come into his home, possessing subtle, intangible weapons he could not cope with: looks and youth and sophistication and, above all, a communion with Ellen born in a time which, Brody knew, Ellen wished had never ended. Where previously he had felt Ellen was trying to use Hooper to impress other summer people, now he felt she was trying to impress Hooper herself. He didn't know why. Maybe he was wrong. After all, Ellen and Hooper had known each other long ago. Perhaps he was making too much of two friends simply trying to get to know one another again. Friends? Christ, Hooper had to be ten years younger than Ellen, or almost. What kind of friends could they have been? Acquaintances. Barely. So why was she putting on her supersophisticated act? It demeaned her, Brody thought; and it demeaned Brody that she should try, by posturing, to deny her life with him.

"Fuck it," he said aloud. He stood up, opened a dresser drawer, and rooted through it until he found Ellen's jewelry box. He took out the silver chain, closed the drawer, and walked into the hall. He poked his head into the boys' rooms and said, "Let's go, troops," and then he walked downstairs.

Ellen and Hooper were sitting at opposite ends of the couch, and as Brody walked into the living room, he heard Ellen say, "Would you rather that I not call you Matthew?"

Hooper laughed and said, "I don't mind. It does sort of bring back memories, and despite what I said the other day, there's nothing wrong with that."

The other day? Brody thought. In the hardware store? That must have been some conversation. "Here," he said to Ellen, handing her the chain.

"Thank you," she said. She unclasped the pearls and tossed them onto the coffee table. "Now, Matthew, show me how this should go." Brody picked the string of pearls off the table and put them in his pocket.

The boys came downstairs single file, all dressed neatly in sport shirts and slacks. Ellen snapped the silver chain around her neck, smiled at Hooper, and said, "Come here, boys. Come meet Mr. Hooper. This is Billy Brody. Billy's fourteen." Billy shook hands with Hooper. "And this is Martin Junior. He's twelve. And this is Sean. He's nine . . . almost nine. Mr. Hooper is an oceanographer."

"An icthyologist, actually," said Hooper.

"What's that?" said Martin Junior.

"A zoologist who specializes in fish life."

"What's a zoologist?" asked Sean.

"I know that," said Billy. "That's a guy who studies animals."

"Right," said Hooper. "Good for you."

"Are you going to catch the shark?" asked Martin.

"I'm going to try to find him," said Hooper. "But I don't know. He may have gone away already."

"Have you ever caught a shark?"

"Yes, but not one as big as this."

Sean said, "Do sharks lay eggs?"

"That, young man," said Hooper, "is a good question, and

a very complicated one. Not like a chicken, if that's what you mean. But yes, some sharks do have eggs."

Ellen said, "Give Mr. Hooper a chance, boys." She turned to Brody. "Martin, could you make us a drink?"

"Sure," said Brody. "What'll it be?"

"A gin and tonic would be fine for me," said Hooper.

"What about you, Ellen?"

"Let's see. What would be good? I think I'll just have some vermouth on the rocks."

"Hey, Mom," said Billy, "what's that around your neck?"

"A shark tooth, dear. Mr. Hooper gave it to me."

"Hey, that's really cool. Can I look?"

Brody went into the kitchen. The liquor was kept in a cabinet over the sink. The door was stuck. He tugged at the metal handle, and it came off in his hand. Without thinking, he pegged it into the garbage pail. From a drawer he took a screwdriver and pried open the cabinet door. Vermouth. What the hell was the color of the bottle? Nobody ever drank vermouth on the rocks. Ellen's drink when she drank, and that was rarely, was rye and ginger. Green. There it was, way in the back. Brody grabbed the bottle, twisted off the cap, and sniffed. It smelled like one of those cheap, fruity wines the winos bought for sixty-nine a pint.

Brody made the two drinks, then fashioned a rye and ginger for himself. By habit, he began to measure the rye with a shot glass, but then he changed his mind and poured until the glass was a third full. He topped it off with ginger ale, dropped in a few ice cubes, and reached for the two other glasses. The only convenient way to carry them in one hand was to grip one with the thumb and last three fingers of his hand and then support the other against the first by sticking his index finger down the inside of the glass. He took a slug of his own drink and went back into the living room.

Billy and Martin had crowded onto the couch with Ellen and Hooper. Sean was sitting on the floor. Brody heard Hooper say something about a pig, and Martin said, "Wow!"

"Here," said Brody, handing the forward glass—the one with his finger in it—to Ellen.

"No tip for you, my man," she said. "It's a good thing you decided against a career as a waiter."

Brody looked at her, considered a series of rude remarks, and settled for, "Forgive me, Duchess." He handed the other glass to Hooper and said, "I guess this is what you had in mind."

"That's great. Thanks."

"Matt was just telling us about a shark he caught," said Ellen. "It had almost a whole pig in it."

"No kidding," said Brody, sitting in a chair opposite the couch.

"And that's not all, Dad," said Martin. "There was a roll of tar paper, too."

"And a human bone," said Sean.

"I said it looked like a human bone," said Hooper. "There was no way to be sure at the time. It might have been a beef rib."

Brody said, "I thought you scientists could tell those things right on the spot."

"Not always," said Hooper. "Especially when it's only a piece of a bone like a rib."

Brody took a long swallow of his drink and said, "Oh."

"Hey, Dad," said Billy. "You know how a porpoise kills a shark?"

"With a gun?"

"No, man. It butts him to death. That's what Mr. Hooper says."

"Terrific," said Brody, and he drained his glass. "I'm going to have another drink. Anybody else ready?"

"On a weeknight?" said Ellen. "My."

"Why not? It's not every night we throw a no-kidding, go-to-hell dinner party." Brody started for the kitchen but was stopped by the ringing of the doorbell. He opened the door and saw Dorothy Meadows, short and slight, dressed, as usual, in a dark blue dress and a single strand of pearls. Behind her was a girl Brody assumed was Daisy Wicker—a tall, slim girl with long, straight hair. She wore slacks and sandals and no makeup. Behind her was the unmistakable bulk of Harry Meadows.

"Hello, there," said Brody. "Come on in."

"Good evening, Martin," said Dorothy Meadows. "We met Miss Wicker as we came into the driveway."

"I walked," said Daisy Wicker. "It was nice."

"Good, good. Come on in. I'm Martin Brody."

"I know. I've seen you driving your car. You must have an interesting job."

Brody laughed. "I'd tell you all about it, except it would probably put you to sleep."

Brody led them into the living room and turned them over to Ellen for introduction to Hooper. He took drink orders— Bourbon on the rocks for Harry, club soda with a twist of lemon for Dorothy, and a gin and tonic for Daisy Wicker. But before he fixed their drinks, he made a fresh one for himself, and he sipped it as he prepared the others. By the time he was ready to return to the living room, he had finished about half his drink, so he poured in a generous splash of rye and a dash more ginger ale.

He took Dorothy's and Daisy's drinks first, and returned to the kitchen for Meadows' and his own. He was taking one last swallow before rejoining the company, when Ellen came into the kitchen.

"Don't you think you better slow down?" she said.

"I'm fine," he said. "Don't worry about me."

"You're not being exactly gracious."

"I'm not? I thought I was being charming."

"Hardly."

He smiled at her and said, "Tough shit," and as he spoke, he realized she was right: he had better slow down. He walked into the living room.

The children had gone upstairs. Dorothy Meadows sat on the couch next to Hooper and was chatting with him about his work at Woods Hole. Meadows, in the chair opposite the couch, listened quietly. Daisy Wicker was standing alone, on the other side of the room, by the fireplace, gazing about with a subdued smile on her face. Brody handed Meadows his drink and strolled over next to Daisy.

"You're smiling," he said.

"Am I? I didn't notice."

"Thinking of something funny?"

"No. I guess I was just interested. I've never been in a policeman's house before."

"What did you expect? Bars on the windows? A guard at the door?"

"No, nothing. I was just curious."

"And what have you decided? It looks just like a normal person's house, doesn't it?"

"I guess so. Sort of."

"What does that mean?"

"Nothing."

"Oh."

She took a sip of her drink and said, "Do you like being a policeman?"

Brody couldn't tell whether or not there was hostility in the question. "Yes," he said. "It's a good job, and it has a purpose to it."

"What's the purpose?"

"What do you think?" he said, slightly irritated. "To uphold the law."

"Don't you feel alienated?"

"Why the hell should I feel alienated? Alienated from what?"

"From the people. I mean, the only thing that justifies your existence is telling people what not to do. Doesn't that make you feel freaky?"

For a moment, Brody thought he was being put on, but the girl never smiled or smirked or shifted her eyes from his. "No, I don't feel freaky," he said. "I don't see why I should feel any more freaky than you do, working at the whatchamacallit."

"The Bibelot."

"Yeah. What do you sell there anyway?"

"We sell people their past. It gives them comfort."

"What do you mean, their past?"

"Antiques. They're bought by people who hate their present and need the security of their past. Or if not theirs, someone else's. Once they buy it, it becomes theirs. I bet that's important to you, too."

"What, the past?"

"No, security. Isn't that supposed to be one of the heavy things about being a cop?"

Brody glanced across the room and noticed that Meadows'

glass was empty. "Excuse me," he said. "I have to tend to the other guests."

"Sure. Nice talking to you."

Brody took Meadows' glass and his own into the kitchen. Ellen was filling a bowl with tortilla chips.

"Where the hell did you find that girl?" he said. "Under a rock?"

"Who? Daisy? I told you, she works at the Bibelot."

"Have you ever talked to her?"

"A little. She seems very nice and bright."

"She's a spook. She's just like some of the kids we bust who start smart-mouthing us in the station." He made a drink for Meadows, then poured another for himself. He looked up and saw Ellen staring at him.

"What's the matter with you?" she said.

"I guess I don't like strange people coming into my house and insulting me."

"Honestly, Martin. I'm sure there was no insult intended. She was probably just being frank. Frankness is in these days, you know."

"Well, if she gets any franker with me, she's gonna be out, I'll tell you that." He picked up the two drinks and started for the door.

Ellen said, "Martin . . ." and he stopped. "For my sake . . . please."

"Don't worry about a thing. Everything'll be fine. Like they say in the commercials, *calm down.*"

He refilled Hooper's drink and Daisy Wicker's without refilling his own. Then he sat down and nursed his drink through a long story Meadows was telling Daisy. Brody felt all right—pretty good, in fact—and he knew that if he didn't have anything more to drink before dinner, he'd be fine.

At 8:30, Ellen brought the soup plates out from the kitchen and set them around the table. "Martin," she said, "would you open the wine for me while I get everyone seated?"

"Wine?"

"There are three bottles in the kitchen. A white in the icebox and two reds on the counter. You may as well open them all. The reds will need time to breathe."

"Of course they will," Brody said as he stood up. "Who doesn't?"

"Oh, and the *tire-bouchin* is on the counter next to the red."

"The what?"

Daisy Wicker said, "It's *tire-bouchon*. The corkscrew."

Brody took vengeful pleasure in seeing Ellen blush, for it relieved him of some of his own embarrassment. He found the corkscrew and went to work on the two bottles of red wine. He pulled one cork cleanly, but the other crumbled as he was withdrawing it, and pieces slipped into the bottle. He took the bottle of white out of the refrigerator, and as he uncorked it he tangled his tongue trying to pronounce the name of the wine: Montrachet. He arrived at what seemed to him an acceptable pronunciation, wiped the bottle dry with a dish towel, and took it into the dining room.

Ellen was seated at the end of the table nearest the kitchen. Hooper was at her left, Meadows at her right. Next to Meadows, Daisy Wicker, then an empty space for Brody at the far end of the table, and, opposite Daisy, Dorothy Meadows.

Brody put his left hand behind his back and, standing over Ellen's right shoulder, poured her a glass of wine. "A glass of Mount Ratchet," he said. "Very good year, 1970. I remember it well."

"Enough," said Ellen, tipping the mouth of the bottle up. "Don't fill the glass all the way."

"Sorry," said Brody, and he filled Meadows' glass next.

When he had finished pouring the wine, Brody sat down. He looked at the soup in front of him. Then he glanced furtively around the table and saw that the others were actually eating it: it wasn't a joke. So he took a spoonful. It was cold, and it didn't taste anything like soup, but it wasn't bad.

"I love gazpacho," said Daisy, "but it's such a pain to make that I don't have it very often."

"Mmmm," said Brody, spooning another mouthful of soup.

"Do you have it very often?"

"No," he said. "Not too often."

"Have you ever tried a G and G?"

"Can't say as I have."

"You ought to try one. Of course, you might not enjoy it since it's breaking the law."

"You mean eating this thing is breaking the law? How? What is it?"

"Grass and gazpacho. Instead of herbs, you sprinkle a little grass over the top. Then you smoke a little, eat a little, smoke a little, eat a little. It's really wild."

It was a moment before Brody realized what she was saying, and even when he understood, he didn't answer right away. He tipped his soup bowl toward himself, scooped out the last little bit of soup, drained his wine glass in one draft, and wiped his mouth with his napkin. He looked at Daisy, who was smiling sweetly at him, and at Ellen, who was smiling at something Hooper was saying.

"It really is," said Daisy.

Brody decided to be low-keyed—avuncular and nonetheless annoyed, but low-keyed, so as not to upset Ellen. "You know," he said, "I don't find . . ."

"I bet Matt's tried one."

"Maybe he has. I don't see what that . . ."

Daisy raised her voice and said, "Matt, excuse me." The conversation at the other end of the table stopped. "I was just curious. Have you ever tried a G and G? By the way, Mrs. Brody, this is terrific gazpacho."

"Thank you," said Ellen. "But what's a G and G?"

"I tried one once," said Hooper. "But I was never really into that."

"You must tell me," Ellen said. "What is it?"

"Matt'll tell you," said Daisy, and just as Brody turned to say something to her, she leaned over to Meadows and said, "Tell me more about the water table."

Brody stood up and began to clear away the soup bowls. As he walked into the kitchen, he felt a slight rush of nausea and dizziness, and his forehead was sweating. But by the time he put the bowls into the sink, the feeling had passed.

Ellen followed him into the kitchen and tied an apron around her waist. "I'll need some help carving," she said.

"Okeydoke," said Brody, and he searched through a drawer for a carving knife and fork. "What did you think of that?"

"Of what?"

"That G and G business. Did Hooper tell you what it is?"

"Yes. That was pretty funny, wasn't it? I must say, it sounds tasty."

"How would you know?"

"You never know what we ladies do when we get together over at the hospital. Here, carve." With a two-tine serving fork, she hefted the lamb onto the carving board. "Slices about three quarters of an inch thick, if you can, the way you'd slice a steak."

That Wicker bitch was right about one thing, Brody thought as he slashed the meat: I sure as shit feel alienated right now. A slab of meat fell away, and Brody said, "Hey, I thought you said this was lamb."

"It is."

"It isn't even done. Look at that." He held up the piece he had sliced. It was pink and, toward the middle, almost red.

"That's the way it's supposed to be."

"Not if it's lamb, it isn't. Lamb's supposed to be cooked through, well done."

"Martin, believe me. It's all right to cook a butterfly lamb sort of medium. I promise you."

Brody raised his voice. "I'm not gonna eat raw lamb!"

"Ssshhh! For God's sake. Can't you keep your voice down?"

Brody said in a hoarse whisper, "Then put the goddam thing back till it's done."

"It's done!" said Ellen. "If you don't want to eat it, don't eat it, but that's the way I'm going to serve it."

"Then cut it yourself." Brody dropped the knife and fork on the carving board, picked up the two bottles of red wine, and left the kitchen.

"There'll be a slight delay," he said as he approached the table, "while the cook kills our dinner. She tried to serve it as it was, but it bit her on the leg." He raised a bottle of wine over one of the clean glasses and said, "I wonder why you're not allowed to serve red wine in the same glass the white wine was."

"The tastes," said Meadows, "don't complement each other."

"What you're saying is, it'll give you gas." Brody filled the six glasses and sat down. He took a sip of wine, said, "Good," then took another sip and another. He refilled his glass.

Ellen came in from the kitchen carrying the carving board. She set it on the sideboard next to a stack of plates. She returned to the kitchen and came back, carrying two vegetable dishes. "I hope it's good," she said. "I haven't tried it before."

"What is it?" asked Dorothy Meadows. "It smells delicious."

"Butterfly lamb. Marinated."

"Really? What's in the marinade?"

"Ginger, soy sauce, a whole bunch of things." She put a thick slice of lamb, some asparagus and summer squash on each plate, and passed the plates to Meadows, who sent them down and around the table.

When everyone had been served and Ellen had sat down, Hooper raised his glass and said, "A toast to the chef."

The others raised their glasses, and Brody said, "Good luck."

Meadows took a bite of meat, chewed it, savored it, and said, "Fantastic. It's like the tenderest of sirloins, only better. What a splendid flavor."

"Coming from you, Harry," said Ellen, "that's a special compliment."

"It's delicious," said Dorothy. "Will you promise to give me the recipe? Harry will never forgive me if I don't give this to him at least once a week."

"He better rob a bank," said Brody.

"But it is delicious, Martin, don't you think?"

Brody didn't answer. He had started to chew a piece of meat when another wave of nausea hit him. Once again sweat popped out on his forehead. He felt detached, as if his body were controlled by someone else. He sensed panic at the loss of motor control. His fork felt heavy, and for a moment he feared it might slip from his fingers and clatter onto the table. He gripped it with his fist and held on. He was sure his tongue wouldn't behave if he tried to speak. It was the wine. It had to be the wine. With greatly exaggerated precision, he reached forward to push his wine glass away from him. He slid his fingers along the tablecloth to minimize the chances of knocking over the glass. He sat back and took a deep breath. His vision blurred. He tried to focus his eyes on a painting above Ellen's head, but he was distracted by the image of Ellen talking to Hooper. Every time she spoke she touched Hooper's arm—lightly, but, Brody thought, intimately, as if they were sharing secrets. He didn't hear what anyone was saying. The last thing he remembered hearing was, "Don't you think?" How long ago was that? Who had said it? He didn't know. He looked at Meadows, who was talking to Daisy. Then he looked at Dorothy and said thickly, "Yes."

"What did you say, Martin?" She looked up at him. "Did you say something?"

He couldn't speak. He wanted to stand and walk out to the kitchen, but he didn't trust his legs. He'd never make it without holding on to something. Just sit still, he told himself. It'll pass.

And it did. His head began to clear. Ellen was touching Hooper again. Talk and touch, talk and touch. "Boy, it's hot," he said. He stood up and walked, carefully but steadily, to a window and tugged it open. He leaned on the sill and pressed his face against the screen. "Nice night," he said. He straightened up. "I think I'll get a glass of water." He walked into the kitchen and shook his head. He turned on the cold-water tap and rubbed some water on his brow. He filled a glass and drank it down, then refilled it and drank that down. He took a few deep breaths, went back into the dining room, and sat down. He looked at the food on his plate. Then he suppressed a shiver and smiled at Dorothy.

"Any more, anybody?" said Ellen. "There's plenty here."

"Indeed," said Meadows. "But you'd better serve the others first. Left to my own devices, I'd eat the whole thing."

"And you know what you'd be saying tomorrow," said Brody.

"What's that?"

Brody lowered his voice and said gravely, "I can't believe I ate the *whole* thing."

Meadows and Dorothy laughed, and Hooper said, in a high falsetto whine, "No, Ralph, *I* ate it." Then even Ellen laughed. It was going to be all right.

By the time dessert was served—coffee ice cream in a pool

of crème de cacao—Brody was feeling well. He had two helpings of ice cream, and he chatted amiably with Dorothy. He smiled when Daisy told him a story about lacing the stuffing at last Thanksgiving's turkey with marijuana.

"My only worry," said Daisy, "was that my maiden aunt called Thanksgiving morning and asked if she could come for dinner. The turkey was already made and stuffed."

"So what happened?" said Brody.

"I tried to sneak her some turkey without stuffing, but she made a point of asking for it, so I said what the heck and gave her a big spoonful."

"And?"

"By the end of the meal she was giggling like a little girl. She even wanted to dance. To *Hair* yet."

"It's a good thing I wasn't there," said Brody. "I would have arrested you for corrupting the morals of a maiden."

They had coffee in the living room, and Brody offered drinks, but only Meadows accepted. "A tiny brandy, if you have it," he said.

Brody looked at Ellen, as if to ask, Do we have any? "In the cupboard, I think," she said.

Brody poured Meadows' drink and thought briefly of pouring one for himself. But he resisted, telling himself, Don't press your luck.

At a little after ten, Meadows yawned and said, "Dorothy, I think we had best take our leave. I find it hard to fulfill the public trust if I stay up too late."

"I should go, too," said Daisy. "I have to be at work at eight. Not that we're selling very much these days."

"You're not alone, my dear," said Meadows.

"I know. But when you work on commission, you really feel it."

"Well, let's hope the worst is over. From what I gather from our expert here, there's a good chance the leviathan has left." Meadows stood up.

"A chance," said Hooper. "I hope so." He rose to go. "I should be on my way, too."

"Oh, don't go!" Ellen said to Hooper. The words came out much stronger than she had intended. Instead of a pleasant request, they sounded a shrill plea. She was embarrassed, and she added quickly, "I mean, the night is young. It's only ten."

"I know," said Hooper. "But if the weather's any good tomorrow, I want to get up early and get into the water. Besides, I have a car and I can drop Daisy off on my way home."

Daisy said, "That would be fun." Her voice, as usual, was without tone or color, suggesting nothing.

"The Meadows' can drop her," Ellen said.

"True," said Hooper, "but I really should go so I can get up early. But thanks for the thought."

They said their good-byes at the front door—perfunctory compliments, redundant thanks. Hooper was the last to leave, and when he extended his hand to Ellen, she took it in both of hers and said, "Thank you *so* much for my shark tooth."

"You're welcome. I'm glad you like it."

"And thank you for being so nice to the children. They were fascinated to meet you."

"So was I. It was a little weird, though. I must have been about Sean's age when I knew you before. You haven't changed much at all."

"Well, *you've* certainly changed."

"I hope so. I'd hate to be nine all of my life."

"We'll see you again before you go?"

"Count on it."

"Wonderful." She released his hand. He said a quick good night to Brody and walked to his car.

Ellen waited at the door until the last of the cars had pulled out of the driveway, then she turned off the outside light. Without a word, she began to pick up the glasses, coffee cups, and ashtrays from the living room.

Brody carried a stack of dessert dishes into the kitchen, set them on the sink, and said, "Well, that was all right." He meant nothing by the remark, and sought nothing more than rote agreement.

"No thanks to you," said Ellen.

"What?"

"You were awful."

"I was?" He was genuinely surprised at the ferocity of her attack. "I know I got a little queasy there for a minute, but I didn't think—"

"All evening, from start to finish, you were awful."

"That's a lot of crap!"

"You'll wake the children."

"I don't give a damn. I'm not going to let you stand there and work out your own hang-ups by telling me I'm a shit."

Ellen smiled bitterly. "You see? There you go again."

"*Where* do I go again? What are you talking about?"

"I don't want to talk about it."

"Just like that. You don't want to talk about it. Look . . . okay, I was wrong about the goddam meat. I shouldn't have blown my stack. I'm sorry. Now . . ."

"I said I don't want to talk about it!"

Brody was ready for a fight, but he backed off, sober enough to realize that his only weapons were cruelty and innuendo, and that Ellen was close to tears. And tears, whether shed in orgasm or in anger, disconcerted him. So he said only, "Well, I'm sorry about that." He walked out of the kitchen and climbed the stairs.

In the bedroom, as he was undressing, the thought occurred to him that the cause of all the unpleasantness, the source of the whole mess, was a fish: a mindless beast that he had never seen. The ludicrousness of the thought made him smile.

He crawled into bed and, almost simultaneous with the touch of his head to the pillow, fell into a dreamless sleep.

A BOY AND his date sat drinking beer at one end of the long mahogany bar in the Randy Bear. The boy was eighteen, the son of the pharmacist at the Amity Pharmacy.

"You'll have to tell him sometime," said the girl.

"I know. And when I do, he's gonna go bullshit."

"It wasn't your fault."

"You know what he'll say? It must have been my fault. I must have done something, or else they would have kept me and canned somebody else."

"But they fired a lot of kids."

"They kept a lot, too."

"How did they decide who to keep?"

"They didn't say. They just said they weren't getting

enough guests to justify a big staff, so they were letting some of us go. Boy, my old man is gonna go right through the roof."

"Can't he call them? He must know somebody there. I mean, if he says you really need the money for college . . ."

"He wouldn't do it. That'd be begging." The boy finished his beer. "There's only one thing I can do. Deal."

"Oh, Michael, don't do that. It's too dangerous. You could go to jail."

"That's quite a choice, isn't it?" the boy said acidly. "College or jail."

"What would you tell your father?"

"I don't know. Maybe I'll tell him I'm selling belts."

8

BRODY AWOKE WITH a start, jolted by a signal that told him something was wrong. He threw his arm across the bed to touch Ellen. She wasn't there. He sat and saw her sitting in the chair by the window. Rain splashed against the windowpanes, and he heard the wind whipping through the trees.

"Lousy day, huh?" he said. She didn't answer, continuing to stare fixedly at the drops sliding down the glass. "How come you're up so early?"

"I couldn't sleep."

Brody yawned. "I sure didn't have any trouble."

"I'm not surprised."

"Oh boy. Are we starting in again?"

Ellen shook her head. "No. I'm sorry. I didn't mean anything." She seemed subdued, sad.

"What's the matter?"

"Nothing."

"Whatever you say." Brody got out of bed and went into the bathroom.

When he had shaved and dressed, he went down to the kitchen. The boys were finishing their breakfast, and Ellen was frying an egg for him. "What are you guys gonna do on this crummy day?" he said.

"Clean lawnmowers," said Billy, who worked during the summer for a local gardener. "Boy, do I hate rainy days."

"And what about you two?" Brody said to Martin and Sean.

"Martin's going to the Boys' Club," said Ellen, "and Sean's spending the day at the Santoses'."

"And you?"

"I've got a full day at the hospital. Which reminds me: I won't be home for lunch. Can you get something downtown?"

"Sure. I didn't know you worked a full day Wednesdays."

"I don't, usually. But one of the other girls is sick, and I said I'd fill in."

"Oh."

"I'll be back by suppertime."

"Fine."

"Do you think you could drop Sean and Martin off on your way to work? I want to do a little shopping on my way to the hospital."

"No problem."

"I'll pick them up on my way home."

Brody and the two younger children left first. Then Billy, wrapped from head to foot in foul-weather gear, bicycled off to work.

Ellen looked at the clock on the kitchen wall. It was a few minutes to eight. Too early? Maybe. But better to catch him now, before he went off somewhere and the chance was lost. She held her right hand out in front of her and tried to steady her fingers, but they quivered uncontrollably. She smiled at her nervousness and whispered to herself, "Some swinger you'd make." She went upstairs to the bedroom, sat on the bed, and picked up the green phone book. She found the number for the Abelard Arms Inn, put her hand on the phone, hesitated for a moment, then picked up the receiver and dialed the number.

"Abelard Arms."

"Mr. Hooper's room, please. Matt Hooper."

"Just a minute, please. Hooper. Here it is. Four-oh-five. I'll ring it for you."

Ellen heard the phone ring once, then again. She could hear her heart beating, and she saw the pulse throb in her right wrist. Hang up, she told herself. Hang up. There's time.

"Hello?" said Hooper's voice.

"Oh." She thought, Good God, suppose he's got Daisy Wicker in the room with him.

"Hello?"

Ellen swallowed and said, "Hi. It's me. . . . I mean it's Ellen."

"Oh, hi."

"I hope I didn't wake you."

"No. I was just getting ready to go downstairs and have some breakfast."

"Good. It's not a very nice day, is it?"

"No, but I don't really mind. It's a luxury for me to be able to sleep this late."

"Can you . . . will you be able to work today?"

"I don't know. I was just trying to figure that out. I sure can't go out in the boat and hope to get anything done."

"Oh." She paused, fighting the dizziness that was creeping up on her. Go ahead, she told herself. Ask the question. "I was wondering . . ." No, be careful; ease into it. "I wanted to thank you for the beautiful charm."

"You're welcome. I'm glad you like it. But I should be thanking you. I had a good time last night."

"I did . . . we did, too. I'm glad you came."

"Yes."

"It was like old times."

"Yes."

Now, she said to herself. Do it. The words spilled from her mouth. "I was wondering, if you can't do any work today, I mean if you can't go out in the boat or anything, I was wondering if . . . if there was any chance you'd like to . . . if you're free for lunch."

"Lunch?"

"Yes. You know, if you have nothing else to do, I thought we might have some lunch."

"We? You mean you and the chief and me?"

"No, just you and I. Martin usually has lunch at his desk. I don't want to interfere with your plans or anything. I mean, if you've got a lot of work to do . . ."

"No, no. That's okay. Heck, why not? Sure. What did you have in mind?"

"There's a wonderful place up in Sag Harbor. Banner's. Do you know it?" She hoped he didn't. She didn't know it either, which meant that no one there would know her. But she had heard that it was good and quiet and dark.

"No, I've never been there," said Hooper. "But Sag Harbor. That's quite a hike for lunch."

"It's not bad, really, only about fifteen or twenty minutes. I could meet you there whenever you like."

"Any time's all right with me."

"Around twelve-thirty, then?"

"Twelve-thirty it is. See you then."

Ellen hung up the phone. Her hands were still shaking, but she felt elated, excited. Her senses seemed alive and incredibly keen. Every time she drew a breath she savored the smells around her. Her ears jingled with a symphony of tiny house sounds—creaks and rustles and thumps. She felt more intensely feminine than she had in years—a warm, wet feeling both delicious and uncomfortable.

She went into the bathroom and took a shower. She shaved her legs and under her arms. She wished she had bought one of those feminine hygiene deodorants she had seen advertised, but, lacking that, she powdered herself and daubed cologne behind her ears, inside her elbows, behind her knees, on her nipples, and on her genitals.

There was a full-length mirror in the bedroom, and she stood before it, examining herself. Were the goods good enough? Would the offer be accepted? She had worked to keep in shape, to preserve the smoothness and sinuousness of youth. She could not bear the thought of rejection.

The goods were good. The lines in her neck were few and barely noticeable. Her face was unblemished and unscarred. There were no droops or sags or pouches. She stood straight and admired the contours of her breasts. Her waist was slim, her belly flat—the reward for endless hours of exercise after each child. The only problem, as she assessed her body critically, was her hips. By no stretch of anyone's imagination were they girlish. They signaled motherhood. They were, as Brody once said, breeder's hips. The recollection brought a quick flash of remorse, but excitement quickly nudged it aside. Her legs were long and—below the pad of fat on her rear—slender. Her ankles were delicate, and her feet—with the toenails neatly pruned—were perfect enough to suit any pediphile.

She dressed in her hospital clothes. From the back of her closet she took a plastic shopping bag into which she put a pair of bikini underpants, a bra, a neatly folded lavender summer dress, a pair of low-heeled pumps, a can of spray deodorant, a plastic bottle of bath powder, a toothbrush and a tube of toothpaste. She carried the bag to the garage, tossed it into the back seat of her Volkswagen beetle, backed out of the driveway, and drove to the Southampton Hospital.

The dull drive increased the fatigue she had been feeling for hours. She had not slept all night. She had first lain in bed, then sat by the window, struggling with all the twistings of emotion and conscience, desire and regret, longing and recrimination. She didn't know exactly when she had decided on this manifestly rash, dangerous plan. She had been thinking about it—and trying not to think about it—since the day she first met Hooper. She had weighed the risks and, somehow, calculated that they were worth taking, though she was not entirely sure what she could gain from the adventure. She knew she wanted change, almost any change. She wanted to be assured and reassured that she was desirable—not just to her husband, for she had grown complacent about that, but to the people she saw as her real peers, the people among whom she still numbered herself. She felt that without some remedy, the part of herself that she most cherished would die. Perhaps the past could never be revived. But perhaps it could be recalled physically as well as mentally. She wanted an injection, a transfusion of the essence of her past, and she saw Matt Hooper as the only possible donor. The thought of love never entered her mind. Nor did she want or anticipate a relationship either profound or enduring. She sought only to be serviced, restored.

She was grateful that the work assigned her when she arrived at the hospital demanded concentration and conversation, for it prevented her from thinking. She and another volunteer changed the bedding of the elderly patients for whom the hospital community was a surrogate—and, in some cases, final—home. She had to remember the names of children in distant cities, had to fashion new excuses for why they hadn't written. She had to feign recollection of the plots of television shows and speculate on why such-and-such a character had left his wife for a woman who was patently an adventuress.

At 11:45, Ellen told the supervisor of volunteers that she didn't feel well. Her thyroid was acting up again, she said, and she was getting her period. She thought she'd go lie down for a while in the staff lounge. And if a nap didn't help, she said, she'd probably go home. In fact, if she wasn't back on the job by 1:30 or so, the supervisor could assume she had gone home. It was an explanation that she hoped was vague enough to discourage anyone from actively looking for her.

She went into the lounge, counted to twenty, and opened the door a crack to see if the corridor was empty. It was; most of the staff were in, or on their way to, the cafeteria on the other side of the building. She stepped into the corridor, closed the door softly behind her, and hurried around a corner and out a side door of the hospital that led to the staff parking lot.

She drove most of the way to Sag Harbor, then stopped at a gas station. When the tank was full and the gas paid for, she asked to use the ladies' room. The attendant gave her the key, and she pulled her car around to the side of the station, next to the ladies' room door. She opened the door, but before going into the ladies' room she returned the key to the attendant. She walked to her car, removed the plastic bag from the back seat, entered the ladies' room, and pushed the button that locked the door.

She stripped, and standing on the cold floor in her bare feet, looking at her reflection in the mirror above the sink, she felt a thrill of risk. She sprayed deodorant under her arms and on her feet. She took the clean underpants from the plastic bag and stepped into them. She shook a little powder into each cup of the bra and put it on. She took the dress from the bag, unfolded it, checked it for wrinkles, and slipped it over her head. She poured powder into each of her shoes, brushed off the bottom of each foot with a paper towel, and put on the shoes. Then she brushed her teeth and combed her hair, stuffed her hospital clothes into the plastic bag, and opened the door. She looked both ways, saw that no one was watching her, then stepped out of the ladies' room, tossed the bag into the car, and got in.

As she drove out of the gas station, she hunched down in her seat so the attendant, if he should chance to notice her, would not see that she had changed clothes.

It was 12:20 when she arrived at Banner's, a small steak-and-seafood restaurant on the water in Sag Harbor. The parking lot was in the rear, for which she was grateful. On the off-chance that someone she knew might drive down the street in Sag Harbor, she didn't want her car in plain view.

One reason she had picked Banner's was that it was known as a favorite nighttime restaurant for yachtsmen and summer people, which meant that it probably had little luncheon trade. And it was expensive, which made it almost certain that no year-round residents, no local tradesmen, would go there for lunch. Ellen checked her wallet. She had nearly fifty dollars—all the emergency cash she and Brody kept in the house. She made a mental note of the bills: a twenty, two tens, a five, and three ones. She wanted to replace exactly what she had taken from the coffee can in the kitchen closet.

There were two other cars in the parking lot, a Chevrolet Vega and a bigger car, tan. She remembered that Hooper's car was green and that it was named after some animal. She left her car and walked into the restaurant, holding her hands over her head to protect her hair from the light rain.

The restaurant was dark, but because the day was gloomy it took her eyes only a few seconds to adjust. There was only one room, with a bar on the right as she walked in and about twenty tables in the center. The left-hand wall was lined with eight booths. The walls were dark wood, decorated with bull-fight and movie posters.

A couple—in their late twenties, Ellen guessed—was having a drink at a table by the window. The bartender, a young man with a Vandyke beard and a button-down shirt, sat by the cash register reading the New York *Daily News.* They were the only people in the room. Ellen looked at her watch. Almost 12:30.

The bartender looked up and said, "Hi. Can I help you?"

Ellen stepped to the bar. "Yes . . . yes. In a minute. But first I'd like . . . can you tell me where the ladies' room is?"

"End of the bar, turn right. First door on your left."

"Thank you." Ellen walked quickly down the length of the bar, turned right, and went into the ladies' room.

She stood in front of the mirror and held out her right hand. It trembled, and she clenched it into a fist. Calm down, she said to herself. You have to calm down or it's no use. It's lost. She felt that she was sweating, but when she put a hand inside her dress and felt her armpit, it was dry. She combed her hair and surveyed her teeth. She remembered something a boy she had once gone out with had said: Nothing turns my stomach faster than seeing a girl with a big piece of crud between her teeth. She looked at her watch: 12:35.

She went back into the restaurant and looked around. Just the same people, the bartender, and a waitress standing at the bar, folding napkins.

The waitress saw Ellen come around the corner of the bar and she said, "Hello. May I help you?"

"Yes. I'd like a table, please. For lunch."

"For one?"

"No. Two."

"Fine," said the waitress. She put down a napkin, picked up a pad, and walked Ellen to a table in the middle of the room. "Is this all right?"

"No. I mean, yes. It's fine. But I'd like to have that table in the corner booth, if you don't mind."

"Sure," said the waitress. "Any table you like. We're not exactly full." She led Ellen to the table, and Ellen slipped into the booth with her back to the door. Hooper would be able to find her. If he came. "Can I get you a drink?"

"Yes. A gin and tonic, please." When the waitress left the table, Ellen smiled. It was the first time since her wedding that she had had a drink during the day.

The waitress brought the drink, and Ellen drank half of it immediately, eager to feel the relaxing warmth of alcohol. Every few seconds, she checked the door and looked at her watch. He's not going to come, she thought. It was almost 12:45. He got cold feet. He's scared of Martin. Maybe he's scared of me. What will I do if he doesn't come? I guess I'll have some lunch and go back to work. He's got to come! He can't do this to me.

"Hello."

The word startled Ellen. She hopped in her seat and said, "Oh!"

Hooper slid into the seat opposite her and said, "I didn't mean to scare you. And I'm sorry I'm late. I had to stop for gas, and the station was jammed. The traffic was terrible. And so much for my excuses. I should have left more time. I *am* sorry." He looked into her eyes and smiled.

She looked down at her glass. "You don't have to apologize. I was late myself."

The waitress came to the table. "Can I get you a drink?" she said to Hooper.

He noticed Ellen's glass and said, "Oh, sure, I guess so. If you are. I'll have a gin and tonic."

"I'll have another one," said Ellen. "This one's almost finished."

The waitress left, and Hooper said, "I don't normally drink at lunch."

"Neither do I."

"After about three drinks I say stupid things. I never did hold my liquor very well."

Ellen nodded. "I know the feeling. I tend to get sort of . . ."

"Impetuous? So do I."

"Really? I can't imagine you getting impetuous. I thought scientists weren't ever impetuous."

Hooper smiled and said histrionically, "It may seem, madam, that we are wed to our test tubes. But beneath the icy exteriors there beat the hearts of some of the most brazen, raunchy people in the world."

Ellen laughed. The waitress brought the drinks and left two menus on the edge of the table. They talked—chatted, really—about old times, about people they had known and what those people were doing now, about Hooper's ambitions in icthyology. They never mentioned the shark or Brody or Ellen's children. It was an easy, rambling conversation, which suited Ellen. Her second drink loosened her up, and she felt happy and in command of herself.

She wanted Hooper to have another drink, and she knew he was not likely to take the initiative and order one. She picked up one of the menus, hoping that the waitress would notice the movement, and said, "Let me see. What looks good?"

Hooper picked up the other menu and began to read, and after a minute or two, the waitress strolled over to the table. "Are you ready to order?"

"Not quite yet," said Ellen. "It all looks good. Are you ready, Matthew?"

"Not quite," said Hooper.

"Why don't we have one more drink while we're looking?"

"Both?" said the waitress.

Hooper seemed to ponder for a moment. Then he nodded his head and said, "Sure. A special occasion."

They sat in silence, reading the menus. Ellen tried to assess how she felt. Three drinks would be a fairly heavy load for her to carry, and she wanted to make sure she didn't get fuzzy-headed or fuzzy-tongued. What was that saying, about alcohol increasing the desire but taking away from the performance? But that's just with men, she thought. I'm glad I don't have to worry about *that*. But what about him? Suppose he can't . . . Is there anything I can do? But that's silly. Not on two drinks. It must take five or six or seven. A man has to be incapacitated. But not if he's scared. Does he look scared? She peeked over the top of her menu and looked at Hooper. He didn't look nervous. If anything, he looked slightly perplexed.

"What's the matter?" she said.

He looked up. "What do you mean?"

"Your eyebrows were all scrunched up. You looked confused."

"Oh, nothing. I was just looking at the scallops, or what they claim are scallops. The chances are they're flounder, cut up with a cookie cutter."

The waitress brought their drinks and said, "Ready?"

"Yes," said Ellen. "I'll have the shrimp cocktail and the chicken."

"What kind of dressing would you like on your salad? We have French, Roquefort, Thousand Island, and oil and vinegar."

"Roquefort, please."

Hooper said, "Are these really bay scallops?"

"I guess so," said the waitress. "If that's what it says."

"All right. I'll have the scallops, and French dressing on the salad."

"Anything to start?"

"No," said Hooper, raising his glass. "This'll be fine."

In a few minutes, the waitress brought Ellen's shrimp cocktail. When she had left, Ellen said, "Do you know what I'd love? Some wine."

"That's a very interesting idea," Hooper said, looking at her. "But remember what I said about impetuousness. I may become irresponsible."

"I'm not worried." As Ellen spoke, she felt a blush crawl up her cheeks.

"Okay, but first I better check the treasury." He reached in his back pocket for his wallet.

"Oh no. This is my treat."

"Don't be silly."

"No, really. I asked you to lunch." She began to panic. It had never occurred to her that he might insist on paying. She didn't want to annoy him by sticking him with a big bill. On the other hand, she didn't want to seem patronizing, to offend his virility.

"I know," he said. "But I'd like to take *you* to lunch."

Was this a gambit? She couldn't tell. If it was, she didn't want to refuse it, but if he was just being polite . . . "You're sweet," she said, "but . . ."

"I'm serious. Please."

She looked down and toyed with the one shrimp remaining on her plate. "Well . . ."

"I know you're only being thoughtful," Hooper said, "but don't be. Didn't David ever tell you about our grandfather?"

"Not that I remember. What about him?"

"Old Matt was known—and not very affectionately—as the Bandit. If he was alive today, I'd probably be at the head of the pack calling for his scalp. But he isn't, so all I had to worry about was whether to keep the bundle of money he left me or give it away. It wasn't a very difficult moral dilemma. I figure I can spend it as well as anyone I'd give it to."

"Does David have a lot of money, too?"

"Yes. That's one of the things about him that's always baffled me. He's got enough to support himself and any number of wives for life. So why did he settle on a meatball for a second wife? Because she has more money than he does. I don't know. Maybe money doesn't feel comfortable unless it's married to money."

"What did your grandfather do?"

"Railroads and mining. Technically, that is. Basically, he was a robber baron. At one point he owned most of Denver. He was the landlord of the whole red-light district."

"That must have been profitable."

"Not as much as you'd think," Hooper said with a laugh. "From what I hear, he liked to collect his rent in trade."

That might be a gambit, Ellen thought. What should she say? "That's supposed to be every schoolgirl's fantasy," she ventured playfully.

"What is?"

"To be a . . . you know, a prostitute. To sleep with a whole lot of different men."

"Was it yours?"

Ellen laughed, hoping to cover her blush. "I don't remember if it was exactly that," she said. "But I guess we all have fantasies of one kind or another."

Hooper smiled and leaned back in his chair. He called the waitress over and said, "Bring us a bottle of cold chablis, would you please?"

Something's happened, Ellen thought. She wondered if he could sense—smell? like an animal?—the invitation she had extended. Whatever it was, he had taken the offensive. All she had to do was avoid discouraging him.

The food came, followed a moment later by the wine. Hooper's scallops were the size of marshmallows. "Flounder," he said after the waitress had left. "I should have known."

"How can you tell?" Ellen asked. Immediately she wished she hadn't said anything. She didn't want to let the conversation drift.

"They're too big, for one thing. And the edges are too perfect. They were obviously cut."

"I suppose you could send them back." She hoped he wouldn't; a quarrel with the waitress could spoil their mood.

"I might," said Hooper, and he grinned at Ellen. "Under

different circumstances." He poured Ellen a glass of wine, then filled his own and raised it for a toast. "To fantasies," he said. "Tell me about yours." His eyes were a bright, liquid blue, and his lips were parted in a half smile.

Ellen laughed. "Oh, mine aren't very interesting. I imagine they're just your old run-of-the-mill fantasies."

"There's no such thing," said Hooper. "Tell me." He was asking, not demanding, but Ellen felt that the game she had started demanded that she answer.

"Oh, you know," she said. Her stomach felt warm, and the back of her neck was hot. "Just the standard things. Rape, I guess, is one."

"How does it happen?"

She tried to think, and she remembered the times, when, alone, she would let her mind wander and conjure the carnal images. Usually she was in bed, often with her husband asleep beside her. Sometimes she found that, without knowing it, she had been rubbing her hand over her vagina, caressing herself.

"Different ways," she said.

"Name one."

"Sometimes I'm in the kitchen in the morning, after everybody has left, and a workman from one of the houses next door comes to my back door. He wants to use the phone or have a glass of water." She stopped.

"And then?"

"I let him in the door and he threatens to kill me if I don't do what he wants."

"Does he hurt you?"

"Oh no. I mean, he doesn't stab me or anything."

"Does he hit you?"

"No. He just . . . rapes me."

"Is it fun?"

"Not at first. It's scary. But then, after a while, when he's . . ."

"When he's got you all . . . ready."

Ellen's eyes moved to his, reading the remark for humor, irony, or cruelty. She saw none. Hooper ran his tongue over his lips and leaned forward until his face was only a foot or so from hers.

Ellen thought: The door's open now; all you have to do is walk through it. She said, "Yes."

"Then it's fun."

"Yes." She shifted in her seat, for the recollection was becoming physical.

"Do you ever have an orgasm?"

"Sometimes," she said. "Not always."

"Is he big?"

"Tall? Not . . ."

They had been speaking very softly, and now Hooper lowered his voice to a whisper. "I don't mean tall. Is he . . . you know . . . big?"

"Usually," said Ellen, and she chuckled. "Huge."

"Is he black?"

"No. I've heard that some women have fantasies about being raped by black men, but I never have."

"Tell me another one."

"Oh no," she said, laughing. "Now it's your turn."

They heard footsteps and turned to see the waitress approaching their table. "Is everything all right?" she said.

"Fine," Hooper said curtly. "Everything's fine." The waitress left.

Ellen whispered, "Do you think she heard?"

Hooper leaned forward. "Not a chance. Now tell me another one."

It's going to happen, Ellen thought, and she felt suddenly nervous. She wanted to tell him why she was behaving this way, to explain that she didn't do this all the time. He probably thinks I'm a whore. Forget it. Don't get sappy or you'll ruin it. "No," she said with a smile. "It's your turn."

"Mine are usually orgies," he said. "Or at least threesies."

"What are threesies?"

"Three people. Me and two girls."

"Greedy. What do you do?"

"It varies. Everything imaginable."

"Are you . . . big?" she said.

"Bigger every minute. What about you?"

"I don't know. Compared to what?"

"To other women. Some women have really tight ones."

Ellen giggled. "You sound like a comparison-shopper."

"Just a conscientious consumer."

"I don't know how I am," she said. "I haven't anything to compare it to." She looked down at her half-eaten chicken, and she laughed.

"What's funny?" he asked.

"I was just wondering," she said, and her laughter built. "I was just wondering if—oh, Lord, I'm getting a pain in my side —if chickens have . . ."

"Of course!" said Hooper. "But talk about a tightie!"

They laughed together, and when the laughter faded, Ellen impulsively said, "Let's make a fantasy."

"Okay. How do you want to start?"

"What would you do to me if we were going to . . . you know."

"That's a very interesting question," he said with mock gravity. "Before considering the what, however, we'd have to consider the where. I suppose there's always my room."

"Too dangerous. Everybody knows me at the Abelard. Anywhere in Amity would be too dangerous."

"What about your house?"

"Lord, no. Suppose one of my children came home. Besides . . ."

"I know. No desecrating the conjugal sheets. Okay, where else?"

"There must be motels between here and Montauk. Or even better, between here and Orient Point."

"Fair enough. Even if there's not, there's always the car."

"In broad daylight? You *do* have wild fantasies."

"In fantasies, anything is possible."

"All right. That's settled. So what would you do?"

"I think we should proceed chronologically. First of all, we'd leave here in one car. Probably mine, because it's least known. And we'd come back later to pick up yours."

"Okay."

"Then while we were driving along . . . no, even before that, before we left here, I'd send you into the ladies' room and tell you to take off your panties."

"Why?"

"So I could . . . explore you while we're on the road. Just to keep the motors running."

"I see," she said, trying to seem matter-of-fact. She felt hot, flushed, and sensed that her mind was floating somewhere apart from her body. She was a third person listening to the conversation. She had to fight to keep from shifting on the Leatherette bench. She wanted to squirm back and forth, to move her thighs up and down. But she was afraid of leaving a stain on the seat.

"Then," said Hooper, "while we were driving along, you might be sitting on my right hand and I'd be giving you a massage. Maybe I'd have my fly open. Maybe not, though, because you might get ideas, which would undoubtedly cause me to lose control, and *that* would probably cause a massive accident that would leave us both dead."

Ellen started to giggle again, imagining the sight of Hooper lying by the side of the road, stiff as a flagpole, and herself lying next to him, her dress bunched up around her waist and her vagina yawning open, glistening wet, for the world to see.

"We'd try to find a motel," said Hooper, "where the rooms are either in separate cabins or at least not butted right up against each other, wall to wall."

"Why?"

"Noise. The walls are usually made of Kleenex and spit, and we wouldn't want to be inhibited by the thought of a shoe salesman in the next room pressing his ear to the wall and getting his kicks listening to us."

"Suppose you couldn't find a motel like that."

"We would," said Hooper. "As I said, in a fantasy anything is possible."

Why does he keep saying that? Ellen thought. He can't really be playing a word game, working up a fantasy he has no intention of fulfilling. Her mind scrambled for a question to keep the conversation alive. "What name would you register us under?"

"Ah yes. I'd forgotten. These days I can't conceive of anyone getting uptight about something like this, but you're right: we should have a name, just in case we ran into an old-fashioned innkeeper. How about Mr. and Mrs. Al Kinsey. We could say we were on an extended field trip for research."

"And we'd tell him we'd send him an autographed copy of our report."

"We'd dedicate it to him!"

They both laughed, and Ellen said, "What about after we registered?"

"Well, we'd drive to wherever our room was, scout around to see if anyone seemed to be in the rooms nearby—unless we had a cabin to ourselves—and then go inside."

"And then?"

"That's when our options broaden. I'd probably be so turned on that I'd grab you, let you have it—maybe on the bed, maybe not. That time would be my time. Your time would come later."

"What do you mean?"

"The first time would be out of control—a slam-bam-thank-you-ma'am deal. After that, I'd have more control, and the second time I could prepare you."

"How would you do that?"

"With delicacy and finesse."

The waitress was approaching the table, so they sat back and stopped talking.

"Will there be anything else?"

"No," said Hooper. "Just the check."

Ellen assumed that the waitress would return to the bar to total the bill, but she stood at the table, scribbling and carrying her ones. Ellen slid to the edge of the seat and said as she stood up, "Excuse me. I want to powder my nose before we go."

"I know," said Hooper, smiling.

"You do?" said the waitress as Ellen passed her. "Boy, that's what marriage will do for you. I hope nobody ever knows me that well."

ELLEN ARRIVED HOME a little before 4:30. She went upstairs, into the bathroom, and turned on the water in the tub. She took off all her clothes and stuffed them into the laundry hamper, mixing them with the clothes already in the hamper. She looked in the mirror and examined her face and neck. No marks.

After her bath, she powdered herself, brushed her teeth, and gargled with mouthwash. She went into the bedroom, put on a fresh pair of underpants and a nightgown, pulled back the bedclothes and climbed into bed. She closed her eyes, hoping that sleep would pounce upon her.

But sleep could not overpower a memory that kept sliding into her mind. It was a vision of Hooper, eyes wide and staring—but unseeing—at the wall as he approached climax. The eyes seemed to bulge until, just before release, Ellen had feared they might actually pop out of their sockets. Hooper's teeth were clenched, and he ground them the way people do during sleep. From his voice there came a gurgling whine, whose tone rose higher and higher with each frenzied thrust. Even after his obvious, violent climax, Hooper's countenance had not changed. His teeth were still clenched, his eyes still fixed on the wall, and he continued to pump madly. He was oblivious of the being beneath him, and when, perhaps a full minute after his climax, Hooper still did not relax, Ellen had become afraid—of what, she wasn't sure, but the ferocity and intensity of his assault seemed to her a pursuit in which she was only a vehicle. After a while, she had tapped him on the back and said softly, "Hey, I'm here too," and in a moment his eyelids closed and his head dropped to her shoulder. Later, during their subsequent coupling, Hooper had been more gentle, more controlled, less detached. But the fury of the first encounter still lingered disturbingly in Ellen's mind.

Finally, her mind gave in to fatigue, and she fell asleep.

Almost instantly, it seemed, she was awakened by a voice that said, "Hey there, are you okay?" She opened her eyes and saw Brody sitting on the end of the bed.

She yawned. "What time is it?"

"Almost six."

"Oh-oh. I've got to pick up Sean. Phyllis Santos must be having a fit."

"I got him," said Brody. "I figured I'd better, once I couldn't reach you."

"You tried to reach me?"

"A couple of times. I tried you at the hospital at around two. They said they thought you'd come home."

"That's right. I did. I felt awful. My thyroid pills aren't doing what they should. So I came home."

"Then I tried to reach you here."

"My, it must have been important."

"No, it was nothing important. If you must know, I was calling to apologize for whatever I did that got you upset last night."

A twinge of shame struck Ellen, but it passed, and she said, "You're sweet, but don't worry. I'd already forgotten about it."

"Oh," said Brody. He waited a moment to see if she was going to say anything else, and when it was clear she wasn't, he said, "So where were you?"

"I told you, here!" The words came out more harshly than she had intended. "I came home and went to bed, and that's where you found me."

"And you didn't hear the phone? It's right there." Brody pointed to the bed table near the other side of the bed.

"No, I . . ." She started to say she had turned the phone off, but then she remembered that this particular phone couldn't be turned off all the way. "I took a pill. The moaning of the damned won't wake me after I've taken one of those pills."

Brody shook his head. "I really am going to throw those damn things down the john. You're turning into a junkie." He stood and went into the bathroom.

Ellen heard him flip up the toilet seat and begin to urinate —a loud, powerful, steady stream that went on and on and on. She smiled. Until today, she had assumed Brody was some kind of urinary freak: he could go for almost a day without urinating. Then, when he did pee, he seemed to pee forever. Long ago, she had concluded that his bladder was the size of a watermelon. Now she knew that huge bladder capacity was simply a male trait. Now, she said to herself, I am a woman of the world.

"Have you heard from Hooper?" Brody called over the noise of the endless stream.

Ellen thought for a moment about her response, then said, "He called this morning, just to say thank you. Why?"

"I tried to get hold of him today, too. Around midday and a

couple of times during the afternoon. The hotel said they didn't know where he was. What time did he call here?"

"Just after you left for work."

"Did he say what he was going to be doing?"

"He said . . . he said he might try to work on the boat, I think. I really don't remember."

"Oh. That's funny."

"What is?"

"I stopped by the dock on my way home. The harbor master said he hadn't seen Hooper all day."

"Maybe he changed his mind."

"He was probably shagging Daisy Wicker in some hotel room."

Ellen heard the stream slow, then dwindle into droplets. Then she heard the toilet flush.

9

ON THURSDAY MORNING Brody got a call summoning him to Vaughan's office for a noon meeting of the Board of Selectmen. He knew what the subject of the meeting was: opening the beaches for the Fourth of July weekend that would begin the day after tomorrow. By the time he left his office for the town hall, he had marshaled and examined every argument he could think of.

He knew his arguments were subjective, negative, based on intuition, caution, and an abiding, gnawing guilt. But Brody was convinced he was right. Opening the beaches would not be a solution or a conclusion. It would be a gamble that Amity —and Brody—could never really win. They would never know for certain that the shark had gone away. They would be living from day to day, hoping for a continuing draw. And one day, Brody was sure, they would lose.

The town hall stood at the head of Main Street, where Main dead-ended and was crossed by Water Street. The building was a crown at the top of the T formed by Main and Water streets. It was an imposing, pseudo-Georgian affair—red brick with white trim and two white columns framing the entrance. A World War II howitzer sat on the lawn in front of the town hall, a memorial to the citizens of Amity who had served in the war.

The building had been given to the town in the late 1920s by an investment banker who had somehow convinced himself that Amity would one day be the hub of commerce on eastern Long Island. He felt that the town's public officials should work in a building befitting their destiny—not, as had been the case until then, conducting the town's business in a tiny suite of airless rooms above a saloon called the Mill. (In February, 1930, the distraught banker, who had proved no more adept at predicting his own destiny than Amity's, tried, unsuccessfully, to reclaim the building, insisting he had intended only to loan it to the town.)

The rooms inside the town hall were as preposterously grandiose as the exterior. They were huge and high-ceilinged, each with its own elaborate chandelier. Rather than pay to remodel the interior into small cubicles, successive Amity administrations had simply jammed more and more people into each room. Only the mayor was still permitted to perform his part-time duties in solitary splendor.

Vaughan's office was on the southeast corner of the second floor, overlooking most of the town and, in the distance, the Atlantic Ocean.

Vaughan's secretary, a wholesome, pretty woman named Janet Sumner, sat at a desk outside the mayor's office. Though he seldom saw her, Brody was paternally fond of Janet, and he was idly mystified that—aged about twenty-six—she was still unmarried. He usually made a point of inquiring about her love life before he entered Vaughan's office. Today he said simply, "Are they all inside?"

"All that's coming." Brody started into the office, and Janet said, "Don't you want to know who I'm going out with?"

He stopped, smiled, and said, "Sure. I'm sorry. My mind's a mess today. So who is it?"

"Nobody. I'm in temporary retirement. But I'll tell you one thing." She lowered her voice and leaned forward. "I wouldn't mind playing footsie with that Mr. Hooper."

"Is he in there?"

Janet nodded.

"I wonder when he was elected selectman."

"I don't know," she said. "But he sure is cute."

"Sorry, Jan, he's spoken for."

"By who?"

"Daisy Wicker."

Janet laughed.

"What's funny? I just broke your heart."

"You don't know about Daisy Wicker?"

"I guess I don't."

Again Janet lowered her voice. "She's queer. She's got a lady roommate and everything. She's not even AC-DC. She's just plain old DC."

"I'll be damned," said Brody. "You sure do have an interesting job, Jan." As he entered the office, Brody said to himself: Okay, so where the hell *was* Hooper yesterday?

As soon as he was inside the office, Brody knew he would be fighting alone. The only selectmen present were longtime friends and allies of Vaughan's: Tony Catsoulis, a builder who looked like a fire hydrant; Ned Thatcher, a frail old man whose family had owned the Abelard Arms Inn for three generations; Paul Conover, owner of Amity Liquors; and Rafe Lopez (pronounced *loaps*), a dark-skinned Portuguese elected to the board by, and a vocal defender of, the town's black community.

The four selectmen sat around a coffee table at one end of the immense room. Vaughan sat at his desk at the other end of the room. Hooper stood at a southerly window, staring out at the sea.

"Where's Albert Morris?" Brody said to Vaughan after perfunctorily greeting the others.

"He couldn't make it," said Vaughan. "I don't think he felt well."

"And Fred Potter?"

"Same thing. There must be a bug going around." Vaughan stood up. "Well, I guess we're all here. Grab a chair and pull it over by the coffee table."

God, he looks awful, Brody thought as he watched Vaughan drag a straight-back chair across the room. Vaughan's eyes were sunken and dark. His skin looked like mayonnaise. Either he's got some fierce hangover, Brody decided, or else he hasn't slept in a month.

When everyone was seated, Vaughan said, "You all know why we're here. And I guess it's safe to say that there's only one of us that needs convincing about what we should do."

"You mean me," said Brody.

Vaughan nodded. "Look at it from our point of view, Martin. The town is dying. People are out of work. Stores that were going to open aren't. People aren't renting houses, let alone buying them. And every day we keep the beaches closed, we drive another nail into our own coffin. We're saying, officially, this town is unsafe: stay away from here. And people are listening."

"Suppose you do open the beaches for the Fourth, Larry," said Brody. "And suppose someone gets killed."

"It's a calculated risk, but I think—we think—it's worth taking."

"Why?"

Vaughan said, "Mr. Hooper?"

"Several reasons," said Hooper. "First of all, nobody's seen the fish in a week."

"Nobody's been in the water, either."

"That's true. But I've been on the boat looking for him every day—every day but one."

"I meant to ask you about that. Where were you yesterday?"

"It rained," said Hooper. "Remember?"

"So what did you do?"

"I just . . ." He paused momentarily, then said, "I studied some water samples. And read."

"Where? In your hotel room?"

"Part of the time, yeah. What are you driving at?"

"I called your hotel. They said you were out all afternoon."

"So I was out!" Hooper said angrily. "I don't have to report in every five minutes, do I?"

"No. But you're here to do a job, not go galavanting around all those country clubs you used to belong to."

"Listen, mister, you're not paying me. I can do whatever the fuck I want!"

Vaughan broke in. "Come on. This isn't getting anybody anywhere."

"Anyway," said Hooper, "I haven't seen a trace of that fish. Not a sign. Then there's the water. It's getting warmer every day. It's almost seventy now. As a rule—I know, rules are made to be broken—great whites prefer cooler water."

"So you think he's gone farther north?"

"Or out deeper, into colder water. He could even have gone south. You can't predict what these things are going to do."

"That's my point," said Brody. "You can't predict it. So all you're doing is guessing."

Vaughan said, "You can't ask for a guarantee, Martin."

"Tell that to Christine Watkins. Or the Kintner boy's mother."

"I know, I know," Vaughan said impatiently. "But we have to do something. We can't sit around waiting for divine revelation. God isn't going to scribble across the sky, 'The shark is gone.' We have to weigh the evidence and make a decision."

Brody nodded. "I guess. So what else has the boy genius come up with?"

"What's the matter with you?" said Hooper. "I was asked for my opinion."

"Sure," said Brody. "Okay. What else?"

"What we've known all along. That there's no reason for that fish to hang around here. I haven't seen him. The Coast Guard hasn't seen him. No new reef has popped up from the bottom. No garbage scows are dumping stuff into the water. No extraordinary fish life is around. There's just no reason for him to be here."

"But there never has been, has there? And he was here."

"That's true. I can't explain it. I doubt if anyone can."

"An act of God, then?"

"If you like."

"And there's no insurance against acts of God, is there, Larry?"

"I don't know what you're getting at, Martin," said Vaughan. "But we've got to make a decision. As far as I'm concerned, there's only one way to go."

"The decision's been made," said Brody.

"You could say that, yes."

"And when someone else gets killed? Who's taking the blame this time? Who's going to talk to the husband or the mother or the wife and tell them, 'We were just playing the odds, and we lost'?"

"Don't be so negative, Martin. When the time comes—*if* the time comes, and I'm betting it won't—we'll work that out then."

"Now, goddammit! I'm sick of taking all the shit for your mistakes."

"Wait a minute, Martin."

"I'm serious. If you want the authority for opening the beaches, then you take the responsibility, too."

"What are you saying?"

"I'm saying that as long as I'm chief of police in this town, as long as I'm supposed to be responsible for public safety, those beaches will not be open."

"I'll tell you this, Martin," said Vaughan. "If those beaches stay closed over the Fourth of July weekend, you won't have your job very long. And I'm not threatening. I'm telling you. We can still have a summer. But we have to tell people it's safe to come here. Twenty minutes after they hear you won't open the beaches, the people of this town will impeach you, or find a rail and run you out on it. Do you agree, gentlemen?"

"Fuckin' A," said Catsoulis. "I'll give 'em the rail myself."

"My people got no work," said Lopez. "You don't let them work, you're not gonna work."

Brody said flatly, "You can have my job any time you want it."

A buzzer sounded on Vaughan's desk. He stood up angrily and crossed the room. He picked up the phone. "I told you we didn't want to be disturbed!" he snapped. There was a moment's silence, and he said to Brody, "There's a call for you. Janet says it's urgent. You can take it here or outside."

"I'll take it outside," Brody said, wondering what could be urgent enough to call him out of a meeting with the selectmen. Another attack. He left the room and closed the door behind him. Janet handed him the phone on her desk, but before she could depress the flashing button to release it from "hold," Brody said, "Tell me: Did Larry ever call Albert Morris and Fred Potter this morning?"

Janet looked away from him. "I was told not to say anything about anything to anybody."

"Tell me, Janet. I need to know."

"Will you put in a good word for me with Golden Boy in there?"

"It's a deal."

"No. The only ones I called were the four in there."

"Push the button." Janet pushed the button, and Brody said, "Brody."

Inside his office, Vaughan saw the light stop flashing, and he gently eased his finger off the receiver hook and placed his hand over the mouthpiece. He looked around the room, searching each face for a challenge. No one returned his gaze —not even Hooper, who had decided that the less he was involved in the affairs of Amity, the better off he would be.

"It's Harry, Martin," said Meadows. "I know you're in a meeting and I know you've got to get back to it. So just listen. I'll be brief. Larry Vaughan is up to his tail in hock."

"I don't believe it."

"Listen, I said! The fact that he's in debt doesn't mean anything. It's who he's in debt to that matters. A long time ago, maybe twenty-five years, before Larry had any money, his wife got sick. I don't remember what she had, but it was serious. And expensive. My memory's a little hazy on this, but I remember him saying afterward that he had been helped out by a friend, gotten a loan to pull him through. It must have been for several thousand dollars. Larry told me the man's name. I wouldn't have thought anything about it, but Larry said something about the man being willing to help out people in trouble. I was young then, and I didn't have any money either. So I made a note of the name and stuck it away in my files. It never occurred to me to look it up again until you asked me to start snooping. The name was Tino Russo."

"Get to the point, Harry."

"I am. Now jump to the present. A couple of months ago, before this shark thing ever began, a company was formed called Caskata Estates. It's a holding company. At the beginning, it had no real assets. The first thing it bought was a big potato field just north of Scotch Road. When the summer didn't shape up well, Caskata began to buy a few more properties. It was all perfectly legitimate. The company obviously has cash behind it—somewhere—and it was taking advantage of the down market to pick up properties at low prices. But then—as soon as the first newspaper reports about the shark thing came out—Caskata really started buying. The lower real estate prices fell, the more they bought. All very quietly. Prices are so low now that it's almost like during the war, and Caskata's still buying. Very little money down. All short-term promissory notes. Signed by Larry Vaughan, who is listed as

the president of Caskata. The executive vice-president of Caskata Estates is Tino Russo, who the *Times* has been listing for
years as a second-echelon crumb in one of the five Mafia families in New York."

Brody whistled through his teeth. "And the sonofabitch
has been moaning about how nobody's been buying anything
from him. I still don't understand why he's being pressured to
open the beaches."

"I'm not sure. I'm not even sure he's still being pressured.
He may be arguing out of personal desperation. I imagine he's
way overextended. He couldn't buy anything more no matter
how low the prices go. The only way he can get out without
being ruined is if the market turns around and the prices go
up. Then he can sell what he's bought and get the profit. Or
Russo can get the profit, however the deal's worked out. If
prices keep going down—in other words, if the town is still
officially unsafe—his notes are going to come due. He can't
possibly meet them. He's probably got over half a million out
now in cash down payments. He'll lose his cash, and the
properties will either revert to the original owners or else get
picked up by Russo if he can raise the cash. I don't imagine
Russo would want to take the risk. Prices might keep going
down, and then he'd take a bath along with Vaughan. My
guess is that Russo still has hopes of big profits, but the only
way he has a chance of getting them is if Vaughan forces the
beaches open. Then, if nothing happens—if the shark doesn't
kill anybody else—before long prices will go up and Vaughan
can sell out. Russo will take his cut—half the gross or whatever—and Caskata will be dissolved. Vaughan will get what's
left, probably enough to keep him from being ruined. If the
shark does kill someone else, then the only one who gets
screwed is Vaughan. As far as I can tell, Russo doesn't have a
nickel in cash in this outfit. It's all—"

"You're a goddamned liar, Meadows!" Vaughan's voice
shrieked into the phone. "You print one word of that crap and
I'll sue you to death!" There was a click as Vaughan slammed
down the phone.

"So much for the integrity of our elected officials," said
Meadows.

"What *are* you going to do, Harry? Can you print anything?"

"No, at least not yet. I can't document enough. You know as well as I do that the mob is getting more and more involved in Long Island—the construction business, restaurants, everything. But it's hard as hell to prove an actual illegality. In Vaughan's case, I'm not sure there's anything illegal going on, in the strict sense of the word. In a few days, with a little more digging, I should be able to put together a piece saying that Vaughan has been associating with a known mobster. I mean a piece that will hold up if Vaughan ever did try to sue."

"It sounds to me like you've got enough now," said Brody.

"I have the knowledge, but not the proof. I don't have the documents, or even copies of them. I've seen them, but that's all."

"Do you think any of the selectmen are in on the deal? Larry loaded this meeting against me"

"No. You mean Catsoulis and Conover? They're just old buddies who owe Larry a favor or two. If Thatcher's there, he's too old and too scared to say a word against Larry. And Lopez is straight. He's really concerned about jobs for his people."

"Does Hooper know any of this? He's making a pretty strong case for opening the beaches."

"No, I'm pretty sure he doesn't. I only wrapped it up myself a few minutes ago, and there are still a lot of loose threads."

"What do you think I ought to do? I may have quit already. I offered them my job before I came out to take your call.

"Christ, don't quit. First of all, we need you. If you quit, Russo will get together with Vaughan and handpick your successor. You may think all your troops are honest, but I'll bet Russo could find one who wouldn't mind exchanging a little integrity for a few dollars—or even just for a shot at the chief's job."

"So where does that leave me?"

"If I were you, I'd open the beaches."

"For God's sake, Harry, that's what they want! I might as well go on their payroll."

"You said yourself that there's a strong argument for opening the beaches. I think Hooper's right. You're going to have to open them sometime, even if we never see that fish again. You might as well do it now."

"And let the mob take their money and run."

"What else *can* you do? You keep them closed, and Vaughan'll find a way to get rid of you and he'll open them himself. Then you'll be no use whatever. To anybody. At least this way, if you open the beaches and nothing happens, the town might have a chance. Then, maybe later, we can find a way to pin something on Vaughan. I don't know what, but maybe there'll be something."

"Shit," said Brody. "All right, Harry, I'll think about it. But if I open them, I'm gonna do it my way. Thanks for the call." He hung up and went into Vaughan's office.

Vaughan was standing at the southerly window, his back to the door. When he heard Brody walk in, he said, "The meeting's over."

"What do you mean, over?" said Catsoulis. "We ain't decided a fuckin' thing."

Vaughan spun around and said, "It's over, Tony! Don't give me any trouble. It'll work out the way we want. Just give me a chance to have a little chat with the chief. Okay? Now everybody out."

Hooper and the four selectmen left the office. Brody watched Vaughan as he ushered them out. He knew he should feel pity for Vaughan, but he couldn't suppress the contempt that flowed over him. Vaughan shut the door, walked over to the couch, and sat down heavily. He rested his elbows on his knees and rubbed his temples with his fingertips. "We were friends, Martin," he said. "I hope we can be again."

"How much of what Meadows said is true?"

"I won't tell you. I can't. Suffice it to say that a man once did a favor for me and now he wants me to repay the favor."

"In other words, all of it."

Vaughan looked up, and Brody saw that his eyes were red and wet. "I swear to you, Martin, if I had any idea how far this would go, I'd never have gotten into it."

"How much are you into him for?"

"The original amount was ten thousand. I tried to pay it back twice, a long time ago, but I could never get them to cash my checks. They kept saying it was a gift, not to worry about it. But they never gave me back my marker. When they came to me a couple of months ago, I offered them a hundred thousand dollars—cash. They said it wasn't enough. They didn't want the money. They wanted me to make a few investments. Everybody'd be a winner, they said."

"And how much are you out now?"

"God knows. Every cent I have. More than every cent. Probably close to a million dollars." Vaughan took a deep breath. "Can you help me, Martin?"

"The only thing I can do for you is put you in touch with the D.A. If you'd testify, you might be able to slap a loan-sharking rap on these guys."

"I'd be dead before I got home from the D.A.'s office, and Eleanor would be left without anything. That's not the kind of help I meant."

"I know." Brody looked down at Vaughan, a huddled, wounded animal, and he did feel compassion for him. He began to doubt his own opposition to opening the beaches. How much of it was the residue of prior guilt, how much fear of another attack? How much was he indulging himself, playing it safe, and how much was prudent concern for the town? "I'll tell you what, Larry. I'll open the beaches. Not to help you, because I'm sure if I didn't open them you'd find a way to get rid of me and open them yourself. I'll open the beaches because I'm not sure I'm right anymore."

"Thanks, Martin. I appreciate that."

"I'm not finished. Like I said, I'll open them. But I'm going to post men on the beaches. And I'm going to have Hooper patrol in the boat. And I'm going to make sure every person who comes down there knows the danger."

"You can't do that!" Vaughan said. "You might as well leave the damn things closed."

"I can do it, Larry, and I will."

"What are you going to do? Post signs warning of a killer shark? Put an ad in the newspaper saying 'Beaches Open— Stay Away'? Nobody's going to go to the beach if it's crawling with cops."

"I don't know what I'm going to do. But something. I'm not going to make believe nothing ever happened."

"All right, Martin." Vaughan rose. "You don't leave me

much choice. If I got rid of you, you'd probably go down to the beach as a private citizen and run up and down yelling 'Shark!' So all right. But be subtle—if not for my sake, for the town's."

Brody left the office. As he walked down the stairs, he looked at his watch. It was past one o'clock, and he was hungry. He went down Water Street to Loeffler's, Amity's only delicatessen. It was owned by Paul Loeffler, a classmate of Brody's in high school.

As Brody pulled open the glass door, he heard Loeffler say, ". . . like a goddam dictator, if you ask me. I don't know what's his problem." When he saw Brody, Loeffler blushed. He had been a skinny kid in high school, but as soon as he had taken over his father's business, he had succumbed to the terrible temptations that surrounded him for twelve hours of every day of every week, and nowadays he looked like a pear.

Brody smiled. "You weren't talking about *me*, were you, Paulie?"

"What makes you think that?" said Loeffler, his blush deepening.

"Nothing. Never mind. If you'll make me a ham and Swiss on rye with mustard, I'll tell you something that will make you happy."

"That I have to hear." Loeffler began to assemble Brody's sandwich.

"I'm going to open the beaches for the Fourth."

"That makes me happy."

"Business bad?"

"Bad."

"Business is always bad with you."

"Not like this. If it doesn't get better soon, I'm gonna be the cause of a race riot."

"What do you mean?"

"I'm supposed to hire two delivery boys for the summer. I'm committed. But I can't afford two. Let alone I don't have enough work for two, the way things are. So I can only hire one. One's white and one's black."

"Which one are you hiring?"

"The black one. I figure he needs the money more. I just thank God the white one isn't Jewish."

BRODY ARRIVED HOME at 5:10. As he pulled into the driveway, the back door to the house opened, and Ellen ran toward him. She had been crying, and she was still visibly upset.

"What's the matter?" he said.

"Thank God you're home. I tried to reach you at work, but you had already left. Come here. Quick." She took him by the hand and led him past the back door to the shed where they kept the garbage cans. "In there," she said, pointing to a can. "Look."

Brody removed the lid from the can. Lying in a twisted heap atop a bag of garbage was Sean's cat—a big, husky tom named Frisky. The cat's head had been twisted completely around, and the yellow eyes overlooked its back.

"How the hell did that happen?" said Brody. "A car?"

"No, a man." Ellen's breath came in sobs. "A man did it to him. Sean was right there when it happened. The man got out of a car over by the curb. He picked up the cat and twisted its head until the neck broke. Sean said it made a horrible snap. Then he dropped the cat on the lawn and got back in his car and drove away."

"Did he say anything?"

"I don't know. Sean's inside. He's hysterical, and I don't blame him. Martin, what's *happening*?"

Brody slammed the top back on the can. "Goddamn sonof-*abitch*!" he said. His throat felt tight, and he clenched his teeth, popping the muscles on both sides of his jaw. "Let's go inside."

Five minutes later, Brody marched out the back door. He tore the lid off the garbage can and threw it aside. He reached in and pulled out the cat's corpse. He took it to his car, pitched it through the open window, and climbed in. He backed out of the driveway and screeched away. A hundred yards down the road, in a burst of fury, he turned on his siren.

It took him only a couple of minutes to reach Vaughan's house, a large, Tudor-style stone mansion on Sprain Drive, just off Scotch Road. He got out of the car, dragging the dead cat by one of its hind legs, mounted the front steps, and rang the bell. He hoped Eleanor Vaughan wouldn't answer the door.

The door opened, and Vaughan said, "Hello, Martin. I . . ."

Brody raised the cat and pushed it toward Vaughan's face. "What about this, you cocksucker?"

Vaughan's eyes widened. "What do you mean? I don't know what you're talking about."

"One of your friends did this. Right in my front yard, right in front of my kid. They murdered my fucking cat! Did you tell them to do that?"

"Don't be crazy, Martin." Vaughan seemed genuinely shocked. "I'd never do anything like that. Never."

Brody lowered the cat and said, "Did you call your friends after I left?"

"Well . . . yes. But just to say that the beaches would be open tomorrow."

"That's all you said?"

"Yes. Why?"

"You lying fuck!" Brody hit Vaughan in the chest with the cat and let it fall to the floor. "You know what the guy said after he strangled my cat? You know what he told my eight-year-old boy?"

"No. Of course I don't know. How would I know?"

"He said the same thing you did. He said: 'Tell your old man this—"Be subtle." ' "

Brody turned and walked down the steps, leaving Vaughan standing over the gnarled bundle of bone and fur.

10

FRIDAY WAS CLOUDY, with scattered light showers, and the only people who swam were a young couple who took a quick dip early in the morning just as Brody's man arrived at the beach. Hooper patrolled for six hours and saw nothing. On Friday night Brody called the Coast Guard for a weather report. He wasn't sure what he hoped to hear. He knew he should wish for beautiful weather for the three-day holiday weekend. It would bring people to Amity and if nothing happened, if nothing was sighted, by Tuesday he might begin to believe the shark had gone. If nothing happened. Privately, he would have welcomed a three-day blow that would keep the beaches clear over the weekend. Either way, he begged his personal deities not to let anything happen.

He wanted Hooper to go back to Woods Hole. It was not just that Hooper was always there, the expert voice to contradict his caution. Brody sensed that somehow Hooper had come into his home. He knew Ellen had talked to Hooper since the party: young Martin had mentioned something about the possibility of Hooper taking them on a beach picnic to look for shells. Then there was that business on Wednesday. Ellen had said she was sick, and she certainly had looked worn out when he came home. But where had Hooper been that day? Why had he been so evasive when Brody had asked him about it? For the first time in his married life, Brody was wondering, and the wondering filled him with an uncomfortable ambivalence—self-reproach for questioning Ellen, and fear that there might actually be something to wonder about.

The weather report was for clear and sunny, southwest winds five to ten knots. Well, Brody thought, maybe that's for the best. If we have a good weekend and nobody gets hurt, maybe I can believe. And Hooper's sure to leave.

Brody had said he would call Hooper as soon as he talked to the Coast Guard. He was standing at the kitchen phone. Ellen was washing the supper dishes. Brody knew Hooper was staying at the Abelard Arms. He saw the phone book buried beneath a pile of bills, note pads, and comic books on the kitchen counter. He started to reach for it, then stopped. "I have to call Hooper," he said. "You know where the phone book is?"

"It's six-five-four-three," said Ellen.

"What is?"

"The Abelard. That's the number: six-five-four-three."

"How do you know?"

"I have a memory for phone numbers. You know that. I always have."

He did know it, and he cursed himself for playing stupid tricks. He dialed the number.

"Abelard Arms." It was a male voice, young. The night clerk.

"Matt Hooper's room, please."

"You don't happen to know the room number, sir?"

"No." Brody cupped his hand over the mouthpiece and said to Ellen, "You don't happen to know the room number, do you?"

She looked at him, and for a second she didn't answer. Then she shook her head.

The clerk said, "Here it is. Four-oh-five."

The phone rang twice before Hooper answered.

"This is Brody."

"Yeah. Hi."

Brody faced the wall, trying to imagine what the room looked like. He conjured visions of a small dark garret, a rumpled bed, stains on the sheets, the smells of rut. He felt, briefly, that he was going out of his mind. "I guess we're on for tomorrow," he said. "The weather report is good."

"Yeah, I know."

"Then I'll see you down at the dock."

"What time?"

"Nine-thirty, I guess. Nobody's going to go swimming before then."

"Okay. Nine-thirty."

"Fine. Oh hey, by the way," Brody said, "how did things work out with Daisy Wicker?"

"What?"

Brody wished he hadn't asked the question. "Nothing. I was just curious. You know, about whether you two hit it off."

"Well . . . yeah, now that you mention it. Is that part of your job, to check on people's sex lives?"

"Forget it. Forget I ever mentioned it." He hung up the phone. Liar, he thought. What the hell is going on here? He turned to Ellen. "I meant to ask you, Martin said something about a beach picnic. When's that?"

"No special time," she said. "It was just a thought."

"Oh." He looked at her, but she didn't return the glance. "I think it's time you got some sleep."

"Why do you say that?"

"You haven't been feeling well. And that's the second time you've washed that glass." He took a beer from the refrigerator. He yanked the metal tab and it broke off in his hand. "Fuck!" he said, and he threw the full can into the wastebasket and marched out of the room.

SATURDAY NOON, BRODY stood on a dune overlooking the Scotch Road beach, feeling half secret agent, half fool. He was wearing a polo shirt and a bathing suit: he had had to buy one specially for this assignment. He was chagrined at his white legs, nearly hairless after years of chafing in long pants. He wished Ellen had come with him, to make him feel less conspicuous, but she had begged off, claiming that since he wasn't going to be home over the weekend, this would be a good time to catch up on her housework. In a beach bag by Brody's side were a pair of binoculars, a walkie-talkie, two beers, and a cellophane-wrapped sandwich. Offshore, between a quarter and half a mile, the *Flicka* moved slowly eastward. Brody watched the boat and said to himself: At least I know where *he* is today.

The Coast Guard had been right: the day was splendid—cloudless and warm, with a light onshore breeze. The beach was not crowded. A dozen teen-agers were scattered about in their ritual rows. A few couples lay dozing—motionless as corpses, as if to move would disrupt the cosmic rhythms that generated a tan. A family was gathered around a charcoal fire in the sand, and the scent of grilling hamburger drifted into Brody's nose.

No one had yet gone swimming. Twice, different sets of parents had led their children to the water's edge and allowed them to wade in the wavewash, but after a few minutes—bored or fearful—the parents had ordered the children back up the beach.

Brody heard footsteps crackling in the beach grass behind him, and he turned around. A man and a woman—in their late forties, probably, and both grossly overweight—were struggling up the dune, dragging two complaining children behind them. The man wore khakis, a T-shirt, and basketball sneakers. The woman wore a print dress that rode up her wrinkled thighs. In her hand she carried a pair of sandals. Behind them Brody saw a Winnebago camper parked on Scotch Road.

"Can I help you?" Brody said when the couple had reached the top of the dune.

"Is this the beach?" said the woman.

"What beach are you looking for? The public beach is—"

"This is it, awright," said the man, pulling a map out of his pocket. He spoke with the unmistakable accent of the Queens Borough New Yorker. "We turned off Twenty-seven and followed this road here. This is it, awright."

"So where's the shark?" said one of the children, a fat boy of about thirteen. "I thought you said we were gonna see a shark."

"Shut up," said his father. He said to Brody, "Where's this hotshot shark?"

"What shark?"

"The shark that's killed all them people. I seen it on TV—on three different channels. There's a shark that kills people. Right here."

"There *was* a shark here," said Brody. "But it isn't here now. And with any luck, it won't come back."

The man stared at Brody for a second and then snarled, "You mean we drove all the way out here to see this shark and he's gone? That's not what the TV said."

"I can't help that," said Brody. "I don't know who told you you were going to see that shark. They don't just come up on the beach and shake hands, you know."

"Don't smart-mouth me, buddy."

Brody stood up. "Listen, mister," he said, pulling his wallet from the belt of his bathing suit and opening it so the man could see his badge. "I'm the chief of police in this town. I don't know who you are, or who you think you are, but you don't march onto a private beach in Amity and start behaving like a bum. Now state your business or beat it."

The man stopped posturing. "Sorry," he said. "It's just after all that goddam traffic and the kids screaming in my ear, I thought at least we'd get a look at the shark. That's what we come all the way out here for."

"You drove two and a half hours to see a shark? Why?"

"Something to do. Last weekend we went to Jungle Habitat. We thought maybe this weekend we'd go to the Jersey Shore. But then we heard about the shark out here. The kids never seen a shark before."

"Well, I hope they don't see one today, either."

"Shit," said the man.

"You said we'd see a shark!" whined one of the boys.

"Shut your mouth, Benny!" The man turned back to Brody. "Is it okay if we have lunch here?"

Brody knew he could order the people down to the public beach, but without a resident's parking sticker they would have to park their camper more than a mile from the beach, so he said, "I guess so. If somebody complains, you'll have to move, but I doubt anyone will complain today. Go ahead. But don't leave anything—not a gum wrapper or a matchstick—on the beach, or I'll slap a ticket on you for littering."

"Okay." The man said to his wife, "You got the cooler?"

"I left it in the camper," she said. "I didn't know we'd be staying."

"Shit." The man trudged down the dune, panting. The woman and her two children walked twenty or thirty yards away and sat on the sand.

Brody looked at his watch: 12:15. He reached into the beach bag and took out the walkie-talkie. He pushed a button and said, "You there, Leonard?" Then he released the button.

In a moment the reply came back, rasping through the speaker. "I read you, Chief. Over." Hendricks had volunteered to spend the weekend on the public beach, as the third point in the triangle of watch. ("You're getting to be a regular beach bum," Brody had said when Hendricks volunteered. Hendricks had laughed and said, "Sure, Chief. If you're going to live in a place like this, you might as well become a beautiful people.")

"What's up?" said Brody. "Anything going on?"

"Nothing we can't handle, but there is a little problem. People keep coming up to me and trying to give me tickets. Over."

"Tickets for what?"

"To get onto the beach. They say they bought special tickets in town that allow them to come onto the Amity beach. You should see the damn things. I got one right here. It says "Shark Beach. Admit One. Two-fifty." All I can figure is some sharpie is making a pretty fine killing selling people tickets they don't need. Over."

"What's their reaction when you turn down their tickets?"

"First, they're mad as hell when I tell them they've been taken, that there's no charge for coming to the beach. Then they get even madder when I tell them that, ticket or no ticket, they can't leave their cars in the parking lot without a parking permit. Over."

"Did any of them tell you who's selling the tickets?"

"Just some guy, they say. They met him on Main Street, and he told them they couldn't get on the beach without a ticket. Over."

"I want to find out who the hell is selling those tickets, Leonard, and I want him stopped. Go to the phone booth in the parking lot and call headquarters and tell whoever answers that I want a man to go down to Main Street and arrest that bastard. If he comes from out of town, run him out of town. If he lives here, lock him up."

"On what charge? Over."

"I don't care. Think of something. Fraud. Just get him off the streets."

"Okay, Chief."

"Any other problems?"

"No. There are some more of those TV guys here with one of those mobile units, but they're not doing anything except interviewing people. Over."

"About what?"

"Just the standard stuff. You know: Are you scared to go swimming? What do you think about the shark? All that crap. Over."

"How long have they been there?"

"Most of the morning. I don't know how long they'll hang around, especially since no one's going in the water. Over."

"As long as they're not causing any trouble."

"Nope. Over."

"Okay. Hey, Leonard, you don't have to say 'over' all the time. I can tell when you're finished speaking."

"Just procedure, Chief. Keeps things clear. Over and out."

Brody waited a moment, then pushed the button again and said, "Hooper, this is Brody. Anything out there?" There was no answer. "This is Brody calling Hooper. Can you hear me?" He was about to call a third time, when he heard Hooper's voice.

"Sorry. I was out on the stern. I thought I saw something."

"What did you see?"

"Nothing. I'm sure it was nothing. My eyes were playing tricks on me."

"What did you *think* you saw?"

"I can't really describe it. A shadow, maybe. Nothing more. The sunlight can fool you."

"You haven't seen anything else?"

"Not a thing. All morning."

"Let's keep it that way. I'll check with you later."

"Fine. I'll be in front of the public beach in a minute or two."

Brody put the walkie-talkie back in the bag and took out his sandwich. The bread was cold and stiff from resting against the ice-filled plastic bag that contained the cans of beer.

By 2:30, the beach was almost empty. People had gone off to play tennis, to sail, to have their hair done. The only ones left on the beach were half a dozen teen-agers and the family from Queens.

Brody's legs had begun to sunburn—faint red blotches were surfacing on his thighs and the tops of his feet—so he covered them with his towel. He took the walkie-talkie out of the bag and called Hendricks. "Anything happened, Leonard?"

"Not a thing, Chief. Over."

"Anybody go swimming?"

"Nope. Wading, but that's about it. Over."

"Same here. What do you hear about the ticket seller?"

"Nothing, but nobody's giving me tickets anymore, so I guess somebody ran him off. Over."

"What about the TV people?"

"They're gone. They left a few minutes ago. They wanted to know where you were. Over."

"What for?"

"Beats me. Over."

"Did you tell them?"

"Sure. I didn't see why not. Over."

"Okay. I'll talk to you later." Brody decided to take a walk. He pushed a finger into one of the pink blotches on his thigh. It turned stark white, then flushed angry red when he removed his finger. He stood, wrapped his towel around his waist to keep the sun from his legs, and, carrying the walkie-talkie, strolled toward the water.

He heard the sound of a car engine, and he turned and walked to the top of the dune. A white panel truck was parked on Scotch Road. The black lettering on its side said, "WNBC-TV News." The driver's door opened, and a man got out and trudged through the sand toward Brody.

As the man drew closer, Brody thought he looked vaguely familiar. He was young, with long, curly hair and a handlebar moustache.

"Chief Brody?" he said when he was a few steps away.

"That's right."

"They told me you'd be here. I'm Bob Middleton, Channel Four News."

"Are you the reporter?"

"Yeah. The crew's in the truck."

"I thought I'd seen you somewhere. What can I do for you?"

"I'd like to interview you."

"About what?"

"The whole shark business. How you decided to open the beaches."

Brody thought for a moment, then said to himself, What the hell: a little publicity couldn't hurt the town, now that the chances of anything happening—today, at least—are pretty slim. "All right," he said. "Where do you want to do it?"

"Down on the beach. I'll get the crew. It'll take a few minutes to set up, so if you have something to do, feel free. I'll give a yell when we're ready." Middleton trotted away toward the truck.

Brody had nothing special to do, but since he had started to take a walk, he thought he might as well take it. He walked down toward the water.

As he passed the group of teen-agers, he heard a boy say, "What about it? Anybody got the guts? Ten bucks is ten bucks."

A girl said, "Come on, Limbo, lay off."

Brody stopped about fifteen feet away, feigning interest in something offshore.

"What for?" said the boy. "It's a pretty good offer. I don't think anybody's got the guts. Five minutes ago, you were all telling me there's no *way* that shark's still around here."

Another boy said, "If you're such hot shit, why don't you go in?"

"I'm the one making the offer," said the first boy. "Nobody's gonna pay *me* ten bucks to go in the water. Well, what do you say?"

There was a moment's silence, and then the other boy said, "Ten bucks? Cash?"

"It's right here," said the first boy, shaking a ten-dollar bill.

"How far out do I have to go?"

"Let's see. A hundred yards. That's a pretty good distance. Okay?"

"How do I know how far a hundred yards is?"

"Guess. Just keep swimming for a while and then stop. If it looks like you're a hundred yards out, I'll wave you back."

"You've got a deal." The boy stood up.

The girl said, "You're crazy, Jimmy. Why do you want to go in the water? You don't need ten dollars."

"You think I'm scared?"

"Nobody said anything about being scared," said the girl. "It's unnecessary, is all."

"Ten bucks is never unnecessary," said the boy, "especially when your old man cuts off your allowance for blowing a little grass at your aunt's wedding."

The boy turned and began to jog toward the water. Brody said, "Hey!" and the boy stopped.

"What?"

Brody walked over to the boy. "What are you doing?"

"Going swimming. Who are you?"

Brody took out his wallet and showed the boy his badge. "Do you want to go swimming?" he said. He saw the boy look past him at his friends.

"Sure. Why not? It's legal, isn't it?"

Brody nodded. He didn't know whether the others were out of earshot, so he lowered his voice and said, "Do you want me to order you not to?"

The boy looked at him, hesitated for a moment, then shook his head. "No, man. I can use the ten bucks."

"Don't stay in too long," said Brody.

"I won't." The boy scampered into the water. He flung himself over a small wave and began to swim.

Brody heard footsteps running behind him. Bob Middleton dashed past him and called out to the boy, "Hey! Come back!" He waved his arms and called again.

The boy stopped swimming and stood up. "What's the matter?"

"Nothing. I want to get some shots of you going into the water. Okay?"

"Sure, I guess so," said the boy. He began to wade back toward the shore.

Middleton turned to Brody and said, "I'm glad I caught him before he got too far out. At least we'll get *somebody* swimming out here today."

Two men came up beside Brody. One was carrying a 16 mm camera and a tripod. He wore combat boots, fatigue trousers, a khaki shirt, and a leather vest. The other man was shorter and older and fatter. He wore a rumpled gray suit and carried a rectangular box covered with dials and knobs. Around his neck was a pair of earphones.

"Right there's okay, Walter," said Middleton. "Let me know when you're ready." He took a notebook from his pocket and began to ask the boy some questions.

The elderly man walked down to Middleton and handed him a microphone. He backed up to the cameraman, feeding wire off a coil in his hand.

"Anytime," said the cameraman.

"I gotta get a level on the kid," said the man with the earphones.

"Say something," Middleton told the boy, and he held the microphone a few inches from the boy's mouth.

"What do you want me to say?"

"That's good," said the man with the earphones.

"Okay," said Middleton. "We'll start tight, Walter, then go to a two-shot, okay? Give me speed when you're ready."

The cameraman peered into the eyepiece, raised a finger, and pointed it at Middleton. "Speed," he said.

Middleton looked at the camera and said, "We have been here on the Amity beach since early this morning, and as far as we know, no one has yet dared venture into the water. There has been no sign of the shark, but the threat still lingers. I'm standing here with Jim Prescott, a young man who has just decided to take a swim. Tell me, Jim, do you have any worries about what might be swimming out there with you?"

"No," said the boy. "I don't think there's anything out there."

"So you're not scared."

"No."

"Are you a good swimmer?"

"Pretty good."

Middleton held out his hand. "Well, good luck, Jim. Thanks for talking to us."

The boy shook Middleton's hand. "Yeah," he said. "What do you want me to do now?"

"Cut!" said Middleton. "We'll take it from the top, Walter. Just a sec." He turned to the boy. "Don't ask that, Jim, okay? After I thank you, just turn around and head for the water."

"Okay," said the boy. He was shivering, and he rubbed his arms.

"Hey, Bob," said the cameraman. "The kid ought to dry off. He can't look wet if he isn't supposed to have been in the water yet."

"Yeah, you're right," said Middleton. "Can you dry off, Jim?"

"Sure." The boy jogged up to his friends and dried himself with a towel.

A voice beside Brody said, "What's goin' on?" It was the man from Queens.

"Television," said Brody. "They want to film somebody swimming."

"Oh yeah? I should of brought my suit."

The interview was repeated, and after Middleton had thanked the boy, the boy ran into the water and began to swim.

Middleton walked back to the cameraman and said, "Keep it going, Walter. Irv, you can kill the sound. We'll probably use this for B-roll."

"How much do you want of this?" said the cameraman, tracking the boy as he swam.

"A hundred feet or so," said Middleton. "But let's stay here till he comes out. Be ready, just in case."

Brody had become so accustomed to the far-off, barely audible hum of the *Flicka*'s engine that his mind no longer registered it as a sound. It was as integral a part of the beach as the wave sound. Suddenly the engine's pitch changed from a low murmur to an urgent growl. Brody looked beyond the swimming boy and saw the boat in a tight, fast turn—nothing like the slow, ambling sweeps Hooper made in his normal patrol. He put the walkie-talkie to his mouth and said, "You see something, Hooper?" Brody saw the boat slow, then stop.

Middleton heard Brody speak. "Give me sound, Irv," he said. "Get this, Walter." He walked to Brody and said, "Something going on, Chief?"

"I don't know," said Brody. "That's what I'm trying to find out." He said into the walkie-talkie, "Hooper?"

"Yes," said Hooper's voice, "but I still don't know what it is. It was that shadow again. I can't see it now. Maybe my eyes are getting tired."

"You get that, Irv?" said Middleton. The sound man shook his head: no.

"There's a kid swimming out there," said Brody.

"Where?" said Hooper.

Middleton shoved the microphone at Brody's face, sliding it between his mouth and the mouthpiece of the walkie-talkie. Brody brushed it aside, but Middleton quickly jammed it back to within an inch of Brody's mouth.

"Thirty, maybe forty yards out. I think I better tell him to come in." Brody tucked the walkie-talkie into the towel at his waist, cupped his hands around his mouth, and called, "Hey out there! Come on in!"

"Jesus!" said the sound man. "You damn near blew my ears out."

The boy did not hear the call. He was swimming straight away from the beach.

The boy who had offered the ten dollars heard Brody's call, and he walked down to the water's edge. "What's the trouble now?" he said.

"Nothing," said Brody. "I just think he'd better come in."

"Who are you?"

Middleton stood between Brody and the boy, flipping the microphone back and forth between the two.

"I'm the police chief," Brody said. "Now get your ass out of here!" He turned to Middleton. "And you keep that fucking microphone out of my face, will you?"

"Don't worry, Irv," said Middleton. "We can edit that out."

Brody said into the walkie-talkie, "Hooper, he doesn't hear me. You want to toot in here and tell him to come ashore?"

"Sure," said Hooper. "I'll be there in a minute."

The fish had sounded now, and was meandering a few feet above the sandy bottom, eighty feet below the *Flicka*. For hours, its sensory system had been tracking the strange sound above. Twice the fish had risen to within a yard or two of the surface, allowing sight and smell and nerve canals to assess the creature passing noisily overhead. Twice it had sounded, compelled neither to attack nor move away.

Brody saw the boat, which had been facing westward, swing toward shore and kick up a shower of spray from the bouncing bow.

"Get the boat, Walter," said Middleton.

Below, the fish sensed a change in the noise. It grew louder, then faded as the boat moved away. The fish turned, banking as smoothly as an airplane, and followed the receding sound.

The boy stopped swimming, raised his head, and looked toward shore, treading water. Brody waved his arms and yelled, "Come in!" The boy waved back and started for shore. He swam well, rolling his head to the left to catch a breath, kicking in rhythm with his arm strokes. Brody guessed he was sixty yards from shore and that it would take him a minute or more to reach the beach.

"What's goin' on?" said a voice next to Brody. It was the man from Queens. His two sons stood behind him, smiling eagerly.

"Nothing," said Brody. "I just don't want the boy to get out too far."

"Is it the shark?" asked the father of the two boys.

"Hey, neat," said the other boy.

"Never mind!" said Brody. "Just get back up the beach."

"Come on, Chief," said the man. "We drove all the way out here."

"Beat it!" said Brody.

At fifteen knots, it took Hooper only thirty seconds to cover the couple of hundred yards and draw near the boy. He stopped a few yards away, letting the engine idle in neutral. He was just beyond the surf line, and he didn't dare go closer for fear of being caught in the waves.

The boy heard the engine, and he raised his head. "What's the matter?" he said.

"Nothing," said Hooper. "Keep swimming."

The boy lowered his head and swam. A swell caught him and moved him faster, and with two or three more strokes he was able to stand. The water was up to his shoulders, and he began to plod toward shore.

"Come on!" said Brody.

"I am," said the boy. "What's the problem, anyway?"

A few yards behind Brody, Middleton stood with the microphone in his hand. "What are you on, Walter?" he said.

"The kid," said the cameraman, "and the cop. Both. A two-shot."

"Okay. You running, Irv?"

The sound man nodded.

Middleton spoke into the microphone: "Something is going on, ladies and gentlemen, but we don't know exactly what. All we know for sure is that Jim Prescott went swimming, and then suddenly a man on a boat out there saw something. Now Police Chief Brody is trying to get the boy to come ashore as fast as possible. It could be the shark, but we just don't know."

Hooper put the boat in reverse, to back away from the waves. As he looked off the stern, he saw a silver streak moving in the gray-blue water. It seemed part of the wave-motion, but it moved independently. For a second, Hooper did not realize what he was seeing. And even when the realization struck, he did not see the fish clearly. He cried, "Look out!"

"What is it?" yelled Brody.

"The fish! Get the kid out! Quick!"

The boy heard Hooper, and he tried to run. But in the chest-deep water his movements were slow and labored. A swell knocked him sideways. He stumbled, then stood and leaned forward.

Brody ran into the water and reached out. A wave hit him in the knees and pushed him back.

Middleton said into the microphone, "The man on the boat just said something about a fish. I don't know if he means a shark."

"Is it the shark?" said the man from Queens, standing next to Middleton. "I don't see it."

Middleton said, "Who are you?"

"Name's Lester Kraslow. You want to interview me?"

"Go away."

The boy was moving faster now, pushing through the water with his chest and arms. He did not see the fin rise behind him, a sharp blade of brownish gray that hovered in the water.

"There it is!" said Kraslow. "See it, Benny? Davey? It's right there."

"I don't see nothin'," said one of his sons.

"There it is, Walter!" said Middleton. "See it?"

"I'm zooming," said the cameraman. "Yeah, I've got it."

"Hurry!" said Brody. He reached for the boy. The boy's eyes were wide and panicked. His nostrils flared, bubbling mucus and water. Brody's hand touched the boy's, and he pulled. He grabbed the boy around the chest, and together they staggered out of the water.

The fin dropped beneath the surface, and following the slope of the ocean floor, the fish moved into the deep.

Brody stood in the sand with his arm around the boy. "Are you okay?" he said.

"I want to go home." The boy shivered.

"I bet you do." Brody started to walk the boy to where his friends were standing, but Middleton intercepted them.

"Can you repeat that for me?" said Middleton.

"Repeat what?"

"Whatever you said to the boy. Can we do that again?"

"Get out of my way!" Brody snapped. He took the boy to his friends, and said to the one who had offered the money, "Take him home. And give him his ten dollars." The boy nodded, pale and scared.

Brody saw his walkie-talkie wallowing in the wavewash. He retrieved it, wiped it free of water, pushed the "talk" button, and said, "Leonard, can you hear me?"

"I read you, Chief. Over."

"The fish has been here. If you've got anybody in the water down there, get them out. Right away. And stay there till we get relief for you. Nobody goes near the water. The beach is officially closed."

"Okay, Chief. Was anybody hurt? Over."

"No, thank God. But almost."

"Okay, Chief. Over and out."

As Brody walked back to where he had left his beach bag, Middleton called to him, "Hey, Chief, can we do that interview now?"

Brody stopped, tempted to tell Middleton to go fuck himself. Instead, he said, "What do you want to know? You saw it as well as I did."

"Just a couple of questions."

Brody sighed and returned to where Middleton stood with his camera crew. "All right," he said, "go ahead."

"How much have you got left on your roll, Walter?" said Middleton.

"About fifty feet. Make it brief."

"Okay. Give me speed."

"Speed."

"Well, Chief Brody," said Middleton, "that was a lucky break, wouldn't you say?"

"It was very lucky. The boy might have died."

"Would you say that's the same shark that killed the people?"

"I don't know," said Brody. "I guess it must be."

"So where do you go from here?"

"The beaches are closed. For the time being, that's all I can do."

"I guess you'd have to say that it isn't yet safe to swim here in Amity."

"I'd have to say that, that's right."

"What does that mean for Amity?"

"Trouble, Mr. Middleton. We are in big trouble."

"In retrospect, Chief, how do you feel about having opened the beaches today?"

"How do I *feel*? What kind of question is that? Angry, annoyed, confused. Thankful that nobody got hurt. Is that enough?"

"That's just fine, Chief," Middleton said with a smile. "Thank you, Chief Brody." He paused, then said, "Okay, Walter, that'll wrap it. Let's get home and start editing this mess."

"What about a close?" said the cameraman. "I've got about twenty-five feet left."

"Okay," said Middleton. "Wait'll I think of something profound to say."

Brody gathered up his towel and his beach bag and walked over the dune toward his car. When he got to Scotch Road, he saw the family from Queens standing beside their camper.

"Was that the shark that killed the people?" asked the father.

"Who knows?" said Brody. "What's the difference?"

"Didn't look like much to me, just a fin. The boys was kind of disappointed."

"Listen you jerk," Brody said. "A boy almost got killed just now. Are you disappointed that didn't happen?"

"Don't give me that," said the man. "That thing wasn't even close to him. I bet the whole thing was a put-on for them TV guys."

"Mister, get out of here. You and your whole goddam brood. Get 'em out of here. Now!"

Brody waited while the man loaded his family and their gear into the camper. As he walked away, he heard the man say to his wife, "I figured all the people would be snot-noses out here. I was right. Even the cops."

AT SIX O'CLOCK, Brody sat in his office with Hooper and Meadows. He had already talked to Larry Vaughan, who called—drunk and in tears—and muttered wildly about the ruination of his life. The buzzer on Brody's desk rang, and he picked up the phone.

"Fellow named Bill Whitman to see you, Chief," said Bixby. "Says he's from the *New York Times*."

"Oh, for . . . Okay, what the hell. Send him in."

The door opened, and Whitman stood in the doorway. He said, "Am I interrupting something?"

"Nothing much," said Brody. "Come on in. You remember Harry Meadows. This is Matt Hooper, from Woods Hole."

"I remember Harry Meadows, all right," said Whitman. "It was thanks to him that I got my ass chewed from one end of Forty-third Street to the other by my boss."

"Why was that?" said Brody.

"Mr. Meadows conveniently forgot to tell me about the attack on Christine Watkins. But he didn't forget to tell his readers."

"Must have slipped my mind," said Meadows.

"What can we do for you?" said Brody.

"I was wondering," said Whitman, "if you're sure this is the same fish that killed the others."

Brody gestured toward Hooper, who said, "I can't be positive. I never saw the fish that killed the others, and I didn't really get a look at the one today. All I saw was a flash, sort of silvery gray. I know what it was, but I couldn't compare it to anything else. All I have to go on is probability, and in all probability it's the same fish. It's too farfetched—for me, anyway—to believe that there are two big man-eating sharks off southern Long Island at the same time."

Whitman said to Brody, "What are you going to do, Chief? I mean, beyond closing the beaches, which I gather has already been done."

"I don't know. What *can* we do? Christ, I'd rather have a hurricane. Or even an earthquake. At least after they happen, they're over and done with. You can look around and see what's been done and what has to be done. They're events, something you can handle. They have beginnings and ends. This is crazy. It's as if there was a maniac running around loose, killing people whenever he felt like it. You know who he is, but you can't catch him and you can't stop him. And what makes it worse, you don't know why he's doing it."

Meadows said, "Remember Minnie Eldridge."

"Yeah," said Brody. "I'm beginning to think she may have something, after all."

"Who's that?" said Whitman.

"Nobody. Just some nut."

For a moment there was silence, an exhausted silence, as if everything that needed to be said had been said. Then Whitman said, "Well?"

"Well what?" said Brody.

"There must be someplace to go from here, something to do."

"I'd be happy to hear any suggestions. Personally, I think we're fucked. We're going to be lucky if there's a town left after this summer."

"Isn't that a bit of an exaggeration?"

"I don't think so. Do you, Harry?"

"Not really," said Meadows. "The town survives on its summer people, Mr. Whitman. Call it parasitic, if you will, but that's the way it is. The host animal comes every summer, and Amity feeds on it furiously, pulling every bit of sustenance it can before the host leaves again after Labor Day. Take away the host animal, and we're like dog ticks with no dog to feed on. We starve. At the least—the very least—next winter is going to be the worst in the history of this town. We're going to have so many people on the dole that Amity will look like Harlem." He chuckled. "Harlem-by-the-Sea."

"What I'd give my ass to know," said Brody, "is why us? Why Amity? Why not East Hampton or Southampton or Quogue?"

"That," said Hooper, "is something we'll never know."

"Why?" said Whitman.

"I don't want to sound like I'm making excuses for mis-judging that fish," said Hooper, "but the line between the nat-ural and the preternatural is very cloudy. Natural things oc-cur, and for most of them there's a logical explanation. But for a whole lot of things there's just no good or sensible an-swer. Say two people are swimming, one in front of the other, and a shark comes up from behind, passes right beside the guy in the rear and attacks the guy in front. Why? Maybe they smelled different. Maybe the one in front was swimming in a more provocative way. Say the guy in back, the one who wasn't attacked, goes to help the one who was attacked. The shark may not touch him—may actually avoid him—while he keeps banging away at the guy he did hit. White sharks are supposed to prefer colder water. So why does one turn up off the coast of Mexico, strangled by a human corpse that he couldn't quite swallow? In a way, sharks are like tornadoes. They touch down here, but not there. They wipe out this house but suddenly veer away and miss the house next door. The guy in the house that's wiped out says, 'Why me?' The guy in the house that's missed says, 'Thank God.'"

"All right," said Whitman. "But what I still don't get is why the shark can't be caught."

"Maybe it can be," said Hooper. "But I don't think by us. At least not with the equipment we have here. I suppose we could try chumming again."

"Yeah," said Brody. "Ben Gardner can tell us all about chumming."

"Do you know anything about some fellow named Quint?" said Whitman.

"I've heard the name," Brody said. "Did you ever look into the guy, Harry?"

"I read what little there was. As far as I know, he's never done anything illegal."

"Well," said Brody, "maybe it's worth a call."

"You're joking," said Hooper. "You'd really do business with this guy?"

"I'll tell you what, Hooper. At this point, if someone came in here and said he was Superman and he could piss that shark away from here, I'd say fine and dandy. I'd even hold his dick for him."

"Yeah, but . . ."

Brody cut him off. "What do you say, Harry? You think he's in the phone book?"

"You really are serious," said Hooper.

"You bet your sweet ass. You got any better ideas?"

"No, it's just . . . I don't know. How do we know the guy isn't a phony or a drunk or something?"

"We'll never know till we try." Brody took a phone book from the top drawer of his desk and opened it to the Qs. He ran his finger down the page. "Here it is. 'Quint.' That's all it says. No first name. But it's the only one on the page. Must be him." He dialed the number.

"Quint," said a voice.

"Mr. Quint, this is Martin Brody. I'm the chief of police over in Amity. We have a problem."

"I've heard."

"The shark was around again today."

"Anybody get et?"

"No, but one boy almost did."

"Fish that big needs a lot of food," said Quint.

"Have you seen the fish?"

"Nope. Looked for him a couple times, but I couldn't spend too much time looking. My people don't spend their money for looking. They want action."

"How did you know how big it is?"

"I hear tell. Sort of averaged out the estimates and took off about eight feet. That's still a piece of fish you got there."

"I know. What I'm wondering is whether you can help us."

"I know. I thought you might call."

"Can you?"

"That depends."

"On what?"

"On how much you're willing to spend, for one thing."

"We'll pay whatever the going rate is. Whatever you charge by the day. We'll pay you by the day until we kill the thing."

"I don't think so," said Quint. "I think this is a premium job."

"What does that mean?"

"My everyday rate's two hundred a day. But this is special. I think you'll pay double."

"Not a chance."

"Good-bye."

"Wait a minute! Come on, man. Why are you holding me up?"

"You got no place else to go."

"There are other fishermen."

Brody heard Quint laugh—a short, derisive bark. "Sure there are," said Quint. "You already sent one. Send another one. Send half a dozen more. Then when you come back to me again, maybe you'll even pay triple. I got nothing to lose by waiting."

"I'm not asking for any favors," Brody said. "I know you've got a living to make. But this fish is killing people. I want to stop it. I want to save lives. I want your help. Can't you at least treat me the way you treat regular clients?"

"You're breaking my heart," said Quint. "You got a fish needs killing, I'll try to kill it for you. No guarantees, but I'll do my best. And my best is worth four hundred dollars a day."

Brody sighed. "I don't know that the selectmen will give me the money."

"You'll find it somewhere."

"How long do you think it'll take to catch the fish?"

"A day, a week, a month. Who knows? We may never find him. He may go away."

"Don't I wish," said Brody. He paused. "Okay," he said finally. "I guess we don't have any choice."

"No, you don't."

"Can you start tomorrow?"

"Nope. Monday's the earliest. I got a party tomorrow."

"A party? What do you mean, a dinner party?"

Quint laughed again, the same piercing bark. "A charter party," he said. "You don't do much fishing."

Brody blushed. "No, that's right. Can't you cancel them? If we're paying all that money, it seems to me we deserve a little special service."

"Nope. They're regular customers. I couldn't do that to them or I'd lose their business. You're just a one-shot deal."

"Suppose you run into the big fish tomorrow. Will you try to catch him?"

"That would save you a lot of money, wouldn't it? We won't see your fish. We're going due east. Terrific fishing due east. You oughta try it sometime."

"You had it all figured out, right?"

"There's one more thing," said Quint. "I'm gonna need a man with me. I lost my mate, and I wouldn't feel comfortable taking on that big fish without an extra pair of hands."

"Lost your mate? What, overboard?"

"No, he quit. He got nerves. Happens to most people after a while in this work. They get to thinking too much."

"But it doesn't happen to you."

"No. I know I'm smarter 'n the fish."

"And that's enough, just being smarter?"

"Has been so far. I'm still alive. What about it? You got a man for me?"

"You can't find another mate?"

"Not this quick, and not for this kind of work."

"Who are you going to use tomorrow?"

"Some kid. But I won't take him out after a big white."

"I can understand that," said Brody, beginning to doubt the wisdom of approaching Quint for help. He added casually, "I'll be there, you know." He was shocked by the words as soon as he said them, appalled at what he had committed himself to do.

"You? Ha!"

Brody smarted under Quint's derision. "I can handle myself," he said.

"Maybe. I don't know you. But you can't handle a big fish if you don't know nothing about fishing. Can you swim?"

"Of course. What has that got to do with anything?"

"People fall overboard, and sometimes it takes a while to swing around and get to 'em."

"Don't worry about me."

"Whatever you say. But I still need a man who knows something about fishing. Or at least about boats."

Brody looked across his desk at Hooper. The last thing he wanted was to spend days on a boat with Hooper, especially in a situation in which Hooper would outrank him in knowledge, if not authority. He could send Hooper alone and stay ashore himself. But that, he felt, would be capitulating, admitting finally and irrevocably his inability to face and conquer the strange enemy that was waging war on his town.

Besides, maybe—over the course of a long day on a boat—Hooper might make a slip that would reveal what he had been doing last Wednesday, the day it rained. Brody was becoming obsessed with finding out where Hooper was that day, for whenever he allowed himself to consider the various alternatives, the one on which his mind always settled was the one he most dreaded. He wanted to *know* that Hooper was at the movies, or playing backgammon at the Field Club, or smoking dope with some hippie, or laying some Girl Scout. He didn't care what it was, as long as he could know that Hooper had not been with Ellen. Or that he had been. In that case . . . ? The thought was still too wretched to cope with.

He cupped his hand over the mouthpiece and said to Hooper, "Do you want to come along? He needs a mate."

"He doesn't even have a mate? What a half-assed operation."

"Never mind that. Do you want to come or not?"

"Yes," said Hooper. "I'll probably live to regret it, but yes. I want to see that fish, and I guess this is my only chance."

Brody said to Quint, "Okay, I've got your man."

"Does he know boats?"

"He knows boats."

"Monday morning, six o'clock. Bring whatever you want to eat. You know how to get here?"

"Route 27 to the turnoff for Promised Land, right?"

"Yeah. It's called Cranberry Hole Road. Straight into town. About a hundred yards past the last houses, take a left on a dirt road."

"Is there a sign?"

"No, but it's the only road around here. Leads right to my dock."

"Yours the only boat there?"

"Only one. It's called the *Orca*."

"All right. See you Monday."

"One more thing," said Quint. "Cash. Every day. In advance."

"Okay, but how come?"

"That's the way I do business. I don't want you falling overboard with my money."

"All right," said Brody. "You'll have it." He hung up and said to Hooper, "Monday, six A.M., okay?"

"Okay."

Meadows said, "Do I gather from your conversation that you're going, too, Martin?"

Brody nodded. "It's my job."

"I'd say it's a bit beyond the call."

"Well, it's done now."

"What's the name of his boat?" asked Hooper.

"I think he said *Orca*," said Brody. "I don't know what it means."

"It doesn't *mean* anything. It *is* something. It's a killer whale."

Meadows, Hooper, and Whitman rose to go. "Good luck," said Whitman. "I kind of envy you your trip. It should be exciting."

"I can do without excitement," said Brody. "I just want to get the damn thing over with."

At the door, Hooper turned and said, "Thinking of orca reminds me of something. You know what Australians call great white sharks?"

"No," said Brody, not really interested. "What?"

"White death."

"You had to tell me, didn't you?" Brody said as he closed the door behind them.

He was on his way out when the night desk man stopped

him and said, "You had a call before, Chief, while you were inside. I didn't think I should bother you."

"Who was it?"

"Mrs. Vaughan."

"*Mrs.* Vaughan!" As far as Brody could remember, he had never in his life talked to Eleanor Vaughan on the telephone.

"She said not to disturb you, that it could wait."

"I'd better call her. She's so shy that if her house was burning down, she'd call the fire department and apologize for bothering them and ask if there was a chance they could stop by the next time they were in the neighborhood." As he walked back into his office, Brody recalled something Vaughan had told him about Eleanor: whenever she wrote a check for an even-dollar amount, she refused to write "and 00/100." She felt it would be an insult, as if she were suggesting that the person who cashed the check might try to steal a few cents.

Brody dialed the Vaughans' home number, and Eleanor Vaughan answered before the phone had rung once. She's been sitting right by the phone, Brody thought. "Martin Brody, Eleanor. You called."

"Oh yes. I do hate to bother you, Martin. If you'd rather—"

"No, it's perfectly okay. What's on your mind?"

"It's . . . well, the reason I'm calling *you* is that I know Larry talked with you earlier. I thought you might know if . . . if anything's wrong."

Brody thought: She doesn't know anything, not a thing. Well, I'm damned if I'm going to tell her. "Why? What do you mean?"

"I don't know how to say this exactly, but . . . well, Larry doesn't drink much, you know. Very rarely, at least at home."

"And?"

"This evening, when he came home, he didn't say anything. He just went into his study and—I think, at least—he drank almost a whole bottle of whiskey. He's asleep now, in a chair."

"I wouldn't worry about it, Eleanor. He's probably got things on his mind. We all tie one on now and then."

"I know. It's only . . . something *is* wrong. I can tell. He hasn't acted like himself for several days now. I thought that perhaps . . . you're his friend. Do you know what it could be?"

His friend, Brody thought. That's what Vaughan had said, too, but he had known better. "We used to be friends," he had said. "No, Eleanor, I don't," he lied. "I'll talk to him about it, though, if you like."

"Would you, Martin? I'd appreciate that. But . . . please . . . don't tell him I called you. He's never wanted me to meddle in his affairs."

"I won't. Don't worry. Try to get some sleep."

"Will he be all right in the chair?"

"Sure. Just take off his shoes and throw a blanket over him. He'll be fine."

PAUL LOEFFLER STOOD behind the counter of his delicatessen and looked at his watch. "It's quarter to nine," he said to his wife, a plump, pretty woman named Rose, who was arranging boxes of butter in a refrigerator. "What do you say we cheat and close up fifteen minutes early?"

"After a day like today I agree," said Rose. "Eighteen pounds of bologna! Since when have we ever moved eighteen pounds of bologna in one day?"

"And the Swiss cheese," said Loeffler. "When did we ever run out of Swiss cheese before? A few more days like this I could use. Roast beef, liverwurst, everything. It's like everybody from Brooklyn Heights to East Hampton stopped by for sandwiches."

"Brooklyn Heights, my eye. Pennsylvania. One man said he had come all the way from Pennsylvania. Just to see a fish. They don't have fish in Pennsylvania?"

"Who knows?" said Loeffler. "It's getting to be like Coney Island."

"The public beach must look like a dump."

"It's worth it. We deserve one or two good days."

"I heard the beaches are closed again," said Rose.

"Yeah. Like I always say, when it rains it pours."

"What are you talking about?"

"I don't know. Let's close up."

Part Three

11

THE SEA WAS as flat as gelatin. There was no whisper of wind to ripple the surface. The sun sucked shimmering waves of heat from the water. Now and then, a passing tern would plunge for food, and rise again, and the wavelets from its dive became circles that grew without cease.

The boat sat still in the water, drifting imperceptibly in the tide. Two fishing rods, in rod-holders at the stern, trailed wire line into the oily slick that spread westward behind the boat. Hooper sat at the stern, a twenty-gallon garbage pail at his side. Every few seconds, he dipped a ladle into the pail and spilled it overboard into the slick.

Forward, in two rows that peaked at the bow, lay ten wooden barrels the size of quarter kegs of beer. Each was wrapped in several thicknesses of three-quarter-inch hemp, which continued in a hundred-foot coil beside the barrel. Tied to the end of each rope was the steel head of a harpoon.

Brody sat in the swiveled fighting chair bolted to the deck, trying to stay awake. He was hot and sticky. There had been no breeze at all during the six hours they had been sitting and waiting. The back of his neck was already badly sunburned, and every time he moved his head the collar of his uniform shirt raked the tender skin. His body odor rose to his face and, blended with the stench of the fish guts and blood being ladled overboard, nauseated him. He felt poached.

Brody looked up at the figure on the flying bridge: Quint. He wore a white T-shirt, faded blue-jean trousers, white socks, and a pair of graying Top-Sider sneakers. Brody guessed Quint was about fifty, and though surely he had once been twenty and would one day be sixty, it was impossible to imagine what he would look like at either of those ages. His present age seemed the age he should always be, should always have been. He was about six feet four and very lean—perhaps 180 or 190 pounds. His head was totally bald—not shaven, for there were no telltale black specks on his scalp, but as bald as if he had never had any hair—and when, as now, the sun was high and hot, he wore a Marine Corps fatigue cap. His face, like the rest of him, was hard and sharp. It was ruled by a long, straight nose. When he looked down from the flying bridge, he seemed to aim his eyes—the darkest eyes Brody had ever seen—along the nose as if it were a rifle barrel. His skin was permanently browned and creased by wind and salt and sun. He gazed off the stern, rarely blinking, his eyes fixed on the slick.

A trickle of sweat running down Brody's chest made him stir. He turned his head, wincing at the sting in his neck, and tried to stare at the slick. But the reflection of the sun on the water hurt his eyes, and he turned away. "I don't see how you do it, Quint," he said. "Don't you ever wear sunglasses?"

Quint looked down and said, "Never." His tone was completely neutral, neither friendly nor unfriendly. It did not invite conversation.

But Brody was bored, and he wanted to talk. "How come?"

"No need to. I see things the way they are. That's better."

Brody looked at his watch. It was a little after two: three or four more hours before they would give up for the day and go home. "Do you have a lot of days like this?" The excitement and anticipation of the early morning had long passed, and Brody was sure they would not sight the fish that day.

"Like what?"

"Like this. When you sit all day long and nothing happens."

"Some."

"And people pay you even though they never catch a thing."

"Those are the rules."

"Even if they never get a bite?"

Quint nodded. "That doesn't happen too often. There's

generally something that'll take a bait. Or something we can stick."

"Stick?"

"With an iron." Quint pointed to the harpoons on the bow.

Hooper said, "What kinds of things do you stick, Quint?"

"Anything that swims by."

"Really? I don't—"

Quint cut him off. "Something's taking one of the baits."

Shading his eyes with his hand, Brody looked off the stern, but as far as he could see, the slick was undisturbed, the water flat and calm. "Where?" he said.

"Wait a second," said Quint. "You'll see."

With a soft metallic hiss, the wire on the starboard fishing rod began to feed overboard, knifing into the water in a straight silver line.

"Take the rod," Quint said to Brody. "And when I tell you, throw the brake and hit him."

"Is it the shark?" said Brody. The possibility that at last he was going to confront the fish—the beast, the monster, the nightmare—made Brody's heart pound. His mouth was sticky-dry. He wiped his hands on his trousers, took the rod out of the holder, and stuck it in the swivel between his legs.

Quint laughed—a short, sour yip. "That thing? No. That's just a little fella. Give you some practice for when your fish finds us." Quint watched the line for a few more seconds, then said, "Hit it!"

Brody pushed the small lever on the reel forward, leaned down, then pulled back. The tip of the rod bent into an arc. With his right hand, Brody began to turn the crank to reel in the fish, but the reel did not respond. The line kept speeding out.

"Don't waste your energy," said Quint.

Hooper, who had been sitting on the transom, stood up and said, "Here, I'll tighten down the drag."

"You will not!" said Quint. "You leave that rod alone."

Hooper looked up, bewildered and slightly hurt.

Brody noticed Hooper's pained expression, and he thought: What do you know? It's about time.

After a moment, Quint said, "You tighten the drag down too far and you'll tear the hook out of his mouth."

"Oh," said Hooper.

"I thought you was supposed to know something about fishing."

Hooper said nothing. He turned and sat down on the transom.

Brody held on to the rod with both hands. The fish had gone deep and was moving slowly from side to side, but it was no longer taking line. Brody reeled—leaning forward and cranking quickly as he picked up slack, hauling backward with the muscles in his shoulders and back. His left wrist ached, and the fingers in his right hand began to cramp from cranking. "What the hell have I got here?" he said.

"A blue," said Quint.

"He must weigh half a ton."

Quint laughed. "Maybe a hundred fifty pounds."

Brody hauled and leaned, hauled and leaned, until finally he heard Quint say, "You're getting there. Hold it." He stopped reeling.

With a smooth, unhurried motion, Quint swung down the ladder from the flying bridge. He had a rifle in his hand, an old army M-1. He stood at the gunwale and looked down. "You want to see the fish?" he said. "Come look."

Brody stood, and reeling to take up the slack as he walked, he moved to the side of the boat. In the dark water the shark was acrylic blue. It was about eight feet long, slender, with long pectoral fins. It swam slowly from side to side, no longer struggling.

"He's beautiful, isn't he?" said Hooper.

Quint flicked the rifle's safety to "off," and when the shark moved its head to within a few inches of the surface, he squeezed off three quick shots. The bullets made clean round holes in the shark's head, drawing no blood. The shark shuddered and stopped moving.

"He's dead," said Brody.

"Shit," said Quint. "He's stunned, maybe, but that's all." Quint took a glove from one of his hip pockets, slipped his right hand into it, and grabbed the wire line. From a sheath at his belt he took a knife. He lifted the shark's head clear of the water and bent over the gunwale. The shark's mouth was open two or three inches wide. Its right eye, partly covered by a white membrane, gazed blankly at Quint. Quint jammed the knife into the shark's mouth and tried to pry it open farther, but the shark bit down, holding the blade in its small triangular teeth. Quint pulled and twisted until the knife came free. He put it back in its sheath and took a pair of wire cutters from his pocket.

"I guess you're paying me enough so I can afford to lose a hook and a little leader," he said. He touched the wire cutters to the leader and was about to snip it. "Wait a minute," he said, putting the cutters back in his pocket and taking out his knife. "Watch this. This always gives the folks a boot." Holding the leader in his left hand, he hoisted most of the shark out of the water. With a single swift motion he slit the shark's belly from the anal fin to just below the jaw. The flesh pulled apart, and bloody entrails—white and red and blue—tumbled into the water like laundry falling from a basket. Then Quint cut the leader with the wire snips, and the shark slid overboard. As soon as its head was beneath the water, the shark began to thrash in the cloud of blood and innards, biting any morsel that passed into its maw. The body twitched as the shark swallowed, and pieces of intestines passed out the hole in the belly, to be eaten again.

"Now watch," said Quint. "If we're lucky, in a minute other blues'll come around, and they'll help him eat himself. If we get enough of them, there'll be a real feeding frenzy. That's quite a show. The folks like that."

Brody watched, spellbound, as the shark continued to nibble at the floating guts. In a moment he saw a flash of blue rise from below. A small shark—no more than four feet long—snapped at the body of the disemboweled fish. Its jaws closed on a bit of flapping flesh. Its head shook violently from side to side, and its body trembled, snakelike. A piece of flesh tore away, and the smaller shark swallowed it. Soon another shark appeared, and another, and the water began to roil. Flecks of blood mingled with the drops of water that splashed on the surface.

Quint took a gaff from beneath the gunwale. He leaned overboard, holding the gaff poised like an ax. Suddenly he lunged and jerked backward. Impaled on the gaff hook, squirming and snapping, was a small shark. Quint took the

knife from its sheath, slashed the shark's belly, and released
it. "Now you'll see something," he said.

Brody couldn't tell how many sharks there were in the
explosion of water. Fins crisscrossed on the surface, tails
whipped the water. Amid the sounds of splashes came an occasional grunt as fish slammed into fish. Brody looked down
at his shirt and saw that it was spattered with water and
blood.

The frenzy continued for several minutes, until only three
large sharks remained, cruising back and forth beneath the
surface.

The men watched in silence until the last of the three had
vanished.

"Jesus," said Hooper.

"You don't approve," said Quint.

"That's right. I don't like to see things die for people's
amusement." Quint snickered, and Hooper said, "Do you?"

"It ain't a question of liking it or not. It's what feeds me."

Quint reached into an ice chest and took out another hook
and leader. The hook had been baited before they left the
dock—a squid skewered and tied to the shaft and barb of the
hook. Using pliers, Quint attached the leader to the end of the
wire line. He dropped the bait overboard, fed out thirty yards
of line, and let it drift into the slick.

Hooper resumed his routine of ladling chum into the water. Brody said, "Anybody want a beer?" Both Quint and
Hooper nodded, so he went below and took three cans from a
cooler. As he left the cabin, Brody noticed two old, cracked,
and curling photographs thumbtacked to the bulkhead. One
showed Quint standing hip-deep in a pile of big, strange-look-
ing fish. The other was a picture of a dead shark lying on a
beach. There was nothing else in the photograph to compare
the fish to, so Brody couldn't determine its size.

Brody left the cabin, gave the others their beers, and sat
down in the fighting chair. "I saw your pictures down there,"
he said to Quint. "What are all those fish you're standing in?"

"Tarpon," said Quint. "That was a while back, when I did
some fishing in Florida. I never seen anything like it. We must
have got thirty, forty tarpon—big tarpon—in four nights' fishing."

"And you kept them?" said Hooper. "You're supposed to throw them back."

"Customers wanted 'em. For pictures, I guess. Anyway, they don't make bad chum, chopped up."

"What you're saying is, they're more use dead than alive."

"Sure. Same with most fish. And a lot of animals, too. I never did try to eat a live steer." Quint laughed.

"What's the other picture?" said Brody. "Just a shark?"

"Well, not *just* a shark. It was a big white—about fourteen, fifteen feet. Weighed over three thousand pounds."

"How did you catch it?"

"Ironed it. But I tell you"—Quint chuckled—"for a while there it was a question of who was gonna catch who."

"What do you mean?"

"Damn thing attacked the boat. No provocation, no nothing. We were sitting out here minding our own business, when whamo! It felt like we was hit by a freight train. Knocked my mate right on his ass, and the customer started screaming bloody murder that we were sinking. Then the bastard hit us again. I put an iron in him and we chased him—Christ, we must have chased him halfway across the Atlantic."

"How could you follow him?" Brody asked. "Why didn't he go deep?"

"Couldn't. Not with that barrel following him. They float. He dragged it down for a little while, but before too long the strain got to him and he came to the surface. So we just kept following the barrel. After a couple hours we got another two irons in him, and he finally came up, real quiet, and we throwed a rope round his tail and towed him to shore. And all the time that customer's going bullshit, 'cause he's sure we're sinking and gonna get et up.

"You know the funniest thing? When we got the fish back and we was all tied up safe and sound and not likely to sink, that dumb fuck of a customer comes up to me and offers me five hundred bucks if I'll say he caught the fish on hook and line. Iron holes all over it, and he wants me to swear he caught it on hook and line! Then he starts giving me some song and dance about how I ought to cut my fee in half because I didn't give him a chance to catch the fish on hook and line. I told him that if I had let him try, I'd be out one hook, three hundred yards of wire line, probably one reel and one rod, and definitely one fish. Then he says what about all the valuable publicity I'll be getting from a trip *he's* paying for. I told him he could give me the money and keep the publicity and try to spread it on a cracker for himself and his wife."

"I wondered about that hook-and-line business," said Brody.

"What do you mean?"

"What you were saying. You wouldn't try to catch the fish we're after on a hook and line, would you?"

"Shit, no. From what I hear, the fish that's been bothering you makes the one we got look like a pup."

"Then how come the lines are out?"

"Two reasons. First, a big white might just take a little squid bait like that. It'd cut the line pretty quick, but at least we'd know he was around. It's a useful telltale. The other reason is, you never know what a chum slick will bring around. Even if your fish doesn't show up, we might run into something else that'll take the bait."

"Like what?"

"Who knows? Maybe something useful. I've had swordfish take a drifting squid, and with all the federal bullshit about mercury no one's catching them commercially anymore, so you can get two fifty a pound for broadbill in Montauk. Or maybe just something that'll give you a boot in the ass to catch, like a mako. If you're paying four hundred bucks, you might as well have some fun for your money."

"Suppose the big white did come around," said Brody. "What would be the first thing you'd do?"

"Try to keep him interested enough so he'd stick around till we could get at him. It's no big trick; they're pretty stupid fish. It depends on how he finds us. If he pulls the same crap the other one did and attacks the boat, we'll just start pumping irons into him as fast as we can, then pull away from him and let him wear himself down. If he takes one of the lines, there'll be no way to stop him if he wants to run. But I'll try to turn him toward us—tighten the drag way down and take the risk of tearing loose. He'll probably bend the hook out pretty quick, but we might get him close enough for an iron. And once I've got one iron in him, it's only a matter of time.

"Most likely, the way he'll come will be following his nose —right up the slick, either on the surface or just below. And that's where we'll have a little trouble. The squid isn't enough to keep him interested. Fish that size'll suck a squid right down and not even know he's et it. So we'll have to give him something special that he can't turn down, something with a big ol' hook in it that'll hold him at least until we can stick him once or twice."

"If the hook's too obvious," said Brody, "won't he avoid the bait altogether?"

"No. These things don't have the brains of a dog. They eat anything. If they're feeding, you could throw a bare hook down at 'em and they'll take it if they see it. A friend of mine had one come up once and try to eat the outboard motor off his dinghy. He only spat it out 'cause he couldn't get it down in one swallow."

From the stern, where he was ladling chum, Hooper said, "What's something special, Quint?"

"You mean that special treat he can't turn down?" Quint smiled and pointed to a green plastic garbage can nestled in a corner amidships. "Take a look for yourself. It's in that can. I've been saving it for a fish like the one we're after. On anything else it'd be a waste."

Hooper walked over to the can, flipped the metal clasps off the sides, and lifted the top. His shock at what he saw made him gasp. Floating vertically in the can full of water, its lifeless head swaying gently with the motion of the boat, was a tiny bottle-nosed dolphin, no more than two feet long. Sticking out from a puncture on the outside of the jaw was the eye of a huge shark hook, and from a hole in the belly the barbed hook itself curled forward. Hooper clutched the sides of the can and said, "A baby."

"Even better," Quint said with a grin. "Unborn."

Hooper gazed into the can for a few more seconds, then slammed the top back on and said, "Where did you get it?"

"Oh, I guess about six miles from here, due east. Why?"

"I mean how did you get it?"

"How do you think? From the mother."

"You killed her."

"No." Quint laughed. "She jumped into the boat and swallowed a bunch of sleeping pills." He paused, waiting for a laugh, and when none came he said, "You can't rightly buy them, you know."

Hooper stared at Quint. He was furious, outraged. But he said only, "You know they're protected."

"When I fish, son, I catch what I want."

"But what about laws? Don't—"

"What's your line of work, Hooper?"

"I'm an icthyologist. I study fish. That's why I'm here. Didn't you know that?"

"When people charter my boat, I don't ask questions about them. But okay, you study fish for a living. If you had to work for a living—I mean the kind of work where the amount of money you make depends on the amount of sweat you put in —you'd know more about what laws really mean. Sure, those porpoise are protected. But that law wasn't put in to stop Quint from taking one or two for bait. It was meant to stop big-time fishing for them, to stop nuts from shooting them for sport. So I'll tell you what, Hooper: You can bitch and moan all you want. But don't tell Quint he can't catch a few fish to help him make a living."

"Look, Quint, the point is that these dolphins are in danger of being wiped out, extinguished. And what you're doing speeds up the process."

"Don't give me that horseshit! Tell the tuna boats to stop snaring porpoise in their nets. Tell the Jap long-liners to stop hookin' 'em. They'll tell you to go take a flying fuck at the moon. They got mouths to feed. Well, so do I. Mine."

"I get your message," said Hooper. "Take it while you can, and if after a while there's nothing left, why, we'll just start taking something else. It's so stupid!"

"Don't overstep, son," said Quint. His voice was flat, tone-less, and he looked directly into Hooper's eyes.

"What?"

"Don't go calling me stupid."

Hooper hadn't intended to give offense, and he was surprised to find offense taken. "I didn't mean that, for God's sake. I just meant . . ."

On his perch midway between the two men, Brody decided it was time to stop the argument. "Let's drop it, Hooper, okay?" he said. "We're not out here to have a debate on ecology."

"What do you know about ecology, Brody?" said Hooper. "I bet all it means to you is someone telling you you can't burn leaves in your backyard."

"Listen, you. I don't need any of your two-bit, rich-kid bullshit."

"So that's it! 'Rich-kid bullshit.' That rich-kid stuff really burns your ass, doesn't it?"

"Listen, damn you! We're out here to stop a fish from killing people, and if using one porpoise will help us save God knows how many lives, that seems to me a pretty good bargain."

Hooper smirked and said to Brody, "So now you're an expert on saving lives, are you? Let's see. How many could have been saved if you'd closed the beaches after the . . ."

Brody was on his feet moving at Hooper before he consciously knew he had left his chair. "You shut your mouth!" he said. Reflexively, he dropped his right hand to his hip. He stopped short when he felt no holster at his side, scared by the sudden realization that if he had had a pistol he might have used it. He stood facing Hooper, who glowered back at him.

A quick, sharp laugh from Quint broke the thread of tension. "What a pair of assholes," he said. "I seen that coming since you came aboard this morning."

12

THE SECOND DAY of the hunt was as still as the first. When they left the dock at six in the morning, a light southwest breeze was blowing, promising to cool the day. The passage around Montauk Point was choppy. But by ten the breeze had died, and the boat lay motionless on the glassy sea, like a paper cup in a puddle. There were no clouds, but the sun was dulled by a heavy haze. Driving to the dock, Brody had heard on the radio that the pollution in New York City had reached a crisis stage —something about an air inversion. People were falling sick, and of those who were sick already, or very old, some were dying.

Brody had dressed more sensibly today. He wore a white, short-sleeved shirt with a high collar, light cotton trousers, white socks, and sneakers. He had brought a book along to pass the time, a sex mystery borrowed from Hendricks, called *The Deadly Virgin.*

Brody did not want to have to fill time with conversation, conversation that might lead to a repeat of yesterday's scene with Hooper. It had embarrassed him—Hooper, too, he thought. Today they seldom spoke to one another, directing most of their comments at Quint. Brody did not trust himself to feign civility with Hooper.

Brody had observed that in the mornings, Quint was quiet —tight and reserved. Words had to be wrung from him. But as the day wore on, he loosened up and became more and more loquacious. As they had left the dock that morning, for in-

stance, Brody had asked Quint how he knew what spot to pick
to wait for the fish.

"Don't," said Quint.

"You don't know?"

Quint moved his head once from left to right, then back
again.

"Then how do you choose a place?"

"Just choose one."

"What do you look for?"

"Nothing."

"You don't go by the tide?"

"Well, yeah."

"Does it matter whether the water's deep or shallow?"

"Some."

"How so?"

For a moment, Brody thought Quint would refuse to answer. He stared straight ahead, eyes fixed on the horizon.
Then he said, as if it were a supreme effort, "Big fish like that
probably won't be in too shallow water. But you never know."

Brody knew he should drop the subject and leave Quint in
peace, but he was interested, so he asked another question. "If
we find that fish, or if he finds us, it'll be luck, won't it?"

"Sort of."

"Like a needle in a haystack."

"Not quite."

"Why not?"

"If the tide's running good, we can put out a slick that'll
cover ten miles and more by the end of the day."

"Would it be better if we stayed the night out here?"

"What for?" said Quint.

"To keep the slick going. If we can spread ten miles in a
day, we could make it more than twenty miles long if we
stayed out all night."

"If a slick gets too big, it's no good."

"Why?"

"Gets confusing. If you stayed out here a month, you could
cover the whole fuckin' ocean. Not much sense in that." Quint
smiled, apparently at the thought of a chum slick covering the
whole ocean.

Brody gave up and read *The Deadly Virgin.*

By noon, Quint had opened up. The lines had been in the slick for over four hours. Though no one had specifically assigned him the task, Hooper had taken up the chum ladle as soon as they began to drift, and now he sat at the stern, methodically scooping and dumping. At about ten o'clock, a fish had taken the starboard line and had caused a few seconds of excitement. But it turned out to be a five-pound bonito that could barely get its mouth around the hook. At ten-thirty, a small blue shark took the port line. Brody reeled it in, Quint brought it to gaff, slit its stomach open, and released it. The shark nibbled feebly at a few pieces of itself, then slipped into the deep. No other sharks came around to feed.

At a little after eleven, Quint spied the scythed dorsal fin of a swordfish coming toward them up the slick. They waited silently, begging the fish to take a bait, but it ignored both squid and cruised aimlessly sixty yards off the stern. Quint jiggled one of the baits—tugging the line to make the squid move and seem alive—but the swordfish wasn't impressed. Finally, Quint decided to harpoon the fish. He turned on his engine, told Brody and Hooper to reel in the lines, and drove the boat in a wide circle. One harpoon dart was already attached to the throwing pole, and a line-covered barrel stood ready at the bow. Quint explained the pattern of attack: Hooper would drive the boat. Quint would stand at the end of the pulpit in the bow, holding the harpoon over his right shoulder. As they came upon the fish, Quint would point the harpoon left or right, depending on which way he wanted the boat to turn. Hooper would turn the boat until the harpoon was again pointing straight ahead. It was like following a compass heading. If all went well, they would be able to creep up on the fish, and Quint could plunge the iron off his right shoulder—a throw of about twelve feet, almost straight down. Brody would stand at the barrel, making sure the line was kept clear as the fish sounded.

All did go well until the last moment. Moving slowly, with the engine sound barely above a murmur, the boat closed on the fish, which lay resting on the surface. The boat had a sensitive helm, and Hooper was able to follow Quint's directions precisely. Then, somehow, the fish sensed the presence of the boat. Just as Quint raised his arm to cast the iron, the fish lurched forward, thrust its tail, and darted for the bottom. Quint threw, yelling "Prick!" and missed by six feet.

Now they were back at the head of the slick again.

"You asked yesterday if we have many days like this," Quint said to Brody. "It's not often we string two of them together. We should of at least had a bunch of blue sharks by now."

"Is it the weather?"

"Could be. Makes people feel shitty enough. Maybe fish, too."

They ate lunch—sandwiches and beer—and when they were finished, Quint checked to see if his carbine was loaded. Then he ducked into the cabin and returned, holding a machine Brody had never seen before. "Still got your beer can?" Quint asked.

"Sure," said Brody. "What do you want it for?"

"I'll show you." The device looked like a potato-masher hand grenade—a metal cylinder with a handle at one end. Quint pushed the beer can down into the cylinder, turned it till there was a click, and took a .22 blank cartridge from his shirt pocket. He slipped the blank into a small hole at the base of the cylinder, then turned the handle until there was another click. He handed the device to Brody. "See that lever there?" he said, pointing to the top of the handle. "Point the thing up to the sky, and when I tell you, push that lever."

Quint picked up the M-1, released the safety, raised the rifle to his shoulder, and said, "Now."

Brody flipped the lever. There was a sharp, high report, a mild kick, and the beer can was launched from his hand straight up into the air. It spun, and in the bright sunlight it shone like a sparkler. At the height of its track—the split-second point when it hung suspended in air—Quint fired. He aimed low, to catch the can as it started down, and he hit its bottom. There was a loud *whang*, and the can cartwheeled down into the water. It did not sink immediately, but floated at a cockeyed angle, bobbing on the surface.

"Want to try?" said Quint.

"You bet," said Brody.

"Remember to try to catch it right at the top and lead it a little bit low. If you go for it in full rise or full fall, you've got to lead by a whole lot, and it's much harder. If you miss it, drop your sights, lead it again, and squeeze off another round."

Brody exchanged the launcher for the M-1 and stationed himself at the gunwale. As soon as Quint had reloaded the launcher, Brody shouted, "Now!" and Quint released the can. Brody fired once. Nothing. He tried again at the top of the arc. Nothing. And he led it by too much as it fell. "Boy, that's a bitch," he said.

"Takes some getting used to," said Quint. "See if you can hit it now."

The can floated upright in the still water, fifteen or twenty yards from the boat. Half of it was exposed above water. Brody aimed—consciously a hair low—and squeezed the trigger. There was a metallic *plop* as the bullet hit the can at the water line. The can vanished.

"Hooper?" said Quint. "There's one can left, and we can always drink more beer."

"No thanks," said Hooper.

"What's the problem?"

"Nothing. I just don't want to shoot, that's all."

Quint smiled. "You worried about the cans in the water? That's an awful lot of tin we're dropping into the ocean. Probably rust and sink to the bottom and clutter up everything down there."

"That's not it," said Hooper, careful not to rise to Quint's bait. "It's nothing. I just don't feel like it."

"Afraid of guns?"

"Afraid? No."

"Ever shot one?"

Brody was fascinated to see Quint press, and pleased to see Hooper squirm, but he didn't know why Quint was doing it. Maybe Quint got ornery when he was bored and wasn't catching fish.

Hooper didn't know what Quint was doing either, but he didn't like it. He felt he was being set up to be knocked down. "Sure," he said. "I've shot guns before."

"Where? In the service?"

"No. I . . ."

"Were you in the service?"

"No."

"I didn't think so."

"What's that supposed to mean?"

"Christ, I'd even bet you're still a virgin."

Brody looked at Hooper's face to see his response, and for a split second he caught Hooper looking at him.

Then Hooper looked away, his face beginning to redden. He said, "What's on your mind, Quint? What are you getting at?"

Quint leaned back in his chair and grinned. "Not a thing," he said. "Just making a little friendly conversation to pass the time. Mind if I take your beer can when you're through? Maybe Brody'd like to take another shot."

"No, I don't mind," said Hooper. "But get off my back, will you?"

For the next hour they sat in silence. Brody dozed in the fighting chair, a hat pulled down over his face to protect it from the sun. Hooper sat at the stern, ladling and occasionally shaking his head to keep awake. And Quint sat on the flying bridge, watching the slick, his Marine Corps cap tilted back on his head.

Suddenly Quint said—his voice flat, soft, matter-of-fact— "We've got a visitor."

Brody snapped awake. Hooper stood up. The starboard line was running out, smoothly and very fast.

"Take the rod," Quint said. He removed his cap and dropped it onto the bench.

Brody took the rod out of the holder, fit it between his legs, and held on.

"When I tell you," said Quint, "you throw that brake and hit him." The line stopped running. "Wait. He's turning. He'll start again. Don't want to hit him now or he'll spit the hook." But the line lay dead in the water, limp and unmoving. After several moments, Quint said, "I'll be goddamned. Reel it in."

Brody cranked the line in. It came easily, too easily. There was not even the mild resistance of the bait.

"Hold the line with a couple fingers or it'll snarl," said Quint. "Whatever that was took the bait gentle as you please. Must have kissed it off the line."

The line came clear of the water and hung at the tip of the

rod. There was no hook, no bait, no leader. The wire had been neatly severed. Quint hopped down from the flying bridge and looked at it. He felt the end, ran his fingers around the edges of the break, and gazed out over the slick.

"I think we've just met your friend," he said.

"What?" said Brody.

Hooper jumped down off the transom and said excitedly, "You've got to be kidding. That's terrific."

"That's just a guess," said Quint. "But I'd bet on it. This wire's been chewed clean through. One try. No hesitation. No other marks on it. The fish probably didn't even know he had it in his mouth. He just sucked the bait in and closed his mouth and that did it."

"So what do we do now?" said Brody.

"We wait and see if he takes the other one, or if he surfaces."

"What about using the porpoise?"

"When I know it's him," said Quint. "When I get a look at him and know the bastard's big enough to be worth it, then I'll give him the porpoise. They're garbage-eating machines, these fish, and I don't want to waste a prize bait on some little runt."

They waited. There was no movement on the surface of the water. No birds dived, no fish jumped. The only sound was the liquid plop of the chum Hooper ladled overboard. Then the port line began to run.

"Leave it in the holder," said Quint. "No sense in getting ready if he's going to chew through this one, too."

Adrenaline was pumping through Brody's body. He was both excited and afraid, awed by the thought of what was swimming below them, a creature whose power he could not imagine. Hooper stood at the port gunwhale, transfixed by the running line.

The line stopped and went limp.

"Shit," said Quint. "He done it again." He took the rod out of the holder and began to reel. The severed line came aboard exactly as had the other one. "We'll give him one more chance," said Quint, "and I'll put on a tougher leader. Not that that'll stop him if it's the fish I think it is." He reached into the ice chest for another bait and removed the wire leader. From a drawer in the cockpit he took a four-foot length of three-eighths-inch chain.

"That looks like a dog's leash," said Brody.

"Used to be," said Quint. He wired one end of the chain to the eye of the baited hook, the other to the wire line.

"Can he bite through that?"

"I imagine so. Take him a little longer, maybe, but he'd do it if he wanted to. All I'm trying to do is goose him a little and bring him to the surface."

"What's next if this doesn't work?"

"Don't know yet. I suppose I could take a four-inch shark hook and a length of no-shit chain and drop it overboard with a bunch of bait on it. But if he took it, I wouldn't know what to do with him. He'd tear out any cleat I've got on board, and until I see him I'm not going to take a chance and wrap chain around anything important." Quint flipped the baited hook overboard and fed out a few yards of line. "Come on, you bugger," he said. "Let's have a look at you."

The three men watched the port line. Hooper bent down, filled his ladle with chum, and tossed it into the slick. Something caught his eye and made him turn to the left. What he saw sucked from him a throaty grunt, unintelligible but enough to draw the eyes of the other two men.

"Jesus Christ!" said Brody.

No more than ten feet off the stern, slightly to the starboard, was the flat, conical snout of the fish. It stuck out of the water perhaps two feet. The top of the head was a sooty gray, pocked with two black eyes. At each side of the end of the snout, where the gray turned to cream white, were the nostrils—deep slashes in the armored hide. The mouth was open not quite halfway, a dim, dark cavern guarded by huge, triangular teeth.

Fish and men confronted each other for perhaps ten seconds. Then Quint yelled, "Get an iron!" and, obeying himself, he dashed forward and began to fumble with a harpoon. Brody reached for the rifle. Just then, the fish slid quietly backward into the water. The long, scythed tail flicked once—Brody shot at it and missed—and the fish disappeared.

"He's gone," said Brody.

"Fantastic!" said Hooper. "That fish is everything I

thought. And more. He's fantastic! That head must have been four feet across."

"Could be," said Quint, walking aft. He deposited two harpoon barbs, two barrels, and two coils of rope in the stern. "In case he comes back," he said.

"Have you ever seen a fish like that, Quint?" said Hooper. His eyes were bright, and he felt ebullient, vibrant.

"Not quite," said Quint.

"How long, would you say?"

"Hard to tell. Twenty feet. Maybe more. I don't know. With them things, it don't make much difference over six feet. Once they get to six feet, they're trouble. And this sonofabitch is trouble."

"God, I hope he comes back," said Hooper.

Brody felt a chill, and he shuddered. "That was very strange," he said, shaking his head. "He looked like he was grinning."

"That's what they look like when their mouths are open," said Quint. "Don't make him out to be more than he is. He's just a dumb garbage bucket."

"How can you say that?" said Hooper. "That fish is a beauty. It's the kind of thing that makes you believe in a god. It shows you what nature can do when she sets her mind to it."

"Horseshit," said Quint, and he climbed the ladder to the flying bridge.

"Are you going to use the porpoise?" said Brody.

"No need. We got him on the surface once. He'll be back."

As Quint spoke, a noise behind Hooper made him turn. It was a swishing noise, a liquid hiss. "Look," said Quint. Heading straight for the boat, thirty feet away, was a triangular dorsal fin more than a foot high, knifing the water and leaving a rippled wake. It was followed by a towering tail that swatted left and right in tight cadence.

"It's attacking the boat!" cried Brody. Involuntarily, he backed into the seat of the fighting chair and tried to draw away.

Quint came down from the flying bridge, cursing. "No fucking warning this time," he said. "Hand me that iron."

The fish was almost at the boat. It raised its flat head,

gazed vacantly at Hooper with one of its black eyes, and
passed under the boat. Quint raised the harpoon and turned
back to the port side. The throwing pole struck the fighting
chair, and the dart dislodged and fell to the deck.

"Cock*sucker!*" shouted Quint. "Is he still there?" He
reached down, grabbed the dart, and stuck it back on the end
of the pole.

"Your side, your side!" yelled Hooper. "He's passed this
side already."

Quint turned back in time to see the gray-brown shape of
the fish as it pulled away from the boat and began to dive. He
dropped the harpoon and, in a rage, snatched up the rifle and
emptied the clip into the water behind the fish. "Bastard!" he
said. "Give me some warning next time." Then he put the rifle
down and laughed. "I suppose I should be grateful," he said.
"At least he didn't attack the boat." He looked at Brody and
said, "Gave you a bit of a start."

"More 'n a bit," said Brody. He shook his head, as if to
reassemble his thoughts and sort out his visions. "I'm still not
sure I believe it." His mind was full of images of a torpedo
shape streaking upward in the blackness and tearing Christine Watkins to pieces; of the boy on the raft, unknowing,
unsuspecting, until suddenly seized by a nightmare creature;
and of the nightmares he knew would come to him, dreams of
violence and blood and a woman screaming at him that he
killed her son. "You can't tell me that thing's a fish," he said.
"It's more like one of those things they make movies about.
You know, the monster from twenty million fathoms."

"It's a fish, all right," said Hooper. He was still visibly excited. "And what a fish! Damn near *megalodon.*"

"What are you talking about?" said Brody.

"That's an exaggeration," said Hooper, "but if there's
something like this swimming around, what's to say
megalodon isn't? What do you say, Quint?"

"I'd say the sun's got to you," said Quint.

"No, really. How big do you think these fish grow?"

"I'm no good at guessing. I'd put that fish at twenty feet, so
I'd say they grow to twenty feet. If I see one tomorrow that's
twenty-five feet, I'll say they grow to twenty-five feet. Guessing
is bullshit."

"How big *do* they grow?" Brody asked, wishing immediately that he hadn't said anything. He felt that the question subordinated him to Hooper.

But Hooper was too caught up in the moment, too flushed and happy, to be patronizing. "That's the point," he said. "Nobody knows. There was one in Australia that got snarled in some chains and drowned. He was measured at thirty-six feet, or so said the reports."

"That's almost twice as big as this one," said Brody. His mind, barely able to comprehend the fish he had seen, could not grasp the immensity of the one Hooper described.

Hooper nodded. "Generally, people seem to accept thirty feet as a maximum size, but the figure is fancy. It's like what Quint says. If they see one tomorrow that's sixty feet, they'll accept sixty feet. The really terrific thing, the thing that blows your mind, is imagining—and it could be true—that there are great whites way down in the deep that are a hundred feet long."

"Oh bullshit," said Quint.

"I'm not saying it's so," said Hooper. "I'm saying it could be so."

"Still bullshit."

"Maybe. Maybe not. Look, the Latin name for this fish is *Carcharodon carcharias*, okay? The closest ancestor we can find for it is something called *Carcharodon megalodon*, a fish that existed maybe thirty or forty thousand years ago. We have fossil teeth from *megalodon*. They're six inches long. That would put the fish at between eighty and a hundred feet. And the teeth are exactly like the teeth you see in great whites today. What I'm getting at is, suppose the two fish are really one species. What's to say *megalodon* is really extinct? Why should it be? Not lack of food. If there's enough down there to support whales, there's enough to support sharks that big. Just because we've never seen a hundred-foot white doesn't mean they couldn't exist. They'd have no reason to come to the surface. All their food would be way down in the deep. A dead one wouldn't float to shore, because they don't have flotation bladders. Can you imagine what a hundred-foot white would look like? Can you imagine what it could do, what kind of power it would have?"

"I don't want to," said Brody.

"It would be like a locomotive with a mouth full of butcher knives."

"Are you saying this is just a baby?" Brody was beginning to feel lonely and vulnerable. A fish as large as what Hooper was describing could chew the boat to splinters.

"No, this is a mature fish," said Hooper. "I'm sure of it. But it's like people. Some people are five feet tall, some people are seven feet tall. Boy, what I'd give to have a look at a big *megalodon.*"

"You're out of your mind," said Brody.

"No, man, just think of it. It would be like finding the Abominable Snowman."

"Hey, Hooper," said Quint, "do you think you can stop the fairy tales and start throwing chum overboard? I'd kind of like to catch a fish."

"Sure," said Hooper. He returned to his post at the stern and began to ladle chum into the water.

"You think he'll come back?" said Brody.

"I don't know," said Quint. "You never know what these bastards are going to do." From a pocket he took a note pad and a pencil. He extended his left arm and pointed it toward shore. He closed his right eye and sighted down the index finger of his left hand, then scribbled something on the pad. He moved his hand a couple of inches to the left, sighted again, and made another note. Anticipating a question from Brody, Quint said, "Taking bearings. I want to see where we are, so if he doesn't show up for the rest of today, I'll know where to come tomorrow."

Brody looked toward shore. Even shading his eyes and squinting, all he could see was a dim gray line of land. "What are you taking them on?"

"Lighthouse on the point and the water tower in town. They line up different ways depending where you are."

"You can see them?" Brody strained his eyes, but he saw nothing more distinct than a lump in the line.

"Sure. You could too, if you'd been out here for thirty years."

Hooper smiled and said, "Do you really think the fish will stay in one place?"

"I don't know," said Quint. "But this is where we found him this time, and we didn't find him anywhere else."

"And he sure as hell stayed around Amity," said Brody.

"That's because he had food," said Hooper. There was no irony in his voice, no taunt. But the remark was like a needle stabbing into Brody's brain.

They waited for three more hours, but the fish never returned. The tide slackened, carrying the slick ever slower.

At a little after five, Quint said, "We might as well go in. It's enough to piss off the Good Humor man."

"Where do you think he went?" said Brody. The question was rhetorical; he knew there was no answer.

"Anywhere," said Quint. "When you want 'em, they're never around. It's only when you don't want 'em, and don't expect 'em, that they show up. Contrary fuckers."

"And you don't think we should spend the night, to keep the slick going."

"No. Like I said, if the slick gets too big, it's no good. We don't have any food out here. And last but not least, you're not paying me for a twenty-four-hour day."

"If I could get the money, would you do it?"

Quint thought for a moment. "Nope. It's tempting, though, 'cause I don't think there's much chance anything would happen at night. The slick would be big and confusing, and even if he came right up alongside and looked at us, we wouldn't know he was there unless he took a bite out of us. So it'd be taking your money just to let you sleep on board. But I won't do it, for two reasons. First off, if the slick did get too big, it would screw us up for the next day. Second, I like to get this boat in at night."

"I guess I can't blame you," said Brody. "Your wife must like it better, too, having you home."

Quint said flatly, "Got no wife."

"Oh. I'm sorry."

"Don't be. I never saw the need for one." Quint turned and climbed the ladder to the flying bridge.

Ellen was fixing the children's supper when the doorbell rang. The boys were watching television in the living room, and she called to them, "Would somebody please answer the door?"

She heard the door open, heard some words exchanged, and, a moment later, saw Larry Vaughan standing at the kitchen door. It had been less than two weeks since she had last seen him, yet the change in his appearance was so startling that she couldn't help staring at him. As always, he was dressed perfectly—a two-button blue blazer, button-down shirt, gray slacks, and Gucci loafers. It was his face that had changed. He had lost weight, and like many people who have no excess on their bodies, Vaughan showed the loss in his face. His eyes had receded in their sockets, and their color seemed to Ellen lighter than normal—a pasty gray. His skin looked gray, too, and appeared to droop at the cheekbones. His lips were moist, and he licked them every few seconds.

Embarrassed when she found herself staring, Ellen lowered her eyes and said, "Larry. Hello."

"Hello, Ellen. I stopped by to . . ." Vaughan backed up a few steps and peered into the living room. "First of all, do you suppose I could have a drink?"

"Of course. You know where everything is. Help yourself. I'd get it for you, but my hands are covered with chicken."

"Don't be silly. I can find everything." Vaughan opened the cupboard where the liquor was kept, took out a bottle, and poured a glass full of gin. "As I started to say, I stopped by to say farewell."

Ellen stopped shuffling pieces of chicken in the frying pan and said, "You're going away? For how long?"

"I don't know. Perhaps for good. There's nothing here for me anymore."

"What about your business?"

"That's gone. Or it soon will be."

"What do you mean, gone? A business doesn't just go away."

"No, but I won't own it anymore. What few assets there are will belong to my . . . partners." He spat the word and then, as if to cleanse his mouth of its unpleasant residue, took a long swallow of gin. "Has Martin told you about our conversation?"

"Yes." Ellen looked down at the frying pan and stirred the chicken.

"I imagine you don't think very highly of me anymore."

"It's not up to me to judge you, Larry."

"I never wanted to hurt anybody. I hope you believe that."

"I believe it. How much does Eleanor know?"

"Nothing, poor dear. I want to spare her, if I can. That's one reason I want to move away. She loves me, you know, and I'd hate to take that love away . . . from either of us." Vaughan leaned against the sink. "You know something? Sometimes I think—and I've thought this from time to time over the years—that you and I would have made a wonderful couple."

Ellen reddened. "What do you mean?"

"You're from a good family. You know all the people I had to fight to get to know. We would have fit together and fit in Amity. You're lovely and good and strong. You would have been a real asset to me. And I think I could have given you a life you would have loved."

Ellen smiled. "I'm not as strong as you think, Larry. I don't know what kind of . . . asset I would have been."

"Don't belittle yourself. I only hope Martin appreciates the treasure he has." Vaughan finished his drink and put the glass in the sink. "Anyway, no point in dreaming." He walked across the kitchen, touched Ellen's shoulder, and kissed the top of her head. "Good-bye, dear," he said. "Think of me once in a while."

Ellen looked at him. "I will." She kissed his cheek. "Where are you going?"

"I don't know. Vermont, maybe, or New Hampshire. I might sell land to the skiing crowd. Who knows? I might even take up the sport myself."

"Have you told Eleanor?"

"I told her we might be moving. She just smiled and said, 'Whatever you wish.'"

"Are you leaving soon?"

"As soon as I chat with my lawyers about my . . . liabilities."

"Send us a card so we'll know where you are."

"I will. Good-bye." Vaughan left the room, and Ellen heard the screen door close behind him.

When she had served the children their supper, Ellen went upstairs and sat on her bed. "A life you would have loved,"

Vaughan had said. What would a life with Larry Vaughan have been like? There would have been money, and acceptance. She would never have missed the life she led as a girl, for it would never have ended. There would have been no craving for renewal and self-confidence and confirmation of her femininity, no need for a fling with someone like Hooper.

But no. She might have been driven to it by boredom, like so many of the women who spent their weeks in Amity while their husbands were in New York. Life with Larry Vaughan would have been life without a challenge, a life of cheap satisfactions.

As she pondered what Vaughan had said, she began to recognize the richness of her life: a relationship with Brody more rewarding than any Larry Vaughan would ever experience; an amalgam of minor trials and tiny triumphs that, together, added up to something akin to joy. And as her recognition grew, so did a regret that it had taken her so long to see the waste of time and emotion in trying to cling to her past. Suddenly she felt fear—fear that she was growing up too late, that something might happen to Brody before she could savor her awareness. She looked at her watch: 6:20. He should have been home by now. Something has happened to him, she thought. Oh please, God, not him.

She heard the door open downstairs. She jumped off the bed, ran into the hall and down the stairs. She wrapped her arms around Brody's neck and kissed him hard on the mouth.

"My God," he said when she let him go. "That's quite a welcome."

13

"YOU'RE NOT PUTTING that thing on my boat," said Quint.

They stood on the dock in the brightening light. The sun had cleared the horizon, but it lay behind a low bank of clouds that touched the eastern sea. A gentle wind blew from the south. The boat was ready to go. Barrels lined the bow; rods stood straight in their holders, leaders snapped into eyelets on the reels. The engine chugged quietly, sputtering bubbles as tiny waves washed against the exhaust pipe, coughing diesel fumes that rose and were carried away by the breeze.

At the end of the dock a man got into a pickup truck and started the engine, and the truck began to move slowly off down the dirt road. The words stenciled on the door of the truck read: Woods Hole Oceanographic Institute.

Quint stood with his back to the boat, facing Brody and Hooper, who stood on each side of an aluminum cage. The cage was slightly over six feet tall and six feet wide and four feet deep. Inside, there was a control panel: atop were two cylindrical tanks. On the floor of the cage were a scuba tank, a regulator, a face mask, and a wet suit.

"Why not?" said Hooper. "It doesn't weigh much, and I can lash it down out of the way."

"Take up too much room."

"That's what I said," said Brody. "But he wouldn't listen."

"What the hell is it anyway?" said Quint.

"It's a shark cage," said Hooper. "Divers use them to pro-tect themselves when they're swimming in the open ocean. I had it sent down from Woods Hole—in that truck that just left."

"And what do you plan to do with it?"

"When we find the fish, or when the fish finds us, I want to go down in the cage and take some pictures. No one's ever been able to photograph a fish this big before."

"Not a chance," said Quint. "Not on my boat."

"Why not?"

"It's foolishness, that's why. A sensible man knows his limits. That's beyond our limits."

"How do you know?"

"It's beyond any man's limits. A fish that big could eat that cage for breakfast."

"But *would* he? I don't think so. I think he might bump it, might even mouth it, but I don't think he'd seriously try to eat it."

"He would if he saw something as juicy as you inside."

"I doubt it."

"Well, forget it."

"Look, Quint, this is a chance of a lifetime. Not just for me. I wouldn't have thought of doing it until I saw the fish yesterday. It's unique, at least in this hemisphere. And even though people have filmed great whites before, no one's ever filmed a twenty-foot white swimming in the open ocean. Never."

"He said forget it," said Brody. "So forget it. Besides, I don't want the responsibility. We're out here to kill that fish, not make a home movie about it."

"What responsibility? You're not responsible for me."

"Oh yes I am. The town of Amity is paying for this trip, so what I say goes."

Hooper said to Quint, "I'll pay you."

Quint smiled. "Oh yeah? How much?"

"Forget it," said Brody. "I don't care what Quint says. *I* say you're not bringing that thing along."

Hooper ignored him and said to Quint, "A hundred dollars. Cash. In advance, the way you like it." He reached into his back pocket for his wallet.

"I said no!" said Brody.

"What do you say, Quint? A hundred bucks. Cash. Here it is." He counted five twenties and held them out to Quint.

"I don't know." Then Quint reached for the money and said, "Shit, I don't suppose it's my business to keep a man from killing himself if he wants to."

"You put that cage on the boat," Brody said to Quint, "and you don't get your four hundred." If Hooper wants to kill himself, Brody thought, let him do it on his own time.

"And if the cage doesn't go," said Hooper, "I don't go."

"Fuck yourself," said Brody. "You can stay here, for all I care."

"I don't think Quint would like that. Right, Quint? You want to go out and take on that fish with just you and the chief? You feel good about that?"

"We'll find another man," said Brody.

"Go ahead," Hooper snapped. "Good luck."

"Can't do it," said Quint. "Not on this short notice."

"Then the hell with it!" said Brody. "We'll go tomorrow. Hooper can go back to Woods Hole and play with his fish."

Hooper was angry—angrier, in fact, than he knew, for before he could stop himself, he had said, "That's not all I might . . . Oh, forget it."

For several seconds, a leaden silence fell over the three men. Brody stared at Hooper, unwilling to believe what he had heard, uncertain how much substance there was in the remark and how much empty threat. Then suddenly he was overcome by rage. He reached Hooper in two steps, grabbed both sides of his collar, and rammed his fists into Hooper's throat. "What was that?" he said. "What did you say?"

Hooper could hardly breathe. He clawed at Brody's fingers. "Nothing!" he said, choking. "Nothing!" He tried to back away, but Brody gripped him tighter.

"What did you mean by that?"

"Nothing, I tell you! I was angry. It was something to say."

"Where were you last Wednesday afternoon?"

"Nowhere!" Hooper's temples were throbbing. "Let me go! You're choking me!"

"Where were you?" Brody twisted his fists tighter.

"In a motel! Now let me go!"

Brody eased his grip. "With who?" he said, praying to himself, God, don't let it be Ellen; let his alibi be a good one.

"Daisy Wicker."

"Liar!" Brody tightened his grip again, and he felt tears begin to squeeze from his eyes.

"What do you mean?" said Hooper, struggling to free himself.

"Daisy Wicker's a goddam lesbian! What were you doing, knitting?"

Hooper's thoughts were fogging. Brody's knuckles were cutting off the flow of blood to his brain. His eyelids flickered and he began to lose consciousness. Brody released him and pushed him down to the dock, where he sat, sucking air.

"What do you say to that?" said Brody. "Are you such a hotshot you can fuck a lesbian?"

Hooper's mind cleared quickly, and he said, "No. I didn't find out until . . . until it was too late."

"What do you mean. You mean she went with you to a motel and then turned you down? No dyke is gonna go to any motel room with you."

"She did!" said Hooper, desperately trying to keep pace with Brody's questions. "She said she wanted . . . that it was time she tried it straight. But then she couldn't go through with it. It was awful."

"You're bullshitting me!"

"I'm not! You can check with her yourself." Hooper knew it was a weak excuse. Brody could check it out with no trouble. But it was all he could think of. He could stop on the way home that evening and call Daisy Wicker from a phone booth, beg her to corroborate his story. Or he could simply never return to Amity—turn north and take the ferry from Orient Point and be out of the state before Brody could reach Daisy Wicker.

"I will check," said Brody. "You can count on it."

Behind him, Brody heard Quint laugh and say, "That's the funniest thing I ever did hear. Tried to lay a lesbian."

Brody tried to read Hooper's face, searching for anything that might betray a lie. But Hooper kept his eyes fixed on the dock.

"Well, what do you say?" said Quint. "We going today or not? Either way, Brody, it'll cost you."

Brody felt shaken. He was tempted to cancel the trip, to return to Amity and discover the truth about Hooper and Ellen. But suppose the worst was true. What could he do then? Confront Ellen? Beat her? Walk out on her? What good would that do? He had to have time to think. He said to Quint, "We'll go."

"With the cage?"

"With the cage. If this asshole wants to kill himself, let him."

"Okay by me," said Quint. "Let's get this circus on the road."

Hooper stood and walked to the cage. "I'll get in the boat," he said hoarsely. "If you two can push it over to the edge of the dock and lean it toward me, then one of you come down into the boat with me, we can carry it over into the corner."

Brody and Quint slid the cage across the wooden boards, and Brody was surprised at how light it was. Even with the diving gear inside, it couldn't have weighed more than two hundred pounds. They tipped it toward Hooper, who grabbed two of the bars and waited until Quint joined him in the cockpit. The two men easily carried the cage a few feet and pushed it into a corner under the overhang that supported the flying bridge. Hooper secured it with two pieces of rope.

Brody jumped aboard and said, "Let's go."

"Aren't you forgetting something?" said Quint.

"What?"

"Four hundred dollars."

Brody took an envelope from his pocket and handed it to Quint. "You're going to die a rich man, Quint."

"That's my aim. Uncleat the stern line, will you?" Quint uncleated the bow and midships spring lines and tossed them onto the dock, and when he saw that the stern line was clear, too, he pushed the throttle forward and guided the boat out of the slip. He turned right and pushed the throttle forward, and the boat moved swiftly through the calm sea—past Hicks Island and Goff Point, around Shagwong and Montauk points. Soon the lighthouse on Montauk Point was behind them, and they were cruising south by southwest in the open ocean.

Gradually, as the boat fell into the rhythm of the long ocean swells, Brody's fury dulled. Maybe Hooper was telling the truth. It was possible. A person wouldn't make up a story that was so easy to check. Ellen had never cheated on him before, he was sure of that. She never even flirted with other men. But, he told himself, there's always a first time. And once again the thought made his throat tighten. He felt jealous and injured, inadequate and outraged. He hopped down from the fighting chair and climbed up to the flying bridge.

Quint made room on the bench for Brody, and Brody sat down next to him. Quint chuckled. "You boys almost had a no-shit punch-up back there."

"It was nothing."

"Looked like something to me. What is it, you think he's been poking your wife?"

Confronted with his own thoughts stated so brutally, Brody was shocked. "None of your damn business," he said.

"Whatever you say. But if you ask me, he ain't got it in him."

"Nobody asked you." Anxious to change the subject, Brody said, "Are we going back to the same place?"

"Same place. Won't be too long now."

"What are the chances the fish will still be there?"

"Who knows? But it's the only thing we can do."

"You said something on the phone the other day about being smarter than fish. Is that all there is to it? Is that the only secret of success?"

"That's all there is. You just got to outguess 'em. It's no trick. They're stupid as sin."

"You've never found a smart fish?"

"Never met one yet."

Brody remembered the leering, grinning face that had stared up at him from the water. "I don't know," he said. "That fish sure looked mean yesterday. Like he meant to be mean. Like he knew what he was doing."

"Shit, he don't know nothing."

"Do they have different personalities?"

"Fish?" Quint laughed. "That's giving them more credit than they're due. You can't treat 'em like people, even though I guess some people are as dumb as fish. No. They do different things sometimes, but after a while you get to know everything they *can* do."

"It's not a challenge, then. You're not fighting an enemy."

"No. No more 'n a plumber who's trying to unstick a drain.

Maybe he'll cuss at it and hit it with a wrench. But down deep he don't think he's fighting some*body*. Sometimes I run into an ornery fish that gives me more trouble than other ones, but I just use different tools."

"There are fish you can't catch, aren't there?"

"Oh sure, but that don't mean they're smart or sneaky or anything. It only means they're not hungry when you try to catch 'em, or they're too fast for you, or you're using the wrong bait."

Quint fell silent for a moment, then spoke again. "Once," he said, "a shark almost caught *me*. It was about twenty years ago. I had a fair-size blue shark to gaff and he gave a big yank and hauled me overboard with him."

"What did you do?"

"I come up over that transom so fast I don't think my feet touched anything between water and deck. I was lucky I fell over the stern, where it's fairly low down, near the water. If I'd of fallen over amidships, I don't know what I would've done. Anyway, I was out of that water before the fish even knew I was in it. He was busy trying to shake the gaff."

"Suppose you fell over with this fish. Is there anything you could do?"

"Sure. Pray. It'd be like falling out of an airplane without a parachute and hoping you'll land in a haystack. The only thing that'd save you would be God, and since He pushed you overboard in the first place, I wouldn't give a nickel for your chances."

"There's a woman in Amity who thinks that's why we're having trouble," said Brody. "She thinks it's some sort of divine retribution."

Quint smiled. "Might be. He made the damn thing, I suppose He can tell it what to do."

"You serious?"

"No, not really. I don't put much stock in religion."

"So why do you think people have been killed?"

"Bad luck." Quint pulled back on the throttle. The boat slowed and settled in the swells. "We'll try to change it." He took a piece of paper from his pocket, unfolded it, read the notes, and sighting along his outstretched arm, checked his bearings. He turned the ignition key, and the engine died.

There was a weight, a thickness, to the sudden silence. "Okay, Hooper," he said. "Start chuckin' the shit overboard."

Hooper took the top off the chum bucket and began to ladle the contents into the sea. The first ladleful spattered on the still water, and slowly the oily smear spread westward.

By ten o'clock a breeze had come up—not strong, but fresh enough to ripple the water and cool the men, who sat and watched and said nothing. The only sound was the regular splash as Hooper poured chum off the stern.

Brody sat in the fighting chair, struggling to stay awake. He yawned, then recalled that he had left the half-read copy of *The Deadly Virgin* in a magazine rack below. He stood, stretched, and went down the three steps into the cabin. He found the book and started topside again, when his eye caught the ice chest. He looked at his watch and said to himself, the hell with it; there's no time out here.

"I'm going to have a beer," he called. "Anybody want one?"

"No," said Hooper.

"Sure," said Quint. "We can shoot at the cans."

Brody took two beers from the chest, removed the metal tabs, and started to climb the stairs. His foot was on the top step when he heard Quint's flat, calm voice say, "There he is."

At first, Brody thought Quint was referring to him, but then he saw Hooper jump off the transom and heard him whistle and say, "Wow! He sure is!"

Brody felt his pulse speed up. He stepped quickly onto the deck and said, "Where?"

"Right there," said Quint. "Dead off the stern."

It took Brody's eyes a moment to adjust, but then he saw the fin—a ragged, brownish-gray triangle that sliced through the water, followed by the scythed tail sweeping left and right with short, spasmodic thrusts. The fish was at least thirty yards behind the boat, Brody guessed. Maybe forty. "Are you sure it's him?" he said.

"It's him," said Quint.

"What are you going to do?"

"Nothing. Not till we see what he does. Hooper, you keep ladling that shit. Let's bring him in here."

Hooper lifted the bucket up onto the transom and scooped the chum into the water. Quint walked forward and fastened a harpoon head to the wooden shaft. He picked up a barrel and put it under one arm. He held the coiled rope over his other arm and clutched the harpoon in his hand. He carried it all aft and set it on the deck.

The fish cruised back and forth in the slick, seeming to search for the source of the bloody miasma.

"Reel in those lines," Quint said to Brody. "They won't do any good now we've got him up."

Brody brought in the lines one by one and let the squid bait fall to the deck. The fish moved slightly closer to the boat, still cruising slowly.

Quint set the barrel on the transom to the left of Hooper's bucket and arranged the rope beside it. Then he climbed up on the transom and stood, his right arm cocked, holding the harpoon. "Come on," he said. "Come on in here."

But the fish would come no closer than fifty feet from the boat.

"I don't get it," said Quint. "He should come in and take a look at us. Brody, take the cutters out of my back pocket and clip off those squid bait and throw 'em overboard. Maybe some food'll bring him in. And splash the hell out of the water when you throw 'em. Let him know something's there."

Brody did as he was told, slapping and roiling the water with a gaff, always keeping the fin in sight, for he imagined the fish suddenly appearing from the deep and seizing him by the arm.

"Throw some other ones while you're at it," said Quint. "They're in the chest there. And throw those beers over, too."

"The beers? What for?"

"The more we can get in the water, the better. Don't make no difference what it is, so long as it gets him interested enough to want to find out."

Hooper said, "What about the porpoise?"

"Why, Mr. Hooper," said Quint. "I thought you didn't approve."

"Never mind that," Hooper said excitedly. "I want to see that fish!"

"We'll see," said Quint. "If I have to use it, I will."

The squid had drifted back toward the shark, and one of

the beers bobbed on the surface as it slowly faded aft of the boat. But still the fish stayed away.

They waited—Hooper ladling, Quint poised on the transom, Brody standing by one of the rods.

"Shit," said Quint. "I guess I got no choice." He set the harpoon down and jumped off the transom. He flipped the top off the garbage can next to Brody, and Brody saw the lifeless eyes of the tiny porpoise as it swayed in the briny water. The sight repelled him, and he turned away.

"Well, little fella," said Quint. "The time has come." From the lazaret he took a length of dog-leash chain and snapped one end of it into the hook eye protruding from beneath the porpoise's jaw. To the other end of the chain he tied a length of three-quarter-inch hemp. He uncoiled several yards of the rope, cut it, and made it fast to a cleat on the starboard gunwale.

"I thought you said the shark could pull out a cleat," said Brody.

"It might just," said Quint. "But I'm betting I can get an iron in him and cut the rope before he pulls it taut enough to yank the cleat." Quint took hold of the dog chain and lifted the starboard gunwale and set it down. He climbed onto the transom and pulled the porpoise after him. He took the knife from the sheath at his belt. With his left hand he held the porpoise out in front of him. Then, with his right, he cut a series of shallow slashes in the porpoise's belly. A rank, dark liquid oozed from the animal and fell in droplets on the water. Quint tossed the porpoise into the water, let out six feet of line, then put the rope under his foot on the transom and stepped down hard. The porpoise floated just beneath the surface of the water, less than six feet from the boat.

"That's pretty close," said Brody.

"Has to be," said Quint. "I can't get a shot at him if he's thirty feet away."

"Why are you standing on the rope?"

"To keep the little fella where he is. I don't want to cleat it down that close to the boat. If he took it and didn't have any running room, he could thrash around and beat us to pieces." Quint hefted the harpoon and looked at the shark's fin.

The fish moved closer, still cruising back and forth but

closing the gap between itself and the boat by a few feet with every passage. Then it stopped, twenty or twenty-five feet away, and for a second seemed to lie motionless in the water, aimed directly at the boat. The tail dropped beneath the surface; the dorsal fin slid backward and vanished; and the great head reared up, mouth open in a slack, savage grin, eyes black and abysmal.

Brody stared in mute horror, sensing that this was what it must be like to try to stare down the devil.

"Hey, fish!" Quint called. He stood on the transom, legs spread, his hand curled around the shaft of the harpoon that rested on his shoulder. "Come see what we've got for you!"

For another moment the fish hung in the water, watching. Then, soundlessly, the head slid back and disappeared.

"Where'd he go?" said Brody.

"He'll be coming now," said Quint. "Come, fish," he purred. "Come, fish. Come get your supper." He pointed the harpoon at the floating porpoise.

Suddenly the boat lurched violently to the side. Quint's legs skidded out from under him, and he fell on his back on the transom. The harpoon dart separated from the shaft and clattered to the deck. Brody tumbled sideways, grabbed the back of the chair, and twirled around as the chair swiveled. Hooper spun backward and slammed into the port gunwale.

The rope attached to the porpoise tautened and shivered. The knot by which it was secured to the cleat tightened so hard that the rope flattened and its fibers popped. The wood under the cleat began to crack. Then the rope snapped backward, went slack, and curled in the water beside the boat.

"I'll be fucked!" said Quint.

"It was like he knew what you were trying to do," said Brody, "like he knew there was a trap set for him."

"Goddammit! I never have seen a fish do that before."

"He knew if he knocked you down he could get to the porpoise."

"Shit, he was just aiming for the porpoise, and he missed."

Hooper said, "Aiming from the opposite side of the boat?"

"Well, it don't make no never-mind," said Quint. "Whatever he did, it worked."

"How do you think he got off the hook?" said Brody. "He didn't pull the cleat out."

Quint walked over to the starboard gunwale and began to pull in the rope. "He either bit right through the chain, or else . . . uh-huh, that's what I figured." He leaned over the gunwale and grabbed the chain. He pulled it aboard. It was intact, the clip still attached to the eye of the hook. But the hook itself had been destroyed. The steel shaft no longer curled. It was nearly straight, marked by two small bumps where once it had been tempered into a curve.

"Jesus Christ!" said Brody. "He did that with his mouth?"

"Bent it out nice as you please," said Quint. "Probably didn't slow him down for more than a second or two."

Brody felt light-headed. His fingertips tingled. He sat down in the chair and drew several deep breaths, trying to stifle the fear that was mounting inside him.

"Where do you suppose he's gone?" said Hooper, standing at the stern and looking at the water.

"He's around here somewhere," said Quint. "I imagine he'll be back. That porpoise wasn't any more to him than an anchovy is to a bluefish. He'll be looking for more food." He reassembled the harpoon, recoiled the rope, and set them on the transom. "We're just gonna have to wait. And keep chumming. I'll tie up some more squid and hang 'em overboard."

Brody watched Quint as he wrapped twine around each squid and dropped it overboard, attached to the boat at cleats, rod-holders, and almost anything else around which he could tie a knot. When a dozen squid had been placed at various points and various depths around the boat, Quint climbed to the flying bridge and sat down.

Hoping to be contradicted, Brody said, "That sure does seem to be a smart fish."

"Smart or not, I wouldn't know," said Quint. "But he's doing things I've never seen a fish do before." He paused, then said—as much to himself as to Brody—"but I'm gonna get that fucker. That's one thing for sure."

"How can you be sure?"

"I know it, that's all. Now leave me be."

It was a command, not a request, and though Brody wanted to talk—about anything, even the fish itself, as long as he could steer his mind away from the image of the beast lurking in the water below him—he said nothing more. He looked at his watch: 11:05.

They waited, expecting at any moment to see the fin rise off the stern and cut back and forth through the water. Hooper ladled chum, which sounded to Brody, every time it hit the water, like diarrhea.

At eleven-thirty, Brody was startled by a sharp, resonant *snap.* Quint leaped down the ladder, across the deck, and onto the transom. He picked up the harpoon and held it at his shoulder, scanning the water around the stern.

"What the hell was that?" said Brody.

"He's back."

"How do you know? What was that noise?"

"Twine snapping. He took one of the squid."

"Why would it snap? Why wouldn't he chew right through it?"

"He probably never bit down on it. He sucked it in, and the twine came tight between his teeth when he closed his mouth. He went like this, I imagine"—Quint jerked his head to the side—"and the line parted."

"How could we hear it snap if it snapped under water?"

"It didn't snap under water, for Christ sake! It snapped right there." Quint pointed to a few inches of limp twine hanging from a cleat amidships.

"Oh," said Brody. As he looked at the remnant, he saw another piece of twine—a few feet farther up the gunwale—go limp. "There's another one," he said. He stood and walked to the gunwale and pulled in the line. "He must be right underneath us."

Quint said, "Anybody care to go swimming?"

"Let's put the cage overboard," said Hooper.

"You're kidding," said Brody.

"No, I'm not. It might bring him out."

"With you in it?"

"Not at first. Let's see what he does. What do you say, Quint?"

"Might as well," said Quint. "Can't hurt just to put it in the water, and you paid for it." He put down the harpoon, and he and Hooper walked to the cage.

They tipped the cage onto its side, and Hooper opened the top hatch and crawled through it. He removed the scuba tank, regulator, face mask, and neoprene wet suit, and set them on the deck. They tipped the cage upright again and slid it across the deck to the starboard gunwale. "You got a couple of lines?" said Hooper. "I want to make it fast to the boat." Quint went below and returned with two coils of rope. They tied one to an after cleat, one to a cleat amidships, then secured the ends to the bars on top of the cage. "Okay," said Hooper. "Let's put her over." They lifted the cage, tipped it backward, and pushed it overboard. It sank until the ropes stopped it, a few feet beneath the surface. There it rested, rising and falling slowly in the swells. The three men stood at the gunwale, looking into the water.

"What makes you think this'll bring him up?" said Brody.

"I didn't say 'up,' " said Hooper. "I said 'out.' I think he'll come out and have a look at it, to see whether he wants to eat it."

"That won't do us any damn good," said Quint. "I can't stick him if he's twelve feet under water."

"Once he comes out," said Hooper, "maybe he'll come up. We're not having any luck with anything else."

But the fish did not come out. The cage lay quietly in the water, unmolested.

"There goes another squid," said Quint, pointing forward. "He's there, all right." He leaned overboard and shouted, "God damn you, fish! Come out where I can have a shot at you."

After fifteen minutes, Hooper said, "Oh well," and went below. He reappeared moments later, carrying a movie camera in a waterproof housing, and what looked to Brody like a walking stick with a thong at one end.

"What are you doing?" Brody said.

"I'm going down there. Maybe that'll bring him out."

"You're out of your goddam mind. What are you going to do if he does come out?"

"First, I'm going to take some pictures of him. Then I'm going to try to kill him."

"With what, may I ask?"

"This." Hooper held up the stick.

"Good thinking," Quint said with a derisive cackle. "If that doesn't work you can tickle him to death."

"What is that?" said Brody.

"Some people call it a bang stick. Others call it a power head. Anyway, it's basically an underwater gun." He pulled both ends of the stick, and it came apart in two pieces. "In here," he said, pointing to a chamber at the point where the stick had come apart, "you put a twelve-gauge shotgun shell." He took a shotgun shell from his pocket and pushed it into the chamber, then rejoined the two ends of the stick. "Then, when you get close enough to the fish, you jab it at him and the shell goes off. If you hit him right—in the brain's the only sure place—you kill him."

"Even a fish that big?"

"I think so. If I hit him right."

"And if you don't? Suppose you miss by just a hair."

"That's what I'm afraid of."

"I would be, too," said Quint. "I don't think I'd like five thousand pounds of pissed-off dinosaur trying to eat me."

"That's not my worry," said Hooper. "What concerns me is that if I miss, I might drive him off. He'd probably sound, and we'd never know if he died or not."

"Until he ate someone else," said Brody.

"That's right."

"You're fucking crazy," said Quint.

"Am I, Quint? You're not having much success with this fish. We could stay here all month and let him eat your bait right out from under us."

"He'll come up," said Quint. "Mark my words."

"You'll be dead of old age before he comes up, Quint. I think this fish has you all shook. He's not playing by the rules."

Quint looked at Hooper and said evenly, "You telling me my business, boy?"

"No. But I am telling you I think this fish is more than you can handle."

"That right, boy? You think you can do better 'n Quint?"

"Call it that if you want. I think I can kill the fish."

"Fine and dandy. You're gonna get your chance."

Brody said, "Come on. We can't let him go in that thing."

"What are *you* bitchin' about?" said Quint. "From what I seen, you just as soon he went down there and never come up. At least that'd stop him from—"

"Shut your mouth!" Brody's emotions were jumbled. Part of him didn't care whether Hooper lived or died—might even relish the prospect of Hooper's death. But such vengeance would be hollow—and, quite possibly, unmerited. Could he really wish a man dead? No. Not yet.

"Go on," Quint said to Hooper. "Get in that thing."

"Right away." Hooper removed his shirt, sneakers, and trousers, and began to pull the neoprene suit over his legs. "When I'm inside," he said, forcing his arms into the rubber sleeves of the jacket, "stand up here and keep an eye. Maybe you can use the rifle if he gets close enough to the surface." He looked at Quint. "You can be ready with the harpoon . . . if you want to."

"I'll do what I'll do," said Quint. "You worry about yourself."

When he was dressed, Hooper fit the regulator onto the neck of the air tank, tightened the wing nut that held it in place, and opened the air valve. He sucked two breaths from the tank to make sure it was feeding air. "Help me put this on, will you?" he said to Brody.

Brody lifted the tank and held it while Hooper slipped his arms through the straps and fastened a third strap around his middle. He put the face mask on his head. "I should have brought weights," said Hooper.

Quint said, "You should have brought brains."

Hooper put his right wrist through the thong at the end of the power head, picked up the camera with his right hand, and said, "Okay." He walked to the gunwale. "If you'll each take a rope and pull, that'll bring the cage to the surface. Then I'll open the hatch and go in through the top, and you can let the ropes go. It'll hang by the ropes. I won't use the flotation tanks unless one of the ropes breaks."

"Or gets chewed through," said Quint.

Hooper looked at Quint and smiled. "Thanks for the thought."

Quint and Brody pulled on the ropes, and the cage rose in the water. When the hatch broke the surface, Hooper said,

"Okay, right there." He spat in the face mask, rubbed the saliva around on the glass, and fit the mask over his face. He reached for the regulator tube, put the mouthpiece in his mouth, and took a breath. Then he bent over the gunwale, unlatched the top of the hatch and flipped it open. He started to put a knee on the gunwale, but stopped. He took the mouthpiece out of his mouth and said, "I forgot something." His nose was encased in the mask, so his voice sounded thick and nasal. He walked across the deck and picked up his trousers. He rummaged through the pockets until he found what he was looking for. He unzipped his wetsuit jacket.

"What's that?" said Brody.

Hooper held up a shark's tooth, rimmed in silver. It was a duplicate of the one he had given Ellen. He dropped it inside his wet suit and zipped up the jacket. "Can't be too careful," he said, smiling. He crossed the deck again, put his mouthpiece in his mouth, and kneeled on the gunwale. He took a final breath and dove overboard through the open hatch. Brody watched him go, wondering if he really wanted to know the truth about Hooper and Ellen.

Hooper stopped himself before he hit the bottom of the cage. He curled around and stood up. He reached out the top of the hatch and pulled it closed. Then he looked up at Brody, put the thumb and index finger of his left hand together in the okay sign, and ducked down.

"I guess we can let go," said Brody. They released the ropes and let the cage descend until the hatch was about four feet beneath the surface.

"Get the rifle," said Quint. "It's on the rack below. It's all loaded." He climbed onto the transom and lifted the harpoon to his shoulder.

Brody went below, found the rifle, and hurried back on deck. He opened the breach and slid a cartridge into the chamber. "How much air does he have?" he said.

"I don't know," said Quint. "However much he has, I doubt he'll live to breathe it."

"Maybe you're right. But you said yourself you never know what these fish will do."

"Yeah, but this is different. This is like putting your hand in a fire and hoping you won't get burned. A sensible man don't *do* it."

Below, Hooper waited until the bubbly froth of his descent had dissipated. There was water in his mask, so he tilted his head backward, pressed on the top of the faceplate, and blew through his nose until the mask was clear. He felt serene. It was the pervasive sense of freedom and ease that he always felt when he dived. He was alone in the blue silence speckled with shafts of sunlight that danced through the water. The only sounds were those he made breathing—a deep, hollow noise as he breathed in, a soft thudding of bubbles as he exhaled. He held his breath, and the silence was complete. Without weights he was too buoyant, and he had to hold on to the bars to keep his tank from clanging against the hatch overhead. He turned around and looked up at the hull of the boat, a gray body that sat above him, bouncing slowly. At first, the cage annoyed him. It confined him, restricted him, prevented him from enjoying the grace of underwater movement. But then he remembered why he was there, and he was grateful.

He looked for the fish. He knew it couldn't be sitting beneath the boat, as Quint had thought. It could not "sit" anywhere, could not rest or stay still. It had to move to survive.

Even with the bright sunlight, the visibility in the murky water was poor—no more than forty feet. Hooper turned slowly around, trying to pierce the edge of gloom and grasp any sliver of color or movement. He looked beneath the boat, where the water turned from blue to gray to black. Nothing. He looked at his watch, calculating that if he controlled his breathing, he could stay down for at least half an hour more.

Carried by the tide, one of the small white squid slipped between the bars of the cage and, tethered by twine, fluttered in Hooper's face. He pushed it out of the cage.

He glanced downward, started to look away, then snapped his eyes down again. Rising at him from the darkling blue— slowly, smoothly—was the shark. It rose with no apparent effort, an angel of death gliding toward an appointment foreordained.

Hooper stared, enthralled, impelled to flee but unable to move. As the fish drew nearer, he marveled at its colors: the flat brown-grays seen on the surface had vanished. The top of the immense body was a hard ferrous gray, bluish where dappled with streaks of sun. Beneath the lateral line, all was creamy, ghostly white.

Hooper wanted to raise his camera, but his arm would not obey. In a minute, he said to himself, in a minute.

The fish came closer, silent as a shadow, and Hooper drew back. The head was only a few feet from the cage when the fish turned and began to pass before Hooper's eyes—casually, as if in proud display of its incalculable mass and power. The snout passed first, then the jaw, slack and smiling, armed with row upon row of serrate triangles. And then the black, fathomless eye, seemingly riveted upon him. The gills rippled—bloodless wounds in the steely skin.

Tentatively, Hooper stuck a hand through the bars and touched the flank. It felt cold and hard, not clammy but smooth as vinyl. He let his fingertips caress the flesh—past the pectoral fins, the pelvic fins, the thick, firm genital claspers—until finally (the fish seemed to have no end) they were slapped away by the sweeping tail.

The fish continued to move away from the cage. Hooper heard faint popping noises, and he saw three straight spirals of angry bubbles speed from the surface, then slow and stop, well above the fish. Bullets. Not yet, he told himself. One more pass for pictures. The fish began to turn, banking, the rubbery pectoral fins changing pitch.

"What the hell is he doing down there?" said Brody. "Why didn't he jab him with the gun?"

Quint didn't answer. He stood on the transom, harpoon clutched in his fist, peering into the water. "Come up, fish," he said. "Come to Quint."

"Do you see it?" said Brody. "What's it doing?"

"Nothing. Not yet, anyway."

The fish had moved off to the limit of Hooper's vision—a spectral silver-gray blur tracing a slow circle. Hooper raised his camera and pressed the trigger. He knew the film would be worthless unless the fish moved in once more, but he wanted to catch the beast as it emerged from the darkness.

Through the viewfinder he saw the fish turn toward him. It moved fast, tail thrusting vigorously, mouth opening and closing as if gasping for breath. Hooper raised his right hand to change the focus. Remember to change it again, he told himself, when it turns.

But the fish did not turn. A shiver traveled the length of its body as it closed on the cage. It struck the cage head on, the snout ramming between two bars and spreading them. The snout hit Hooper in the chest and knocked him backward. The camera flew from his hands, and the mouthpiece shot from his mouth. The fish turned on its side, and the pounding tail forced the great body farther into the cage. Hooper groped for his mouthpiece but couldn't find it. His chest was convulsed with the need for air.

"It's attacking!" screamed Brody. He grabbed one of the tether ropes and pulled, desperately trying to raise the cage.

"God damn your fucking soul!" Quint shouted.

"Throw it! Throw it!"

"I can't throw it! I gotta get him on the surface! Come up, you devil! You prick!"

The fish slid backward out of the cage and turned sharply to the right in a tight circle. Hooper reached behind his head, found the regulator tube, and followed it with his hand until he located the mouthpiece. He put it in his mouth and, forgetting to exhale first, sucked for air. He got water, and he gagged and choked until at last the mouthpiece cleared and he drew an agonized breath. It was then that he saw the wide gap in the bars and saw the giant head lunging through it. He raised his hands above his head, grasping at the escape hatch.

The fish rammed through the space between the bars, spreading them still farther with each thrust of its tail. Hooper, flattened against the back of the cage, saw the mouth reaching, straining for him. He remembered the power head, and he tried to lower his right arm and grab it. The fish thrust again, and Hooper saw with the terror of doom that the mouth was going to reach him.

The jaws closed around his torso. Hooper felt a terrible pressure, as if his guts were being compacted. He jabbed his fist into the black eye. The fish bit down, and the last thing Hooper saw before he died was the eye gazing at him through a cloud of his own blood.

"He's got him!" cried Brody. "Do something!"

"The man is dead," Quint said.

"How do you know? We may be able to save him."

"He is dead."

Holding Hooper in its mouth, the fish backed out of the cage. It sank a few feet, chewing, swallowing the viscera that were squeezed into its gullet. Then it shuddered and thrust forward with its tail, driving itself and prey upward in the water.

"He's coming up!" said Brody.

"Grab the rifle!" Quint cocked his hand for the throw.

The fish broke water fifteen feet from the boat, surging upward in a shower of spray. Hooper's body protruded from each side of the mouth, head and arms hanging limply down one side, knees, calves, and feet from the other.

In the few seconds while the fish was clear of the water, Brody thought he saw Hooper's glazed, dead eyes staring open through his face mask. As if in contempt and triumph, the fish hung suspended for an instant, challenging mortal vengeance.

Simultaneously, Brody reached for the rifle and Quint cast the harpoon. The target was huge, a field of white belly, and the distance was not too great for a successful throw above water. But as Quint threw, the fish began to slide down into the water, and the iron went high.

For another instant, the fish remained on the surface, its head out of water, Hooper hanging from its mouth.

"Shoot!" Quint yelled. "For Christ sake, shoot!"

Brody shot without aiming. The first two shots hit the water in front of the fish. The third, to Brody's horror, struck Hooper in the neck.

"Here, give me the goddam thing!" said Quint, grabbing the rifle from Brody. In a single, quick motion he raised the rifle to his shoulder and squeezed off two shots. But the fish, with a last, vacant gaze, had already begun to slip beneath the surface. The bullets plopped harmlessly into the swirl where the head had been.

The fish might never have been there. There was no noise, save the whisper of a breeze. From the surface the cage seemed undamaged. The water was calm. The only difference was that Hooper was gone.

"What do we do now?" said Brody. "What in the name of

God can we do now? There's nothing left. We might as well go back."

"We'll go back," said Quint. "For now."

"For now? What do you mean? There's nothing we can do. The fish is too much for us. It's not real, not natural."

"Are you beaten, man?"

"I'm beaten. All we can do is wait until God or nature or whatever the hell is doing this to us decides we've had enough. It's out of man's hands."

"Not mine," said Quint. "I am going to kill that thing."

"I'm not sure I can get any more money after what happened today."

"Keep your money. This is no longer a matter of money."

"What do you mean?" Brody looked at Quint, who was standing at the stern, looking at the spot where the fish's head had been, as if he expected it to reappear at any moment clutching the shredded corpse in its mouth. He searched the sea, craving another confrontation.

Quint said to Brody, "I am going to kill that fish. Come if you want. Stay home if you want. But I am going to kill that fish."

As Quint spoke, Brody looked into his eyes. They seemed as dark and bottomless as the eye of the fish. "I'll come," said Brody. "I don't guess I have any choice."

"No," said Quint. "We have no choice." He took his knife from its sheath and handed it to Brody. "Here. Cut that cage loose and let's get out of here."

WHEN THE BOAT was tied up at the dock, Brody walked toward his car. At the end of the dock there was a phone booth, and he stopped beside it, prompted by his earlier resolve to call Daisy Wicker. But he suppressed the impulse and moved on to his car. What's the point? he thought. If there was anything, it's over now.

Still, as he drove toward Amity, Brody wondered what Ellen's reaction had been when the Coast Guard had called her with the news of Hooper's death. Quint had radioed the Coast Guard before they started in, and Brody had asked the duty officer to phone Ellen and tell her that he, at least, was all right.

By the time Brody arrived home, Ellen had long since finished crying. She had wept mechanically, angrily, grieving not so much for Hooper as in hopelessness and bitterness at yet another death. She had been sadder at the disintegration of Larry Vaughan than she was now, for Vaughan had been a dear and close friend. Hooper had been a "lover" in only the most shallow sense of the word. She had not *loved* him. She had used him, and though she was grateful for what he had given her, she felt no obligation to him. She was sorry he was dead, of course, just as she would have been sorry to hear that his brother, David, had died. In her mind they were both now relics of her distant past.

She heard Brody's car pull into the driveway, and she opened the back door. Lord, he looks whipped, she thought as she watched him walk toward the house. His eyes were red and sunken, and he seemed slightly hunched as he walked. She kissed him at the door and said, "You look like you could use a drink."

"That I could." He went into the living room and flopped into a chair.

"What would you like?"

"Anything. Just so long as it's strong."

She went into the kitchen, filled a glass with equal portions of vodka and orange juice, and brought it to him. She sat on the arm of his chair and ran her hand over his head. She smiled and said, "There's your bald spot. It's been so long since I touched your bald spot that I'd forgotten it was there."

"I'm surprised there's any hair left at all. Christ, I'll never be as old as I feel today."

"I'll bet. Well, it's over now."

"I wish it was," said Brody. "I truly do wish it was."

"What do you mean? It is over, isn't it? There's nothing more you can do."

"We're going out tomorrow. Six o'clock."

"You're kidding."

"I wish I was."

"Why?" Ellen was stunned. "What do you think you can do?"

"Catch the fish. And kill it."

"Do you believe that?"

"I'm not sure. But Quint believes it. God, how he believes it."

"Then let him go. Let him get killed."

"I can't."

"Why not?"

"It's my job."

"It is *not* your job!" She was furious, and scared, and tears began to well behind her eyes.

Brody thought for a moment and said, "No, you're right."

"Then *why*?"

"I don't think I can tell you. I don't think I know."

"Are you trying to prove something?"

"Maybe. I don't know. I didn't feel this way before. After Hooper was killed, I was ready to give up."

"What changed your mind?"

"Quint, I guess."

"You mean you're letting him tell you what to do?"

"No. He didn't tell me anything. It's a feeling. I can't explain it. But giving up isn't an answer. It doesn't put an end to anything."

"Why is an end so important?"

"Different reasons, I think. Quint feels that if he doesn't kill the fish, everything he believes in is wrong."

"And you?"

Brody tried to smile. "Me, I guess I'm just a screwed-up cop."

"Don't joke with me!" Ellen cried, and tears spilled out of her eyes. "What about me and the children? Do you want to get killed?"

"No, God no. It's just . . ."

"You think it's all your fault. You think you're responsible."

"Responsible for what?"

"For that little boy and the old man. You think killing the shark will make everything all right again. You want revenge."

Brody sighed. "Maybe I do. I don't know. I feel . . . I believe that the only way this town can be alive again is if we kill that thing."

"And you're willing to get killed trying to—"

"Don't be stupid! I'm not willing to get killed. I'm not even willing—if that's the word you want to use—to go out in that goddam boat. You think I like it out there? I'm so scared every minute I'm out there I want to puke."

"Then *why go?*" She was pleading with him, begging. "Can't you ever think of anybody but yourself?"

Brody was shocked at the suggestion of selfishness. It had never occurred to him that he was being selfish, indulging a personal need for expiation. "I love you," he said. "You know that . . . no matter what."

"Sure you do," she said bitterly. "Oh, sure you do."

They ate dinner in silence. When they were finished, Ellen picked up the dishes, washed them, and went upstairs. Brody walked around the living room, turning out lights. Just as he reached for the switch to turn off the hall light, he heard a tap on the front door. He opened it and saw Meadows.

"Hey, Harry," he said. "Come on in."

"No," said Meadows. "It's too late. I just wanted to drop this by." He handed Brody a manila envelope.

"What is it?"

"Open it and see. I'll talk to you tomorrow." Meadows turned and walked down the path to the curb, where his car was parked, lights on and motor running.

Brody shut the door and opened the envelope. Inside was a proof of the editorial page of the next day's *Leader*. The first two editorials had been circled in red grease pencil. Brody read:

A NOTE OF SORROW . . .

In the past three weeks, Amity has suffered through one horrible tragedy after another. Its citizens, and its friends, have been struck down by a savage menace that no one can deter, no one can explain.

Yesterday another human life was cut short by the Great White Shark. Matt Hooper, the young oceanographer from Woods Hole, was killed as he tried to kill the beast singlehandedly.

People may debate the wisdom of Mr. Hooper's daring attempt. But call it brave or foolhardy, there can be no debate about the motive that sent him on his fatal mission. He was trying to help Amity, spending his own time and money in an effort to restore peace to this despairing community.

He was a friend, and he gave his life so that we, his friends, might live.

. . . AND A VOTE OF THANKS

Ever since the marauding shark first came to Amity, one man has spent his every waking minute trying to protect his fellow citizens. That man is Police Chief Martin Brody.

After the first attack, Chief Brody wanted to inform the public of the danger and close the beaches. But a chorus of less prudent voices, including that of the editor of this newspaper, told him he was wrong. Play down the risk, we said, and it will disappear. It was we who were wrong.

Some in Amity were slow to learn the lesson. When, after repeated attacks, Chief Brody insisted on keeping the beaches closed, he was vilified and threatened. A few of his most vocal critics were men motivated not by public-spiritedness but personal greed. Chief Brody persisted, and, once again, he was proven right.

Now Chief Brody is risking his life on the same expedition that took the life of Matt Hooper. We must all offer our prayers for his safe return . . . and our thanks for his extraordinary fortitude and integrity

Brody said aloud, "Thank *you*, Harry."

AROUND MIDNIGHT, THE wind began to blow hard from the northeast, whistling through the screens and soon bringing a driving rain that splashed on the bedroom floor. Brody got out of bed and shut the window. He tried to go back to sleep, but his mind refused to rest. He got up again, put on his bathrobe, went downstairs to the living room, and turned on the television. He switched channels until he found a movie—*Weekend at the Waldorf*, with Ginger Rogers. Then he sat down in a chair and promptly slipped into a fitful doze.

He awoke at five, to the whine of the television test pattern, turned off the set, and listened for the wind. It had moderated and seemed to be coming from a different quarter, but it still carried rain. He debated calling Quint, but thought, no, no use: we'll be going even if this blows up into a gale. He went upstairs and quietly dressed. Before he left the bedroom, he looked at Ellen, who had a frown on her sleeping face. "I do love you, you know," he whispered, and he kissed her brow. He started down the stairs and then, impulsively, went and looked in the boys' bedrooms. They were all asleep.

14

WHEN HE DROVE up to the dock, Quint was waiting for him—a tall, impassive figure whose yellow oilskins shone under the dark sky. He was sharpening a harpoon dart on a Carborundum stone.

"I almost called you," Brody said as he pulled on his slicker. "What does this weather mean?"

"Nothing," said Quint. "It'll let up after a while. Or even if it doesn't, it don't matter. He'll be there."

Brody looked up at the scudding clouds. "Gloomy enough."

"Fitting," said Quint, and he hopped aboard the boat.

"Is it just us?"

"Just us. You expecting somebody else?"

"No. But I thought you liked an extra pair of hands."

"You know this fish as well as any man, and more hands won't make no difference now. Besides, it's nobody else's business."

Brody stepped from the dock onto the transom, and was about to jump down to the deck when he noticed a canvas tarpaulin covering something in a corner. "What's that?" he said, pointing.

"Sheep." Quint turned the ignition key. The engine coughed once, caught, and began to chug evenly.

"What for?" Brody stepped down onto the deck. "You going to sacrifice it?"

Quint barked a brief, grim laugh. "Might at that," he said. "No, it's bait. Give him a little breakfast before we have at him. Undo my stern line." He walked forward and cast off the bow and spring lines.

As Brody reached for the stern line, he heard a car engine. A pair of headlights sped along the road, and there was a squeal of rubber as the car stopped at the end of the pier. A man jumped out of the car and ran toward the *Orca*. It was the *Times* reporter, Bill Whitman.

"I almost missed you," he said, panting.

"What do you want?" said Brody.

"I want to come along. Or, rather, I've been ordered to come along."

"Tough shit," said Quint. "I don't know who you are, but nobody's coming along. Brody, cast off the stern line."

"Why not?" said Whitman. "I won't get in the way. Maybe I can help. Look, man, this is news. If you're going to catch that fish, I want to be there."

"Fuck yourself," said Quint.

"I'll charter a boat and follow you."

Quint laughed. "Go ahead. See if you can find someone foolish enough to take you out. Then try to find us. It's a big ocean. Throw the line, Brody!"

Brody tossed the stern line onto the dock. Quint pushed the throttle forward, and the boat eased out of the slip. Brody looked back and saw Whitman walking down the pier toward his car.

The water off Montauk was rough, for the wind—from the southeast now—was at odds with the tide. The boat lurched through the waves, its bow pounding down and casting a mantle of spray. The dead sheep bounced in the stern.

When they reached the open sea, heading southwest, their motion was eased. The rain had slacked to a drizzle, and with each moment there were fewer whitecaps tumbling from the top of waves.

They had been around the point only fifteen minutes when Quint pulled back on the throttle and slowed the engine.

Brody looked toward shore. In the growing light he could see the water tower clearly—a black point rising from the gray strip of land. The lighthouse beacon still shone. "We're not out as far as we usually go," he said.

"No."

"We can't be more than a couple of miles offshore."

"Just about."

"So why are you stopping?"

"I got a feeling." Quint pointed to the left, to a cluster of lights farther down the shore. "That's Amity there."

"So?"

"I don't think he'll be so far out today. I think he'll be somewhere between here and Amity."

"Why?"

"Like I said, it's a feeling. There's not always a why to these things."

"Two days in a row we found him farther out."

"Or he found us."

"I don't get it, Quint. For a man who says there's no such thing as a smart fish, you're making this one out to be a genius."

"I wouldn't go that far."

Brody bristled at Quint's sly, enigmatic tone. "What kind of game are you playing?"

"No game. If I'm wrong, I'm wrong."

"And we try somewhere else tomorrow." Brody half hoped Quint would be wrong, that there would be a day's reprieve.

"Or later today. But I don't think we'll have to wait that long." Quint cut the engine, went to the stern, and lifted a bucket of chum onto the transom. "Start chummin'," he said, handing Brody the ladle. He uncovered the sheep, tied a rope around its neck, and lay it on the gunwale. He slashed its stomach and flung the animal overboard, letting it drift twenty feet from the boat before securing the rope to an after cleat. Then he went forward, unlashed two barrels, and carried them, and their coils of ropes and harpoon darts, back to the stern. He set the barrels on each side of the transom, each next to its own rope, and slipped one dart onto the wooden throwing shaft. "Okay," he said. "Now let's see how long it takes."

The sky had lightened to full, gray daylight, and in ones and twos the lights on the shore flicked off.

The stench of the mess Brody was ladling overboard made his stomach turn, and he wished he had eaten something—anything—before he left home.

Quint sat on the flying bridge, watching the rhythms of the sea.

Brody's butt was sore from sitting on the hard transom, and his arm was growing weary from the dipping and emptying of the ladle. So he stood up, stretched, and, facing off the stern, tried a new scooping motion with the ladle.

Suddenly he saw the monstrous head of the fish—not five feet away, so close he could reach over and touch it with the ladle—black eyes staring at him, silver-gray snout pointing at him, gaping jaw grinning at him. "Oh, God!" Brody said, wondering in his shock how long the fish had been there before he had stood up and turned around. "There he is!"

Quint was down the ladder and at the stern in an instant. As he jumped onto the transom, the fish's head slipped back into the water and, a second later, slammed into the transom. The jaws closed on the wood, and the head shook violently from side to side. Brody grabbed a cleat and held on, unable to look away from the eyes. The boat shuddered and jerked each time the fish moved its head. Quint slipped and fell to his knees on the transom. The fish let go and dropped beneath the surface, and the boat lay still again.

"He was waiting for us!" yelled Brody.

"I know," said Quint.

"How did he—"

"It don't matter," said Quint. "We've got him now."

"*We've* got *him*? Did you see what he did to the boat?"

"Give it a mighty good shake, didn't he?"

The rope holding the sheep tightened, shook for a moment, then went slack.

Quint stood and picked up the harpoon. "He's took the sheep. It'll be a minute before he comes back."

"How come he didn't take the sheep first?"

"He got no manners," Quint cackled. "Come on, you motherfucker. Come and get your due."

Brody saw fever in Quint's face—a heat that lit up his dark eyes, an intensity that drew his lips back from his teeth in a crooked smile, an anticipation that strummed the sinews in his neck and whitened his knuckles.

The boat shuddered again, and there was a dull, hollow thump.

"What's he doing?" said Brody.

Quint leaned over the side and shouted, "Come out from under there, you cocksucker! Where are your guts? You'll not sink me before I get to you!"

"What do you mean, sink us?" said Brody. "What's he doing?"

"He's trying to chew a hole in the bottom of the fucking boat, that's what! Look in the bilge. Come out, you godforsaken sonofabitch!" Quint raised high his harpoon.

Brody knelt and raised the hatch cover over the engine room. He peered into the dark, oily hole. There was water in the bilges, but there always was, and he saw no new hole through which water could pour. "Looks okay to me," he said. "Thank God."

The dorsal fin and tail surfaced ten yards to the right of the stern and began to move again toward the boat. "There you come," said Quint, cooing. "There you come." He stood, legs spread, left hand on his hip, right hand extended to the sky, grasping the harpoon. When the fish was a few feet from the boat and heading straight on, Quint cast his iron.

The harpoon struck the fish in front of the dorsal fin. And then the fish hit the boat, knocking the stern sideways and sending Quint tumbling backward. His head struck the footrest of the fighting chair, and a trickle of blood ran down his neck. He jumped to his feet and cried, "I got you! I got you, you miserable prick!"

The rope attached to the iron dart snaked overboard as the fish sounded, and when it reached the end, the barrel popped off the transom, fell into the water, and vanished.

"He took it down with him!" said Brody.

"Not for long," said Quint. "He'll be back, and we'll throw another into him, and another, and another, until he quits. And then he's ours!" Quint leaned on the transom, watching the water.

Quint's confidence was contagious, and Brody now felt ebullient, gleeful, relieved. It was a kind of freedom, a freedom from the mist of death. He yelled, "Hot shit!" Then he noticed the blood running down Quint's neck, and he said, "Your head's bleeding."

"Get another barrel," said Quint. "Bring it back here. And don't fuck up the coil. I want it to go over smooth as cream."

Brody ran forward, unlashed a barrel, slipped the coiled rope over his arm, and carried the gear to Quint.

"There he comes," said Quint, pointing to the left. The barrel came to the surface and bobbed in the water. Quint pulled the string attached to the wooden shaft and brought it aboard. He fixed the shaft to the new dart and raised the harpoon above his head. "He's coming up!"

The fish broke water a few yards from the boat. Like a rocket lifting off, snout, jaw, and pectoral fins rose straight from the water. Then the smoke-white belly, pelvic fin, and huge, salamilike claspers.

"I see your cock, you bastard!" cried Quint, and he threw a second iron, leaning his shoulder and back into the throw. The iron hit the fish in the belly, just as the great body began to fall forward. The belly smacked the water with a thunderous boom, sending a blinding fall of spray over the boat. "He's done!" said Quint as the second rope uncoiled and tumbled overboard.

The boat lurched once, and again, and there was the distant sound of crunching.

"Attack me, will you?" said Quint. "You'll take no man with you, uppity fuck!" Quint ran forward and started the engine. He pushed the throttle forward, and the boat moved away from the bobbing barrels.

"Has he done any damage?" said Brody.

"Some. We're riding a little heavy aft. He probably poked a hole in us. It's nothing to worry about. We'll pump her out."

"That's it, then," Brody said happily.

"What's what?"

"The fish is as good as dead."

"Not quite. Look."

Following the boat, keeping pace, were the two red wooden barrels. They did not bob. Dragged by the great force of the fish, each cut through the water, pushing a wave before it and leaving a wake behind.

"He's chasing us?" said Brody.

Quint nodded.

"Why? He can't still think we're food."

"No. He means to make a fight of it."

For the first time, Brody saw a frown of disquiet on Quint's face. It was not fear, nor true alarm, but rather a look of uneasy concern—as if, in a game, the rules had been changed without warning, or the stakes raised. Seeing the change in Quint's mood, Brody was afraid.

"Have you ever had a fish do this before?" he asked.

"Not like this, no. I've had 'em attack the boat, like I told you. But most times, once you get an iron in 'em, they stop fighting you and fight against that thing stickin' in 'em."

Brody looked astern. The boat was moving at moderate speed, turning this way and that in response to Quint's random turning of the wheel. Always the barrels kept up with them.

"Fuck it," said Quint. "If it's a fight he wants, it's a fight he'll get." He throttled down to idling speed, jumped down from the flying bridge and up onto the transom. He picked up the harpoon. Excitement had returned to his face. "Okay, shit-eater!" he called. "Come and get it!"

The barrels kept coming, plowing through the water—thirty yards away, then twenty-five, then twenty. Brody saw the flat plain of gray pass along the starboard side of the boat, six feet beneath the surface. "He's here!" he cried. "Heading forward."

"Shit!" said Quint, cursing his misjudgment of the length of the ropes. He detached the harpoon dart from the shaft, snapped the twine that held the shaft to a cleat, hopped down from the transom, and ran forward. When he reached the bow, he bent down and tied the twine to a forward cleat, unlashed a barrel, and slipped its dart onto the shaft. He stood at the end of the pulpit, harpoon raised.

The fish had already passed out of range. The tail surfaced twenty feet in front of the boat. The two barrels bumped into the stern almost simultaneously. They bounced once, then rolled off the stern, one on each side, and slid down the sides of the boat.

Thirty yards in front of the boat, the fish turned. The head raised out of the water, then dipped back in. The tail, standing like a sail, began to thrash back and forth. "Here he comes!" said Quint.

Brody raced up the ladder to the flying bridge. Just as he got there, he saw Quint draw his right arm back and rise up on tiptoes.

The fish hit the bow head on, with a noise like a muffled explosion. Quint cast his iron. It struck the fish atop the head, over the right eye, and it held fast. The rope fed slowly overboard as the fish backed off.

"Perfect!" said Quint. "Got him in the head that time."

There were three barrels in the water now, and they skated across the surface. Then they disappeared.

"God *damn!*" said Quint. "That's no normal fish that can sound with three irons in him and three barrels to hold him up."

The boat trembled, seeming to rise up, then dropped back. The barrels popped up, two on one side of the boat, one on the other. Then they submerged again. A few seconds later, they reappeared twenty yards from the boat.

"Go below," said Quint, as he readied another harpoon. "See if that prick done us any dirt up forward."

Brody swung down into the cabin. It was dry. He pulled back the threadbare carpet, saw a hatch, and opened it. A stream of water was flowing aft beneath the floor of the cabin. We're sinking, he told himself, and the memories of his childhood nightmares leaped into his mind. He went topside and said to Quint, "It doesn't look good. There's a lot of water under the cabin floor."

"I better go take a look. Here." Quint handed Brody the harpoon. "If he comes back while I'm below, stick this in him for good measure." He walked aft and went below.

Brody stood on the pulpit, holding the harpoon, and he looked at the floating barrels. They lay practically still in the water, twitching now and then as the fish moved about below. How do you die? Brody said silently to the fish. He heard an electric motor start.

"No sweat," said Quint, walking forward. He took the harpoon from Brody. "He's banged us up, all right, but the pumps should take care of it. We'll be able to tow him in."

Brody dried his palms on the seat of his pants. "Are you really going to tow him in?"

"I am. When he dies."

"And when will that be?"

"When he's ready."

"And until then?"

"We wait."

Brody looked at his watch. It was eight-thirty.

For three hours they waited, tracking the barrels as they moved, ever more slowly, on a random path across the surface of the sea. At first they would disappear every ten or fifteen minutes, resurfacing a few dozen yards away. Then their submergences grew rarer until, by eleven, they had not gone under for nearly an hour. By eleven-thirty, the barrels were wallowing in the water.

The rain had stopped, and the wind had subsided to a comfortable breeze. The sky was an unbroken sheet of gray.

"What do you think?" said Brody. "Is he dead?"

"I doubt it. But he may be close enough to it for us to throw a rope 'round his tail and drag him till he drowns."

Quint took a coil of rope from one of the barrels in the bow. He tied one end to an after cleat. The other end he tied into a noose.

At the foot of the gin pole was an electric winch. Quint switched it on to make sure it was working, then turned it off again. He gunned the engine and moved the boat toward the barrels. He drove slowly, cautiously, prepared to veer away if the fish attacked. But the barrels lay still.

Quint idled the engine when he came alongside the barrels. He reached overboard with a gaff, snagged a rope, and pulled a barrel aboard. He tried to untie the rope from the barrel, but the knot had been soaked and strained. So he took his knife from the sheath at his belt and cut the rope. He stabbed the knife into the gunwale, freeing his left hand to hold the rope, his right to shove the barrel to the deck.

He climbed onto the gunwale, ran the rope through a pulley at the top of the gin pole and down the pole to the winch. He took a few turns around the winch, then flipped the starter switch. As soon as the slack in the rope was taken up, the boat heeled hard to starboard, dragged down by the weight of the fish.

"Can that winch handle him?" said Brody.

"Seems to be. It'd never haul him out of the water, but I bet it'll bring him up to us." The winch was turning slowly, humming, taking a full turn every three or four seconds. The rope quivered under the strain, scattering drops of water on Quint's shirt.

Suddenly the rope started coming too fast. It fouled on the winch, coiling in snarls. The boat snapped upright.

"Rope break?" said Brody.

"Shit no!" said Quint, and now Brody saw fear in his face. "The sonofabitch is coming up!" He dashed to the controls and threw the engine into forward. But it was too late.

The fish broke water right beside the boat, with a great rushing whoosh of noise. It rose vertically, and in an instant of horror Brody gasped at the size of the body. Towering overhead, it blocked out the light. The pectoral fins hovered like wings, stiff and straight, and as the fish fell forward, they seemed to be reaching out to Brody.

The fish landed on the stern of the boat with a shattering crash, driving the boat beneath the waves. Water poured in over the transom. In seconds, Quint and Brody were standing in water up to their hips.

The fish lay there, its jaw not three feet from Brody's chest. The body twitched, and in the black eye, as big as a baseball, Brody thought he saw his own image reflected.

"God damn your black soul!" screamed Quint. "You sunk my boat!" A barrel floated into the cockpit, the rope writhing like a gathering of worms. Quint grabbed the harpoon dart at the end of the rope and, with his hand, plunged it into the soft white belly of the fish. Blood poured from the wound and bathed Quint's hands.

The boat was sinking. The stern was completely submerged, and the bow was rising.

The fish rolled off the stern and slid beneath the waves. The rope, attached to the dart Quint had stuck into the fish, followed.

Suddenly, Quint lost his footing and fell backward into the water. "The knife!" he cried, lifting his left leg above the surface, and Brody saw the rope coiled around Quint's foot.

Brody looked to the starboard gunwale. The knife was there, embedded in the wood. He lunged for it, wrenched it free, and turned back, struggling to run in the deepening water. He could not move fast enough. He watched in helpless terror as Quint, reaching toward him with grasping fingers, eyes wide and pleading, was pulled slowly down into the dark water.

For a moment there was silence, except for the sucking sound of the boat slipping gradually down. The water was up to Brody's shoulders, and he clung desperately to the gin pole. A seat cushion popped to the surface next to him, and Brody grabbed it. ("They'd hold you up all right," Brody remembered Hendricks saying, "if you were an eight-year-old boy.")

Brody saw the tail and dorsal fin break the surface twenty yards away. The tail waved once left, once right, and the dorsal fin moved closer. "Get away, damn you!" Brody yelled.

The fish kept coming, barely moving, closing in. The barrels and skeins of rope trailed behind.

The gin pole went under, and Brody let go of it. He tried to kick over to the bow of the boat, which was almost vertical now. Before he could reach it, the bow raised even higher, then quickly and soundlessly slid beneath the surface.

Brody clutched the cushion, and he found that by holding it in front of him, his forearms across it, and by kicking constantly, he could stay afloat without exhausting himself.

The fish came closer. It was only a few feet away, and Brody could see the conical snout. He screamed, an ejaculation of hopelessness, and closed his eyes, waiting for an agony he could not imagine.

Nothing happened. He opened his eyes. The fish was nearly touching him, only a foot or two away, but it had stopped. And then, as Brody watched, the steel-gray body began to recede downward into the gloom. It seemed to fall away, an apparition evanescing into darkness.

Brody put his face into the water and opened his eyes. Through the stinging saltwater mist he saw the fish sink in a slow and graceful spiral, trailing behind it the body of Quint— arms out to the sides, head thrown back, mouth open in mute protest.

The fish faded from view. But, kept from sinking into the deep by the bobbing barrels, it stopped somewhere beyond the reach of light, and Quint's body hung suspended, a shadow twirling slowly in the twilight.

Brody watched until his lungs ached for air. He raised his head, cleared his eyes, and sighted in the distance the black point of the water tower. Then he began to kick toward shore.

For the Squid Squads

1979

*Billy Mac, Garbage Bob,
The Duke, Columbus Mould,
Captain Fathom*

1990

*George Bell, Clayton Benchley,
Nat Benchley, Adrian Hooper,
Kyle Jachney, Stan Waterman,
Michele Wernick, Donald Wesson,
John Wilcox*

*And, of course, for the Tuckers:
Teddy, Edna and Wendy*

"She [Scylla] has twelve splay feet and six lank scrawny necks. Each neck bears an obscene head, toothy with three rows of thick-set crowded fangs blackly charged with death. . . . Particularly she battens on humankind, never failing to snatch up a man with each of her heads from every dark-prowed ship that comes."

—HOMER, *The Odyssey*

Part One

1

It hovered in the ink-dark water, waiting.

It was not a fish, had no air bladder to give it buoyancy, but because of the special chemistry of its flesh, it did not sink into the abyss.

It was not a mammal, did not breathe air, so it felt no impulse to move to the surface.

It hovered.

It was not asleep, for it did not know sleep, sleep was not among its natural rhythms. It rested, nourishing itself with oxygen absorbed from the water it pumped through the caverns of its bullet-shaped body.

Its eight sinuous arms floated on the current; its two long tentacles were coiled tightly against its body. When it was threatened or in the frenzy of a kill, the tentacles would spring forward, like tooth-studded whips.

It had but one enemy: All the other creatures in its world were prey.

It had no sense of itself, of its great size or of the fact that its capacity for violence was unknown in other creatures of the deep.

It hung more than half a mile below the surface, far beyond the reach of any sunlight, yet its enormous eyes registered faint glimmers, generated, in terror or excitement, by other, smaller hunters.

Had it been observable to the human eye, the animal would have been seen as purplish maroon, but that was now, at rest. When aroused, it would change color again and again.

The only element of the sea that the animal's sensory system monitored constantly was temperature. It was most comfortable in a range between 40 and 55 degrees Fahrenheit, and as it drifted with the currents and encountered thermoclines and upwellings that warmed or cooled the water, it moved up or down.

It sensed a change now. Its drift had brought it to the scarp of an extinct volcano, which rose like a needle from the ocean canyons. The sea swept around the mountain, and cold water was driven upward.

And so, propelled by its tail fins, the beast rose slowly in the darkness.

Unlike many fish, it did not need community; it roamed the sea alone. And so it was unaware that many more of its kind existed than had ever existed before. The balance of nature had been disrupted.

It existed to survive. And to kill.

For, peculiarly—if not uniquely—in the world of living things, it often killed without need, as if Nature, in a fit of perverse malevolence, had programmed it to that end.

2

From afar, the boat might have been a grain of rice on a vast field of blue satin.

For days, the wind had blown steadily from the southwest. Now, in the past few hours, it had faded—withered, retreated —and the stillness was uncertain, as if the wind were catching its breath and shuffling like a weary fighter before deciding where to launch its next assault.

Howard Griffin sat in the cockpit, one bare foot resting on a spoke of the wheel. The boat, deprived of the driving force of the wind, rocked gently in the long swells.

Griffin glanced up at the flapping sails, then checked his watch and cursed himself for a fool. He hadn't counted on this, hadn't anticipated a calm. He had plotted their course, their schedule, on the presumption of southerly winds.

Naïve. Stupid. He should have known better than to try to outguess the weather.

They were already hours behind schedule, thanks to having spent the entire morning in the Royal Navy Dockyard waiting for a customs officer to finish showing an apprentice how properly to search a fifty-two-foot Hatteras for contraband.

They should have been well at sea by now. Instead, as Griffin turned and looked back off the fantail, he could see the tall channel marker at the end of Eastern Blue Cut, a white speck glistening in the oblique light of the lowering sun.

He heard the kettle whistling below, and after a moment his wife came up through the hatch and handed him a cup of tea. He smiled his thanks and, as the thought suddenly came into his mind, he said, "You look terrific."

Startled, Elizabeth smiled back. "You're not so bad yourself."

"I'm serious. Six months on a boat, I don't know how you do it."

"A delusion." She bent down and kissed the top of his head. "Your standards have gone to hell."

"Smell good, too." Soap and air and skin. He looked at her legs, the color of oiled oak, not a stretch mark or a varicose vein to betray age or two children born more than fifteen years ago, just a single white scar where she had barked her shin against a concrete post one night down in the Exumas. He looked at her feet, brown and knobby and callused. He loved her feet.

"How am I ever gonna wear shoes again?" she said. "Maybe I'll get a job at the Barefoot Bank and Trust Company."

"If we ever get there." He gestured at the luffing mainsail.

"The wind'll go round again."

"Maybe. But we don't have time." He leaned forward, toward the ignition key, to turn on the engine.

"Don't."

"You think I like it? The man's gonna be at the dock Monday morning, and we better be there too."

"One second." She held up a hand, staying him. "Just let me check."

Griffin shrugged and sat back, and Elizabeth went below. He heard a burst of static as she adjusted the radio, then Elizabeth's voice as she spoke into the microphone. "Bermuda Harbour Radio, Bermuda Harbour Radio, Bermuda Harbour Radio . . . this is the yacht *Severance*."

"Yacht *Severance*, Bermuda Harbour Radio . . ." came back a voice from fifteen miles to the south. "Go to six-eight, please, and stand by."

"*Severance* going to six-eight," Elizabeth said, and there was silence.

Griffin heard a little splash off the stern of the boat. He looked overboard and saw half a dozen gray chubs swarming on a patch of yellow sargasso weed, competing for the tiny shrimps and other creatures that took shelter among the floating stalks and bladders. He liked sargasso weed, as he liked shearwaters, which spoke to him of freedom, and sharks, which spoke to him of order, and dolphins, which spoke to him of God. Sargasso weed spoke to him of life. It traveled on the water, pushed by the wind, bearing food for small animals, which became food for larger animals, and so on up the food chain.

"Yacht *Severance,* Bermuda Harbour Radio . . . go ahead."

"Yes, Bermuda. We're sailing north for Connecticut. We'd like to get a weather forecast. Over."

"Right, *Severance.* Barometer three-oh-point-four-seven and steady. Wind southwest ten to fifteen, veering northwest. Seas three to six feet tonight and tomorrow, with winds northwest fifteen to twenty. Scattered showers possible over open water. Over."

"Many thanks, Bermuda. *Severance* standing by on sixteen."

Elizabeth reappeared through the hatch and said, "Sorry."

"Me too."

"This wasn't the way it was supposed to end."

"No."

What was supposed to happen, how they had envisioned their return, was that they would ride a south wind all the way up the coast, and when they cleared Montauk Point, with Fishers Island ahead and Stonington Harbor just beyond, they'd run up all the burgees and pennants and flags from all the countries and yacht clubs and marinas they'd visited in the last half-year. When they reached the Stonington breakwater, the wind would back a little bit around to the east so they could march triumphant down the harbor with everything flying proud and beautiful. Their kids would be waiting on the dock with Elizabeth's mother and Griffin's sister and her kids, and they'd have a bottle of champagne and then strip the boat of all their personal things and turn it over to the broker for sale.

One chapter of their life would end, and the next would begin. With all flags flying.

"There's still hope," Griffin said. "This time of year, a

northwest wind doesn't last." He paused. "It better not, or we'll run out of fuel and tack back and forth till we die of old age."

He turned the key and pushed the button that started the engine. The four-cylinder diesel wasn't particularly noisy, but it sounded to him like a locomotive. It wasn't particularly dirty, but it smelled to him like midtown Manhattan.

Elizabeth said, "God, I hate that thing!"

"It's a machine. How can you hate a machine? I don't like it, but I can't hate it. You can't hate a machine."

"I can so. I'm a terrific-looking person. You said so yourself. It's in the Constitution: Terrific-looking people can hate whatever they want." She grinned and went forward to haul in the jib.

"Think positively," he called after her. "We've had a lot of sailing. Now we'll do a little motoring."

"I don't *want* to think positively. I want to be angry and disappointed and spoiled. And I'd appreciate it if you'd be angry too."

"What do I have to be angry about?" When he saw that the jib was down, Griffin put the boat in gear and pointed the bow into the breeze, which had begun to freshen. The oily calm had been wiped off the swells and replaced by the dappling of little waves. "I'm shacked up with the most beautiful crazy woman in the Atlantic, I've got a boat worth enough money to let me spend a year looking for a decent job, and I'm getting horny. What more could a guy ask?"

Elizabeth came aft and started on the mainsail. "So that's the bottom line, is it? You want to fool around."

"That I do," Griffin said. He stood and helped her with the big sail, steering with his foot to keep the bow pointed to windward. "But there's one tiny little problem."

"What's that?" She stood on one foot and let the toes of the other trace a circle on Griffin's calf.

"Someone to drive the boat."

"Turn on the automatic pilot."

"Great idea . . . if we had one."

"Yeah. I thought maybe saying the words would make one happen."

"You are disturbed," he said. "Gorgeous but nuts." He

leaned between folds of the sail and kissed her. Then he reached for a length of bungee cord to secure the sail. His foot slipped off the wheel, and the boat yawed off the wind. A wave struck the starboard quarter and splashed cold spray down Elizabeth's legs. She yelped.

"Nice work," she said. "You sure know how to drown romance."

Griffin spun the wheel to starboard and brought the bow back into the wind. The boat's motion was uncomfortable now, as it plowed into the short, choppy seas. He said, "Maybe we should wait for a fairer breeze."

"Well . . . it's nice to know your heart's in the right place." She smiled at him and wiggled her butt and went below.

Griffin looked to the west. The sun had reached the horizon and was squashing into an orange ball as it slipped off the edge of the world.

The bow dipped under a wave, rose up and slapped the next wave hard. Spray flew aft like a chill rain. Griffin shivered, and was about to call out to Elizabeth, to ask for his slicker, when she reappeared, wearing her own slicker and carrying a cup of coffee.

"Let me take her for a while," she said. "You get some sleep."

"I'm all right."

"I know, but if the wind doesn't go round, this is bound to be a long night." She slipped around the wheel, into the seat beside him.

"Okay," he said, and he lifted one of her hands off the wheel and kissed it.

"What was that for?"

"Change of command. Old sea custom. Always kiss the hand of your relief."

"I like that."

He stood up, ducked under the boom and went to the hatch. "Wake me if the wind dies," he said.

Below, he consulted with the loran, took its numbers to a chart on the gimballed table in the cabin and pinpointed their position. He used a ruler to draw a pencil line from their position to Montauk Point, then matched the line to the compass rose on the chart.

He poked his head up through the hatch and said, "Three-three-oh oughta do it." In the past few minutes the sky had darkened so that the light from the binnacle now cast a reddish glow under Elizabeth's chin. Her yellow slicker shone orange, and her auburn hair shimmered like charcoal embers.

"You *are* beautiful," Griffin said, and he backed down into the cabin and went into the head. As he peed, he listened to the engine and to the sounds of the water rushing by the wooden hull. His ears were alert to strange noises, but he heard none.

He walked forward, peeled off his shirt and shorts and tucked himself into one of the two small bunks in the fo'c'sle. In port, they slept together in the after cabin, but at sea it was better for whichever one was sleeping to sleep forward, to keep in touch with the motion of the boat, to sense a change in the weather, a shift in the wind, just in case. . . .

The pillow smelled of Elizabeth.

He slept.

THE ENGINE DRONED ON. Injectors pumped fuel into the cylinders, pistons compressed the fuel to combustion, and a thousand explosions every minute turned the shaft that held the propeller that drove the boat north into the night.

A pump drew seawater through a fitting in the hull and passed it through the engine, cooling it, and fed it aft to be flushed overboard with the engine's exhaust.

The engine was not old, had had less than seven hundred hours on it when they bought the boat, and Griffin had nursed it like a cherished child. But the exhaust pipe was harder to tend. It exited the engine compartment aft and nestled tightly beside the propeller shaft, under the floor of the after cabin. It was of steel, good steel, but for a thousand hours or more of engine use it had carried tons of salt water and acrid gases. And when the engine was not running, when the boat was sailing or tied to a dock, salt residue and molecules of corrosive chemicals had lain in the exhaust pipe and begun gradually to eat away at the steel.

The minuscule hole in the exhaust pipe could have been there for weeks. They had had fair winds all the way up from the Bahamas and had used the engine only to power in and out of St. George's Harbour and Dockyard, and routine pumping of the bilges would have removed any excess water. But now, with the engine running steadily and the heat-exchanger pump working full time and the boat punching into the sea rather than sailing gently with it, thus stressing its innards, the hole was growing. Bits of rusted metal flaked away from its edges, and before long it was the diameter of a pencil.

Water that had dripped into the bilges now flowed.

ELIZABETH STEERED WITH her feet and leaned back against the cushions in the cockpit. To her left, in the west, all that remained of the day was a sliver of violet on the rim of the world. To her right, a crescent moon was rising, casting a streak of gold that tracked her on the surface of the sea.

No souls, she thought as she looked at the moon. It was an Arab idea—she had read of it in *The Discoverers*, one of a score of books she had for years been meaning to read and had at last devoured in these past six months—and she decided she liked it: The new moon was an empty celestial vessel setting out on a month's journey to collect the souls of the departed, and as the days passed it swelled and swelled until, finally, engorged with souls, it disappeared to deposit its cargo in heaven, then reappeared, an empty vessel, and began again.

One reason she liked the conceit of a ship of souls was that for the first time in her life she was beginning to think she understood what a soul was. She was not a profound person, had always deflected serious conversations before they could plumb too deeply. Besides, she and Griffin had always been too busy living to pause and reflect.

He had been on the fast track at Shearson Lehman Brothers, she in the private banking division of Chemical Bank. The eighties had been a time when they had gathered toys: a million-dollar apartment, a half-million-dollar house in Stonington, two cars with heated seats and light bulbs in the backseat ashtrays. The money came in, the money went out:

twenty thousand dollars for private-school tuition, fifteen thousand a year for eating out a couple times a week, twenty thousand for vacations, fifty thousand for maintenance and upkeep.

Twenty thousand here, twenty thousand there—they used to joke—and pretty soon you're talking about real money.

It *was* a joke, because the money just kept coming in.

And then one day the tap was turned off. Griffin was laid off. A week later, Elizabeth was given a choice: half time at half salary, or quit.

Griffin's settlement would have allowed them to live for a year, no frills, while he looked for another job. But another job (undoubtedly at less money) would have meant climbing onto the same treadmill, a few paces back of the pack.

The other option was to take their severance money and buy a boat and see if, in fact, there was more to the world than *confit de canard* and designer fizzy water.

They kept the house in Stonington, sold the apartment in New York and put the proceeds in a trust to fund the children's education.

They were free, and with freedom came excitement and fear and—day after day, almost minute after minute—discovery. Discovery about themselves, about each other, about what was important and what was dispensable.

It could have been a disaster, two people confined twenty-four hours a day to a space forty feet long by twelve feet wide, and for the first couple of weeks they wondered. They got in each other's way and carped about this and that.

But then they became competent, and with competence came self-assurance, and with self-assurance, self-esteem and appreciation for one another's strengths.

They fell in love again, and, just as important, came to like themselves again.

They had no idea what they would do when they got home. Maybe Griffin would try for another job in the money business, though from everything they'd read—mostly in the Caribbean edition of *Time*—the money business was in the dumper. Maybe he'd try to find work in a boatyard. He loved tinkering, didn't even mind varnishing and sewing sails.

And she? Maybe she'd teach sailing, maybe try to join the

staff of an environmental group. She had been horrified by
what they had seen of the destruction of the reefs in the Bahamas and of the wildlife in the Windwards and Leewards. They
had snorkeled over barren bottoms littered with the sea-
bleached shells of dead conchs and the shattered carapaces of
spiny lobsters. Around island after island they had seen the
ocean environment despoiled and destroyed. And because
they had had time to think and observe, they had come to
understand more fully the cycle of poverty breeding ignorance
breeding poverty breeding ignorance. She had concluded that
there might be something she could do, could contribute—as
a researcher or a lobbyist. She still had contacts with a lot of
the rich people she had dealt with at Chemical.

It didn't matter. They'd find something. And whatever they
found would be better than what had been before, for they
were new people.

It had been a wonderful trip, with not a single regret.

Well, that wasn't quite true. There was one regret—that
they had had to turn on the engine. She hated its relentless
rumble, the absurd gurgle as the exhaust pipe dipped in and
out of the water, the vile smell of the fumes eddying over the
stern and swirling in the cockpit.

THE HOLE IN the exhaust pipe had begun to grow, as tiny bits of
rusty, weakened metal had flaked away. With each surge of
the boat, with each slight heave from side to side, there was
movement, not only of the hull but of everything within it—
not much, not noticeable, but enough to cause strain, enough
to aggravate weakness.

An eye could not have seen the hole grow, but now, as the
boat's bow stuttered between two short, choppy seas, the exhaust pipe was seized by a slight torsion. It buckled and tore,
and then all the water from the cooling pump poured into the
bilges. And because the pipe was broken, when the boat's
stern dipped and the exhaust outlet submerged, there was
nothing to keep the sea from rushing in.

ELIZABETH WAS SLEEPY. The boat's motion was the worst kind of soporific: staccato enough to be unpleasant but not violent enough to force her to stay alert. Perhaps she should wake Griffin.

She looked at her watch. No. He'd been asleep for only an hour and a half. Let him have another half hour. Then he'd be fresh and she could get some sleep.

She slapped herself in the face and shook her head.

She decided to sing. Impossible to fall asleep singing. Scientific fact. So she sang the first few bars of "What Are You Doing the Rest of Your Life?"

A wave lapped over the stern of the boat and soaked her.

No problem. The water wasn't cold. It would—

A *wave*? How does a wave come over the stern of a boat when you're heading into the sea?

She turned and looked.

The stern was four inches from being awash. As she watched, it dipped again, and more water rushed aboard and spread over the cushions.

Adrenaline shot up her back and down her arms. She sat still for a moment, willing herself to stay calm, to gather data. The annoying gurgle from the exhaust pipe has stopped. Fumes no longer swirled over the stern. The seas on either side of the boat looked higher. The boat's motion was sluggish, wallowing, ass-heavy.

She reached forward of the wheel, lifted a plastic cover and flicked the switch that turned on the bilge pump. She heard the electric motor start, but something was wrong with the sound. It was distant, faint and laboring.

"Howard!" she shouted.

No answer.

"Howard!"

Nothing.

A length of bungee cord was looped over the boom, and she hooked each end around a spoke of the wheel, securing it, and went down through the hatch.

A stench of exhaust fumes choked her and burned her eyes. It was coming up through the floor.

"Howard!"

She looked into the after cabin. Six inches of water covered the carpet.

Griffin was in a dark, foreboding dream when he heard his name called from what seemed a great distance. He willed himself awake, sensing that something was wrong, wrong with him, for his head hurt, his mouth tasted foul, he felt drugged.

"What is it?" he said, and he rolled his legs over the edge of the bunk. He looked aft and saw, through a bluish haze, Elizabeth running toward him and shouting something. What was she saying?

"We're sinking!"

"Come on. . . ." He blinked, shook his head. Now he could smell the exhaust, recognize the taste.

Elizabeth peeled back the carpet in the main cabin and lifted the hatch covering the engine compartment. By now Griffin was standing over her. They saw that the engine was half underwater. The batteries were still dry, but the water rose as they watched.

Griffin heard sloshing in the after cabin, saw the water and knew what had happened. He said, "Shut down the engine."

"What?"

"Now!"

Elizabeth found the lever and choked off the engine. The rumbling died, and with it the circulating pump. No new water was being forced aboard, and they could hear the comforting electric whine of the bilge pump.

But there was still an open wound in the stern.

Griffin grabbed two dish towels from the sink and a shirt from a hook, and he handed them to Elizabeth. "Stick these up the exhaust pipe. Tight. Tight as you can."

She ran up through the hatch.

Griffin reached into a drawer and found a crescent wrench. He knelt on the deck and adjusted the wrench to one of the bolts holding the batteries to their mounts. If he could get the batteries out of the engine compartment, raise them a couple of feet, a foot even, he could give the bilge pump time to stop the water from rising. He had meant to move the batteries, after he read a cautionary article in one of the boating magazines about how dangerously dependent modern boats had become on sophisticated electronics. But that would have involved some reconstruction beyond his talents, which would have meant dealing with island labor, which would have delayed them.

Delayed them from what?

He cursed and heaved against the first bolt. It was corroded, and the wrench skidded off.

With its way gone, the boat slewed broadside to the sea and fell into a rhythm of steep, jerky rolls. A cupboard door flew open, and a stack of plates skidded out and crashed to the deck.

He tightened the wrench and leaned on the handle. The bolt moved. He managed half a turn, then the wrench handle butted against the bulkhead. He yanked the wrench off, refitted it and turned again. The water rose.

In the cockpit, Elizabeth lay face down on the fantail, spread-legged, her feet braced against the roll. One of the dish towels was balled in her fist, and she felt along the hull for the two-inch opening in the exhaust outlet. She could barely reach it with the tips of her fingers, and she tried to jam the towel inside. The pipe was too big, the towel too thin. It slipped out of the hole and floated away.

She heard a new sound, and paused to decipher it. It was the sound of silence. The bilge pump had stopped.

Then she heard Griffin's voice below. "Bermuda Harbour Radio . . . this is the yacht *Severance* . . . Mayday, Mayday, Mayday . . . we are sinking . . . our position is . . . *Fuck!*"

Elizabeth pulled the shirt from under her chest and balled it with the second dish towel, and again felt for the hole in the stern.

The boat yawed. Water rushed over the stern, and she skidded. Her feet lost their grip. She was falling. Her arms flailed.

A hand grabbed her and pulled her back, and Griffin's voice said, "Never mind."

"Never *mind*!? We're sinking!"

"Not anymore." His voice was flat. "We've sunk."

"No. I don't—"

"Hey," he said, and he gathered her to him and held her

head against his chest and stroked her hair. "The batteries're gone. The pump's gone. The radio's gone. She's gone. What we've got to do is get the hell off before she slips away. Okay?"

She looked up at him and nodded.

"Good." He kissed her head. "Get the EPIRB."

Griffin went forward and uncovered the raft lashed to the cabin roof. He checked to make sure all its cells were inflated, checked the rubberized box screwed to the deck plates, to reassure himself that no one in some out-island port had stolen their flares or fishing lines or cans of food. He felt his belt to make sure his Swiss Army knife was secure in its leather case.

A five-gallon plastic jug of fresh water was tied to the boat's railing, and he untied it and set it in the raft. He debated going below to retrieve the small outboard motor stowed forward, then decided: Forget it. He didn't want to be caught below when the boat sank.

As he undid the last of the raft's lashings, Griffin felt a weird satisfaction: He wasn't panicking. He was acting precisely as he should—methodically, rationally, thoroughly.

Keep it up, he told himself. Keep it up. And maybe you've got a chance.

Elizabeth came forward. She carried the plastic bag containing the boat's papers, their passports and cash, and in her other hand the EPIRB, the emergency beacon, a red box covered with yellow Styrofoam, with a retractable antenna on one end.

The deck was awash now, and it was easy for them to heave the raft over the low railing into the sea. He held the raft with one hand and with the other steadied her as she jumped aboard. When she was seated in the bow, he stepped off the sailboat's deck and dropped into the stern of the raft. He sat, flicked on the switch on the EPIRB, pulled out the antenna and fitted the device into an elastic strap on one of the rubber cells.

Because the raft was light and the northwest wind was brisk, it moved quickly away from the crippled sailboat.

Griffin took Elizabeth's hand, and they watched in silence.

The sailboat was a black silhouette against the stars. The stern sank lower, then slowly disappeared. Then, suddenly, the bow rose up like a rearing horse and slipped backward down into the abyss. Enormous bubbles rushed to the surface and burst with muffled booms.

Griffin said, "Jesus . . ."

3

IT WAS ALERT, had been for several moments, and its sensory receptors were processing signals of increasing danger.

Something large was approaching, from above, from where its enemy always came. It could feel vast quantities of water being displaced, feel the pressure waves.

It prepared to defend itself. Chemical triggers fired throughout the great body, sending fuel to the masses of flesh. Chromatophores ignited within the flesh, and its color changed from maroon to a lighter, brighter red—not a blood-red, for so permeated was its blood with hemocyanin that it was in fact green, but a red designed by Nature purely for intimidation.

It withdrew and cocked its two longest, whiplike arms, then turned and backed around to face the direction from which its enemy was coming.

It was not capable of fear; it did not consider flight.

But it was confused, for the signals from its enemy were unusual. There was no acceleration, no aggression. Most of all, there were none of the normal sounds of its enemy echolocating, no clicks or pings.

Whatever was coming moved erratically at first and then angled downward without pause.

Whatever it was, it passed and continued into the deep, trailing strange noises. Creaks and pops. Dead sounds.

The creature's color changed again, and its arms uncocked and unfurled with the sea.

Random drift had brought it to within a hundred feet of

the surface, and its eyes gathered flickering shimmers of silver from the stars. Because light could signal prey, it allowed itself to rise toward the source.

When it was twenty feet from the surface and its motion was beginning to be affected by the roll above, it sensed something new—a disturbance, an interruption in the flow of the sea, moving and yet not moving, floating with the current, on the water but not part of it.

Two impulses drove the creature now, the impulse to kill and the impulse to feed. Hunger dominated, a hunger that had become more and more urgent as it searched in vain for prey in the deep. Once, hunger had been a simple cue, a signal to feed, and it had responded routinely, feeding at will. But now food was a quest, for prey had become scarce.

Again the animal was alert: not to defend itself, but to attack.

4

THEY HAD NOT spoken.

Griffin had fired a flare, and, holding hands, they had watched the yellow arc and the burst of orange brilliance against the black sky.

Then they had returned their gaze to the spot where the boat had been. A few bits of flotsam had drifted by—a seat cushion from the cockpit, a rubber fender—but now there was nothing, no sign that the boat had ever existed.

Elizabeth felt a tightness, a rigidity, in Griffin's hand, and she cupped it in both of hers and said, "What are you thinking?"

"I was doing the old 'if only' routine."

"What?"

"You know: if only we'd left a day earlier or a day later, if only the wind hadn't gone around, if only we hadn't had to start the engine . . ." He paused, and then his voice was bitter. ". . . if only I hadn't been too goddam lazy to get underneath the floor and check that pipe . . ."

"Don't do this, Howard."

"No."

"It wasn't anybody's fault."

"I suppose." She was right. Or even if she wasn't, what he was doing was useless. Worse than useless.

"Hey!" he said, forcing brightness. "I just thought of something. Remember when Roger sold us the insurance? Remember we wanted the cheapest policy we could get, and he said no, we could never rebuild a wooden boat that big these days for anything like that amount, and he made us go the whole way? Remember that?"

"I guess."

"Sure you do. The point is, the boat is insured for four hundred and fifty thousand dollars. We could *never* get that on a sale."

Elizabeth knew what he was doing. She was glad, and she was about to say something, when the raft dipped off the top of a wave and slid into a trough.

They were capsizing. She knew it, they couldn't stop it. She screamed.

Then the raft evened out and bobbed gently up the next wave.

"Hey," Griffin said, and he edged over to her and put his arm around her shoulders. "It's okay. We're fine."

"No," she said into his chest. "We're not fine."

"Okay, we're not fine. What are you scared of?"

"What am I scared of?" she snapped at him. "We're in the middle of the ocean in the middle of the night in a raft the size of a bottle cap . . . and you ask what am I scared of? How about *dying*?"

"Dying from what?"

"For God's sake, Howard . . ."

"I'm serious. Let's talk about it."

"I don't want to talk about it."

"You got something better to do? Come on." He kissed her head. "Let's bring the demons out and crush them."

"Okay." She took a deep breath. "Sharks. Call me a wimp, but I'm terrified of sharks."

"Sharks. Good. Okay. We can forget about sharks."

"*You* can, maybe."

"No. Listen. The water's cold. The Japanese and the Koreans have fished most of them out anyway. And if some big shark does come around, as long as we stay in the raft we don't look, smell or feel like anything he's used to eating. What else?"

"Suppose a storm . . ."

"Okay. Weather. Not a problem. The forecast is good. We're not in hurricane season. Even if a northeaster does come up, this raft is next thing to unsinkable. Worst can happen, it tips over. If it does, we right it again."

"And float around till we starve to death."

"Not gonna happen." Griffin was pleased, for he found that the more he talked, the more he was able to push his own fears away. "One, the wind is pushing us back toward Bermuda. Two, there are ships in and out of here every day. Three, worst case, by Monday afternoon the kids and what's-his-name from the brokerage will report us missing, and Bermuda Harbour Radio knows all about us. But it won't get to that. This baby is beeping its heart out for us." He patted the EPIRB. "First plane that goes over will call out the cavalry. Probably already has."

Elizabeth was silent for a moment, then said, "You believe all that?"

"Sure I believe all that."

"And you're not scared."

He hugged her and said, "Sure I am."

"Good."

"But if you don't do something with fear—talk it away, change it—it eats you up."

She put her head down into his chest and breathed through her nose. She smelled salt and sweat . . . and comfort. She smelled twenty years of her life.

"So . . ." she said. "You want to fool around?"

"Right!" he laughed. "Capsize in a fit of passion."

They stayed like that, huddled together, as the raft drifted slowly south on the breeze. Overhead, stars seemed to dance in crazy unison, twisting and dipping with the motion of the raft but always moving inexorably westward.

After a while, Griffin thought Elizabeth had fallen asleep. Then he felt tears on his chest.

"Hey," he said. "What is it?"

"Caroline," she replied. "She's so young. . . ."

"Don't, hon. Please . . ."

"I can't help it."

"You should try to sleep."

"Sleep!?"

"Okay, then. Let's play Botticelli."

She sighed. "Okay. I'm thinking of . . . a famous *M*."

"*M.* Let's see. Is he a . . . famous French—"

Elizabeth suddenly started. She sat up and turned toward the bow. "What was that?"

"What was what?"

"That scraping noise."

"I didn't hear anything."

"Like fingernails."

"Where?"

She crawled forward and touched the rubber on the forward-most cell of the raft. "Right here. Like fingernails scraping on the rubber."

"Something from the boat, maybe. Forget it. A piece of wood. All sorts of floating crap out here. Could've been a flying fish. Sometimes they'll come right in the boat."

"What's that smell?"

"What smell?" Griffin took a deep breath, and now he did smell it. "Ammonia?"

"That's what I thought."

"Something from the boat."

"Such as?"

"How do I know? We had a bottle under the sink. . . . Unless something's spilled in here." He turned and faced the stern of the raft and unzipped the lid of the rubberized box. It was too dark to see, so he bent over to smell inside the box.

He heard a noise like a grunt, and the raft bounced and lurched to one side. He was knocked off his knees, and the tins in the box rattled together, and the deck plates beneath him creaked and squealed against the rubber, and he heard some vague splashing sounds—probably of the raft slapping against confused wavelets.

"Hey!" He steadied himself with one hand on each side of the raft. "Careful there."

There was no alien odor in the box. He zipped it closed. "Nothing." But the smell of ammonia was stronger now. He turned back to face the bow. "I don't know what—"

Elizabeth was gone.

Gone. Just . . . gone.

He had a split second's sensation that he had gone mad, that he was hallucinating, that none of this was happening, that none of it had ever happened, that he would soon awake in a hospital after a month-long coma induced by an automobile accident or a lightning strike or a slab of cornice fallen from an office building.

He called out, "Elizabeth!" The word was swallowed by the breeze. He called again.

He sat back and took a deep breath and closed his eyes. He felt dizzy and nauseated, and his pulse thundered in his ears.

After a moment, he opened his eyes again, expecting to see her sitting in the bow and eyeing him quizzically, as if wondering if he'd had a fit.

He was still alone.

He got to his knees and hobbled around the entire raft, hoping—imagining—that she had fallen overboard and was clinging to a dangling loop of lifeline.

No.

He sat back again.

Okay, he thought. Okay. Let's look at this rationally. What are the possibilities? She jumped overboard. She suddenly went out of her mind and decided to swim to shore. Or to kill herself. Or . . . or what? She was kidnapped by terrorists from the Andromeda Galaxy?

He screamed her name again, and again.

He heard a scraping noise, felt something touch the rubber beneath his buttocks.

She was there! Under the raft! She must have fallen over and gotten tangled in something, maybe some debris from the sailboat, and now she was under the raft fighting for air.

He leaned over the side and stretched his arms under the raft, feeling for her hair, her foot, her slicker . . . anything.

He heard the scraping noise again, behind him.

He withdrew his arm and shoved himself back inside the raft and looked forward.

In the yellow-gray light from the sliver of moon he saw something move on the front of the rubber raft. It seemed to be clawing its way up the rubber, scrambling to come aboard.

A hand. It had to be a hand. She had freed herself from the tangle and now, exhausted, half-drowned, was struggling to climb aboard.

He flung himself forward and reached out, and when his fingers were an inch or two away from it—so close that he could feel its radiant coolness—he realized that it wasn't a hand, that it wasn't human.

It was slimy and undulant, an alien thing that moved toward him, reaching for him.

He recoiled and scrambled toward the stern of the raft. He skidded, fell. The shift of his weight caused the bow to rise up, and he knew a second of relief as the thing disappeared.

But then he watched, horrified, as it reappeared and inched upward until finally it was entirely atop the rubber cell. It straightened up, fanned out, looking now, he thought, like a giant cobra. Its surface was crowded with circles, each quivering with a life of its own and dripping water like ghastly spittle.

Griffin screamed. No word, no oath, no curse or plea, just a visceral shriek of terror, outrage, disbelief.

But the thing kept moving forward, always forward, compressing itself into a conical mass and slithering toward him, walking, it seemed, on its writhing circles; and as each circle touched the rubber it made a rasping sound, as if it contained claws.

It continued to come. It did not hesitate or pause or explore. It came as if it knew that what it was searching for was there.

Griffin's eyes fell on the oar in the raft, tucked under the cells on the starboard side. He grabbed it and held it like a baseball bat, and he raised it above his head and waited to see if the thing would come closer.

He braced himself on his knees, and when he judged that the moment had come he shouted, "Son of a *bitch!*" and slammed the oar down upon the advancing thing.

He was never to know whether the oar struck the thing or whether, somehow, the thing had anticipated it. All he would know was that the oar was torn from his hands and held aloft and crushed and rejected, cast away into the sea.

Now the thing, sensing exactly where Griffin was, moved more rapidly along the rubber.

Griffin stumbled backward, fell into the stern. He pushed himself back, and back, and back, desperate to squeeze into the tiny space between the cells and the deck plates. He reached—insanely, ridiculously—for his Swiss Army knife, fumbling with the snap on the leather case and mewling a litany of "Oh God . . . oh Jesus . . . oh God . . . oh Jesus."

The thing hovered over him, twitching and spraying him with drops of water. Each of its circles twisted and contorted itself as if in hungry competition with its neighbors, and in the center of each was a curved hook which, as it reflected rays of moonlight, resembled a golden scimitar.

That was the last Griffin knew, save for pain.

5

WHIP DARLING TOOK his cup of coffee out on the veranda, to have a look at the day.

The sun was about to come up; already there was a pink glow in the eastern sky, and the last of the stars had faded. Soon, a slice of orange would appear on the horizon, and the sky would pale and the wind would make up its mind what it was going to do.

Then he'd make up his mind, too. He should put to sea, try to raise something worth a few dollars. On the other hand, if he stayed ashore, there was always work to do on the boat.

The wind had gone around during the night. When he had come up from the dock at twilight, the boats anchored in the bay had been facing south. Now their bows were a phalanx arrayed to the northwest. But there were no teeth to the wind; it was little more than a gentle breeze. Any less, and the boats would have lain scatterways and swung with the tide.

He saw a splash in the bay, then another, and heard a fluttering sound: baitfish, a school of fry running for their lives and skittering over the glassy surface.

Mackerel? Jacks? Little puppy sharks finishing their dawn patrol before returning to the reefs?

Mackerel, he decided, from the vigor of the swirls and the relentlessness of the chase.

He loved this time of day, before the din of traffic began across in Somerset, and the growl of sightseeing boats in the bay and all the other noises of humanity. It was a time of peace and promise, when he could gaze at the water and let his memory dwell on what had been, and his imagination on what might yet be.

The screen door swung open behind him, and his wife, Charlotte—barefoot and wearing the summer cotton night-gown that showed the shadow of her body—came out with her cup of tea and, as she did every morning, stood beside him so close that he could smell the spice of sleep in her hair. He put an arm around her shoulder.

"Mackerel in the bay," he said.

"Good. First time in . . . what?"

"Six weeks or more."

"You going out?"

"I expect so. Chasing rainbows is more entertaining than chipping paint."

"You never can tell."

"No." He smiled. "And there's always hope. Anyway, I want to retrieve the aquarium's lines."

He finished his coffee, poured the dregs onto the grass, and as he turned to go inside, the first rays of the sun flashed over the water and bounced off the whitewashed house. He looked at the dark blue shutters, paint flaking, slats cracked and sagging.

"Lord, this house is a mess."

"They want two hundred apiece to do the shutters," said Charlotte, "three thousand for the lot."

"Thieves," he said, and he held the door for her.

"I suppose we could ask Dana. . . ." She paused.

"Not a chance, Charlie. No more. She's done enough."

"She *wants* to help. It's not like—"

"We're not there yet," he said. "Things aren't that bad."

"Maybe not yet, William." She went into the house. "But almost."

" 'William' now, is it?" he said. "It's pretty early in the day for your heavy artillery."

William Somers Darling was named after the Somers who settled Bermuda by shipwreck in 1609. Sir George Somers had been on his way to Virginia when his *Sea Venture* struck Bermuda, which Darling regarded as a triumph of seaman-ship, since to hit Bermuda in the middle of a billion square miles of Atlantic Ocean was akin, he felt, to breaking one's leg by tripping over a paper clip on a football field. Still, Somers wasn't the first or the last: It was a safe guess that the twenty-two square miles of Bermuda were ringed by more than three hundred shipwrecks.

Most Bermudians, black and white, were named after one or another of the early settlers—Somers, Darling, Trimingham, Outerbridge, Tucker and a dozen more. The names harkened to history, rang with tradition. And yet, as if in rebellion against mother-country pretension, most Bermudians, black and white, soon cast off one or two of their names and assumed a nickname that had to do with something they looked like or something they'd done or some affliction.

Darling's nickname was "Buggywhip," in commemoration of the weapon with which his father had regularly thrashed him.

His friends called him Whip, and so did Charlotte, except when they argued or discussed something she considered too serious for levity. Then she called him William.

He was a fisherman, or, rather, he had been; now he was an ex-fisherman, for being a fisherman in Bermuda had become about as practical a profession as trying to be a ski instructor in the Congo. It was hard to make a living catching something that wasn't there.

They could live comfortably if not lavishly on twenty or twenty-five thousand dollars a year. They owned the house—it had been in his family, free and clear, since before the American Revolution. Upkeep, including cooking gas and insurance and electricity, cost five or six thousand dollars a year. Boat maintenance, which he and his mate, Mike Newstead, did themselves, cost another six or seven thousand dollars. Food and clothing and all the other magical incidentals that appeared from nowhere and ate money, consumed the rest.

But twenty thousand dollars might as well have been a million, because he wasn't making it. This year was half gone, and so far he'd made less than seven thousand dollars.

His daughter, Dana, was working downtown in an accounting firm, making good money instead of going to college, and she tried to help. Darling had refused, more brusquely than he meant to but unable to articulate the confusion of love and shame that his child's offer had triggered in him.

For a while, Dana had succeeded in stealing some of their bills from their mailbox and paying them herself. When, inevitably, she had been discovered and confronted, she had advanced the matter-of-fact defense that since the house was going to be hers one day, she saw no reason why she shouldn't contribute to its maintenance, especially since the alternative was for them to go to the bank for mortgage money, which would only burden her with payments later on.

The argument had slipped away from reason into dark regions of trust and mistrust and had ended in hurt and anger.

Maybe Charlotte was right. Maybe things *were* that bad. Darling had seen a folder from the bank in a pile of mail on the kitchen table, but before he could ask about it, it had vanished, and he had put it out of his mind. But now he forced himself to wonder: Was she already talking about mortgages or loans? Would they have to let the bank get its hooks into them?

No. He wouldn't let it happen. There had to be ways. The Newport-Bermuda race was coming up in ten days, and a friend in the dive business was overbooked for charters during the layover and had asked Darling to pick up a few for him. They'd be good for a thousand dollars apiece, maybe five thousand in all.

Then there was the aquarium retainer, which paid his fuel costs in exchange for his bringing them exotic animals he fished up from the deep. At four dollars a gallon he burned up thirty-two dollars' worth of fuel every hour he was away from the dock. The aquarium also paid a bonus if he caught something spectacular. He never knew what he'd catch. There were common things down there, like little toothless sharks with catlike eyes, and rare things, like anglerfish, which lured their prey with bioluminescent dorsal stalks and ate it with needle teeth that seemed to be made of crystal. He knew that in the abyss there were unknown critters, too, animals no one had ever seen. Those were the challenge.

Finally, there was always the chance—about as long as winning the Irish Sweepstakes, but never mind, a chance—that he'd find a shipwreck with some goodies on it.

In the kitchen, he ate a banana while he warmed up some of last night's barracuda. There were two barometers on the wall, and he consulted both. One was a standard aneroid instrument with two pointers, one of which you set by hand, the other responding to atmospheric pressure. He tapped the glass. No change.

The other barometer was a tube of shark-liver oil. In good weather the oil was clear, a light amber color. In times of change or dropping pressure, the oil clouded. His faith was in the shark-oil barometer, for it wasn't a machine, and he distrusted machines. Machines were made by man, and man was a chronic screwup. Nature rarely made mistakes.

The oil was clear.

He decided to go to sea. Maybe there was a robust grouper out there waiting to be caught, a wanderer from times gone by. A hundred-pound fish could net him four or five hundred dollars. Maybe he'd run into a school of tuna.

Maybe . . .

Darling's mate, Mike Newstead, showed up a little after seven. Darling liked to joke that a geneticist would have prized Mike as the ultimate Bermudian, for he contained every ethnic strain ever represented in the colony. He had the short, curly hair of a black, the dark red skin of an Indian—a memento of eighteenth-century Tories bringing Mohawk Indians to the island as slaves—the bright blue eyes of an Englishman (but almond-shaped like an Asian's), and the taciturn resignation of a Portuguese. He was thirty-six, five years younger than Darling, but he looked ageless. His face had always been sharp-featured and deeply furrowed, as if hacked from some mountain stone. A stranger might have guessed his age at anything from thirty to fifty.

Some people still referred to him, behind his back, as Tutti-Frutti, but nobody called him that to his face anymore, for he stood six foot four and weighed well over 220 pounds, not a gram of which was fat. Though Mike was slow to anger, he was said to possess an explosive temper that was kept in check by his diminutive Portuguese wife, and by Darling, whom he loved.

Darling considered him the perfect mate. Mike didn't like to make decisions, but rather preferred to be told what to do. He responded instantly and unquestioningly to commands— as long as he respected his commander. He didn't talk much— he barely spoke, in fact—and if he had any opinions, he kept them to himself. He communicated most intimately and joyfully with Darling's most hated enemies: machines. Utterly unschooled, he seemed to intuit the workings of engines and motors, be they powered by diesel oil, gasoline, kerosene, air or electricity. He talked to them, soothed them, cajoled them and seduced them into doing what he wanted.

Darling poured Mike some coffee, and they went outside and stood on the dock and watched a cormorant wheeling over the bay in search of food.

"I guess we'll go pull the aquarium's traps," Darling said. "We leave 'em down too long, critters might die or get eaten . . . traps could break away."

"Aye."

"Might take along some bait . . . just in case."

Mike nodded, finished his coffee and went to the freezer in the toolshed to fetch some mackerel for bait.

Darling boarded the boat and started the big Cummings diesel and let it warm up.

The *Privateer* was a shrimp dragger that Darling had bought at a yard in Houma, Louisiana, and had converted to an all-purpose Bermuda workboat. Her name back then had been *Miss Daisy*, but he had known at first sight she was not a Miss Daisy. She was big and broad and strong, steel-plated, steel-bulkheaded, steel-decked, a safe, stable platform that rode good weather comfortably and challenged bad weather with defiance, slamming into the seas as if daring them to hole her or pop her rivets.

She'll knock you down, he'd say, but she'll never drown you.

She had a dry and roomy house, two compressors, two generators and racks for twenty scuba tanks.

Darling was as superstitious as the next man, but he defended himself against the offense of changing the boat's name by declaring that since she had been misnamed to begin with, all he had done was give her her right name.

Still, just to be on the safe side, on the bulkhead inside the wheelhouse he had nailed a little obeah figurine from Antigua, and in times of trial—such as the day when a small cyclone made up directly over Bermuda and the wind went from 8 to 120 knots in five minutes and blew like the howling hounds of hell for an hour—he'd give it a rub.

Mike hopped aboard and cast off fore and aft. Darling put the boat in gear and eased out of Mangrove Bay and around the point to Blue Cut.

Settling himself onto a hatch cover in the stern, Mike muttered at a recalcitrant pump motor as he cradled it in his lap.

Darling had set the aquarium's line to the northwest, about six miles offshore, in five hundred fathoms of water. He could have found five hundred fathoms closer on the south shore, for there the reefs ended and deep water began only a mile or two from land. But for some reason the creatures that interested the aquarium seemed to live only off the northwest edge.

Now, as they cruised among the reefs, the water was calm but with enough of a ripple to cut the glare and give definition to the different colors of the corals, which gave Darling leave to wander away from the cut and thread his way through the high heads. There was truth to the old rule that the darker something was, the deeper it was, so as long as he could see the yellow villains beneath the surface, he could avoid them.

Standing on the flying bridge, cooled by the northwest breeze and warmed by the young sun, Whip Darling felt himself a happy man. He could forget, for a moment, that he didn't have any money, and could dream dreams of vast wealth. He allowed himself to fantasize about stacks of silver coins and serpentine chains of gold. Sure, it was fantasy, but it was reality, too, it had been known to happen: the Tucker treasure, the Fisher treasure from the *Atocha*, the billion-dollar bonanza from the *Central America*. Who could say it couldn't happen again?

And gold and silver weren't the only treasures waiting to be discovered. There were animals, unknown and unimagined, especially in the deep, that might change people's ideas about everything from biology to evolution, that might give clues to cures for everything from arthritis to cancer. Finding one or two of these creatures wouldn't fill Darling's pocket-book, but they were the things that nourished his spirit.

His gaze drifted from the white sand holes to the crevices in patches of reef, and always his eyes searched for the telltale signs of a shipwreck that could be as old as the time of the first James.

Nobody knew when the first ship had come to grief on the Bermuda volcano: at least as far back as Elizabeth, because there was evidence that a hapless Spaniard had passed an unplanned holiday there during the reign of the Virgin Queen. The man had spent a lot of time and trouble carving an inscription on a rock that was still legible: F.T. 1543.

Bermuda had always been a ship trap, and it still was, even with all the modern miracles like RDF, loran and satellite navigation, because the volcano, albeit extinct, protruded from the bottom of the sea like a wand full of electromagnetic anomalies. Machines, electronic or magnetic, seized up and went berserk around Bermuda. Nothing worked, not reliably. Compasses reeled back and forth like drunks. A mariner who asked a loran where he was might well be told he was in the mountains above Barcelona.

The whims of the Bermuda volcano helped spawn the legends of the Bermuda Triangle, for when the mind of man got hold of a nugget of truth and twisted it into a pretzel of fancy, it conjured up everything from Atlantis to UFOs to omnivorous monsters living in the core of the planet.

Darling didn't object to people indulging themselves in nonsense about the Bermuda Triangle, but it seemed to him a waste of time. If people would make an effort to learn about the wonders that *did* exist, he thought, their appetite for dragons would be well satisfied. Seventy percent of the earth's surface was covered by water, and ninety-five percent of that seventy percent had never been explored by anybody. Instead, man kept spending billions of dollars to explore places like Mars and Neptune, to a point where it was an established fact that we already knew more about the back side of the moon than we did about three-quarters of our own home. Crazy.

Even he—a nobody in a tiny, pissant corner of nowhere—had in his twenty-five years on the ocean seen enough to know that the sea sheltered ample dragons to fuel the nightmares of the entire human race: thirty-foot sharks that lived in the mud, crabs as big as motorcars, finless fish with heads like horses, viper eels that ate anything including each other, fish that went fishing with little lanterns that hung down off their eyebrows, and so on.

These days, the Bermuda ship trap snared one or two victims every couple of years, usually a Liberia- or Panama-registered tanker, owned by a partnership of dentists or podiatrists from someplace like Altoona, Pa., whose Taiwanese captain spoke not a word of English. He would leave Norfolk, say, and set his course for the Straits of Gibraltar and turn on his automatic pilot. Then he'd go below to drink tea or have a nap or get a shiatsu massage, without bothering to notice an insignificant blip on his chart some six hundred miles to the east of North Carolina.

A couple of nights later, the airwaves would suddenly be flooded with S.O.S. calls. Sometimes, if the night was still and clear, Darling had only to walk out his back door and look to the north or northwest, and there on the horizon would be the lights of the stranded vessel.

His first thought always was, Lord, don't let her be laden with oil. His second was, If she has got oil, Lord, don't let her have a hole in her.

Back in the old days, the reefs were capturing so many ships that an industry arose of people who made their living rowing out and salvaging stricken ships. Some weren't content to wait; they wanted to make their luck, and they'd wave phony lights to lure ships onto the reefs.

Darling had always been amused by what he regarded as a nice irony: Mariners had made Bermuda a ship trap. They could have avoided Bermuda; the trouble was, they needed it.

Until the 1780s, there was no such thing as reliable longitudinal navigation. Sailors could tell their latitude by the angle of the sun off the horizon, had been doing it for a thousand years with cross-staffs, astrolabes, octants and sextants. But to tell where they were on the east-west axis they needed an accurate—truly accurate—chronometer. And there wasn't one.

Bermuda was a known fixed point in the ocean, and once they found it, they knew exactly where they were. And so, they would leave the West Indies or Hispaniola or Havana and sail north in the Gulf Stream, then northeast, until they reached 32 degrees north latitude. Then they would turn east and look for Bermuda, which would give them the course to set for home.

But if they ran into a storm, with winds so fierce and seas so high that they couldn't see, or if there was a fog, or if their navigator was a bit addled, by the time they finally did see Bermuda, the chances were they would be *on* Bermuda.

Charlotte had once read Darling a line a poet wrote: ". . . many a midnight ship and all its shrieking crew." He liked the words, because they spawned in him a vision of what it must have been like aboard one of the old-timers facing doom: sailing along, safe as a bird on the wing, the sounder up in the bow dropping his lead and getting no bottom, then all of a sudden—what's that?—the sound of surf—*surf*? how can there be surf in the middle of the ocean?—and they strain their eyes but they can't see, and the boom of the surf grows louder—and then the sounding lead does find a bottom, and there's that moment of horror when they know. . . .

TODAY, DARLING SAW no signs of shipwreck in the shallow water, but what he did see—for it was all he saw—drew the happiness out of him like a syringe pulling blood: one parrotfish, a needlelike garfish tail-walking across the surface, half a dozen flying fish that spooked away from the boat's bow, and a few meandering breams.

Reefs that had once teemed with life were as empty as a train station after a bomb scare.

He felt as if he were witnessing a funeral for a way of life . . . his way of life.

Soon the shallows sloped away, to forty feet, sixty feet, a hundred feet, and he stopped looking at the bottom and began to search for his buoy.

It was where he had left it, which half surprised him, because over the past year or two desperate fishermen had begun to abandon the code of honor that said, No man touches another man's pots. And even without human intervention, the baits were so deep that some great survivor could have taken and run with them—a six-gill shark, perhaps, or a big-eyed thresher—and dragged the traps miles away before breaking loose.

"Coming up on it," Darling called down to Mike, who put his pump motor aside and reached for the boat hook.

The orange-and-white buoy slid down the side of the boat, and when it reached the stern, Mike snagged it and pulled it aboard and walked it forward and wrapped the rope around the winch.

Darling put the boat in neutral, letting it wallow in the gentle sea, and came down from the flying bridge.

"Go you," Mike said, and Darling pushed the lever and turned on the winch, and as the rope began to come up, Mike fed it into a fifty-five-gallon plastic drum.

They had put down three thousand feet of polyethylene rope, with the buoy on top and twenty-five pounds of sash weights to keep it on the bottom. Starting at two thousand feet, they had attached, at every hundred-foot interval, a twenty-foot length of forty-eight-strand stainless-steel airplane cable, and at the end of each cable was one of the aquarium's gimmicks. Some were small wire boxes, some were contraptions of fine-mesh net. Most had bits of gurry inside to attract whatever creatures lived down in the dark. Because Darling didn't know—nobody knew—what those creatures might be or what they liked to eat, he had indulged his theory about ocean scavengers—whatever stinks most works best—and had baited the traps with the rankest, rottenest flesh he could find.

Into a few of the traps he had put no bait at all, just Cyalume chemical lights, following another of his theories—that light was such a novelty in a world of perpetual night that some animals might be drawn to it out of curiosity.

His hope was to bring the animals up alive and keep them alive in a cold-water tank on the boat. Every week or so, a scientist from the aquarium would come to examine the catch, and the creatures that were rare or unknown he would take back to study in the laboratory in Flatts.

Darling estimated that twenty percent of the animals survived the trip and the transfer to the aquarium—not a great number, perhaps, but as good a cheap way as possible to gather new species.

And it paid his fuel bills, which really mattered these days.

Darling held the lever and kept his eye on the rope. It was taut, squeaking and spitting water, but it should be, considering the weight of half a mile of rope and twenty-five pounds of lead and the traps and the cables and the baits.

He put his foot on the bulwark to steady himself against the wallow and looked over the side, down into the blue gloom, hoping to see some big fish cruising by.

Not bloody likely, he thought. If there were any such left in the sea, they had long since departed Bermuda.

"Something's not right," Mike said. He had a hand on the rope, feeling the tension with his fingertips.

"What?"

"She's stuttery. Feel." Mike passed the rope to Darling and stepped back to take the winch lever from him.

Darling felt the rope. It was trembling erratically. There was a thud to it, like an engine misfiring.

The rope was marked in hundred-fathom sections, and as the third mark passed, Darling held up a hand, telling Mike to slow the winch, and bent over the side to see the first trap come into view. If it was fouled around the rope, he wanted to clear it before it banged against the boat. Some of the tiny abyssal animals were so delicate that any slight trauma would kill them.

He saw the glint of the first stainless-steel swivel holding the length of cable, saw the cable, and then . . . nothing.

The trap was gone.

Impossible. The only animal large enough to take it was a shark, but there was nothing in the trap to interest a shark. And if one of them had taken a run at it, he would have taken the whole rig with him, rope and all. There was no way a shark could have broken the cable.

He let the winch bring the cable up to him, and he unsnapped it from the rope and looked at the end. Then he held it up to Mike.

"Busted?" Mike asked.

"No. If she'd popped, the strands'd be all frizzy, like a head of hair when you stick your finger in a light socket. Look: These strands are still as tight as in the factory."

"So?"

Darling held the end of the cable close to his eyes. It had been sheared off, cut as clean as if by a scalpel. There were no gnaw marks, no worry marks.

"Bit," he said. "Bit clean through."

"Bit?"

Darling looked out over the water. "What in the name of Christ has a mouth that can bite through forty-eight strands of stainless steel?"

Mike said nothing. Darling gestured for him to start the winch again, and in a moment the second cable came up.

"Gone," he said, for that trap had vanished, too, that cable bitten through.

"Gone," he said again as the next cable appeared, and the next and the next. They were all gone.

Now he saw the sash weights coming, and there was something strange about them, so he told Mike to stop the winch, and he pulled the last of the rope up by hand.

"Sweet Jesus," he said. "Look here."

One of the traps had been wrapped around the weights, embedded into them so hard it was as if everything had been melted together in a furnace.

They pulled the gnarled mass up and set it on the deck; it was a confusion of steel reinforcing rod, wire and lead.

Mike stared at it for a long moment, then said, "Jesus, Whip. What kind of sumbitch do that?"

"No man, for sure," said Darling. "No animal, neither. At least, no animal I've ever seen."

6

THEY DIDN'T SPEAK as they disassembled the rig, coiling the lengths of cable and securing them with twist ties, discarding the chemical lights, jamming the final fathoms of rope into the plastic drum.

Darling was running through the catalog of creatures in his head, trying to think of what might have the power and the inclination to destroy that rig.

He even considered Mike's thought that it might have been a man, some fisherman who was angry, resentful, jealous— although what Whip Darling had these days that anybody'd be jealous of he couldn't imagine. Or maybe just somebody bent on destruction for its own sake. No. He didn't think that any man could do it, and he was certain that nobody'd bother. There was no logic to it.

So what did that leave? What could have bitten through a cable woven of forty-eight strands of stainless steel?

Part of him hoped that they'd never know.

He wasn't a stranger to the fact that Nature had a dark side. Once, more than two decades ago, he had been crew on a tanker off South Africa when, out of nowhere—an easy sea and a steady barometer—had come a rogue wave that had put a hundred-foot wall of water in front of the ship. The captain had never seen such a thing, no one on board ever had, and because they didn't know what to do they steamed directly into the wall of water, which closed over the ship, drowning it, sending it plunging to the bottom. If Darling hadn't been sent up to the crow's nest three minutes earlier to fetch something, he would have gone down with the ship. Instead, he had washed overboard and drifted on a hatch cover for two days until a coastal freighter picked him up.

Another time, in Australia, he and some mates had jumped ship after discovering that the captain was addicted to ouzo and boys, and had embarked on a feckless treasure hunt in the outback. They had met up with a family on holiday in a little caravan, and one afternoon they came back to find the whole family dead, killed by a taipan, a snake that attacks for the sake of attacking, that kills for the sake of the kill.

Darling had gradually concluded that Nature wasn't to be trusted; often enough, she revealed a sinister side.

Mike had had no such experiences, and he was not happy with the unknown. He didn't mind so much not having answers himself, but he didn't like it when Whip didn't have them. He hated to hear Whip say, "I don't know." He preferred the security of knowing that somebody was in charge, somebody knowledgeable.

So now he was worried.

Darling saw the signs of anxiety. Mike refused to look him in the eye; he was coiling the lengths of cable too meticulously. Darling knew he would have to ease the man's misery.

"I take it back," Darling said. "I think it was a shark."

"What makes you think so?" Mike asked, wanting to believe, but needing some convincing.

"Had to be. I just remembered, *National Geographic*, some sharks can put out twenty tons per square inch when they bite. That'd be more than enough to cut those cables."

"Why wouldn't he run with it?"

"Wouldn't have to. No hooks in it. He just swims round and round and bites the wires off one by one." Darling was even beginning to convince himself.

Mike thought for a moment, then said, "Oh."

Darling looked up at the sky. He felt an odd desire, a desire to quit and go home. But the sun was still climbing, it wasn't yet noon, and he'd already burned up twenty-five or thirty dollars' worth of fuel. If they went home now, he'd be out of pocket fifty bucks with nothing to show for it but an awkward explanation to the aquarium. And so he forced himself to say, "What say we try for a day's pay?"

Mike said, "Good enough," and together they began to rig a deep line with some big baited hooks.

Maybe they'd catch something worth selling, maybe just something worth eating. Even if they just caught *some*thing, it would be better than heading back to the dock and acknowledging another day's defeat.

The thought depressed him. These days, the act of fishing itself, which once had been enjoyable even when he was skunked, had become depressing. He likened it to journeying back to the place where you were raised, where you had had good times and good memories, and finding that it had been paved over and made into a parking lot.

All fishing did nowadays was remind him of how good things used to be.

He had read all the old accounts of what Bermuda had been like when the first settlers arrived. The island was overrun then by birds and pigs. The birds belonged, and some of them, like the cahows, were so dumb that they'd land on people's heads and wait to be grabbed and put into the cook pot. The pigs didn't belong. Some had been put ashore by ships' captains, in anticipation of a time when castaways would need nourishment. Others swam ashore from shipwrecks, and they thrived on birds and eggs.

But what had entranced the old-timers, what accounted for the almost religious enthusiasm in their accounts, was the sea life. Everything was around Bermuda, everything from turtles to whales, and in numbers inconceivable to people from the Old World, where even by the seventeenth century a great many species had been slaughtered almost to extinction.

Darling wasn't one to indulge in weepy bushwa about the good old days. He saw change as inevitable and destruction as part of it, especially when man got into the mix, and that was the way things were.

But what did infuriate him, what shamed and disgusted him, was the change he had seen in Bermuda in only twenty years. By his reckoning, Bermuda had been ruined in the lifetime of a house cat.

In the late sixties and early seventies, he could still go out on the reefs and catch his dinner. There were lobsters under every rock, schools of parrotfish, angelfish, triggerfish, surgeonfish, damselfish, hogfish, porgies, even occasional groupers. When he worked on a shipwreck, goatfish dug in the sand beside him, rays skittered across the bottom, and there was always the tiny danger that some nearsighted wrasse would take a bite from his earlobe. More than once, reef sharks had chased him off a wreck, nibbling at the tips of his flippers.

Just over the edge in deeper water were whole colonies of groupers—Nassau groupers, spotted groupers, black groupers and now and then a 500- or 600-pound jewfish. There were moray eels and tiger sharks, bull sharks and hinds and snappers. Turtles poked their heads up like little children swimming on the surface.

And in the deep, to put out a slick and drift was an invitation to excitement. Wahoo fought with barracudas for the bait. Bonitos and Alison tuna swarmed around the back of the boat. Billfish cruised the slick, their dorsal fins cutting the water like scythes, and the big, fast pelagic sharks flashed beneath the boat and showed off the shiny blue of their backs.

A good day was a thousand pounds of rockfish and a thousand more of tuna, and the hotels took pride in listing the prime special of the day as fresh Bermuda fish.

No more. Some of the hotels still listed Bermuda fish, but not with pride, for what they served now, all that was left, was trash, the fish that had survived because nothing wanted them. If a fisherman caught a grouper of any size, it was an event that made the paper.

Bermuda's ocean was one step from being as lifeless as the western eddies of Long Island Sound.

Darling listened with bitter amusement to the explanations of the fishermen. Pollution! they cried, and to that he replied: Bullshit.

What had killed Bermuda's fishing industry—he believed, he knew, he felt he could document—was fishermen. Not only Bermuda fishermen, but the species in general. People. People who weren't content with making a living and wanted to make a killing, treating the ocean as if it were a deep pit to be strip-mined. He had even given them a scientific name: *Homo assholus.*

Well, they'd made a killing all right, but not the way they thought.

And the chief villain was a piece of equipment they had invented: the fish trap.

In times past, fishermen had *fished*—with hand lines—and what limited their catch was their grit. They stopped when they fell down in a stupor, their hands swollen like a convention of sausages.

Then someone thought of putting down wire cages with bait inside and buoys to the surface. The fish would swim in and, thanks to the construction of the traps, not be able to find their way out again.

Soon, everybody was putting traps down, as many as they wanted. There was supposed to be a limit, but nobody paid any attention to it.

And did they catch fish! So many fish that they threw away all but the best—dead or dying, but who cared?—and if the price went down because there were too many, why, no sweat, they just caught more.

Darling had never used traps, didn't like them, not from some high moral purpose but because to him trapping wasn't fishing, it was killing and scooping up, not entertaining in the least. And, he thought, if you can't enjoy what you do for a living, then find something else to do. He had no intention of ending his days sitting in the yard with a cat in his lap and a bird on his shoulder, telling visitors that he had lived a long life and had hated every minute of it.

The first problem with the traps was that they did their job too well. They caught everything—big, small, young, old, pregnant, whatever. A hand-line fisherman could pick and choose among his catch and put back fish that were too small or too young or too loaded with roe or simply not what he was fishing for. But with traps, by the time the fish had been jammed together in the wire for a few days, and bruised and shocked and scarred and abused by one another and by the cage itself, they had little chance of surviving even if the fishermen took the trouble to put them back, which most of them didn't.

The second problem was lost traps. If the buoy broke away or the rope chafed off or a storm sea pushed the trap over the edge into the deep and it sank beyond reach, the trap would

keep on killing. The fish inside would die and become bait for
more fish, which would come in and be trapped and die and
become bait for more fish, forever and ever, amen.

Everybody had a remedy. They tried biodegradable string
to hold the traps' doors shut, even biodegradable doors, on
the theory that if a trap got lost, eventually the material would
rot away and the door would open and the fish could get out.
But "eventually" was so long in coming that whole generations of animals could be wiped out before the doors would
magically pop open.

Darling had found lost traps on the bottom that looked
like a Tokyo subway car at rush hour, jampacked with everything from eels to parrotfish to octopus to crabs. The sight
saddened and enraged him, for while he was not a sentimen-
talist about death, this was death to no purpose whatever—an
ultimate waste. More than once, he had stopped the boat and
lost time and money diving down to deep traps and slashing
off the floating lines and cutting away the doors with wire
snips. The perplexed, exhausted and wounded prisoners—
some with scales scraped away by the wire, some with open
sores from frantic fights—would meander within the now-
open trap for several moments, as if unable to believe their
sudden good fortune, and only when he moved away would
they seem to share some silent cue and burst free.

Finally, in 1990, about ten years too late, the Bermuda government had outlawed trap fishing and paid off the island's
seventy-eight commercial fishermen—richly enough, Darling
thought, though the fishermen complained loudly that the
amounts were too paltry to compensate them for the loss of a
God-given right.

The sanctimonious outcry against the loss of rights infuriated Darling. *What* rights? Where was it written that any man
had a right to kill off all the fish in Bermuda? By such logic,
he felt, bank robbery should be a protected profession: If a
man has a right to feed his family, and if what he does costs
an insurance company a few hundred thousand dollars a year,
well, that's the cost of freedom.

Now that traps were outlawed, the hope was that the fish
would come back, but Darling had his doubts. Bermuda was
not like the Bahamas, a chain of seven hundred islands that

had a chance to replenish each other if one or another was fished out—though some Bahamians seemed even more hell-bent than Bermudians on destroying themselves. They had taken to fishing with Clorox: pump a little into a reef, and all the fish and lobsters come out in the open where they're easy to scoop up. Of course, Clorox killed the reef, too, all of it, forever. But a man had to make a living.

Bermuda was a single rock in the middle of nowhere. What was there was there, and what wasn't never would be.

And as if man weren't working fast enough to turn Bermuda into a wasteland, Nature was throwing her wrecking ball at the island. Darling had a friend, Marcus Sharp, stationed at the U.S. Navy base, who knew something about meteorology and had showed him some NOAA figures concluding that the water temperature around Bermuda had risen by two degrees in the last twenty years.

Some scientists said it was because of the burning down of the Amazon jungle and the burning up of too much fossil fuel. Others said it was part of a natural rhythm, like the coming and going of the ice ages. But the reason wasn't as important as the fact: It was happening.

To a man in a city, two degrees might be nothing. To corals in the sea, two degrees spelled the difference between life and death. Ten percent of Bermuda's corals were already dead. Darling saw the evidence every day—big patches of bleached reef, like a boneyard. If ten percent became twenty percent, if then *all* the corals disappeared, gradually Bermuda would erode away, for corals were the island's shield against the open ocean.

Coral polyps weren't the only animals affected by the temperature rise. Some creatures had vanished, some had gone deeper, and some new ones had sprung up. There was a new burrower, for example—a microscopic worm or louse that lived in the sand. When divers disturbed the sand, the burrowers were liberated, and they fixed themselves to human skin and dug in. They excreted a poison that caused pustulant sores and an infernal itching that lasted for a week.

The last horse in the troika of destruction was the foreigners. While Bermudians were killing off their reef fish, the Japanese and the Koreans were massacring the deep-water species. They were out there every day, setting thirty-mile-long nets to intercept the migrators, and they were getting everything: tuna and billfish, mackerel and wahoos, sharks and bonitos and jacks and porpoises.

Those fishermen who didn't use nets used long lines—miles and miles of line, with baited hooks every few feet, which accomplished the same thing: They killed everything, without selection or discrimination.

Darling thought of it as equality of slaughter.

Fishing had once given Darling a feeling of vitality, an appreciation of and wonder at the richness and diversity of life.

Now all it made him think of was death.

It took them an hour to bait and set their deep line. When it was down, Darling snapped a rubber buoy into a loop at the end of the line and tossed it overboard, letting it drift with the tide as the breeze pushed the boat to the southeast.

Mike opened a tin of Polish ham and a bottle of Coke and took them aft and sat on the hatch cover and tinkered some more with the pump motor.

Darling went into the wheelhouse and ate an apple while he listened to the radio to hear if anyone was catching anything anywhere. One captain reported that he had raised a shark. Another, a charter-boater way out on Challenger Bank, had caught a few Alison tuna. No one else had seen a thing.

The sun had just begun to slide westward off its peak when they pulled in the line. They took turns—one on the winch, the other feeling the line—and exchanged hopeful guesses.

"Feel him?"

"Coupla coneys."

"Gummy shark, maybe."

"Tapioca fish."

"I say a pair of snappers."

"Don't you wish. . . ."

The eight hooks had caught two small red snappers, their eyes popped and their bladders squeezed out through their mouths by the sudden loss of pressure. Darling tossed them into the bait box and looked at the sky, then at the sea. Not a fin, not a feeding bird. Nothing. "Well, then, to hell with it," he said, and he wiped his hands on his pants and went forward to start the engine.

He was about to step inside the cabin when he heard Mike say, "Look there." He was pointing to the southern sky.

A navy helicopter was heading their way from the south.

"Wonder where he's going," Darling said.

"Nowhere. They never do. Just loggin' time."

"Maybe." Darling waved as the helicopter passed overhead and continued northward. Mike was probably right. Except for occasional search-and-rescue jobs, there was so little work for navy pilots that they often had to fly back and forth around the island just to keep up their proficiency and their flying hours.

But this pilot wasn't idling, he was heading north into the vast nowhere, and with speed on too.

"I don't know," Darling said. "Unless he's late for supper up in Nova Scotia, I'd say he's on a mission with some clout to it."

He turned into the wheelhouse and picked up the radio microphone.

"Huey One . . . Huey One . . . Huey One . . . this is *Privateer* . . . come back. . . ."

7

LIEUTENANT MARCUS SHARP had been shooting baskets that Friday
—fantasizing himself in a *mano a mano* with Larry Bird—
when the operations officer called him inside and said that a
British Airways pilot on his way to Miami had picked up an
emergency signal twenty miles north of Bermuda.

The pilot hadn't seen anything, the ops officer said, which
wasn't surprising considering that he was traveling more than
five hundred miles an hour more than six miles above the
ocean, but the signal had been loud and clear on his VHF
radio. Someone was in trouble down there.

The guys in the tower at the naval air station had checked
with Miami, Atlanta, Raleigh/Durham, Baltimore and New
York to see if any planes were overdue. Then ops had called
Bermuda Harbour Radio and asked for any reports of vessels
missing, overdue or in distress.

Everything seemed copacetic, but they couldn't take a
chance—they had to follow up on the signal.

Sharp had quickly showered and pulled on his flight suit,
while the operations officer had rounded up a co-pilot and a
rescue diver for him and made sure one of the helicopters was
gassed up. Then he had scribbled down the coordinates reported in by the B.A. pilot, stuffed a chocolate bar and some
gum into his pockets and trotted across the apron to the waiting chopper.

As he had lifted off from Kindley Field and banked around
to the north, for the first time in weeks Marcus Sharp felt
alive. His juices were flowing, his pulse was up, he was inter-

ested, he had a goal to focus on. Something was happening—
not much, not exactly what he'd call action, but *anything* was
better than the nothing that had become his routine.

Maybe, he thought as he corrected his course to the northwest, maybe they'd actually find someone in the water, someone in danger. Maybe they'd even have to accomplish something . . . for a change.

Sharp's problem wasn't only that he was bored. It was
more complicated than that, worse than boredom: He had a
weird, amorphous sense that he was dying, not physically but
in other, less tangible, ways. He had always needed adventure,
courted danger, thrived on—felt he could not survive without
—change. And life had always provided nourishment enough.

The navy recruiter at Michigan State had recognized the
need in Sharp for action and had played to it. Here was a kid
who had broken both legs—one skiing, one hang-gliding—and
yet had persisted in both sports; a certified scuba diver since
the age of fourteen whose hero was not Jacques Cousteau but
Peter Gimbel, the man who had made the first underwater
films on great white sharks and the wreck of the *Andrea
Doria;* a dreamer who wanted to build an ultralite airplane
and fly it across the country; a restless quester whose ambition was to affirm himself not by accumulating wealth but by
testing his own limits. On the navy's psychological-profile test,
he had listed three men he admired: Ernest Hemingway, The-
odore Roosevelt and James Bond—all "because they were do-
ers, not observers, they *lived* their lives." (Sharp noted that,
like him, the navy wasn't persnickety about making distinc-
tions between legend and reality.)

The recruiter persuaded Marcus that the navy offered him
a chance to spend his career doing what others could hope to
do only on occasional vacations. He could pick his specialty,
change it regularly, "stretch his envelope" on the sea and in
the sky and, in the process—almost incidentally—contribute
to the nation's defense.

He signed up before graduation and, in June of 1983, he
entered Officer Candidate School in Newport, Rhode Island.

The first few years met all his expectations. He became
expert in underwater demolition. He qualified as a helicopter
pilot. He served a stint of sea duty and actually saw combat, in

Panama. When his mind caught up with his body and he developed adult interests, he spent a year studying meteorology and oceanography on an exchange tour in Halifax.

Life for Sharp was rich, varied and fun.

But in the past year and a half, variety and fun had ceased to satisfy.

Part of his problem, he knew, was an unwillingness to confront the specter of becoming a grown-up. He was twenty-nine and hadn't given much thought to thirty, certainly hadn't been afraid of it, until a few months before, when he had been rejected in his application to join the navy's elite, high-risk, high-demand amphibious guerrillas, the SEALs. He was too old.

But at the core of his discontent lay the only thing close to tragedy that Marcus Sharp had ever known.

He had fallen in love with a United Airlines flight attendant, a skier and scuba diver, and they had been all over the world together. They were young and immortal. Marriage was a possibility but not a necessity. They lived in and for the present.

And then one September day in 1989, they were snorkeling off a beach in North Queensland. They had heard routine warnings about dangerous animals, but they hadn't been worried. They had been swimming with sharks and rays and barracudas; they could take care of themselves. The sea was a world not of danger but of adventure and discovery.

They had seen a turtle swimming by, and they had followed it, trying to keep up with it. The turtle had slowed and opened its mouth, as if to eat something, though they saw nothing, and they glided up to it, entranced by its grace and efficiency in the water.

Karen had reached out to touch it, to stroke its shell, and as Sharp watched she suddenly convulsed and arched her back and clawed at her breast. Her snorkel slipped from her mouth. Her eyes went wide and she screamed, tearing at her own flesh.

Sharp grabbed her and pulled her to the surface and tried to get her to speak, but all she could do was shriek.

By the time he got her to shore, she was dead.

The turtle had been feeding on sea wasps, box jellyfish all

but invisible in the water, colonies of nematocysts so toxic that a brush with them could stop a human heart. And so it had.

When Karen had been buried in Indiana and Sharp's grief had begun to scar over, he had found himself possessed by darker thoughts, thoughts of the randomness of fate. It wasn't a matter of injustice or unfairness—he had never thought of life as fair or unfair; it simply *was*. But fate was capricious. They were not immortal; nothing was forever.

He had become plagued by the emptiness of his life, the lack of focus. He had done many things, but to no purpose.

He had an image of himself as a steel ball on a pinball machine, popping in and out of one hole after another, going nowhere.

The navy had given him the best billet available, a two-year tour in Bermuda—sunny, comfortable, undemanding and only two hours from the U.S. mainland. Quiet, however, was not what Sharp needed. He needed action, but now action alone wasn't enough: There had to be a point, a purpose to it.

In Bermuda, he had found nothing much to do except shuffle papers and occasionally fly around in a helicopter and hope that someone needed rescuing.

From time to time, he thought of quitting the navy, but he had no idea what he would do. Civilian life had few slots for helicopter pilots expert in blowing up bridges.

Meanwhile, he volunteered for any task that would keep his mind off himself.

HE WAS HEADING northwest now, intending to set a search pattern from the northwest to the north to the northeast and then the east, all on the north side of the island. He turned his UHF radio to 243.0 and his VHF to 121.5, the two frequencies over which emergency equipment broadcast. He flew at five hundred feet.

Six miles off the island, where the reefs ended and the water changed from dappled turquoise to deep cerulean, he heard a beep—very faint, very distant, but persistent. He looked at the co-pilot, tapped his earphones, and the co-pilot nodded and gave him a thumbs-up sign. Sharp scanned his instruments, turning the helicopter slowly from side to side until he found the direction in which the beeping from his radio direction finder was loudest. He took a bearing from the compass.

Then a voice came over his marine radio.

"Huey One . . . Huey One . . . Huey One . . . this is *Privateer* . . . come back."

"*Privateer* . . . Huey One . . ." Sharp smiled. "Hey, Whip . . . where you at?"

"Right underneath you, lad. Don't you keep your eyes on the road?"

"Had my eyes on the future."

"Going for an outing?"

"B.A. pilot picked up an EPIRB signal a while ago. You hear anything?"

"Not a peep. How far out?"

"Ten, fifteen miles. I've got it on one-twenty-one-five now. Whatever it is, northwest wind's pushing it back this way."

"Maybe I'll chase your wake."

Sharp hesitated, then said, "Okay, do that, Whip. Who knows? Might use your help."

"Done and done, Marcus. *Privateer* standing by."

Good, Sharp thought. If there was a boat sinking out there, Whip would arrive a lot faster than any vessel summoned from the base. If it was an abandoned boat, a lifeboat, say, SOP would call for him to put a diver down to investigate. The weather was decent, but putting a diver down from a helicopter in the open ocean under any conditions involved risk. He wouldn't hesitate to go himself, but he didn't relish putting a nineteen-year-old down into the sea all alone. Whip could check it out for him while he went in search of floaters. If they found people, alive or dead, he'd have to put the diver down, and he wanted the boy to be fresh.

Besides, maybe there'd be something worthwhile for Whip if nobody claimed it. A raft. A radio. A flare gun. Something worth selling or using, something to get Whip money or save him money. And Sharp knew Whip needed it.

Besides, Sharp thought, I owe him one.

One? Hell, he owed Whip Darling about a hundred.

Whip had saved Sharp's sanity, at a time when there was a

better-than-even chance of his becoming a blob, an addict of entertainments like *Surf Nazis Must Die* and *Amazon Women on the Moon*. His weekends had become unbearable. He had dived with every commercial tour group on the island, ridden a motorbike around every square inch of the place, visited every fort and museum, spent money in every saloon—he had no moral objection to becoming a drunk, but he had no tolerance for liquor and didn't like the taste of it—and seen every movie in the base video store except those involving the ax murder of baby-sitters. He read for hours every day, till his eyes rebelled and his ass atrophied. He was on the brink of doing the unthinkable—taking up golf—when he met Whip at a base function.

He had listened, fascinated, to Whip's discourse on the techniques of discovering shipwrecks and had asked enough intelligent questions to secure an invitation to come out on the boat some Sunday . . . which had quickly become every Sunday and most Saturdays. As he listened to Whip, he learned, and, curiously, he found himself becoming ashamed of his education. For, here was a man with six years' schooling who had taught himself to be not just a fisherman and a diver but a historian and a biologist and a numismatist and . . . well, a walking encyclopedia of the sea.

Sharp had offered to contribute to the cost of Darling's fuel and been turned down; he had offered to help paint the boat and been accepted, which pleased him because it made him feel like a participant instead of a parasite. Then Whip had shown him photographs of what old shipwrecks looked like from the air, and suddenly—as if a door had cracked open, lighting a corner of his mind he had not known was there—he saw the prospect of new interests, new goals.

Whip taught him not to look for the classic fairy-tale image of a shipwreck—the ship upright and ready on its keel, sails rigged, tricorn-hatted skeletons sitting where they died gambling over a stack of doubloons. The old ships had been wooden, and, for the most part, the ones that hit Bermuda sank in shallow water. Storm seas broke them to pieces, and centuries of moving water had dispersed them and pressed them into the bottom, and the bottom had absorbed them and corals grew on them, taking the dead to their bosoms.

There were three main telltales, Whip had said, to a shipwreck on the bottom. When a ship was driven over the reefs—flung by the wind, shoved by a following sea—it would crush the reef, kill the fragile corals and leave a scrub mark that, from a couple of hundred feet in the air, would look like a giant tire track.

A sharp eye might see a cannon or two, overgrown and coral-encrusted and looking like not much more than an unlikely mass in an unnaturally straight line. There was truth to the old saying that nature doesn't like straight lines. But the presence of a cannon didn't always mean the ship itself was nearby, because when a vessel was in its last throes, often the crew would heave everything heavy overboard to keep her from capsizing. It was possible to find a cannon here, an anchor there, and no ship at all if the sea had carried her miles away before slamming her down and busting her to bits in her last resting place.

What *was* a dead giveaway—visible from the air but most difficult to identify—was a ballast pile, for Whip insisted that where a ship dropped her ballast was where she had died. Yes, her deck might have drifted away, or her rigging, carrying a survivor or two, but her heart and soul—her cargo, her treasure—lay with her ballast. Usually, the old-timers ballasted with river rocks from the Thames or the Ebro or one of the other rivers near their home ports. The rocks were smooth and round and small enough for a man to lift. Think of cobblestones, Whip told Sharp, because all the cobblestones in places like Nantucket had been ballast stones, carried in the bowels of a ship to keep her upright on her way over from England, then replaced with barrels of oil for the journey home.

So what Sharp conditioned himself to look for was a gathering of very round stones all piled together, often in a white sand hole between dark coral heads, for Whip had taught him that an old ship would have struck the coral head and stuck there until another sea came along and broke her loose and cast her innards into the sand, which would embrace them and cover them over.

Now Sharp never missed a chance to fly, and whenever he flew—whether supposedly to keep his hours up, or to train new pilots, or to test new equipment—he always kept an eye out for shipwrecks. He flew as low as possible, yawing back and forth to keep the sun's rays at a cutting angle through the shallow seas, and if one of his crew ever asked what the hell he was doing, he would reply with something vague like, Putting her through her paces.

So far, he had found two ballast piles, two shipwrecks. One, Whip said, had been explored in the sixties. One was new. They'd go have a dig on it one of these days.

THE BEEPING WAS loud and regular now, and Sharp could see something yellow sliding up and down the rolling seas. He pushed the collective-power-control lever down, and dropped the helicopter to a hundred feet.

It was a raft, small and empty and apparently undamaged. He circled it, careful to stay high enough so that the downdraft from his rotors didn't start it spinning or capsize it off the top of a wave.

"*Privateer* . . . Huey One . . ."

"Yeah, Marcus . . ." came Whip's voice.

"It's a raft. Nobody aboard. Just a raft. Could've fallen off a boat. Some of those EPIRBs are salt-water activated."

"Whyn't you let me pick it up with my davit? I'll cruise around, see if there's any swimmers, then bring it to shore. Nobody has to get wet."

"You got it. It's three-four-oh from where you were. Should be here in an hour or so. Meantime, we'll set a search grid and swing back and forth till fuel sends us home."

"Roger that, Marcus."

"False alarm, I guess. But the land of the free and the home of the brave is grateful to you anyway, Whip."

"My pleasure. *Privateer* standing by. . . ."

8

"MAYBE THE DAY isn't a dead loss after all," Darling said as he climbed the ladder to the flying bridge.

"Why's that?" Mike was stowing the last of the coiled wire leaders.

"Got us a chance to pick up a raft. If she's a Switlik and nobody's name's on her, there's a couple thousand, maybe more."

"Somebody'll claim it. They always do."

"Probably . . . the way our luck's been running."

They raised the raft in less than an hour, and Darling made a slow circle around it, studying it like a specimen on a laboratory slide.

"Switlik," he said, pleased.

"Looks brand-new off the shelf, like nobody was ever on it."

"That, or they were rescued right quick." Darling saw none of the normal signs that people had spent time in the raft: no dirt, no scuff marks from rubber shoes, no fish blood from anything they'd caught, no bits of clothing.

"Sharks got 'em?" Mike said.

Darling shook his head. "Shark would've bit through the rubber, collapsed one of the cells, maybe burred it with his skin. You'd see it."

"What, then?"

"Whale, maybe." Darling kept circling as he pondered that possibility. Killer whales had been known to attack rafts, dinghies, even big boats. Nobody knew why, because they'd never gone on and attacked the people; there had never been a true case of an orca eating a human being. Perhaps they just got to playing with a raft and, like a kid who had grown too fast, they didn't know their own strength.

Humpback whales had killed people, but always by accident. They had come up to rafts out of curiosity, to see what they were, and gotten underneath and given a flip with their tails, and people had been flung to death.

"No," Darling said, dismissing the thought. "Everything would be upside down and akimbo."

Mike said, "Could be she just slipped off the deck and fell in the ocean."

"Then what turned on the EPIRB?" Darling pointed to the Styrofoam-cased beacon. "That's not automatic. Somebody turned it on."

"Maybe a ship picked the folks up and they forgot to turn it off."

"And nobody bothered to report in to Bermuda?" Darling paused. "Gun to my head, I'd say their boat sank out from under 'em, and they tossed the raft in the sea and jumped for it and missed and drowned themselves."

Mike seemed to like that answer, so Darling didn't articulate the hazy idea he had of another option. No point in stirring up bad thoughts in Mike. Besides, speculation was usually bullshit.

"Well, the good news is," Darling said, "she's a brand-spanking-new Switlik, worth enough to keep the wolves at bay for a little while."

They snagged the raft with a grappling hook, fixed the rope to the block-and-tackle rig on the davit, turned on the winch and hauled it aboard.

Mike knelt down and poked around, opening the supply box in the bow, feeling under the rubber cells.

"Best turn off the EPIRB," Darling said as he removed the hook and coiled the rope. "Don't want a lot of pilots baffled by emergency signals when they should be caring for their hangovers."

Mike flicked the switch on the beacon and pushed the antenna back inside. He stood up. "Nothing. Nothing missing, nothing wrong."

"No." But something was bothering Darling, and he continued to stare at the raft, comparing the inventory of what he saw to what he knew he should be seeing.

The oar. That was it. There wasn't any. Every raft carried at least one oar, and this one had been meant to have oars; there were oarlocks. But no oar.

And then, as the boat shifted slightly, his eye was attracted to sunlight glinting off something on one of the rubber cells. He bent over and put his face close to the rubber. There were scratch marks, as if a knife had cut the rubber but hadn't gone all the way through, and around each scratch mark, shining in the sun, was a patch of some kind of slime. He touched his fingers to the slime and raised them to his nose.

"What?" Mike said.

Darling hesitated, then decided to lie. "Sunburn oil. Poor buggers were worried about their tans."

He had no idea what it was. It stank of ammonia.

Darling called Sharp on the radio and told him he had the raft and intended to keep searching, a bit farther to the north. A person in the water, alive or dead, had no sail area, so he or she wouldn't have traveled nearly as far as the raft had—might, in fact, have moved in the opposite direction from the raft, depending on the current.

And so they drove north for an hour—ten miles, more or less—then turned south and began to zigzag from southwest to southeast. Mike stood on the bow, his eyes on the nearby surface and the few feet below it, while Darling scanned the distance from the flying bridge.

They had just turned eastward, away from the sun, when Mike called out, "There!" and pointed off the port side.

Twenty or thirty yards away, something big and glisteny was floating in a tangle of sargasso weed.

Darling slowed and turned toward it. As they closed on it, they saw that the thing, whatever it was, was not man-made. It bobbed slowly and had a wet sheen and quivered like Jell-O.

"What the hell is *that?*" said Mike.

"Looks like a six-foot jellyfish snarled itself in the weed."

"Damn! Don't want to run into him."

Darling put the boat in neutral and watched from the flying bridge as the thing slid down the side. It was a huge clear jelly oblong, with a hole in the middle, and it appeared to have some sort of life, for it rotated as if to expose new parts of itself to the sunlight every few seconds.

Mike said, "No jellyfish *I've* ever seen."

"No," Darling agreed. "Beats me. Spawn of some kind, I guess."

"Want to pick some up?"

"What for?"

"The aquarium?"

"No. They never asked me for spawn. If it *is* spawn, let's let the critters live, whatever they are."

Darling resumed his course to the southeast. By the time they reached the area where they had recovered the raft, they had found two seat cushions and a rubber fender.

"Wonder why Marcus didn't see these," Mike said as he brought the fender aboard. "It's not like they were underwater."

"A helicopter is a wonderful contraption, but you got to fly it *real* slow over open water or you overwhelm the scanners in the human eye." Darling looked out over the water. There were no signs of life, present or past. "That's it, then."

He took a bearing on the dim hump in the distance called Bermuda, and headed for home.

By six o'clock, they had left the deep behind, the ocean swell had faded and the water's color had changed from blued steel to dark green. From the flying bridge they could see sand holes on the bottom and dark patches of grass and coral.

"Who's that?" Mike asked, pointing to a boat silhouetted against the lowering sun.

Darling shaded his eyes and looked at the boat, appraising the rake of the bow and the shape of the house and the size of the cockpit.

"Carl Frith," he said.

"Hell's he doing? Trolling?"

"In the shallows? Not bloody likely."

They kept looking. They could see movement aboard the boat, which rolled as if it were taking on weight and then rolled back as if releasing it.

"You don't think . . . ?" Mike began. "Nah, he's not that stupid."

"Stupid? Maybe not," Darling said as he turned toward the boat and pushed his throttle forward. "But how about greedy?"

Mike glanced over at Darling. There was a set to Whip's jaw, a cold and squinty hardness to his eyes.

Carl Frith had been a trap fisherman, and one of the noisiest protesters when traps were outlawed. He was always bleating about freedom, independence and the rights of man, despite having received over $100,000 from his settlement with the government—enough for any man, Darling thought, enough to let him change over to line fishing or charter fishing or start another business altogether. But it was beginning to look as if Carl Frith wanted to have it both ways.

Because they were approaching from the northwest, upwind, they got to within a hundred yards of Frith before he heard *Privateer*'s engine. They had a clear view of him reaching underwater with his boat hook and snagging the sunken buoy, pulling the rope up to his winch, hauling the big fish trap aboard his boat, opening the door and emptying the catch into the fish hold.

"Miserable sonofabitch," Darling said.

"Gonna run him down?"

"Gonna fillet the bastard."

"Good enough."

Darling felt a rage rising in the pit of his stomach. He didn't care that what Frith was doing was illegal: As far as Darling was concerned, most laws were whores assigned to serve politicians. What burned him—outraged him, sickened him—was the mindless selfishness of the man, the headlong rush at destruction and waste. And it wasn't only that Frith was still trap fishing, he was using submerged buoys so that the marine police wouldn't see them on the surface. A passing boat might catch the buoy in its propeller and cut it away, or a storm might shift the trap so Frith couldn't find it. Either way, the trap would be lost on the bottom, where day after day, week after week, it would kill and kill and kill.

Frith heard him coming now. He had a trap hung over the side, and as soon as he turned and saw *Privateer* bearing down on him, he pulled a knife from a sheath at his belt and cut the rope holding the trap, and the trap splashed into the water and sank away.

Darling kept up speed until he was ten yards from Frith's small boat, and then he turned sharply and pulled back on the throttle, throwing a wake that slammed into Frith's boat and staggered the man.

"Hey!" Frith shouted. "What you think you're doin'?"

Darling let his boat wallow beside Frith's. He leaned on the railing of the flying bridge and looked down. Frith was in his fifties, big-bellied and bald. His skin was as dark and worn as an old saddle, his teeth yellow from nicotine.

Darling said, "Just come by to see what you're up to, Carl."

"None of your concern."

"Wouldn't be fishing, would you?"

"Don't worry about it."

"Wouldn't be *trap* fishing?"

"Piss off, Whip."

"Let's see, Carl . . ." Darling's smile was icy. "I expect you're getting mostly . . . what? . . . parrotfish and breams. Right?"

Frith said nothing.

Darling turned to Mike. "Have a look, Michael, see what he's got."

Mike started down the ladder from the flying bridge. Frith pulled his knife and held it up. "Nobody comes aboard my boat."

From his perch on the ladder, Mike leaned over and looked down into Frith's fish hold. Then he looked up at Darling and nodded.

Darling kept smiling and said, "Parrotfish and breams. Gonna cut 'em up and sell 'em to the hotels, right, Carl? Sell 'em as fresh Bermuda fish? Get maybe a couple bucks a pound?"

"You can't prove anything," Frith said. He spread his arms and gestured at the empty cockpit. "Traps? Where do you see traps?"

"I don't have to prove anything, Carl, I'm not gonna report you."

"Oh." Frith relaxed. "Well, then . . ."

Mike looked startled, but he kept quiet.

"You know what parrotfish and breams do, Carl? They eat the algae that grow on the corals, they clean the reefs. Without them, the coral suffocate and die."

"Come on, Whip . . . one man, a few traps, don't make—"

"Sure, Carl." Darling let his smile fade. "One man who took a hundred thousand dollars from the government and gave his word he'd stop fishing, one man who doesn't need the money but's too pigheaded to do anything else, one man who doesn't give a shit . . ."

"Hey, fuck you, Whip."

"No, Carl," Darling said. "Fuck *you.*" He spun his wheel to the right and leaned on his throttle, and *Privateer* jumped ahead and to the right, slamming into Frith's boat, its steel bow shearing off Frith's wooden swim step.

Frith screamed, "Hey! Goddam—"

Darling kept turning, his bow pushing Frith's stern around. Frith ran forward and turned the key and pushed the button to start his engine. The engine coughed, protested, turned over.

Darling reversed his engine, backed around and aimed his bow at Frith's stern. He struck Frith's fantail, crushing it.

Then Frith was in gear, pulling away, trying to escape.

Mike climbed the ladder and stood beside Darling on the flying bridge. "Gonna sink him?"

"He's gonna sink himself." Darling looked back into the sun: It was still well above the horizon, still a brilliant yellow ball.

Frith fled, heading east. Darling stayed ten yards behind, threatening collision but not forcing it, heading Frith off whenever he tried to turn, pressing him ever eastward.

"I don't get it," Mike said.

"You will."

"You're driving him to the cut."

"Not exactly *to* it."

Mike thought for a moment, and then he got it, and he smiled.

For five more minutes Darling chased Frith, always checking the sun behind him and the reefs ahead. Then, gently, he pulled back on his throttle. *Privateer* slowed, and Frith gradually drew away.

Frith looked back and saw that he was gaining. He shouted something that was snatched away by the wind, and he threw Darling the finger.

Darling pulled his throttle back into neutral, and *Privateer* stopped. "Bye, Carl," he called. "Have a nice day." He pointed off the bow. Not five feet away, barely covered by water, was the first of a ragged phalanx of yellow coral heads.

"Think it'll work?" Mike said. "He knows these reefs."

"No man knows these reefs, Michael, if he can't see."

CARL FRITH DODGED one coral head, then another.

Take it easy, he told himself. You may only draw three feet, but some of these buggers aren't a foot deep.

He throttled back, slowing down, letting his breath catch up with his heart.

Damn him, the self-righteous bastard. Who was Whip Darling to tell a man how to make a living? Whip wasn't doing such a good job of it himself, from what he'd heard. You'd think he'd have some sympathy. Parrotfish important? Breams? That was a laugh. They were trash fish, everybody knew that.

Whip was just pissed off 'cause he hadn't had any traps to stiff the government for.

Never mind. No problem. Whip had said he wasn't about to report him, and, whatever else there was about Whip, he was a man of his word. He wanted this to be personal, Frith would keep it personal. He'd go out one day and maybe just cut away Whip's buoys, all that horseshit he did for the aquarium. Not even man's work.

Anyway, it was obvious Whip wasn't too serious, or he would've done more than just chase him up into the shallows. No big deal. All he had to do was turn around and . . .

Frith looked to the west. He couldn't see anything, just the blinding yellow flashes of the sun on the dappled sea. No definition to the water, no coral heads, nothing. It was like looking at a sheet of tinfoil at high noon.

He realized he was trapped. He couldn't go eastward because there the coral heads actually broke water. He couldn't go west because he couldn't see: Blind, he was guaranteed to tear the bottom out of his boat. And the tide was falling, he remembered that from this morning when he had checked the tide tables to be sure he could find his buoys.

He could wait till sunset—and what? Try it in the dark? Forget it.

He'd have to wait till morning. He'd put his anchor down and wait, have a beer and a sleep and . . .

But he didn't dare. If the wind came up, he might be forced to move in the middle of the night. What was the wind supposed to do? He hadn't bothered to check, it hadn't seemed important.

He couldn't see Whip's boat: It was out there somewhere in the sunlight. He shouted, "God damn you! . . ."

DARLING WATCHED FRITH's boat slow down, then stop. He imagined Frith thinking everything was fine, then turning around and looking into the sun.

"He'll wait till morning," Mike said.

"Not Carl. He hasn't got the patience."

They stayed for a few more minutes, drifting at the edge of the shallow reef.

"Maybe you're right," Darling said, and he reached for his throttle.

Just then, they heard Frith's engine roar.

"Nope," Mike said, grinning.

They listened to the sound of the engine across the still water, heard it rev up then die off, advancing and retreating.

"He's searching," Darling said. "Like a blind man."

A moment later they felt a little tremor in their feet, sent by the water through the *Privateer*'s steel plates, and then they heard a low grinding kind of noise, followed suddenly by the yowl of Frith's engine.

"He did it," Darling said, and he laughed and slapped Mike on the shoulder. "Ran himself up on that reef, hard and fast."

"Want me to call the police?" Mike asked. "They can send the rubber boat."

"Let him swim. He could use the workout." Darling turned his boat to the west. "Besides, we got a duty to do."

"What's that?"

"Wreck the bastard's traps."

"He'll report us," Mike said. Then he paused. "No, now I think of it, I don't guess he will."

BY THE TIME Darling rounded the point into Mangrove Bay, the blue of the sky was fast turning violet, and the departed sun had tinted the western clouds the color of salmon.

A single light bulb burned on the dock, and beneath it, moored to a piling, was a white twenty-five-foot outboard motorboat with the word POLICE stenciled on the side in foot-high blue letters.

"Christ," Mike said, "he's reported us already."

"I doubt it," said Darling. "Carl's a fool, but he's not crazy."

Two young policemen stood on the dock, one white, one black, both wearing uniform shirts, shorts and knee socks. They watched as Darling eased the boat against the dock, and they passed Mike the bow and stern lines.

Darling knew the policemen, had no problem with them—no more than he had with the marine police in general, whom he regarded as ill-trained, underequipped and overburdened. These two he had taken to sea with him on their days off, had helped them learn to read the reefs, had shown them short-cuts to the few deep-water channels in and out of Bermuda.

Still, he chose to remain on the flying bridge, sensing instinctively that altitude reinforced his authority.

He leaned on the railing and raised a finger and said, "Colin . . . Barnett . . ."

"Hey, Whip . . ." Colin, the white cop, said.

Barnett said, "Come aboard?"

"Come ahead," said Darling. "What brings you fellas out of a night?"

"Hear you found a raft," Barnett said.

"True enough."

Barnett stepped aboard and pointed to the raft lying athwart the cockpit. "That it?"

"That's the one."

Barnett shone a flashlight on the raft and leaned down to it. "Lord, it stinks!"

Colin stayed where he was and said hesitantly, "Whip . . . we gotta take it."

Darling paused. "Why's that? Somebody claim to have lost it?"

"No . . . not exactly."

"Then it's mine, isn't it? . . . First law of salvage: finders keepers."

"Well . . ." Colin seemed uneasy. He looked at his feet. "Not this time."

"That so." Darling waited, feeling a roil of anger in his stomach, fighting it down. "What, then?"

"Dr. St. John," Colin said. "He wants it."

"Dr. St. John." Now Darling knew he was bound to lose, and his temper was bound to win. "I see."

Liam St. John was one of the few men in Bermuda whom Darling took the trouble to loathe. A second-generation Irish immigrant, he had gone away to school in Montana and graduated from some diploma mill that awarded him a doctorate. Exactly what the doctorate was in, nobody knew and he never said. All anybody knew for certain was that little Liam had left Bermuda pronouncing his name "Saint John" and had returned pronouncing it (and insisting everyone else do, too) "SINjin."

Armed with an alphabet appended to his name, St. John had rallied a few powerful friends of his parents and besieged the government, arguing that certain disciplines, such as maritime history and wildlife management, were being grossly mishandled by amateurs and should be turned over to certified, qualified experts—which meant him, since he was the only status-Bermudian with a doctorate in anything other than medicine. Never mind that his degree was in an unknown field, probably something utterly useless like Druid combs.

The politicians, who were unconcerned with shipwrecks and nettled by loudmouthed fishermen, were pleased to remove both from their agendas, and for Dr. Liam St. John, Ph.D., they created the new position of minister of cultural heritage. They didn't bother with a precise job description, which suited St. John just fine, for he defined and expanded the job as he went along, assuming more and more authority and enforcing rules and regulations of his own making.

As far as Darling was concerned, all St. John and his regulations had done was turn hundreds of Bermudians into criminals. He had decreed, for example, that no one was permitted to touch any shipwreck without first securing a license from him and agreeing to pay one of his staff two hundred dollars a day to supervise work on the wreck. The result was that nobody ever reported finding anything, and if they did dig up some coins or artifacts, gold earrings or Spanish pottery, they hid them until they could smuggle them out of Bermuda.

Thanks to the minister of cultural heritage, Bermuda's heritage was being sold in galleries on Madison Avenue in New York.

Scientists who had once regarded Bermuda as a prime deep-water laboratory, a unique speck of land in the mid-Atlantic, no longer bothered to come, because St. John insisted that all discoveries be turned over to and examined by his staff, who prepared papers (always pedestrian, usually erroneous) for him to deliver at academic conclaves.

For almost a year, Darling and his diver friends had fantasized about ways to get rid of St. John. Someone had suggested reporting a shipwreck find and taking St. John to have a look at it and then sinking the boat. (It was said that St. John didn't know how to swim.) The idea was vetoed, largely on the grounds that St. John would never go himself: He'd send one of his stooges.

Someone else suggested they just kill him—hit him on the head and dump him in the deep. But although everyone agreed that the result was desirable, no one volunteered to do the deed.

Darling wouldn't have been surprised, however, if it were to happen some night—if St. John were simply to vanish. Nor would he have been crestfallen at the news.

"Colin," he said, "I want you to do me a favor."

"Name it."

"You go back and tell Dr. St. John that I'll give him the raft . . ."

"Okay."

". . . if he'll come over here himself and let me shove it up his ass."

"Oh." Colin looked at Barnett, then at his feet again, then, reluctantly, at Darling. "You know I can't do that, Whip."

"Then we got us a problem, don't we, Colin? 'Cause there's something else you can't do, and that's take the raft."

"But we *have* to!" There was a wailing note in Colin's voice.

Barnett stepped away from the raft and came forward and stood at the bottom of the ladder, looking up.

As Darling looked down at him, he saw movement in the shadows aft. It was Mike, moving silently toward the rack where they kept the clubs and gaff hooks for subduing big fish.

"Whip," Barnett said, "you don't want to do this."

"That raft is mine, Barnett, and you know it." Darling wanted to say more, wanted to say that it wasn't a matter of the raft, wasn't even just a matter of principle, it was also a matter of the two or three or four thousand dollars, dollars that could make a difference, dollars he was not going to let Liam St. John steal from him. But he said none of it; he was not about to whine to a policeman.

"Not if St. John wants to study it like he says."

"Prick doesn't want to study it. He wants to keep it. He knows what it's worth."

"That's not what he says."

"And since when has he become a frigging paragon of truthfulness?"

"Whip . . ." Barnett sighed. Something made him look aft —a glimmer of light, maybe, or a sound—and he saw Mike standing in the darkness, holding across his chest a three-foot gaff with a honed four-inch hook on the end. "You know what we're gonna have to do."

"Yep. Go back and tell Dr. St. John to suck eggs."

"No. We're gonna go back and get a dozen more coppers and come back and take the raft."

"Not without somebody getting bruised."

"That may be, Whip, but think about it: That happens, you're gonna end up in jail, we're gonna end up with the raft, and who's gonna get the last laugh? Doctor St.-fucking-John."

Darling looked away, across the dark water of Mangrove

Bay, at the lights of the cars crossing Watford Bridge, at the glow of lanterns on the veranda of Cambridge Beaches, the hotel nearby, where some bygone singer was warbling along with the band, telling the world he did it His Way.

Darling wanted to fight, wanted to rage and defy and storm around. But he swallowed it, because he knew Barnett was right.

"Barnett," he said at last, and he started down the ladder, "you are the soul of wisdom."

Barnett looked over at Colin, who let out a big breath and smiled back at him.

"Dr. *SINjin* wants my raft," Darling said as he strode aft and took the gaff from Mike, "Dr. *SINjin* shall have my raft."

He stepped over to the raft and raised the gaff above his shoulder and slashed downward at the bow. The hook plunged through the rubber, and, with a pop and a hiss, the cell collapsed.

"Whoops!" Darling said, "sorry," and he dragged the raft toward the bulwark. He slammed the hook into another cell, and it deflated, and he hauled the sagging rubber up onto the bulwark. Something small fell from the raft and hit the steel deck with a click and rattled away. He withdrew the hook and stepped back and drove it through the aftermost cell. He yanked upward and held the raft in the air over the police boat. The muscles in his shoulders were afire, and the sinews in his neck stuck out like wires.

"Whoops!" he said again, and he dropped the raft into the police boat, where it landed in a heap of hissing rubber. He turned back to the two policemen and dropped the gaff on the deck and said, "There. Dr. St. John can have his bloody raft."

The policemen looked at one another. "Okay," said Colin, as he quickly stepped off onto the dock. "We'll tell Dr. St. John that's how you found it."

"Right," said Barnett, and he followed Colin. "Looks to me like a shark got it."

"And there *was* a sea on," Colin said. "You couldn't go into the water after it, sharks all around. . . . 'Night, Whip."

Darling watched as the policemen piled the raft in the stern of their boat and started their motor and backed away into the darkness. He felt drained and slightly nauseated, half-pleased with himself and half-ashamed.

"There's always the dive charters during the big race lay-over," Mike said. "They'll turn us a pretty dollar."

"Sure," said Darling. "Sure."

As THEY CLEANED up the boat, stowing gear and swabbing down the deck, Darling felt something small and sharp under his foot. He picked it up and looked at it, but the light was bad, so he dropped it into his pocket.

"See you in the morning?" Mike said when he was ready to go ashore.

"Right. We'll give the aquarium the bad news, see if they want to trust us with more gear. If not, we'll start chipping paint."

"'Night, then."

Darling followed Mike up the path to the house, waited till Mike had started his motorbike and driven away, then shut off the outside lights and went inside.

He poured himself a couple of fingers of dark rum and sat in the kitchen. He debated turning on the news but decided not to: All news was bad news, by definition, otherwise it wasn't worth putting on the TV. And he didn't need any more bad news.

Charlotte came in, smiled and sat down across the counter from him. She took a sip from his glass, then reached for one of his hands and held it between hers.

"That was childish," she said quietly.

"You saw?"

"Police don't stop by every evening."

He shook his head. "Whoreson Irish bastard."

"What did you accomplish?"

"D'you know how sick it makes me feel to feel so helpless? I had to do *something*."

"Did it make you feel better?"

"Sure."

"Really?"

"Sort of . . ." He looked at her. She was smiling. "Okay, you're right. I'm an old fart with a baby's brain."

"Well . . . you're cute anyway." She leaned across the counter and took his chin and drew him toward her.

As he rose up to kiss her, something stabbed him in the thigh, and he yipped and jerked backward and fell into his seat.

"What?" she said.

"I've been punctured." He reached into his pocket and pulled out the thing he had stepped on and put it on the counter.

It was a crescent-shaped hook, not of steel but of some hard, shiny, bony substance.

"What have I gone and stabbed myself with now?" He picked it up and pressed it into the counter, trying to bend it. It wouldn't bend.

"It looks like a claw," said Charlotte. "Tiger, maybe. Or even a fang. Where'd you find it?"

"Fell out of that raft," he said. He hesitated as he recalled the marks he had seen on the raft, like cuts in the rubber. He looked at Charlotte, then at the thing, and he frowned and said, "What the hell . . . ?"

9

IT HUNG IN the deep and waited.

Motionless, invisible in the blackness, it searched with its senses for the vibrations that would signal the approach of prey.

It was accustomed to being served, for the cold, nutrient-rich water at a thousand feet had always been host to countless animals of all sizes. It had never known, never needed, patience, for food had always been abundant. It had been able to nourish its great body by reflex, without struggle or severe exertion.

Its skills were those of a killer, not a hunter, for it had never needed to hunt.

But now the rhythmic cycles that propelled the creature through life had been disrupted. Food was no longer abundant. Because it had no capacity for reason, knew no past and no future, it was confused by the discomfort caused by the unfamiliar sensation of hunger.

Instinct was telling it to hunt.

It felt an interruption in the flow of the sea, a sudden irregular static in the water's pulse.

Prey. In numbers. Passing by.

They were not near, they were somewhere distant, somewhere above.

The creature drew quantities of water through the muscular collar of its mantle, then expelled it through the funnel in its belly, driving itself up and backward with the force of a racing locomotive.

It homed on the signals and thrust itself through the water with spasmodic expulsions from its funnel. It recognized the signature of the signals: fish, many fish, many big fish.

Chemicals coursed through its flesh, altering its colors.

When it judged itself close enough, it spun and faced the direction where its prey should be. Its huge eyes registered a flash of silver, and it lashed out with its whips. The clubs at the ends of the whips fastened on flesh, their toothed circles tore at it, the crescent-shaped hooks erect within each circle slashed it to shreds. Within seconds, all that remained of the fish was a shower of scales and a billow of blood.

The creature's hunger was not allayed, however—it was increased. It needed more, much more.

But the pressure wave generated by the displacement of so much water by the movement of a body so huge had alarmed the school of bluefin tuna, and they had fled in phalanx.

And so the searching whips found nothing. The shorter arms at the base of its body gradually ceased moving; the gnashing beak closed its jaws and withdrew into the body cavity.

Hunger now consumed the creature, but exhaustion also restrained it. Vast amounts of energy had been expended, and yet it had found too little with which to fuel its enormous needs.

It drifted, hungry and confused.

The bottom far below was ridged, and the current that swept up from the abyss propelled the creature slowly along a slope to a plateau at five hundred feet. The cool water eddied here, so the creature rose no farther.

On another slope, up ahead, was something large and unnatural, something that its senses told it was dead, except for the routine life forms that grew upon it.

The creature ignored it, and waited, gathering strength.

10

LUCAS COVEN WAS so annoyed, and so impatient to get this day over and done with, that he put his boat in gear and leaned on the throttle before the winch had the anchor snugged up. He heard the big steel flukes thud against the hull, and he could envision the nasty gouges in the fiberglass, which made him even angrier.

He was always doing this, getting himself in over his head and then, captive of his bullheaded pride, refusing to back off. He was a fisherman, for God's sake—had been, anyway—so where did he get off playing Jacques bloody Cousteau?

It was his mouth that betrayed him every time. He swore that if he made it through today without a calamity or a lawsuit, he'd never go into a bar again—or, if he did, he'd sew his lips together and drink his vodka through a straw.

Once clear of Ely's Harbour, he turned south. He looked down from the flying bridge to make sure his two passengers hadn't fallen overboard or speared one another or dropped something serious on a foot. They were down there on the stern assembling their diving gear—compasses, knives, computers, octopus regulators, buoyancy vests, still cameras, video cameras—good God, they had enough gear to equip an astronaut for a month on the back side of the moon.

They had said they were expert divers, had insisted on showing him their Advanced Open-Water cards. But in Lucas's mind, people who decked themselves out in all that machinery weren't divers, they were shoppers. Sure, diving could be complicated, if you wanted to mess with all that chemistry, but it didn't have to be. A savvy person made it simple: Wear a bathing suit so nothing grabs you by the balls, flippers for your motor, a mask so you can see, a tank of air to breathe, a few pounds of lead to keep you down, a depth gauge in case you get absentminded.

Besides, that girl, Susie, looked like she didn't *need* gear— she had a set of lungs on her that should take her to a thousand feet on a single breath. Gear just spoiled the picture, covered up all the golden-brown skin, the mane of yellow hair that when he first saw it had made him catch his breath. She was a prime candidate for that *Sports Illustrated* special issue.

But they were high-tekkies, these two. Like most everybody these days, they relied on electronic doodads to do their work for them. Common sense and gut instincts were becoming a thing of the past.

Well, he hoped one of them, the boy or the girl, still had a ration of common sense, because where they were going, the only thing the costly toys might do was provide a record for the coroner.

That thought brought Lucas another fit of anger. Maybe he'd pay someone to remove his vocal cords.

His first mistake had been to go to the Hog Penny Pub for his five o'clock smile. He never went to any of the tourist bars on Front Street: The drinks were overpriced and undergenerous. But a pretty girl had stopped on her motorbike to ask him directions, and she'd said she went to the Hog Penny every day, and why didn't he come by for a drink later on, and so he'd shaved his face and changed his shirt and dropped by. Naturally, the girl never did.

His second mistake had been to hang around long enough to destroy a twenty-dollar bill, because even at tourist prices, twenty dollars bought him enough fuel to generate heat in his belly and tamp down his native quietness.

His third—and by far most serious—mistake had been to put his mouth where it didn't belong, into a conversation between two young people he didn't know.

He'd been dazzled by the girl from the moment he saw her, but he had no ambitions about her because the boy she was with was just as good-looking as she was, in his way, just as tall and blond and tan. Lucas imagined them to be a matched pair from some scientific stud farm, programmed to breed a race of beauties. They looked so much alike, they could have been brother and sister . . .

. . . which, he later learned, was exactly what they were: twins, just out of college, down here staying in their parents' house out by the Mid-Ocean Club. He gathered that their father was some big-shot tycoon in the broadcast business up in the States.

Because Dr. Smirnoff had Lucas well in tow by now and was deluding him that he was as smooth as Tom Cruise, Lucas began to fancy that he might actually have a chance with this heart-stopper. Her get up alone should have been warning enough: No girl with a real-gold Rolex watch, a gold pinky ring and one of those five-dollar golf shirts with the fifty-dollar polo player on it—let alone the satin skin and teeth as perfect as piano keys—was likely to give a thought to some scraunchy, ragged-haired boat-jockey in tattered jeans. But Dr. Smirnoff was driving.

They were consulting a set of decompression tables, wondering aloud if they should have decompressed after their last dive and planning how deep they could go on tomorrow's dives—all of which should have rung alarm bells in Lucas's head since, first of all, no visitors were ever taken on deep dives in Bermuda and, second, deep diving wasn't something sensible people did by choice.

Lucas didn't say a thing while the two discussed the depths of the various shipwrecks they had been on, comparing the *Constellation* to *l'Herminie,* the *North Carolina* to the *Virginia Merchant.* None of them lay deeper than forty feet—breathhold range for anybody but a consumptive. He wasn't tempted to correct them when they talked about the *Cristóbal Colón* versus the *Pollockshields,* two iron ships so shallow you had to take care not to hit them with the boat.

He had found his opening when the boy—Scott, his name was—said something like, "The boat guy said the deepest wreck around's the *Pelinaion.*"

"Where is it?" asked Susie. "Will he take us to it?"

Lucas leaned forward and turned his head toward them and said, " 'Scuse me. None of my business, but I'm afraid somebody's pulling your chain."

"Really?" Susie's eyes opened wide, and Lucas decided that she had the longest eyelashes he'd ever seen.

"Yep. Like I say, none of my business, but I hate to see you get a bum steer."

"What is, then?" said Scott. "The deepest wreck."

"The deepest shipwreck in Bermuda," Lucas said with a smile, *so* charming, pleased to find that his mouth was working even though his lips felt kind of numb, "is the *Admiral Durham*. It's off the South Shore. Leastways, the deepest one anybody's ever seen."

"How deep is that?" Scott had a look that said he didn't believe a word of this but that he had nothing better to do just now than humor Lucas Coven.

"She starts at a hundred and ninety, then angles down the slope to about three hundred."

Susie said, "Wow!"

Scott said, "Gimme a break. . . ."

Looking back, Lucas wished he'd said something terminal like, "Piss off, Junior," something that would have sunk the expedition right then and there.

But Susie had given Scott a punch on the shoulder and said, "Scott! Listen, for once in your life," which meant she was interested.

So Lucas had let his mouth keep running.

"She ran up on the South Shore in a storm and hung there a day or more while they tried to pull her off. They got her free okay, but she was holed so bad that before they could patch her she filled up and went, slid back down the hill."

"And you've seen it," Scott said.

"Once, years back. She's not so easy to find."

"What was it like?" Susie asked, all eager.

"Gets your blood to racing. I call her the Widowmaker." He didn't, but it sounded good. "For a long time you don't see anything at all. Then all of a sudden she looms up out of the deep, and your first thought is, Man, I must be narcked. 'Cause what you see is a great iron ship that looks to be sailing right up at you. Then, what downright convinces you that you've got the vapors is that there's this no-kidding locomotive train engine lying right beside her, fallen off the bow. Just about the time your head clears, it's time to go. You only get about five minutes at that depth."

"I don't believe it," said Scott.

Lucas said, "That's your privilege," and motioned for a re-fill.

Susie put a hand on Lucas's arm, actually touched him, and, with a glance at her brother that told him to keep quiet, said, "Our treat," and gestured to the bartender to give them a couple of beers and Lucas another vodka.

That was the moment when Lucas knew he had them. And because he was enjoying himself and trying to figure out where to take Susie when they managed to ditch Scott, he didn't think the time would come when he wished he hadn't.

When the drinks came, Susie said, "Excuse us a minute," and she took Scott's arm and led him off by some empty tables. They stayed over there, whispering, for three or four minutes, gesturing at one another, and when they came back it was Scott who started the ball rolling.

There had been no stopping it.

Did Lucas think he could find the *Admiral Durham* again?

Probably, with the new electronics on the boat.

Would he be willing to try?

What for?

Because (Susie said) they were bored with the diving around Bermuda; they'd seen nearly everything, and they wanted to get some *real* diving in before the summer was gone and they were both trapped indoors in jobs or grad school or whatever. Also, they couldn't go to some other island to dive right now, because they were waiting for their parents to come down from New York.

Well . . . he didn't know, he was pretty busy.

They'd make it worth his while.

He had to be honest with them, he said, he had a charter party on hold for tomorrow. (*Charter party!* Where had he come up with *that?* He'd never taken a charter party out in his life; he had no idea what you did with one or how much you charged them.) He wished he could help them, they seemed like nice kids and all, but he couldn't sacrifice that charter fee.

And how much was that?

Well . . . full day . . . fifteen hundred (a fat figure, plucked out of the air).

No problem. In fact, if he could guarantee to put them on the shipwreck, they'd pay two thousand. But if he didn't find it (Scott was playing Mr. Big-Time Hard-Nose), they'd ride for free.

Fair enough, but Lucas had to ask, were they sure they were up to a two-hundred-foot dive? Ever done it before? Did they know about the bends, which could cripple or kill them; about nitrogen narcosis, the notorious "rapture" that could cause them to lose their bearings . . . about all the other stuff that happened at depth?

Oh sure, they were supercareful, they knew all the chemistry and physics. And if they hadn't actually gone to two hundred feet before, they'd both been down well over a hundred (Scott was positive, Susie pretty sure), and there wasn't really that much difference, was there, only nine or ten stories of an office building.

And three more atmospheres of pressure, Lucas thought— three steps up on the squeeze ladder, three times the chance of a mishap that could end in a funeral. But he didn't say anything because by now he was convinced Susie had eyes for him, and besides, Scott was running on about their expertise.

Scott listed all the places they'd dived and in what kinds of weather. They brandished their C-cards and logbooks listing every time they'd gotten their feet wet.

Okay, then, he'd take them, but he'd have to send them down the anchor line alone, he couldn't go with them 'cause he didn't have a mate and he couldn't leave the boat unmanned—safety was his first concern, he had a reputation around the island. 'Cause if the boat should happen to break away, they didn't want to have to swim to shore after a two-hundred-foot dive . . . unless they cared to spring for another couple of hundred to hire a mate for the day.

Susie said, Gosh, they didn't need a nursemaid, they'd swim right down the old anchor line, take a lot of pictures and be back before he knew it.

Scott said, So let's raise a glass to the dive of a lifetime.

And they had done just that, several glasses, in fact, until the time came when Lucas decided to make his move on Susie and suggested they slip away for a quiet dinner somewhere.

She had laughed at him—not a nasty laugh but a kind of sweet motherly laugh that he couldn't get mad at—and ruffled his hair and said, See you tomorrow.

LUCAS GAVE SOUTHWEST Breaker a wide berth. There was no breeze to speak of, just a light sou'westerly, but the sea still boiled around the treacherous fang of rock sticking up from the bottom, yearning to puncture passersby.

Fresh air cleared Lucas's head, a handful of peppermints killed the taste of rot in his mouth and a breakfast beer restored him to where he could look on the bright side of things.

Two thousand dollars was more than he could make in a month netting flying fish or helping a chummy haul water.

Maybe the kids had done some bragging, maybe they had too much faith in all their Mickey Mouse gear, but they certainly were being careful, checking and rechecking every hose and fitting.

He could tell, looking down at them, that they were nervous, which was healthy. They might eat up air so fast they'd never get near the bottom, but that wasn't his worry.

The day was looking promising, after all. With luck, he could be back at the dock by lunchtime. If they were successful, if he gave them the dive of a lifetime, Susie might yet come around. You never knew.

The reef line was close on the South Shore, deep water came fast, so it wasn't long before Lucas started looking to array his landmarks. He had written them down—no reason, but now a piece of good luck—the one and only time he'd been out to this wreck, which had to be ten years ago.

There was a purple house with twin tall casuarinas directly behind it. His eye was supposed to line up those trees straight as a rifle sight, at the same time triangulating so that the main building of the peach-colored cottage colony to the westward sat at the feet of Gibbs Hill Lighthouse.

The tide was running offshore, so Lucas drove a little bit to sea, then turned and pointed the bow at the shore while he powered slowly up and adjusted the landmarks.

Landmarks weren't foolproof, though, with a shipwreck this deep. You couldn't see it from the surface, you had to take your marks after you'd swum up from it, and maybe by then the boat had swung at anchor.

And close wasn't good enough with the *Admiral Durham.* The light was dim down there, visibility probably no more than thirty or forty feet at best, and with five minutes' bottom time—which meant five minutes from the time you left the surface till the time you started up from the bottom—you didn't have leisure to go hunting around. Lucas had to anchor *on* it, drop the hook on the deck and let it drag along till it found a purchase on a rail or some chain or maybe even that rusty old commode that squatted on the foredeck, the one he'd had his picture taken sitting on.

He switched on his fish-finder and set the depth of its read and shaded the screen with his hand. The readout of lines and lumps showed nothing, a void, between the surface and the bottom. He turned the wheel, nosing the boat a couple of points to port, then a couple to starboard, and suddenly it was there, a giant hulk rising up from the bottom.

Lucas jockeyed the boat until the hulk was dead center on the screen. Then he nudged forward a hair, enough to compensate for the current gripping the anchor and bowing the line, and pushed the button that released the anchor.

He closed his eyes and wished the anchor all the way down, seeing it in his mind dropping through the darkening blue and striking steel with a hearty clang.

11

THE CREATURE WAS in a state close to hibernation. Its respiration —the ingestion and expulsion of water—had slowed to fifteen cycles per minute. Its color had dulled to a grayish brown. Its arms and whips floated freely, like gigantic snakes.

And it was gaining strength, as if sucking sustenance from the cool and silent darkness.

Suddenly the silence was broken by sound vibrations, which showered down upon it and were amplified by the salt water. To a human ear, the sound would have been thick, resonant, metallic, the sound of solid steel striking hollow steel with weight and velocity.

To the creature, the sound was unknown . . . alien and alarming, and so its respiration increased, quickly doubled. Its arms curled, its whips cocked. Its color changed, brightened, brown hues vanishing, replaced by purples and reds.

It located the noise as coming from above, so it began to rise up the slope toward the large and unnatural and lifeless thing it had sensed there earlier.

The sound began again, but altered, a series of short staccato bumps. Then it stopped altogether.

The creature moved toward the unnatural thing, then hovered over it, searching for the source of the sound. Any sound, any change whatever in the normal rhythms of the sea, could mean prey.

And the need that was overwhelming it, now that it was moving and consuming energy, was hunger.

12

LUCAS STOOD ON the bow and let the anchor rope run through his hands until he saw the piece of tape marking fifty fathoms. Then he took a turn around a cleat and watched the swing of the bow and the angle of the rope. If he gave it too little scope, there was a risk that it would pull the anchor free; too much, and traveling time for the divers would be too long and they'd run out of air.

Might as well give them a sporting chance, he thought, now that the two thousand dollars was as good as in his pocket.

When he was satisfied with the set, he cleated off the rope and went aft. "Dive, dive, dive!" he said, grinning at Scott and Susie, who looked like heroes from one of those comic books.

They were wearing matching wetsuits, blue with yellow chevrons the color of their blond hair, and strapped to their legs were red-handled knives big enough to fell a buffalo. Their Italian flippers were so long that the kids looked like some kind of weird mutant ducks. Both of them were lashed up with straps, buckles and snaps.

"You're sure you found the *Durham*?" said Scott.

"You didn't hear the anchor bong on the deck down there?"

They didn't know whether to believe him or not, so they just smiled, both looking antsy.

Lucas ushered them down onto the swim step off the stern. Susie's tan seemed to have faded, and her face had taken on an ashy hue.

"You okay?" Lucas asked, touching her arm.

"Yes . . . I guess."

"You don't have to go. There's no shame."

"We're going," Scott said. "She'll be fine."

Lucas looked at Susie, who nodded.

"It's your party." Serious now, Lucas said, "Swim on the surface up to the anchor line. Get a grip on it and check everything out and wait till you're all calm and cool. I don't care if it takes a week, there's no rush, I don't want you going down there all anxious. When you're ready, one of you go first, the other right behind, and I tell you, *fire* for the bottom, don't dally. You got precious little time as it is. Any spare time you got, use it to come up nice and slow."

They nodded and cleaned their masks and put them on. Lucas passed them their cameras: a video in a housing for Scott, a Nikonos V for Susie.

They gave one another the thumbs-up sign.

"Hey!" said Lucas, and they looked up at him. "One last thing: Don't go frightening anything down there." He smiled, to show he was making a little joke.

They didn't smile back.

As soon as they hit the water, they inflated their vests and lay on their backs and kicked against the tide toward the bow of the boat.

Lucas walked forward and stood looking down as they gathered at the anchor line. They fiddled with this and checked that and said something back and forth. Then they put their mouthpieces in, vented their vests and dropped beneath the surface.

Lucas looked at his watch: 10:52. By eleven o'clock he'd either be two thousand dollars richer or in a mess he didn't want to think about.

THE CREATURE HAD twice covered the length and breadth of the large, unnatural thing. The sound vibrations had ceased, and no other signs of prey had followed.

Its eyes registered faint light above. Here the cool water was blending with warmer, so it moved away from the unnatural thing and began to drop back into the darkness.

But then it sensed movement again, something coming closer, and a sound that signaled a life form.

It dropped back atop the unnatural thing, its great body resting in shadows, waiting.

As the movement drew near and the rasping sound of living things respiring grew louder, the creature's color began to change.

SCOTT PULLED HIMSELF down the anchor rope hand over hand, the video camera snapped to his weight belt trailing behind him. He was in dim nothingness now, surrounded by blue. He paused to check his air gauge—2,500 pounds, plenty—and his depth gauge—120 feet. He saw no shipwreck below him, no bottom.

The feeling was eerie, lonely, but not frightening, for there was solace in the tautness of the anchor line. *Some*thing was down there; the anchor had caught in it. If it was the shipwreck, fine; if not, well . . . they'd save two thousand dollars. He still hadn't figured out how to explain to the old man the thousand-dollar cash advances he and Susie had each taken on their credit cards.

Where was Susie?

Scott turned and looked back up the anchor line. She was way above, hanging on the rope at fifty or sixty feet—afraid, maybe, or having trouble with her ears.

There was nothing he could do for her. As long as she was above him, she'd be okay. Coven could look after her.

He rinsed a patch of fog from his mask, tipped downward and kicked for the bottom.

At 160 feet he saw it, and his breath caught. It was exactly as Coven had described it—a ghost ship seeming to sail right up at him, enormous beyond imagining. And lying on the bottom beside the starboard bow, like a wounded behemoth staring blankly with its cyclopean eye, was the blunt face of a locomotive.

Fantastic!

He wanted to stop his descent long enough to unsnap the video camera from his belt, switch on its light and adjust its settings. But though he kicked hard, thrusting upward with his flipper blades, he felt himself continuing to sink. He was overweighted for this depth: His neoprene suit had compressed, lost its buoyancy, and he was too heavy, descending too fast. He pressed the button that shot air into his vest, and once again he was nearly neutral in the water. He checked his air gauge—1,800 pounds—and told himself to control his breathing.

Then he aimed his camera at the bow of the ship, pressed the trigger and let himself drift gradually downward.

IT WAS ALIVE, whatever this thing was, and slow and clumsy.

And it was coming.

The creature cocked its whips and fluttered its tail fins and, very slowly, began to move out of the shadows toward the prey.

SCOTT DROPPED DOWN onto the bow of the ship. He was still breathing too fast, he could hear his heart, but he didn't care. This was incredible! The size of it!

He found something to wrap his legs around, to steady himself—it was a *toilet*, for God's sake, right here on the deck! —and he brought the camera's viewfinder up to his mask, trying somehow to get it all in frame.

His world became a tiny square with a green light in one corner and some numbers on the bottom.

He felt a change in the rhythm of the water around him, but he didn't turn to look: It had to be a blip in the current, or perhaps Susie arriving nearby.

He saw a vague, shadowy movement at the farthest left edge of the frame, but he assumed it was an illusion caused by the dappled light.

Something touched him. He jerked, turned, but all he could see was a blur of purple.

And then the something had him around the chest and was squeezing.

He dropped the camera, twisted around, but the something kept squeezing. Now there were stabbing things in it, like knives. He heard a crack—his ribs, breaking like sticks of kindling.

The last thing he saw, in his mask, was a bubble of blood.

SUSIE COULD SEE nothing above, nothing below. She was fighting to stay in control, not to panic. Why hadn't Scott waited for her? They were supposed to go down together. Lucas had insisted; they had agreed. But no, Scott had gone off on his own. Impatient, selfish. As usual.

She checked her air gauge—1,500 pounds—and her depth gauge—110 feet. She'd never make it. She was gasping, and she could envision air disappearing with every breath. She felt surrounded, compressed, imprisoned. She couldn't even make it to the surface. She was going to die!

Stop it! she told herself. Everything's fine. *You're* fine.

She clung to the anchor line and closed her eyes, willing herself to take slow, deep breaths. Oxygen nourished her, her brain cleared, panic subsided.

She opened her eyes and looked at her air gauge again: 1,450 pounds.

She decided to drop down the line another fifty feet. Maybe she could at least see the shipwreck from there. Then she'd start up.

Still clutching the rope, she let herself fall. A hundred and twenty feet, 130, 140, then . . . what was that? Something was moving below. Something was coming up at her.

It had to be Scott. He had seen the wreck and taken his pictures and was already on the way back.

She'd never get to see it. She'd have to settle for Scott's description—endlessly repeated, inevitably embellished. She'd have to endure his sly asides about this being a "man's dive, too tough for the girls."

Too bad, but . . .

This moving thing, this purplish thing, it wasn't Scott rising at her. It was huge, so huge it couldn't possibly be alive. But what was it? What could it—

Her last sensation was surprise.

LUCAS LOOKED AT his watch: 10:59. They'd better be on their way up in the next sixty seconds. If not, he'd have to get on the radio and find out where the nearest decompression chamber was. Because these two were gonna be bent up like corkscrews.

That is, unless they never got there at all, chickened out, maybe hung at 150 feet or so, from where they could just see the shipwreck. It was common enough: Big ships underwater freak a lot of people.

That was it, had to be. They'd gotten halfway down and decided this was out of their league after all. They were at 125, 150. They could stay another five minutes.

11:02.

He lay on the bow and shaded his eyes and stared hard down the anchor line, looking for even a glimmer of one of those snazzy wetsuits.

He heard a noise down aft. *Jesus!* Stupid bastards had come up away from the anchor line, probably run out of air and shot for the surface. Be lucky if one of them didn't have an embolism.

Or maybe they'd been decompressing at ten or twenty feet, then come up under the boat. Sure. Made sense.

But why hadn't he seen them? The water was clear as gin.

He stood up and started aft. The noise was still going on, a weird noise, a wet, sucking kind of noise.

Now he smelled something.

Ammonia. *Ammonia?* Here?

As he edged along the side of the cabin, the boat suddenly heaved sharply to starboard.

Christ! What was that?

He heard wood crack and splinter.

The boat was listing badly now, he had to struggle to keep his footing. He jumped down into the cockpit. The gin pole was gone, snapped off three feet above the deck.

He looked over the transom, and what he saw froze him and drove the breath from him. It was an eye, an eye as big as the moon, bigger even, in a field of quivering slime the color of arterial blood.

He shouted—not words, just noise—and snapped upright,

to flee the eye. He lurched to the right, took a step, but the boat heaved again, and he was thrown backward. His knees struck the transom, his arms flailed out and he tumbled overboard.

13

MARCUS SHARP CHECKED his fuel gauges and saw that in another fifteen or twenty minutes he'd have to turn back to the base.

He had been aloft for a couple of hours, ostensibly on a routine training patrol, in fact trying to spot shipwrecks. He had circled the island, flown low over the reefs in the north and northwest, looking for ballast piles. He had spotted the known wrecks, the *Cristóbal Colón* and the *Caraquet*, but nothing new.

He had hoped to find a virgin wreck for Whip, preferably a late-sixteenth-century Spanish ship laden with ingots and gold chains and perhaps some uncut emeralds. But he'd settle for anything old and untouched, to replenish Whip's rapidly depleting reserves of enthusiasm, hope and money.

Sharp was feeling guilty, because he'd all but promised Whip he could keep that raft, and he'd heard that the police had confiscated it, on the orders of that self-important little shit, St. John.

And it *was* Sharp's fault, at least partly, because—as Captain Wallingford had pointed out in his most patronizing way—Sharp had had no authority to deputize Whip Darling to do anything, let alone to give Darling what amounted to evidence. The logic of Sharp's defense had failed to move Wallingford, who had subjected him to a half-hour lecture on the proper behavior for American servicemen stationed in foreign countries.

Now Sharp was cruising along the South Shore, off Elbow Beach. He could see scores of people frolicking in the surf, and a few snorkelers offshore exploring the wreck of the *Pollockshields*.

Shark bait, Sharp thought . . . if there are any sharks left.

The *Pollockshields* had been a menace for generations. An iron steamer loaded with World War I ammunition, she had sunk on the shallow reefs in 1915. Though much of the ammunition was still live, that wasn't the problem. The iron was. Snorkelers came out from Elbow Beach and poked around the wreck and got caught in the waves that broke over it, and sometimes they were slammed up against the sharp shards of iron. They'd be cut and bleeding and forced to swim hundreds of yards back to shore, through the calm, murky shallows that were the hunting grounds of reef sharks—or, rather, had been.

At five hundred feet, Sharp made a slow circle over the snorkelers, reassuring himself that no dark shadows were lurking nearby, and then he banked off to the west.

Whip had said a friend of a friend had been poring through the Archives of the Indies in Seville, looking for details of a Spanish fleet that had sunk off Dominica in 1567, when he had seen a reference—almost a parenthesis—about one of the ships being separated from the others early in the voyage and running up on the south side of Bermuda.

Looking for that lost lamb was a shot in the dark, but what the hell . . . he had nothing better to do.

Sharp's co-pilot, a lieutenant junior grade named Forester, finished the copy of *People* he'd been reading and said, "I gotta take a fearsome leak."

"Almost home," Sharp said.

He was about to give up, to gain altitude and turn back to the northeast, when his radio came alive.

"Huey One . . . Kindley . . ."

"Go ahead, Kindley. . . ."

"Feel like a little flake patrol, Lieutenant?"

"If it doesn't take more'n ten minutes. Otherwise Forester busts a gut and we all swim home. What's up?"

"A woman called the cops, said she saw a boat go to pieces a mile south of Sou'west Breaker."

"Go to pieces? What did she mean, blow up?"

"No, that's the strange part. She said she was looking

through her telescope for humpback whales—sometimes she can see 'em from her house—and she saw this fishing boat, thirty-five or forty feet she says, just . . . go to pieces. No flame, no smoke, no nothing. It came apart."

"Sure . . . fat chance. Okay, I'll have a look," Sharp said. "It's on the way home anyway."

He pressed his stick to the left, and the helicopter banked off to the south.

Forester said, "Make it fast, or I'm gonna pee in my pants."

"Grab it and strangle it," Sharp said. "That's an order."

Sharp left Southwest Breaker to his right, so that the sun was almost directly overhead and slightly behind him, and there was no glare on the water. He could see perfectly.

But there was nothing to see.

He flew south for two minutes, then turned southeast. Nothing. Nothing floated, nothing bobbed, nothing broke the endless roll of the blue swells.

"Kindley . . . Huey One . . ." Sharp said into his radio. "I gotta break off. Nothing down there."

"Come on home, Huey One. Probably nothing to it."

Sharp turned east.

"Hey!" Forester said, and he tapped the Plexiglas beside him and pointed downward.

Sharp banked to the left and looked. He saw two white rubber fenders, then some planks, then, half-submerged, looking like a white blanket covered with blue haze, the entire roof of a boat's cabin.

"Can't stop now," Sharp said, "or we'll be down there with it." He set his course at 040, straight for the base.

He had crossed the reef line and was about to be over land when he looked to his right and saw the *Privateer* chugging slowly westward along the shore.

Go home, he told himself, don't do this. You don't need to give Wallingford an excuse to chew your ass a second time.

Then he thought, Screw Wallingford. Sharp had been chewed out by some of the greats, and Wallingford was decidedly junior varsity. What else could they do to him, bring him up for a Captain's Mast? So what? He was formulating new priorities, and the navy was slipping down the list fast.

He pressed the "talk" button on his microphone and said,

"Privateer . . . Privateer . . . Privateer . . . This is Huey One. . . ."

DARLING WAS IN the wheelhouse, drinking a cup of tea and wondering how much he could get if he sold his Masonic bottle— it was a good bottle, rare, 170 years old—when the call came over Channel 16.

He picked up the microphone from its hook. *"Privateer* . . . go to twenty-seven, Marcus."

"Going to twenty-seven . . .''

"More bullshit?" Mike said.

"Wasn't his fault about the raft," said Darling. "He tried to do us a good turn."

"Privateer . . . Huey One . . ." said Sharp. "Whip, there's a boat wrecked about two miles dead ahead of you, call it two-three-zero from where you are. Mile and a half off the beach."

"Wrecked how?"

"Don't know. There's wreckage on and under the surface. I haven't got fuel left to look for survivors. Police boat's probably on the way, but you're closest."

"Roger that, Marcus. I'll go check it out." Darling started to hang up, but then a kindness occurred to him, and he pushed the button again and said, "Hey, Marcus . . . probably be going out this weekend, if you're interested."

There was relief in Sharp's voice as he replied, *"I'll* say . . . that is, if they don't have me swabbing latrines."

DARLING REPLACED THE microphone on its hook, dialed the radio back to Channel 16 and said to Mike, "See? Do a good turn for a friend and they give you a reaming. Hell of a note." He pushed his throttle forward and watched the tachometer needle rise from 1,500 rpms to 2,000.

"Why'd the navy get on Marcus's case?" asked Mike.

"Why d'you think? 'Cause the earl of fucking St. John got on theirs."

Darling was finding himself so angry so often these days that he was beginning to wonder about himself. He'd have to be careful not to let himself slip over the edge into paranoia.

He and Mike had returned the damaged gear to the aquarium and had explained what little they knew about what had happened to it. Darling had begun to outline how he thought new gear might be improved, when the deputy director—a slight, nervous black man whose Vandyke beard, Darling had always believed, was a disguise for his mousy personality—had said, "I'm afraid not."

"Afraid not what?"

"We'll be . . . ah . . . terminating our agreement with you."

"*What?* Why?"

"Well, this was . . . ah . . ." He wouldn't look at Darling. "Expensive equipment . . . after all."

"Sharks are big animals . . . *after all.* . . . Jesus, Milton, if you want me to hang the gear at ten feet, sure, nothing'll touch it. But you want me to hang it down where the action is, maybe actually catch something interesting, there are risks. That's the whole point."

"Yes, but . . . I'm afraid that's that."

"Who's gonna catch your critters for you?"

"Well . . . that's yet to be decided."

Darling had taken a deep breath and closed his eyes, trying to suppress the rage—and the fear, he had to admit—at the thought of eight hundred dollars a month vanishing into the ether.

"It's St. John, isn't it? . . ."

Milton had looked away, at the telephone, as if praying for it to ring. "I don't—"

"Wildlife management. He's decided wildlife management takes in the aquarium, too . . . right?"

"You're jumping to—"

"He's gonna take *my* eight hundred a month and go out with a dip net and a case of Budweiser, and when he doesn't come back with shit, he can blame it on the oil spills off California." Darling was right, he knew it.

Milton was sweating; his eyes darted from side to side. "For heaven's sake, Whip . . ."

"You're right, Milton, I'm overreacting." He had walked to the door and opened it. He could see Mike outside, talking to a tortoise so old it was said to have been a gift to Bermuda from Queen Victoria. "But you know what? I feel sorrier for you. I may not make much of a living, but at least I don't have to earn my pay by kissing the ass of that Irish lizard."

Darling was convinced that St. John saw him as a threat to his power, a rebel against the construction of his little empire. St. John was determined to bring Darling to heel . . . or to destroy him.

And what rankled Darling, what ate away at his guts, was the fact—more evident day by day—that St. John was succeeding. He had all the weapons.

"THERE," SAID MIKE, pointing to some floating wood. It was about three by five feet, with a patch of indoor-outdoor carpeting nailed to it and two short lengths of chain dangling from it.

"Swim step," Darling said. "Bring it aboard."

Mike went outside, grabbed the boat hook and went aft, while Darling climbed the ladder to the flying bridge.

From up here, twelve feet above the surface, he could see debris everywhere, some a foot underwater, some bobbing on the surface. There were fenders, planks, cushions, life jackets.

The water was patched with rainbow slicks: oil that had leaked from the engine as the boat sank.

"Sling it all aboard," he called down to Mike.

For an hour he cruised among the debris, as Mike grabbed piece after piece of flotsam and tossed it into the cockpit.

"Want that too?" Mike said, pointing to a white wooden rectangle, twelve feet wide by fifteen feet long, that hung a foot or two beneath the surface.

"No, that's his roof," Darling said from the flying bridge. Then something came to him, and he said, "Hang on," and he put the boat in neutral, letting it drift, and went down the ladder. He picked up a four-pronged grapnel attached to twenty feet of rope, and he tossed the hook at the wood. He let it drop till it caught the far edge, then he hauled back on it, dragging the corner of the roof out of water. He had a glimpse of pea-soup green on the underside of the roof.

"It's Lucas Coven's boat," he said, letting the wood fall back, coiling the rope as he brought the hook aboard.

"How d'you know that?"

"I saw him painting the boat last spring. He was doing the whole inside of the house in baby-shit green. Said he'd got the paint on sale."

"What the hell was he doing out here?"

"You know Lucas," Darling said. "Probably had some half-ass scheme to make two dollars in a hurry."

They had known Lucas Coven for more than twenty years and always thought of him as suffering from a case of the "almosts": everything Coven did he could almost make a living at, almost but not quite. He couldn't afford enough fish traps to cover his boat expenses, and when traps were outlawed he had no other trade. He'd do anything for a few bucks —haul water, paint houses, build docks—but he never stuck with anything long enough to make a steady go of it.

"How do you make two dollars out here? Nothing here."

"No," Darling agreed. "Nothing but the *Durham.*"

"Nobody dives on the *Durham* . . . nobody with sense."

"Right again. Let's have a look." Darling picked up a rubber fender. There were no marks on it, no scratches, no scars, no burns.

"He had a GM in her, didn't he?" Mike said.

"Yeah. Six-seventy-one."

"So that didn't blow him up. Propane stove?"

"Maybe. But Christ, they'd've heard that bang all the way in St. George's." Darling picked up a section of planking with a brass screw-cap countersunk in it.

"So what blew him up? He carry explosives?"

Darling said, "Nothing blew him up. Look here. No char, no smoke, no disintegration like you'd see in an explosion." He put his nose to the wood. "No stink. You'd smell it if there'd been heat to it." He tossed the wood onto the deck. "He was busted up . . . somehow."

"By what? Nothing out here for him to hit."

"I don't know. Killer whales? This was a wooden boat."

"Killer whales!? In hailing distance of the beach?"

"*You* come up with something, then." Darling felt anger welling up again. Mike always wanted answers, and it seemed he had fewer and fewer of those. "What else? UFOs? Martians? The frigging Tooth Fairy?" He dropped the wood onto the deck.

"Hey, Whip . . ." Mike said.

Annoyed now with himself, Darling said, "Shit!" and kicked a life jacket, which rose off the deck and would have gone overboard if Mike hadn't caught it.

Mike was about to toss it aside when he noticed something. "What's this?"

Darling looked. The orange cloth covering the kapok had been shredded, and the buoyant material beneath was exposed. There were two marks in it, circles, about six inches in diameter. The rim of each circle was ragged, as if it had been cut by a rasp, and in the center was a deep slash.

"For God's sake," Darling said. "Looks like a scuttle."

"Sure." Mike thought Darling was joking. An octopus? "Moby-bleeding-scuttle," he said. "Besides, you ever seen a scuttle with teeth in its suckers?"

"No." Mike was right. The suckers on an octopus's arms were soft, pliable. A man could unwrap them from around his arm as easily as removing a bandage.

But what was it, then? It was an animal, for certain. This boat hadn't blown up, hadn't hit anything, hadn't been struck by lightning, hadn't magically disintegrated. It had come up against something and been destroyed.

Darling tossed the life jacket onto the deck and kicked some pieces of wood aside to clear his way forward. One of the planks struck the steel bulwark, and as it fell back to the deck something dropped out of it and landed with a click.

It was a claw, like the other one, crescent-shaped, two inches long and sharp as a razor.

He looked overboard, at the still water. But the water wasn't really still, it was alive, and, as if to remind Darling, it sent a gentle swell at him that heaved the boat upward.

As the boat settled again, something floated out from underneath it: rubber, blue with a yellow chevron on either side.

A wetsuit hood.

Darling picked up the boat hook and dipped it overboard and scooped up the hood. It came up like a cup, full of water, and in the water were two little black-and-yellow-striped fish: sergeant majors. They were feeding on something.

Darling held the hood in his hand. A smell rose from it, sharp and acrid. Like ammonia.

His body was shadowing the hood, so he turned into the sun and let light fall into the dark pocket.

What the fish were feeding on looked like a big marble.

Mike came up behind Darling and looked over his shoulder. "What've you— Holy sweet Jesus!" Mike gasped. "Is that human?"

"It is," said Darling, and he stood aside to let Mike retch into the sea.

14

THE WOMAN WATCHED through her telescope until her head ached and her vision began to blur. She had seen the navy helicopter come and go, and seen Whip Darling show up in that ramshackle *Privateer*. But where were the police? She had done her civic duty by reporting what she saw; the least the police could do was follow up.

Now it looked as if someone were throwing up over the side. Probably hung over. Fishermen were all the same: fish all day and drink the night away.

If the police weren't going to respond, perhaps she should call the newspaper. Sometimes reporters were more diligent than the police. The only reason she hadn't called the paper earlier was that she was worried that one of her humpbacks might have wrecked the boat—by accident, of course—and an ignorant reporter might be tempted to say bad things about whales. But she had looked and looked, and seen no sign of whales, no spouting, no flukes, so it was probably safe by now to call the paper.

THE REPORTER STARED at the flashing light on his telephone as he hurried to pull a notepad from his desk drawer, and blessed his luck. He had been trying to find this woman for an hour, ever since he had heard the first reports on the newsroom's police-band radio, but Harbour Radio had refused to give him her name.

This story could be his ticket out of the trenches, his passport to the big time. He had spent the past three years writing on numbing topics like the fish-trap controversy and the rise in import duties, and he had begun to despair that he'd never get off this godforsaken rock. The problem with Bermuda was that nothing ever happened here, at least nothing of interest to the wire services or the news magazines or the television networks.

But this was different. Deaths at sea, especially deaths under mysterious circumstances, were dynamite. If he could play up the mystery, maybe impose a Bermuda Triangle slant on it, he might catch the eye of the AP or the Cleveland *Plain Dealer* or, dream of dreams, *The New York Times*.

He had about given up on the woman and was on his way out the door to go to Somerset, to wait for Whip Darling, when the switchboard operator had relayed the call.

He pushed the flashing button and said, "Brendan Eve, Mrs. Outerbridge. Thank you for calling."

He listened for a few minutes, then said, "You're sure it didn't explode?"

Again she talked, and again he listened. Lord, but the woman could talk! By the time she had finished, he saw that he had scribbled four pages of notes. He could write a treatise on the history of humpback whales.

But there had been nuggets of value in the woman's monologue. He noticed that there was one phrase he had written down several times, and he underlined it: "sea monster."

Part Two

15

DOCTOR HERBERT TALLEY hunched his shoulders and shielded his face against the wind, a roaring northeaster that drove salt water off the ocean and blended it with rain, creating a brackish spray that burned leaves brown. He stepped in a puddle and felt icy water slop over his shoe tops and seep between his toes.

It might as well be winter. The only difference between summer and winter in Nova Scotia was that by winter all the leaves had been blown away.

He crossed the quadrangle, stopped at Commons to pick up his mail and climbed the stairs to his tiny office. He was winded by the exertion, which annoyed, but didn't surprise, him. He wasn't getting enough exercise. He wasn't getting *any* exercise. The weather had been so vile for so long that he hadn't been able to swim or jog. He had taken pride in being a young fifty, but he was beginning to feel like an old fifty-one.

He vowed to start exercising tomorrow, even in a whole gale. He had to. To go to flab would be to admit defeat, to accept the loss of his dreams, to resign himself to whiling away his days as a teacher. Some might say that academia was the graveyard of science, but Herbert Talley wasn't ready to be buried just yet.

Days like today didn't help. A grand total of six students had showed up for his lecture on cephalopods: six stuporous summer-school students, misfits who had been denied their diplomas until they passed their science requirement. He had done his best to infuse them with his enthusiasm. He was among the world's leading experts on cephalopods, and he found it incredible that they couldn't share his appreciation of the wondrous head-foots. Perhaps the fault lay in him. He was an impatient teacher, who preferred showing to instructing, doing to telling. On field trips and expeditions he was a wizard. But there weren't any more expeditions, not with the economy of the Western world about to implode.

Talley's office had room for a desk and a desk chair, a lounge chair and reading lamp, a bookcase and a table for his radio. One wall was taken up with a *National Geographic* map of the world, which Talley had dotted with pushpins representing events in malacology: expeditions of which he was keeping track, sightings of rare species, depredations by pollution and cyclical calamities like red tides and toxic algae blooms, which could be natural or man-made. The other walls contained his framed degrees, awards, citations and photographs of the celebrities of his field: octopus and squid and oysters and clams and conchs and cowries and chambered nautiluses.

Talley hung his hat and raincoat on the back of the door, turned on the radio, plugged in the electric kettle for water for tea and sat with his airmail copy of *The Boston Globe*, the only newspaper he had access to that recognized the existence of issues other than fishing and petty crime.

There was no news, really, at least nothing to excite an aging malacologist stuck in the wilds of Nova Scotia. Everything was more of the same.

Lulled by Bruno Walter's soothing rendition of Beethoven's Sixth Symphony and by the patter of rain and the whisper of wind, warmed by his tea, Talley struggled to stay awake.

Suddenly his eyes snapped open. A phrase—one phrase out of all the thousands of words on the enormous page in his lap —had infiltrated his doziness and imprinted itself on his mind. It had awoken him like an alarm.

Sea monster.

What about it? What sea monster?

He scanned the page, couldn't find it, ran down each column top to bottom, and then . . . there it was, a tiny item on the bottom of the page, a filler, what was called boilerplate.

THREE DIE AT SEA

Bermuda (AP)—Three persons died yesterday when their boat sank from unknown causes off the shore of this island colony in the Atlantic Ocean. The victims included the two children of media magnate Osborn Manning.

There was no evidence of explosion or fire, and some local residents speculated that the boat had been struck by lightning, though no electrical storms had been reported in the area.

Others, recalling the mysteries of the Bermuda Triangle, blamed the incident on a sea monster. The only clues noted by police were strange marks on wooden planks and an odor of ammonia in some of the debris.

Talley held his breath. He read the item again, and again. He rose from his chair and went to the wall map. His pushpins were color-coded, and he searched for red ones. There were only two, both off Newfoundland, both marked with reference dates from the early 1960s. Off Bermuda there was nothing.

Until now.

Obviously, the reporter hadn't known what he was writing about. He had gathered facts and lumped them together, not realizing that he was inadvertently including the key to the puzzle.

Ammonia. Ammonia was the key. Talley felt a thrill of discovery, as if he had suddenly stumbled upon a new species.

This species wasn't new, however; it was Talley's old nemesis, his quarry, a creature he had spent a large part of his professional life seeking, a creature he had written books about.

He tore the item from the paper and read it again. "Can it be?" he said aloud. "Merciful God, please let it be. After all these years. And, it's time."

It was true, it had to be. There was nothing else it could be. And it was only a thousand miles away, a couple of hours away by air, waiting for him.

But as quickly as he had become elated, he was overcome

by gloom. He had to get to Bermuda, but how? He must mount a search, a proper scientific search, but how would he pay for it? The university was funding nothing these days; grant money had vanished. He had no cash of his own, and no family to borrow from.

He had a vision of himself as a mountain climber, with the summit of his aspirations suddenly appearing through a break in the clouds. He would have to struggle to reach it, but struggle he would.

He *had* to. If he missed this chance, he would be acknowledging that he was the most contemptible of academic frauds, a reciter of other people's data, an amalgamator of other people's theories.

The solution was simple enough: money, the world was full of money. How could he get some of it?

From the radio came the strains of music he knew but couldn't name, a lilting melody, a song, haunting and sad but somehow hopeful too. What was it? The blank in his memory annoyed him, so he pushed from his mind all thoughts of money and concentrated on identifying the piece.

The song ended, there was a brief pause, and then another song began—equally haunting, equally hopeful—and Talley knew what it was: Mahler's *Kindertotenlieder*, the song cycle about the death of children. A nice irony, Talley thought, that from the most ghastly of tragedies could come a wondrous masterpiece. It would take a spiritual giant to create beauty out of the death of children.

Children . . .

He stopped breathing.

There it was. His answer.

He took the newspaper clipping from his pocket and smoothed it on the desk before him. Manning, he read . . . "media magnate Osborn Manning."

He picked up the telephone and asked the operator for Directory Assistance for New York City.

Osborn Manning sat in his office and tried to focus on a report from one of his vice presidents. The news was good. With the economy heading for the dumper, people weren't willing to pay seven dollars for a movie or fifty for the theater, weren't taking Sunday drives of visiting amusement parks. They were opting for cheap entertainment, his entertainment, cable television. Subscriptions were up across the country, and his people had been able to buy half a dozen new franchises at distress prices, from operators who couldn't keep up with their bank debt. Manning had no bank debt. He had seen the troubles coming, and had concluded that in the nineties, cash would be king. He had sold off most of his marginal companies in late '88, at the top of the market, and now he had more cash than many emerging nations.

So what? Would cash bring back his kids? Would cash make his wife whole? He hadn't known how much his family mattered to him, until he lost it. Could cash restore a family?

Cash couldn't even buy him revenge, and revenge was one thing he craved, as if it could help expiate his sin of being a distant, almost an absentee, father. In his private, unspoken yearnings, he wished his children had been murdered by some hophead. Then he could have killed the hophead himself, or hired someone to do it.

But he didn't even have the luxury of imagining revenge, for he had no idea what had killed his children. No one knew. Freak accident. Terribly sorry. Pain gnawed at his stomach, a spasm flashed from just below his rib cage down into his bowels. Maybe he was getting an ulcer. Good, he thought. He deserved it.

He tossed the report aside, leaned back in his chair and looked out the window at the sprawl of Central Park. The late-day sun was glittering gold off the windows on Fifth Avenue. It was a view he loved, or, used to love. He didn't care anymore.

The intercom buzzed on his desk. He spun around and punched a button and said, "Dammit, Helen, I told you I—"

"Mr. Manning . . . it's about the children."

"What about them?" And then, to see what the words felt like in his mouth, he added, "They're dead."

There was a pause, and in his mind's eye Manning saw his secretary swallow.

"Yes, sir," she said. "But there's this Canadian scientist on the phone."

"Who?"

"A man who says he knows what killed the children."

Manning suddenly felt cold. He couldn't speak.

"Mr. Manning . . . ?"

He reached for the phone, and he saw that his hand was shaking.

16

THEY HAD RESTED, mother and calf, on the surface of the sea with the others in the small pod, since the sun had lowered into the western sky and the moon had appeared as a pale wafer in the east.

It was a daily gathering, fulfilling a need for socialization. No matter where they were, no matter how dispersed during the day, as night began to fall the pod came together, not to feed, not to breed, but to experience the comfort of community.

In times past, long ago but still within the memory of the eldest of the pod, there had been many more of them. There was no questioning, for these whales with the largest brains on earth did not question, they accepted. They accepted their smaller numbers, would accept the inevitable further shrinkage, would accept even when the pod was perhaps reduced to two or three.

But these sophisticated brains, unique among animals, did recognize loss, did know sadness, did, in their way, feel. And accept though they might, they also lamented.

Now, as darkness fell, the pod disbanded. In ones and twos and threes they moved slowly apart and drew breaths through the tops of their heads, a chorus of hollow sighs; they filled their enormous lungs and dove into the darkness. Instinct drove them north, and north they would go, until months from now the planet's rhythms shifted and sent them south again.

Mother and calf dove as one; only a few months ago, this

would have been impossible. When the calf was younger, its lungs were still developing, and they had lacked the capacity to sustain an hour-long dive into the deep. But now the calf was two years old, had grown to twenty-five feet long and more than twenty tons of weight. The teeth in its lower jaw had erupted into pointed cones efficient for gripping and scooping. The calf had ceased to nurse and now it fed on live prey.

As they dove in the black water, propelling themselves with powerful sweeps of their horizontal tails, from their blunt foreheads they emitted the pings and clicks of sonar impulses that, on return, would identify prey.

THE CREATURE HUNG in the dark, doing nothing, anticipating nothing, fearing nothing, letting itself be carried by the current. Its arms and whips floated loose, undulating like snakes; its fins barely moved, yet kept it stable.

Suddenly it was struck a blow, and another, and what passed for hearing in the creature registered a sharp and penetrating ping. Its arms withdrew, its whips coiled and cocked.

Its enemy was coming.

THE SONAR RETURN was unmistakable: prey. The mother thrust downward with her tail, accelerating, pulling away from her calf as she drove herself ever deeper.

The calf strove to keep up, and with its striving—though as yet it had no sense of this, felt no urgency—it was consuming oxygen too fast.

Though the prey was already located and had made no effort to escape, the mother's brain fired sonar missiles again and again, for it had determined that this was to be the calf's first mature kill. The prey was large and must be stunned by sonar hammers before the calf could set upon it.

BESIEGED, THE CREATURE recoiled. Chemical triggers fired, nourishing the flesh, galvanizing it and streaking it with luminescence. As if in contradiction of the color display, other reflexes voided a sac within the body cavity, flushing a cloud of black ink into the black water.

Blows struck it again and again, pounding the flesh, confusing the small brain.

Defense impulse changed to attack impulse. It turned to fight.

As THE MOTHER closed in on the prey, she slowed, permitting the calf to draw even, then to pass her. She unleashed a final burst of sonar blows, then swerved and began to circle the prey.

The calf plunged downward, excited by the prospect of the kill, impelled by a million years of imprinting.

It opened its mouth.

THE CREATURE FELT the pressure wave, was driven backward by it. The enemy was upon it.

It lashed out with its whips. They flailed blindly, then found flesh, hard and slick. Automatically they surrounded it and their circles fastened to it and their hooks dug in.

The muscles in the whips tightened, drawing the enemy to the creature and the creature to the enemy, like two boxers in a clinch.

THE CALF CLOSED its mouth on . . . nothing. It was perplexed. Something was wrong. It felt pressure behind its head, confining it, slowing its movement.

It struggled, pumping with its tail, corkscrewing, frantic to rid itself of whatever was holding it down.

Now its lungs began to send out signals of need.

THE MOTHER CIRCLED, alarmed, sensing danger to her calf but incapable of helping it. She knew aggression, she knew defense, but in the programming of her brain there was no code for response to a threat to another, even to her own offspring. She made noises—high-pitched, desperate and futile.

THE CREATURE HELD on, anchored to its enemy. The enemy thrashed, and from its motion the creature sensed a change in the balance of the battle: No longer was its enemy the aggressor; it was trying to escape.

Though here in the absence of light there were no colors, the chemicals in the body of the beast changed their composition from defense to attack.

The more its enemy struggled to rise, the more the creature drew water into its body and expelled it through the funnel beneath its belly, forcing itself and its enemy down into the abyss.

THE CALF WAS drowning. Deprived of oxygen, the musculature in its tissue shut down bit by bit. An unknown agony coursed through its lungs. Its brain began to die.

It stopped struggling.

THE CREATURE FELT its enemy stop struggling and begin to sink. Though it still clutched the flesh, gradually the creature released the tension and let itself fall with its kill, slowly spiraling.

The whips tore away a chunk of blubber and fed it to the arms, which passed it back to the snapping protuberant beak.

THE MOTHER, CIRCLING, followed her calf with sonar pings. She sent clicks and whistles of distress, a bleat of helpless despair.

At last her lungs, too, were exhausted, and, with a final sonic burst, she thrust up toward the life-giving air above.

17

MARCUS SHARP SAT on the beach and wished he were somewhere else. He couldn't remember the last time he had gone to a beach, probably not since the times with Karen. He didn't like beaches much; he didn't like sitting on sand and watching water while his skin fried in the tropical sun. A misguided impulse, born of desperate frustration, had led him to jump on his motorbike and drive the fifteen miles from the base to Horseshoe Bay.

It was a Saturday; he was off duty and had hoped to go diving with Whip Darling. But when he had called at eight that morning, Darling had told him that he and Mike intended to chip paint all day. Sharp had offered to help, but Darling had said no, they'd be working in a tight hold in the stern of the boat, nowhere near big enough for three people.

Sharp had read for an hour and then, at eleven o'clock, had found himself scanning the titles in the video store. He had looked at his watch and realized, with a feeling of depression bordering on nausea, that in order to get through the rest of Saturday he would have to rent not one, not two, but at least three movies.

This is your life? he had said to himself. Deciding between *National Lampoon's Christmas Vacation* and *Look Who's Talking*? Is all that's left to you a choice between spending your time with an infantile adult or a smart-ass infant? What would Karen say? She'd say, Live, Marcus. Go rob a bank, fly a plane, trim your toenails, *any*thing. Just do *some*thing!

He had walked out of the video store and tried to find a

tennis game, but all the tennis players he knew were playing soccer, and he didn't like the game: It was all technique with little result; he liked high-scoring games. He had called a couple of dive-tour operators; the boats had all left for the day. He had volunteered to take a helicopter up; none was available.

So he had gone to the beach, impelled, he guessed, by some vague hope that he might meet a girl worth talking to, having lunch with, maybe even making a date with to go dancing. Not that he knew how to dance, but anything was better than sitting around the Bachelor Officers Quarters watching reruns of *Cagney & Lacey*.

It had been a mistake. As he sat on the beach and watched children frolic in the wave wash and couples stroll along and families picnic under palm trees, he had felt more and more lonely, more and more hopeless. He wondered if there were any singles clubs on the island. Maybe he should become a lush and join Alcoholics Anonymous, just for the company.

He had seen two girls with potential, American tourists, pretty and vivacious, wearing bikinis brief enough to stir interest but not so brief as to announce that they were on the prowl. They had even stopped and spoken to him. Why, he wasn't certain; possibly because he looked safe: thirtyish, and obviously not a self-styled stud, what with his workingman's tan—all white except for his arms and face. One had fair skin and red hair, the other was deeply tanned and raven-haired.

He had wanted to talk to them; his mind had flooded with conversational gambits—the navy, helicopters, shipwrecks, diving, Bermuda. But he was out of practice in the dating game, and after he had answered their questions about moderately priced restaurants in Hamilton, he had let them get away. Within five minutes, of course, he had thought of several stratagems that might have intrigued them, and he cursed himself as a dim-witted fool.

Perhaps they'd go in the water, and he'd have a second chance. He'd go in nearby and, as the locals would say, have a go at chatting them up.

Then he thought: Why bother? What would it accomplish? He didn't feel driven by his glands. He didn't feel driven by anything.

And that, brother, he had concluded, is your problem.

Sharp looked at the water and saw, a hundred yards off-shore, a wind-surfer trying valiantly to catch a puff of breeze and sail a few feet. But there was no breeze, so he kept top-pling over backward and dragging the sail down on top of him.

Sharp wondered how deep the water was out where the guy was wind-surfing. Whatever had destroyed that boat and killed the divers was in deep water.

Sharp found it interesting that there had been no panic, especially after the paper had quoted that dippy woman word for word and included all her idiotic claims about a sea mon-ster. People were still swimming, still sailing, still wind-surf-ing. He had been in his teens when *Jaws* had swept the States, and he had vivid memories of parents refusing to let their children get their feet wet, of beaches being closed and of otherwise rational adults declining to swim in water over their heads . . . in lakes.

Perhaps the current lack of panic could be attributed to lack of knowledge. No one knew what kind of thing might be out there, but it wasn't a shark and it wasn't a whale, so there wasn't even credible speculation. Sharp suspected that Whip would have an idea, but Whip wasn't a man to make guesses. Guesses, Whip would say, were a waste of time and energy.

Sharp was hungry, and so he got to his feet and started toward the concession stand. He was about to turn into the trees when he saw the two American girls. They were tying their hair back with rubber bands. They saw him watching them, and they waved at him, ran into the water and began to swim.

Okay, he thought, what the hell. . . . He'd wait till they stopped swimming, then he'd go in and swim out to them and try to think of something clever to say.

When they were thirty or forty yards offshore, the girls stopped and treaded water. Their heads were three or four feet apart, and they were talking and laughing.

Sharp walked down to the water's edge. He saw one of the girls wave, and he waved back.

The girl waved again, with both hands, and then she disap-peared underwater, and now the other one was waving, too, and shouting. No, not shouting, Sharp realized. Screaming.

"Omigod," he said, and he took a couple of running steps and dove into waist-deep water and swam, sprinting. He churned the water, breathing only every third or fourth stroke.

He looked up to get his bearings; he was almost there. He saw the redheaded girl flailing and shrieking, and every time she raised her arms out of the water she'd sink. The other girl was trying to get to her, to get under her windmilling arms, to grab her and stop her hysterics.

Sharp swam up behind the redhead and pinned her arms to her sides and wrapped his arms around her and leaned back, kicking to keep himself afloat and her head out of water. He looked for the shark, the barracuda, the man-o'-war. He looked for blood.

"I've got you," he said. "You're okay. Calm down, it's okay."

The girl's shrieks were subsiding now into sobs.

"Are you hurt? What happened?"

The other girl said, "She just all of a sudden started screaming and waving her arms."

Sharp felt the girl relax, and he released his grip and put a hand under her back to keep her afloat.

"Something . . ." she said.

"Bit you?" Sharp asked.

". . . horrible and slimy and gross . . ."

"What, stung you?"

"No, it . . ." She rolled over and clung to Sharp, weeping and almost sinking him.

Sharp said, "Let's get you to shore." He took one of her arms, and gestured for the other girl to take the other arm. Together they sidestroked toward shore, holding the girl between them. Soon they could touch bottom.

The girl said, "I'm okay. I just . . . it was . . ." She looked at Sharp and, trying to smile, said, "Thanks."

"Back in a minute," Sharp said, and he turned toward deep water and swam an easy breaststroke. When he gauged that he had reached the spot where the girls had been, he stopped swimming and spun in a slow circle, searching the water. He didn't know what he was looking for. Box jellyfish didn't exist in Bermuda; there were no sea wasps. Besides, the girl was unhurt, just scared. There were Portuguese men-o'-war, but they were unmistakable: Their purple bladders floated on the surface. He supposed there were big, harmless jellyfish that hung under the surface, but she'd have seen them, parts of them would have stuck to her.

He started for the shore, slowly, breaststroking, and then his hand touched something; he jerked upward, backpedaled. He looked at the water where his hand had been. There, a foot underwater, was something creamy white and roundish, about the size of a watermelon. Gingerly, he reached forward and touched it. It was slimy, ragged, pulpy. It felt like rotten meat. He put his hand under it. The underside was hard and slick. He brought it to the surface, and as soon as the air touched it, his nostrils were assailed by a vile smell of putre-faction that made his eyes water.

It wasn't meat, it was fat. Blubber. Pinkish white and shredded.

He rolled it over. The skin side was blue-black and newly scarred, near the middle, with a circle, five or six inches across, of what looked like cuts. In the center of the circle was a single deep gash that went all the way through the skin and into the blubber. On one of the edges was half of another circle.

"Sweet Jesus . . ." Sharp said.

Pushing the thing ahead of him, he swam to shore.

On the beach, the children were gathered around some-thing that had washed up. They were prodding it with a stick and pushing one another toward it and saying "Yuk!" and "Gross!"

Sharp looked at it and realized that it was another piece of blubber, smaller, with two half-circles, one on either end.

As he turned away, a parent came up to the children and saw what they had and said, "Holy shit!" and then called, "Hey, Nelson, come looka this!"

Sharp held the thing as far away from his face as he could. The girls were sitting together, the redhead wrapped in a towel, the other's arm around her shoulder.

"She's okay," said the dark-haired girl, smiling and adding,

"We want to thank you. Can we—" The breeze carried the stench of Sharp's prize to her. "What's *that*?"

"Gotta go," Sharp said. He scooped up his towel, wrapped the blubber in it, put on his sunglasses and walked up to the lot where he had left his motorbike.

18

DARLING AND MIKE were on their knees in the after hold of the *Privateer*, sanding away the rough edges around the paint they had chipped. They wore surgical masks to keep the paint dust out of their lungs, and goggles to protect their eyes.

Darling had owned the boat for six years, and the hull had held up well. There weren't any significant leaks, even around the stuffing box, but the hold trapped humidity, and humidity and salt air eventually ate through everything.

He was in a foul mood. He hated chipping paint, would much prefer to have let the yard do it when the boat was hauled out for bottom-painting in the fall. But the yard was charging forty dollars per man-hour, and Darling was beginning to wonder if he'd even be able to afford to have the boat pulled up on the slip so *he* could paint the bottom.

He felt the boat dip slightly as a weight came aboard, heard footsteps on the deck above. He looked up and saw Sharp standing by the open hatch. "Hey, Marcus . . ."

"Sorry to interrupt."

"Don't be. I'd welcome Lucifer himself to get me away from this godforsaken work."

"Could you look at something for me?"

"You bet." Darling removed his mask and goggles and started up the ladder.

Mike kept sanding until Darling said, "Come look, Michael boy. Don't miss a chance for a breather."

Sharp had set the bundle on a cutting table amidships and was standing away from it, to avoid the smell.

As Darling approached, the stench hit him, and he said, "Christ, lad! What you brung me, something dead?"

"Very," Sharp said, and he told Darling what had happened at Horseshoe Bay.

Darling held an end of the towel while Mike unrolled it. Flies materialized from nowhere, and two gulls that had been sitting on the water rose up and began to circle over the boat.

"Whale," Mike said.

Darling nodded. "Young, too."

"What tells you that?" Sharp asked.

"The blubber's thin; he hasn't got his full ration yet. See how it goes to pink after a few inches?"

Mike said, "Sperm whale?"

"I warrant."

"Prop got him?"

"No," Sharp said. "Turn it over."

Darling used a knife blade to flip the blubber. In the direct sunlight, the circle of marks shone like a necklace, and putrid flesh was oozing out of the slash in the center.

Mike and Darling looked at each other, then Darling said softly, "Son of a bitch . . ." He walked into the cabin, reached up on a shelf for something, then came back holding an amber-colored crescent claw. He slid the claw into the slash in the blue-black skin. It fit perfectly.

"Son of a bitch . . ." he said again.

Sharp said, "What is it, Whip? What did this?"

"I hope it isn't what I think it is," Darling said.

"What?"

Darling pointed to the blubber and said to Mike, "Drop that mess over the side, let the breams have a feed." Then he turned to Sharp. "Come on."

"Where to?"

"Need to consult a book or two."

As Darling led the way up the path to his house, he noticed his daughter's car in the driveway. "Dana's here," he said. "Wonder what about."

Sharp had never been inside Darling's house before, and he looked quickly around. It was a classic eighteenth-century Bermuda house, built like an upside-down ship. Sturdy wooden knees supported the ceilings; twelve-by-twelve beams braced the walls. The chests, cabinets, tables and floors were all of wide-board Bermuda cedar, relics of the days before the blight that killed all the cedar trees. The rooms were cool and dark and redolent of the rich spiciness of cedar.

The two women sitting in the dining room jumped when they saw Darling in the doorway.

The younger woman—tanned and sharp-featured, with sun-bleached hair—quickly shuffled the papers on the table before her, covering some with others.

Darling didn't seem to notice. He said, "Hey, Lizard," and went to her and kissed her on the cheek. "What brings you up here?"

"Plotting and planning," she said. "What else?"

"That's the way, keep the bastards at bay. You know Marcus Sharp? Marcus, this is Dana."

"Know *of* you," said Dana, and she smiled and shook Sharp's hand.

"Nice to meet you," Sharp said. He thought Dana looked uneasy, awkward. She kept her back to the table, blocking the pile of papers.

Darling led Sharp through the living room to a small room beyond, lined with bookcases and furnished only with a huge cedar desk and two chairs.

"I should be ashamed," Darling said as he turned on a light.

"Why?"

"Putting my faith in science. The only thing scientists admit is what they know. What they don't know—what might be, all the stuff in the realm of the possible but unproven—they dismiss as myth."

Sharp let his eyes scan the titles on the shelves. It seemed that every book ever written about the sea was here, from Rachel Carson to Jacques Cousteau, Samuel Eliot Morison to Mendel Peterson, Peter Freuchen to Peter Matthiessen. And not only books about the sea, but books on coins, ceramics, glassware, shipwrecks, treasure, weaponry.

"Now let's see." Darling pulled a large cased volume from a shelf, and read the title aloud: *"Mysteries of the Sea."* He removed the case, and opened the book.

"About ten years ago," he said as he leafed through the

pages, "I was on a boat in the Sea of Cortez with some aquarium people from California, helping them gather strange critters. One night, we saw some Mexicans fishing with lights, and we cruised over to have a look. They were jigging for big squid. Humboldt squid, four or five feet long, fifty or sixty pounds. I'd never seen the big ones before, so I decided to get in the water with them. As soon as my mask cleared, one of the bastards made a run at me. I swatted at him, and faster than I could believe, one of his whips shot out and grabbed my wrist. I thought a hundred needles were stabbing me. I punched him in the eye, and he let go, and I started up, figuring this wasn't a healthy place to be. Then all of a sudden I felt myself being dragged down. *Three* of the goddam things had me, and they were yanking me down into the gloom. I tell you, the Lord must have a special place in His heart for stupid Bermudians, 'cause everything they grabbed broke away: one of my flippers, my depth gauge, a collecting bag. I took off for the surface. For some reason, they didn't chase me, and I got back on the boat. But I had nightmares for a month."

"Jesus," Sharp said.

Darling turned a page, then said, "There," and pushed the book toward Sharp.

"What's *that*?" Sharp asked as he stared at the picture on the page. It was a nineteenth-century woodcut of a hideous creature, a prehistoric-looking beast with a huge bulbous body that ended in a tail shaped like an arrowhead. It had eight writhing arms, two whips twice the length of the body and two gigantic eyes. In the picture, the beast was rising up out of the sea and destroying a sailing ship. Bodies were flying from the wreckage, and a woman, her eyes wide with terror, was hanging from the creature's beak.

"That," Whip said, "is the granddaddy of the critter that grabbed me. It's *Architeuthis dux*, the oceanic giant squid."

"Talk about nightmares. It can't be real . . . can it?"

"It's real, all right, rare but real." Darling paused. "In fact, Marcus, it's more than real. It's out there now. It's here."

Sharp looked at Darling. "Come on, Whip. . . ." he said.

"You don't believe me?" Darling said. "Okay. Maybe you'll believe Herman Melville." He reached up and pulled out a copy of *Moby-Dick*, and flipped through the pages until he found the one he wanted. Then he read aloud: " '. . . we now gazed at the most wondrous phenomenon which the secret seas have hitherto revealed to mankind. A vast pulpy mass, furlongs in length and breadth, of a glancing cream-color, lay floating on the water, innumerable long arms radiating from its centre, and curling and twisting like a nest of anacondas, as if blindly to clutch at any object within reach.' "

As Darling closed the book, Sharp said, "Whip, *Moby-Dick* is fiction."

"Not altogether. The whale is fact, based on a real incident that happened to a ship called the *Essex.*"

"Still . . ."

"You want facts? Okay, we'll find you facts." Darling pulled out another book, and squinted as he read the faded lettering on the spine. "The Last Dragon," he said, "by Herbert Talley, Ph.D. This should do it." Years before, he had turned pages down as marks, and he opened the book to the first mark. "Giant squid have been written about since the sixteenth century, maybe even earlier. You've heard the word *kraken?* It's Swedish for 'uprooted tree.' That's what people thought the monsters looked like, with all those tentacles snaking around like roots. Nowadays, scientists like the word *cephalopod,* which is a pretty good description."

"Why?" asked Sharp. "What's it mean?"

" 'Head-footed.' It's 'cause their arms, what people thought were their feet, spring right out from their head." He turned to another mark. "Here, Marcus," he said. "One of the buggers came up in the Indian Ocean and dragged down a schooner called the *Pearl,* just like in that woodcut. Killed everybody. There were more than a hundred witnesses." Darling slapped the book. "Damn," he said. "I can't believe I didn't figure this out sooner. It's so obvious. There's *nothing* else that could have torn up our gear like that. Nothing else. No shark that's ever swum is big enough and mean enough to break a thirty-eight-foot boat into splinters." He paused. "And nothing else is so all-out, bone-deep evil."

"But, Whip. Look at the date." Sharp pointed at the book. "Eighteen seventy-four. That's not today."

"Marcus, those marks on the whale skin, you saw for yourself." Darling took one of the claws from his pocket and held it up. "What kind of beast has knives like that?" Darling felt a growing sense of urgency. Suppose he was right. Suppose what was out there was a giant squid. What could they possibly do? Catch it? Hardly. Kill it? How? But if they didn't kill it, what could they do—what could anybody do—to get rid of it?

He pulled more books down from the shelf, handed a few to Sharp, then sat on the couch and opened one. "Read," he said. "We better learn everything we can about this beast."

They pored through Darling's books about the sea. The references to giant squid were sketchy and often contradictory, some experts claiming that the animals grew no bigger than fifty or sixty feet long, others insisting that hundred-footers, or bigger, swam in all the oceans of the world. Some said that the sucker disks of giant squid contained teeth and hooks; some said they contained one or the other; some said neither. Some said that they had photophores in their flesh, which made them glow with bioluminescence; some said they didn't.

"Nobody can agree about anything," Sharp said after he had read for a while. "That's the bad news. The good news is that all the recorded attacks on people took place in the last century."

"No," said Darling, and he passed the Talley book to Sharp. "With this beast, it looks like there is no good news."

Sharp glanced at the open page. "Shit," he said. "Nineteen forty-one?"

"And not far from here, either. Twelve torpedoed sailors in a lifeboat. It was overloaded, and a couple of them had to hang overboard. The first night, in pitch-darkness, there was a scream, and one of the men was gone. Second night, same thing. So now they all crowded into the boat. The third night, they heard a scratching noise on the gunwale, and they smelled something. Well, it seems that the giant squid that had been following them—staying down during the day and coming up at night—was feeling around with one of his whips. It touched one of the men, snapped around him fast as lightning and hauled him overboard. Now they knew what it was, and the next night they were ready for it, so when the whip came up and started hunting, they jumped on it and cut it off, but not before one of the men got beat up pretty bad.

The squid went away, never came back. The guy who got beat up, they found he'd had pieces of flesh torn away the size of an American quarter. They figure the animal was . . . what?"

Sharp ran his finger down the page. "Twenty-three feet," he said. "The size of a big station wagon."

Darling thought for a moment, then said, "How big would you say those marks on that whale skin were?"

"Five inches?"

"Judas Priest." Darling stood up. "This goddam squid may be as big as a blue whale."

"A blue whale!" Sharp said. "For crissakes, Whip, that's twice as big as your boat. It's bigger than a goddam dinosaur. A blue whale's the biggest animal that's ever been."

"In body mass, yes, but maybe not in length. And sure as hell not in nastiness."

As THEY HEADED back outside, they passed the dining room, and Charlotte looked up and said, "Whip, what's this about a giant squid?"

"Giant squid? What are you, some kind of psychic?"

"It was on the radio just now. Somebody found something on a beach, and one of the scientists at the aquarium said—"

"Yes, Charlie," Darling said. "It looks like we've got ourselves a giant squid."

"They're having a big meeting about it tomorrow night. Down at the lodge hall. Fishermen, divers, sailboat types. The whole island's in an uproar."

"I don't wonder."

"How big is a thing like that?"

"Big."

"William," Charlotte said, and she rose from the table and came over and took Darling's arm. "Promise me."

"Come on, Charlie. Nobody but a horse's ass would make a run at a beast like that."

"Like Liam St. John, for instance."

"What do you mean?"

"St. John said on the radio that he's going to catch it. To save Bermuda. He says he and what he called his 'people' know how to do it."

"Fat bloody chance," Darling said. "Dr. St. John's gonna end up in the belly of the beast, and good riddance." He leaned over and kissed her and looked beyond at the pile of papers on the table. "What are you girls doing, taking over General Motors?"

"Nothing," Charlotte said, and she kissed him back. "Go away." She started toward the table, stopped and said, "You had a call."

"Who from? What'd they want?"

"They didn't say. Foreigners. The one I talked to sounded Canadian. They just wanted to know if you were available."

"Available for what?" Darling said. "Never mind, I can guess. If they call again, you can tell 'em I *was* available, until about ten minutes ago. Now, all of a sudden, I think I've retired."

19

WHAT A JOKE, Darling thought as he left the lodge hall. They had called it an island forum, but it had really been nothing but a charade, a vehicle for the premier, Solomon Tucker, to show the citizenry that he was concerned, without ever having to do anything. Not that there was anything anybody could do; but the premier hadn't gone so far as to admit that: Like most politicians, he'd retreated from here to Christmas, without actually surrendering.

Everybody had been allowed to blow off steam and offer cockamamy suggestions for dealing with a monster that few people had ever heard of and nobody had ever seen. Now, if things calmed down and returned to normal, old Solly could credit "democracy in action"; if things got worse, he could lay off at least half the blame on the people, who had been asked to participate but hadn't had any solutions. He was a winner either way.

Darling took a deep breath of night air and decided to walk home. It was only a couple of miles, and he needed the exercise after sitting for two hours. He figured the meeting would go on for at least another hour, with people squabbling over how to phrase the warnings that would have to be issued.

It was probably too late to worry. Thanks to Liam St. John and his everlasting crusade for personal publicity, this morning's paper had carried the headline MONSTER IS GIANT SQUID, ST. JOHN CONFIRMS. By now, that news would be burning up the wires all around the world.

Some people had voiced the hope that the Newport-to-Bermuda race, which was already under way, wouldn't be affected, but the part of it that benefited Bermuda already had been. Hotel reservations were down; caterers were finding themselves with no affairs to cater; taxi drivers were sitting idle, playing cribbage on the hoods of their cabs.

Even Darling himself had managed to lose a pile of money he didn't have. Halfway through the meeting, Ernest Chambers, the diver who had offered Darling charter work during the race layover, had jumped to his feet and announced that two-thirds of his dive trips had been canceled, and what was the government going to do about it.

Predictably, Liam St. John had waited till things seemed at an impasse before he rose from his seat in the row of cabinet ministers and, after a vain attempt to make himself appear taller than his five feet four by fluffing up his helmet of pumpkin-colored curls, asked for public support for his plan of action.

Since nobody knew enough about the monster to pass judgment on St. John's plan, a clamor had gone up to get Darling to say what he thought about it. After all, somebody had pointed out, "Whip's caught at least one of everything God ever put in the ocean around here."

And Darling had told them what he'd read, and his conclusions: that the appearance of a giant squid around Bermuda was probably a fluke, a natural accident; that since boats and human beings weren't its normal food, in all likelihood it would eventually go away; and that to set out to catch or destroy it was pointless, because in his opinion no one could do it, Dr. St. John's ambitious plan notwithstanding. In sum, Darling had said, leave it alone for a while and wait.

St. John had termed Darling's approach "do-nothing defeatism," and that had set off a new round of circular arguing.

As Darling had left, elbowing through the crowd of standees, he had heard someone mention issuing a formal Notice to Mariners, someone else suggest a press release pointing out that more people were killed every year by bee stings than by all sea creatures put together, and the premier announce the formation of a committee to explore options—to be chaired by Dr. St. John.

Darling walked along the road to Somerset, and thought

about what to do. Part of the problem with all those people, he decided, was modern times. Back in the old days, they would have accepted the advent of something like *Architeuthis* without question. The unexplainable and unpreventable were part of life, and people learned to live with them. Not anymore. People were spoiled; they couldn't accept a situation that demanded patience and offered no easy solutions.

As he came to a narrow part of the road, buttressed on both sides by high limestone walls, a car approached from behind. He stepped off the pavement and backed against the wall to let the car pass, but as it passed him, it slowed and stopped just ahead.

Now what? he thought. He looked at the trunk of the car and saw a BMW insignia. Somebody rich . . . and foolish: In a country with a speed limit of 20 mph, a BMW wasn't transportation, it was a trophy.

A man got out of the passenger's side and started back toward him. "Captain Darling?" he said.

Darling saw a tweed jacket and tan-colored pants and low-topped walking boots, but he couldn't see the man's face. "Do I know you?" he said.

"My name is Dr. Herbert Talley, Captain."

Talley, Darling thought. Talley. There was something familiar about that name, but he couldn't place it. "Doctor of what?"

"Malac— . . . well, squid, Captain. Doctor of squid, you could say."

"You don't have to talk down to me. I know the word 'malacology.'"

"Sorry. Of course. Could we give you a lift home?"

"I'm happy to walk," Darling said, and he started around the car, but then he remembered, and he stopped and said, "Talley. Dr. Talley. You wrote that book, right? *The Last Dragon.*"

Talley smiled and said, "Yes. I did."

"Good book. Full of facts. At least, I took 'em for facts."

"Thank you. Ah . . . Captain . . . we'd like to talk to you. Could you spare us a few minutes?"

"Talk about what?"

"About *Architeuthis.*"

An alarm bell rang in the back of Darling's brain: This must be the man who had telephoned. Charlotte had said he sounded Canadian, and Talley's pronunciation of the word 'about,' as if it were 'a boat,' was a dead giveaway. He said, "I've said all I have to say."

"Perhaps you could listen, then, just for a few minutes . . . a drink?"

"Who's 'we'?"

Talley gestured toward the car. "Mr. Osborn Manning." When Darling said nothing, seeming not to register, Talley said, "Manning . . . the father of the—"

"Oh yeah. Sorry."

"We . . . he . . . we would appreciate a word with you."

Darling hesitated, wishing Charlotte were with him. He wasn't good at fencing with slick people. On the other hand, he didn't want to be rude, not to a man who had just lost both his children. What would *he* feel like if Dana were eaten by some . . . thing? He couldn't imagine and didn't want to try. Finally, he said, "No harm, I guess."

"Fine," Talley said, holding open the back door of the car. "There's a nice hotel around the—"

Darling shook his head. "Go up the road a hundred yards, pull in under a sign that says 'Shilly's.' I'll meet you there."

"We'll drive you."

"I'll walk." Darling stepped around the car.

"But—"

"Shilly's," Darling said, and kept walking.

Shilly's had once been a one-pump gas station; then, in succession, a discotheque, a boutique and a video-rental store. Now it was a one-room restaurant, owned by a retired shark fisherman. It advertised itself as "the home of Bermuda's famous conch fritters," which was a local joke since Bermuda's conchs had been fished out years ago. If pressured, Shilly would serve a patron something he called fried fish, but he made his living purveying cheap booze. The skeleton of the old gas pump still stood in the parking lot, painted purple.

Darling could have let them take him up to the hotel; he had nothing against hotels. But they would have been comfortable there, and he didn't want them to feel comfortable.

He wanted them to be on edge, and to make the conversation short and to the point.

As he turned into the parking lot, he saw that the BMW was parked between two battered vans.

He walked into Shilly's and stood for a moment, letting his eyes adjust to the darkness. He smelled stale beer and cigarette smoke and the spicy, sweet aroma of marijuana. A dozen men crowded around the snooker table, shouting and placing bets. A few others argued over an ancient pinball machine. They were hard men, all of them, with short fuses. Every one was black.

There were several empty tables near the door, but Talley and Manning were standing together in a corner, as if they had been sent there as punishment by a teacher.

An enormous man, black as a Haitian and broad as a linebacker, slid off a barstool and ambled over to Darling. "Whip . . ." he said.

"Shilly . . ."

"They with you?" Shilly tipped his head toward the corner.

"They are."

"Good enough." Shilly lumbered to the corner and let his face crack into a grin. "Gentlemen," he said, "please be seated." He pulled a chair out from the nearest table and held it for Manning.

When they were seated, Shilly said, "What's your pleasure?"

Manning said, "I'd like a Stolichnaya on the—"

"Rum or beer."

"Make it three Dark and Stormys, Shilly," Darling said.

"You got it," Shilly said, and turned back to the bar.

Darling looked at Osborn Manning, who appeared to be in his early fifties. He was impeccably tended: His nails were polished, his hair perfectly shaped. His blue suit looked as if it had been pressed while he waited to be seated. His white shirt was starched and spotless, his blue silk tie held in place by a gold pin.

But it was Manning's eyes that Darling couldn't stop looking at. In the best of times they would have seemed sunken: His forehead stopped in a shelf of bone over his eyes, and his brows were thick and dark. But now they looked like two black tunnels, as if the eyes themselves had disappeared.

Maybe it's just dark in here, Darling thought. Or maybe that's what grief does to a man.

Manning noticed Darling staring at him, and he said, "Thank you for coming."

Darling nodded and tried to think of something civil to say, but couldn't come up with anything better than, "No problem."

"Do you live nearby?" Talley asked, making conversation.

"Close enough." Darling nodded at the north wall. "Across Mangrove Bay."

Shilly brought the drinks, and Talley took a gulp and said, "Splendid." Darling watched Manning's reaction as he took a sip: He winced but suppressed a grimace. To a mouth used to vodka and ice, Darling thought, rum and ginger beer must taste like anchovies with peanut butter.

There was an awkward silence then, as if Talley and Manning didn't know how to begin. Darling had a fair notion of what they wanted of him, and he had to force himself to resist the temptation to tell them to cut to the chase, get to the bottom line. But he didn't want to seem eager; over the years, he had made quite a few dollars by keeping his mouth shut and listening. At the very least, he always learned something.

Manning sat stiffly, his suit coat buttoned, his hands folded in front of him, and stared at the light of the single candle on the table.

What the hell, Darling thought, no harm in being polite. He said to Manning, "Sorry about your youngsters."

"Yes," was all Manning said.

"I can't imagine what . . . we have a daughter . . . it must be . . ." He didn't know what else to say, so he shut up.

Manning looked away from the candle and raised his head toward them. His eyes still seemed hidden back in their caves.

"No you can't, Captain. You can't imagine. Not till it happens to you." Manning shifted in his seat. "You know the worst feeling I ever had up to then? It was when they were applying to college. It was the first time my children were ever threatened by something I couldn't protect them from. Their lives, their futures, were in the hands of strangers I had no

control over. I've never felt so frustrated in my life. One day I
found I was losing the sight in one eye. I went to doctors, had
all manner of tests, nothing was wrong. But I *was* losing the
sight in that eye. Then I was playing squash with a friend, and
I told him about it—an excuse, I suppose, for why I was losing
so badly—and he said that when his kids had applied to college, he had developed ulcerative colitis. What I had was hysterical blindness. As soon as they were accepted into schools,
it went away. I swore then that nothing like that would ever
happen again." He squeezed his hands together and shook his
head. "You want to know what the feeling is like? I feel like
I'm dead."

Talley took another gulp of his drink and said, "Captain
Darling, we liked what you said at the meeting."

"You were there? Why?"

"In the back of the room. We wanted to see how people are
reacting to all this."

"That's easy," Darling said. "They're scared to death. One
step short of panic. They see their world being threatened by
something they can't even understand, much less do anything
about."

"But you're not . . . scared, I mean."

"You heard what I said back there. It's like anything else
big and awful in nature. You leave it alone, it'll leave you
alone." He thought of Manning's children, and added, "Generally . . . as a rule."

"That doctor back there. St. John . . . he's a fool."

"That's one way to put it."

"But there is something I disagree with you on. What's
happening here is not an accident."

"What is it, then?"

Darling saw Talley glance at Manning, then Talley said,
"Tell me, Captain, what do you know about *Architeuthis*?"

"What I read, what you wrote, other stuff. Not a whole
lot."

"What do you *think* about it?"

Darling paused. "Whenever I hear talk about monsters," he
said, "I think about *Jaws*. People forget *Jaws* was fiction,
which is another word for . . . well, you know, B.S. As soon
as that picture came out, every boat captain from here to

Long Island and down to South Australia started fantasizing about thirty- and forty- and fifty-foot white sharks. My rule is, when someone tells me about a critter as big as a tractor-trailer truck, I right away cut a third or a half off what he says."

"Sound," said Talley, "very sound. But—"

"But," Darling said, "with this beast, seems to me when you hear stories about him, the smart thing to do is not cut anything off. The smart thing to do is double 'em."

"Exactly!" Talley said. His eyes were bright, and he leaned toward Darling, as if pleased to have discovered a kindred spirit. "I told you I'm a malacologist, but my specialty is teuthology . . . squid . . . specifically *Architeuthis*. I've spent my life studying them. I've used computers, made graphs, dissected tissue, smelled it, tasted it—"

"*Tasted* it? What's it taste like?"

"Ammonia."

"Ever seen a live one?"

"No. Have you?"

"Never," Darling said. "And I'd like to keep it that way."

"The more I studied, the more I realized how little anybody knows about the giant squid. Nobody knows how big they grow, how old they get, why they strand sometimes and wash up dead . . . not even how many species there are: People say three, some say nineteen. It's a classic example of the old saw The more you know, the more you realize how little you really know." Talley stopped, looking embarrassed, and said, "Sorry. I get carried away. I can cut this short if you—"

"Go on," said Manning. "Captain Darling has to know."

They're setting me up, Darling thought: They're trolling for me, teasing me like I was a hungry marlin.

"I have a theory," Talley said, "as good as most and better than some. Up to the middle of the last century, nobody quite believed in the existence of *Architeuthis*, or of *any* giant squid. The few sightings were dismissed as the rantings of sailors gone mad. All of a sudden in the 1870s there was a rash of sightings and strandings and even attacks on boats, and—"

"I read about them," Darling said.

"The point is, there were so many witnesses that for the first time people believed them. Then it all stopped again, until the early 1900s, when, for no reason, there were more sightings and strandings. I wondered if there was a pattern, so I collected reports of every sighting and every stranding, and I fed them into the computer with all the data on major weather events, current shifts and so forth, and I told the computer to find some rhyme or reason to it.

"The computer's answer was that the pattern of sightings and strandings coincided with cyclical fluctuations in branches of the Labrador Current, the big cold-water funnel that sweeps up the whole Atlantic coast. For most of the cycle, *Architeuthis* is never seen, alive or dead. But in the first few years of the change, for whatever reason—water temperature, food supply, I don't pretend to know—the beast shows up."

"How long are the cycles?" Darling asked.

"Thirty years."

"And the last one began in . . ." He knew the answer before the words were out of his mouth.

"Nineteen sixty . . . ran through sixty-two."

"I see."

"Yes," Talley said. "You do see. It's here because it's time." Talley leaned forward, his hands on the table. "But the truth is, I can give you a volume of facts, and document them for you, and not for a second can I tell you *why* they're so. Some people think *Architeuthis* may get trapped in warm-water currents and suffocate for lack of oxygen and die and wash ashore. Other people think it could be *cold* water that gets him, water less than, say, minus ten degrees centigrade. Nobody knows."

This man, Darling thought, is in love with giant squid. "Doc," he said, "this is all very interesting, but it doesn't say a lick about why the beast is suddenly eating people."

"But it does!" Talley said, and he leaned farther forward. "*Architeuthis* is what we call an adventitious feeder. He feeds by accident, he eats whatever's there. His normal diet—I've looked in their stomachs—is sharks, rays, big fish. But he'll eat *any*thing. Let's say that cyclical currents are bringing him up from the two-, three-thousand-foot level where he usually stays. And let's say he's finding that his usual food sources are gone. You'd know about this, Captain. From what I hear, Bermuda's almost fished out. And let's say all he's finding to eat is—"

There was a sharp *snap!* that sounded like a rifle shot, and something flew past Darling's face.

Osborn Manning had been clutching his plastic swizzle stick so hard that it shattered. "Sorry," he said. "Excuse me."

"No," said Talley. *"I'm* sorry. Lord . . ."

"Doc," Darling said after a pause, "there's one thing you haven't talked about—Nature's number one rule, balance. When there get to be too many sea lions, up jump the white sharks to keep 'em down. When there get to be too many people, up jumps some plague like the Black Death. Seems to me, this critter being around here is saying nature's out of whack. Why?"

"I have a theory," Talley said. "Nature's not out of whack, people have *put* nature out of whack. There's only one animal that preys on *Architeuthis,* and that's the sperm whale. Man has been killing off the sperm whales—they could already be practically extinct. So it's possible that more and more giant squid are surviving, and now they're showing up. Here."

"You mean you think there's more than *one?*"

"I don't know. My guess is not, because there's not enough food to support more than one. But I could be wrong."

More questions crowded into Darling's mind, more theories swam around and tried to coalesce. Suddenly he realized that he was taking the bait, and he forced himself to back off, to prevent Talley from setting a hook in him.

He made a show of looking at his watch, then pushed his chair back from the table. "It's late," he said, "and I get up early."

"Ah . . . Captain . . . ," Talley said, ". . . the thing is, this animal can be caught."

Darling shook his head. "No one ever has."

"Well, no, not a true *Architeuthis.* Not alive."

"What makes you think you can?"

"I know we can."

"Why in God's name do you want to?"

Talley started. *"Why?* Why *not?* It's unique. It's—"

Manning interrupted. "Captain Darling," he said, "this . . . this creature, this beast . . . it killed my children. My only children. It has destroyed my life . . . our lives. My wife has been sedated since . . . she tried to—"

"Mr. Manning," Darling said. "This beast is just an animal. It—"

"It is a sentient being. Dr. Talley has told me . . . and I believe . . . that it knows a form of rage, it knows vengeance. Well, so do I. Believe me. So do I."

"It's still just an animal. You can't take revenge on an animal."

"Yes I can."

"But why? What good will it—"

"It's something I can do. Would you have me sit back and blame fate and say, 'That's the way it goes'? I will not. I will kill this beast."

"No you won't. All you'll succeed in doing is—"

Talley said, "Captain, we can. It *can* be caught."

"If you say so, Doctor. But leave me out of it."

Manning said, "How much do you charge for a day's charter?"

"I don't—"

"How much?"

Here we go, Darling thought. I never should have come here. "A thousand dollars," he said.

"I'll give you five thousand dollars a day, plus expenses."

When, after a moment, Darling hadn't replied, Talley said, "This isn't only personal, Captain. This animal *must* be caught."

"Why? Why not just let it go away?"

"Because you were wrong about another thing back at the meeting: It won't stop. It will go on killing people."

"Five minutes ago that was a theory, Doc. Now it's a fact, is it?"

"A probability," Talley acknowledged. "If it's found a food source, I see no reason why it will move on. And I don't believe there's a living thing out there that can stop it."

"Well, neither can I. Get someone else."

"There *is* no one else," Manning said. "Except that jackass St. John . . ."

". . . with his master plan," Talley broke in. "Does that man truly think he can catch *Architeuthis* by throwing explosives in the ocean? It's ridiculous . . . a game of blindman's bluff!"

Darling shrugged. "He'll get his name in the papers. Look, Mr. Manning, you've got all that money, you can hire yourself some big-time experts, bring in a ship."

"Don't think I didn't try. You think I want to work with you . . . with locals? I know islanders, Captain, I know Bermudians." Manning put his elbows on the table and leaned toward Darling. His voice was low, but its tone had an intensity that made it seem like a shout. "I've had a house here for years. I know all about small islands and small minds; I know how you people strut around and bray about your independence; I know what you think about foreigners. As far as you're concerned, I'm just another rich Yankee asshole."

Talley looked stricken. Darling leaned back, smiled and said to Manning, "You do have a way with words."

"I'm tired of this crap, Captain. Here's the way it is: I could have chartered a boat, there were people up and down the coast dying to come. But your pigheaded government has so many rules and regulations, so many permits and licenses, so many fees and duties, that it would have taken months to set it up. So I have to use locals, and that means using you. You're the best. As I see it, we've got only one problem, you and I, and that's money. I haven't come up with the right figure yet. Tell me, then. Tell me your price."

Darling looked at him for a long moment, then he said, "Let me tell you how *I* see it, Mr. Manning. You are rich and you are a Yankee, but I don't hold those against you. What makes you an asshole is that you think money will bring your children back. You think killing the beast will. Well, it won't. You can't buy yourself peace."

"I have to try, Captain."

"Okay," Darling said. "You've laid down your cards; here are mine. I've got two hundred and fifty thousand dollars wrapped up in my boat, and, no question, I could use your money. But the only other asset I've got is wrapped up in these clothes, and if I lose that asset, my personal worth is zero." He stood up. "So thanks but no thanks." He nodded at Talley, and walked out.

"Think about it, Captain," Manning called after him.

WHEN DARLING HAD gone, Talley finished his drink, sighed and said, "I must say, Osborn, you were—"

"Don't tell me how to do business," Manning said. "Charm wouldn't have worked any better. We understand one another, Darling and I. We may not like one another, but we understand one another." He signaled to Shilly for the check.

Talley was furious. This couldn't be happening. Everything had gone so well. He had a blank check from Manning, had meshed his own obsession with Manning's and had created a common purpose. He could buy anything he wanted, and had: the best equipment, the newest, the most sophisticated.

Best of all, he had a plan.

But now the final thing he needed, the last cog in his elaborate machine, was not available.

He had to hide his discouragement from Manning, in case it might become contagious. If Manning canceled his check, thirty years of research, of hopes, of dreams, would vanish like steam.

They did not speak again until they were in the parking lot, and then Manning said, "How much do we know about Darling?"

"Just reputation. He's the best around."

"No . . . about *him* . . . personally."

"Nothing."

"Nose around, see what you can learn. There's not a man alive who doesn't have enemies. Find one. Throw money at him. Tell him you want to know everything there is to know: dirt, gossip, lies, rumors. Start with the fishermen. Small community, no work, no money . . . I'll bet they're worse than actors—they'll sell their own mothers for the chance to ruin a competitor."

"You want to destroy the man? Why?"

"No. I want to control him, but I can't until I know what there is to know. Old truism, Talley: Knowledge is power. I'll go downtown in the morning, talk to some people, cash a few chips."

"Talk about what?"

"Weaknesses . . . liabilities. Another old truism: Every

man has his price. All we have to do is find Darling's, and then he's ours."

CHARLOTTE WAS WAITING in the kitchen when Darling arrived home. When he had finished telling her about the evening, she kissed him and said, "I'm proud of you."

"Five thousand a day." Darling shook his head. "I could've gotten ten days' work out of it, maybe more."

"Yes, but then . . . ?"

Darling put an arm around her. "You could've thrown me a hell of a funeral."

Charlotte didn't smile. She looked up at him and said, "Just remember your promise, William. Don't get involved with people who've got nothing to lose."

20

THE WHEEL WAS huge, and it took both hands and all her concentration to control it. It was a circle of stainless steel, four feet across, and it seemed to have a life of its own, wanting to yank away from her and let the boat fall off the wind and wallow. It reminded her of an unruly horse. The answer was to show it who was boss; then it would behave.

Katherine wasn't about to make a mistake now, not after waiting for three days and nights for the chance to take the helm, listening to her father and Timmy and David and the others talk about how tough the boat was to steer in a quartering sea, how it took a man's strength to control the boat, how they should wait for the wind to die down and the conditions to be just right . . . blah, blah, blah.

She sat up straight and braced her knees against the wheel post and gripped the wheel so tightly that her fingers began to cramp. The muscles in her arms already ached, and soon, she knew, they would begin to sting.

Timmy lounged on the cushions beside her. Up forward, David and Peter were sprawled on the deck, working on their tans. They had nothing to do now, on a broad reach, except wait until it was time for the next watch to take over.

"Come off a bit," said Timmy.

"Why?"

" 'Cause there's a flutter of luff in the main." Timmy pointed to the top of the mainsail. "Jeez . . . why do you think?"

She looked up, squinting at the brilliance of the white sail against the blue sky. Timmy was right, which annoyed her; it was something she should have seen herself. Or heard. Noticed, anyway. But the luff was so tiny, so insignificant, that she couldn't believe it would make a difference.

She heaved on the wheel, turning it to the right, until she saw the trailing edge of the sail stop quivering. The boat heeled to starboard, and she had to brace herself with her feet.

"That's got it," Timmy said.

"Thank heavens. I'm sure glad you saw that. Now we'll win for sure."

"Hey, Kathy . . . it's a *race*."

"Could've fooled me."

There wasn't another boat in sight. How many had started? Fifty? A hundred? She had no idea. Enough so that the starting line had looked like a riot, with boats zigzagging back and forth and people yelling at each other and horns blowing. But as the hours had passed, the numbers had seemed to shrink: fewer and fewer boats nearby, then fewer and fewer in sight, as if one by one they were being swallowed up by the sea. She knew that all that was happening was that each captain was trying his own strategy, going off on his own tacks, using computers and experience and guesswork and, for all she knew, voodoo to find the perfect combination of wind and tide and current that would give him an edge.

Still, it was eerie to be alone on the ocean like this. The boat was almost fifty feet long, and down below it seemed as big as a house, but up here—with the waves on either side and the horizon stretching forever and the sky completely empty— it felt as tiny as a bug on a carpet.

Her father stuck his head up through the hatch. "How's it going, Muffin?"

She had begged him to call her Katherine. Just for this trip. Or Kathy. Anything but Muffin.

"Fine, Daddy."

"How's she doing, Tim?"

Be nice, she prayed. Don't be a typical shithead brother.

"Pretty good . . ." Tim said.

Thank you . . .

". . . only a little absentminded now and then."

Shithead!

"We just raised Bermuda on the radar . . . edge of the fifty-mile ring."

"Great!" Katherine said, hoping that was the right thing to say.

"Sure is. Means we can cruise right along all night, and if we're lucky hit the channel just after daybreak. We don't want to try it in the dark."

"God, no," said Tim. "Remember last year?"

"Don't remind me."

Of course, Katherine thought. Last year. When I wasn't there. That's when the excitement always happens: when I'm not there.

Her father started to pull his head back, then stopped and said, "Funny thing . . . Bermuda Harbour Radio's broadcasting a Notice to Mariners about some animal that's attacking boats."

"A whale?" Katherine said. "Maybe it's sick."

"I don't know, I think they're just trying to juice up tourism, play on the Bermuda Triangle thing. Anyway, no point taking chances. Put your lifeline on whenever you move around."

"Daddy, it's not even rough."

"I know, Muffin, but better safe than sorry." He smiled. "I promised your mother I'd take extra-special care of you." He gestured to Tim, then backed down into the cabin.

Tim sat up, reached over to Katherine's life jacket, unwrapped her jury-rigged lifeline and snapped it into the steel ring on the wheel post.

"What about yours?" she said. "You're not even wearing a life jacket."

"I've done this race three times," Tim said. "I think I know how to walk around a boat."

"So do I!"

"Argue with Dad, then, not me. I'm just following orders." Tim smiled at her and lay back on the cushions.

She flexed her fingers to quell the cramps, and shifted her weight to try to ease the strain on her arms and shoulders. She wasn't wearing a watch, had no idea how much longer she had to wrestle with this stupid wheel. Not too much longer, she hoped, or she'd have to ask Tim to take over for her, and he'd make some crack that would put her down—nothing mean, really, just some dumb macho remark.

She wasn't a quitter. She had pleaded to come on this trip, and she was determined to do her share, including standing watches. She knew that her brothers had argued against her coming along, and that if her mother hadn't sat her father down and had a heart-to-heart talk with him about fairness and equality and all the rest, she'd be back in Far Hills teaching tennis to ten-year-olds. She owed it to her mother, and to herself, to prove that she could be an asset, not a liability.

But she couldn't wait for it to be over, to get to Bermuda and spend a couple of days lying on the beach and tooling around on a motorbike, while her father and the others talked sailing over drinks at the Yacht Club—no, the *Dinghy* Club, they called it here. Cute.

Then she'd fly home, that had been the deal. Thank God.

She couldn't fathom the mystique of big-boat sailing, although she feigned enthusiasm and tried her best to master obscure terms like "klew cringle" and "running backstay."

She enjoyed day sailing in small boats at the shore. It was fun to spend a couple of hours on the water, racing against friends, yahooing around, sometimes even capsizing—but then going home to a hot shower and decent food and a good night's sleep.

But this: This was a marathon of boredom, discomfort and fatigue. Nobody slept more than four or five hours a day. Nobody bathed. She had tried to take a shower once, but had fallen down twice and cut her head on the soap dish, so had resigned herself to sponging off whatever she could reach whenever she could. Everything felt soggy. Everything stank of salt and mold. The entire belowdecks smelled like a giant wet sneaker. You needed a graduate degree in engineering to operate the toilets. Both of them clogged at least once a day, and blame inevitably fell on Katherine and the only other female on board, David's stuck-up girlfriend Evan . . . as if girls somehow conspired against marine plumbing. Katherine had been appointed "assistant chief cook and bottle washer," which turned out to be a bad joke because how can you cook anything decent when the whole boat is always tilted at an angle so you can barely stand up? All she had been able to do was keep hot coffee and soup available day and night, and sandwich makings in a Tupperware bowl in the sink for whoever wanted something more.

She wouldn't have minded any of the bad stuff if there had been enough good stuff to compensate, but as far as she could tell, ocean racing—in good weather, at least—consisted of a lot of talk, a lot of sitting around, and about half an hour a day of frantic action, during which her contribution was to stay out of the way.

Katherine had concluded that it must all have something to do with male bonding, and while she was glad to have seen it firsthand, she would be perfectly happy henceforth to hear about it and to smile politely at her brothers' tales of heroics on the high seas.

Her arms and shoulders were shrieking now; she had no choice; she'd have to turn the wheel over to Tim.

But then suddenly—blessedly—the watch changed. Her father and her uncle Lou came up through the hatch to relieve her and Tim, and Lou's two boys went forward to replace David and Peter.

"Good job, sweetheart," her father said as he slid behind the wheel. "Right on course."

"You have any idea how we're doing?" Tim asked.

"Hard to tell. I think we've got a shot at second or third in our class. Lot of boats on the radar, but I can't tell what they are."

Katherine unsnapped her lifeline from the steel ring and went below. She took off her life jacket and tossed it on her bunk. Tim squeezed by her and went forward into the fo'c'sle and flung himself on one of the bunks. Didn't even take his shoes off. No wonder the place smelled like a gym.

Katherine decided to have a cup of soup and read for a while, until she fell asleep. Nothing else to do.

She heard her father shout, "Ready about!" Footsteps hammered on the fiberglass overhead. She gripped the railing of the top bunk, where Evan was asleep and snoring like a chain saw, and braced herself.

"Hard alee!" called her father, and the boat righted itself and hung there for a second and then, as the boom came around and the sail caught the wind with a *whump!*, it heeled to port. There was a clatter of crockery in the sink, as dirty cups shifted and tumbled over one another.

She should wash the cups. That was her job. But it was Evan's job, too, and Evan hadn't bothered, she'd just gone to sleep. To heck with it; she'd wash them later. She rinsed one cup and poured some soup for herself and drank it down.

On her way back to her bunk, she stopped and looked at the radar screen. It glowed like a green video game. A yellow line swept clockwise in a circle, flashing golden blips that she knew were other boats. At the top of the screen was a ragged smear.

Hello, Bermuda, she thought. Save some sun for me. And maybe, while you're at it, a good-looking lifeguard. One who hates sailboats.

She was glad she had looked—it made her feel less alone.

She lay down in her bunk and turned on the little reading light over her head and picked up her copy of Anne Rice's *The Mummy*—her mother's choice for her, and perfect for a trip like this: romantic, scary, long enough to last several days and easy to pick up and put down without losing the plot. She found her place. Ramses had brought Cleopatra back to life, and Cleopatra was making out with every man she met and then killing him, and . . .

She had to go to the john. She sighed and got up and walked aft, past the chart table, and opened the door to the head. The smell assaulted her, worse than the public johns in Penn Station. She didn't have to look, but she did, and sure enough, it was clogged. She stepped on the flush pedal and gave the pump handle one try, but the sound—a strangled gurgle—warned her against trying again.

She went forward to the other head. There was a piece of masking tape on the door, with OUT OF ORDER on it in marking pen.

Swell.

She went back to her bunk and opened the drawer beneath it and fetched her emergency john: an empty quart mayonnaise jar.

Then she returned to the after head and held her breath as

she peed in the jar, thinking only: Please let tomorrow come, let me go to sleep and not wake up till we're at the dock.

When she had finished, she screwed the top tight and started up through the hatch.

"Life jacket," her father said.

"I'm just . . ." She showed him the jar.

"Both now?"

"Uh-huh. Again."

"Lord . . . well, we'll fix 'em when we get in."

Uncle Lou said, with a little snicker, "Ladies . . ."

"Uncle Lou . . ." Katherine said. "I wasn't great at biology, but I think men go to the john, too . . . sometimes."

"I stand corrected," Uncle Lou said, smiling.

"Here," said her father, and he held his hand out to take the jar.

"I'll do it," she said.

"Muffin . . ."

"I'll *do* it."

"Then put your life jacket on."

"Daddy . . . Oh, all right." She backed down the ladder and went to her bunk and got her life jacket. She was angry, embarrassed, annoyed. Nobody else was wearing a life jacket, and they were running around the deck like monkeys. She wanted to take three steps to empty a jar overboard, and he was making her dress up like an astronaut.

She put the life jacket on and thought, Who's being dumb now? Why don't you let him throw it over for you? Because. Because what? Because it's . . . private. Stupid. He used to change your diapers. Never mind, too late now.

She went up through the hatch and stepped around the wheel and started forward on the leeward side of the boat. The sun was low in the western sky, low enough so that the ocean swells blocked it, and here, further shaded by the big sail, the light was as dim as evening.

"Snap in," her father said.

"Yes, sir." She snapped the lifeline onto the quarter-inch cable connecting two stanchions.

"I know you find this hard to believe, but I'm not being a pain just to amuse myself."

"No, sir." She knew she sounded petulant, but she couldn't help it.

She unscrewed the cap of the jar and, her knees braced against a stanchion, leaned out to empty the jar. The jar was big for her hand, and as she upended it, it slipped. Reflexively, she reached for it with her other hand, and she dropped the cap, and she lunged to grab that, too, and then suddenly there was a little stutter in the wind, a puff that pushed the boat farther over. And then suddenly there was nothing supporting her legs, and because most of her weight was overboard she lost her balance and fell, somersaulting.

In that split second, she knew that the lifeline would stop her and swing her back into the boat, and she tensed and raised her hands to her head. There was a jolt as the lifeline caught. She heard herself screaming, and something else, a weird tearing noise, and then, when she should have felt herself slamming against the side of the boat, she felt . . . water.

She was underwater, upside down, and then the life jacket righted her and she bobbed to the surface. She couldn't see— her hair was in her eyes. She wiped it away, and still she couldn't see anything but water, great undulating swells of blue-black water.

This couldn't be! What had happened? She looked down at her life jacket, and there was a jagged hole where the lifeline had torn away.

She could hear her father shouting, and other people too, a jumble of words, so she used her hands to turn herself around, and there, silhouetted against the setting sun, was the top of the mast, heading away from her, the sail flapping, the voices growing fainter.

A swell rose beneath her and carried her high on its crest, and now she could see all of the mast and even the top of the cabin. She screamed, but she felt—no, she *knew*—that the wind was snatching her words away and flinging them eastward into the night.

The swell passed her, and she slid into the trough, and now she saw none of the boat, not even the top of the mast.

She felt something in the water that encased her, a pulsing, very faint, but definite.

The engine. They'd turned on the engine. Good. Now they could maneuver, and find her fast. Fast. Before night fell.

Another swell came, and from its crest she saw the mast again, looking farther away, and all the lights were on it—masthead light, running lights, anchor lights—so she would be able to see it.

She screamed again and waved her arms, but they couldn't hear her now. Of course they couldn't, not with the engine on.

Why did they keep moving away from her? Why didn't they turn around?

Then the boat did turn, its bow slewing to the right; it began to circle back to her. Good. They'd find her now.

The swell dropped her into a trough, where she could see nothing but water.

If she couldn't see them, how could they see her? They stuck up fifty feet. How far did she stick up? Two feet?

Save your strength, she thought. Don't scream, don't flail around till you're on the top of a wave, where they can see you.

A swell raised her up, and she saw the boat, almost all of it . . . but it was moving away from her, in a different direction! She screamed.

As that swell dropped her down again, she turned her head to the west. The sun was gone, leaving only an orange glow on the horizon, and pink-rimmed clouds against the darkening sky. Overhead she could see stars.

It would be dark soon. They had to find her . . . *had* to . . . or . . .

Don't even think about it.

God, it was cold! How could she be so cold so soon? She'd only been in the water a few minutes, but her arms and legs were trembling, and her throat and jaw were quivering so badly that she had trouble breathing.

IT FLOATED IN the cool middle layer of the ocean water, unthreatened, unperturbed, drifting.

It had fed recently, gorging itself, so for now it felt no urgency to hunt.

It was existing, merely existing.

And then, from somewhere far away, it felt the thrum of a pulse, faint waves that coursed through the water and tapped at its flesh.

Curious rather than concerned, it fluttered its tail fins and slowly rose.

Had it encountered warmer water, it would have stopped, for comfort was its only imperative. But the cool layer continued, and so it allowed itself to rise.

It sensed light now, and the pulse was nearer, and there was something else, something apart from the pulse, disturbing the water above.

Something alive.

A SWELL LIFTED Katherine, and when she reached the crest she saw the boat, the whole boat—nearby!—a dark shape against the twilight sky, with the white and red and green lights shining from the mast.

She screamed and waved her arms, then slid off the crest and back into the trough again.

They hadn't seen her, hadn't heard her. *Why?* They were so close! She had heard *them,* had heard the engine and even maybe a voice.

She was downwind, that was why. Sound was carrying from them to her but not from her to them.

Dark. It was dark, almost night. And cold. And deep. How deep? Forever deep.

Now, at last, terror struck her, a true gut primal fear that flooded through her veins and tore at every nerve ending.

Her father had talked of monsters, and now she knew they were going to get her. Nightmare images flashed into her mind, images she hadn't had in years, since she was six or eight, all the beasts that had lived under her bed and in the closet and in the rustling trees outside her window. Always her mother had come into her room and comforted her, told her everything was fine, the monsters were make-believe.

But nobody rushed to comfort her now. Make-believe was real.

She felt so alone, a loneliness she had never known existed, as if she were the only living thing on the planet.

Thoughts tumbled over one another in her head: Why had she insisted on coming on this trip? Why hadn't she let her father empty the jar for her? Why, why, why?

She tried to pray, but all she could think of was, Now I lay me down to sleep. . . .

She was going to die.

No!

She screamed again—not on purpose, not to be noticed, but the scream of a living being protesting death.

She was carried to the top of another crest, and saw that the boat was there, even closer, but something was different. It wasn't moving; it had stopped. She could hear no engine noise.

As she slid into the trough, she heard a voice: her father, talking through a loud-hailer.

"Katherine, can you hear me? We can't see you, but we've turned off the engine, turned off everything, so we'll be able to hear you. If you can hear me, as soon as I stop, you scream, honey, scream for all you're worth, okay? . . . Now scream!"

She thought: He called me Katherine.

She screamed.

IT WAS ONE hundred feet below the surface. It hovered, letting its senses gather information.

The pulse from above had stopped, but there was disturbance on the surface, and something small, moving.

The living thing.

Slowly, it rose.

"I HEAR YOU, Katherine! Again! Again!"

She screamed again, her voice scratchy, not as loud, but she summoned all her strength and forced herself to scream again, and again.

A swell caught her, and from its crest she saw a searchlight swinging toward her. She prayed she wouldn't drop away until it had found her, but she was dropping, dropping. She waved her arms. It was going to miss her!

At the last instant, the light caught her upraised hands—

she saw the beam illuminate her grasping fingers—and stopped swinging, and she heard the voice on the loud-hailer cry, "Got you!"

Then she heard the engine start again.

THE PULSE HAD begun again . . . closer, more distinct, moving toward the small living thing.

Excited now, it rose, and its color changed. It was excited not by hunger, not by a sense of an impending battle or an imminent threat, but by a desire to kill.

It began to feel the swells, for it was near the surface.

WHEN KATHERINE REACHED the top of a swell, the light hit her face and blinded her. But the boat was there, she could feel the beat of the engine, she could smell the exhaust.

Something splashed beside her, something big, and she felt an arm around her waist and heard a voice say, "I've got you . . . it's okay . . . it's okay."

Timmy. She wrapped her arms around him, and then she felt herself being pulled, and her hand touched the hard side of the boat.

IT WAS THERE, the living thing, directly above, thrashing.

A wounded animal.

Prey.

More than prey.

Food.

The creature drew a mass of water into the caverns of its body and expelled it through the funnel in its belly, and it shot upward.

HANDS GRABBED KATHERINE and pulled so hard she thought her arms might come out of their sockets, but then she was in her father's embrace, and he was crushing her against him and saying, "Oh, sweetheart . . . oh baby . . . oh Muffin . . ."

Other hands pulled Timmy aboard, and he fell onto the deck, coughing.

Then someone said, "What's that smell?"

She heard the clunk of the engine's gears engaging, and she felt the boat begin to move.

Then, as her father carried her to the after hatch, voices:

"Hey, look!"

"What?"

"Back there."

"Where?"

"Something in the water."

"I don't see anything."

"There! Right there!"

"What? What is it?"

"I don't know. Something."

"Probably just our wake."

"No, I don't think so."

"It's nothing. We've got her back. Forget it."

THE PULSE WAS fading again, the living thing was gone.

The creature wallowed in the swells and scanned the water with one of its mammoth yellow-white eyes. It raised its whips and swept them across the surface, searching. But it found nothing, and so it sank back into the deep.

WRAPPED IN BLANKETS, Katherine lay in her bunk, and let her father feed her soup. He was laughing and crying at the same time, and his hand shook so that finally she took the soup from him and fed herself.

Evan had taken her clothes off for her—not so stuck-up anymore, in fact rather nice—and washed her off with hot water and given her one of her own sweat suits.

Timmy stopped by on his way to the shower and didn't say anything, just bent down and kissed her forehead.

David and Peter and Uncle Lou, everybody, came in one at a time and said something, and there wasn't a condescending remark among them.

She felt like a celebrity, and she liked it. For once, she had a story she could tell, when everybody else was boasting. For once, the excitement had included her.

Her eyes drooped. She thought she'd like to sleep all the way to Bermuda.

21

As WHIP DARLING took a breath, he realized that the air was coming slowly, reluctantly, as if he were sucking on an empty soda bottle. His tank was almost out. He might get one more breath, two at most, before he'd have to surface.

Never mind, he was only five feet down. If he drew a vacuum, he'd spit out the mouthpiece and exhale and go up.

But he didn't want to have to go up now and change tanks and come back down, just to finish this stupid, cussed job that should have taken twenty minutes and was already into its second hour. Replacing the government buoys was easy; anyone who could master a pair of pliers could do it; he'd done it a hundred times. All you had to do was unshackle the buoy from the chain, put a temporary float on the chain, haul the buoy aboard, drop the replacement buoy overboard, shackle it on the chain and retrieve your float. Piece of cake.

Not this time. First, Mike had given him the wrong size shackle for the chain, then the wrong size pin for the shackle. Then Darling had dropped the correct pin and had had to go up to find another one, because Mike was so rattled about Darling being down there alone that he couldn't find his ass with both hands. Then, while Darling was aboard looking for the pin, Mike had dropped the boat hook with which he was holding the buoy, so the buoy had drifted away on the tide and they'd had to haul the anchor and chase it, because no one man was going to dive in and drag a three-hundred-pound steel buoy that wanted to travel.

It should have been Mike down here anyway, and Darling

passing him the proper equipment piece by piece—and it *would* have been Mike if Darling hadn't decided that Mike was so obviously panicked about being chewed on by some great villain that he might forget to breathe and have an embolism and die. And so Darling had decided to do the job himself.

He held his breath and set the pin to the shackle and whacked it with the hammer. In the water, the hammer moved in slow motion, and most of its force was spent before it struck, so he had to hit the pin again. His vision was distorted by the water and the mask and the bouncing around of the buoy, so he hit the pin awry, and it skipped off the shackle and tumbled away, down into the blue.

Darling shouted "Shit!" into his mouthpiece as he watched it fall. He took his final breath from the tank, sucking in every last atom of air, and pulled the spare pin from the waistband of his bathing suit. He struck it with the hammer, and it slid in like a sharp knife into fresh fish. He spun it tight with pliers, then looked around below, to make sure nothing was cruising in the gloom that might make a run at him as he surfaced. He spat out his mouthpiece and exhaled and kicked upward into the sun.

Mike was waiting on the dive step. "Done?" he asked as he took Darling's tank and weight belt and hauled them up onto the deck.

Darling nodded and pulled himself up onto the dive step and lay facedown, catching his breath.

"What are we doing out here, Michael?" he said when finally he could speak. "We should be sitting in a condo in Vero Beach, drinking Pink Ladies and watching the sunset, instead of casting ourselves into the sea and damn near drowning, all for a measly five-dollar bill."

"It pays the fuel."

"Barely," Darling said, and thought to add something nice to make Mike feel better about not doing the diving himself. "Only thanks to you."

Mike had determined that with some minor fiddling with the engine, he could make it run fine on a mixture of diesel oil and kerosene, which brought the cost of fuel down by more than a third. And that meant that they could actually make a couple of dollars from crappy jobs like this.

Darling hadn't had to work on the government's buoys in years, had hoped he'd never have to again. But when he had heard that the government wanted to change one of the major channel buoys and was letting the job out for bids, he had gotten into the bidding and, to his amazement—embarrassment, almost—found himself the low bidder.

Now they were doing the job, for $500, and because they were running on cheaper fuel they might actually clear $250 on the day—not exactly ransom money, but better than sitting around the yard counting the hairs on the neighbor's cat.

There was no other work, at least not work Darling would do. The aquarium retainer was gone, and the race layover had passed without a single dive charter for anybody, because as soon as the racers had hit shore and seen that article in *Newsweek*, with the picture of the giant squid from the Museum of Natural History in New York, they had concluded that diving was out . . . even on the shallow reefs, where the worst thing likely to happen was a coral cut on the knee. It had been nearly two weeks since anybody had seen a sign of the squid, and still not a single diver had gone into the water.

It made no sense, but then, Darling thought, lots of things didn't. Soon enough, there'd be reports of people refusing to take showers for fear that a giant squid would come out of the shower head or up the drain and eat them.

Other people were getting work, though. One of the glass-bottom boats had painted a new name on its transom, SQUID HUNTER, and was taking tourists out to the edge of the reefs and letting them peer into a hundred feet of water, while the captain, dressed up like Indiana Jones, scared the bejesus out of them with bullshit broadcasts over his P.A. system in his best Vincent Price voice.

It was nonsense, but Darling didn't fault the man; he'd had to do something. Some of the boats that took out snorkelers might as well have been in dry dock. Visitors were afraid to get near the water, and they weren't about to pay thirty dollars to ride around and be told what they should be seeing.

An enterprising gift-shop owner was already selling a line of squid-theme jewelry, junk made from seashells and silver wire. And there was talk that one of the fishermen was making a fortune catching little school squid and freezing them and casting them into blocks of Lucite and selling them as Genuine Miniature Bermuda Triangle Monsters.

Representatives of the far-out environmental groups had arrived, and were going door to door raising money for their Save the Squid campaign. Darling had been asked to be a local spokesman for the campaign, but he had refused, on the grounds that *Architeuthis* was doing a fine job of saving itself without any help from him or anyone else.

The Save-the-Squidders hadn't been in Bermuda for forty-eight hours before they got into a fight with the opposition, some big-time sport fishermen who were sending their Rybovitches and Hatterases and Merritts down from all points westward to go monster fishing. A couple of them had gotten impatient waiting for their boats and had tried to charter Darling, but he'd turned them down, same as he'd turned down Manning and Dr. what's-his-name . . . Talley.

Sometimes he regretted turning down Talley, especially days like today, when his mouth ached from biting on a regulator mouthpiece, when he was frozen like a Popsicle and whipped to the point of coma . . . all for a couple of hundred bucks that he'd have to split with Mike.

But, as the saying went, Talley and Manning were folks to feed with a long spoon. Charlotte had pointed out that each in his own way was the most dangerous kind of person to get mixed up with: A person who has nothing to lose. Darling had never stopped to think exactly what *was* worth risking his life for, outside of Charlotte and Dana, but he knew for sure it wasn't some creature that ate people for breakfast and boats for lunch.

Besides, he wasn't totally out of hope. A restaurant down in town needed its dock repaired, and if he landed the job it could be a week's work at a thousand a day. He'd heard that the telephone company might be wanting a cable laid . . . scut work, pumping mud to dig a trench to lay the cable in, but honest work that paid some bills without destroying anything.

That was all he wanted . . . work. He didn't know how Charlotte was keeping food on the table and the lights turned on and the insurance paid up, but she was, somehow.

Darling washed the salt off in the shower, and put on a

pair of shorts, while Mike stowed the dive gear and fried a mackerel from the cold box. They'd been meaning to use the mackerel as bait, but since there wasn't anything around to catch, they figured they might as well eat it.

After lunch, they cruised southwest along the outer edge of the reefs, meandering toward home. Darling intended to stop at the town dock on the way and submit his bill to Marine & Ports. He had a friend there who had promised to pay him in cash.

"Look there," Mike said, pointing down from the flying bridge. Two snappers were floating belly-up, and the boat passed between them.

A moment later, they saw two more, then a porgy and an angelfish and four or five sergeant majors. All dead, all bloated.

"What the hell's going on?" Darling said.

They heard a noise then, in the distance, a deep, resonant *ka-WHUMP*, and they felt a thud through the steel at their feet, as if someone were hammering on the hull with a maul.

Then, half a mile ahead and to the right, in deep water, they could see a boat, and in front of the boat a torrent of spray descending onto what looked like a hump of ocean water. As they watched, the hump withdrew, absorbed by the sea, and the spray became a white smear on the surface.

Mike picked up the binoculars and focused on the boat. "It's the aquarium's boat," he said.

"Christamighty," said Darling. "Liam's gone and got himself a permit to bomb the beast."

HERBERT TALLEY LICKED the salt spray off his sunglasses and wiped them on his shirttail. He found the little gray fish that had been blown out of the water and had struck him in the back of the head, and he tossed it overboard where the others —the dozens, the scores, that had been killed by the concussion—were bobbing to the surface, their white bellies turned to the sun.

"That was close," he said, and he restrained himself from using the other words he wanted to say, words like "fool" and "idiot."

"Not really, Doctor," said St. John, whose curls, water-soaked and blast-blown, hung like jungle weeds down the sides of his head. "I've made a study of explosives. We were quite safe."

St. John looked over the side, shading his eyes to see down beneath the layer of dead fish. He straightened up, took a step forward and shouted to his men in the bow, "Rig another one! And set this one for a hundred fathoms."

The helmsman, a muscle-bound graduate student who looked like the star of a sex-and-surfers movie, stuck his head out of the cabin and said, "How far do we go to find a hundred fathoms?"

"Use the fathometer, for God's sake. You know how, don't you? . . . Or do I have to do everything?"

"We just blew it out."

"Go that way, then!" St. John said, and he waved his arm in the general direction of darker water.

When he turned back to Talley, he said, "You agree that when we kill the animal, it will float."

"If," Talley said. "If you kill the animal. Yes." Agree? Talley had told St. John, who hadn't known the first thing about the biology of *Architeuthis*.

"Even when we blow it to shreds?"

"Yes." Talley saw no point in qualifying his assertion, since St. John seemed to have about as much chance of killing *Architeuthis* as a ten-year-old had of hitting a sparrow with a slingshot.

"It'll come to the surface even from a hundred fathoms . . . six hundred feet?"

"From anywhere. As I told you, the ammonia content of the flesh makes it lighter than seawater. It will float, just like oil, just like—"

"I know, I know," St. John said, and he turned away toward the bow.

Talley swallowed bile, and tried to think how to escape from this diminutive bully who was treating him like an apprentice. He should never have accepted St. John's invitation to come along.

On the phone, however, St. John had been polite, receptive, even eager to have Talley observe his attempt to kill the giant squid. He had welcomed Talley aboard the thirty-five-foot aquarium boat, had introduced him to his crew of four—including the young man in charge of explosives, who looked nauseated, either from nervousness or anticipatory seasickness—and then proceeded to lecture Talley about the subject that Talley had made his life's work, a lecture laced with pseudofacts gleaned, Talley imagined, from comic books, horror movies and supermarket tabloids.

When Talley had contradicted one of St. John's putative facts—not rudely, not didactically, he had simply stated that there was no conclusive evidence to affirm St. John's assertion that there were only three species of *Architeuthis,* that many scientists believed there could in fact be as many as nineteen species, all with subtly different characteristics—St. John's response had been a curt "Ridiculous!" and he had changed the subject, convincing Talley that he had no interest in learning anything, and that he expected Talley only to approve and applaud whatever he did.

The amazing thing was that St. John was so ignorant of how ignorant he was; he truly believed the nonsense he purveyed. It was as if his brain gathered data from all sources —the reliable, the marginal and the fantastic—and selected that which it liked and discarded all the rest and molded its own gospel truth.

St. John had stayed away from Talley for most of the voyage, had instructed Talley to stay aft—"where it's safe"—while he lectured his crew about giant squid and underwater explosives. The only reason he had bothered to say anything else to Talley—and it hadn't been phrased as a question but as a speculative musing about the flotation of certain kinds of flesh— was that one of his crew had wondered how they would know if they had killed the monster because if it didn't have a swim bladder it would probably sink to the bottom . . . wouldn't it?

St. John had looked stricken until Talley had volunteered that *Architeuthis* flesh had positive buoyancy, information that St. John had then passed along as if it had sprung whole from the cornucopia of his mind.

Talley didn't mind feeding St. John data. By now, all he

wanted to do was to get off this boat, before St. John pulled some boner that blew them all to bits.

If only he and Manning had been able to charter a boat of their own. They had tried, but there was nothing of suitable size available except an old ferry that needed a complete overhaul. There were a few medium-size government boats, but as they inquired about each, they encountered bureaucratic confusions, all concocted, Talley was becoming convinced, by St. John, who wanted the creature to himself.

Manning had made another attempt to arrange for a boat from the States, but traveling time and clearances and inspections and duties threatened to keep them landlocked for most of the year.

Meanwhile, Talley knew, his one chance, perhaps the only chance he would ever have, to see and study and film the animal that had obsessed him for thirty years, was fading with every passing day. Seasonal changes in currents and water temperature and the flow of the Gulf Stream might encourage *Architeuthis* to move on.

Their only hope, clearly, was Whip Darling. From what they had heard about him and learned from their conversation with him, they knew that he was the perfect man for the job: expert, ingenious, sensible, tough and determined. His boat was perfect, too. Talley and Manning had rented a punt and rowed across Mangrove Bay one evening, after seeing Darling and his wife leave their home in a taxi. They had boarded the boat in the long shadows of twilight, had studied its broad stern, which was obviously capable of holding huge reels of cable, its engine and the shelves of spare parts, had approved of the lifting gear and the hauling gear, even the rake of the bow and the cast of the bottom, which spoke of the boat's ruggedness and stability.

They had debated trying to buy the boat from Darling, but from a few artificially casual conversations with the staff at Cambridge Beaches, and with workers at the boatyard, Talley had learned that boat and man were inseparable. Buying the boat was the same thing as buying the man, and the man had made it clear he was not for sale.

They had yet to discover a weakness in Darling that they could exploit, but Manning wasn't about to give up. He insisted that, given enough time, he could find an Achilles' heel in a saint. He still had a few more acquaintances to talk to, a few more favors to call in.

Talley, on the other hand, could think of no one else to question, nothing else to try. He had one other person to meet, this evening, but he assumed that the conversation would produce nothing but a request for money in exchange for a promise of juicy gossip about Darling. There had been a few of those, but Talley had declined to pay until he heard the information, and in no instance had the dirt been worth a dime.

Then he had gotten a phone call last night from someone who said his name was Carl Frith, and that he was a fisherman. He said he had heard that Talley was nosing around about Whip Darling, and maybe he could help. The only reason Talley hadn't refused the meeting outright was that Frith had begun by saying he didn't want any money. All he wanted was justice . . . whatever that meant.

"Set!" called a voice from the bow.

St. John said to the helmsman, "Are we in position?"

"Yes, sir."

"How far are we from the charge?"

"About a hundred yards."

"Get closer. I want to be sure the signal reaches."

"But—"

"Get closer, damn it! You want it to work, don't you? . . . Or don't you?"

"Yes, sir." As the helmsman put the boat in gear and gave it power, Talley moved as far aft as he could. He tapped the fiberglass and wondered if it had any flotation built into it.

Then St. John shouted, "Fire!" and the crewman turned the switch on the firing box.

For a moment nothing happened, there was only silence, and then there was a sound of rumbling and a sensation as if a giant hand had grabbed the boat and was trying to lift it into the sky. And then the water erupted around them.

Finally the boat fell back, and the spray dissipated, and St. John came aft and leaned over the side. Little fish—pink and red and gray and brown—floated to the surface.

"Deeper," he said. "He must be down deeper. We'll have to try to go deeper."

The helmsman stepped out of the cabin and said, "Doctor. Ned says we've sprung a leak."

"A leak? Where?"

"The glass cracked. In the viewing ports down below."

"Why did you get us so close?"

"What? You told me—"

"The safety of this vessel is your responsibility. If you thought it was dangerous to get so close, you had an obligation to refuse."

The helmsman just stared at him.

"Idiot!" St. John said, and he started forward. "How serious is the leak?"

"Maybe we should start home, just in case."

"Nonsense. Fix it with epoxy," St. John said, and he disappeared inside the cabin.

Talley thought, Great, now we're going to sink, and I'll probably drown out here in the middle of nowhere. He looked around in the cockpit, searching for something that might float. He saw a wooden hatch cover, and unhooked it so it would float free if the stern went underwater. He looked toward shore, estimating how far it was. . . . Three miles? Four? He couldn't tell, but it seemed a long, long way.

Then, as he turned back, he saw a boat in the near distance. It wasn't doing anything, it was just there, its bow pointed this way. It was a big boat.

Be thankful, he thought. At least maybe someone will come to save you.

He heard their engine drop into gear and felt the boat labor into a turn and begin to head for shore.

St. John came out of the cabin, sweating, and his face had a purplish tinge to it, either from exertion or rage.

"There's a boat over there," Talley said. "Perhaps we should—"

"I see it." St. John banged on the cabin bulkhead and shouted, "Hey!"

The helmsman stuck his head out the door. "Yes, sir?"

"You see that boat over there? Call them on the radio and tell them to follow us in."

"*Tell* them, Doctor?"

"Yes, Rumsey . . . *tell* them. Tell them who we are and tell them to follow us in, in case we need help. They'll do it. You can bet on it."

"Yes, sir." As the helmsman backed into the cabin, St. John said, "Do you recognize them?"

"Yes, sir."

"Who is it?"

"*Privateer* . . . it's Whip Darling."

"Oh," St. John said, and he hesitated for a second before adding, "forget it."

"Sir?"

"Forget it. Don't call them. Just get us home."

The helmsman frowned, then shrugged and went inside.

"Look how she's riding," Mike said.

"*Low* . . ." Darling said. "She's holed herself."

"Want to follow 'em in?"

"They want help, they can call us," Darling said. "I'd like that, but I don't think Liam would."

He put the wheel hard over, pushed the throttle forward and headed for the marker that signaled Western Blue Cut. He stayed in deep water, and for several minutes the bow of the boat shed the corpses of small fish.

Mike said, "He sure blowed everything to ratshit."

"It's a shame being dumb isn't a crime," Darling said, "or we could lock that man up for life."

"What was he using?"

Darling shrugged. "I don't imagine *he* knew. Long as it went *bang*, that's all he cared. Water gel . . . C-4 . . . maybe plain old dynamite."

"You don't just buy that stuff at the grocery store."

"Sure you do. Look at all the powder we've got. All you have to say is you need to blast for a dock or a foundation. The permit man never takes into account the asshole factor."

"Still, makes you wonder. . . . Hey!" Mike had been looking to the north, and he was pointing at something shiny floating between two swells.

Darling swung the wheel, and the boat rocked as it took the waves on its port quarter.

"Be damned," Darling said as they neared the floating thing. "More of that spawn . . . if that's what it is."

It was another of the gelatinous doughnuts, an oblong measuring six or eight feet by two or three feet, undulating, with a hole in its center.

Darling put the boat in neutral and leaned on the railing of the flying bridge and looked down.

"I'd say it was whale spew," he said. "You know . . . ambergris . . . that is, if there were any whales left around."

"It's not dark enough," Mike said. "And it doesn't stink."

"No . . . gotta be spawn, but spawn of what I'm damned if I know." Darling paused. "We should take some back for that Dr. Talley to have a look at."

"Want me to dip it up?"

"Why not?"

Mike went down the ladder, found the long-handled dip net and went aft, where the boat's combing was low and he could reach the water easily.

Darling turned the boat in a tight circle and maneuvered it so that the mass of jelly slid close down its side.

Mike leaned overboard and scooped with the net. As he touched the jelly, it fragmented.

"Damn," he said. "She come apart."

"Get any of it?"

"Lemme try again."

Darling backed down, and Mike held the handle of the net and stretched his arm out.

As the net touched water, something grabbed it, and pulled. Mike's shins struck the low bulwark, and because too much of his weight was outboard, he started to fall.

"Hey!" he yelled, flailing with his free hand but finding only air.

"Let it go!" shouted Darling, but Mike didn't. As if his hand were welded to it, he clutched the aluminum handle of the dip net, and was pulled overboard. His body turned half a somersault and he landed in the water on his back. Only then did he let go of the net.

Darling ran to the back of the flying bridge and half jumped, half slid down the ladder and hurried aft. The boat was already out of gear, so Mike was in no danger from the propeller, but Darling was worried he might panic and swallow water and drown himself.

And panicked Mike was. He forgot how to swim. He screamed incoherently and windmilled with his arms . . . not five feet from the stern of the boat.

Darling grabbed a rope, cleated one end and held up the other. "Michael!" he shouted.

But Mike didn't hear him, he just kept thrashing and screaming.

Darling coiled the loose rope and aimed it at Mike's head and threw it. It hit him in the face, but Mike ignored it, until his hands found it and, in reflex, fastened on. Then Darling pulled him to the dive step at the stern of the boat, bent down and grabbed him by the collar and hauled him up onto the step.

Mike lay there, whimpering and spitting water. Then he coughed and gasped and rose to his knees and said, "Fuck this."

"Why, Michael," Darling said, smiling. "It was just a big old turtle, that's all. I saw him . . . must've decided to fight you for the spawn."

"Fuck him. Fuck you. Fuck everything. Forever."

Darling laughed. "You okay?"

"I'm gonna go be a taxi driver."

When Mike had wrung out his clothes and wrapped a towel around himself, Darling returned to the wheel and circled around to where the dip net was floating on the surface. He put the boat in neutral and let its momentum carry it over to the net. He snagged it with the boat hook and brought it aboard.

The turtle had torn a hole in the netting, but a few globs of jelly clung to some of it. Darling held one of the globs to the sunlight and looked closely. There were little things inside, too small to make out. He debated scraping it off the netting and storing it in a jar, but there probably wasn't enough of it to be worthwhile. So he washed the jelly away in the water, dropped the net on the deck and went up to the flying bridge.

A few minutes later, when Darling had turned into the mouth of Western Blue Cut, Mike appeared on the flying bridge with two cups of tea.

"I don't like this," Mike said, handing Darling one of the cups.

"Falling overboard can mess up your day."

"No, I mean everything. Everything's making me go apeshit. I've been overboard before and I've never gone apeshit."

"Don't let it get to you. Everybody has a bad day."

"Everybody doesn't go apeshit, though. Friggin' critter's got me spooked. I half wish Liam *would* blow the bugger up. Who'd have thought a fuckin' squid could make me mental?"

"Stop it, or you *will* make yourself mental . . . talk yourself right into it."

"Can't do what's already done."

Darling looked at Mike, huddled in a towel, his hands shaking, and he thought: This thing has opened a dark door inside this young man. It's weird how things we don't understand can arouse demons we don't even know we have.

THEY WERE WELL up in the shallows, with the fortress of Dockyard looming to the left and the pink cottages of Cambridge Beaches peeking through the casuarinas to the right, when Mike, who was leaning on the railing and facing aft, said, "Never seen that fella before."

Darling looked back. To the north, at least three miles away, approaching the entrance to the deep North Channel, was a small ship, no more than 120 to 150 feet long, with a white hull and a single black stack.

"He's not local," said Mike.

"Not hardly."

"Not navy neither. It looks like one of those private research vessels."

Darling picked up the binoculars, braced his elbows on the railing and focused on the ship. He could see a lifeboat suspended from davits on the starboard side, and, aft of the cabin, a huge steel crane. On a cradle beneath the crane was something oval, something with portholes in it.

"I'll be damned, Michael," Darling said. "Whoever he is, he's got a submersible, one of those little submarines, mounted on his stern."

Part Three

22

CAPTAIN WALLINGFORD WAS hunched over his desk, signing requisition forms, when Marcus Sharp arrived, rapped twice on the doorjamb and said, "Captain?"

"Sharp. What is it?" Wallingford spoke without looking up. "No, wait, don't tell me. You've heard the scuttlebutt that there's a research vessel here, loaded with space-age search gear, including a state-of-the-art, two-million-dollar submersible, and they've come to look for the giant squid. You've heard that we're going to put a navy man on that ship and in the submersible when they go down, and you've come to volunteer. You think you're the best man for the job." Wallingford looked up and smiled. "Well?"

"I . . . yes. Sir." Sharp stepped into the office and stood before the captain's desk.

"Why you, Sharp? You're a chopper jockey, not a submariner. And why should I send an officer, why not just a seaman? All I need down there is a pair of eyes, somebody to make sure these turkeys don't poke around where they shouldn't, or screw up one of the navy's acoustical cables by accident."

"I'm a diver, sir," Sharp said. "I know what the underwater looks like. I know what all that sensitive equipment of ours looks like down there. I might be able to see things other people wouldn't." He paused. "I've had UDT training."

"UDT training?" said Wallingford. "Christ, Sharp, these people aren't here to blow anything up. They're magazine hotshots who want to be the first to take pictures of a live giant squid . . . a squid that, from what I hear, is probably a thousand miles away from here by now."

"What's the deal with the Bermuda government? I'd've thought the last thing Bermuda wanted was any more publicity."

"Money. What else? Bermuda's hurting. Tourism is in the dumper. Hotels are in trouble, restaurants are in trouble, sport fishing has pretty well stopped. The diving business is *out* of business. When these people from *Voyager—*"

"*Voyager?*"

"It's the magazine. It's new, started by some guy in the ball-bearing business with a ton of money. They had their brand-new Finnish submersible down in the Cayman Islands, taking pictures of weird things in deep water, and when they heard about the squid up here, they saw it as a chance for a coup—a scoop that might catapult 'em into the league with *National Geographic*. The *Geographic* doesn't have a submersible. Nobody does, no Americans anyway, except the navy, and we only have one that's worth a damn. At any rate, Bermuda said to itself, Hey, why not let them in? If they find the squid, fine, maybe they can figure out a way to kill it. If not, let them spend their time and money looking around, and when they don't find the squid, we can publicize the hell out of the fact that the thing is gone, and tell the world Bermuda's safe again."

"Where does the navy fit in? I mean, these are Bermuda waters, this seems—"

"Where do we *fit?* Sharp, come on. . . . Bermuda *has* no waters. These are NATO waters by law. But the fact is, they're American. Every drop. Do you really think the Bermudians put down all those sonar trackers? Do you think the Bermudians laid all those cables, the ones that keep track of Soviet subs? This is America out here, Sharp. And when the Pentagon heard about this deal, about that ship with all the high-tech gear, they were all over me like sweat, to make sure I got a U.S. Navy man on the ship and on the submersible. Nobody, I don't care if they're American citizens or Munchkins, nobody is gonna poke around our deep-water assets without our being right beside him, looking over his shoulder."

Wallingford leaned back in his chair. "So there it is,

Sharp," he said. "Now, as for you, why would you want to go down in that thing? You think you'll spot some shipwrecks for your pal Whip Darling?"

"No, sir," Sharp said quickly, embarrassed. It had never occurred to him that Wallingford knew about his using helicopter time to cruise above the reefs and look for wrecks. He should have realized it, however, since he was never alone on the chopper, there was always at least one person with him, and the navy base was a tiny community full of people with plenty of time to gossip. "What would be the point?" he added. "Even if I saw something at five hundred or a thousand feet, there'd be no way to recover it."

"What is it, then?" said Wallingford. "What makes you want to go half a mile down into the ocean, with people you don't know, in a little steel coffin, to look for something that probably isn't there and might kill you if it is?"

"Because . . ." Sharp hesitated, knowing that most people would have trouble understanding his reasoning. "It's something I've never done before. I want to see what it's like."

"You've never been to the moon before, either. Would you go to the moon if somebody asked you?"

"Yes, sir. Yes, I surely would."

"God almighty, Sharp," Wallingford said, shaking his head. "Okay, you've got it. Be at Dockyard at sixteen hundred. They're gonna go out and anchor tonight, and put the sub down first thing tomorrow."

"Thank you, sir," said Sharp. "How official is this? Should I wear a uniform?"

"No. But take a sweater and some warm socks. I hear it's cold three thousand feet down there in the dark."

"Yes, sir." Sharp saluted and turned to go.

"Sharp," Wallingford said, stopping him at the door.

"Sir?"

"I was gonna send you, even if you hadn't volunteered." Wallingford grinned. "I just wanted to hear you make your case."

BACK IN HIS quarters, Sharp packed an overnight bag, and threw in a Walkman, a few tapes and a book. By the time he had taken a shower and put on a pair of jeans and a denim shirt, it was nearly 1500. Dockyard was at the other end of Bermuda, an hour away by motorbike, so he picked up his bag and started out of the room. At the door he remembered that he had been scheduled to go diving the next day with Darling, and so he went back inside and picked up the phone.

Darling's wife answered, and before Sharp could leave a message she said Whip was down on the boat and she'd go fetch him. While he waited, Sharp wondered whether he should tell Darling where he was going. Knowing the navy's passion for secrecy, he assumed that this trip was classified, even though it involved a national magazine that planned to document it on film. But the navy liked to classify everything, from the number of potatoes bought for the mess to the price paid for enlisted men's socks.

Screw secrecy, he decided. The odds were good that Darling knew all about it anyway.

"Glad you called, Marcus," Darling said when he picked up the phone. "I was gonna call you. How about a rain check for tomorrow's diving? There's a bunch of people here from some magazine who want to put a submarine down to take pictures of the squid. They've hired me as escort."

"You're going? What do you mean, escort?"

"They don't know where to look for the thing. They don't know where the drop-off is, or where the bottom shelves off, or where the deep begins. They've got a fathometer and a side-scan sonar, and if they took the time they could find out for themselves. But that boat must cost ten thousand a day to run, so they see using me as a shortcut."

"And you agreed to go? I thought—"

"Marcus. It's a thousand dollars a day. But all I'll do is show 'em where to go, tell 'em where to aim their cameras and float around over their submarine in case it has to surface away from the ship." Darling laughed. "You can be damn sure I'm not going down in that sub."

"Whip," Sharp said, and he paused, feeling his enthusiasm begin to ebb. "I'm supposed to go with them."

"You? What for?"

"The navy's worried that they'll snoop around our sonar gear, maybe decide to justify their expenses by doing a story

on how much money we're wasting monitoring Soviet submarines that don't exist."

"What makes Wallingford so sure they won't find the
squid?"

"The navy thinks it's gone away," Sharp said. "So do the
people from the Oceanographic Administration and Scripps."

"Well, I don't. Neither does Talley, or he would have gone
back to Canada. No, it's likely that the critter is down there,
Marcus. I'm pretty sure he's down there somewhere." For a
moment there was silence on the line, then Darling said, "You
said you were going with them. You don't mean you're going
down in that submarine."

"Sure," Sharp said. "That's the whole point."

"Don't."

"I have to, Whip."

"No you don't, Marcus." Darling paused, then said,
"There's one thing we both have to remember: There's a big
difference between being brave and being foolish."

23

THE ROYAL NAVY Dockyard had been built in the nineteenth century by convicts—called "transports," for they had been transported out from England and housed in prison hulks grounded on the muddy bottom of Grassy Bay. Its stone walls were more than ten feet thick, its cobbled streets had been paved by hand. It occupied the entire northern end of Ireland Island, and had once been a civilization unto itself. There had been barracks for hundreds of soldiers, cook houses, jail cells, sail lofts, chandleries, rope lockers and armories.

Now, as Sharp walked along the quay toward the little ship tied to the dock, a dock that still occasionally sheltered British and American ships-of-the-line, he passed boutiques, cafés, souvenir shops, a museum.

Lettering on the transom identified the ship as the *Ellis Explorer,* from Fort Lauderdale. Measuring his paces, Sharp walked along the dock beside the ship. She was 150 feet long, more or less, and most of her was open stern. About halfway between the fantail and the cabin, the submersible rested on its cradle, covered by a tarpaulin. Clearly, the ship was brand-new, built, he guessed after appraising its sleek lines, in Holland or Germany, and it was meticulously tended. There wasn't a speck of rust on the hull, not a chip or a scuff mark on the paint. Ropes on the deck were perfectly coiled, and the steel-and-aluminum superstructure gleamed in the afternoon sun. Whoever owns this vessel, he thought, isn't worried about money.

A woman stood in the bow, tossing pieces of bread to a school of little fish.

"Hello," Sharp said.

She turned to him and said, "Hi." She was in her late twenties, tall and lithe and deeply tanned. She wore cutoff jeans, a man's Oxford shirt with its tails tied at her waist and a Rolex diver's watch. Her sun-bleached brown hair was cut short and swept back from her face. A pair of sunglasses hung from a cord around her neck.

"I'm Marcus Sharp. . . . Lieutenant Sharp."

"Oh," she said. "Right. Come on aboard."

Sharp walked up the gangway and stepped onto the deck.

"I'm Stephanie Carr," the woman said, smiling and holding out her hand. "I take pictures." She led him aft, into the cabin.

The cabin was large and comfortably furnished. There were two folding tables on gimbals, two vinyl-covered sofas bolted to the deck, a stack of plastic chairs, racks of paperback books and, on a shelf, a television set and VCR. Steps led up to the bridge forward and down to the galley and the staterooms aft.

A short, wiry man with a crew cut, who might have been anywhere between thirty and forty-five, sat on the deck and watched a tape of a James Bond movie.

"That's Eddie," Stephanie said. "He drives the sub. Eddie, this is Marcus."

Eddie gestured distractedly and said, "Hey."

Sharp noticed that one of the tables was littered with cameras, strobes, light meters and boxes of film. "Do you have a writer with you?" he asked Stephanie.

"No," she said. "I do it all. Besides, if we get pictures of this monster, no one's going to care about words." She pointed to the staircase aft. "There are a couple of empty cabins below. You can put your stuff wherever you want."

Sharp tossed his bag onto a chair. "Who's Ellis?" he said. "The name—*Ellis Explorer*."

"Barnaby Ellis . . . Ellis Bearings . . . the Ellis Foundation . . . Ellis Publications. The bearings funded the foundation, the foundation owns the boat. When one of the publications needs the boat, they borrow it from the foundation."

"You work for him?"

"No, I'm free lance. I work for the *Geographic*, for *Traveler*, for whoever wants to pay me."

"Hey, navy man," a voice called down from the bridge.

"Come meet Hector," Stephanie said, and she led the way up onto the bridge.

Hector appeared to be in his mid-forties. He was dark-skinned and beefy, and he wore a starched white shirt with captain's shoulder boards, creased black trousers and spit-shined black shoes. He was working with a pencil and a ruler on a chart of the waters around Bermuda. "This Darling," he said, "he tells me to go anchor out here"—he tapped a spot on the chart—"but out here there's no bottom."

"Did he talk you through it?" Sharp asked.

"Every step. Around the point here, north from here to the buoy, then northwest to here. But the chart says there's no bottom till five hundred fathoms. I can't anchor in five hundred fathoms."

"Do what he says," said Sharp. "If he says there's a bottom there, there's a bottom there. It may be a sea mount, it may be a ledge. It may be part of the shelf."

"But the chart—"

"Captain," Sharp said, "in Bermuda, if I had to choose between some mapmaker from Coast and Geodetic Survey and Whip Darling, I'd go with Whip Darling every time."

IT WAS AFTER five when they left the point at Dockyard behind and headed north toward the channel markers. Sharp and Stephanie stood on the observation deck atop the cabin and watched the little puffs of cumulus cloud change color as the lowering sun struck them from different angles.

"Where do you live?" Sharp asked.

"San Francisco, sort of. But nowhere, really. I keep a tiny apartment there, just to have a place to come back to, but I'm away ten or eleven months a year."

"So you're not married."

"Hardly," she said, smiling. "Who'd have me? He'd never see me. When I got started in this business—fresh out of college, I was working for a little paper in Kansas, and I moonlighted wildlife pictures—I knew I'd have to make a choice. I knew I couldn't have it both ways. A lot of my friends are photographers who specialize in what I do—sports, adventure, animals—and of the ones who get married, ninety percent get divorced."

"Is it worth it?"

"It has been. I've been everywhere in the world, my passport's as thick as the phone book. I've met a lot of people, done a lot of crazy things, photographed everything from tigers to army ants. But I'm beginning to get tired of it. Now and then, I think about settling down. But every time I do, the phone rings, and I'm off to somewhere new." She waved her hand at the sea, and said, "Like now."

"How much do you know about giant squid?"

"Nothing. Well, almost nothing. I read a couple of articles on the way over. I gather that nobody's ever gotten a picture of one, and that's enough for me; it isn't often one of us gets to do something that's never been done before."

"There's a reason, you know. They're rare, and they're dangerous."

"Well," she said, "that's the fun of it, right? Look at it this way, Marcus. We're getting paid to do what other people couldn't do if they had all the money in the world: take chances and make discoveries. It's called living."

As Sharp looked at her, he suddenly felt a stab of pain that he hadn't felt in many months, the pain of remembering Karen.

"I TELL YOU," Hector said, pointing at the fathometer, "there's no bottom here." A faint orange light whirled on a circular screen, blipping brighter as it passed the mark for 480 fathoms.

"Are you sure you're in the right place?" Sharp asked.

"The SatNav says I'm on the money, right where he said."

Sharp looked out the window. There was nothing in the color of the water that suggested a shallow spot; the sea was a uniform gray, like burnished steel. "Drop the anchor," he said.

"Easy for you to say, navy man," said Hector. "It's not your two grand worth of anchor and chain."

"Drop it. If you lose it, I'll dive it up for you myself." Sharp smiled.

Hector looked at him, then said, "Shit," and pushed the button that released the anchor. They heard a splash, followed by the rattle of chain through the hawsehole in the bow. A crewman in a striped matelot shirt stood on the forepeak and watched the chain plummet.

"Mind if I turn on your side-scan?" Sharp asked.

"Go ahead."

Sharp turned the switch on the side-scan sonar and pressed his face to the rubber gasket. The gray screen brightened, and a white line appeared, created by reflected sonar impulses, showing the contour of the bottom more than half a mile away. Where is it? he wondered. Where's the secret shelf that'll snag the anchor before it disappears into the deep?

He heard Hector say, "I'll be damned," and just then a tiny white stroke appeared on the top left corner of the sonar screen, reflecting a little outcropping from the cliff. The rattle of the anchor chain stopped.

"Two hundred and ten feet," Hector said. "How the hell did Darling know that?"

"Twenty-five years at sea out here, that's how," Sharp said. "Whip knows every pimple on the ledge; and he knew how the tide would carry your anchor."

"Does he know where this giant squid is?"

"Nobody knows that," Sharp said, and he went down the steps into the cabin.

THEY HAD DINNER in the cabin: microwaved hamburgers, steamed pasta and salad. When they had washed the dishes, Eddie and the two crewmen gathered around the TV and watched a tape of *The Hunt for Red October*, and Hector returned to the bridge.

Stephanie poured coffee for herself and Sharp, took a cigarette from one of her camera bags and led him outside onto the open stern. The moon was so bright that it extinguished the stars around it; the sea was as flat as glass.

"What about you?" she asked him. "Are you married?"

"No," Sharp said, and then—he wasn't sure why—he told her about Karen.

"That's rough," she said when he had finished. "I don't think I could deal with that kind of pain."

Before Sharp could say anything else, they heard Hector shout, "Hey, navy man!" from the bridge.

They walked forward along a passageway on the port side and up four steel steps to the outside door of the bridge.

"Come here," Hector said.

Sharp stepped inside the bridge. In darkness, it looked like an abandoned nightclub, for the only lights were the red and green and orange glows from the electronic gear.

"What do you make of that?" Hector said, and he gestured at the side-scan sonar.

"Of what?"

"We've been swinging at anchor. I think maybe we swung ourselves right overtop a shipwreck."

As he bent to the machine, Sharp thought what a nice irony it would be if they did discover an old wreck, unseen and untouched for hundreds of years. They had the submersible, so they could reach the wreck, photograph it, perhaps even recover something from it. Whip would be amazed.

Sharp closed his eyes, then opened them again and let them focus on the gray screen. He knew that side-scan sonar images could be remarkably accurate, if the object being drawn was in good shape, alone and on a flat bottom. He had seen a side-scan picture in *National Geographic* of a ship that had sunk in the Arctic. The ship sat upright on the bottom, its masts and superstructure clearly visible, looking as if it were about to sail away. But that ship had sunk at anchor in three hundred feet of water. If there was a ship here, it had tumbled for half a mile, probably breaking apart as it fell. It might be nothing more than a heap of scrap.

What he saw was a shapeless smear. He looked at the calibration numbers on the side of the screen: The smear seemed to be twenty or thirty meters long, possibly the right size for a shipwreck.

"It could be," he said.

"Have a look at it from the sub tomorrow," said Hector. "A

lot of ships were lost around here during the war. Maybe it's one of them. Give me the loran numbers, will you?"

Sharp stepped away from the sonar screen and crossed the bridge to the loran. He read the numbers aloud to Hector, who scribbled them on a piece of paper.

None of them looked at the sonar screen again. If they had, they would have seen a change in the shapeless smear. They would have seen some lines fade, others appear, as the thing three thousand feet beneath them began to move.

24

KAREN'S ARMS WERE out, reaching for him; her eyes pleaded for
help, and she was screaming, but in a language he couldn't
understand. He tried to reach her, but his legs wouldn't work.
He felt as if he were slogging through transparent mud or
being held back by something that forced him to move in slow
motion. The closer he got, the farther away she seemed. And
then something was chasing her, something he couldn't see
but that must be huge and terrifying, for her fear became
panic and her screams grew louder. All of a sudden she disappeared, and the thing chasing her was gone, too, and all that
was left was a loud, piercing buzz.

Sharp awoke, and for a moment he didn't know where he
was. The bed was small, not his, and the light was dim. Only
the buzz remained, an urgent summons from somewhere near
his head. He rolled over and saw an intercom phone on the
bulkhead. He picked up the phone and mumbled his name.

"Rise and shine, Marcus," said Stephanie. "Time to go."

As he hung up, Sharp felt a rush of adrenaline. He had
volunteered for this, but what yesterday had seemed exciting
was fast becoming frightening. He had never ridden in a submarine, let alone a submarine a third the size of a subway car.
He didn't like crowded elevators—who did?—and he felt uneasy in interior cabins on ships. He suddenly wondered if he
would discover he was a closet claustrophobe.

Well, he thought, you'll soon find out.

As he shaved and dressed in jeans, a shirt, wool socks and
a sweater, his apprehension gave way once again to excite-

ment. At least this was action, a challenge. At least this was something new. As Stephanie would say, this was living.

The sun had barely cleared the horizon when Sharp arrived in the cabin and poured himself a cup of coffee. Through the windows in the rear of the cabin he saw Eddie and one of the crewmen removing the tarpaulin from the submersible. Stephanie was on the afterdeck, mounting a video camera in an underwater housing. Then, as his gaze wandered to the right, he saw that the *Privateer* was tied to the port side of the ship. He started out of the cabin, but stopped when he heard Darling's voice behind him, up on the bridge, talking to Hector.

"Morning, Marcus," Darling said when Sharp appeared on the bridge. "Are you sure you still want to go down there and freeze your buns off?"

"Yes," Sharp said. "I'm sure."

Darling turned to Hector and said, "I'll have my mate hang off a ways till you launch, then he'll track the sub on my gear."

Sharp said, "What are you gonna do, Whip?"

"Keep an eye on you, Marcus," Darling said, and he smiled. "You're too valuable to lose." He left the bridge and walked aft to talk to Mike on the *Privateer*.

Sharp carried his coffee down to the stern. At the top of a ladder he met Stephanie on her way up, and she gestured for him to follow her through a watertight door above the main cabin and aft of the bridge.

It was the control room for the submersible, and it was dark, lit only by a red bulb in the overhead and by four television monitors that were showing color bars. One of the crewmen, whom Sharp remembered as Andy, sat before a panel dotted with colored lights and keyboard buttons, wearing a headset and a microphone.

"Andy keeps tabs on all our systems," Stephanie said. "Your friend Whip will be in here with him—we can talk to him anytime."

Sharp pointed at the TV monitors. "The submersible is hard-wired to the surface?"

"Everything's videotaped, for the foundation. One fiber-optic cable does it all. I've got video cameras inside and outside the sub, plus my still cameras. Can I give you a camera? We'll be at different portholes, we may see different things."

"Sure," Sharp said, "if you've got a real idiot-proof camera. What do you want pictures of? Gorgonian corals? Algae growth?"

"No way." Stephanie grinned. "Monsters. Nothing but monsters. Great big ones."

AT CLOSE RANGE, the submersible looked to Sharp like a giant antihistamine capsule, a Dristan with arms. Each arm had steel pincers on the end, and mounted between them was a video camera in a globular housing.

The sun was higher now, and there wasn't a breath of breeze. Perspiration poured from Sharp as he lowered himself through the round hatch in the top of the submersible. The crewman manning the crane gave him a thumbs-up sign, and he smiled wanly in reply.

Stephanie was already inside, as was Eddie, wearing a down vest and crouching forward to check his switches and gauges.

The interior of the capsule was a tube, twelve feet long, six feet wide and five feet high. There were three small portholes, one in the bow for Eddie, one on either side for Stephanie and Sharp. A square cushion sat on the steel deck before Sharp's porthole, and he dropped to his knees and crawled to the cushion. He found that he could sit with his legs curled beneath him, or kneel with his face pressed to the porthole, or lie with his feet raised. But there was no way he could straighten out.

What would happen if he got a cramp? How would he shake it out? Don't think about it, he told himself. Just *do* it.

"How long does it take to get to the bottom?" he asked.

"Half an hour," said Stephanie. "We drop at a hundred feet a minute."

Not too bad. He could survive for an hour, anyway. "And how long do we spend down there?"

"Up to four hours."

"Four hours!" Never, Sharp thought. Not a chance.

He heard the hatch slam above him, and a metallic hiss as it was dogged down.

Stephanie passed him a small 35-mm camera with a wide-angle lens, and said, "All loaded and ready to go. Just push the button."

Sharp tried to take the camera, but it slipped from his sweaty palms, and Stephanie caught it an inch above the steel deck. "You look like death," she said.

"No kidding." Sharp wiped his hands on his trousers and took the camera from her.

"What are you worried about? This is a state-of-the-art deep boat, and Eddie is a state-of-the-art pilot." She smiled. "Right, Eddie?"

"Fuckin' A," Eddie said. He mumbled something into the microphone suspended from his headset, and suddenly the capsule jerked and began to rise as the crane lifted it off its cradle and swung it out over the side of the ship. For a moment it yawed back and forth like an amusement-park ride, and Sharp had to brace himself to keep from being tossed across the deck. Then it dropped slowly until it thudded into the water, and its motion changed to a gentle rocking.

Sharp looked through the porthole and saw the sea lapping at the glass. From overhead came the metallic sound of the shackle being released from the submersible's lifting ring.

The capsule began to sink. Water now covered the portholes. Sharp pushed his cheek to the glass and rolled his eyes upward, straining for one last glance at sunlight. Refracted through the moving water, the blue of the sky and the white of the clouds and the gold of the sun danced together hypnotically.

Then the colors faded, replaced by a monochromatic blue mist. All noise ceased, except for the soft whirring of the electric motor aboard the submersible.

The world had been swallowed by the sea.

Sweat was quickly evaporating from Sharp's forehead and from under his arms and down his back, and he felt chilly. In less than a minute, the temperature had dropped something like thirty degrees. And yet he was still sweating, not from heat but from fear, and the creeping onset of claustrophobia.

He looked through the porthole and saw that the blue outside was fast deepening to violet. He dared his eyes to wander downward. Rays of sunlight seemed to struggle to light the water, but they were dispersed and consumed. Below, blue yielded to black, and all was night.

They fell slowly, seeing nothing, hearing nothing, feeling nothing. Then Sharp realized he was taking comfort in the nothingness, for he began to recall the tales Darling had told him about what lived down here in this night, this dark. And he shivered.

25

SHARP WAS FREEZING. His wool socks were soaked with the condensation on the inside of the steel capsule. Up on the surface, the wetness had felt cool and comfortable, but now, although the condensation had evaporated, his socks had not dried. His toes were numb, the soles of his feet itched. He put his hands beneath his sweater and tucked them under his arms, and leaned away from the porthole to look over Eddie's shoulder at his gauges. The outside temperature was 4 degrees centigrade, about 40 degrees Fahrenheit. Inside it wasn't much warmer, just above 50. They were at two thousand feet, and falling.

Into his microphone Eddie said, "Activating illumination," and he flicked a switch. Two 1,000-watt lamps on top of the submersible flashed on, casting a flood of yellow that penetrated fifteen or twenty feet before being swallowed by the blackness.

And then a universe of life exploded before Sharp's eyes. Tiny planktonic animals swirled in and out of the light, a living snowstorm of sea life. An infinitesimal shrimp adhered to his porthole and began to march purposefully across the glass. Something resembling a gray-and-red ribbon with yellow eyes and a pompadour of tiny spikes wriggled up to the porthole, fluttered before it for a moment, then darted away.

"Look," Eddie said, pointing out his porthole. Sharp craned to see, but whatever it was, was gone. He returned to his own porthole, and a moment later he could see it—it appeared, serenely circling the capsule, a creation of some disturbed imagination.

It was an anglerfish: round, bulbous and brownish yellow, trailing short, mucous fins. Its eyes protruded like blue-green sores, it had fangs like needles of diamond, its flesh was crisscrossed with black veins. It looked like a cyst with teeth. Where its nose should have been was a white stalk, and atop the stalk, glowing like a beacon, was a light.

Sharp had seen pictures of anglerfish. They used their stalks as lures, dangling the lights before their gaping mouths to attract curious and unwary prey.

Because there was nothing in the background to compare it to, Sharp had no idea how far away the fish was, or how big.

"What do you think?" he asked Eddie, and he held his hands a couple of feet apart.

Eddie grinned, and held up his hand and spread his thumb and index finger: The fish was four inches long, at most.

Sharp heard the motor drive on Stephanie's camera firing frame after frame. She was holding the lens against her porthole, and rotating the f-stop ring, hoping by random shooting to get a good exposure.

"I thought you only wanted monsters," Sharp said.

"What do you think these are?" Stephanie pointed out her porthole. "Good God, look at that!"

Sharp saw a flicker of yellow pass Stephanie's porthole. He turned back and waited for the animal to make its way around the capsule.

This creature seemed to have no fins; it might have been a yellow arrow, save that its entire digestive system, gut and stomach, hung down from a pouch and trailed along, pulsing. Its lower jaw was studded with pinprick teeth, and its black, milk-white eyes stuck out of its head like round buttons.

Soon, other animals swarmed around the capsule, drawn by the light, inquisitive and unafraid. There were snakelike creatures that seemed to trail hairs along their backs; large-eyed eels with lumps on their heads that looked like tumors; translucent globes that seemed to be all mouth.

Sharp started as Darling's voice suddenly boomed over the speaker inside the capsule. "You've got yourself a bloody zoo down there, Marcus," he said. "If the aquarium ever comes to its senses, I know where to drop my traps next time."

"Wait'll they see these pictures, Whip," Sharp said. "They'll come back to you on their hands and knees."

Forgetting his fear, ignoring the cold, Sharp picked up the camera Stephanie had given him, and adjusted its focus. He knelt on the cushion, and waited for the next miniature mystery to swim by.

26

MIKE SLAPPED HIMSELF in the face, and the sting roused him for a moment. But as soon as his eyes returned to the screen of the fish-finder, he felt his lids begin to droop. He stood up, stretched, yawned and looked out the window. The ship was about a quarter of a mile away, and behind it he saw the gray lump of Bermuda. Otherwise, from horizon to horizon the sea was empty.

Whip had told him to keep his eyes glued to the fish-finder —he called it the poor man's side-scan sonar—and for more than an hour Mike had. But the image hadn't changed at all: There was the line that delineated the bottom, and just above it the little dot of the meandering submersible. Nothing else. Not a broken smear that would signal a school of fish, certainly not the solid mark of something big and dense, like a passing whale.

Normally, Mike wouldn't have liked being left alone on the boat, but this was different: There was a ship nearby, and Whip was on it, and all the action was half a mile away and didn't involve him. He had nothing to do but watch, and report in if he saw something. Best of all, he had no decisions to make.

He didn't just feel calm, he felt hypnotized, not only by the static screen but also because the sea rocked the *Privateer* with such subtle gentleness that before he knew what was happening, he had twice found himself lulled to sleep. He might not have woken up at all if his head hadn't banged against the bulkhead.

The radio crackled to life, and Mike heard Whip's voice: *"Privateer . . . Privateer . . . Privateer . . .* come back."

Mike picked up the microphone, pushed the "talk" button and said, "Go ahead, Whip."

"How you doing, Michael?"

" 'Bout to fall dead asleep. This is worse than watching paint dry."

"Nothing's going on—take a breather."

"I'll do that," Mike said. "Make some coffee, go out in the fresh air and fiddle with that whoreson pump."

"Leave the volume up and the door open, so you'll hear me if I call."

"Roger that, Whip. Standing by."

Mike replaced the microphone on its hook. He looked at the fish-finder one more time, saw that the image hadn't changed and went below.

In the wheelhouse, the fish-finder continued to glow. For several moments, the image stayed as steady as if it were a still picture. Then, on the right side of the screen, about a third of the way up from the bottom, a new mark appeared. It was solid, a single mass, and slowly it began to move across the screen, toward the submersible.

27

THERE HAD BEEN a change in the creature. Until now, as it had grown and matured, it had lived adventitiously, drifting with the currents, eating whatever food came its way. But food was no longer plentiful; passivity could not guarantee survival.

Its instincts had not changed—they were genetically programmed, immutable—but its impulse for survival had altered. It had started to become more active in its responses to its environment.

It could no longer live as a scavenger; it had been forced to become a hunter.

Hovering now at the confluence of two currents that swept around the volcano, the creature grew agitated; something was intruding, disturbing the normal rhythms of the sea.

It sensed a change in its surroundings, as if energy had suddenly surged into its world. There was a faint but persistent pulsing in the water; small animals darted back and forth, flashing bioluminescence; larger ones traveled nearby, subtly altering the water pressure.

The small and relatively weak human eye could not have perceived any light at all, but the creature's enormous eyes were suffused with rod cells that gathered and registered even the smallest scintilla of light.

Now it perceived more than a scintilla. Somewhere in the distance below there was a great light, moving, emitting the pulsing sound, galvanizing other animals.

The creature had not eaten in days, and though it did not respond to time, it was driven by cycles of need.

It drew water in through its body cavity and expelled it through its funnel, aiming for the source of light.

It began to hunt.

28

"YOU LOOK COLD, Marcus," Stephanie said.

Sharp nodded. "You got that right," he said. His arms were crossed over his chest, his hands tucked into his armpits, but still he couldn't stop shivering. "How come you're not?"

"I've got a layer of wool over a layer of silk over a layer of cotton." She turned to Eddie. "Where's the coffee?"

Eddie pointed and said, "In the box there."

Stephanie reached over, opened a plastic box and took out a thermos bottle. She poured the top full of coffee and passed it to Sharp.

The coffee was strong, sour-bitter, unsweetened and harsh, but as it pooled in his stomach, Sharp welcomed the warmth. "Thanks," he said.

He looked at his watch. They had been down for nearly three hours, drifting at twenty-five hundred feet, about five hundred feet over the bottom, and they had seen nothing but the small, strange creatures that gathered curiously around the capsule and then vanished into the darkness.

"What say I put her down on the bottom?" Eddie said into his microphone.

Darling's voice came over the speaker. "Might's well," he said. "Maybe you'll see a shark."

Eddie pushed the control stick forward, and the capsule began to drop.

The bottom was like pictures Sharp had seen of the surface of the moon: barren, dusty, undulating. The submersible pushed a slight pressure wave before it, and mud rose up and billowed away as the machine moved along.

Suddenly Eddie straightened up and said, "Christ!"

"What?" Sharp said. "What is it?"

Eddie pointed at Sharp's porthole, and so Sharp shaded his eyes and pressed his face to the glass.

Snakes, Sharp thought at first. A million snakes. All swarming on a dead body.

And then, as he watched, he thought: No, they can't be snakes, they're eels. But no, not eels either—they had fins. They were fish, some kind of weird fish, writhing and twisting and tearing at flesh. Bits of flesh broke loose and floated away, and were instantly mobbed and ingested and reduced to molecules by other, smaller scavengers.

One of the eely, snakelike things detached itself from its food and backed away and, confused or enraged by the lights, attacked the submersible. It thrust its face at Sharp's porthole and thrashed, as if to suck the entire machine into its belly. The face became nothing but a mouth, and around its edges were rasping teeth and a probing tongue. The body twisted like a corkscrew, frantic to force the face to drill a hole in the prey.

A hagfish, Sharp realized, one of the nightmare demons that bored holes in larger animals and gnawed the life out of them.

Eddie swung the submersible over the gnarled ball of hagfish, pressed its bow among them, driving them away, and then Sharp could see what they had been feeding on.

"A sperm whale!" he said. "It's the lower jaw of a sperm whale. Do you see that, Whip?"

"Yes," Darling's voice said, sounding flat and distant.

"What the hell kills a sperm whale?"

Darling didn't answer, but in the silence, Sharp suddenly thought: *I* know. And he began to sweat. He strained his eyes to see beyond the perimeter of light. Fish darted back and forth, not fading from view but suddenly appearing and disappearing, phantoms that crossed the rim of light. He was comforted by them and by what they signaled: Whip had once said that as long as fish were around, you didn't have to worry about sharks, because, long before a man could, the fish read the electromagnetic impulses that warned of a shark's intention to attack. It was when the fish vanished that you worried.

On the other hand, Sharp reminded himself, *Architeuthis* isn't a shark. He raised his camera to the porthole.

29

THE CREATURE'S EYES gathered more and more light; its other senses recorded the increased vibrations in the water. Something was there, not far away, and it was moving.

Its olfactories detected no signs of life, no confirmation of prey. If it had been less hungry, the creature might have been more cautious, might have hung back in the darkness and waited. But its body's needs were impelling the brain to be reckless, so it continued to move toward the source of the light.

Soon it saw the lights, little pinpoints of brightness piercing the black, and throughout its body it felt the thrumming vibrations emanating from the thing.

Motion meant life; vibrations meant life. And so, although it had yet to perceive the scent of life, it determined that the thing was alive.

It attacked.

30

"THE THING'S NOT down here," Eddie said. "We're going up." He pulled back on the control stick.

Sharp looked at the digital depth readout on the console in front of Eddie. It was calibrated in meters, and as Sharp watched, the numbers changed—ever so slowly, he thought, and he tried to will the numbers to flash faster—from 970 meters to 969. He sighed and massaged his toes, and wondered if they were frostbitten.

Suddenly the capsule jolted and yawed to one side. Sharp was knocked off his knees, and he grabbed for a handhold. The capsule righted itself and continued upward.

"What the hell was that?" Sharp said.

Eddie didn't answer. He was hunched forward, his shoulders tensed.

Stephanie's back was pressed against the bulkhead, her hands braced on the deck. "What was it, Eddie?" she said.

"I didn't see," Eddie said. "It felt like we hit an air pocket, or like a ship passed overhead."

"You mean a current?"

Over the speaker Darling's voice said, "Not a chance. There *are* no currents down there." He paused. "Something's out there."

As Darling's words registered with Sharp, he suddenly felt a weight like a sack of rocks in his stomach. Oh God, he thought. Here we go.

He saw that his camera had tumbled across the deck, and now, as he retrieved it and checked its settings and adjusted the focus, he found that his fingers weren't working very well. They were trembling, and each one seemed to be independent and to defy the messages from his brain. A drop of sweat fell from the tip of his nose onto the lens, and he wiped it away with the tail of his shirt.

He looked over at Stephanie. She had her back to him, and her camera lens was against the porthole. She pressed the release button, and the motor drive fired a dozen frames in a couple of seconds. "Take some pictures, Marcus," she said over her shoulder.

"Of what?" Sharp said. "I didn't see anything."

"The lens is wider than your eye. Maybe it'll see something."

Before Sharp could reply, the capsule was jolted again, hard, and it careened to the left. A shadow passed before the lights, dimming them, then disappeared.

"God dammit!" Eddie shouted, and he fought the stick, righting the capsule.

Sharp put his camera to the porthole and pressed the shutter release, advanced the film and shot again.

The capsule was rising again. Sharp looked at the readout: 960 meters, 959, 958 . . .

31

THE GIANT SQUID rushed through the darkness, seized by parox-
ysms of frustrated rage. Its whips lashed out, hooks erect,
then recoiled and lashed out again, as if trying to flay the sea
itself. Its colors flashed from gray to brown to maroon to red
to pink, then back to an ashy white.

It had passed once over the lighted thing, appraising it;
then it had tried to kill it, although the signs of life the thing
emitted were vague and uncertain.

The thing had been hard, an impenetrable carapace, and it
had fought back with vigorous movement and alien sounds.

Because its attack had created no encouraging spoor of
blood or torn flesh, the squid had not pressed the attack. It
had moved on in search of other nourishment.

But its cells were not accustomed to being denied; its digestive juices had begun to flow in anticipation. Now they
were causing the creature pain, confusion and rage.

Seeking food, any food, it rushed through the water, moving slowly upward, far behind the retreating lighted thing, not
pursuing it but following it nevertheless.

32

"THAT WAS *SOMETHING*," Stephanie said as she pulled herself up through the open hatch and sat on its rim. She grinned down at Darling and Hector, who stood below on the ship's deck.

Sharp squeezed through the hatch and sat beside her. He took a deep breath, savoring the fresh air. Savoring safety.

"Did you see it?" Hector asked.

"We saw about a million of the weirdest things in the world," said Stephanie. "Things I never even imagined, let alone photographed, before."

"No, I mean the thing that knocked you around down there? What rocked the boat?"

"I don't know, I didn't really see it." She looked at Sharp. "Did you?"

"No," Sharp said, looking at Darling. "Did you get anything on the video, Whip?"

"Just a shadow," Darling said, and he began to walk around the submersible, examining it, touching the paint here and there.

Eddie, who had exited the capsule first and was helping the two crewmen secure it to its cradle, said, "Whatever it was, it didn't want to tackle the sub. It had a look at us and kept on truckin'."

"Maybe," said Darling. He had stopped in his circuit of the capsule, and he was touching something.

Sharp leaned over the side and looked where Whip's fingers were rubbing the paint. He saw five ragged scratch marks, two or three feet long; something had slashed through the paint and exposed bare metal beneath. "It's the squid, isn't it," he said.

Darling nodded and said, "Looks like it to me."

"Well, if it was," Eddie said, "he gave us a once-over and took off."

"We'll be ready for him next time," said Stephanie. "I'm going to readjust the video cameras." She pulled her legs out of the hatch, slid down off the capsule and said to Eddie, "What's your turnaround time?"

"Four hours," Eddie replied, looking at his watch. "We should be ready to go down again at about three-thirty, four o'clock."

Not me, Sharp thought, I've had enough excitement for one day. "I'll stay topside," he said. "I can see plenty on the TV screens to keep the navy happy."

"You couldn't go even if you wanted to, navy man," said Hector. "You've already been bumped."

"By whom?"

When Hector didn't answer, Sharp looked at Darling and saw a look of disgust on his face. Then Darling turned away and spit over the side of the ship.

33

HERBERT TALLEY WATCHED the ramshackle pickup truck head off down the driveway, then he turned and went into the house. He crossed the living room, walked down a hallway and opened the door to Manning's bedroom. "Wake up, Osborn," he said. The room smelled of night breath and stale brandy, and Talley went to the far wall, opened the curtains and raised the window.

Manning groaned and said, "What time is it?"

"Nearly noon. Meet me on the terrace."

While Manning brushed his teeth and poured himself a cup of coffee, Talley stood on the terrace and gazed across Castle Harbour. At the airport a mile away a 747 lumbered in for a landing, and when the pilot reversed his engines, the shriek was so loud that the spoon trembled on Talley's saucer. What was it about Tucker's Town, Talley wondered, that enticed the rich and famous to buy and refurbish huge houses practically on top of one another for the privilege of enduring deafening noise twenty times a day? Exclusivity, he decided; the gate at the end of the lane and the sign that said PRIVATE.

Manning came out from the kitchen, carrying his coffee and wearing a bathrobe. "What's up?" he said.

"That fisherman, Frith. He was just here. He overheard some interesting radio chatter about half an hour ago, between a research vessel and the navy base. A Lieutenant Sharp was reporting in."

"And?" Manning was edgy and impatient, and his hangover didn't help. When he saw Talley pause and smile, he barked, "Dammit, Herbert, stop playing games. What's going on?"

"The ship is called the *Ellis Explorer*. It's got a submersible on board. It's here looking for *Architeuthis*. I think they found it, even though they don't know for sure."

"Ellis," Manning said. "Barnaby Ellis?"

"I don't know, I guess so. But the point is, Osborn, I think the squid is still here and still hungry. And there's a ship out there with the equipment and capability to take people down to it. On that sub we could see it, study it, film it, learn about it. And you could kill it, if . . ." Talley paused.

"If what?" Manning said.

"If we can get on board. You have power, Osborn. Now's the time to use it."

Manning hesitated, thought for a moment, then got up and went indoors. Talley heard him punching numbers into a telephone.

Talley walked to the edge of the terrace and looked down at the big oval swimming pool. A scuba tank lay beside the pool, rigged with backpack and regulator. Talley could see that it had been there for days, if not weeks, for it was covered with pine needles, and a salamander had made a home among its straps. He wondered if the tank had been used by one of Manning's children, and if Manning had left it there as a kind of bleak memorial.

Talley had begun to feel restless. Manning was spending his evenings with a brandy bottle, and Talley sensed that his passionate anger was being transformed by inaction and frustration into despair.

He heard Manning talking into the phone, and he thought, Good; maybe this will get things going again.

When Manning came back, he said, "It's all set. I talked to Barnaby himself. The ship is here for one of his magazines. He agreed to bump his people and give us a crack at it tomorrow."

"Tomorrow?" Talley said. "Why not today? Frith said they've got a dive scheduled for this afternoon."

"The sub is filled. The Bermuda government's got someone on it this afternoon. It seems they've got a plan to kill the squid."

"How?" Talley suddenly felt sick. "How do they think they're going to kill that beast?"

"I have no idea," Manning said, "but I wouldn't worry about it."

"How can you be so nonchalant? You've spent—"

"I'd say their chances are about one in a million."

"Why?"

"Because the chief squid hunter they're sending is your friend Liam St. John."

34

SHARP AND DARLING stood on the observation deck and watched St. John unload his gear from the aquarium boat. There were four aluminum cases, two boxes of fresh fish and a modified fish trap, about three feet square, made of chicken wire and steel reinforcing rod.

St. John consulted with Eddie and Stephanie. Then Eddie called the two crewmen over, and they hauled the cases to the submersible and began to fasten the wire cage to the top of the submersible, forward of the hatch.

Stephanie climbed the ladder to the observation deck. "This should be interesting," she said. "He's even got Hector jazzed, and that takes some doing." She pointed to the after-deck, and they saw Hector following St. John around, asking questions.

Darling looked at Stephanie, and after a moment he said, "Sometimes there's a reason certain things haven't ever been done, and that's because they can't be done."

"I know," Stephanie said, "but this doesn't look to me like an impossibility. Just a long shot."

Sharp said, "So you think he's got a chance?"

"A chance, yes. And he's sure got enough bait. A hundred pounds of fresh tuna should attract anything that lives down there, and keep it busy long enough for us to do what we have to do."

"How does he think he's gonna kill it?" Darling asked.

"With two weapons," Stephanie said, gesturing at the mechanical arms of the submersible. "Both are attached to the sub's arms, and he can work them from inside the capsule. One's a spear gun loaded with a syringe of strychnine, enough to kill a dozen elephants. The other's like a diver's bang-stick —it fires a twelve-gauge shotgun shell, loaded with globs of mercury that disperse like poisonous shrapnel. I don't know that much about giant squid, but it seems to me he's got enough firepower to kill it two or three times over. Eddie thinks so, too."

"I can see how you think it all makes sense," Darling said, "but what you haven't calculated is that this beast doesn't know sense. It doesn't play by our rules. It *makes* the rules."

"He's taken that into account."

"How?"

"If the weapons don't kill it, he thinks the squid might wrap itself around the capsule, and then it can be brought to the surface on the cables, and killed up here."

"My God, girl," Darling said. "That's like trying to catch a tiger by sticking your arm in his mouth and shouting, 'I've got him!' Don't you know what kind of beast this is?"

"He can't crush the submersible," Stephanie said. "I think it sounds like a pretty good idea."

"Well, I think it sounds like damn foolishness," said Darling, and he left the deck.

"Don't go down," Sharp said to Stephanie when Darling had gone. "Let St. John try it alone. You can go the next time."

"You're nice to care, Marcus," she said, and she touched his cheek. "But I want to go. That's what I'm here to do."

DARLING ENTERED THE bridge, asked Hector's permission to use the radio and called over to the *Privateer*, which by now had drifted a mile to the north.

It took Mike several moments to respond. Darling assumed he had been out on the stern, napping or working on his pump.

"Just checking in, Michael," he said. "You staying awake?"

"Barely. Okay with you if I put a line down, try to catch me some snappers?"

"Sure, but drive the boat over here first. Get within a couple hundred yards, then kill the engine and let her drift. That way you'll be in position to track the sub."

"Okay. When are they putting it down?"

"In about an hour. And, Michael, once it's down there, try not to nod off. I want you wide awake and firing on all cylinders, in case you're needed."

"Roger that, Whip," Mike said. *"Privateer* standing by."

35

MIKE TOOK THE boat out of gear and let it settle. He looked across the still water and tried to gauge his distance from the ship. A hundred and fifty yards, he guessed, maybe two hundred. Just about right. He turned off the engine.

He took the binoculars off the shelf in front of the wheel and focused them on the submersible. The hatch was open, and people were still fooling with the sub's mechanical arms. He had plenty of time.

He went aft and cut up the mackerel he'd put out in the sun to thaw. He rigged two hooks on a line, put half the mackerel on each, then tied a two-pound weight to the end of the line and tossed the rig overboard. He let the line run through his fingers until he judged that the hooks were about a hundred feet down. Then he stopped it and stood with his hip against the bulwark, holding the line in his fingertips and jigging it every few seconds, to create the illusion of a wounded fish.

He saw at his feet the bucket that the mackerel had been in. It was half-full of bloody water, scales and bits of flesh. He picked up the bucket, tossed its contents overboard and watched a little slick of blood and oil begin to spread behind the boat.

When after five minutes he hadn't had a nibble, it occurred to him that if there were any fish around, they might be far above or far below his bait. The fish-finder was still on; he might as well take advantage of it, see if it could give him any clues. He cleated the line off and went forward, into the wheelhouse.

The screen was a mess, he'd never seen a pattern like this before. If he hadn't known for a fact that he was in three thousand feet of water, he'd have sworn the boat was aground. It looked as if some of the impulses sent out by the fish-finder were bouncing off something right beneath the boat, while others were getting through but being deflected on their way into the deep. The pattern was shimmery and indistinct.

Maybe something had gotten caught in the through-hull fitting that held the machine's transponder. When they got to shore, he'd put on a scuba tank and go under the boat and have a look. Or maybe the machine itself had broken down. These days, with everything made of chips and circuit boards and invisible magic things that could only be understood by Japanese people with microscopes, there was no way a normal man could look at a piece of electronics and make a decent diagnosis.

He decided that when he'd finished fishing, when the sub was down, he'd pull the machine apart and see if the problem was something simple, like a loose wire.

He went back to the stern and uncleated his line, and right away could tell that something was wrong with it; it was too light. The weight was gone, and probably the hooks and bait as well.

He cursed and began to reel in the line.

36

THE CREATURE BLEW a volume of water from its funnel and propelled itself through the blue water, searching for the faint
trail of food scent that it had found, then lost, then found,
then lost again.

It was not comfortable this close to the surface, was not
accustomed to warm water and would not have been up here
if hunger had not driven it. It had found two bits of food and
had consumed them, and then it had rested in the cool
shadow of something above. But it had felt itself tapped by a
barrage of annoying impulses from that thing above, and so
after a moment it had moved again.

It plunged from blue water to violet, then rose once more
onto the terrain of blue.

It found nothing.

The higher it went, however, the closer to the surface it
rose, the more promising the water seemed. There was no
substance, but there were hints that tantalized the squid, as if
the water near the surface contained the residue of food.

It rose still higher, close to something dark above, and
soared directly beneath it, pushing a vast mass of water before
and above itself.

37

GODDAM PUPPY SHARKS, Mike thought as he examined the end of the monofilament line. Leave a line cleated for one minute, and they sneak up on you and bite it the hell off.

The boat rose beneath him, as if lifted by a sudden sea, and he raised his eyes from the line and looked at the flat water. It was weird how ground swells could appear like that, out of nowhere. In the distance, he saw the crane on the *Ellis Explorer* pick the submersible up from its cradle and swing it out over the side of the ship.

How long did they say it took the submersible to get to the bottom? Half an hour? He still had time to put another line down. But this time he wouldn't leave it, he'd keep it in his fingers, and if some puppy shark wanted to make a run at it, he'd get the surprise of his life.

Mike took a new wire leader off the midships hatch cover, leaned back against the bulwark and held the eye of the swivel on the end of the leader up to his face so he could see to thread the monofilament through it. He missed on his first try. Getting old, he thought, soon be needing granny glasses.

There was a vague noise behind him, a squishing kind of noise. Part of his mind registered the noise, but he was concentrating on threading the monofilament through the eye of the swivel.

The line slid through the hole. "Gotcha," Mike said.

He heard the squishing noise again, closer this time, and there was a sound of scratching. He started to turn toward it.

There was a smell to it, too, a familiar smell, but he couldn't quite place it.

And then suddenly Mike's world went dark. Something had him around the chest and head, something tight and wet. Mike's hands grabbed at it, then slipped off, as the thing that had him began to squeeze. He felt a pain as if a thousand ice picks were piercing his flesh.

As his feet lifted off the deck and he felt himself dragged through the air, he realized what had happened.

38

ANDY SAT AT the console in the control room. Darling stood behind him, wearing a headset, and Sharp stood beside Darling.

Because only two television cameras were in use, two of the four monitors were blank. The third showed the inside of the capsule: Eddie holding the stick and looking out his porthole, St. John testing the manipulators of the arms, Stephanie adjusting the lens of one of her cameras. The fourth monitor showed the scene outside the capsule: the bright aura from the lamps, the shower of plankton, and evanescent swirls of red as the eddying currents swept fish blood from the wire cage. Now and then, a small fish flashed before the camera, frantic with frustration at being unable to squeeze through the wire mesh and get to the source of the tantalizing spoor.

"Twenty-eight hundred," Andy said. "They're nearly there."

Soon they saw the bottom rise up. The turbulence of the submersible's propeller stirred the mud and caused a cloud that dimmed the video camera's lens.

The capsule settled, and the cloud cleared.

Suddenly a shadow passed over the bottom, disappeared and passed again, going the other way.

"Shark," said Darling. "Liam didn't figure on sharks. It'll probably go for his bait."

The image on the monitor jiggled as the capsule shook.

"What's that?" they heard St. John say.

"A shark, Doctor," Andy said into his microphone. "Just a shark."

"Well, do something!" said St. John.

Darling laughed. "We're half a bloody mile away, Liam. What do you want us to do?"

Andy pushed a button, then grabbed a control lever. The monitor of the exterior camera seemed to track outward, then it turned and faced upward. Now they could see the wire cage.

"It's a six-gill shark," Darling said. "Rare enough."

It was chocolate brown, with a bright green eye and six rippling gill slits. It was small, less than twice the size of the cage, but tenacious. It bit down on the corner of the cage and rolled its body, first one way, then the other, trying to tear a hole in the wire. Smaller fish hovered in the background, like vultures waiting to claim their share of the prize.

"Why haven't the fish taken off?" Sharp asked. "I thought they stayed away from feeding sharks."

"He's focused," Darling said, "and not on them. They can tell. He's sending out electromagnetic signals they can read clear as day. If he gets pissed off and turns on 'em, or another one comes by and gets jealous, *then* watch 'em scatter."

On the other monitor they saw St. John crawl forward and take the handles that operated one of the mechanical arms. Recessed in the control panel was a four-inch black-and-white monitor showing the image seen by the outside camera. Consulting it like a surgeon performing an arthroscopy, St. John pulled one handle, and the arm flexed; he pushed the other handle, and the arm rose and turned, pointing its needle toward the wire cage.

"Uh-oh," Darling said. He pressed the "talk" button and spoke into his microphone. "Don't do it, Liam. Leave the bloody shark alone."

St. John's voice came over the speaker. "Why should I let the shark take all the bait?"

"Listen. He can't take your cage. A six-gill doesn't have big rippers for teeth. He'll worry it and bend it, but he can't wreck it."

"So *you* say."

Darling sighed, searched for another tack, then said, "Look, Liam, you want to kill yourself, that's your business, but you got two other people down there with you maybe not so eager to play harps."

They saw Stephanie move toward St. John, and heard her say, "Doctor, if we waste one of your weapons on a shark, we're cutting our odds in half."

"Don't worry, Miss Carr," St. John said. "We'll still have plenty left to do the job."

On one monitor they saw St. John push a button; on the other they saw a burst of bubbles as the dart fired from the spear gun and struck the shark just behind its gill slits.

For a few seconds, the shark seemed to take no notice of the sting. Then suddenly its body arched, its tail and pectoral fins stiffened and its mouth jerked away from the cage and gaped. Rigid and quivering, it hung suspended in the water and then, like a fighter plane peeling away from formation, it banked to the right, rolled over, bounced once on the side of the capsule and fell into the mud.

The smaller fish closed in then, curiously circling the corpse before they turned back to the food in the wire cage.

One of the video monitors showed Stephanie pressing her camera against the porthole and snapping pictures.

"Won't a dead shark just bring *more* sharks?" Sharp asked.

"No," said Darling. "Sharks are strange that way. They'll kill each other, but if one of their own dies, they stay away. It's like they can read their own death in it." Darling paused and looked at the monitor. "Some things can't deal with death," he said. "Others thrive on it."

39

THE SQUID HAD fed, but after so long a deprivation, the protein it had consumed had not satisfied its hunger but rather had tantalized it, spurring a craving for more. And so the beast continued to hunt.

Suddenly, its senses were assaulted by new, conflicting signals—signals of food: of live prey, dead prey, of light, movement, sound. And so it began to charge back and forth, confused, defensive, ravenous, aggressive.

It moved upward in the water, seeking the source of the conflict, but it found nothing. And so it drifted downward, perceiving the soft bottom beneath it.

The rods in its eyes detected twinkles of bioluminescence from small animals nearby; it ignored them. Then more light flooded in, and more. Agitated, sensing both opportunity and danger, it drew water into its body and expelled it, propelling itself across the bottom.

As the beast drew closer to the source of light, the light became harsh, repellent. Reflex told it to retreat into the darkness, but its olfactory sensors began to receive strong, overwhelming waves of food spoor: fresh kill, rich and nourishing.

Hunger drove it onward.

It rose off the bottom, above the light, and let itself be carried into the darkness behind the light. It settled there, where signals of threat had disappeared, and it could concentrate on the scent of prey below.

It descended.

40

SHARP YAWNED, STRETCHED and shook his head; he was having trouble staying awake. They had been watching for over an hour, and there had been no movement on either monitor. It was hypnotic, like watching test patterns.

In the submersible, Stephanie, St. John and Eddie had hardly spoken and barely moved. Stephanie had taken a few pictures of the strange animals that swarmed around her porthole, but now she just knelt and watched.

St. John looked up at the video camera in the submersible, and he said, "What's the time?"

"Ninety minutes gone," Andy said into his microphone.

St. John nodded and resumed staring out his porthole.

The exterior camera had been readjusted, and it showed the body of the dead shark, belly-up in the mud. Earlier, a hagfish had darted in and tried to bore a hole in the shark, but the skin was too tough, and the hagfish had given up and gone in search of easier prey.

The door to the control room opened, and Darling entered, carrying two cups of coffee. He passed one to Sharp and said, "I couldn't find any proper cream, so . . . holy shit!"

"What?" Sharp said, and he followed Darling's eyes to the monitors.

"The fish. They're gone."

As Darling put on a headset and fumbled for the "talk" button on the microphone, Sharp realized what he meant: No abyssal creatures were patrolling the edge of darkness, no small fish hovered over the dead shark, no tiny scavengers gulped the bits of tuna that floated down from the wire cage.

"Liam!" Darling shouted into the microphone. "Look out!"

St. John started at the sound of the voice, and he looked around, but saw nothing. "Look out for—?"

There was a hollow sound then, a scraping, a crunch almost like the sound of a ship running aground. Then the capsule was jerked up and tilted forward. The interior camera showed Stephanie and St. John being hurled into Eddie, and all of them tumbling over the control panel. The exterior camera showed nothing but mud.

Eddie cursed, St. John grabbed the handles for the mechanical arm and tried to work them. "The arm's stuck in the mud!" he yelled.

"Put power to her!" Darling said to Eddie. "That beast won't like the propeller."

They saw Eddie pull back on the stick and apply power, and they heard the submersible's motor whine, then shriek as it raced.

The capsule tilted up; the mechanical arm came free.

"The camera!" St. John said.

Eddie reached for the controls for the outside camera as St. John flexed and raised the mechanical arm, his finger poised over the firing button.

The monitor showed the camera tracking out and turning: Mud gave way to water, then to a blur on the side of the capsule, then to . . .

"What the hell is that?" Sharp said.

The camera showed a field of circles, pinkish gray, each quivering on its own stalk, each apparently rimmed with teeth and each containing an amber-colored claw.

"Bad news, is what that is," said Darling, and he shouted into his microphone, "Fire it, Liam!"

Then, as the camera was ripped from its mounts, the screen went blank.

THE CREATURE CRUSHED the camera in its whip and cast it away.

Then it turned back to the shredded remains of the food,

its eight short arms scratching and clawing as it searched for more to feed to the snapping beak. But there was no more.

The creature was confused, for the spoor of food was everywhere, permeating the water. All its senses told it there was food; its hunger demanded food. But where was it?

It perceived a large, hard carapace, and associated it with the scent of food. It encircled the thing with its whips and set about to destroy it.

"I CAN'T SEE!" St. John shouted. "Where did it go?"

"Fire it, Liam!" Darling shouted. "Fire the dart! The bastard's so big you can't miss."

They saw St. John push the button to fire the dart. "It didn't fire!" he cried, and he pushed the button again, and again.

Stephanie yelled, "Look!" She was pointing out her porthole. "In the mud. The spear gun. The thing tore it *off*."

The capsule shuddered then, and rolled from side to side. St. John skidded and fell on top of Stephanie; Eddie hung on to the controls. The images through the portholes flashed and changed like pieces of glass in a kaleidoscope: mud, water, light, darkness.

Again the capsule shuddered, and there were screeching sounds.

Watching the single television monitor, Sharp felt sick with helplessness. "We've got to *do* something!" he said.

"Like what?" Darling asked.

"Bring it up. Start the winch. Maybe the motion will scare it off."

"It'd take ten minutes to reel in the slack in the cable," Darling said. "And they don't have ten minutes. Whatever's gonna happen is gonna happen now."

THE CREATURE SOUGHT weakness. There was weakness somewhere. There was weakness in all prey.

The thing was less than half the creature's size, and although it was strong and dense, it did not struggle. The creature lifted it easily in its two long whips and turned it, probing for a soft spot, a crack. Then it drew the thing in to its eight short arms and clutched it. It opened its beak and let its tongue search the skin. The tongue traveled slowly: licking, probing, rasping.

"WHAT'S THAT NOISE?" St. John hissed. It sounded as if a coarse file were scraping at the hull.

The capsule was upside down now, and the three of them knelt on the overhead and braced themselves with their hands.

"It's playing with you," Darling said over the mike. "Like a cat with a toy. With any luck, it'll get bored and leave you be."

St. John tilted his head, apparently listening for another sound. "Our motor's quit," he said.

"As soon as the critter lets you go, we'll winch you up. Won't be long now."

Sharp waited until Darling had released the "talk" button, then said, "You believe that?"

Darling paused before he said, "No. The sonofabitch is gonna find a way in."

THE TONGUE SNAKED across the skin, examining texture, seeking difference. But the skin was all the same: hard, tasteless, dead. The tongue speeded up, impatient as it licked.

A signal flashed across its brain and vanished.

The tongue stopped, retreated, began to lick again, slower. There. The signal reappeared, steady.

The texture here was different: smoother, thinner.

Weaker.

STEPHANIE MUST HAVE heard a noise behind her, for they saw her turn and look at her porthole. What she saw made her scream and back away.

St. John looked, and gasped.

"What?" Darling said.

"I think . . ." St. John said. "A tongue."

Andy changed the angle of the camera in the submersible

and focused on the porthole. Then they could see it, too: a tongue. It licked in circles, covering the glass with pink flesh. Then it withdrew and changed its shape into a cone and tapped at the glass. It made a sound like a hammer driving carpet tacks.

Then the tongue receded, and for a moment the porthole was blanketed in black. There was the sound of a deafening screech.

St. John grabbed a flashlight from a clip on the bulkhead and shined it on the porthole.

They could see only part of it, for it was bigger than the porthole, much bigger: a curved, scythelike beak, amber-colored, its sharply pointed end pressing on the glass.

Stephanie flattened herself against the opposite bulkhead, while St. John knelt mutely and held the flashlight pointed at the porthole. Eddie turned his face to the camera and said, "God damn!"

There was a cracking noise then, and in a fraction of a second, an explosion of water, a booming sound, and screams . . . and then silence, as the monitor went dead.

They all continued mutely to stare at the blank screen.

41

As SOON AS Darling got into the taxi, he took off his tie and stuffed it into his jacket pocket. He felt as if he were suffocating. He rolled the window down and let the breeze wash over his face.

He hated funerals. Funerals and hospitals. It wasn't only because they were associated with sickness and death; they also represented the ultimate loss of control. They were evidence of the flaw inherent in the precept that guided his life: that a smart and careful man could survive by calculating his risks and never overstepping the line. Hospitals and funerals were proof that the line sometimes moved.

Besides, he believed that funerals didn't do a damn thing for the dead; they were for the living.

Mike had agreed with him. They had made a pact long ago that if one of them died, the other would bury him at sea with no ceremony whatsoever. Well, Mike had been buried at sea, all right, but not the way they had planned.

It had been a small funeral, just family and Darling, with a few words from a Portuguese preacher and a couple of songs. There had been no questions, no recriminations, no discussion of what had happened. On the contrary, in fact, Mike's widow and her two brothers and two sisters had made a special effort to comfort Darling.

Which, of course, had made him feel even worse.

He hadn't told them the truth about how Mike had died. He and Sharp were the only ones who knew the truth, and there was no way anyone would ever suspect different. They had seen no point in painting pictures for the family that would haunt their dreams for the rest of their lives. So Darling had said that Mike had fallen overboard and drowned; that he must have struck his head on the dive step as he fell and knocked himself out.

They had told that tale to the authorities, too, with no conscience about suppressing evidence. There was enough carnage visible on the videotapes to satisfy all the ghouls. One more victim wouldn't make any difference.

When Darling had gotten no answer to his calls to the *Privateer*, he had been ready to chew Mike's ass from here to Sunday for falling asleep on watch. He and Sharp had borrowed Hector's Zodiac and sped across the half-mile of open water to the drifting boat. Sharp had been still in shock; he had ridden in the boat like a zombie. But when they had found Mike missing, he had quickly come around.

For the first fifteen or twenty minutes, they were convinced that Mike *had* fallen overboard. They had noted the run of the tide and the drift of the boat, and had used the quick, maneuverable little Zodiac to search a mile or more of ocean. But then they had decided that they needed the distance and perspective that the height of the *Privateer*'s flying bridge would give them, and they had returned to the boat. As they approached along the starboard side, they had seen scratch marks in the paint.

And then, when they had climbed aboard and run their hands along the bulwark, they had felt a telltale slime, and smelled a telltale odor.

Darling hadn't been on the boat when the accident happened, and there probably was nothing he could have done even if he *had* been there. But he heaped blame on himself. Even though he knew it was mostly irrational, he also knew there was a kernel of justification to it. Mike had never been one to make decisions on his own; he had relied on Whip to tell him the right thing to do; he had never liked being alone on the boat, and Whip had known it.

Stop it, Darling told himself. There's no point to this.

The taxi driver had the radio on, and the midafternoon newscast began, with more gloomy news about the Bermuda economy. In the week since the submersible disaster, tourism had dropped almost fifty percent.

People were pressuring the government to do something to get rid of the beast, but nobody had any concrete suggestions, and the government continued to consult with scientists from California and Newfoundland, who couldn't reach a consensus. Eventually, they all predicted hopefully, the giant squid would just go away.

Nobody wanted to tangle with the beast anymore—nobody, that is, except that Dr. Talley and Osborn Manning. They had written to Darling, tried to call, sent him wires, every damn thing. They had even tried to convince him that he had some sort of responsibility to help them kill the creature, that it was both a symbol and a symptom of the imbalance of nature, and that destroying it would somehow begin to put things right again. They had upped their ante to a point where, if Darling had a mind to take them out on his boat for up to ten days, he could clear $100,000. His response had been simple enough: What good is $100,000 to a dead man?

It hadn't been difficult to refuse their bait, for as he saw it, each of them was, in his own way, the next thing to nuts. Manning was crazed by his personal vendetta, Talley by a need to prove that his life had been worth something. They didn't have a full deck between them.

He understood that they had even approached the navy. According to Marcus, Manning had contacted a U.S. senator, who had contacted the Defense Department, which had asked for Captain Wallingford's thoughts on how the beast might be caught and eliminated. The request had made Wallingford extremely anxious, partly because he regarded any questions from the Pentagon as criticism, and partly because he was a coward: He didn't want to displease a senator who might someday have a say in whether or not he got to trade in his silver eagle for a silver star. And so Wallingford had taken out his anxiety on Marcus, whom he had tried somehow to blame for the entire fiasco.

But the investigation had cleared Sharp, and had laid official blame on the easiest of all targets, the dead: Liam St. John, who had concocted what, in retrospect, was now considered a reckless scheme, and Eddie, who had agreed to go along with it.

As the taxi turned onto Cambridge Road, the newscast ended, and Darling noted that the word "squid" hadn't been mentioned once.

His own concern was to find an immediate way to make a living. He had decided that the time had come at last to sell his cherished Masonic bottle, and the dealer in Hamilton had told him there was some interest in it. If a couple of collectors could be encouraged to bid against each other, he might get a few thousand dollars for it. He knew that Charlotte had written to Sotheby's some time ago, to inquire about including her coin collection, inherited from her father, in one of their auctions. He thought he might go through the artifacts in the house and see if there was anything else rare enough to be worth selling. He hated to do it, it was like selling pieces of his past, or of himself, but he had no choice.

He did have one practical hope, however: The aquarium had called, and they were interested in discussing a new retainer agreement. Now that St. John was gone, they could make decisions based on practicality instead of ego. That might pay for some fuel.

Still, he and Charlotte couldn't eat fuel.

THE CHAIN WAS across the dirt road to Darling's house, and he paid the driver, got out of the taxi, unhooked the chain and let it fall.

As he started toward the house, he saw Dana's car in the driveway. What was she doing here this early in the day? Wasn't she working? *Some*body had to work in this family. He grimaced, and thought: Great, you're one tiny step away from being a true parasite.

Then he heard a voice: "Captain Darling?"

He turned and saw Talley and Manning walking down the road toward him. Manning was in front, immaculate in a gray suit, a blue shirt and a striped tie, and carrying a briefcase; Talley followed, looking, Darling thought, nervous and uneasy.

"What do you want?" Darling said.

"We want to talk to you," Manning said.

"I've got nothing to say." Darling turned back toward the house.

"Talk to us now, Captain," Manning said, "or you'll talk to the law later."

Darling stopped. "The law?" he said. "What law? You got nothing better to do than threaten people?"

"I didn't threaten anybody, Captain. I stated a fact."

"Okay. Say your piece and go along."

"May we perhaps"—Manning gestured at the house—"go to the house and discuss this like—"

"I'm not a civilized person, Mr. Manning. I'm a pissed-off fisherman who's sick to death of having people tell me—"

"As you wish, Captain. Dr. Talley and I have already made you what we think is a generous offer for your help. In light of recent events, however, we are prepared to increase that offer."

"Jesus *Christ*, man, do you still not have any idea what it is you want to go up against? Don't you know—"

"Yes, Captain, we do. But the fact is, we believe we can kill the squid. Not the two of us, not you alone, but the three of us together."

"*Kill* it? You might get to see it, but it'll be the last thing you'll ever see. Kill it? Not a chance. I don't see how anyone's gonna better that beast."

"Captain," Talley said, "let me—"

"Shut up, Herbert," Manning snapped. "Words won't convince him." He turned back to Darling. "A final offer, Captain. If you will take us out to hunt for the giant squid, I will pay you two hundred thousand dollars. If we don't find it, if it has gone away, if we fail to kill it, the money is yours to keep. Your only obligation is to make a good-faith effort."

"You still think money can do it," said Darling. "Well, it can't. Go get drunk, if that'll help you. Say some prayers for your children, give your money to a good cause in their name. At least that's worth something."

Manning looked at Talley, and Darling saw Talley close his eyes and expel a breath.

"That's your last word?" Manning said.

"First, last . . . call it what you want."

"I'm sorry, Captain, you leave me no choice. We need you. You're the only person with the skill, the knowledge and the boat. So . . ." Manning hesitated, then continued. "Here it is: I must tell you that within ten days of close-of-business today, you are to deliver to me a certified check for twelve thousand dollars. If you fail to make the deadline, you will then have thirty days to move yourself and your belongings out of your house."

Darling stared at Manning, and let the words rerun in his mind. Then he looked at Talley, who was staring at the ground.

"Wait a second," Darling said. He couldn't have heard right; there had to be a mistake. "Let me get this straight. I give you twelve thousand dollars for not taking you to sea, or you kick me out of my house."

"Correct. You see, Captain, I own your house . . . or, to be precise, I will very soon."

Darling laughed. "Right. Next, you'll tell me you're my great-great-grandfather and you built it for me back in 1770." As he turned away he said, "You folks are smoking some powerful weed."

"Captain . . ." Manning had taken a manila folder from his briefcase, and he held a piece of paper out to Darling. "Read this."

The paper was in legalese, full of *wherefores* and *party of the first parts,* and the only elements Darling could parse were the name of the house, its location, an assignment of something or other to Osborn Manning, and some numbers. Maybe Charlotte could make sense of it. "I'll have to get my specs," he said.

"By all means. But why don't I tell you the substance? Your wife has been borrowing money, using the house as collateral. She is nearly three months behind in the payments and has twice been notified that she is in danger of default. I bought the note from the lender. In ten days, I will foreclose on the note."

"Bullshit," Darling said, staring at the paper. The paper couldn't say all that, because it couldn't have happened. "Piece of paper doesn't mean a thing. Charlie wouldn't have done that. Not ever."

"She did it, Captain."

"Bull*shit*," Darling said again, and he turned back toward the house, clutching the paper.

CHARLOTTE AND DANA were sitting together at the kitchen counter.

The screen door slammed behind Darling, and he marched in from the hallway. "You won't believe what that . . ." He stopped when he saw their faces. They had both been crying, and now, seeing him, they began to weep again. "No," he said. "No." And then, "Why?"

"Because we had to live, William."

"We were living. We had food, we had fuel."

"We had food because Dana brought us food. How was I supposed to pay our electricity? How was I supposed to pay the house taxes? When the freezer broke and all your bait melted, how was I supposed to get that fixed? And the crack in the cistern . . . we would have had no water. Our insurance was about to be canceled. They were going to cut off our gas." Charlotte wiped her eyes and looked at him. "What the hell do you think we've been *living* on all these months?"

"But . . . I mean . . . there were things we could sell. The coins . . ."

"I sold them. And the three-mold bottles, and the Bellarmine jug, and . . . all of it. There was nothing more."

"I'll go talk to the bank. For God's sake, Derek can't just—"

"It wasn't the bank," said Dana. "They wouldn't give you a mortgage. You had no steady income. I offered to co-sign the note. They still wouldn't do it."

"Who lent the money, then?"

"Aram Agajanian," said Charlotte.

"Agajanian!" Darling shouted. "That pervert?" Aram Agajanian was a recent immigrant to Bermuda who had made a fortune producing soft-core pornography for Canadian cable-television systems and had chosen Bermuda as a tax haven. "Why did you go to *him*?"

"Because he offered. Dana had done the accounts for one of his companies, and she asked him a couple of questions about securing loans, and . . . well, he offered."

"Christ!" Darling said, turning to Dana. "You had to hang out our dirty laundry in front of that Armenian star-fucker?"

"You want me to say I'm sorry, Daddy? Well, I am. I'm sorry. There. Does that make you feel better?" Dana was struggling not to sob. "But the fact is, he offered. No strings, no payment schedule. Pay it when you can, he said. I never thought he'd sell the note. He didn't want to."

"Why did he?"

"I think Mr. Manning made him one of those offers you can't refuse. Mr. Manning owns a lot of cable companies."

"How did Manning find out about it?"

"Agajanian thinks it must have been from Carl Frith."

"*What?!* Is there anybody on this island who *doesn't* know?" Darling heard himself shouting. "How did *he* find out?"

"He was working on Agajanian's dock, and he must have overheard something."

"Wonderful . . . great." Darling felt betrayed and confused. He looked around and, for no reason, touched one of the walls. "Two hundred and twenty years," he said.

"It's just a house, William," Charlotte said. "We'll find somewhere else to live. Dana wants us to move in with her. For a while. It's just a house."

"No, Charlie, it's not. It's not just a house. It's more than two centuries of Darlings. It's our family." He looked at his wife and his daughter. "It was passed on to me, and if I have one obligation in this life, it's to keep passing it on for the future."

"Let it go, William. We're alive, we're together. That's all that counts."

"Like hell," Darling said, and he turned and left the room. "Like bloody hell."

42

WHEN DARLING RETURNED to the end of his driveway, he found the tableau unchanged: Talley still paced and fidgeted; Manning still stood like a Bond Street mannequin.

Darling motioned for them to follow him, and as he led them down the driveway, he imagined Manning was gloating, and he had to fight to keep from spinning on the man.

He gestured for them to sit at a table on the porch.

"You're pretty sure that beast is still around, then," he said to Talley.

"Yes."

"Why's that?"

"Because nothing's changed yet. The seasons haven't changed, currents haven't changed, there have been no major storms. I got figures from NOAA last night, and they think— it's an educated guess—that the Gulf Stream won't begin its seasonal shift for maybe a month." Talley could feel his enthusiasm returning, erasing his embarrassment at being party to Manning's extortion. "Meanwhile, *Architeuthis* is finding food —not its normal food, but food. There's been no reason for it to leave."

"There was no reason for him to come, either."

"Yes, but it did, it's here. The important thing to remember, Captain, is not to make *Architeuthis* into a demon. It—not *he, it*—is an animal, not a devil. It has its own cycles, it responds to natural rhythms. I think it's hungry and confused. It's not finding its normal prey. I think I can coax it to respond to an illusion of normalcy."

"Whatever the hell that means."

"Leave that to me."

"And you truly believe you can get the best of this thing?"

"I think so, yes."

"Before it kills everybody?"

"Yes. Yes, I do."

"How?"

Talley hesitated. "I'll tell you . . . soon."

"Is it a state secret or something?"

"No. I'm sorry, I'm not playing games. The means depend on the circumstances, on how the animal behaves. It may . . . there's a chance . . . what I want to try to do is make it destroy itself."

Darling looked at Manning, and saw him staring, stone-faced, at the bay, as if these details bored him.

"Sure, Doc," Darling said. "It may take off and fly to Venus, too, but I wouldn't count on it. I think I've got a right to—"

"No, Captain," Manning said, suddenly interested again. There was a thin smile on his lips. "You have no rights. You have a duty: to drive the boat and to help us."

"Now, Osborn . . ." Talley said, "I don't think—"

"Why not, Herbert? We're not civilized people here; Captain Darling said so himself, and I respect him for it. Politeness is deceptive, and it wastes time. Better that we all know exactly where we stand, right from the start."

Darling felt a sharp pain behind his eyes, sparked, he knew, by rage and a feeling of impotence. He pressed his temples, trying to squeeze the pain away. He wanted to hit Manning, but Manning was correct: He had found Darling's price, and had bought him, and there was no point in pretending otherwise.

Darling said, "When do you want to go?"

"As soon as we can," Manning replied. "All we have to do is load up the gear."

"I'll have to get fuel, food. We could go tomorrow."

"Fuel," Manning said, and he reached into his briefcase and brought out a banded packet of hundred-dollar bills. "Ten thousand enough for starters?"

"Should do."

"Now, the terms." Manning snapped his briefcase shut.

"Dr. Talley is confident that he'll be able to locate and attract the squid within seventy-two hours, so you'll provision the boat for three days. Whether or not we catch the animal, on our return, I'll destroy the note and pay you the balance of the two hundred thousand. Your net, after securing your house, should be somewhere over a hundred thousand." He stood up. "Agreed?"

"No," Darling said.

"What do you mean, 'No'?"

"Here are *my* terms," Darling said, looking at Manning. "You'll burn the note now, in front of me. Before we leave the dock, you'll give me fifty thousand dollars in cash, which will stay ashore here, with my wife. The balance in her name in escrow in the bank, in case we don't come back."

Manning hesitated, then opened his briefcase again and took out the note and a gold Dunhill lighter. "You're an honorable man, Captain," he said as he held the note out over the lawn and touched the flame to it. "We know that much about you. But so am I. Once a deal is done, I don't quibble. You shouldn't distrust me."

"This has nothing to do with trust," Darling said. "I want to provide for my wife."

DARLING WATCHED TALLEY and Manning walk away up the drive and turn into the parking lot at Cambridge Beaches, then he put the stack of bills into his pocket and went down the path to the boat. He started the engine and climbed up to the flying bridge, and he was about to put the boat in gear when he suddenly remembered that it was still tied to the dock.

He felt as if somebody had punched him in the stomach, and he blew out a breath and leaned on the railing. It was the first real evidence he'd had that Mike was gone. He stayed there for a few moments, until the feeling passed, then went below and untied the lines.

As he rounded the corner out of Mangrove Bay on his way to the fuel pumps at Dockyard, Darling tried to think of somebody he could hire as a mate. He had no reason to believe that Talley and Manning knew anything about setting rigs or keeping the boat pointed into the wind or any of the scores of other chores involved in running a boat.

No, he concluded, there was nobody. He had friends and acquaintances who were capable and might even be willing, but he wasn't about to ask them. He wasn't about to be responsible for another death.

He'd do it alone. Well, not quite alone. He had one ally, in a box down in the hold, and he'd use it if he had to.

One chance, Mr. Manning, he thought. I'm giving you one chance. And if you screw up, I'm gonna blow that motherfucker to kingdom come.

IT TOOK DARLING almost three hours to pump two thousand gallons of diesel fuel and seven hundred gallons of fresh water into the tanks on the *Privateer,* and to buy six bags of groceries: fresh and dried fruits and vegetables, corned beef, canned tuna, blocks of cheddar cheese, loaves of bread, stew meat and a variety of beans. By the time they'd eaten all that food, he figured, they'd either be home or they'd be dead.

When he returned to his dock, evening was coming on. He removed extraneous gear from the boat: broken traps, scuba tanks, parts of a dismantled compressor. He came across the pump Mike had been working on. He held it in his hands and looked at it, and he thought he could feel Mike's energy in it.

Don't be stupid, he said to himself, and he put the pump ashore.

CHARLOTTE WAS IN the kitchen, doing what she always did when things were bad and she didn't know what else to do: cooking. She had roasted an entire leg of lamb and made a salad big enough to feed a regiment.

"Company coming?" Darling said, and he went to her and kissed the back of her neck.

"After twenty-one years," she said, "you'd think I would have known what you'd do."

"I even surprised myself. Until today, I thought there were only two things in the world that really mattered to me." Darling reached into the refrigerator for a beer. "I wonder what my old man would say."

"He'd say you're a damn fool."

"I doubt it. He was a big one for roots—that's why they all loved this house. It was their roots. It's our roots, too."

"What about *us*?" Charlotte turned to face him, and there were tears in her eyes. "Aren't we roots enough, Dana and I?"

"We wouldn't *be* us without this house, Charlie. What would we be, living in a condo downtown or taking up Dana's spare room? Just a couple of old farts waiting for the sun to set. That's not us."

The phone rang down the hall, and Darling answered it, told the caller to piss off and returned to the kitchen. "A reporter," he said. "I guess there's no such thing as an unlisted number."

"Marcus called earlier," said Charlotte.

"Did you tell him what's going on?"

"I did. I thought maybe he could think of a way to stop you."

"And could he?"

"Of course not. He thinks you walk on water."

"He's a good lad."

"No, just another damn fool."

Darling looked at her back. "I love you, Charlie," he said. "I don't say it too often, but you know I do."

"Not enough, I guess."

"Well . . ." He sighed, wishing he could think of comforting words to weave.

"Or is it *you* you don't love enough?" Charlotte said, whipping gravy into a froth.

That was the strangest question Darling had ever heard. What did it mean, loving himself? What kind of person loved himself? He couldn't think of an answer, so he turned on the television to get the weather forecast.

They left the television on while they ate, letting the local newscaster fill the silence, for they both sensed that there was nothing more to say, and that any attempts at conversation would result in words they would regret.

After supper, Darling went out onto the lawn and looked at the bay. There was still some light—the soft violet that ushers in the night—and he could see two egrets standing like sentries in the shallows by the point, perhaps hoping for a twilight meal of mullet. A gentle fluttering sound, like the opening of a paper fan, heralded the arrival of a school of fry, skittering in flight across the glassy water.

When he was a child, he had spent his evenings watching the bay, as enraptured by it as other children were by radio or television, for from the bay came sounds, and sometimes sights, that excited his imagination as vividly as had any ever fabricated on a soundstage. Marauding barracuda slashed through schools of mackerel, and the water boiled with a bloody foam. Sharks came, too, sometimes singly, sometimes in twos or threes, their dorsal fins slicing the surface as they calmly cruised in search of prey, exercising some primal rite of plunder. Crabs scuttled on the beach sands; turtles exhaled like tiny bellows; irate kiskadees chastised one another in the treetops.

The bay was life and death, and it had given him a feeling of peace and security he could not articulate. It carried with it the reassurance of continuity.

There was still life in the bay, though less, still much to love.

The crown of a full moon peeked above the trees in the east, and cast arrows of gold that flashed on the egrets and lit them like golden statues.

"Charlie," Darling called, "come look."

He heard her footsteps in the house, but they stopped at the screen door. "No," she said.

"Why not?" he asked.

She didn't answer. Instead, she thought to herself, Oh William, you look like an old Indian, sitting on a hillside, getting ready to die.

Part Four

43

DARLING WAS AWAKENED by the sound of the wind whistling through the casuarinas behind the house. It was still dark, but he didn't need to see to know the weather; his ears told him that the wind was out of the northwest and blowing fifteen to twenty knots. At this time of year, a northwest wind was an unstable wind, so before long it should shift, either back around to the southwest and settle down, or veer into the northeast and crank up into a little gale. He half hoped for a gale: Maybe a rough ride would make Manning and Talley get sick and decide to quit.

Not a chance, he thought. Those two were in the grip of forces they probably didn't understand and certainly couldn't defy, and nothing short of a hurricane would put them off.

Charlotte lay on her side, curled up like a little girl and breathing deeply. He bent down and kissed the back of her neck, inhaling her aroma and holding his breath, as if trying to carry the memory of her with him.

By the time he had shaved and made coffee and heated up some of last night's lamb, the sky was lightening in the east and the kiskadees were gathering in the poinciana tree to announce the advent of day.

He stood on the lawn and looked at the sky. There was still a stiff breeze on; low clouds were being shoved to the southeast. But a ridge of high cirrus was creeping northward, signaling that the wind would soon shift back to the south. By noon, the chop would be gone from the shallow water and the swell would have faded from the deep.

The boat was straining against its lines, rocking gently. He was about to step aboard, when suddenly he sensed that someone was there, in the cabin. He wasn't sure why he knew, so he stopped and listened. Over the routine noises of the lines creaking and water lapping against the hull, he heard breathing sounds.

Some damn reporter, he thought, one of those smart-ass kids who think that "no" means "try harder" and that they've got a God-given right to invade a man's privacy.

He crossed the gangplank and stepped down onto the steel deck and said, "By the time I count three, your ass better be up and ashore, or you're goin' for a long, long swim." Then he stepped over the threshold into the cabin, said, "One . . ." and saw Marcus Sharp sit up with a start and strike his head on the upper bunk.

Sharp yawned, rubbed his head, smiled and said, "Morning, Whip . . ."

"Well, I'll be damned," Darling said. "To what do I owe the pleasure?"

"I thought maybe you could use some help today."

"I'd welcome a pair of friendly hands, that's for sure, but what does Uncle Sam have to say about this?"

"Uncle Sam sent me . . . sort of. Scientists from all over the country—all over the *world*—have been trying to goose the navy into launching an expedition to hunt for the squid, but the navy claims it doesn't have the money. I think the truth is that the navy doesn't want to tackle something they don't know anything about, and run the risk of looking foolish. Anyway, they've been getting on Wallingford's case, as if *he's* supposed to come up with some magic formula. When I told him you were going out, he thought it would look good to have the navy go too, sort of show the flag—that is, me. I'm supposed to make it look as if Wallingford is actually doing something." Sharp paused. "I tried to call. I thought you wouldn't . . . I hope you don't mind."

"Hell no. But look, Marcus, I want you to know up front what you're signing on for. These folks—"

"I've seen the beast, Whip. Or almost."

"Okay, then. You've had demolition training, right?"

"A year."

"Good. We're gonna need it." Darling smiled. "Meantime, first thing to do is make some coffee."

AT SIX-THIRTY, they cast off and motored slowly across the bay to the town dock, where Talley and Manning waited beside a rented pickup truck piled high with cases. Talley wore a windbreaker, khaki pants and short rubber boots. Manning looked as if he had stepped from the pages of a catalog: Topsider boat shoes, pleated trousers, a beige shirt with a club logo on the breast and a crisp new Gore-Tex foul-weather jacket.

"What's all that crap for?" Darling asked from the flying bridge while Sharp tied the boat to the dock. "You aiming to build yourselves a skyscraper?"

Neither of them answered, and Darling realized there was tension between them. Curious, he thought: What now? They've gotten their way, everything should be peachy.

They unloaded twenty-two cases in all, placing them aboard the boat under Talley's supervision. He wanted some of them inside the cabin, protected from the weather, but most were stacked on the afterdeck.

When all the cases were aboard, Manning reached inside the cab of the truck and brought out a long case. From the way Manning carried it, Darling could see that it was heavy, and from the care he took not to bang it on anything, he could tell that it was precious.

"What's that?" Darling asked him.

"Never mind," Manning said, and he disappeared into the cabin.

Is that so? Darling said to himself. Well, we'll see about that.

A van from the local television station wheeled around the corner at the end of the lane and stopped at the edge of the dock. A reporter got out, followed by a cameraman who scrambled to assemble his equipment.

"Captain Darling?" called the reporter. "Can we talk to you, please? For ZBM."

"No," Darling said from the flying bridge.

"Just for a minute." The reporter looked behind him to

make sure the cameraman was ready and rolling. "You're going out after the monster. What makes you—"

"No we're not. Hell, son, nobody in his right mind would do that." He looked aft and said to Sharp, "Cast her off, Marcus," and when he saw that the last of the lines were aboard, he put the boat in gear and began to move slowly through the dozens of boats moored in the bay.

He waited until he was sure that they were out of earshot of the dock, and then he leaned over the side of the flying bridge and said, "Mr. Manning, would you come up here a second?"

Manning climbed the ladder and walked forward and said impatiently, "What is it?"

"What's in the case?"

"I told you all you need to know."

"Uh-huh," Darling said. "I see." A hundred yards dead ahead, a sixty-foot schooner lay broadside to their path, flanked by two fifty-foot fishing boats. "Okay, then . . ." He reached over and grabbed one of Manning's hands and put it on the wheel. "Here you go."

Then he turned and walked off the flying bridge and headed for the ladder.

"What are you doing?" Manning shouted.

"Gonna take a nap."

"*What!?*"

"It's your show; you run it."

"Come back here!" Manning cried, looking ahead. The schooner was fifty yards away now, and they were closing on it. He had nowhere to turn; there were boats on all sides.

Darling started down the ladder. "Call me when we get there," he said.

Manning pulled back on the throttle and spun the wheel, but the boat didn't stop; it yawed; it was aimed directly at the schooner. He jerked the throttle back, and the boat rumbled into reverse and began to back toward the stern of a fishing boat. "What do you *want?*" he shouted.

Darling said, "You want to run the show, go ahead and run it."

"No!" Manning protested. "I . . . help!" He slammed the throttle forward, and again the bow aimed for the schooner.

Darling waited for another second, until Manning, panicked, flung his hands in the air and lurched backward. Then he took two steps up the ladder, walked quickly across the deck and took the wheel. He spun it, gunned the throttle and, like a tailor threading a needle, nosed the boat between the bow of the schooner and the stern of the fishing boat, missing each by no more than six inches.

"Funny, isn't it?" Darling said when they were clear. "The things money can't buy."

Manning was angry. "That was completely unne—"

"No, it was very necessary," Darling said. "Look, Mr. Manning, we have to work together. We can't have folks running all over the boat with their own agendas. Talley knows the animal but doesn't know anything about the ocean. Marcus knows the ocean but doesn't know the animal. I know something about each, and you, I figure, don't know shit about anything but making money. So: What's in the case?"

Manning hesitated. "A rifle."

"How did you get it in? Bermuda doesn't take kindly to guns."

"Disassembled. I spread the pieces around in Talley's cases. It would have taken an armorer to put the puzzle together."

"What kind of rifle?"

"A Finnish assault rifle. A Valmet. It usually shoots a standard NATO seven-point-sixty-five-millimeter cartridge."

"What do you mean, 'usually'? You've had something done to it?"

"To the bullets, yes. The clips are loaded so that every third bullet is a phosphorous tracer, and the others are filled with cyanide slugs."

"And you think you can kill the beast with that."

"That's our arrangement. Talley will find it, do whatever studies he wants, and then I'll kill it."

"It has to be you."

"Yes."

Darling thought for a moment, then said, "Do you really think there's anything you can do for your kids at this point?"

"It has nothing to do with them, not anymore. It has to do with me. This is something I have to do."

"I see," Darling said with a sigh. "Okay, Mr. Manning, but take a word of counsel: Do it right the first time, 'cause I'm only giving you one chance. Then it's my show, I'm taking over."

"And doing what?"

"I'm gonna blow him into dust. Or try to."

"Fair enough," Manning said. "Want some coffee?"

"Sure. Black."

Manning walked aft toward the ladder, and said, "I'll tell the mate to bring you some."

"The mate, Mr. Manning," Darling said, "is a lieutenant in your United States Navy. Don't tell him; ask him. And say 'please.'"

Manning opened his mouth, closed it. "Excuse me," he said, and he went below.

At the mouth of the bay, Darling turned to the north. As he rounded the point and headed for the cut, he looked back. Between two Norfolk pines on the end of the point stood Charlotte, her nightgown billowing in the breeze. He waved to her, and she waved back, then turned away, and walked up the lawn toward the house.

Sharp brought Darling some coffee and stood beside him on the flying bridge. They looked to the northwest, to the spot at the edge of the deep where the *Ellis Explorer* had anchored.

For a moment, neither of them spoke, then Darling said, "You liked that girl."

"Yes. I even thought . . . well, it doesn't matter."

"Sure it matters."

Talley came up to the bridge and stood to one side. He looked edgy, excited.

"Spend much time at sea, Doc?" Darling asked.

"Some, years ago, collecting octopus. But nothing like this. I've been waiting my whole life for this, for the chance to find a giant squid. It's my dragon."

"It's a dragon now, is it?"

"I think of it that way. That's why I called my book *The Last Dragon*. Man needs dragons, he always has, to explain the unknown. You've seen the old maps. When they drew unknown lands, they'd write 'Here be dragons,' and that said it all. I've spent my life reading and writing books about the dragon. Do you know what a privilege it is to finally get close to one?"

"Seems to me, Doc," Darling said, "there are some dragons better left alone."

"Not to scientists." Talley suddenly pointed and shouted, "Look!"

Half a dozen flying fish scattered away from the bow of the boat, skimming over the water for fifty yards or more before splashing down again. Talley's face lit up with wonder.

They came upon a trail of sargasso weed, floating patches of yellow vegetation, unconnected and yet apparently following one another, like ants, toward the horizon.

"Does it always make a straight line?" Talley asked.

"Seems to. It's a mystery, like that spawn we saw. I can't figure out what that thing is, where it comes from or where it goes."

"What thing? What does it look like?"

Darling described the huge gelatinous oblongs, with the holes in the center, and told him about how they appeared to be rotating, as if to expose all their parts to the sunlight.

Talley asked questions, pressed Darling for details, and with every answer he seemed to grow more excited. "It's an egg sac," he said finally. "Nobody's ever seen one before, at least not in a hundred years. Do you think you can find another one?"

"Never know. I'd never seen *any* till the other day. Now I've seen two. We tried to collect one, but it fell apart."

"It would. And once its matrix broke, its cocoon, the animals inside would die."

"What kind of critters live in a sac like that?"

Talley looked out over the sea, then slowly turned to look at Darling. "What do *you* think, Captain?"

"How should I . . . ?" Then Darling paused, and said, "Jesus Christ! Little baby beasts? In that jelly thing?"

"Hundreds," Talley said. "Maybe thousands."

"But they'll die, right?" Sharp said.

"Normally, yes. Most of them."

Darling said, "Something'll eat them."

"Yes," Talley said. "That is, if there's anything left down there to do that."

44

"HAVE YOU EVER read Homer?" Talley asked as he reached into one of his cases and passed Darling a six-inch stainless-steel hook. "Homer of the wine-dark sea."

"Can't say as I have," Darling said. He fed the barb of the hook through a mackerel, and tossed the fish onto a pile of others.

"You know, the guy who wrote the *Iliad*," Sharp said. He was attaching swivels to the eyes of the hooks, then tying six-foot titanium wire leaders to each swivel.

"The same," Talley said. "There are those who believe, and I'm one, that Homer talked about giant squid three thousand years ago. He called it Scylla, and this is how he described it: 'She has twelve splay feet and six lank scrawny necks. Each neck bears an obscene head, toothy with three rows of thick-set crowded fangs blackly charged with death. . . . Particularly she battens on humankind, never failing to snatch up a man with each of her heads from every dark-prowed ship that comes.'" Talley smiled. "Vivid, don't you think?"

"Sounds to me," Darling said as he snapped wire leaders onto one of Talley's folding umbrella rigs, "like your Homer had himself a twelve-volt imagination." He dragged the umbrella rig across the deck and placed it beside two others.

"Not at all," said Talley. "Imagine being a sailor back then, when dragons and monsters were the answer to everything. Suppose you saw *Architeuthis*. How would you describe it to the people back home? Or even in modern times, suppose you were on a troop transport during World War Two and one attacked your ship. How would you describe a great monster that rose out of nowhere and tried to tear the rudder post off your ship?"

"They did that?" Darling snapped the cap ring on one of the umbrella rigs to a length of cable attached to the nylon rope.

"Several times, off Hawaii."

"Why would a giant squid want to attack a ship?"

"Nobody knows," Talley said. "That's the wonderful thing about—"

Gunfire exploded beside them, thirty shots so fast that the sound was like fabric tearing. They spun and saw Manning standing on the stern, holding his assault rifle. Behind the boat, feathers drifted down among bloody bits of shattered petrel.

"What was that for?" Talley demanded.

"A little practice, Herbert," Manning said, and he popped the empty clip from the rifle and inserted a new one.

It took them an hour to lower the gear, what Talley referred to as Phase One of his operation. From three thousand feet of half-inch rope, six umbrella rigs fanned out at intervals on different levels, each with ten baits on titanium leaders. The wire was unbreakable, the hooks unbendable and four inches across at the base—so big that the only other animal that might be tempted to take one would be a shark. If a shark did get hooked, they reasoned, its struggle would send out distress signals that would add to the lure. And if *Architeuthis* should take one of the baits, it would flail with its many arms and (or so Talley theorized) foul itself onto many more of the hooks until, finally, it would be immobilized.

"How much is the beast likely to weight?" Darling had asked when Talley had outlined his plan.

"There's no telling. I've weighed the flesh of dead ones; it's almost exactly the weight of water. So it's possible that a truly big squid could weigh as much as five or ten tons."

"*Ten tons!* I couldn't put ten tons of dead meat in this boat, and that thing isn't likely to be dead. I might be able to tow ten tons, but—"

"Nobody's asking you to. We'll winch it up, and when Osborn has killed it, I'll cut specimen samples from it."

"With what, your penknife?"

"I saw you have a chain saw below. Does it work?"

"You're ambitious, Doc, I'll give you that," Darling had said. "But suppose the critter doesn't want to play by your rules?"

"It's an animal, Captain," Talley had replied. "Just an animal. Never forget that."

When the rope was down, Darling and Sharp tied three four-foot pink plastic mooring buoys in a line, snapped them to the end of the rope and tossed them overboard.

"What now?" Sharp asked.

"No point in pulling it for a couple of hours," said Darling. "Let's eat."

AFTER LUNCH, TALLEY unpacked some of his cases and set up a video monitor and tested two of his cameras, while Manning sat on one of the bunks and read a magazine. Darling beckoned Sharp to follow him outside. The boat had been drifting with the buoys, but slightly faster, so by now the buoys had fallen a hundred yards astern.

"Doc's right about one thing," Darling said as he watched the buoys from the stern of the boat. "Anything tangles with that rigmarole, it'll know it's hooked."

"I don't think Talley wants to kill it."

"No, the silly bugger just wants to see the damn thing, learn about it. That's the trouble with scientists, they never know when to leave Nature the hell alone."

"Maybe it'll beat itself to death on the line."

"Sure, Marcus," Darling said with a smile. "But just in case the beast has other ideas, let's be ready. Get me the boat hook."

"What for?"

"We're gonna make ourselves a little insurance." Darling climbed down the ladder through the after hatch and disappeared into the hold.

By the time Sharp had found the boat hook on the bow and brought it aft, Darling was standing beside the midships hatch cover and opening a cardboard carton about twice the size of a shoebox. Stenciled on the side of the carton was a single word in a foreign alphabet.

"What's that?" Sharp asked.

Darling reached into the carton and pulled out what looked like a six-inch-long salami, roughly three inches in diameter, covered with a dark red skin of plastic. He held it up to Sharp and smiled. "Semtex," he said.

"Semtex!" said Sharp. "Jesus, Whip, that's terrorist stuff." He had heard of Semtex but never seen any. Manufactured in Czechoslovakia, it was the current explosive-of-choice of the world's most sophisticated terrorists, for it was extremely powerful, malleable and, best of all, stable. It would take a stupid man, and clumsy as well, to set it off by mistake. The cassette player that had blown up Pan Am 103 had been packed with Semtex. "Where did you get it?"

"If people knew what was flying around the world with them, Marcus, they'd never leave home. It came with a shipment of compressor parts I'd ordered from Germany; it must have just been an accident in packing. Lord knows where it was supposed to go. I didn't know what the hell it was at first, and neither did the customs inspector, but I figured why give away something that might be useful someday, so I told him it was a lubricant. He didn't care. It wasn't till a couple weeks later that I saw a picture of Semtex in a book and realized, holy shit, that's what I had stowed up in the garage." Darling turned the end of the salami toward Sharp. It was the color of eggnog. "We've got enough here to blow the end off Bermuda and send it all the way to Haiti. But we do have one little problem."

"What's that?"

"No detonators. Mike must have put 'em ashore and forgot to bring 'em back. Mike doesn't"—Darling paused, took a breath, then corrected himself—"*didn't* like sailing with things that might sink us."

"We may be able to make one," Sharp said.

"What do you need?"

"Benzine . . . regular gasoline."

"There's a can for the outboard down below."

"Glycerine. You have any Lux flakes?"

"In the galley, under the sink. That it?"

"No, I need a trigger, something to ignite it. Phosphorous would be best. Maybe if you've got a box of kitchen matches, we could—"

"No problem. Manning's got a couple hundred rounds of phosphorous tracers. How many?"

"Just one. A little bit goes a long way. But, Whip . . . I've never done this before. I've read about it, but I've never actually done it."

"I've never chased a ten-ton squid before, either," Darling said.

"IT DOESN'T LOOK like a bomb," Sharp said when they had finished. "More like a piece of cheap fireworks."

"Or a butcher's idea of a practical joke," said Darling. "Think it'll work?"

"It better, hadn't it."

"One consolation, Marcus: If it doesn't, there'll be nobody left around to chew you out."

They had blended the gasoline and the soap flakes into a thick paste, which they pressed, like a wad of gum, to the end of the stick of Semtex. Then Sharp had pried open one of Manning's phosphorous tracer bullets. He worked with his hands in a pan of water, for phosphorous ignites on contact with air, and when he had discarded the lead slug, he had poured the residue of phosphorous and gunpowder and water into a small glass pill bottle, which he had then sealed off and embedded in the paste.

Now they used duct tape to affix the contraption to the end of the ten-foot-long boat hook. Darling lifted the boat hook and shook it to make sure the bomb was secure. "What happens if he swallows it before he breaks the pill bottle?" he asked.

"It won't go off," Sharp said. "If air doesn't get to the phosphorous, it won't ignite. If it doesn't ignite, it won't trigger the rest of the detonator. It'll be a dud."

"So you want me to make the thing bite it."

"Just for a second, Whip. Then jump, or—"

"I know, I know. With any luck, Talley's plan will work and

we won't need it." Darling paused. "Of course, with *real* luck, we won't find the bastard to begin with."

He climbed to the flying bridge, went forward to the wheel, turned the boat to the south and began to look for the floating buoys. It had taken them an hour to rig the explosive and bolt a rod holder to the railing in which to stow the boat hook upright, out of harm's way. He hadn't worried about the buoys, hadn't thought about them.

He was surprised to find that he didn't see them right away. The boat couldn't have drifted more than half a mile from the buoys, and on a clear day like this, those big pink balls should have been visible for at least a mile. Still, he knew exactly where they were; he had taken landmarks when he dropped them. There was probably more of a swell on than he'd realized, and they were in a trough. He'd pick them up in a minute.

But he didn't. Not in a minute or two or three. By the time he had been heading south for five minutes, he knew from his landmarks that he was beyond the spot where he had left them.

They were gone.

He picked up the binoculars and focused them on a trail of sargasso weed. If the buoys had drifted with the tide, they'd be going in the same direction as the weed, so with his eyes he followed the trail all the way to the horizon. Nothing.

He heard footsteps behind him, then Manning saying, "Have you lost them?"

"No," Darling said. "I just haven't found 'em yet."

"God dammit! If you hadn't wasted so much time—"

Darling held up a hand, suddenly tensing; he had heard something, or felt something, sensed something.

The feeling was coming through his feet, he realized, faint and far below, a weird thumping sensation. Almost like a distant explosion.

"What in God's name are you—"

Now Darling recognized it, even though he could hardly believe it. "Sonofabitch!" he said, and he shouldered Manning aside and went to the railing and looked down into the bottomless blue.

It came into view then, the only one left intact, and it was rushing for the surface like a runaway missile. It broke water with a loud, sucking *whoosh* sound, and flew half a dozen feet into the air, spraying them, before it settled back onto the surface and bobbed there, trailing beneath it the burst tatters of the two other buoys.

Talley and Sharp had heard the commotion and come out of the cabin, and by the time Darling reached the deck Sharp had snagged the rope with a grapnel and was hauling the buoy aboard. Darling unsnapped the buoy, tossed the rope aside, then wrapped the rope around the winch and turned it on.

"Is it him?" Manning said. "Is it the squid?"

The rope was quivering and shedding drops of water. Darling felt it with his fingertips. "I can't say, Mr. Manning, but I'll tell you this much: Anything strong enough to yank the stretch out of half a mile of poly rope, plus sink three mooring buoys each designed to float half a ton—sink 'em so deep that two of 'em bust—that is one humongous motherfucker." Darling leaned over the side, then said, "I can't tell if he's still there or not."

"If he was hooked," Talley said, "he's there. He can't break those wires or bend the hooks."

"Never say never, Doc, not when you're dealing with something that's off the scale." Then Darling said to Sharp, "Get a knife, Marcus, and use the stone on it till it's like a razor. Then come and stand right beside me."

Sharp went into the cabin, and Talley followed and began to load his video camera.

"A knife, Captain?" said Manning. "What for?"

"If this is a real monster, if he's half the size Doc says he might be—and if there's even a spark of life left in him—I'm gonna cut the line and let the bastard go."

"Like hell you are. Not before I get a shot at him."

"We'll see."

"We certainly will," Manning said, and he headed down into the cabin.

TALLEY SET A tripod on the flying bridge and mounted his video camera on it, while Manning positioned himself against the railing, his rifle loaded with a thirty-round banana clip and held against his chest. Below, Darling ran the winch as Sharp fed the rope into a plastic drum.

When the drum was half-full, Darling reached out and strummed the rope with his fingers. Then he stopped the winch and wrapped a hand around the rope and tugged on it.

"It's gone," he said. "If it was ever there. It's gone now, there's nothing on this rope but rope."

"It can't be!" Talley said.

"We'll know in a minute," Darling said, and he started the winch again.

"He wasn't really hooked, then."

"You mean he pulled those buoys down just for sport?"

The first of the umbrella rigs came up, and Sharp lifted it aboard. The baits were there, whole, untouched. A moment later the second rig came up, then the third. Nothing had eaten any of them.

As the fourth umbrella rig came into view, Sharp held up a hand, and Darling slowed the winch.

"Lord," Sharp said, reaching for the rig, "this thing looks like it was run over by a train."

The rig had been crushed, and its wires had been wrapped tight around the rope. Intertwined with the rope and wires were strands of a white musclelike fiber. Two of the baits were whole, still secured to the hooks, but the other baits were gone, and nothing was left of the hooks but a couple of inches of gnarled shaft.

Talley's camera was running, his eye pressed to the viewfinder. Darling held one of the hooks up for the camera. "Can't bend 'em out, huh? Can't bust 'em off? Well, Doc, whatever's down there didn't just bend 'em out, he *bit* 'em off."

Sharp plucked some of the white fibers from the rig, and they left a pungent stench on his fingers. He grimaced and wiped his hands on his trousers.

"It's *Architeuthis*," Talley said. "Smell the ammonia. He left us his calling card." He turned off the camera.

"Don't other things stink of ammonia?" Darling asked.

"Not like *Architeuthis* does, Captain. It's his signature, and it's the main reason we know anything about him. Nobody has seen a live one, not in this century, except for one that killed some people in the 1940s, and that was in the dark and they never really saw it. But people have seen dead ones; two washed up off Newfoundland in the sixties. The reason they washed up instead of sinking—they're not like fish, they don't have swim bladders—is that their flesh is full of ammonium ions, and the specific gravity of ammonium ions is slightly less than that of seawater. It's one-point-oh-one against one-point-oh-two-two, if you care. I saw the dead ones, Captain, and they didn't just smell of ammonia, they *reeked* of it." Talley turned to Manning and grinned. "It's him, Osborn. He's here, no question. We've found him."

"Listen, Doc," Darling said, "either you're crazy or you've been holding out on us. You can't catch a giant squid on a hook. You can't catch him with a submarine. So how in Christ's name do you plan to catch him?"

Talley said, "Living things are driven by two primal instincts, Captain, isn't that correct? The first one is hunger. What's the other?"

Darling looked at Sharp, who shrugged and said, "I don't know. Sex?"

"Yes," Talley said, "sex. I intend to capture the giant squid with sex."

45

TALLEY HAD NUMBERED his cases, and had included detailed descriptions of their contents in the customs manifest. Now he consulted the manifest and, with the help of Sharp and Darling, sorted the cases and arranged them on the afterdeck in a precise order.

Manning stood aside, and stared out at the water. To Darling, he seemed to be reducing himself to a single core, with a single purpose, stripping away the layers of social conditioning and leaving only a naked compulsion to kill. Darling had known people like Manning in the past, people who had lost all regard for safety; there was nothing more dangerous on a boat.

When Talley was satisfied with the arrangement of his cases, he beckoned Darling and Sharp over to a long aluminum box the size of a coffin, which was secured with snap locks. He undid the locks and lifted the lid. "Admit it," he said proudly. "Isn't this the sexiest thing you ever saw?"

Cushioned in foam rubber was what looked to Darling like a six-foot-long bowling pin, made of one of the new plastics and painted bright red. Hundreds of tiny stainless-steel hooks hung from swivels all over it, and a three-inch stainless ring was embedded in its top.

Talley lifted the thing by the ring and passed it to Darling. It couldn't have weighed more than ten pounds, and when Darling tapped it, he heard a hollow sound.

"I give up," Darling said simply, and he handed the thing to Sharp.

"It's genius, pure and simple," Talley said.

"Obviously," said Sharp. "But what *kind* of genius?"

Talley took the thing from Sharp and put a hand on either end and held it up before him. "Think of this," he said, "as the main body, the head and torso, what we call the mantle, of *Architeuthis*. As a general rule, the body of a giant squid—whatever its species, whether it's *dux, japonica* or *sanctipauli* —constitutes about a third of its total length. So this represents an animal whose total length, counting the tentacles and whips, would be about eighteen or twenty feet."

"A baby," Sharp said. "A squirt."

"Not necessarily. In any case, that's not important; the sex drive doesn't notice size. Even if our animal is, as I think it is, four or five times as big as this thing, its impulse will be to breed with this. If the beast is a male, it will want to deposit sperm in here; if it's a female, it will want its eggs fertilized."

"Why the hell would it want to do *anything* with a piece of plastic?" Darling asked.

"That's where the genius comes in." Talley began to unscrew the steel ring. "I've spent years developing a chemical that perfectly replicates the breeding attractant of *Architeuthis*. Over time, I've been able to collect tissue samples from two dead specimens. I removed the oviduct from a large female that had stranded in Nova Scotia, and then two years ago I heard that part of the mantle of a male had washed up on Cape Cod. By the time I got there, there wasn't much left; birds and crabs had been working on it. But part of it had been buried in the sand and protected, and I was able to recover the entire spermatophoral sac. It was over three feet long. For months, I analyzed both parts, male and female, with microscopes and spectrographs and computers. Finally, I was able to synthesize the chemical trigger."

"You're positive?" Darling said. "Have you ever tried it?"

"In the field? No. But in the laboratory, yes. It makes perfect sense scientifically. I won't burden you with the specifics of the science, but just as a dog in heat emits a musk, just as human beings respond to testosterone and the pheromones and all our other hormonal signals, a giant squid responds to chemicals released by others of its species during a period similar to what we mammals call estrus." He put his finger in the hole left by the steel ring. "A vial of liquid poured in here and diluted with seawater will seep out through tiny holes behind each hook. It will create a spoor that will travel for miles. *Architeuthis* will perceive that one of its kind is ready for breeding, and it will be a call of Nature that the beast won't be able to resist."

"Won't he know it's a phony?" Sharp asked.

"No. There's almost no light down there, remember, so it doesn't depend on its eyes for much. We know it can change colors, but we don't know if it can *see* colors, so just to be on the safe side I painted the surrogate red, which we know is one of the colors of excitation. And the surrogate's shape is correct. We'll hang chemical lights beside it, so in case the animal is accustomed to using its eyes for confirmation, they should cast enough of a glow to be convincing." Talley paused. "It may be overkill," he said. "The spoor might work if I let it leak out of a bottle. But making the lure the right shape and the right color didn't cost much and can't hurt. When you play cards with the unknown, it's good to hold as many trumps as you can."

"Okay," Darling said. "So he comes and screws the bejesus out of this thing. Then what?"

"The beast has eight arms and two whips, and it will wrap all of them around the object. It will press its body to it." Talley flipped a few of the little hooks, and they tinkled. "Each one of these will set into its flesh—not enough to alarm it, certainly not enough to cause it pain. But when it tries to get away, it won't be able to. That's when we bring it up, just close enough on the surface for me to take pictures of it, and for Osborn to kill it. Then I'll cut some specimens." Talley looked from Sharp to Darling, and smiled.

"Well, one thing's for sure," Darling said. "By the time he gets up here, that's gonna be one pissed-off squid."

"I don't think so. I think it will be concerned with only one thing: survival. The rapid change in water temperature may stun it, the change in pressure may kill it before it reaches the surface. It may be so exhausted it can't respire. But whatever happens," Talley said, turning and gesturing at Manning, "that's when Osborn takes over."

Manning acknowledged Talley with a curt nod, and gestured with his rifle.

"You know what scares me?" Darling said. "You're too sure of all this. I've seen too many perfect plans go ass-upwards." He turned to Sharp. "Marcus, I'm damn glad we built ourselves that bomb."

"You won't need explosives, Captain," Talley said. "You'll see."

"I hope so. But from what I've seen, this is not a critter to underestimate."

IT TOOK THEM more than three hours to set Talley's rig, which was a masterpiece of complexity, involving thousands of feet of rope, hundreds of feet of cable and a low-light surveillance video camera housed in a Plexiglas sphere the size of a fortune-teller's crystal ball. Talley hadn't realized that objects on long lines underwater tend to spin unpredictably, and had mistakenly assumed that his camera would hang beside the lure and focus on it, so Darling had to fetch his chain saw from below and find a two-by-four, cut it and lash it between the camera and the lure as a connecting brace.

"How long does the camera run for?" Darling asked as Talley plugged the power cord into the battery pack.

"The tape is a hundred twenty minutes long," Talley said, "and the lithium battery in the base will run camera and lights for all of that. But we won't turn it on and leave it—a timer will set it off for one minute every five minutes. Or, I can turn it on whenever I choose from up here."

It was twilight when at last the rig was ready. The wind had died, and the sea was a meadow of steely swells.

Sharp watched a pair of gulls wheel over the stern, looking for an offering of bread or baitfish, and then fly off. As his gaze followed them toward the sunset, he saw something in the distance, something on the surface of the sea. At first he thought he was seeing the splashes of diving birds, but they didn't act like splashes: They lasted too long, and the water flew too high, more like spray. Then he knew.

"Look, Whip," he said, pointing. "Whales."

"Nice," Darling said. "At least there's *some* left."

"What are they, humbacks?"

"No. Sperm whales. Humpbacks don't linger like that, they keep moving. Sperm whales always gather at twilight, I don't know why, maybe to get together for a gam."

Talley looked at the whales, then cupped his hands together and shouted at them, "Go away!"

Darling laughed. "What've you got against whales, Doc?" he asked.

"Nothing. I just don't want them to scare off *Architeuthis*. They eat squid, you know."

"I wouldn't worry about it," Darling said. "I don't know anything God ever made that would scare that beast away. Whales aren't as stupid as us—they know when to leave well enough alone."

Talley went into the cabin, and by the time he came back, the whales had sounded, and the sea had closed over them.

In his hands Talley held a six-ounce vial of clear liquid. At Talley's direction, Darling and Sharp held the lure upright and poured in buckets of seawater. Then Talley unscrewed the cap from the vial, and he held it out to them. "For science," he said.

Darling hesitated, then shrugged and said, "What the hell . . . it's not every day I get to sniff a randy squid." He held Talley's wrist and put his nose to the vial—and felt as if the lining of his nose had caught fire. His eyes watered, his stomach heaved; he staggered backward, coughing.

Talley laughed and said, "What do you make of it?"

"*Make* of it!" Darling choked. "Holy shit! Ammonia, sulfur . . . that stuff the freaks use to give their hearts a trumpeting —amyl nitrate—and something, I don't know, something purely *bad.*"

"Bad?" Talley said. "You mean bad as in evil? There's no such thing as an evil animal."

"That's what *you* say, Doc. Me, I'm beginning to think different."

Talley emptied the vial into the water in the lure and screwed the steel ring tight. They shackled the ring to the cable and then, with Darling holding one end of the two-by-four and Sharp the other, they lowered the rig over the stern and let it go. It floated for a moment, until the last of the air inside the lure was expelled, and then it slipped away in a flurry of bubbles.

Darling and Sharp manned two hand-crank winches clamped on either side of the stern. Simultaneously, they fed first the cables, then the ropes, over into the sea, pausing every twelve feet to allow Talley to secure the camera's cable to the rope.

Then darkness fell; the stars strewed silver glitter on the still ocean, and the rising moon cast a golden path from the eastern horizon to the stern of the boat. From behind them came the warm glow of the cabin lights.

Finally, at nine o'clock, the 480-fathom marks on the ropes slipped through their hands, and they halted the rig, wrapped the ropes around the winches and tied them off to an iron towing post that ran down through the deck and into the keel.

"Want some food, Mr. Manning?" Darling asked as he and Sharp started forward.

Manning shook his head and continued to stare at the water.

Talley sat at the table in the cabin, adjusting the video recorder and the monitor and the control box. Darling walked behind him and looked at the monitor: The lure was in frame, swaying back and forth, and from the hundreds of holes in its skin, shimmering strands of spoor trickled out and trailed off into the blackness.

Darling noticed that Talley was sweating and that his hand shook as he turned the dials on the control box. "Is it getting to you, Doc?" he said. "Sometimes it's better if our dreams don't come true."

"I'm not afraid, Captain," Talley said sharply. "I'm excited. I've been waiting thirty years for this. No, I'm not afraid."

"Well, I am," said Darling, and he stepped up into the wheelhouse. He looked through the windows at the calm night sea. There were no other lights out here, no fishing boats, no passing ships. They were alone. A little frisson passed up his back, and he shook it off.

He turned on the fathometer. A stylus traced a pattern on a sheet of graph paper, and Darling read the depth. The bottom was 3,000 feet away, so if he and Sharp had measured the lines correctly, the lure and camera were suspended 120 feet above it. He started back down into the cabin, then stopped, reached over and switched on the fish-finder and calibrated its reading depth to five hundred fathoms. As the screen warmed up, the bottom glowed as a straight line. Otherwise, it was blank.

"That spoor's driving everything away, from here to the Azores," Darling said as he stepped down into the cabin. "There isn't a porgy or a shark between us and the bottom."

"No," Talley said, "there wouldn't be. They know to stay away." He turned off the camera and set the timer.

Darling walked to the door and flicked a switch beside it. The halogen lamps mounted on the flying bridge flashed on, and the afterdeck was flooded with light. Through the window Darling saw that Manning didn't budge, as if he hadn't noticed the sudden explosion of light. He sat on the midships hatch cover, his shoulders hunched, his rifle cradled in his lap.

Sharp passed Darling a sandwich. He nodded toward Manning and said, "Should I take him one?"

"He's not interested in food," Darling said. "The man's eating himself up inside."

"Osborn is unfortunate," Talley commented as he reached for a piece of bread and some cheese. "He's lost his perspective. Three weeks ago, he was a man who had power and knew how to use it. We made a deal that would give him revenge. He regarded it as a good deal. But now the project has become an obsession."

"Can you blame him?" Sharp asked.

"Of course. He's being irrational."

"Worse than irrational," said Darling. "He's dangerous."

"It'll pass. We'll let him shoot his gun at *Architeuthis*, and he'll be what he has always been: a winner."

"That simple, is it?"

"Animals are predictable, Captain, even the human one."

"Including *Architeuthis*?"

"Oh yes. It's programmed as surely as any machine. Once we know the codes, its behavior is predictable. Absolutely."

BY TEN-THIRTY, the timer had activated the camera a dozen times, and each time they had gathered around the monitor and seen the lure swinging back and forth across the frame, leaking ribbons of spoor. Up-current from the lure, a few tiny crustaceans flashed like fireflies across the screen, leaving afterglows of phosphorescence. Down-current there was nothing but black.

The boat drifted on the calm sea; even lying beam-to, it didn't snap-roll but seemed to rock gently, like a baby's cradle. The cabin lights were a snug orange cocoon that added to the illusion of peace.

"Suppose he doesn't come tonight," Darling said to Talley.

"In the morning, then, or the afternoon. But it will come."

"We might's well get some sleep, then."

"If you can."

"Better had. You too."

Sharp went to the bunk room below. Talley watched the monitor through one more cycle, then lay back on the bench seat and closed his eyes. Darling went outside.

Manning was still sitting on the hatch cover, but he was slumped over, asleep.

Darling checked the ropes; they hung straight down, unmoving, untouched. Then he looked toward shore. The loom of Bermuda was a rosy glow against the black sky, and he could make out the light pattern of the huge Southampton Princess Hotel and the sweeping beam of the lighthouse on Gibbs Hill. They were ten miles away, but he took comfort in the knowledge that home was still there. He thought of Charlotte, in their house, in their bed, and suddenly he was suffused with loneliness.

When he went back inside, the television monitor was running again, casting pale gray shadows on Talley's sleeping face.

Darling climbed up into the wheelhouse and stood quietly, listening to the sounds of the night. The generator purred; the stylus on the fathometer hissed as it tracked the boat's drift along the five-hundred-fathom line; the fish-finder hummed, its screen still showing desolate emptiness. He heard the sound of the water softly caressing the steel hull, and the sound of Talley breathing.

He went into the cabin and lay down on one of the bunks. He longed for sleep, for abstraction from himself, but, exhausted though he was, he was sure that his mind would refuse to retreat into the comfort of numbness. Ever since he had first gone to sea as a boy, whenever he slept on a boat a part of his brain had always stood watch, alert to any change in the wind, to the slightest alteration in the rhythms of the ocean.

The watchman in his head had been on duty in the best of times, when the boat had floated over an apparently infinite resource of life, when being woken in the middle of the night usually signaled promise rather than threat. The watchman hadn't flagged even in recent bad times, when nights were filled mostly with vain hopes.

Darling knew that the watchman would be on duty now, when, for the first time in his life, his most fervent hope was that the sea beneath him would remain a barren, lifeless plain.

His breathing slowed; his brain succumbed to fatigue. The watchman stood guard, a lonely sentry.

46

THE GIANT SQUID expanded its mantle, drew water within and expelled it from the funnel in its belly. It propelled its great mass through the night sea with a force that pushed pressure waves before it and left eddies behind.

Driven by the most basic of all impulses, it rushed in one direction, then stopped, then rushed in another, extending its many senses to gather in more and more of the scattered signals that were exciting it into a frenzy. Its body chemistry was confused, and the chromatophores it triggered changed the creature's flesh color from pale gray to pink to maroon to red, reflecting emotions from anxiety to passion.

The signals it was receiving were partly alien and partly familiar, but its brain registered only that they were irresistible.

And so it rushed on, soaring up and down and side to side, like an aircraft out of control or a gigantic raptor gone berserk.

Suddenly it encountered a stream of the signals; it was a trail, strong and true.

The creature homed in on it, excluding everything else.

47

DARLING AWOKE, WITHOUT knowing what had woken him. He lay quietly for a moment, listening and feeling.

He heard the familiar sounds: the hum of the refrigerator, the scratch of the stylus across the fathometer paper, Talley's breathing. He saw the familiar sights: darkness, relieved only by the faint red glimmer from the binnacle in the wheelhouse. But he felt a difference in the motion of the boat. There was a reluctance, as if the boat were no longer going with the flow of the sea, but rather fighting it.

He rolled off the bunk, walked to the door and stepped outside. The instant his eye caught the movement of the water, he knew what had woken him: The boat was going in the wrong direction.

Something was pulling it backward.

Then he looked at the stern, and saw little waves slapping against it, casting spray. The ropes still angled straight downward, but they were trembling, and even from a distance he could hear the high-pitched squeak of straining fibers.

So, he thought. Here we go.

He ducked back inside and shouted, "Marcus!"

Talley sat up on the bench seat and said, "What?"

"Turn your TV monitor on, Doc," Darling said, then called again, "Marcus! Let's go."

"Why?" Talley was still groggy. "What . . . ?"

"Because we've hooked the sonofabitch, that's why. And he's dragging us backward." Darling reached across Talley and pressed the switch. The monitor flickered, then glowed.

The image was without definition, a swirl of bubbles and shadows, light flashing against darkness—a scene of chaos and violence.

"The lure!" Talley said. "Where's the lure?"

"He's got it," said Darling. "And he's trying to run with it."

Just then, Sharp came up from below, and Darling beckoned to him and went outside.

Manning was standing in the stern, soaked with spray, staring at the thrumming ropes. "Is it . . . ?" he asked.

"Either it's the beast, or we've hooked the devil himself." Darling directed Sharp to the starboard winch while he took the one on the port side, and together they began to wind in the ropes.

For a minute or two, they made no headway; the weight on the winches was too great for them to get traction, so the winch drums skidded under the ropes. The boat continued to move backward, splashing spray as the stern dug into the waves.

Then the ropes suddenly eased, and the boat stopped.

"The strain's gone," Sharp said. "Did it get off?"

"Could be. Or else he's just turning, I can't tell. Keep cranking."

They wound in tandem, retrieving a foot of rope every second, ten fathoms a minute. The muscles in Darling's arms ached, then began to burn, and he switched hands every few turns.

"Whip, he's got to have busted away," Sharp said when the two-hundred-fathom marks on the ropes rolled over the winch drums and tumbled into the coils at their feet. "Must have."

"I don't think so," said Darling. He had a hand on the rope and was feeling it, trying to read it. There was weight to the rope but no strain, pull but no action. "It feels like he's there but not pulling. Maybe taking a breather."

"Or maybe dead," Sharp said, sounding hopeful.

"Keep cranking, Marcus," Darling said.

Talley came out of the cabin. "I can't see anything on the video," he said. "It's a mess."

"Leave it run anyway," said Darling.

"I am." Talley took a position behind them, pressed against

the cabin bulkhead. He had taken another video camera from one of his cases, and he hurried to load a tape and attach a battery.

Suddenly, Sharp said, "Whip! Look . . ." and he pointed. The ropes no longer hung vertically; they had started to move slowly out, away from the boat. Still there was no stutter on the winches; the rope kept coming aboard.

"He's coming up!" Darling shouted, and he thought: He's just like a billfish on a run to breaching; he pulls, stops, gathers strength, and now he's gonna make his move. He looked at Manning and said, "Cock your gun. This is what you've been waiting for." Then he said to Talley, "If you want any pictures, Doc, you better get 'em fast. The beast isn't gonna stay long."

For the next few minutes, no one spoke. To Darling, the silence was like the false calm in the eye of a hurricane.

Darling and Sharp cranked the winch handles, and the rope flowed aboard, then ended, and the big shackles rattled over the bulwarks, followed by the first lengths of cable. "Fifty fathoms, Marcus," Darling said. "Another minute or two."

The cables angled out behind them, not quite horizontal, taut and quivering but still coming aboard. The creature must be nearing the surface now, but they couldn't tell for sure, or how far away it might be, or how far out in the darkness.

They stared at the water off the stern, trying to follow the silver threads of cable, to see beyond the edge of the pool of light cast by the halogen lamps.

"Show yourself, you bastard!" Darling called, and he realized suddenly that his fear had changed. What he was feeling now was not dread or foreboding or horror, but the galvanic fear of meeting an opponent more formidable than any he had ever imagined. It was almost like an electric charge, a healthy fear, he thought, and it blended with the fever of the hunt.

Just then the winches jolted, skidded, and the cable that had just come aboard leaped from its coils on the deck and began to snake overboard.

"What's he doing?" Sharp shouted.

"He's running again!" Darling cried, and he grabbed the winch handle and leaned on it, but the winch refused, the spool spun, the cable kept backing off into the water.

"No!" Manning screamed. "Stop him!"

"I can't!" Darling said. *"Nothing* can."

"You mean you *won't.* You're afraid. I'll show you how." Manning dropped his rifle, reached down into the coil of cable at his feet and grabbed a length of slack.

"Don't!" Darling yelled, and he took a step toward Manning, but before he could stop him, Manning had flung the cable at the iron post that ran down into the keel, looped it around the post and tied it off.

"There," Manning said. The cable continued to run off the stern, buzzing as it passed over the steel bulwark. Manning turned to face the stern, raised his rifle and waited for the creature to rise into his sights. But as he was turning, he slipped, and just then the creature must have accelerated, for suddenly the coils of cables jumped off the deck and flew. As Manning staggered to regain his balance, one of his feet stepped through a snarl of cable, and the cable snapped tight around his thigh, and he was lifted off the deck like a puppet. For a fraction of a second he hung suspended in the lights. He made no sound, and the rifle fell away from his hands.

Then a great force slammed the cables taut, and Manning seemed to fly backward, pulled by his leg, his arms out as if he were doing a swan dive.

Light flashed on Manning's face for an instant, and Darling saw no horror, no agony, no protest—only surprise, as if Manning's last sensation were amazement that fate had had the temerity to thwart him.

The rifle struck the deck and discharged a bullet, which ricocheted off the bulwark and whined away overhead.

Darling thought he saw Manning's leg pull away from his body, for something seemed to fall from the cable. But he heard no splash, for all sounds were overwhelmed by the *sproing!* of the cable setting against the iron post.

Instantly the cable rose to the horizontal, and the boat was dragged backward. Waves splashed against the transom, soaking them.

Then Darling saw the cable rise above the horizontal, and he yelled, "He's up!"

"Where?" Talley cried. "Where?"

They heard a splash then, and a sound like a bellows, and

they smelled a stinging stench. The spray that fell on them suddenly became a rain of black ink.

Darling got to his knees and started to stand, but then he saw, ten or fifteen feet behind the stern, a little flicker of silver, and instinctively he knew what it was: The threads of the cable were snapping and rolling back on themselves.

He shouted, "Duck!"

"What?" said Talley.

Darling dove at him and tackled him to the deck, and as they fell, there was a booming sound from behind the boat, like a magnum pistol being fired in a tunnel, followed instantly by a high-pitched whistle.

A length of cable screamed overhead and shattered the windows in the back of the cabin. The second length followed immediately, and they heard the crash of Talley's camera housing disintegrating against a steel bulkhead.

The boat pitched and yawed for a moment, then settled back into the sea.

"Jesus God . . ." Talley said.

Darling rolled away from him and stood up. He looked aft, out into the darkness. There was no sign that anything had ever been there, no roil of water, no sound. Only the soft whisper of breeze over the silent sea.

48

TALLEY'S FACE WAS the color of cardboard, and as he got up off the deck, he trembled so badly that he could barely stand. "I never thought . . ." he began, but his voice trailed off.

"Forget it," Darling said. He and Sharp were pulling in the skeins of rope that littered the surface beside the boat.

"You were right," Talley said. "All along you were right. There was no way we—"

"Listen, Doc . . ." Darling looked at Talley and thought: The man's in despair; in about a minute, he's gonna collapse. "When we get to shore, there'll be time enough to piss and moan. We'll say nice words for Mr. Manning and do all the proper things. But right now, what I want to do is get us the hell out of here. Go inside and lie down."

"Yes," Talley said. "Right." And he went into the cabin.

When they had hauled the last of the rope aboard, Sharp leaned over the stern and said, "I hope none of that rope's wrapped around the prop."

"You want to go overboard and have a look?" Darling said, starting forward. "*I* don't." Then he added, "Talley was right about one thing—the bastard sure was drawn to the lure. But now, who knows? All I know is, I want to be somewhere else when he figures out he's been had."

In the cabin, Talley was sitting at the table. He had rewound the videotape, and he looked at the monitor as he started to play it back.

"What are you looking for?" Darling asked.

"Anything," Talley said. "Any images at all."

Darling took a step up toward the wheelhouse, and said over his shoulder to Sharp, "Check the oil pressure for me, Marcus."

Sharp opened the engine-room hatch and started below.

Suddenly Talley jolted in his seat and shouted, "Jesus, Mary and Joseph!" His eyes were wide as he stared at the monitor, and he groped blindly for the controls for the recorder.

Sharp and Darling crowded behind Talley as he found the tape controls and pressed the "pause" button.

On the monitor was an image of froth and bubbles. Talley pressed the "frame-advance" button, and the picture jumped. "There's the lure," he said, pointing to a flicker of something dense and shiny. On the black-and-white screen it looked dark gray. In the next frame it had disappeared, then it reappeared at the top of the screen. Talley pointed to the bottom of the screen, and he said, "Now watch."

A grayish hump rose from the bottom of the screen, and, in the staccato pulse of the frame-advance, it seemed to march upward until it covered the entire screen. The frames kept changing, and the gray shade kept climbing. And then the bottom of the screen was invaded by something off-white, curved on top. It moved upward, as if to cover the screen.

The thing must have moved away from the camera, for gradually the image widened out, and the thing showed itself as a perfect off-white circle, and in its center was another perfect circle, blacker than ebony.

"My God," Sharp said. "Is that an *eye*?"

Talley nodded.

"What kind of size?" asked Darling.

"I can't tell," Talley said. "There's nothing to measure it against. But if the focal length of the camera was about six feet, and the eye fills the whole frame, it has to be . . . like so." He held his hands two feet apart. For a moment he gazed at his hands, as if unable to believe the size of the span he had created. Then, in a voice barely above a whisper, he said, "The thing must be ninety feet, perhaps more." He looked up at Darling. "This could be a hundred-foot animal."

"When we get home," Darling said, "we're all gonna get down on our knees and give thanks that we never got any closer to that fucker." Then he turned away and climbed the two steps up into the wheelhouse.

Dawn was breaking. The sky in the east had lightened to a grayish blue, and the advancing sun cast a line of pink on the horizon.

Darling pushed the starter button, and waited to hear the warning bell from the engine room and the rumbling cough as the engine came to life.

But all he heard was a click, then nothing.

He pushed it again. This time, nothing at all. He swore to himself several times, and then whacked the wheel with the heel of his hand, for as soon as he knew that the engine wouldn't start, he knew why it wouldn't start. There was no generator noise: The silence told him that sometime during the night, the generator had run out of fuel. The batteries had taken over automatically, but eventually, after being drained for hours by the lights and the refrigerator and the fathometer and the fish-finder, they had run down. They were still putting out some power, but they couldn't muster the juice to fire up the big diesel engine.

After he had calmed down, he considered which of the two fully charged compressor batteries would be easiest to shift over to the main engine, selected one, and reviewed in his mind the procedure for removing it from its mounts and sliding it through the tangle of machinery in the engine room and mounting it beside the engine.

It was nasty work, but not the end of the world.

As he crossed the wheelhouse on his way down to the engine room, it occurred to him that he should turn off the instruments, to save power. All the kick in the new battery should be directed to igniting the engine. He turned the knob on the fathometer, and the stylus stopped moving. The switch on the fish-finder was farther away. As he reached for it, his eyes glanced at the screen.

It wasn't blank anymore. For a moment, he thought: Good, life is coming back. Then he looked closer, and he realized that he had never seen an image like this on the screen. There weren't the little dots that signaled scattered fish, or the smears that showed schools of larger animals. The image on the screen was a single, solid mass, a mass of something alive. Something rising toward the surface, and rising fast.

49

THE BEAST SHOT upward through the sea like a torpedo. An observer might have thought that it was in retreat, for it moved backward, but it was not retreating. Nature had designed it to move backward with great speed and efficiency. It was attacking, and its triangular tail was like an arrow point, guiding it to its target.

It was over a hundred feet long from the clubs on its whips to the tip of its tail, and it weighed a dozen tons. But it had no concept of its size, or of the fact that it was supreme in the sea.

Its whips were retracted now, its tentacles clustered together like a trailing tail, for it was streamlined for speed.

Its chemistry was agitated, and its colors had changed many times, as its senses struggled to decipher conflicting messages. First there had been the irresistible impulse to breed; then perplexity when it had tried to mate and been unable to; then confusion when the alien thing had continued to emit breeding spoor; then anxiety as it had tried to shed the thing and found it could not, for the thing had attached itself like a parasite; then rage as it had perceived a threat from the thing and proceeded, with its tentacles and its beak, to destroy the threatener.

Now, what remained was rage, and it was rage of a new dimension. The beast's color was a deep, viscous red.

Before, the giant squid had always responded to impulses of rage with instantaneous explosive spasms of destruction, which had consumed the rage. But this time the rage did not abate; it evolved. And now it had a purpose, a goal.

And so the hunter rose, driven to cause not only destruction but death.

50

A THOUSAND FEET, Darling guessed as he calibrated the fish-finder. The thing was at a thousand feet, and it was coming up like a bullet. They had five minutes, no more, probably less.

He jumped down into the cabin. "Get the boat hook, Marcus," he said. "And make sure that detonator's ready to fire."

"What's wrong?" Talley asked.

"The bastard's coming up at us again," said Darling, "and my bloody battery's dead." He disappeared down into the engine room.

SHARP CLIMBED UP to the flying bridge, lifted the boat hook and examined the bomb. The paste of glycerine and gasoline had hardened, but it was still moist, and he smeared it evenly over the top of the explosive. Then he pressed the little glass bottle deeper into the paste, so it couldn't fall out even if the end of the boat hook was waved around.

The device was simple; there was no reason it shouldn't work. As soon as air got to the phosphorous, it would ignite and start an instantaneous chain reaction, setting off the Semtex. All they had to do was make sure that the beast bit down on the bottle, or crushed it in one of its whips.

All they had to do was feed an explosive to a hundred-foot monster, and jump out of the way before they were blown to tatters.

That was all.

Sharp suddenly felt sick. He looked out over the calm sea,

dappled by the rising sun. Everything was peaceful. How did Whip know the creature was coming up? How could he be sure? Maybe what he had seen on the screen was a whale.

Stop it, he told himself. Stop fantasizing and get ready.

It would work. It had to.

DARLING CRAWLED ACROSS the engine room and pushed the heavy twelve-volt battery in front of him. His knuckles were bloody and his legs cramped. When he judged that the battery was close enough for the cables to reach it, he unbolted them from the dead battery, without bothering to remove the dead battery from its mounts. He didn't care if the fresh battery tore itself loose and tumbled around; once he got it to kick over the engine, he wouldn't need it.

He paused long enough to be sure he was attaching the cables to the proper poles—positive to positive, negative to negative—and bolted it down.

Then he got to his feet and raced up the ladder.

51

ITS PREY WAS directly above.

It could see it with its eyes, could feel it with the sensors in its body. It did not pause to analyze the quarry, did not seek signs of life or scent of food.

But because the prey was alien, instinct told the creature to be wary, to appraise it first. And so, as a shark circles unknown objects in the sea, as a whale emits sonar impulses and deciphers the returns, *Architeuthis dux* passed once beneath the quarry and scanned it with its eyes. The force of its passage cast a pressure wave upward.

Then suddenly the prey above it erupted with noise, and began to move.

The beast interpreted the noise and movement as signs of flight. Quickly, it rotated the funnel in its belly, turned in its own length and attacked.

52

WHEN DARLING HAD felt the boat surge beneath him, he had held his breath and pushed the button, and then, a second later, had heard the rumble of the big diesel. He didn't wait for the engine to warm up—he rammed the throttle forward and leaned on it.

At first, the boat leaped forward, and then suddenly it stopped short, as if it were anchored by the stern. It tipped backward; the bow rose, and Darling was thrown back against the bulkhead. Then the boat fell forward again, and nosed into the sea. But still it didn't move.

The pitch of the engine had changed from a roar to a complaining whine. Then it began to sputter. It coughed twice, then died, and the boat lay dead in the water.

Sweet Jesus, Darling thought—the beast has wrecked the propeller, either jammed it or bent it up against the shaft. He felt suddenly cold.

He dropped down into the cabin and went out through the door onto the afterdeck.

Talley was standing by the midships hatch, staring numbly at the sea. When he saw Darling, he said, "Where is he? I thought you said—"

"Right underneath us," Darling said. "He's screwed us good and proper." He went to the stern and looked down over the transom into the water. A few feet beneath the swim step, snaking out from beneath the boat, was the tip of a tentacle.

Standing beside Darling, Talley said, "He must have tried to grab the propeller."

"Now he's lost an arm," said Darling, "maybe that'll discourage him."

"It won't," Talley said. "All it will do is enrage him."

Darling looked up at the flying bridge and saw Sharp standing at the railing, holding Manning's rifle. As he started up the ladder, he heard Talley say, "Captain . . ."

"What?"

"I'm sorry," Talley said. "This was all my—"

"Forget it. Sorry's a waste of time, and we don't have much time. Put on a life jacket."

"Are we sinking?"

"Not yet," Darling said.

The boat hook stood vertically in a rod holder, and Darling removed it and felt its heft.

"I'll do it," Sharp said, gesturing at the bomb on the end of the boat hook.

"No, Marcus," said Darling, and he tried to smile. "Captain's prerogative."

They both looked out over the water then, and as they watched, the sun cleared the horizon and faded from orange to gold, and the color of the sea changed from dead gray to steel blue.

THE BEAST WRITHED in the darkness, berserk with pain and confusion. Green fluid seeped from the stump of its missing tentacle.

It was not disabled—it sensed no loss of power. It knew only that what it had perceived as prey was more than prey. It was an enemy.

The creature rose again toward the surface.

DARLING AND SHARP were gazing off the bow, when suddenly from behind them came Talley's voice, screaming, "No!"

They whirled around and looked at the stern, and they froze.

Something was coming over the bulwark. For a moment it seemed to ooze like a giant purple slug. Then the front of it curled back like a lip, and it began to rise and fan out until it was four feet across and eight feet high, and it blocked the rays of the sun. It was covered with quivering circles, like hungry mouths, and in each one Darling could see a shining amber blade.

"Shoot it, Marcus!" Darling shouted. "Shoot!"

But Sharp stood agape, mesmerized, the rifle useless in his hands. Then, below them, Talley heard something, and he turned to his left, and screamed. Amidships, slithering aboard, was the beast's other whip.

The scream startled Sharp, and he spun and fired three shots. One went high; one struck the bulkhead and ricocheted away; the third hit the club of the whip dead center. The flesh did not react, did not bleed, twitch or recoil. It seemed to swallow the bullet.

More and more of both whips came aboard, writhing like snakes and falling in heaps of purple flesh, each atom of which moved and pulsed and quivered as if it had a goal of its own. They seemed to sense life aboard, and movement, for the clubs bent forward and began to move ahead on their circles, like searching spiders.

Talley seemed paralyzed. He did not flinch, made no move to flee, but stood still, frozen.

"Doc!" Darling shouted. "Get the hell out of there!"

When both whips were heaped in the stern, they stopped moving for a moment, as if the creature were hesitating, and then suddenly both whips expanded with muscle tension, and the stern was pressed downward. Behind the boat, the ocean seemed to rise up, as if giving birth to a mountain. There was a sucking sound, and a roar.

"Jesus Christ!" Darling yelled. "It's coming aboard!" He backed away, holding the boat hook at shoulder level, like a lance.

They saw the tentacles first, seven thrashing arms that grasped the stern and, like an athlete hoisting himself onto a parallel bar, pushed downward to bring the body up.

Then they saw an eye, whitish yellow and impossibly huge, like a moon rising beneath the sun. In its center was a globe of fathomless black.

The stern was forced downward until it was awash. Water

poured aboard and ran forward, flooding into the after hatches.

It's gonna do it, Darling thought. The bastard's gonna sink us. And then pick us off one by one.

The other eye came up now, and as the creature turned its head and faced them, the eyes seemed to fix on them. Between the eyes the arms quivered and roiled, and at the juncture of the arms, like a bull's-eye on a target, the two-foot beak, sharp and protuberant, snapped reflexively, looking to be fed. The sound was of a forest falling in a storm, like great trunks cracking in a roaring wind.

Talley suddenly came to. He turned and ran to the bottom of the ladder and began to climb. He was halfway to the flying bridge when the creature saw him.

One of the whips recoiled, rose in the air and sprang forward, reaching for him. Talley saw it coming, and as he tried to dodge it, his feet skidded off the ladder, and he hung by his hands from one of the rungs. The whip coiled around the ladder, tore it away from the bulkhead and held it suspended over the flying bridge, with Talley dangling from it like a marionette.

"Drop, Doc!" Darling shouted, as the other whip hissed overhead and slashed at Talley.

Talley let go, and fell, his feet struck the outboard lip of the flying bridge, and for a second he teetered there, his arms cartwheeling as he groped for the railing. His eyes were wide, and his mouth hung open. Then, almost in slow motion, he toppled backward into the sea. The whip crushed the ladder and cast it away.

Sharp fired the rifle at the beast until the clip was empty. Tracer bullets streaked into the oozing flesh and vanished.

The tail of the creature thrust forward, driving the body farther up on the boat, driving the stern farther down. The bow rose out of the water, and from below came the sounds of tools and chairs and crockery crashing into steel bulkheads.

"Go, Marcus!" Darling said.

"You go. Let me—"

"*Go*, God dammit!"

Sharp looked at Darling, wanted to speak, but there was nothing to say. He dove overboard.

Darling turned aft. He could barely stand; the deck sloped out from under him, and he crouched, bracing himself with one foot on the railing.

The creature was tearing the boat to pieces. The whips flailed randomly, clutching anything they touched—a drum of rope, a hatch cover, an antenna mast—and crushing it and flinging it into the sea. As it drew air into its mantle and expelled it through its funnel, the creature made sounds like a grunting pig.

And then its rampage ceased, and as if it had suddenly remembered something, the great head, with its face like a nest of vipers, turned toward Darling. The whips lashed out; each one fastened on a steel stanchion on the flying bridge. Darling saw the flesh balloon as the muscles contracted. The whips pulled, and the creature lunged forward.

Darling balanced one foot on the railing and one on the deck, and he raised the boat hook over his head like a harpoon. He tried to gauge how far he was from the beak.

The creature seemed to be falling toward him. The arms reached out. Darling focused only on the gnashing beak, and he struck.

The boat hook was torn from his hands, and he was thrown back against the iron railing. He saw one of the whips raise the boat hook, and drop it into the sea.

His only thought was: I am going to die.

The arms reached for him. He ducked, his feet slipped out from under him, and he fell, skidding over the edge of the flying bridge and dropping onto the sloping afterdeck.

He found himself in waist-deep water. He started to slog toward the railing. If he could get overboard, away from the boat, maybe he could hide in the wreckage, maybe the creature would lose interest, maybe . . .

The beast appeared around the edge of the cabin then, looming above him, its whips waving like dancing cobras. The seven shorter arms, and even the oozing stump of the eighth, reached for him, to push him into the amber beak.

He turned and struggled toward the other side of the boat. One of the arms slapped the water beside him, and he dodged to the side, stumbled and regained his footing. How many steps to go? Five? Ten? He'd never make it. But he kept going, because there was nothing else he could do, and because something deep inside him refused to surrender.

An obstacle blocked him. He tried to push it out of the way, but it was too heavy, it wouldn't move. He looked at it, wondering if he could dive under it. It was the big midships hatch cover, floating. Lying atop it was the chain saw.

Darling didn't consider, didn't hesitate, didn't think. He grabbed the chain saw and pulled the starter cord. It caught on the first try, and the little motor came to life, idling with a minatory growl. He pressed the trigger, and the saw blade spun, shedding drops of oil.

He heard himself say, "Okay," and he turned and faced the beast.

It seemed to pause for a moment, and then, with a grunt of expelled air, it lunged for him.

Darling squeezed the trigger again, and the sound of the saw rose to a shrill screech.

One of the writhing arms flashed before his face, and Darling swung the saw at it. The saw's teeth bit into flesh, and Darling was bathed in a stench of ammonia. The motor labored, seemed to slow, as it might when cutting wet wood, and Darling thought, No! Don't quit, not now!

The pitch of the motor changed again, rose again, and the teeth cut deep, spraying bits of flesh into Darling's face.

The arm severed, and fell away. A sound burst from the beast, a sound of rage and pain.

Another arm assailed Darling, and another, and he slashed with the saw. As the teeth touched each one, the arms flinched and withdrew and then, as if goaded by the creature's frenzied brain, attacked again. A shower of flesh exploded around Darling, and he was drenched with green slime and black ink.

Suddenly he felt something touch one of his legs underwater, and it began to crawl up his leg and circle his waist.

One of the whips had him. He turned, trying to find it, wanting to attack it with the saw before it got a secure grip on him, but in the mass of curling, twisting tentacles he couldn't distinguish it from the arms.

When the whip had circled his waist, it began to squeeze, like a python, and Darling felt a stabbing pain as the hooks in each sucker disk tore into his skin. He felt his feet leave the deck as the whip picked him up, and he knew that once he was in the air, he was as good as dead.

He twisted his body so that he faced the snapping beak. As the whip squeezed and drove the breath from him, Darling leaned toward the beak, holding the saw before him. The beak opened, and for a second Darling could see a flicking tongue within, pink and studded with toothlike rasps.

"Here!" he shouted, and he drove the saw deep into the yawning beak.

The saw stuttered as its teeth failed to slice through the bony beak, and skidded off. As Darling raised the saw again, one of the arms flashed before his face, circled his hands and wrenched the saw from them and flung it away.

Now, Darling thought, now I am truly dead.

The whip squeezed, and Darling sensed that the mist that dimmed his eyes was signaling the onset of oblivion. He felt himself rising, saw the beak reaching for him, smelled a rancid stench.

He saw one of the eyes, dark and blank, relentless.

Then suddenly the beast itself seemed to rise up, as if propelled by a force from below. There was a sound unlike anything Darling had ever heard, a rushing, roaring noise, and something huge and blue-black exploded from the sea, holding the squid in its mouth.

The whip that had him contorted violently, and he felt himself flying, then falling into nothingness.

53

"PULL!" SHARP SHOUTED.

Talley reached into the water and groped for Darling's belt. He found it and pulled, and with Sharp hauling on his arms they brought him aboard the overturned hatch cover. It was awash, but its wood was thick and sound, and it was large enough to hold three of them.

Darling's shirt was in tatters, and streaks of blood criss-crossed his chest and belly where the creature's hooks had torn at his skin.

Sharp touched an artery in Darling's neck. The pulse was strong and steady. "Unless something's busted inside," he said, "he should be okay."

In a dark fog, Darling heard the word "okay," and he felt himself swimming up toward light. He opened his eyes.

"How do you feel, Whip?"

"Like a truck ran over me. A truck full of knives."

Sharp lifted Darling up and supported his back. "Look," he said.

Darling looked around. The motion of the hatch cover made him nauseated, and he shook his head to clear it.

The boat was gone. The animal was gone.

"What was it?" Darling asked. "What did it?"

"One of the sperm whales," said Sharp. "It took the whole damn squid. Bit it off just behind the head."

There was sudden movement in the water, and Darling started.

"It's all right," Talley said. "Just life, just Nature."

The surface of the sea was littered with flesh, masses of it, and each one was being assaulted. The tumult around the boat had been like a dinner bell, summoning creatures both from shallow and from deep. The dorsal fin of a shark crossed the debris. The head of a turtle poked up, looked around, then submerged again. Bonitos rippled the surface as they swarmed on fresh and helpless prey. Triggerfish, yellowtails and jacks ignored one another as they darted through the rich broth.

"Nice," Darling said, and he lay back. "That's the kind of life I like."

"I don't know where we are or where we're going," said Sharp. "I can't see land. I can't see a thing."

Darling wet a finger and held it up. "Home," he said. "Northwest wind. We're going home."

54

IT HAD BEEN created in the abyss, and had remained there for weeks, adhering to a rock overhang on the mountainside. Then it had broken away, as Nature planned it should, and, buoyed by a concentration of ammonium ions, it had begun slowly to drift toward the surface. In times past, it might have been eaten on the way up, for it was a rich food source.

But nothing had attacked it; nothing had shattered its integrity and permitted a rush of seawater that would have killed the tiny creatures within, so it had arrived safely on the surface and bathed itself in the sunlight vital to its survival.

It floated on the still water, oblivious to wind and weather, so thin as to be nearly transparent. But its jelly skin was remarkably strong.

It was oval, with a hole in its center, and it followed eons of genetic instructions and rotated itself in the sun, exposing all of itself to nutrients sent from almost 100 million miles away.

Still, it was vulnerable. A turtle might have fed on it, a passing shark might have slashed at it. Nature had ordained that many of its members would die, feeding other species and maintaining the balance of the food chain.

But since nature itself was out of balance, the gelatinous oblong rotated through days and nights until its cycle was complete. At last, ripe, it broke apart and scattered into the sea thousands of little sacs, each containing a complete creature. As each creature sensed that its time had come for life, it struggled free of its sac and immediately began to search for food.

They were cannibals, these creatures, and those that could turned on their brethren and ate them. But there were so many, and they dispersed so fast in the water, that most survived and dove for the comfort of the cold abyss.

Almost all should have been eaten before they reached the bottom, or the safety of the crevices on the submerged volcano's slopes; at most, one creature in a hundred should have survived.

But the predators were gone, and while a few lone hunters did appear, and took their toll, there were no longer the great gatherings that had once acted as natural monitors. The vast schools of bonito and mackerel, the swarms of small white squid, the pelagic jacks, the herds of tuna, the voracious wahoo and barracuda, all were gone.

And so, by the time the creatures had crossed three thousand feet of open water and taken shelter in the cliffs, nearly ten percent—perhaps a hundred individual animals, perhaps two or three hundred—still lived.

They hovered, each alone, for each was completely self-sufficient, and drew water into their mantles and expelled it from the funnels in their bellies. Their confidence grew with every respiration. Their bodies would mature slowly, and for a year or more they would be wary of other predators. But the time would come when they would sense their uniqueness, their superiority, and then they would venture out.

They hovered, and they waited.

THE GIRL OF
THE SEA OF
CORTEZ

For Kate Medina

ACKNOWLEDGMENTS

I am grateful to ABC's "The American Sportsman" and its producer, John Wilcox, under whose aegis I was introduced to the Sea of Cortez; to Stanton A. Waterman, for taking me along on the voyage and for his sage counsel and fine company; and to Susannah Waterman, whose inspired graphic eye captured the look of the Sea of Cortez.

P.B.

1

THE GIRL LAY on the surface of the sea, looking into the water through a mask, and she was afraid.

She was surprised to feel fear—a true, deep fear that bordered on panic—for not in years had anything in the sea frightened her.

But then, never in her life had she been actively, aggressively menaced by an animal. Creatures had snapped at her, and some had circled her, hungry and curious, but always a show of strength and confidence had sent them on their way in search of more appropriate prey.

But this animal did not seem to want to bite her, or eat her. It looked to her as if it wanted simply to hurt her, to stab her.

It had appeared with magical speed. One moment the girl was gazing into an empty blue haze; the next, she was staring at a sharp and pointed bill of bone that quivered three feet from her chest. The bill swooped back to a broadened base, and ended in two clam-size black eyes as cold as night.

Unlike the other billfish, this one had no fin on its back. It had instead a dorsal sail covering most of its backbone, which could lie flat against the back and be almost invisible or stand in proud display.

Or, when the fish was agitated, as now, the sail pulsed up and down, up and down, as the head of a serpent hypnotizes a rodent.

The fish's tail was like a honed scythe. It twitched once, a shudder passed along the body, and the bill jerked quickly, startling the girl.

She did not know what to do, how to behave. Backing away was no answer: this was not territorial aggression, for this was not a territorial animal. It cruised the deep water of the open sea; it knew no home.

To move suddenly *at* it was no answer: the fish was supremely confident of its superiority over her—in speed and strength and agility—or it would not have approached her. She could not hope to shoo it away.

And to stay where she was seemed to be no answer: apparently she was somehow irritating the fish, for it shook its head, and its spear sliced the water and she felt its force against her chest.

Its long, slim pectoral fins dropped; its back hunched; its tail twitched. Its entire body was a cocked spring, ready, at the release of an inner trigger, to impale her on its bill.

Why?

It could not be pure malice, for her father had taught her that malice did not exist in animals. Animals could be hungry, angry, frightened, hurt, sick, defensive, protective, jealous, careless, or playful—and in any of those states could become vicious or violent—but not malevolent.

What, then? What did it want?

Again the head shook, and the spear slit the water.

She wondered if she could make it to her boat before the fish attacked. She fluttered her fingers and toes, hoping to propel herself backward, inch by inch, closer to her boat.

But how far away was the boat?

She turned her head a half-turn, flicked her eyes over her shoulder, saw the boat, and turned immediately back to face the fish.

It was gone.

She had felt nothing, heard nothing, and now all she could see was the endless blue.

2

THERE WAS NO electricity on the island, and kerosene lamps burned with a thick, greasy smoke that made some people sick, so the old man and the girl chose to sit in a room illuminated only by the light that leaked around the edges of the covered windows. The old man kept the room dark intentionally, had put cloths over the windows, because the slashing rays of the late-afternoon sun coloured the room with contrasts so sharp that they pained his eyes and confused him. He had cataracts in both eyes, and sudden bursts of bright light felt like little explosions in his brain.

The old man's name was Francisco, but everyone called him Viejo, Old Man, even the children who might have called him Grandfather or a pet name, because Viejo was an honour, a title as significant as Excellency or General. To attain old age was a true achievement.

The girl's name was Paloma—Dove—after the morning bird that cooed a prelude to the cock's crow. She was sixteen.

"I don't understand, Viejo," she said. "Nothing like that has ever happened to me before."

"You had never met a bad animal before. Now you have. It had to happen, eventually."

"Forgive me, but . . ." She hesitated. "Papa always told me there was no such thing as a bad animal."

"Your father Jobim was a . . . a curious man." Viejo sought gentle words to describe his son-in-law, rather than those that came quickly to mind. "Of course there are bad animals, just as there are bad people. I am only grateful that the sailfish you met today was not truly bad, or he would have run you through. That happens. Once, many years before you were born . . ."

To forestall the reminiscence, Paloma said, "I don't see why God would create a bad animal. It doesn't make sense."

Viejo pressed his lips together, which Paloma recognized as a sign of pique. He was a fine storyteller, and it was one of the few pleasures that life still permitted him.

"Who says you must understand everything?" Viejo said. "For a human being to try to fathom all of God's works is a waste of time."

Paloma tried to retreat. "I didn't mean . . ."

"What is, is. And one of the things that is, is that there are good things and bad things." He paused. "They tell me you have been interfering with the fishermen again."

"No! I only . . ."

"They say you shout and make a fool of yourself."

"They can think what they please. All I did was ask Jo and Indio and the others why they can't be more careful. They catch everything; they bring back fish they have no use for. They don't kill just for food. That I could understand. The way they fish, someday there will be nothing left."

"No. The sea is forever. And you must learn that man will hunt what he wishes for whatever reason he wishes. His judgements are his own. For example, it has been judged that some animals are good alive *and* dead, like the bonito and the tuna and the grouper. Alive, they feed other animals; dead, they feed people and still more animals, useful animals. Some animals are bad, like the sea snake and the stonefish and the scorpion. All they do is cause pain and death.

"And then there are animals both good and bad, like barracuda—which one day feeds a man handsomely and the next day poisons him—and like sharks. Sharks bring us food and money, true, but now and again they kill people."

"What about an angelfish?" Paloma asked. "What could be good or bad about an angelfish? Or a pufferfish? Indio caught a pufferfish the other day, and you'd think he had caught a marlin. Why? We don't sell them. We don't eat them."

"The fishermen make their living from the sea," said Viejo, "and so they must become one with the sea and all its creatures. Sometimes, the only way to come to know a creature is to catch and kill it."

Because Paloma did not want to distress or offend her grandfather, she did not argue further: his truths were unshakeable. So, all she said was, "Well, I hope nothing ever wants to get to know me that well."

Outside Paloma looked to the western sky. The sun hovered over the horizon, as if about to be sucked beneath the shiny grey water.

She hurried to her rock, a narrow shelf of stone that jutted out over the western tip of the island. She came here at this time every day, and she loved both the place and the time of day, for this was where she felt at peace, close to nature, to life.

There were a few clouds overhead, and the setting sun painted them pink, but the horizon was cloudless, a blade beneath the red fireball that was slowly sliding downward and seeming to squash oblong.

Tonight might be a night for the green flash, she thought, and she steadied her chin in her hands and forced herself not to blink as she fastened her eyes on the vanishing sun. You almost never saw the green flash: the evening had to be clear and almost chilly; no waves of heat could be shimmering up from the water; the horizon had to be sharp and without even a wisp of cloud. And, of course, you had to be there and alert, and you couldn't blink, because the green flash lasted only that tiny bit of a second as the last infinitesimal rim of sun dipped below the horizon. Many times she had missed it by blinking, and in all her life she had seen it only twice—the first time the evening long ago when her father had led her by the hand and shown her this special place.

The bottom of the sun touched the horizon, and Paloma half expected to hear a hiss as the water quenched the fire, or see a cloud of steam explode from the sea. But smoothly and without a sound, it slipped faster and faster out of the sky.

Paloma held her breath and opened her eyes as wide as she could. The last of the sun dropped away and then, as Paloma was beginning to think there would be no green flash tonight, there it was—a shining pinprick of brilliant green, gone so fast that it became a memory at almost the same instant it registered as a sight.

Paloma watched the sky for a moment more, enjoying the changes that happened with such speed only at the beginning and end of the day. The yellow light was fading, following the sun to other parts of the world. The sky overhead was darkening quickly and soon was speckled with stars, and only the faintest splash of pink still touched the clouds.

Paloma felt suddenly calm and happy. Seeing the green flash was supposed to be an omen of good fortune, and though she didn't really believe in omens, surely it was better to have seen it than not to have seen it.

She rose to her knees and was about to leave the rock when a flicker of movement made her look back at the water. What she saw made her stop and stare and catch her breath again.

Rising clear of the water, outlined against the lapis sky, twisting in a spasm of pure pleasure, was an enormous marlin. Its sabre blade sliced through the air, its sickle tail arched upward, and then, in graceful slow motion, the huge body slammed down upon the water.

It was a full second before Paloma heard the heavy, resonant boom, and by then all that remained as testimony to the acrobatics was a spreading ring of ripples on the sea.

That, Paloma thought, was definitely something special. Maybe nature is telling me I *should* believe in omens.

With a feeling of privilege, of being witness to nature revelling in itself, Paloma started for home. As she walked along the path, she looked down and saw her brother, Jo, and his two friends approaching the dock in their skiff.

Paloma could see from the top of the hill that they had had a good day. The bow of their boat was heaped high with fish, a kaleidoscope of glistening colours in the fading light. And Paloma could see, even from where she stood, that they had taken fish indiscriminately: whatever they could catch they had killed. There were angelfish and rockfish, bonitos and jacks, pufferfish and stingrays, and even one of the rare and strange and furtive creatures called guitar sharks—harmless and, to fishermen, useless. Those fish that would not take a hook had been harpooned. Those that had eluded the harpoon had been netted.

As Paloma watched, Jo shut off the outboard motor and guided the wallowing skiff toward the dock, while his mates culled the piles of dead fish with their fingers, throwing overboard those that were not worth selling.

When Paloma had first seen them do this, she had erupted in fury, screaming at Jo, demanding to know why, if they intended to throw back the fish, they didn't do so as soon as they caught them, when the fish still had a chance to live.

If Jo had been startled at her anger, he had nevertheless been forthright in his response. "Early in the day, before we know the size of the catch, any fish is a good fish. By the end of the day, if the catch has been rich we can afford to keep only the good ones. So then we throw the bad ones back."

Paloma had tried to argue, but Jo had walked away, saying that was the way things had always been, and that was the way they would remain.

Now, she watched as the one called Indio picked up a small fish by its eye sockets and waved it at the other mate, Manolo. Though she was still a distance from them and the twilight was deepening, she could tell them apart by the color of their hair. Indio always wore a hat on the boat, so his hair had remained black. Manolo kept his head cool by pouring salt water on it, so his hair had been bleached to a light brown, just as Paloma's own long auburn hair had been bleached nearly blond by salt and sun. Indio said something now and threw the fish at Manolo, who picked up another fish by its tail and whacked Indio on the head with it.

Yowling and cursing, the fishermen flung fish at one another. Most missed their targets and landed in the water, to float there belly up.

To Paloma, striding down the hill, the fight was nauseating, the waste obscene. It offended something deep inside her to see dead animals treated as if they had never been live beings.

She bent over and picked up a rock and called out, "Hey!" The three in the skiff looked up. "If you have to throw things at each other, throw these." And she cocked her arm and threw the rock as hard as she could, hoping it would strike the skiff and knock a hole in it. But the rock flew wide and plopped in the water, and Jo responded by laughing and ticking his thumbnail off his front teeth and pointing at her—the coarsest, most insulting, and most contemptuous gesture he could make.

Paloma turned away.

Her father had explained the problem to her many times, during those early days when she had first complained about the young men who fished without care, taking everything and wasting much. "The sea, this sea, is too rich," he had said. "It has too much life."

She had not understood.

"If fish were in short supply here, fishermen might fish with care, in self-defense, for fear of killing off their livelihood. But here," Papa said, "nature seems to be showing off, proving to us how rich it can be. There is so much here, people see no reason to be careful. One day they will, but by then it may be too late. For now, it is all there to take."

Paloma had loved the sea since the time of her earliest memories. Her father, Jobim, had recognized the affinity between his first-born child and the sea, and had determined to nourish it. When she was a baby, he had bathed her in the sea and taught her to float, and then to swim, and to fear few living things but to respect them all.

And he had captivated her with his descriptions of the things that made their sea, the Sea of Cortez, unique.

The Sea of Cortez itself, he said, existed because of an ancient accident. Ages and ages ago, the peninsula known as Baja California had been part of the Mexican mainland. Then, at some point in prehistory, the plates that fit together to make the earth's surface had realigned themselves and caused what must have been the most spectacular earthquake of all time.

"You know how you take an old, ratty shirt and tear it up the back to make rags?" Jobim had said. "That's what happened to Mexico. It split along its main seam, the San Andreas Fault. And when the seam split there was a big space, and the Pacific Ocean rushed in, and a new sea was born."

The sea had had no name then, of course. Jobim read to her from a book that said it was not until 1536 that the sea was named for the Spanish explorer Hernando Cortez, who discovered Lower California and the sea that separated it from the Mexican mainland.

"Isn't that funny?" he had said. "Doesn't that make you laugh?"

"What?" Paloma wanted very much to share the laugh, but she didn't understand. "What's funny?"

"That they say some Spaniard discovered this place. Your ancestors were here, living and farming and fishing, when the Spaniards were still living in caves and eating bugs. All Cortez did was kill people and go on his way." Papa shook his head. "And for that they named the sea after him."

One book even credited Cortez with naming all of California. According to the story, as they cruised north along the west coast of the American continent, the Spaniards suffered badly from the heat. At one point, Cortez was supposed to have remarked, in Latin, to one of his officers that he found the region to be stinking hot, as hot (*calidus*) as a furnace (*fornax*).

"Nowadays," Jobim had said, "some people don't call it a sea any more. They call if a gulf, the Gulf of California. But it doesn't need a name. It is the sea. There are three things that make up life here: the sea, the land, and the people. They don't need names to separate them." He had smiled. "If you can't tell the difference, life won't be easy for you."

So to Paloma it was, simply, the sea—provider and friend but also tormentor and enemy. For if it gave her most of what she loved in life, it had also taken from her the one thing that she had cherished most in life.

Because of its peculiar combination of mountains and water, extreme dryness and extreme humidity, Pacific Ocean winds and high sierra winds, the Sea of Cortez was a breeding ground for sudden, violent low-pressure weather systems. With no warning at all, a fine day on the sea could turn mean. Over the horizon would race a black swirl of clouds. Beneath and before the clouds, the calm sea would begin to churn. At first, there would be a sound like a distant whisper, but soon it would swell into a horrid, wailing roar.

They were called *chubascos,* and unlike hurricanes and typhoons, they did not come from anywhere: they were created right there, and they lived and died right there. So, even if you had a radio, you could not hear a weather forecast about a *chubasco* approaching.

If you were lucky and were on land, you could fling yourself into a ditch or into the lee of a hill.

If you were unlucky and were on the water, you hoped to be able to notice a few early signs—even one sign, like a subtle shift in the wind or the sudden formation of a tower of black clouds—that would give you time to run for a lee or, at least, to reach open water, where you could face the pounding waves without fear of being driven onto a rocky shore.

If you were so unlucky as to be underwater when the first signs formed, and did not see them until the storm had made up and was almost upon you, and were forced to scramble aboard your boat and start your motor and free your anchor— then all that was left to you was prayer. Sometimes it worked; sometimes it didn't.

Two summers before, after the terrible *"chubasco* of the full moon"—the moon was full and the tides were very high, which meant that the storm-driven water rose higher and did more damage—Paloma's father was found, drowned, washed up on the beach of a nearby island.

That was one reason Paloma tended to question the acceptance, by Viejo and others, that everything mysterious was somehow an integral part of God's master plan.

If anyone or any thing or any force had deliberately willed or caused her father's death, that something would be the focus of her hatred till the day she died. She believed, rather, that Papa's death was an accident, a random blow, something that nothing had ordained or could have prevented. She had conditioned her mind not to think beyond that, about what might lie behind randomness or luck.

AT SUPPER THAT evening, Jo insisted on describing in detail, for Paloma and their mother, each of the triumphs of his day at sea.

He boasted about how many fish they had caught, about how hard the grouper had fought, about how sharks had swarmed around his boat and tried to steal his catch.

Paloma sat silently, knowing that for her to comment could lead only to argument. But Miranda, their mother, smiled and nodded and said, "That's nice."

With a glance at Paloma, Jo said, "I even threw my iron at a manta ray, a giant devilfish. He dodged at the last second and I missed. But then—I swear—he turned and attacked the boat. It's a good thing I was quick, or I would've been rammed and sunk."

Paloma said quietly, "Manta rays don't attack boats."

"*This* one did. This was a real devilfish. I swear."

"Why do you want to harpoon a manta ray? They don't hurt anybody."

"So *you* say! The devilfish is evil! That's why he has horns. He brings the face of evil to the earth."

Paloma said nothing, making a conscious effort to look only at her bowl of fish soup. But she could not resist—it came almost as a reflex—shaking her head as Papa used to, in a way that manifested contempt.

Jo knew the gesture, recognized its origin, and hated it. And so he started to shout. "What do you know? You think you know so much. You don't know anything! The devilfish is evil. Everybody knows that. Everybody but you. You don't know anything."

Miranda recognized the gesture, too, and could see it in Jobim and the conflict he had unknowingly built up between his children. Frightened, she said, "It's possible, Paloma. It could be."

Without looking up from her soup, Paloma said, "No, Mama."

"Don't listen to her," said Jo. "She doesn't know!" He spat toward the fireplace, the way the men of the island did to show that they had won an argument.

"You may think you know, Paloma," Miranda said, still hoping to mediate, to placate both her children, to restore peace to the household. "I know there are times when I think I know something, when maybe I just . . ."

"Mama." Paloma wanted to stop Miranda's compassionate rambling. "Let's leave it."

For a moment, the room was silent.

Then Paloma raised her eyes and looked into the taut,

flushed face of her brother. The arteries on either side of his neck looked as thick as hawsers, and she imagined that she could see them throbbing. His jaws twitched, and his arm—as big around as one of Paloma's thighs—trembled.

She had wanted to avoid enraging Jo by arguing, and instead had enraged him by being silent—a silence that he interpreted as condescension.

Paloma tried to appear completely calm, confident. She hoped that her eyes did not betray her. She knew for sure that if ever he was driven to act out one of the inner tumults that tortured him, and if she happened to be the object of his fury, he could take her apart as easily as he dismantled one of the engines he so loved to tinker with.

Jo was fifteen, seventeen months younger than Paloma, yet he had the physique of a fully developed adult. From hauling lines and nets since he was a young boy, he had developed massive shoulders and arms. He could not wear a standard shirt, for the muscles in his chest and back burst the seams. From balancing in a tipping boat day after day, his calves and thighs were lined with sinews as tough as wire leader. He was short—five feet six—which suited working in boats, for a low center of gravity made quick, efficient movement easy.

A stranger would not have guessed that Paloma and Jo were siblings, or even distant cousins. She was as lithe as he was compact. She was five feet eight inches tall, and though she had not been weighed in several years, she thought that she weighed about 120 pounds. While Jo looked very much of his people—dark of skin and hair and eyes—she did not. Everything about her was light, from her bones to her skin to her hair, for she was not so much of her people as of her father.

And there, she knew, lay the core of the problem between them. Jo felt that it should be he, not she, who was more like their father. After all, was he not a male? Was his name not made from Jobim's? And yet every day, what she said, what she did, her entire manner reminded him of how close Paloma had been to Papa and how far—worse, how increasingly far—he himself had been.

Perhaps worst of all, they both knew that Jo had had a chance to be the one close to Papa. When Paloma was feeling kindly toward Jo, she acknowledged to herself that it would have taken a superhuman boy to be the son Papa wanted. What she was less eager to acknowledge was that she, a girl and a kind of son-by-default, had been taught more patiently, forgiven more kindly, praised more freely.

But once the core of enmity had been established between them, almost every other aspect of their relationship seemed to provide new antagonism. There was, for example, Jo's assumption that upon the death of his father he should become head of the family, an assumption shaken by his knowledge that, while physically capable of almost anything, emotionally he was barely able to take care of himself.

Without another word, Jo rose from the table, turned and left the room.

Miranda looked after him. When he had gone, she turned back and said, "Paloma . . ."

"I know, Mama, I know."

3

FIRST THERE WAS only one, rolling and bucking with the grace and precision of a carousel horse, exhaling a wheezy spray through the hole atop its head, its dorsal fin and glossy back shining in the low morning sun.

It crossed in front of her bow, then leaped clear of the water and dived and passed under the boat and rolled again in front.

Then came another, and another, until there were a dozen, and then a score, and then more than she could count.

They crisscrossed ahead of her boat, four and five and six in phalanx, threading together like fingers, then dispersing, to be replaced by other phalanges on other tacks.

She paddled on, and they came from the rear, leaping along both sides of her boat, as if urging her to gather speed so her boat would make a bow wave for them to ride. But she could make no more than a ripple in the water, so they soared away off to the sides and, in the clicks and chirrups and whistles she could hear clearly, seemed to discuss what game next to play.

They charged her boat in ranks of six and dived beneath it and surfaced on the other side, and in each rank one, only one, would leap *over* the boat, over her, and as its shadow passed it rained droplets on her head.

She laughed and tried with her voice to duplicate the dolphins' chirruping sounds, in faint hope that they would think her one of them and would stay with her. But on some secret signal they ceased their frolicking and faced in a common direction and bounded off across the sea.

Paloma stopped paddling, and watched, thrilled. She felt as if she had been anointed by the dolphins: they had chosen her as their playmate in an interlude in their travels.

It was an omen, like seeing the green flash and the jumping marlin. Perhaps today would be a special day.

As USUAL, PALOMA had awakened just before daybreak, when the sun was sending its first messengers of grey into the blackness of the eastern sky. She splashed water on her face and crept out of the house and trotted along a path to a tor on the cliffs that faced the east.

To most of the islanders, the tor was a pile of rocks, nothing more. From time to time when one of them needed a boulder of a particular size or shape, he would come and take one from the tor, so by now the pile that had once been symmetrical looked like rubble.

But Viejo had told Paloma that the tor was an ancient burial mound—not for their direct ancestors, but for those who had existed back beyond memory. Once, years ago, some scientists had come up from La Paz and sought permission to dig beneath the tor, but the islanders had refused to give consent, and the scientists had gone away.

"I was young, and eager to see what was under the stones," Viejo had said, "but the elders said no, and they were right. We believed that the dead beneath the tor looked after us, protected us from something—from what was a personal matter for each of us. So to let anyone dig it up could only hurt us. If there were bodies under there, and if we disturbed them, that could only be bad for all of us. If there were no bodies, our beliefs would then seem wrong, and our faith would be shaken. So we sent the scientists away, grumbling."

The scientists did, however, leave behind them one small bit of lore which Paloma appreciated. The reason they were confident that the tor was a burial mound, they said, was its location—on the highest point on the easternmost tip of the island. Many ancient peoples believed that they had to be buried facing eastward so they could see the rising sun and benefit from its light. The cruellest thing one could do to a person was to bury him facing westward, for the poor unfortunate was condemned forever to chase the setting sun in search of light.

Knowing this, and more than half believing it, Paloma liked to think that she shared the dawn with the souls of those beneath the tor—especially with her father, who, at his request, had been buried at sea but who also, at Paloma's insistence, had been buried at the moment of daybreak and facing the rising sun.

Slowly the grey sky was suffused with orange, and then the first shimmering line of fire slipped over the lip of the world.

Paloma sat and watched the sea and tried to envision all the things that were happening below the flat, calm surface. She wished she could watch day break from under water, for Jobim had told her that it was the time of most activity in the sea, of movement, change, and feeding.

This was true in all seas, he had said, but particularly true in the Sea of Cortez, because here everything seemed to happen at once and in the same places. As an indirect result of the same tremor that had ripped the shirt of Mexico and created the sea, deep-water fish fed in shallow water, animals that normally never saw light were swept up into bright sunlight, and the whole bustle of the sea was concentrated in a few areas. These areas were called seamounts.

Jobim's knowledge of geology had come from his elders, and from scraps of information gleaned from scientists who stopped occasionally at Santa Maria to study shark specimens. His explanations to Paloma were simple and direct.

Thousands—perhaps millions—of years after the earthquake that created the sea, other shocks and tremors occurred and caused volcanoes to heave up and erupt and, later, to collapse into the sea. Over the ages, some of them had melded back into the sea bottom, but others remained as seamounts—mountains that rose thousands of feet from the bottom of the sea to within fifty or sixty feet of the surface.

The seamounts were a major contributor to the abundance of life in the Sea of Cortez, for they created a kind of natural banquet that attracted animals of every species imaginable.

Deep-water currents that flowed along the bottom of the

sea would strike a seamount and create an "upwelling"—the water would rush upward, carrying with it all the microscopic animals (plankton and tiny shrimps and thousands of other creatures) on which larger animals feed. The larger animals would chase their food into shallower water, and they, in turn, would be pursued by the still larger animals that fed on them.

So around a seamount nature's whole food chain flourished. "You'll see everything, Paloma," Jobim had said before he had taken her diving on a seamount. "Little tiny things that eat great big things, and monsters that eat tiny things; critters that eat plants and critters that eat each other and critters with teeth and critters with filters instead of teeth. And the wonder is, they all get along—even though getting along includes eating one another now and then."

Now Paloma saw it every day—nature's display, its spectacular bazaar—and it was always different.

Jobim had eventually introduced her to a seamount all her own, one never visited by the fishermen because they didn't know it existed. There, only an hour's paddle from Santa Maria Island, she could spend her days watching and swimming with and, in her fancies, imagining herself to be part of, a rich undersea life.

Each morning after breakfast, she walked down to the dock. She pretended to be there to run errands for the fishermen as they prepared for the day's journey; in fact, she was there to see them off, to make sure they left before she did, so there would be no chance they could follow her and discover her private place: in a single morning's fishing they could damage the delicate balance established by nature over countless years.

Jo and the others would never discover Paloma's seamount on their own, for, like almost all the islanders, they adhered strictly to the ancient habits and traditions. They fished the shoals that had always been fished. They did not seek new grounds, and seldom changed their locations by more than a few hundred yards.

One reason they had always confined themselves to the old grounds was that they had never had a need to move: the fishing was always fine, the grounds still yielded well. True, some species—especially the territorial ones, such as groupers—were growing scarce. But if you had a big enough boat, you could balance the marketability of your catch, making up in volume what you lost in quality.

A more compelling reason for staying on the familiar grounds was that Jo and the others had no way of finding new places. He had no depth-finder that could locate a seamount, no electronic fish-finder that would allow him to chase the big schools of jacks. And it would never have occurred to any of them to let themselves be towed behind a boat in the open sea, wearing a face mask so they could spot a seamount from the surface.

They spent their time *on* the sea, never under it; none of the island fishermen stuck his face under water if he could avoid it. They claimed to know how to swim, but most disliked swimming and weren't good at it and went into the water only by accident.

Jo had tried, when Jobim was alive, but he had hated it. From the time when he was eighteen months old and Jobim had pitched him in the water off the dock and told him to swim, he had hated it. It was alien to him, and frightening. He believed there were creatures that wanted to eat him, and that if he was not continually vigilant, the sea itself would consume him. Jobim explained things to him, taught him, cajoled him, bellowed at him—hoping that his son would be different from all the other sons, hoping that through conditioning he could overcome this strange aversion to the place where man was born. But, finally, Jobim had despaired of him, and had turned to Paloma, who did not have to try. For swimming was as natural to her as breathing, and the more he taught her the more she begged to learn.

Of course, the others considered Paloma strange, because no matter where or as what man may have originated, he was a land animal now and there was no practical purpose in putting anything into the sea except a hook or a net.

Paloma did not understand how they could live on the edge of an undiscovered world and have no curiosity about exploring it. Beneath their feet were wonders too exotic for them even to dream of. Secretly, she was glad that they left it all to her.

This morning, Paloma had tried to be more helpful than usual, to send Jo a message of truce. She did not enjoy hurting him. Besides, his foul humors made their mother tense, and when Miranda was tense, the whole house was, too.

But Jo wanted no part of a truce today. He rejected all Paloma's offers of help. When his gear and his mates were aboard, he yanked sharply on the cord of the outboard motor. The cord came off in his hand. Paloma did not laugh, but stood by and tried to appear sympathetic as Jo, for once, restrained himself, rewound the cord, pulled it, and started the motor. Paloma cast off the bowline; Jo pointed the boat toward the rising sun and, squinting, set out for the fishing grounds.

In the old days, the fishermen had fished exclusively for sharks, for one or two sharks could bring the same revenue as hundreds of other fish. The sharks' fins were sold for soup, the meat for food, the liver for vitamins, the hide for leather and abrasives.

But synthetics had cut down the value of a shark by more than three quarters. Now the massive liver was useless because synthetic vitamins had replaced liver oil. The hides brought practically no money; man-made abrasives were cheaper and just as effective and other leathers were easier to cut and process. The fins could still be sold in the Orient, and tourists bought an occasional shark jaw, and a few people would eat shark steaks or shark hash if they couldn't afford something else. But, in general, shark fishing was no longer worthwhile.

So most sharks were taken by accident, when they bit a hook intended to attract something else or wound themselves up in a net, and the fishermen concentrated on the more readily marketable food fish.

Jo and Indio and Manolo would start the day fishing with hand lines. Periodically, they would look through a glass-bottom bucket to see if any big schools were in the neighborhood. If the school fish were there, they would set their net and wait and then gather it, spilling masses of fish into their boat.

If the big boat from La Paz was due that night or the next morning, the fish would be kept cool until they could be dumped into the boat's icehold. If the boat was not due for a few days, the fish would have to be gutted and put on ice on the island, or they would spoil before the boat arrived.

The islanders were at the mercy of the captain of the boat. He told them the price fish would bring in La Paz and the price he would pay them per pound, and they had no choice but to accept his price. But he was not an overly greedy man, and in some rare times when the market was glutted he was known to have paid the islanders too high a price, so they could continue to buy fuel and fruit and vegetables and clothing, and thus there were few serious complaints about him.

Since Paloma was not a fisherman, and not a man, and had no official status in the community, she was not permitted to take up dock space for her little boat. She kept it beneath the dock, where it was out of the way.

When she judged that Jo's boat had travelled a safe distance, she lay on the dock and reached beneath it and pulled out her pirogue. It was eight feet long and two feet wide and, basically, nothing more than a hollow log. It was Paloma's dearest possession.

Her father had made it for her thirteenth birthday. He had ordered the log from La Paz, for there were no trees on Santa Maria, and it had arrived on the boat that came to take away the fish. Then he had built a fire on the log and burned a cavity in it, then attacked it with a chisel and a wooden mallet. Finally, he used coarse dried sharkskin to smooth the wood and erase the splinters.

And all the while he had worked on it, he had never told Paloma who it was for. She had assumed it was for Jo, and she envied him the fun he would have, the places he would go, the things he would learn.

She underestimated her father. When he gave her the pirogue, he said only, "This will give you good times."

This morning, she had tossed a broad-brim hat into the pirogue; later, around midday, when the sun was highest and the temperature over a hundred degrees, to spend more than a few minutes on the water without a hat was to invite a pounding headache and nausea. She had checked her mesh bag to make sure she had all her equipment: her face mask and flippers, a snorkel tube for breathing, her knife—a razor-

sharp, double-edged blade of stainless steel with a rubber hilt
—and a mango for her lunch.

She carried the knife not to defend herself against an animal—before yesterday's encounter with the testy sailfish she
had never felt menaced by anything under the water, and she
reasoned that if a shark was going to bite her it would move
so fast that a knife wouldn't do any good.

The knife was more a tool than a weapon. Its primary use
was to pry oysters free from the rocks on the seamounts and
to open them in her pirogue. Its less common but more important use was precautionary. Over the years, fishermen had
lost a lot of monofilament fishing line. Made of nylon, the line
did not degrade in water; colourless, it was almost impossible
to see under water. The skeins of line gathered in and around
the rocks. Invisible, very strong, anchored to boulders, monofilament line was a trap that could kill a person in a few minutes. If a hand or a foot became entangled, she could not hold
her breath long enough to strip away every thread and wiggle
free. She would have to slash her way out.

Paloma untied the pirogue from the dock and stepped in.
Immediately she dropped to her knees, to keep the boat
steady. She dipped the double-bladed kayak paddle into the
still water, back-paddled away from the dock and turned
west.

Now, AS THE last of the dolphins leaped away out of sight
toward the horizon, Paloma looked around to reorient herself
in the open sea, then dug her paddle into the water and continued toward the seamount.

The highest point on the seamount was not in shallow water—nowhere did it come closer to the surface than forty-five
or fifty feet—so she could not see it from her boat. Nor could
she hope to find it by timing her journey from the dock, for
each day the winds and currents varied a bit from the day
before. If the tide was with her, the trip would take less time;
if against her, more time; if the tide was with her but the wind
was against her, the sea would be rough and hard to paddle
into. A difference of five or ten minutes could mean that she
would miss the seamount entirely, for its summit was less

than an acre around. So Jobim had taught her to locate the seamount by using landmarks.

A few miles to the west there was an island, and on the island grew giant cactus plants. From a distance it appeared that at the very highest point of the island was a particularly tall, thick cactus. But as Paloma paddled closer to the island, her perspective on the cactus would change, and soon she would see that it was not one but two cacti. When she could barely discern a sliver of sky between the two plants, she knew she was on target.

Still, the cactus plants told her only that she had come far enough westward. The wind or the current might have taken her too far north or south. The top of the seamount was a rough oblong that faced east and west, so that its north-south contour was narrower and easy to miss. She had to locate a second landmark that would tell her her north-south position.

As soon as she saw blue sky between the cactus plants, she shifted her gaze to a fishermen's shack at the end of a point of land on a neighboring island. If she was too far north, the shack appeared to be far inland; too far south, it seemed to be floating on the water, disconnected from the land. When the shack was precisely on the point, she knew she was directly over the seamount.

She tossed her anchor overboard and let the rope slip through her fingers. Her "anchor" was nothing but an old rusty piece of iron, called a killick, but it held the small boat as well as a proper anchor would have. And it was expendable. Anchors tended to get caught in the deep crevices in the rocks of the seamount—often in water far too deep for a swimmer to reach them—and then they had to be cut away. Paloma could not have afforded to replace a steel anchor, but there was always another piece of rusted metal to be scavenged.

When the killick had set and Paloma had tied the rope to a cleat on the bow of the pirogue, she dipped her face mask in the water, then spat in it and rubbed the spittle around with her fingertips to keep the glass from fogging (not even her father had been able to explain to her why spit kept glass from fogging, but it worked); then she rinsed it again in salt water. She fitted her knife down the back of her rope belt, slipped her feet into her flippers, adjusted the snorkel tube in the mast strap and, with as little splash as possible, slid over the side.

She kicked gently along the side of the boat until she reached the anchor line. There she paused, looking down through a blue haze streaked with butter-yellow shafts of sunlight, eager for the surprise that always came with the day's first glimpse of life on the seamount.

Sometimes she thought of herself as a sudden, welcome arrival at a big party, where the hundreds of regulars would silently accept her into their midst. Certainly she felt more kinship with the animals of the seamount than with most of the people on Santa Maria, for here all relationships were direct, uncomplicated, trusting.

Usually, though, such fancies embarrassed her, and she swept them from her mind, for Jobim had told her time and again not to think of animals as human beings, not to attribute to them impossible human characteristics, but to regard and respect them as entirely different creatures. Still, once in a while she indulged herself in childish fantasies.

Some days she would see a sailfish, some days a shark, some days a porpoise or a pilot whale. Some days, like today, she saw nothing but haze, for the water was not clear, made dim and murky by vast clouds of plankton and other microscopic animals driven up from the deep. She could see the top of the seamount, a rough plain of rocks and corals, and she could make out the shadowy movement of large animals. But it was all vague and misty.

If nothing would come to the surface, and if she couldn't see well enough from the surface, she had only one choice: she would go down to the bottom.

Most of the islanders, knowing little about swimming, knew even less about diving and virtually nothing about preparing for a long breath-hold descent into the sea. Paloma's training had come from Jobim, who had taken her down in stages of five feet, teaching her how to prepare for each depth, how each depth felt different in her lungs, how to avoid panic. And her training had come as well from four years of practice, and from instinct. She did not think of herself as a good diver, or a not-good diver. She knew only that she could hold her breath long enough to dive to the top of the seamount and spend enough time underwater to have fun—and return to the surface to dive again.

Lying on the water, facedown, with her snorkel poking up behind her head, she took half a dozen deep breaths, each one expanding her lungs further than the one before. After the last breath, she inhaled until she felt she was about to burst, clamped her mouth shut and dived for the bottom. She pulled herself hand over hand down the anchor line and pushed herself with powerful, smooth strokes of her flippers. As she plunged downward, she let little spurts of bubble escape from her mouth, until the feeling in her lungs was comfortable.

She reached the bottom in a few seconds and, to keep herself from floating upward, wrapped her knees around a rock. She felt good, relaxed, her lungs pleasantly full. Time had a way of expanding underwater. She might be able to stay down for only a minute and a half, perhaps two minutes, but because every one of her senses was alert, every sound and sight and feeling registered sharply on her brain. On the surface, two minutes could pass without her noticing anything; down here, everything was an experience, so two minutes could seem as full as an hour.

For the first seconds after her descent, the animals of the seamount retreated, wary of any disturbance in the water and quick to distance themselves from it. Now they began to return, as if accepting Paloma as part of life.

Something slammed her from behind, knocking her forward. She clutched at her rock perch and spun around, one arm up by her face. For a split second, she couldn't see through the cloud of bubbles. If a shark had bumped her, as sometimes they did to test for prey, it would strike again and she would be dead. Whatever it was had not been an accident; accidental collisions underwater were as rare as straight lines in nature.

Arms up, squinting through her bubbles, fighting to suppress panic, Paloma found herself face to face with her assailant. And she laughed into her snorkel.

It was a big grouper—three or four feet long, thirty or thirty-five pounds—and it hovered a foot from her face, its lower jaw pouting out from under the upper, its round eyes staring straight at her, waiting impatiently for her to do what it assumed she had come to do—feed it.

She had fed it often before. There was no mistaking this grouper: it was the only one of its size on this seamount, and it had prominent scars behind one of its gills, mementoes of long-ago narrow escapes from larger predators. Sometimes she brought it bread, which it ate contemptuously, as if doing her a favor; sometimes bits of meat or fish scraps from the dock, which it gobbled up. And sometimes she forgot to bring it anything.

She had resisted giving it a human name, but she could not resist thinking of it in human terms, so she thought of it as Bully, which was apt.

If she had food, she would hold up her fingertips with the food dangling in them, the grouper would charge and she would drop the food into its mouth. It had no desire to bite her fingers, but it was a clumsy eater, consuming anything in its path, and though its teeth were small its jaws were extremely powerful, and a minor slip could result in crushed or shredded fingertips.

Today she had nothing for the grouper, so she held up a closed fist. The animal seemed to understand the gesture, for it made a halfhearted grab for her fist, then turned, flapped its tail in her face and moved off a few yards, there to hover in case she should, after all, produce something edible.

A shadow above crossed one of the chutes of yellow light, and Paloma looked up. One behind another, a procession of hammerhead sharks passed overhead in parade. Their silver-grey bodies were as sleek as bullets, and the sunlight touched the ripples of moving muscle and made them sparkle.

Paloma loved the hammerheads, for they seemed somehow to focus her inchoate thoughts about God and nature. They were a weird and implausible-looking animal—sinuous sledgehammers, with an eye on each end of the hammer's head and a mouthful of teeth beneath—and since once in a great while they had attacked a human and otherwise accomplished absolutely nothing good for man or beast, they must definitely be bad: that, at least, was how Viejo had rated them as living creatures.

And yet, if ever there was an animal that seemed to Paloma

peculiarly blessed, it was the hammerhead. Sharks had for so long been so critical to the island's survival that over the generations facts about them—salted here and there with myths —had been assimilated by most islanders. It was common knowledge, for example, that hammerheads like these had survived, unchanged, for about 30 million years. Except when they were injured or ill, they had no enemies on earth, save man. They had ample food, complete freedom, and sufficient company and kin for whatever their needs might be.

It was Jobim, however, who had given Paloma perspective to add to the facts, who had shown her how perfectly the hammerheads were suited to their lives. They were simple and speedy and efficient, and, he reminded her, unlike man they made neither waste nor war.

So to Paloma, the hammerheads were perfect, and she saw nothing in them but beauty. She wished Viejo could see them from down here, from where they lived in nature. From where he saw them—writhing in agony in a boat or clubbed to death and stinking on a broiling beach—they could only appear grotesque.

Paloma pushed off the rock and swam down a few more feet, into a thin valley between two big boulders. There, in the sand, a triggerfish was darting back and forth, frantic, its tail quivering, its gill flaps fluttering. At first, Paloma thought the triggerfish was wounded, for its movements were erratic and it was encircled by three, then five, then nine or ten other fish, all of which seemed determined to attack it.

A Scotch parrot fish—with tartanlike scales and beaked mouth—charged the smaller triggerfish, which parried with a flurry of twisting bites. The parrot fish retreated.

Immediately an angelfish dashed forward, feinted at the triggerfish, then banked and tried to get at the sand beneath the triggerfish, but it, too, was driven off.

Now Paloma realized what was happening. The triggerfish's egg deposit had been discovered by the other fish in the little valley, and they were ganging up on the triggerfish, trying to divert it long enough for one or another of them to dash in and root out and eat the cache of eggs.

Paloma felt instinctively parental toward the eggs, and so she swam into the midst of the flurry and flashed her hands around; the invaders dispersed. But the triggerfish's natural assumption was that Paloma was another thief, albeit a larger one, and its response was to bite her earlobe.

Paloma moved away, smiling inside but sad because she knew that before long the triggerfish would lose out to the odds. Once an egg deposit was discovered, it was as good as gone. Still, she told herself, that was the way it was supposed to be, an example of nature in balance. If all the eggs of every triggerfish hatched, and all the hatchlings grew to maturity, the sea would be choked with triggerfish.

Now she began to feel the telltale ache in her lungs, the hollow sensation that she imagined as the lungs themselves searching for more bits of air to consume. Her temples began to pound, not painfully but noisily. She pushed off the bottom and kicked easily toward the surface, trailing a stream of bubbles behind.

Her rule was to rest for five or ten minutes between dives, for then she could dive again and again without pain or fatigue. If she did not rest, she found that each successive dive would have to be shorter and the ache in her lungs would be sharper.

So she hung on the anchor line and drew deep breaths of the warm, moist air and occasionally looked under water through her mask to see if anything new or special had arrived in the neighborhood of the seamount.

Perhaps today she would see a golden *cabrío*, the rare, solitary grouper of a yellow so rich and unblemished that when it hung motionless in the water it appeared to be cast of solid gold. Or perhaps there would be a pulsing cloud of barracudas, whose silver backs caught the sunlight and were transformed into a shower of needles.

Once she had even seen a whale shark, but that was an encounter no reasonable person could hope to have again.

Her first reaction had been shock, and then, for a fragment of a second, terror, and then, when she realized exactly what it was, a shiver and tingle and flood of warmth through her stomach.

The whale shark had risen from the bottom, gliding so slowly that it seemed almost to be floating, an animal so huge that in the cloudy water Paloma could not see its head and tail at the same time. But she could determine its color—a speckled, mustardy yellow—and that told her there was no danger. The whale shark ate plankton and tiny shrimps and other minute life.

Jobim had cautioned her that she might see a whale shark out here, had tried to prepare her for the shock she would feel at her first sight of the leviathan.

"There is one way he can hurt you," Jobim had said without a hint of jest.

"Tell me." Paloma imagined stinging spines or molarlike teeth that could crush her bones.

"If you see his mouth open, and you swim to it and you pry open his jaws and you squeeze yourself inside and force the jaws closed behind you."

"Papa!"

"Even then, I don't think he'd like you very much. He'd shake his head and spit you out."

Paloma had jumped on her father and wrapped her arms and legs around him and tried to bite his neck.

When she had positively identified the whale shark, she had swum down to meet this largest of all fish, and just then it had slowed its ambling pace enough so that she could touch the head and run her hand down the endless ridges of the back. It did not show any signs of acknowledging her presence, but continued its lazy cruise, propelled by gentle sweeps of its tail. And when finally Paloma's hand reached the tail, she had hiccoughed in awe, for the tail fin alone was as tall as she was. And as it moved back and forth, it pushed before it a wave of water so powerful that it cast her away in a helpless tumble.

The whale shark had then moved off into the grey-green gloom, relentlessly, seeming almost dutiful—as if programmed to follow a course, or a pattern of courses, set by nature countless millions of years ago.

But today, as Paloma lay on the surface of the sea, with her face in the water, breathing through a rubber tube—wanting to be part of the sea but confined to the world of air—she saw below a scene of routine and undisturbed daily life. It was a life of ceaseless movement, constant vigilance, perpetual caution, and perfect harmony.

A change of pressure told her something was happening, or was about to happen—a slight alteration in the way the water felt around her body. It felt tighter, seemed to press on her, as if something of great mass and size was moving toward her at high speed.

Reflexively, she backpedalled in the water, trying to get away from this thing, whatever it was, that she could feel but couldn't see, that felt as if it was coming closer and closer, for the pressure on her body was beginning to lift her out of the water.

Then she saw it, a black thing.

It was larger than she was, larger even than her boat. It was soaring up at her. It was winged, and the wings swept up and down with such power that everything before and beside them was tossed aside, scattered. She could see a mouth that was a black cavern, and it was flanked by two horns, and the horns were aimed at Paloma, as if to grip her and stuff her into the gaping hole.

It was a manta ray. And even though she knew, rationally, that she had nothing to fear, she felt a rush of panic. Why was it coming straight at her? Why didn't it turn?

Her body was rising higher in the water, driven by the pressure wave forced before the manta. Her breath caught in her throat. Sparks shot through her brain, impelling an action, contradicting the impulse, impelling another action, contradicting that. She was paralyzed.

When it was no more than a few feet from Paloma, the manta tilted its wing and arched its back, changing its angle to display a belly of sheer and shiny white. Five trembling gills were on either side, crescent wings like slices of the winter moon.

The ray rushed up through the water and broke the surface, a perfect triangle of solid flesh that should not be able to fly but was flying, as it broke free of the sea and reached for the sky.

In Paloma's head, sight and feeling gave way to sound, for there was a thick and deafening roar, an enveloping, infernal boom, like the sound the wind makes at the height of a hurricane.

Paloma's head rose with the manta, and her eyes followed

it as it flew high in the air, shedding diamonds of water. At the top of its arc it hung for a fraction of a second, a titan of shimmering black against the sun that rimmed it with a halo of gold.

Then it fell backward, showing its belly; it smashed flat against the pewter sea. The water erupted, and the sound seemed to carry the same reckless violence as a thunderclap that cracks the clouds close by.

Now Paloma could let out her breath, a whoosh of excitement. She had seen mantas jump before—young ones especially, at twilight usually—but always from a distance. They seemed to be flipping in happy somersaults.

But mantas couldn't be "happy". This was what the islanders called an "old" animal, and by "old" they meant low and primitive and stupid. Its cousins were the sharks and the skates and the other rays. The wisdom was that "old" animals could not know pleasure or pain, happiness or distress. Their brains were efficient but small, their capacities limited.

And Paloma agreed with most of this wisdom, for Jobim had taught her that it was wrong ever to think of animals in human terms. It deprived animals of what was most precious about them—their individuality, their place in nature. Jobim had special contempt for people who tried to tame wild animals, to make them pets, to train them to do what he called "people tricks."

It was, he had supposed, a way for people to be less afraid of an animal, for an animal that could be taught to, say, walk on its hind legs or beg for food seemed less wild, less threatening, more human. But it also made the animal seem less whole.

But what, then, was this manta doing? Why had it jumped right beside her, when the sea was empty for miles around? The island wisdom said that mantas jumped out of water only to rid themselves of parasites—small animals that attached themselves to a larger animal and fed on it. Some of these parasites were burrowers, little crabs or snails or worms, that dug holes in the manta and fed on its flesh. Then there were fish called remoras, which had sucker discs on top of their heads by which they fastened themselves to the host animal. They were not parasites but, rather, hitchhikers, for they did no harm to the manta and fed only on scraps of food the manta missed.

According to Jobim, by leaping into the air the manta deprived the parasites of oxygen (for, like fish, the parasites got their oxygen from water, not air), and the sudden shock caused the parasite to let go. If the shock alone did not dislodge the parasites, then being slammed down on the water would surely knock them loose.

Paloma saw the logic in what Jobim had said. But on this manta she had seen no parasites, and in its jumps there was a sense of vigor, of energy, of excitement.

The island wisdom about manta rays had always encouraged Paloma to fear them. Careless sailors and fishermen were said to have been consumed by mantas. Disobedient children were threatened with being cast adrift amid a school of mantas.

And then, Paloma remembered, one day a few months ago she had been diving on the seamount and had seen a manta from the surface. It had been flying through the water with the grace of a hawk, rising and falling on its wind of water. Paloma recalled now how surprised she had been that none of the other creatures on the seamount had acted afraid of the manta. They had not scurried out of its way, had not dashed for cover in the rocks. They had seemed to know that the manta would avoid them—gently lifting a wing to pass over a pair of groupers or dipping it to pass beneath a school of jacks.

On the edge of the seamount that day, beyond a small school of fish, the water had been grey and turbid, signalling the presence of a cloud of plankton swept up into shallow water. The manta had headed for the plankton, and as it approached the cloud, it had surprised Paloma again: its dreadful horns unfurled and showed themselves for what they actually were—floppy fins. The manta had spread the fins and used them like arms, sweeping the plankton-rich water into its mouth.

The manta had made three passes through the cloud of plankton and then, evidently satisfied, had flown up and away.

Now, holding onto her pirogue, feeling her pulse slow and

her breathing become more regular, Paloma waited, her head out of water, to see if today's manta would jump once more. She wanted to see it as it broke the surface, to hear the roar and experience the explosion again.

When, after a few moments, the manta did not reappear, she put her face in the water and turned in a circle. But the manta must have gone off into the deep, for life on the sea- mount had resumed its routine. Paloma decided to dive back down to the bottom.

She took deep breaths and sped down the anchor line. Finding the same rock on the bottom, she locked her legs around it. She half expected things to be different here on the bottom, as if the drama on the surface should have provoked changes below. But all was the same: the same fish patrolled the same rocks, the same eels poked their heads out of the same holes, the same jacks sped by in search of food.

There had been one change which, inevitable though it was, made her feel wistful nonetheless. Nearby, in the little valley, the triggerfish was still darting back and forth, but now the fish was alone. Nothing was taunting it, nothing attacking. And its motion was different from what it had been, less ag- gressive yet more desperate. Such, at least, was Paloma's in- terpretation, for she knew that the triggerfish's eggs had fi- nally been taken and that the fish was searching for them in hopeless frenzy.

Another fish swam slowly before Paloma's mask. It was a fat thing with tiny fins that seemed far too small for its body. She waited until the fish was only a few inches away, then lashed out with both hands and grabbed it around the body. She held it very lightly, anticipating what would happen.

The fish struggled for a second and then, like a balloon, began to inflate. The scales on its back stood on end and be- came stiff white thorns. Its lips pursed and its eyes receded into the swelling body and its fins, which now looked absurdly small, flapped in fury.

Paloma juggled this spiny football on her fingers for a mo- ment, then held its bulbous face to hers. The pufferfish could not struggle long. It had done all it could—become a thor- oughly unappetizing meal—so now it simply stared back at Paloma. Gently, she released it in open water, and it fluttered quickly away. As it neared the shelter of the rocks, gradually it deflated. The thorns on its back lay down and once again became scales. By the time it reached a familiar crevice, it was slim enough to squirt through to safety.

Paloma began to hear anew the distant throbbing in her temples. It was still faint, not urgent; she had plenty of time to get to the surface. But by nature and Jobim's training, she was cautious—better to have more than enough air left when she reached the surface than not enough when she was still far below. And so she kicked off the bottom and rose, facing the hill of rocks and coral.

Ten feet above the bottom, she saw an oyster growing on the underside of a boulder. She reached behind her and slid her knife from her belt and, with a single twist of her wrist, cut the oyster away.

The throbbing in her head was louder now, urging her to hurry up to where she belonged. Often she wished she had gills like a fish and could breathe water. But at times like this, she wanted only one thing: air. She kicked hard, and her strong legs drove her upward with a speed that plastered her hair over the faceplate of her mask.

She popped through the surface, spat, and gulped a breath of air, then clung to the side of the pirogue and drew more breaths until her body was fully nourished with oxygen. Then she dropped the oyster into the pirogue, pulled herself aboard, and lay on the bottom, facing the sun and its warmth.

When she was warm and dry, she used her knife to split the mango and dig out the sweet, juicy fruit. She tossed the mango rind overboard and watched, fascinated, as it was savaged by a school of tiny, yellow-and-black striped fish.

These sergeant-major fish were everywhere, on reefs and rocks, in deep water and shallow. They appeared suddenly, from nowhere, at the slightest trace of food of any kind. They ate fruit, bones, nuts, bread, meat, vegetables, faeces, paper and—now and then—they nibbled on Paloma's toes.

They were daring and fearless and voracious and fast, and the nicest thing Paloma could say about them was that they were so small. A mutant sergeant-major, a specimen of, say, a hundred pounds, would be a genuine horror.

She let her imagination roam further, envisioning a sergeant-major the size of a whale shark, and found herself once again admiring the precision of the balance nature had maintained, over thousands of years, among all its living things.

She picked up the scraggly oyster and held it in one hand. With the other hand, she guided the point of her knife to the rough slit between the two halves of the shell. Oysters weren't like clams, which you could open cleanly and easily, with a cut and a twist and a scoop. Oysters were ragged and sharp and coated with slimy growths, and if you weren't very careful you'd stab yourself in the palm of your hand. And the cut would bleed, so you couldn't dive any more that day, and it would probably get infected so you couldn't go into the water for several days, and it might get so badly infected that you would fall sick and have to go to bed or even on the boat to La Paz to see the doctor.

The point was, best to be careful opening oysters.

Patiently, she pried around the edges of the shell until she found a place where the knife could probe inside. She felt the knife point touch the muscle that held the shell together; slowly she sawed there.

Most people on the island would not eat oysters. They were thought to be unsafe. Some people who had eaten them became violently sick to their stomachs, and over the years a few had died.

The truth was that the only bad oyster was an oyster left too long in the sun. They died soon and spoiled instantly, and a spoiled oyster was a ticket to the hospital in La Paz.

But an oyster fresh from the sea was a delicacy, something cool and rich and salty and pure. Paloma cut through the last bit of muscle and prized open the shell and saw then that this oyster was the greatest delicacy of all.

Inside, nestled in the shimmering grey meat, was the prize. It was misshapen and wrinkled, its color was mottled, and it was only half the size of Paloma's little fingernail. But it was a pearl.

4

PALOMA PLUCKED THE pearl from its shell and let it roll around in the palm of her hand.

Now she had twenty-seven.

It had taken her more than a year to find the others, but her progress had been steady: roughly, an average of two a month. It had been more than six weeks, however, since she had found the last one, and she had begun to wonder. Was it possible that on the whole seamount there were only twenty-six pearl-bearing oysters? She needed at least forty pearls, preferably fifty.

Finding number twenty-seven renewed her hope. She closed her fist around the little pearl and looked at the sky and said, "Thank you."

Her thanks were directed, in a vague but concentrated way, at her father. He was dead, she knew that, but she could not accept the promise that dead meant finished forever. She was lonely for, and needed, her father, and so in her mind she fashioned a presence for him. She did not think of him as alive, exactly, but simply as existing somewhere, still available for her to talk to and ask for help and share private things with. For in all her life he had been the only person she had felt comfortable sharing things with.

The fact that her father was out there somewhere (and it was a fact for her; she felt it strongly) was an enormous help to her. She didn't hear his voice, but he comforted her nevertheless. A sympathetic presence who listened with patience to her problems, he never agreed or disagreed, never criticized or praised. And somehow, being able to explore events and alternatives this way seemed to guide Paloma, help her toward a direction and a solution.

Of course, sometimes she felt foolish, and was glad no one saw her as she seemed to be talking to the sky or the wind or an empty room. But there *was* something there. Whether it was she who willed it there, projected it there, didn't matter; it was there, whatever "it" was. She avoided precise definition, preferring to leave it as a concept amorphous enough so as not to be confining, a spirit, accessible, clear. And while surely she needed her father, she also felt that he needed her, and that they were working as a team.

Shortly before he died, Jobim had recruited Paloma into a conspiracy.

Only a few months from now, Jobim and Miranda would have marked twenty years of marriage. He had wanted to give his wife something special. Since he had no money beyond that which fed and clothed them, he could not buy her something fine. So he had decided he would have to make the gift himself. And whatever he determined to make would have to be made in secret—he could not hope to deceive Miranda as he had deceived Paloma about the pirogue. And if it must be a secret, it must be small enough to conceal.

Yet it could not be a wood carving or a clay figure or a decoration fashioned of seashells. Anyone could carve wood or collect seashells. It had to be something that only he could do, so that for Miranda it would be a gift direct from his heart to hers.

Once he had found the answer, it seemed obvious: pearls, a necklace of natural pearls. Of all the islanders, only he (and, through his teaching, Paloma) pursued the ancient skills of diving for and identifying and collecting and opening pearl oysters. He had maintained the skills only for his own amusement, for pearling was no longer profitable. The pearl bed had been depleted more than a generation ago, but even if they were to come back, the market for natural pearls had all but disappeared. People now preferred cultured pearls; they were rounder, had more luster.

Jobim did not like cultured pearls. "They are prettier, and they do come from the sea, and they make a nice necklace,"

he told Paloma. "But they are not natural. They are man trying to improve on nature. Nature is one miracle after another.
Man can't improve it; he can only change it."

Jobim had found only five pearls before he died, but he had
helped Paloma refine her pearling skills. And so she had taken
upon herself the task of completing the necklace. She and
Jobim had begun something; he had gone away before being
able to complete it; she would complete it for him.

She thought often of how she would give the necklace to
her mother. She didn't want to seem overly sentimental, but,
on the other hand, she wanted to be sure that Miranda knew
the necklace was a gift from Jobim, no matter who had gathered most of the pearls.

One of Jobim's earliest lessons to his children was that
truth was almost always preferable to lies. It was not only a
moral conclusion; truth was usually easier. For one thing, it
was easier to remember. But here the truth was impossible, so
Paloma had decided to weave the simplest lie she could. She
would tell her mother that Jobim had collected the pearls and
had hidden them with the intention of stringing them just
before the anniversary date.

"Thank heavens," Paloma would say. "One day he swore
me to secrecy and told me where they were, in case something
should happen to him."

There would be happiness and sorrow and nostalgia and
tears. The important thing for Paloma was that all the emotion would be directed not at her but at her father—at his
memory or his spirit or whatever image Miranda still held of
him.

Paloma tucked the pearl into a narrow crack in the wood
on one side of the pirogue, so it couldn't roll around or spill
out if the pirogue should tip. Then she lay back to rest for a
few minutes, for she had found that to dive too soon after
eating was to invite a painful knot in her side or, sometimes,
to bring up bile in her throat, which could be very dangerous
and was inevitably very frightening. If bile was rising, vomit
would soon follow behind, and there was nothing worse than
to vomit under water. The gag reflex would force a spasmodic
intake of breath, which would bring saltwater into her lungs,

which would force a violent cough and another breath and would drown her.

She fell asleep. When she awoke no more than half an hour later, she recalled vividly that she had dreamed of a gull flying round and round her pirogue and laughing at her.

It was a recollection more curious than uncomfortable, for she associated nothing whatever with any of her dreams—except those about her father, which were sometimes disturbing when she couldn't separate dream conversations from genuine ones.

Paloma slipped overboard and cleaned her mask. She grabbed the anchor line and took deep breaths and pulled for the bottom. Ten feet from the surface she stopped.

Something was wrong. The seamount had changed. She was disoriented. Was it her eyes? Had more time passed than she realized? Nothing looked the same. An entire section of the seamount seemed covered in black.

She closed her eyes and willed herself to stay calm, to sort through the conflicting images. When she felt more composed, she opened her eyes and looked down again. And then she could see what had perplexed her. Not five feet away was the largest manta ray she had ever seen.

It was like a black cloak, or a big blanket that, from this short distance, blocked out most of her view of the seamount.

It was not only the proximity of the giant that had deceived her; it was also the fact that the animal was not moving at all. It was lying absolutely still in the water, as if suspended from an invisible ceiling. It did not look alive.

But it had to be alive, for how else would it have gotten there? Dead, it would have sunk to the bottom.

She dropped farther down, expecting the animal at any moment to shrug its wing and move away. But the manta continued to hover, motionless.

Her toes were within inches of the manta's back, and now she could see nothing of the seamount below. It was like landing on a black field that extended almost as far as she could see. The ray had to be more than twenty feet across, for she judged that she could have lain down four times across its wings and still not covered them tip to tip.

This is the grandfather of all mantas, she thought. Why is it drifting around? Is it dying?

Paloma had to go up for air. Making as little stir as possible in the water, she floated up. As the distance between her and the manta grew, she gained perspective on the whole animal, and she could see that there was a reason it was not behaving normally. Long, thin things were trailing beneath and behind it.

Her face broke water. She breathed in and out several times, each breath a bit deeper than the last, drew one final breath that seemed to suck air down into her feet, and went down again.

The manta had not moved. This time she approached it from the front, and immediately she saw what was wrong.

Behind the "horn" on the left side, the animal's flesh was torn in a broad, deep gash. Knotted ropes were embedded in the shredded flesh, their ends dangling loose, like tails.

The manta must have become fouled in a fisherman's net, then panicked, and, flailing frantically to get free, driven its great bulk against the taut ropes, forcing them to bite even deeper into its flesh. Finally, it had escaped—undoubtedly, Paloma thought, leaving an angry fisherman to curse his wretched fate and declare that all mantas were devilfish that deserved to die.

But the manta's victory was illusory, for it was bound to die. Paloma had seen many wounded animals—cut or hooked or scraped or bitten—and she knew that in the sea there was no time of truce, there was no mercy.

The wound had weakened the manta, and because the ropes still festered in the open sore there had been no chance for healing to begin. Unable to pursue its food, the manta could not eat as much as it should. The less it ate, the weaker it would become; the weaker it became, the less it could eat.

Before long, the manta would begin to emit the silent signals of distress that would be received and interpreted by every animal on the seamount—especially by the larger animals, the predators.

First would come the tiny, voracious fish, like the sergeant-majors. The signals they interpreted would tell them that it was safe to ravage the bits of dying flesh in the open wound. They would swim in the wound, opening it further.

The manta would grow weaker still. Little by little, it would appear to be, and would become, less and less formidable. Its sensory transmitters, incapable of human guile, would continue to broadcast signals of increasing vulnerability. Inevitably, the manta would be committing inadvertent suicide.

Sharks would begin to gather, circling at a distance, their receivers assessing each new signal, until one of them—particularly hungry, perhaps, or agitated or perhaps simply bold—would break the circle, dart in at the manta and tear away a ragged bite of meat.

The end would come quickly then, in an explosion of blood and a cloud of shreds of skin and sinew.

Paloma could hear the pulse in her temples as she swam down toward the manta. The animal knew she was there—the eye beneath the gaping wound followed her as she drew near—but it did not move.

Her momentum was carrying her past the manta, over its head. She put out a hand to stop herself, and her fingers curled around a hard ledge above the mouth and between the two horns. The flesh there felt firm—like a taut muscle—but slick, for it was coated with a natural mucous slime. The feeling didn't startle Paloma, for she had touched many fish and had felt the same slime. It was a shield against bacteria and other things in the rich saltwater that would cause illness or injury.

Jobim had taught her that if a fish you didn't need was caught in your net, and if you picked it up, intending to release it, you had to be careful that your fingers didn't scrape away the protective coating from the fish's skin. If the slime was removed, a sore might develop on that spot, or a burrowing creature might discover that opening and settle in and begin to gnaw away. A fish that had been handled too much before being released usually didn't survive for long.

Apparently, the manta was no more startled by her touch than was Paloma. It did not bolt from her; it did not twitch or shudder or shake. It didn't move. It just lay there, floating, suspended in midwater.

It has no fear of me, Paloma thought. And why should it?

It knows no enemies. But I am a strange animal and I am touching this manta, and it is not a common occurrence in nature for one wild animal to allow another to touch like this. Still, mantas do put up with remoras stuck onto their bodies and dragging behind. Maybe, as far as this manta knows, I'm just a big remora.

A swift flow of water was holding Paloma horizontal, her flippers fluttering like a flag in a high wind. Somehow, the manta was managing to stay perfectly still in the strong current, without seeming to exert any effort at all. If Paloma were to let go, she would be swept away.

Now she reached with her other hand for the same ledge of muscle, and she tucked her knees up underneath her and knelt on the manta's back. The skin was like a shark's, not really skin but a carpet made up of millions of tiny toothlike things. They all faced to the rear, and so as Paloma's hand stroked the skin from front to back, it felt as smooth as a greased ceramic bowl. But as her knees inched up, back to front, the manta's skin, like coarse sandpaper, abraded them.

The terrible gash in the manta's flesh was beside Paloma's left hand. Some of the knotted ropes were buried several inches deep. Most of the flesh was whitish-grey, but some was pink and some yellow.

Once, the year before Jobim had died, a strange organism had drifted over the seamount and attacked the schooling jacks, causing suppurating sores on their sides. Jobim had caught one of the jacks and shown it to Paloma, pointing out the different flesh tones of the ailing fish: white-grey was healthy, pink was inflamed, and yellow signalled the generation of a pus-like substance that showed that the animal's body had activated its defense mechanisms.

A few of the ropes snaked out of the manta's wound and trailed behind, tugged by the rushing water. Does it feel pain? Paloma wondered. It must. That's probably why it stays so still: movement would tug the ropes harder and make them shift and wiggle, and that would hurt more.

Gripping the ledge tightly with her right hand, she let go with her left and reached for the rope snarled nearest to the surface of the wound. It was a jumble of knots and kinks, and it vibrated as the water flowed through it.

Be quick, Paloma told herself, like when the doctor gives an injection. Grab it, pull it free and cast it away, all before the manta knows what's happening.

She threaded her fingers deep into the mess of rope and made a fist around as much as her hand could grasp. Then she yanked.

It was as if she had thrown a switch that turned the manta on. The animal heaved both wings at once, churning up a maelstrom that threw Paloma off its back and tumbled her into a spinning somersault.

By the time she had righted herself and cleared her mask and waited for the storm of bubbles to dissipate, the manta was flying away into the dark water, ropes fluttering behind. It did not make a sound, but Paloma imagined that she heard an outraged wail of pain.

She kicked toward the surface, trailing some of the ropes in her hand, wishing she had had time to grab more, hoping that by removing some of them she might have increased the manta's chances of survival.

5

THE SUN WAS still high when Paloma left the seamount and started to paddle toward home. She was tired and hungry and cold. But most of all, she was lonely.

It was a curious contradiction that the better her day on the seamount was, the lonelier she felt when it was over, and because today had been particularly exciting, she felt acutely lonely.

The problem was not that her experiences were solitary—she liked being alone—but that there was no one on the island with whom she could share the wonder, the exhilaration, of her day when she got home. There was no friend who would understand, no sister or cousin who would care. In fact, there was no one on the island to whom she had confided the existence of her seamount or what she did all day in her boat.

There were no other girls Paloma's age on the island. Why, no one knew: a quirk of nature. There were plenty of females many years older—women now, with children of their own—and plenty of boys. But no girls. From the moment Paloma had been old enough to know what it was to be alone, she had been alone. Of course, she had her mother, but there were limits to what she felt comfortable talking to her mother about, and there were limits to what Miranda wanted to hear.

Paloma paddled harder, trying to stroke away the loneliness, to ease it with sheer muscle power. And she was trying, as well, to warm up, for gooseflesh had risen on her arms and legs, and the fine yellow hairs were standing on end.

The water never felt cold to her—and it *was* warm, at least

85 degrees—but no matter how warm it felt, it was always cooler than Paloma's body temperature, so spending hours in it sucked the heat from her body and caused its temperature to drop. It was not a dangerous cold—"You can live for a week in this water," Jobim had told her, adding with a grin, "if the sun doesn't cook you or something doesn't eat you." But it was uncomfortable.

She could have combated the cold, however, and eased her hunger, too, by gaining weight. A layer of fat made a fine insulator. But she was reluctant to gain weight, to grow fat, any sooner than necessary. Being fat would slow her down, taking away her agility and worst of all, signal that she was just like all the other women of Santa Maria Island.

For them, fatness seemed to be a natural progression in life. As girls they were slender; in their late teens or early twenties they became robust; in their mid-to-late twenties they were stocky, in their thirties fat and in their forties mountainous. (Paloma's mother was about to turn forty, and over the past few years her figure had gradually disappeared, its contours absorbed into her trunk.) Those who survived into their sixties or seventies often shrank back to whippet thinness.

Paloma saw herself as different. She hoped, prayed, knew that she was special. At least she had been special to her father.

It had been Jobim who made her feel special, who had in effect decreed that she be special. After the second of Jo's accidents underwater, the one that finally convinced Jobim that his son would never be at home in the sea and would instead have to spend his life upon it, after Jobim had begun to tutor Paloma and had discovered how naturally and quickly she took to the sea and had determined that she would become a person *of* the sea, he had told Miranda that their daughter was not to be compelled to follow the normal path to womanhood, was not to be confined to the house and the pots and the washboard. He would take her with him and would teach her things about the sea and would teach her how to learn other things on her own. She would of course contribute to the household eventually, but how and what she would contribute must be left up to her.

Miranda had tried to argue, but Jobim was a man who, when he had made up his mind about something important, tended to reinforce his decision to himself until he became impossible to argue with. And Miranda knew that it was important—even vital—to Jobim that one of his children follow him into the sea.

What Jobim did not know, and what Miranda could not bring herself to tell him, was that by taking Paloma to sea he was taking her forever away from her mother, depriving Miranda of the solace that a daughter was supposed to supply to a woman. He was condemning Miranda to a daily loneliness that would sadden her for the rest of her life, for by the time of Jobim's death, Paloma's independence had been so firmly established that Miranda could not have changed it even if she had tried. Not only did Paloma relish her way of life, but now she felt an obligation to her father to live as he had guided her to. She saw her life as having no limits. Perhaps the limits were there, and if so, someday she would confront them. But not yet.

Paloma recognized, however, that she had responsibilities to her mother, one of which contributed to her decision to return home in the middle of the afternoon. It was important that the people in her mother's world not think that Paloma considered herself too good for everyday chores.

"It is one thing to be quiet and alone and even a bit strange," Viejo had said to her one day. "People will call that growing pains and let it pass. But you must not remove yourself altogether. People will not understand. They will resent you and dislike you, become your enemies, and you do not want any more enemies than necessary."

Paloma did not want any enemies at all. And so, every few days she returned home in time to be with her mother and help her hang out the wash or prepare the meal or clean the house. Almost as important as doing these daughter things was to be seen doing them, for then the other women would cluck and mutter that Paloma was a good girl, after all, that she was sensitive to her mother's great loss, that she might turn out to be a source of comfort in her mother's old age. And so on.

It was a gesture; Paloma knew it and Miranda knew it.

Miranda didn't need help; she felt she didn't have enough to do as it was. But neither did she need the patronizing sympathy of others. Miranda was grateful for the gesture, and for Paloma's presence.

When Paloma reached the dock, Miranda and the other women were washing clothes. Beside the dock was a shelf of flat rocks that led into the water. The women gathered there and soaked their clothes and pounded soap into them with stones and rinsed them. They piled the clean clothes into baskets that would be taken up the hill for a final freshwater rinsing.

Paloma knelt beside Miranda and pounded clothes. No one acknowledged her arrival: the women chattered on around her. They were not ignoring her: to the contrary, they were accepting her—quietly, naturally, as if she had been there all along. It was their gesture to Miranda, for to have greeted Paloma and asked her questions would have directed attention to what was politely regarded as Paloma's peculiarity. No other girl went out on the sea all day long and did God-knows-what.

Sometimes Paloma felt like a person with a chronic affliction, like a spastic tic. People's attitude seemed to be: poor thing, she can't help it, let's just ignore it. It increased her sense of being alone. But in another way she was glad for the treatment, for it reinforced her feeling of being special.

Paloma never volunteered information about what she had seen and done during the day. Most of the women would not have believed her, and that would have embarrassed Miranda. Those that did believe her would not want to hear what she had to say, for it went against all they had been taught about the sea.

From birth, most of the children of the islands were told that the sea was hostile. The people lived from the sea, could not possibly have existed without it, and yet it was viewed not as an ally but as an adversary. The attitude made no sense to Paloma, for she had been taught exactly the opposite, and once she had asked Viejo where the hostility had come from. "It has always been," he said with a shrug. "The sea does not give; man takes from it. Perhaps it began as a way to make man feel stronger, that he has dominion over the sea as well as over the animals."

"I think it's silly," Paloma had said.

"It may be," Viejo had nodded. "But it is the way things are."

To the women who washed and cooked and cleaned and never went on the water, the sea was alien and dangerous, populated by creatures that were ferocious, slimy, poisonous, starved for human flesh. They were comfortable with that view of the sea, and they would not have welcomed contradictions from a young girl.

As excited as Paloma was when she returned to the dock, as tempted to tell everyone what wonders she had encountered today, she restrained herself. She would wait to tell her mother when they were alone.

When the washing was done, Paloma picked up the heavy basket of wet clothes and followed Miranda up the hill. With a hand pump they washed the salt off the clothes, then draped them over a line behind the house.

They worked in silence, but it was busy silence, for Paloma wanted very much to tell her mother about the manta ray and Miranda knew Paloma had something she wanted to say, and that she was trying to find a way to tell her.

Paloma did not want to frighten Miranda, so she could not say how big the manta was, nor how close to it she had gotten —let alone that she had knelt on its back and been tossed off violently. And she had to reassure Miranda that no one else knew what she had been doing, that no one else would know, that it would not become a subject of public gossip. What Paloma did all day every day caused enough chatter; fooling around with a giant devilfish might get her branded as a witch. Miranda had had a husband whose reputation was as a rebel and a troublemaker. She had a son who spent all his time concocting harebrained schemes to make money— enough money to get him off the island and into a technical school in Mexico City, where the Lord alone knew what would happen to him. To add to those two a daughter who was a witch would be altogether too much for her to bear.

By now, the sun had dropped low and had begun to turn red. A light breeze was blowing through the hanging clothes, and the tails of the shirts made soft snapping sounds. Miranda sniffed and nodded and was satisfied; it was a good breeze.

There were three regular breezes that blew over Santa Maria Island. One was bad for drying clothes, one was fair, and one was good. The east wind was bad, because it blew across the dry, dusty eastern part of the island and carried dirt and dust with it. Clothes that had dried in an east wind felt gritty and itchy. Breezes from the west and south were fair. They came over the water. On dry days they carried a faint smell of the sea, but on humid days they were heavy with mist and salt. Clothes took forever to dry, and felt clammy.

This was a breeze from the north. It was dry and fresh and sweet because it had travelled over the highest part of the island, where cacti and wild desert flowers grew. It was a small thing, but Miranda's life was made of small things, good and bad, and because the breeze was good she was pleased.

They walked inside the house and began to prepare the fire for the evening meal.

"I saw a giant manta ray today," Paloma said at last.

"That's nice," said Miranda, without looking up from the fireplace where she was smoothing out the dead ashes before laying new wood.

"It was wounded. I think it got fouled in a fisherman's nets."

Miranda started to say "that's nice" again, but it seemed inappropriate, so all she said was, "Oh?"

"It didn't move well. There were ropes hanging out of the wound. It must have been in very bad pain."

This time Miranda had nothing to say, so she nodded.

"I wanted to help it, but . . ."

"God will take care of it, He will decide." Miranda spoke fast, as if spitting the words out in a rush would add emphasis, would convince Paloma not to meddle. It was like a person in an argument he knows he is losing who decides, as a last recourse, to shout.

"Well then," Paloma said, "He seems to want to let the manta die in agony, or get eaten by sharks."

"If that is His will, so be it."

"So be it," Paloma repeated. She did not intend to argue

with her mother. It was an argument that could have no winners, only losers.

"What fairy tales are you telling now?" It was Jo's voice and it came from behind Paloma.

She spun around. Jo was slouching against the doorway, a smirk on his face.

"Nothing." Paloma could not know how much Jo had overheard, but she did not want to discuss the manta ray with him. A big, wounded animal was something Jo could visualize in only one way: price per pound.

"Giant devilfish, wounded and bleeding, cared for by nurse Paloma," Jo snickered as he came into the room. "Why do you listen to this foolishness, Mama?"

"Now, Jo . . ." Miranda said, and busied herself with the fireplace.

"Sometimes I wonder if you ever leave the dock," Jo said to Paloma. "I think maybe you sit here all day and make up tales."

"Think what you like," Paloma said.

After a moment's pause, Jo asked, "Did you really see a big manta ray?"

"Yes."

"And it didn't attack you?"

"No!"

"It must have been really hurt. Devilfish are mean."

Paloma didn't argue. If Jo wanted to believe that, she would not disrupt his fantasy.

"How big was he?"

"Big," Paloma replied. "Bigger than this room."

Jo whistled. "*He'd* bring a fancy price."

"See, Mama?" Paloma said. "He hears about an injured animal, and right away he wants to kill it."

"Well, Paloma," her mother said, "that is how we live."

"A lot you bring into the house," Jo said. "Have you ever brought home a single fish?" He held up a finger. "One fish? Even one?"

"I . . ."

"You what? You nothing. Where *was* this manta ray?"

Paloma gestured vaguely. "Out there."

"Out where?"

"In the sea."

"I know in the sea. Where in the sea?"

"It doesn't matter. He's gone."

"How do you know?"

"Because I hurt him and he flew away."

"You hurt him how?"

Paloma did not think before she spoke. "I pulled some of the ropes out of his wound and it hurt him."

Miranda stood up. She looked stricken. "You *what*?"

Jo said, "You got that close? I don't believe it."

"Don't believe it then," Paloma said, knowing that Jo believed every word.

"You *what*?" Miranda said again.

"Don't worry, Mama," Paloma said. "There wasn't any danger."

"She's right, Mama," Jo said. "There wasn't any danger, because it didn't happen."

Miranda looked from Jo to Paloma and back again, not knowing what to believe, certain only that she had something to worry about: if Paloma had done what she said, it was right to worry about her safety; if she had not, then a mother should worry about a daughter who makes up stories.

Sensing Miranda's confusion, Paloma said again, "Don't worry, Mama. The important thing is, we're all here and we're all safe."

Because Miranda wanted to believe it, she chose to, and she turned to her work.

Jo did not mention the manta again. During supper, he spoke without bluster about the day's fishing, about what he had caught and what he had hoped to catch, about how it was nice that the price for grouper had risen but the reason it had risen was that the fish were growing scarcer. Or perhaps they had just moved to other grounds.

"Do you see groupers out where you go?" he asked Paloma.

"Some."

"More than before, or less?"

Paloma shrugged. "About the same."

"You ought to bring some home."

"I don't fish."

"I know." Jo paused. "Maybe some day I should come have a look where you are."

Paloma felt all her interior warning systems go off at once, but she forced herself to stay slouched in her chair looking nonchalant. "Wouldn't be worth your time. There's not much there."

"What keeps you going, then?"

"I study different things." She glanced at Jo. "Things Papa wanted me to study."

Jo turned away and said, tight-lipped, "Sure."

After supper, Miranda washed the plates and cups, and Paloma swabbed the table with a wet rag. Jo sat and watched.

At the end of a long silence, Jo said, "I've decided. I'd like you to teach me to dive."

"You would?" It was the first time Jo had ever asked Paloma to teach him anything. "What do you want to dive for? You said yourself it's a waste of time."

"Yeah, well, maybe I've been wrong."

Paloma looked at her mother and said, "I think Jo is sick."

"He asks you to help him," Miranda said sternly. "That is good. Now what do *you* say?"

Paloma looked at Jo. "But you know how to dive. At least, you did once."

"Yeah, well," Jo was blushing. "That didn't work out too well."

Paloma knew the story—how Jobim had led Jo into diving step by step, first in knee-deep water, then in water up to Jo's chin, then in water just over his head, then in water where the bottom was ten or fifteen feet away.

Jo had had all the lessons, knew all the rules, had done everything his father had asked him to do and hated every minute of it. He had felt uncomfortable, unnatural, in the water, and he felt actually threatened by deep water. But he had never dared tell his father, for Jobim's approval was the most important thing in the world. The next most important thing was to be with Jobim, to spend his days with him, and the only way to do that was to dive. So Jo had resolved to force himself.

One day, Jobim had taken Jo into the open sea for the first time. They went to where they could not see bottom, for

Jobim wanted Jo to learn to gauge the depth by the feel of the water pressure on his body and by looking up at the surface from underwater.

They went down the anchor line, and at about forty feet Jo was seized by a fit of claustrophobia. Where some people feel free in open water, Jo felt trapped. The water was pressing on every bit of his body, confining him, suffocating him. There was no land anywhere, not below, not on the sides, not above. Everything was blue and heavy and oppressive. He had to leave.

He had screamed underwater and flailed with his arms and clawed his way up the anchor line. The line caught between his snorkel and his mask. Thrashing to free himself, he twisted the rubber strap even tighter around the line.

Jobim had grabbed him, tried to subdue him, but panic made Jo even stronger than he was normally, and he kicked and punched and tore his father's mask from his face.

Jo might have drowned both of them if Jobim had not felt, blindly, for his son's throat and wrapped his hand around it and squeezed until the boy lost consciousness and could be taken swiftly to the surface.

No, recalling the story of that day, Paloma could not imagine why Jo suddenly wanted to dive again, or why suddenly he thought he could dive without panicking. But she said, "All right. If you want."

"Good. I want to see all the things you see. Tomorrow?"

Paloma spoke quickly. "No, not tomorrow. I've got . . . too many things to do." She had nothing to do, but tomorrow was too soon. She had to have time to think about what Jo could have in mind, for she could not believe that his request meant only what it said. Too many things about it were unlike him.

"Soon, then."

"Yes. Soon."

Jo stood and yawned and said good night and walked through the front door and disappeared into the night. His room was around the corner, connected to the house but separate in that it had its own entrance from outside. That was one of the privileges a boy acquired when, at the age of fourteen, he underwent the elaborate, old-fashioned mystical ritual of becoming a man. As far as Paloma could tell, all the ritual accomplished was to give the boys privileges. It didn't make them men; it called them men.

Paloma and her mother shared a corner of the main room of the house. Neither of them had any privacy in their home at any time of the day or night.

Now Paloma thought how strange it was for Jo to have asked for her help in anything. This was a significant concession: for him to acknowledge that she—a girl—might know more about something worthwhile than he did was remarkable.

She would have to be careful with Jo, take each step cautiously and try to fit it into an overall picture.

She was surprised to find that she truly cared about what these changes in Jo might mean, and she realized it was a reflection of her loneliness, of the quiet desperation she had felt as she paddled home from the seamount that afternoon. To get along with Jo, to establish a relationship, perhaps even to make a friend—that would be a fine thing for Paloma, who had never had a friend.

6

THE LAST TIME the relationship between Paloma and Jo had resembled a friendship had been when Paloma was five and Jo was four: back then, they had played together happily. But soon Jo had found a pack of boys to run with, and Paloma had found herself either taunted or excluded, and she had begun to hate being a girl.

Then Jobim had taken Jo away, and left Paloma to Miranda, to be raised in Miranda's image. The two children had less and less—and finally nothing—in common.

Then had come the break, the reversal from which Jo had not recovered, when Jobim had returned him to Miranda and had taken Paloma with him, to make her the special one.

Still, for a long time Paloma had believed that it was bad to be a girl. For a while, she had dressed like a boy, cut her hair short like a boy's, learned to laugh at jokes directed at her—as if laughing *with* the joke, saying, "Yes, isn't it ridiculous to be a girl? Aren't I foolish? Well, I won't be a girl for long, and then we'll all have a good laugh at what I used to be."

Jobim—as a male who had never wanted to be anything else—could not have understood the depth of anxiety and confusion Paloma was feeling. But he knew generally what was wrong, deduced that it had to come from her being the only girl of her age on the island, and guessed that her feelings about herself and her sex were jumbled, confused.

So one day Jobim had taken Paloma fishing. She was quite young then and had never before been taken to sea. In fact, she had rarely been in Jobim's boat, except for holiday excursions to visit the sealion rookery and a few trips to La Paz.

They were alone in the boat, and Paloma was thrilled. She did not ask why she had been excused from her household chores, or where they were going. She was to be on the sea with Papa, and that was enough. The last thing she could have imagined was that Jobim intended the journey to alter Paloma's view of herself.

The sea was oily calm, so flat that the soft swells looked like bulges in a jelly, and Paloma had been able to kneel on the forward thwart and hang out over the bow of the boat. The sharp wooden prow sliced through the water like a fine blade through flesh. She thought of the surface of the sea as the skin of a huge fish, and of the bow as a knife that was filleting it for market.

Jobim had anchored the boat in what seemed to Paloma to be the middle of the sea. Actually, the boat was directly over the seamount, but Paloma had never yet been under water, so she had no idea that the sea bottom was a landscape of different terrains. As far as she knew, the bottom was distant and dangerous, an unknown country, like death.

Jobim had baited a big hook with half a needlefish, but he did not throw the line overboard. Instead, he handed her a face mask and snorkel and told her to put them on. Then, with his own mask propped up on his forehead, he told Paloma to jump overboard and hang onto the anchor line.

"Here?" Paloma was shocked. "In the middle of the sea? Why?"

"I want to show you something about girls," Jobim had said, and though what he said made no sense to her, she obeyed and slipped over the side.

Jobim jumped into the water and hung beside her, holding the anchor rope in the crook of an elbow so as not to drift away in the current. Slowly he fed the fishing line through his fingers, dropping the baited hook down toward the seamount.

Paloma's first sight of the seamount was breathtaking, a discovery as miraculous as if she had been given a secret glimpse of heaven, for here was a world she had not known existed. It was strange and very active and very silent and (she was surprised when she recalled it later) not at all threatening. It was somehow separate from her world, unquestionably real but wonderfully new, enchanted.

They lay together on the surface, their faces in the water, breathing through the rubber snorkel tubes. Jobim spoke to Paloma by rotating his head a quarter turn, until his mouth was out of the water, and Paloma could hear him clearly without moving: she couldn't tell whether she was receiving the sound of his voice down her snorkel tube and through her mouth or filtered through the few inches of seawater that covered her ears. Neither way made any sense to her, but she didn't care: his words came through distinctly, though they did sound hollow and far away.

The nylon fishing line was soon invisible in the water, but the bait was unmistakable—a white morsel that dangled provocatively just above the bottom and moved, not with its own rhythm like a living thing in harmony with the current, but like a dead thing caught and held.

Small fish approached the bait and hovered around it, seeming to appraise it for delicacy and danger. Jobim had made no attempt to hide the hook, and now and then a glint of steel would flash in a ray of light. Whether the fish were not enticed by the needlefish, or were scared by the hook, Paloma could not tell, but none of them went for the bait.

Then they were gone. The small fish vanished. The bait hung unattended, swaying in the current.

"Where did they go?"

"Watch," Jobim said. "Just watch."

For a moment or two, nothing happened. What had been a bustling community was now a barren plain. Paloma half expected to hear a clap of thunder or see a bolt of lightning, for such a change had to be the result of a natural drama.

And then, from the darkness at the edge of the seamount came the sharks—hammerheads, three of them, one half again as large as the other two: silent searchers moving with a relentless arrogance that broadcast their sovereignty over the seamount. Their bizarre, T-shaped heads swung slowly from side to side, gathering signals from the sea, interpreting them and sending out signals of their own. These soundless impulses preceded them everywhere, giving fair warning of their arrival, allowing all but proper prey to depart in safety.

Jobim jigged the bait, and though Paloma heard nothing new, she could see that the sharks received the message clearly, for they swung, in formation, toward the dangling piece of meat. They circled it once, then again, and then one of the smaller sharks broke the circle and darted in at the bait. Jobim jerked the line, and the bait popped up and away from the shark's mouth.

The three sharks circled again, faster now, each in turn shaking its head with a brusque, annoyed motion. They were perplexed, because something was not as it should be: they were receiving signals that reported dead meat, but the prey was not behaving as if dead.

The second of the two smaller sharks shot forward, and once more Jobim jerked the bait away. This time he did not let it down; he pulled it up toward the surface, challenging the sharks to follow it. Only one did, the largest. The other two hung below, angrily circling nothing.

The big shark did not attack the bait. It followed patiently, with sinuous grace. As it drew near, Paloma saw that this animal, which on the bottom had looked like a good-size fish, was enormous—bigger than she, bigger than Papa, almost as big as Papa's boat.

Paloma was terrified. She trusted Papa totally, knew that she would jump off a mountain or swallow needles if he said she should, but to play games with a big man-eating shark . . .

Unable to take her eyes from the advancing shark, she flailed with her free hand, desperate to grab the gunwale of the boat and pull herself to safety.

"Stop it," Jobim said. "Lie still."

Paloma lay still, but she was sure the shark could hear her heart. Were they like dogs, could they smell fear? She held her breath, hoping to mute the timpani in her chest, but that only made her heartbeat seem louder.

The bait was six or eight feet away, and the shark a foot beyond it. Jobim kept pulling, but now the shark stopped coming. It circled instead, the black eye on the end of its fleshy white "T" watching as Jobim reeled in the bait and, with a single twist, removed the hook from it.

Paloma turned with the shark, rotating like a flower petal

in a tidal eddy, panicked that she might lose sight of the circling hunter: there was something unbearable about knowing that the animal was there and not being able to see it.

A movement below caught her eye. Now the other two sharks were rising. They kept their distance from the larger one, seeming to defer to it, but they were growing bolder. And though they were definitely smaller than the other shark, relativity was the only comfort: her father was six feet tall, and each of these sharks was at least as long as he was tall.

Jobim held the half-needlefish out to the big shark and wiggled it with his fingertips. The circling pattern grew tighter. Now the shark was missing Paloma by only three or four feet as it swept by. The head was shaking actively, the crescent mouth opening and closing in expectant cadence.

Jobim pushed the needlefish out into open water, released it, and quickly drew back his hand. The shark passed by, and the fish disappeared. There had been no snapping, no biting, no shaking of the head. The shark had simply inhaled the needlefish.

It made two more tight turns around Jobim and Paloma, then gradually loosened its pattern, like a spring unwinding. Its black eye never left them, but there was no urgency to its behavior. It was waiting.

Jobim reached inside his shorts, undid a knot and came out with a whole needlefish. Paloma had not seen him do it, but in the boat he must have stuffed a plastic bag of needlefish inside his pants—out of sight of the sharks and, because the neck of the bag was tied off, out of their range of smell.

Immediately, the shark once again swept close by and resumed its tight circling pattern.

This time, Jobim broke the needlefish in two and shook both halves and then dropped them. As they fell, trailing bits of meat and puffs of oil, Jobim tapped Paloma's arm and motioned her to watch.

The smaller sharks sensed the food and rose toward it eagerly, hungrily, their heads shaking quickly. At the same time, the large shark dropped its head and raised its pectoral fins and snapped its tail back and forth, which drove the body downward like a spear.

For a moment, it seemed that the sharks must collide. All

three raced toward the pieces of fish, which continued to fall together.

Paloma saw that the small sharks were bound to win, for the needlefish was falling toward them and away from the bigger shark.

When the pieces of needlefish were no more than a foot from the mouths of each of the smaller sharks—when their victory was inevitable—both, simultaneously and inexplicably, turned away. The big shark soared down upon the pieces of fish, sucking in the first piece then turning away and making a wide circle and letting the second morsel fall—utterly casual, confident that there was no hurry, that the food would be there for the taking—then banking and descending in a dive and gobbling the last bit of food.

The smaller sharks continued downward, away from the large one, away from the food, away from conflict. They shook their heads and hunched their backs and flailed their tails.

They're like puppies, Paloma thought. They're angry and upset and there's nothing they can do about it, so they're running around yapping and chasing their tails.

The big shark returned and began once again to circle. Jobim motioned to Paloma to climb back into the boat. She didn't hesitate. Keeping her eye on the shark, she reached up and gripped the gunwale and pulled herself to the side of the boat. She took a deep breath and tested the firmness of her grasp on the wood. When Jobim had first taught her to swim, he had told her always to get in and out of the water quickly, for it was in the marginal moments—half in, half out of the water—that a person was most vulnerable to shark attack: it was then that the person looked truly like a wounded fish; most of the body was out of the water so it appeared smaller, and what remained in the water (lower legs and feet) kicked erratically and made a commotion like a struggling animal.

She spun, grabbed the gunwale with both hands, hoisted herself out of the water and over the gunwale, and tumbled in a heap to the bottom of the boat. She lay there for a second, breathing heavily, then realized—with a surge of adrenalin that rushed through her arms and pooled warmly in her stomach—that Jobim hadn't followed her. Her mask was still on her face, so she leaned over the side and peered down into the water.

Jobim clung to the anchor line, and he turned with the shark as it circled. Again Paloma thought of dogs—two males, one an intruder into the other's neighbourhood, circling each other, appraising each other, searching for weaknesses.

When the shark was at the most distant point in its circling pattern, on the far side of the boat, Jobim pulled the bag of fish from his shorts and dropped it. The bag sank slowly, yawing like a leaf falling from a tall tree, and Jobim waited until he was sure the shark had seen it. Then as the shark started down after the bag, Jobim pulled himself aboard the boat.

They ate a lunch of mangoes and bananas and a slab of dried, salted *cabrío,* making sure to eat the fish first and the mango last so that the juice from the mango would wash away the thirst caused by the salt in the *cabrío.*

They did not speak while they ate. Paloma didn't know what to say. She was certain she was supposed to have learned something, but she didn't know what it was and she wanted to review everything in her mind before asking any questions. Jobim knew that Paloma was searching for the lesson she was supposed to have learned, and he wanted the experience to ripen in her mind before he explained it.

Jobim rinsed his fingers in the sea and said, "Were you afraid?"

"Yes," said Paloma, and then, worried: "Is that bad?"

Jobim laughed. "Of course not. I don't think there was much danger, but they're fearsome things."

"No danger?" Paloma felt almost disappointed.

"People aren't their normal food. If the water's clear and they can see you, and if you're not bleeding or dead, usually they'll leave you alone."

"Usually," Paloma repeated.

"Usually." Jobim smiled. "Now: do you know what you've learned?"

"No. I know I learned that you don't know what sharks are going to do. I *knew* those two were going to take the needle-fish from the big one, and then they didn't."

"Do you know why?"

"There's a reason?"

"I told you I was going to show you something about girls."
Jobim smiled again. "The big shark was a female, a very
young one. A little girl, as sharks go."

"How do you know?"

"How do I know she's a female? It's almost as it is on
people. On the male you can see what are called claspers.
They secure the connection during breeding. The female
doesn't have any. As for how I know she's young, she had no
scars on her at all. That's as it is with humans, too: the older
you get, the more weather-beaten and cut up and scarred you
are. An old shark looks like Viejo. And an old female shark
has even more scars, because during mating the males prevent the females from throwing them off by biting the females' backs."

"How old was she?"

"I don't know. Three or four years, I guess. Nobody knows
how long they live or what kills them. It's hard to imagine a
shark dying of old age, but maybe it happens."

"What were the other two?"

"Both males, both older. You saw the way they turned and
ran when that young girl came at them." Jobim paused, knowing what was going through Paloma's mind.

She frowned and said, "It doesn't make sense."

"Not to a human, because we've been taught all sorts of
ideas about males and females and the natural order of
things. Males are bigger and do most of the physical work and
support the family and make the decisions and must be
looked up to and obeyed because . . . because why? Because
that's nature? No. Somewhere way back, there must have
been a good reason to make the males dominant. Probably
because they were strong and did the hunting. And when
strength was all there was, the stronger you were, the more
important you were.

"And that's true with a lot of animals—the bigger and
stronger are the most important. With sharks, the females are
almost always bigger and tougher and meaner. Sharks have a
pecking order, just like the chickens at the house. You saw it
right then. When there's food around, the biggest eats first
and eats till it's full. *Then* the others get to feed, but always in
the order of their size and bad temper. That's why you don't

see males and females together very often: the males would starve to death."

"But with people," Paloma said, "females *aren't* the strongest or the toughest or the meanest. They're . . ."

"Who says?" Jobim cut her off. "Strong doesn't only mean biggest; the toughest isn't just the one who can smash something with his bare hands. Strong can mean smart and clever and creative. The toughest can be the one who knows how to survive without wasting energy, or how to swim from here to there against the tide without getting exhausted and drowning.

"Animals have to be what nature made them—big or not, strong or not. That's what sets their place. But people can set their own place. If they don't have one thing, they can make up for it with something else, with knowledge or experience. Do you understand?"

Paloma nodded.

Jobim knelt down beside her and spoke softly. The image of his brown forehead and black eyebrows and broad shoulders framed against the sunlit sky was engraved forever on her mind, the sound of his mellow voice reduced to a hoarse whisper was one she would recall whenever, after his death, she talked to him. "All I want to tell you, all I want today to teach you, is that there are no 'must-bes' in life. Nothing is inevitable.

"You don't *have* to cook the food and sweep the floor and have babies. You are a female, and that is a fine thing. You are a young female, and that is finer still. But the finest thing is that you are a person who can decide for yourself what you want your life to be. You will teach people to respect you for that. More important, you will respect yourself for that, and anyone who doesn't is a fool, to be pitied."

Never, after that day, had Paloma wished to be a boy. She had let her hair grow until it cascaded down her back. She had watched and felt with pride and fascination every change in her body.

A few months after Jobim's death, a big storm blew through, a *chubasco* as big, if not as sudden, as the one that had killed Jobim. (That one had given no warning at all. He had surfaced from a dive to find his boat bucking and heaving in mountainous seas. He must have tried to board it and been knocked unconscious by the motor or the boat, for when he was found dead on the beach, there was a big blue dent in his forehead.) This storm knocked every bush and shrub flat against the ground and lashed the island with blinding, stinging rains.

The first rumblings began in her body almost simultaneously with the onset of the storm, and the cramps seemed to her to be echoing the thunder. She was frightened briefly, for her first thought was that she was becoming violently ill. Then her fear melted into a vague apprehension. Miranda had not warned her about what would happen when the woman change began inside her, had mentioned it only in vague, embarrassed generalities, and had, finally, turned it over to God to deal with. Jobim had done what he could to prepare her, but he could not know what to expect, how she would feel, what exactly would happen to her.

He had prepared her well enough, though, so that soon she felt the comforting conviction that everything that was happening was natural and healthy and—she remembered his word—fine.

She wanted him to know what was happening to her, and how she was responding to it, that she was becoming a woman and was proud of it.

And so, though a squall was driving the rain in horizontal sheets and the wind was whipping around in cyclonic eddies, Paloma fought her way to her rock on the western tip of the island and stood on the rock, naked. She raised her arms to the sky, to Papa, and beamed up at him, radiant with life, and let the rain wash the blood down her legs and over the rock and into the sea.

7

PALOMA DRIED THE last dish, then walked outside into the still night.

For all her delight at being a girl—and her frequent amazement at herself for ever having wanted to be anything else— still Paloma often wished that she could abolish the differences between herself and males. For she was positive that it was this difference (in coincidence with the absence of other girls her age) that made it difficult for her to make friends.

The slightest hint, therefore, that Jo might be undergoing some sort of shift that would make him susceptible to friendship gave Paloma an injection of hope that animated her as much as an adrenaline rush in fright.

As she puttered around the kitchen, she had reprimanded herself for not being more receptive to Jo's new attitude. He had been rather nice tonight, and she had responded sceptically, had put him off. He had given a little something, and she had given nothing.

So she decided she would go to Jo's room, and if he was awake she would tell him that she had been mistaken, that tomorrow would be a good day to teach him to dive.

As she turned the corner around the house, she heard something that made her stop. She waited, then peered around the corner and saw Jo going into his room. He must have gone for a walk, she thought, and she started again for his room. But again she stopped, and this time she wasn't sure why; she knew she didn't want to go on. She was sensing a warning—nothing she could have articulated, but something very strong.

As she stood there, she chided herself for giving in to mystical nonsense. But no matter how foolish it seemed, she could not take another step.

After a few more moments, she returned to the house and went to bed, resolving to let sleep clear her head.

But sleep was a long time coming, for she was an unwilling witness to a pitched battle inside her head—between the half of her mind that wanted a friend and condemned her for being suspicious, and that half that cherished her independence and was suspicious of anyone or anything that might encroach upon it.

By morning, she had decided to give herself the day to settle the conflict in her mind, so although Jo was still being genial, Paloma did not let the mild guilt she felt change her plans.

She accompanied Jo and his friend Indio down the path to the dock, as she did every day. As he untied his boat, Jo said casually, "You want to come with us today?"

"What?" Jo had never invited her into his boat—not for fishing, not for fun, not to gather firewood on one of the nearby islands.

"Manolo is sick."

"Sick with what? He was fine last night."

"I don't know. He says it's his stomach. If it is, I don't want him in the boat."

Paloma was tempted. If she could not make a gesture to Jo, at least she might accept his gesture to her.

But selfishly, she did not want to accept. She had never liked fishing, except with Jobim, and then it wasn't the fishing she liked so much as the being with Papa. Fishing was boring and tiring and painful, for the fishing line always bit through her fingertips and abraded the cuts with salt. Most of all, she disliked fishing because it was killing—for a worthwhile cause sometimes, she had to admit, but still, it was killing. She could not reconcile the communion she felt with the animals on the seamount with the sense of revulsion, of horror, really, she felt on seeing those same animals lifeless and colorless, heaped in the bottom of a boat.

But if Jo needed her help, if they were going to be friends, it would be petty of her to refuse.

"All right," she said.

"Oh." Jo seemed surprised. "I mean, only if you want to."

"If you need the help, I'd like to help."

"Yes. I see." Jo seemed to be searching for something to say. "I don't really need your help, though."

"But I thought Manolo . . ."

"Sure, but . . . I mean . . . Indio and I can . . . Manolo doesn't really . . ." Jo was blushing. "We can manage. I just thought you might . . . I know how you feel about fishing . . . I mean, all we do is kill stuff." Jo grimaced, as if the thought of dead fish nauseated him.

"I know," Paloma said, "but that *is* what we live on. It's time I got tougher about it."

"Okay," Jo said. "Good idea. Only today's not a good day."

"It isn't?"

"No. You said so yourself, remember? We've both got a lot of things to do."

"Yes, but . . ."

"We can manage. Really. You do what you have to do then we'll spend a couple of days together. Maybe more. Maybe one day you can teach me to dive and the next day I'll take you fishing. A deal?"

"Okay." Paloma shrugged. She didn't know if she should say something more. Was she supposed to? Were there customs about this? It had seemed so simple: Jo had asked if she wanted to join them today. More: he had suggested that she could help them, had seemed to be asking for her help. She had said yes, she was willing to help. And then everything had gotten complicated. He had withdrawn the invitation, or denied the request for help—whatever, he was now saying that he didn't want her along, after all.

Or was he being considerate of her? That was what his voice wanted to convey—that he didn't want to be so selfish as to take her away from what she wanted to do. If that truly was his message, if he was being kind, then perhaps she could respond with a kindness, should convince him that what she had to do wasn't very important, that she would gladly put it aside to help him.

But maybe he had changed his mind. If so, she didn't want to force herself on him.

Was this what the beginnings of friendships were like? If so, then maintaining a friendship looked like a full-time job. It was probably worth it, though. The least she could do was learn the tricks and rituals and give it a chance to grow.

And no matter how confusing she found this morning's conversation with Jo, the important thing was that they were being civil to one another. That demonstrated that both of them were willing to try.

Paloma uncleated the bowline and held the bow of the boat away from the dock while Jo and Indio climbed aboard. Then she held the bow from swinging in the tide while Jo tried to start the outboard motor. He pulled the starter cord, and the wheels and gears inside the housing made a purring sound like a feeding cat. He pulled again, and the purring sounded more anxious, then stopped abruptly. Jo cursed the motor and banged on the housing with his fist. Then, with a sigh, he removed the housing and began to tinker with the insides of the motor.

Before, Paloma had watched Jo's rages against the motor with amusement. Now, for the first time, she felt sympathy for him. He knew motors as well as she knew fish—was at home with them, could understand them and talk to them and cajole them into cooperating. But while Paloma's friends flourished in the Sea of Cortez, Jo's friends, the motors, withered and died. This was as hostile an environment as any on earth to an internal-combustion engine. Salt corroded its innards, the sun burned out gaskets and hoses, sand clogged filters and destroyed lubricants.

And there were no expert mechanics, no replacement parts. When a motor broke, you either fixed it yourself, rebuilt the ailing part, or dismantled and cannibalized it for parts to fix some other motor. Paloma remembered seeing Jo spend endless hours with a knife and a piece of truck tire—the tire had been a fender that fell off the boat from La Paz. He had carved and created from the thick rubber a tiny impeller for the outboard motor's water pump.

No wonder Jo wanted to go away to school. He had a gift that was little more than useless here. There were a couple of outboard motors for him to work on, but nothing of size or scope or genuine challenge. He had no way of developing his gift, of honing his skills, of letting his talent earn him money and appreciation. He was like a wonderfully gifted surgeon with no one to practice on.

He took something off the motor, cleaned it, blew on it, screwed it back in and replaced the housing. Then he caressed the motor, said something threatening to it, turned the choke up high, and yanked on the cord. The motor gagged and protested its way to life with a belch of blue-grey smoke.

On other mornings, she would have tossed the bowline loose into the boat, leaving Indio to unsnarl it from the fishing gear. Today she coiled the line carefully and knelt on the dock and handed it to Indio and pushed the bow of the boat around the end of the dock into open water.

Jo headed east, and soon he and Indio and the boat were black silhouettes against the pumpkin sun. Jo waved, Paloma waved back. Then Jo appeared to speak to Indio, and Indio waved, too, which Paloma found curious.

Paloma went back to the house to fetch some feed and a jar of fresh water. Today, for no good reason except to avoid an argument, she let her mother wrap a slice of salted *cabrío* and a tortilla in a piece of paper for her to take along with her mango.

Then she returned to the dock and got in her pirogue and pushed off and paddled westward.

She did not look back, but even if she had, it was unlikely that she would have seen the figure squatting in the bushes at the top of the hill, who was tracking her through a pair of binoculars.

8

MANOLO, SUPPOSEDLY WRITHING with stomach cramps in his bed, had taken several precautions not to be seen. He had removed his silver sacred cross and his brass pinky ring so they would not flash in the sunlight. He had covered himself with leaves and branches. And the pocket mirror he had brought he placed face down in the dirt, until the time came when he would need it.

Now he watched as Paloma paddled toward the west. The heat of the day had not yet arrived, but there was still enough tumult in the interaction of air and water so that, when magnified by his binocular lenses, the atmosphere around Paloma's hat and paddle when she moved emitted a shimmer.

Paloma paddled for a while, then checked her landmarks, dropped her anchor, and held the line in her hands until she felt the iron set in the rocks. Then she put on her mask and fins and snorkel, slid her knife into her belt and slipped overboard.

Not until then did Manolo feel confident enough to step out of the bushes and hold the mirror to the morning sun and flash it twice toward the east.

PALOMA CLEANSED HER mask and blew through her snorkel to clear it. Then she settled down, with one hand on the anchor line, to survey the seamount from one end to the other. With her vision restricted by the sides of her mask and by the turbidity of the water, she could not see a large area at a single glance. In air, with her peripheral vision unhampered and the distances crisp and clear for miles, she could see about 140 degrees. Down here, she could see about 40 degrees with each look, as if she tried to see more, she was certain to miss something.

In practical terms, the difference was that, on the surface she could see everything in the entire circle around her, all the way to the horizon, in a bit more than two looks. Down here, she needed nine full and distinct surveys to see the same circle, and the distance she could see was never more than fifty or sixty feet.

In the first section she concentrated on, she saw nothing but rocks. In the second, a few quickly flickering shadows told her that hammerheads were cruising near the bottom, the colors of their backs melded by the monochromatic seawater into the same mottled green-brown as the stony top of the seamount.

On a conscious level, Paloma was not looking for anything specific; she was doing what she did every day, looking over the seamount to see what was there. But a half-step deeper in her mind, Paloma was looking for the injured manta, hoping —not daring to voice the hope—that it had found its way back to the seamount.

As her eyes moved methodically on through the third, fourth, and fifth sections, hope gave way to resignation: the manta was not there, would not be there, and she had been foolish even to think that it might be there. Mantas were open-sea animals. They cruised ceaselessly, following the food, making their home, like petrels, on the wing. They were not territorial, had no reason to return to a particular area. And even if this manta contradicted the rule and happened to be territorial, Paloma reminded herself, the treatment it had received from her the day before would surely have driven it away.

In the eighth section she saw a manta ray, but it could not be the same one. It was smaller; from here, it looked like a discarded black tricorn hat. She was about to shift her gaze to the last section of the seamount, but her eyes lingered, and then suddenly the scene beneath her took shape and she realized that the ray below *was* the injured manta.

It was distance that had deceived her. The ray was down very deep and perspective had told her the truth; now she could see that small as the manta looked from up here, it dwarfed the terrain around it. Sea fans, half as tall as a man and much wider, looked like postage stamps beside the manta; a passing hammerhead looked no bigger than a spaniel. Also, as she stared down on the animal's back she could see a white slash behind the manta's left horn.

She guessed that the manta was hugging the bottom because there was less current there; the surrounding rocks and valleys would disperse the massive flow of water. And where there was less current there was less tug on the ropes that tore at the manta's already battered flesh.

The manta was hovering in a temporary shelter, where the sea did not aggravate its pain.

That presumed—Paloma checked herself—that a manta felt pain. Jobim had told her that some animals have no sensation similar to what people call pain. They sense by instinct, danger, shock, loss of a limb or of a vital fluid—but not pain. For pain was only a human word for a human feeling. Yet Paloma knew for certain that this animal felt something akin to pain, something that signalled alarm and distress, because yesterday when she had tugged at the ropes in the wound the manta had behaved like a dog that has stepped on a bee.

Paloma also guessed that it was instinct that told the manta it could find shelter in a place of less current and that there was less current near the bottom. Like any animal in pain, humans included, the manta would seek a path of least discomfort. It would move everywhere, into deep water and shallow, close to the seamount and far from it, and where it was most comfortable it would stay.

All of which was fine, Paloma thought, but the manta's quest for comfort posed a problem: she could not possibly help the animal if it was determined to stay at sixty-five or seventy feet. She could make a breath-hold dive that deep, but she could not hope to stay long enough to accomplish anything.

On the surface—but more dramatically underwater—it is a basic truth that the more you attempt to do, the more oxygen you consume. A runner breathes harder than a walker because the runner is using oxygen faster and needs to replenish it faster. Underwater, there is no such thing as breathing harder: you have the oxygen you came down with, and there will be no more until you return to the surface.

The first time Jobim had explained that basic truth to Paloma, she had responded with a weary sigh, as if she felt he was insulting her intelligence. After all, it didn't take a genius to realize that there is no air underwater; that is why you take a deep breath and hold it when you put your head under water.

Later, however, after she had dived many times to many depths and experienced the different ways her body responded to different activities and exertions and pressures and sensations, she knew what her father had meant. You had to know before you dived how far you were going and what you wanted to do. To change your mind at the last minute, far underwater, was to invite confusion, exhaustion, panic and death.

Paloma knew, for example, that she could easily dive down to sixty or seventy feet if all she intended to do was to wrap her legs around a rock and observe the creatures of the seamount—or, at the very most, kick or swim calmly from perch to perch. She knew how to read the signals her body sent her, knew when to respond by starting for the surface. But if she were to go to sixty or seventy feet and were, say, to see a bed of oysters ten feet deeper still, and were to force herself down and begin to hack the oysters free and stuff them in a bag, the signals for immediate ascent would come right away. Because she had gone deeper and exerted herself more than she had intended and had consumed oxygen that should have been left in reserve for the trip to the surface, the signals would already be too late.

She would start up—not in the relaxed, oxygen-efficient way she knew to be best, kicking gently and allowing her body's natural buoyancy to take her up, but struggling frantically, flailing with her arms, scissor-kicking, wasting even more precious oxygen. Long before she would near the surface, the ache in her lungs would change from a dull tightness to a sharp, stabbing flame. Her temples would stop throbbing and would instead thrum in an incessant screech of pain; she would be at the threshold, near explosion.

She would look upward and see a slab of water dozens of feet thick, and at some unknowable moment would realize that she wasn't going to make it.

Starved for oxygen, her brain would begin to shut down. She would lose consciousness. The next thing she would know would be determined entirely by luck.

If she was lucky she would pass out close enough to the surface so that her head would pop free of the water before the breathing reflex commanded her diaphragm to draw a breath. And if she was even luckier, she would rise on her back with her mouth turned upward toward the air instead of on her stomach with her face in the water, so that when her head did pop free and the reflex did command a breath, she would breathe air. After two or three breaths, her brain, like an engine refuelled and reprimed, would reignite her consciousness. She would awaken, and though there would be a blank in her memory, she would soon be fit again and able to resume swimming and diving.

If she was unlucky, her body would try to breathe underwater. Her lungs would expand and inhale salt water. She would cough and gag and inhale and cough and gag and inhale. She would drown.

And when finally she did reach the surface, no one would be there to pound and press her chest and expel the water and breathe life back into her lungs. More and more brain functions would cease, until at last the critical ones that govern respiration and heartbeat would close their circuits forever. She would not awaken. And the next thing she would know would be whatever one knows, if anything, after one has died.

Paloma knew her limits, and knew that to try to help the manta where it now lay was well beyond those limits. So she floated on the surface and waited. The manta did not move, did not flap a wingtip or switch its tail.

Suddenly it occurred to Paloma that the manta was dead. Perhaps it was not hovering above the bottom but was lying *on* the bottom.

No, impossible. If it were dead, other animals would already be feasting on it. That was another of the facts of life: as soon as something died, something else began to eat it.

She recalled once seeing a goat slaughtered. The goat stood, passive and unaware, its tail and ears and lips twitching to keep the flies away. And the flies stayed away. Then the goat's throat was cut. It stood on its feet for a moment, bleeding to death, and must actually have died on its feet, for when at last it toppled over, and before its head had hit the ground, flies were gnawing at its eyes.

Animals knew when animals died, and as yet, nothing was feeding on the manta. So it couldn't be dead.

But it could be dying. Maybe right then, as Paloma watched, life was drifting away from the great animal. She felt helpless and frustrated and angry. She had to help, but she was too far away; she couldn't let the manta die, but there was nothing she could do. Maybe it wasn't dying. Maybe it was resting. Maybe . . .

She had no choice. She had to go down and see for herself.

She took her deep breaths and felt her lungs engage the rhythm of expansion and contraction, and when they were as empty as she could make them she slowly filled them to capacity, shut her mouth and dived for the bottom.

She pulled herself down the anchor line until she was a few feet from the bottom, then released the line and swam over to the manta. It did not budge as she approached.

She saw at once that the manta was not lying on the rocks. It was hovering, as she had first assumed, evidently resting in a quirky swirl of water that flowed steadily over the top of the seamount and over its huge flat wings and permitted it to remain stable.

The manta was so still that it seemed frozen or hypnotized or in hibernation. Paloma swam beneath it—she wanted to look at its gill slits and be sure they were pulsing, however feebly, for that was the most reliable sign that the animal was passing water over its gills and extracting oxygen from it. The big round eye swivelled downward and followed her until she was out of sight beneath a wing.

Paloma swam under the entire breadth of the manta, and it was like being in a cave, for the giant cloak shut out all light from above and cast a blanket of black shadow on the rocks.

The manta's left eye tracked her as she reappeared and swam up over the horn and hung above it, looking down at the deep laceration, with the skeins of rope still floating out like asps among the shreds of flesh.

The wound did not look much different from when she had first seen it. There might be fewer ropes in it—she had removed a few, and a few might have fallen away—but those that remained were as solidly embedded as ever. There were no evident signs of healing. And the fact that the manta preferred to lie quietly, not to swim and feed, told Paloma that it was ill, and very weary. It had no way of knowing that it must eat in order to survive. Its instinctive impulses were weakening and fading.

Left alone, the manta would languish, and left alone it would surely be. Only the whales and dolphins—the so-called higher animals of the sea—actively helped one another. Mothers helped their offspring to breathe, and protected them from predators; the well helped the sick; the young and vital helped the old and feeble; the males deferred in feeding patterns to the young and the females.

Animals of the order of manta rays, however, were solitary in maturity, and therefore, when they were less than healthy, they were very vulnerable. They helped themselves or they died—uncontrollable natural processes either cured or killed them.

Paloma had to surface, yet she lingered for one more moment, feeling indignation—at nature, at fate, at mankind, at fishermen, at whatever had caused this fine animal to be hurt —because the manta was triply helpless: it could not help itself, she could not help it, and nothing else in the sea *would* help it. At the last second before she kicked off from the bottom, Paloma impulsively wrapped her arms round the manta's cephalic fin—the dreaded "horn"—and pushed upward: in desperation, she sought to prod the manta into rising to a depth where she could reach it and do something to help. Then, with the drums pounding in her temples and the ache beginning to sear her lungs, she sped up toward the light.

On the surface she rested, waiting until her breathing had returned to normal and her pulse had quieted to a point where she could no longer hear it or feel it. For good measure, she waited a few minutes more until, from lack of exertion, she shivered: her body had grown cold, and the shiver was its attempt to generate heat. Now she could dive again and exercise with no ill effect.

She put her face in the water and looked down. The manta was gone. First she thought she must be looking in the wrong place. She lifted her head and searched for distant landmarks. Could the boat have swung at anchor, disorienting her? No. Everything was as it had been when she arrived.

She looked again, starting with the first sector, on the far right edge of the seamount, and moving methodically sector by sector toward the left wall that ended in the abyss.

The manta was nowhere.

As she had risen to the surface, it must have fled. Perhaps she had frightened it by grabbing its horn in her arms. But if so, why hadn't it bolted then? Perhaps it had behaved like an opossum—staying dead quiet while she was near and then as soon as she had left and given it what it regarded as a safe margin, it had dashed off to distant refuge.

Paloma felt remorse, condemning herself for driving the manta away when suddenly the giant was soaring toward her, up from the depths like a black bomber flying from the edge of the gloom.

It passed fifteen or twenty feet beneath her as she hung on the anchor line, its wings rising and falling in lazy symmetry. It made a wide, banking circle to the right, ropes fluttering behind, and returned. Then it stopped, directly under Paloma's boat, no more than ten feet beneath her toes.

The pressure wave from the movement of the enormous body through the water made Paloma and her boat bob like toys in a tub.

Paloma did not know why the manta had left the bottom, why it had come into shallow water, why it had stopped beneath her boat. She was tempted, but refused, to settle for the easy answer she knew to be wrong—or, if not absolutely wrong, at least implausible and silly: that is, that the manta knew she was trying to help, that her gentle gesture on the bottom had somehow communicated something, and that the manta had responded like a pet or a child.

But while Paloma did know that all those reasons were not

reasons so much as wishful thoughts, she determined to conclude nothing: the manta was there, and she had to try and help it.

She slid her knife from her belt, took a deep breath and dropped down onto the manta's back.

She braced herself, prepared for the manta to burst to life and speed away, but it did not move. She gripped the lip of solid flesh between the horns and bent to the wound.

One long tail of rope fed out of the wound down the manta's back. The end in the wound was snared in a mess of knots. Gently, Paloma tugged on the rope. A foot or two more came free, and then it pulled tight. The hand that held the lip of flesh felt a shudder course through the manta's body—like a mild electric shock or a series of tiny tics. The shudder subsided, and the manta lay still.

Carefully, with the knife's razor point Paloma cut the rope away and probed the wound, snipping knots and snares, casting away bits of rotten flesh and pieces of soft and flaky rope.

Then, one by one, the alarms in Paloma's body began to sound.

She tried to ignore them all, for she feared that she was causing the manta such discomfort that when she left this time the animal would depart permanently. She did not want to pass out, but she was not afraid that she would: she could make it to the surface in two or three seconds, and she knew she would have much warning before she lost consciousness.

She received that last warning—a tingling in her fingers and toes, a dullness in her shoulders and thighs, a thick feeling in her mouth and throat. She swept down with her arms, scissor-kicked twice with her flippers, and broke through to sunlight.

She held onto the side of the pirogue and gagged and gasped and cursed herself for taking such a chance. But she was unhurt, and she had cut away a lot of the rope. If the manta was gone—well, she had done what she could do, and she hoped that that had been enough so the manta could survive on its own.

When she had rested, she looked down into the water. She expected to have to search for the manta, but it had not moved. It lay still at ten feet.

Paloma breathed deeply and held her breath and was about to plunge back down to the manta, when a new sensation registered in her brain.

At first it was a feeling—a weak vibration—but then, as she concentrated on it, it became a sound. It was a high, very faint buzzing or humming. Still holding her breath, she listened carefully, to make sure she wasn't hearing a sound from within her own head. Then she breathed, to let the sound of her breathing break the monotone of the buzzing, and held her breath again. It was still there; if there was any difference, the sound was a bit louder now.

Paloma knew that even though water was not a particularly good conductor of sound, under water certain sounds were sharper, more audible, more emphatic than they were on the surface. Knocking two stones together, for example, was used as a signal, because if one diver shouted at another underwater, the voice died in his mouth, but if he clicked two stones together, the sound travelled clearly and far.

Whale sounds also travelled vast distances underwater. They were varied, high-pitched clicks and whistles, and when you heard them you often found that the chatty whales or porpoises were so far away that not only could you not see them underwater; you couldn't see them when you raised your head out of water, either.

Certain engine noises could be heard from a long way away. The big, deep-throated diesel engines—called "growlers"—sounded like an army of bears marching across a wooden floor. Usually, you felt a growler coming before you heard it. The turning of the huge propeller would affect the water pressure, and you would feel a thumping on your eardrums or a light tapping on your arms and back. Smaller engines that turned faster made high, buzzing whines.

Paloma did not know the science of why certain sounds travelled under water and others didn't. She assumed it had to do with the quality of the sound, the kind of sound it was. A human voice made a sound that was weak and unfocused. Water dispersed it instantly. A whale's voice was sharp and precise, and it seemed to pierce the water.

Of course, how a sound registered depended a lot on who was listening to it. Jobim had once told Paloma that a human ear was about as efficient as a crystal-set radio he had put together from a kit when he was a boy. It received a very small portion of the signals that were racing through the air all the time.

"We think there is a great silence underwater," he had said, "but the sea is really a very noisy place."

"It isn't noisy," Paloma had insisted. "It's the quietest place in the world."

Jobim had not argued, but on his next trip to La Paz he had bought a dog whistle. He had blown it for Paloma; it made no sound.

"It's broken," she said.

Jobim took her hand and led her next door. Their neighbor's mongrel had had a litter of puppies three weeks earlier. There were six of them, and they were curled in a pile beside the exhausted mother. Jobim handed Paloma the whistle and said, "Blow it gently. They're just beginning to hear, and you don't want to hurt their ears."

Paloma thought this was a joke, and she took a deep breath and was about to blow on the dead whistle with all her might, when Jobim suddenly snatched it from her.

"I'm serious," he said. "Watch."

He put the whistle to his lips and let a feeble wisp of breath escape through it. Paloma heard nothing. But for the heap of drowsy puppies, it was as if a pack of cats had fallen on them from the sky. They struggled to their feet and scrambled over one another, whimpering furiously. They fought to wriggle underneath their mother, whose head was cocked, whose ears were up and whose throat rumbled with a growl of confused menace.

Jobim stopped blowing the whistle, and immediately the puppies relaxed. The mother looked around, decided that the high-pitched alien had departed, and dropped her head to the ground.

"The point is," Jobim had said as he took Paloma home, "just because we can't hear things underwater doesn't mean there aren't sounds underwater." Jobim paused, as if considering whether or not to say what he was about to say. Then he smiled to himself and shrugged. "The same is true with vision."

"What do you mean?"

"The eye is a receiver, too, like the television sets you see in the store windows in La Paz. They receive a kind of signal. Your eye sees a kind of light. But there are kinds of light that your eye doesn't see."

"It doesn't see them, you mean, but they're there?"

Jobim nodded. "Yes. Good for you."

"You mean there are things out there," she waved her arm, "things that *are,* and maybe things that are happening, and I can't see them?"

"Well . . . yes . . . I suppose . . . but no one really knows what . . ."

"I don't want to talk about it," Paloma had said flatly.

Jobim was about to laugh, but he saw that Paloma's jaw was set and her brow was furrowed and she was almost painfully grave, so all he said was "Are you sure?"

Paloma nodded. "It's like infinity. I don't want you ever to talk about infinity again."

"Why not?"

"It scares me and makes me cry."

"All right," Jobim said, and he had squeezed her hand.

Lying on the surface of the water now, listening to the high, buzzing sound, Paloma tried to recall if Jobim had taught her any tricks for judging how far away a sound was. Either he hadn't taught her, or she couldn't remember them, and in any case it didn't matter. She assumed the noise was coming from a boat, probably an outboard, passing in the distance, and if so, it would surely keep on going.

Paloma checked to make sure her knife was secure in her belt, then took her breaths and dropped down to the manta. She saw the big round eye swivel up as she approached and follow her until she had passed out of its range and settled onto the broad black back. As she let herself down slowly, she noticed that her knees were smudged with black. She touched the manta's flesh and looked at her fingers: they were black, too. The manta's protective mucous coating came off on her skin like a black stain.

She turned to the wound; there were very few ropes left, and she was able to reach them with the point of her knife. She removed them all and then, with her fingertips, swabbed at the bits of debris left in the wound. She had to force herself not to think of what it would be like to have someone poking fingers into an open sore of hers, for when the thought first crossed her mind, she nearly fainted.

But the manta did not give any signs of pain, did not flinch or shudder. Either the wound was so deep that it was beyond superficial nervous sensation, or such sensations didn't exist in the manta. Whatever the reason, Paloma was able to clean the wound and cut away all the dangling shreds of putrescent flesh.

The feelings in her head and in her chest told her that she still had some time—half a minute or more—before she would have to surface, so, using her hands as trowels, she began to pack the torn flesh together into the cavity of the wound, pressing it down as if to encourage it to adhere to itself and grow again.

It should have been a silent task, but the flesh as she slapped it sounded like THUCK, and her moving around caused her to emit squeaky streams of bubbles, and the pulse in her temples drummed ever more insistently. And all these sounds, when added to her intense concentration, obliterated the noise of the outboard motor as it approached overhead.

Now she had to surface. She pushed off the manta's back and swept once with her arms and kicked a few times. It was only habit that made her look up: Jobim had taught her always to look up as she ascended from a dive, to avoid knocking her head on the bottom of the boat.

When she did look up, she expected to see the surface or the sky. Instead, all she saw was Jo's face, peering down at her from the surface through a glass-bottom bucket, his grin destroyed by reflection into a gargoyle's leer.

She recoiled, shocked, and looked again to make certain she hadn't imagined it. Then she saw Jo's fingers creep around the edge of his home-made viewing box and wave to her.

9

PALOMA BROKE THROUGH the surface and reached up for the gunwale of her boat. Jo had put a line around her anchor rope, so they were moored together.

He was still looking through the glass-bottom bucket. "Mother of God! What a monster! How did you catch him?"

Indio said, "Let me see."

Paloma's heart was stuttering. She could hear it beat in her chest and feel it in her throat. She took a deep breath and tried to calm herself, for she had to be in control of herself before she could hope to deal with Jo and Indio and—looking so smug, sitting in the bow—the miraculously recovered Manolo. Her first impulse was to shriek at Jo, to lash out at him, for she felt betrayed, even violated.

There were three of them, however, and but one of her, and nothing would be accomplished by a display of rage, except that Jo and his mates would laugh, and she would feel even more humiliated.

"How did you catch him?" Jo asked again.

"I didn't catch him," Paloma said. "He's not caught."

"He's dead, then?"

"No."

Indio was looking through the bucket. "*Look* at 'em all! This place is a fish market! It's a gold mine!"

A surge of nausea swept through Paloma and made her dizzy. Though she still hung in the water, she felt beads of sweat form on her forehead.

"I told you," Jo said to Indio. "I knew she wasn't coming out here to study shrimps."

"You were right."

"You didn't believe me," Jo went on. " 'Let's stay here,' you said. A lot you knew."

"Okay, okay," Indio said. "I said you were right. I admit it. I take it back. Now let's get at 'em!"

As if on cue, Manolo threw a baited hook overboard and fed the weighted line through his fingers.

"Don't!" Paloma shouted.

Manolo laughed. "There are fish down there. Are you saying I can't fish for them? That's what fish are for. To fish for."

"You're wrong." Paloma pulled herself toward the bow of her boat. "You're not so important that God put *any*thing on earth just for you to kill."

With one hand, Paloma grabbed her anchor rope; with the other she reached back into her belt and pulled out her knife and slashed the line that moored the other boat to hers. The line was taut, for the strong tide wanted to pull the boat away, so the sharp blade sliced through the fibres so quickly that they made a popping sound.

Immediately, the bow of Jo's boat swung wide, tangling Manolo's fishing line in the limp mooring line, and the boat slid away downtide.

Furious, Jo leaped to his feet, cursed Paloma, and yanked on the starter cord of his outboard motor. The cord came away in his hand. He cursed the motor, and cursed Paloma again, and the cord, and all boats, and the sea. He rewrapped the cord and pulled a second time, and the motor sputtered and died. He cursed spark plugs and carburetors and gasoline.

Paloma clung to her anchor rope and watched Jo teeter in the stern of his boat and nearly capsize. Then she saw a puff of blue smoke and heard the outboard roar to life and saw the boat swing in a tight circle and head back toward her. Quickly, she pulled herself aboard her own boat, for she knew that Jo's rages were sometimes blind and violent, and he was capable of threatening to run her over with his boat. She didn't believe he would actually do it, but he might hit her by accident.

Aiming directly at Paloma's pirogue, Jo kept his motor at full throttle until he was only ten or twelve feet from her, then cut his power altogether. His boat stopped six inches from Paloma's, and it caused a swell that lifted her boat and tipped it and almost spilled her overboard.

Manolo, cheeks livid with anger, whipped his bow line around her anchor rope and made it fast. His fishing line was wrapped in a tight spiral around the bow line. He tried to unravel it, but every time he freed a loop of fishing line, the loop behind it kinked and doubled. He took a knife from his belt and cut the fishing line and snarled at Jo, "If you can't make her behave, *I* will."

"Don't worry," Jo said. "I'll take care of her."

"Jo, look!" said Indio, who had put the glass-bottom bucket overboard and was surveying the seamount. *"Cabríos.* Dozens of them. And goldens! And jacks! Jesus, a million jacks!"

Jo looked at Paloma and said, mocking her, "Not much out here, eh? Not many groupers. Just the same old stuff. I knew I couldn't trust you."

Paloma was stunned. *"You* couldn't trust *me*? Who was it who said he wanted to learn to dive?"

"I do, I do."

"To study things, to learn about animals."

"I do."

"No. All you want to do is kill things."

"No," Jo said, and he grinned. "I want to kill things and *then* I want to learn things. When I can sell enough fish to get enough money so I can get out of here, then I'll learn things— in Mexico City."

Paloma took the knife from her belt again and moved forward toward the mooring line.

"Paloma," Jo said in a tone reminiscent of Viejo's martyr voice, "don't be so silly."

"Give up, you mean. Let you kill everything here."

"There you go again, exaggerating. Even if I wanted to I couldn't kill everything on this seamount. If we take something, something else comes in to replace it. The sea goes on forever, you ought to know that."

"That's nonsense. You could wipe out the whole place."

"I'm not going to argue with you, but . . . what do you care, anyway? We won't take your precious oysters."

"What? I . . ."

Jo smiled. "Didn't think I knew, did you?"

What does he know? Paloma wondered. He can't know about the necklace. He can't. He'd spoil it. If he knew, he'd find some way to spoil it, just to get back at me for . . . for what? For succeeding where he failed?

Paloma stalled. "Knew what?"

"That you take oysters from here. You're so pure, you never take anything from the sea, sure, sure. Well, I've seen oyster shells in your boat." Jo chuckled. "Or that thing you call a boat." He looked around and was pleased at the appreciative smiles from Indio and Manolo.

"A couple of oysters," she said, relieved, and she added for emphasis, "to eat right here. That's all."

"That's what we want: a few fish to sell. That's all."

"Jo . . ." Paloma hesitated before continuing. "Papa wanted this seamount saved, left as it is. He told me we had a kind of trust, that we had to preserve it. It . . . it was his favorite place."

Jo flushed. "I know that. You think I didn't know that?" The words spilled from his mouth. He turned to Indio and said contemptuously. "Of course I knew that. You heard me say that."

Indio looked quizzically at Jo, but said nothing.

Then Jo glared at Paloma and shouted, "Papa is dead, Paloma! Dead, dead, dead!"

She put her hands to her ears, for she did not want to hear.

"I don't care if he told you to save the whole world! He is dead, and what he said doesn't mean a damn! Do you understand that? Not a God damn! It is what I say that makes a damn, and I say I am more important than your stupid fish!"

There was nothing more Paloma could say, and so she raised her knife to cut the mooring line.

"That won't stop us."

"Yes it will. I'll pull my anchor and go. You'll never find this place again."

"I'll buoy it."

"I'll cut your buoys away."

"I'll take landmarks."

"You?" Paloma sneered. "You couldn't find your way around the house with a landmark. You don't know how."

"I can learn."

Paloma knew he was right. He could learn to take land-marks, and once he had the skill, he could find the seamount as easily as she did.

"Look, Paloma, we don't have to fight like this." Jo was trying to sound reasonable. "We can work it out. We can still be friends."

Paloma had been looking away from him. Now her eyes snapped back to his face, to see if he was purposely mocking her. He was looking intensely sincere.

He said, "I'll make a deal with you."

"What deal?"

"I won't tell anybody about this place. It only makes sense that I'll keep my word; after all, it's good for me, too. We'll fish it with lines only, no nets. Anything we catch that we can't use, we'll throw back."

Paloma saw that Jo's mates were eyeing him as if they thought he had lost his mind, but they stayed silent.

"You have to admit that's fair," Jo said. "I don't *have* to do anything. I could come out here and throw dynamite over-board."

"You could," Paloma agreed. "But you know that if you did"—she hoped her voice had a tone of quiet menace—"I'd get revenge. Somehow, someday, you'd pay."

Jo roared with laughter and slapped Indio on the back, but there was a brittle quality to his laughter, for Paloma was—physically, at least—an unknown and thus an unmeasurable adversary. He was bigger and stronger, but he seemed to sense that she was quicker and smarter, and driven by a pas-sion that gave her courage.

Paloma thought about Jo's "deal" and concluded at once that it was no deal at all; it was a not-very-subtle kind of blackmail. If Paloma agreed to let them fish as often and take as much as they wanted, they would not spoil a good thing by spreading the word to their competitors. If she harassed them by cutting away their bait and their boat and their buoys, they would broadcast the location and its richness.

Worse still, Paloma doubted that they would be able to keep their end of the agreement. It was inevitable that one of them would find himself in a conversation in which he needed something to brag about, a feat that would set him apart from and above his rivals. And once the existence of the seamount was known, its location would follow speedily.

It was also inevitable that before long Jo and his mates would begin to fish with nets. The temptation would become too great to resist. It would be like placing a plate of Easter sweet rolls before the three famished boys and recommending that they eat no more than one apiece because there would be no more when that plate was gone. They would see huge schools of *cabríos* and jacks beneath their boat, and each flashing body would ring in their minds as a silver coin. They would be catching four or six or fifteen fish on their lines, and they would begin to speak of the immense fortune that was swimming away from them because they could not use nets. Then they would agree to try the nets just this once, to see how many fish they could catch—an experiment, they would say, that's all. They would catch hundreds and hundreds, and there would be no satisfying them with less. The seduction would be complete.

They would tell each other (and believe the words) that fishing with nets was fine and just, because God had given man dominion over all the animals.

"What about it?" Jo said. "Do we have a deal?"

Suppose she said no. Suppose she declared open war on them. It was possible that she could make their days on the seamount so miserable that they would leave. It was more likely, though, that their response would be to confide in a few of their friends and bring two or more boats out with them. Paloma would be overwhelmed. They would begin to use nets; life on the seamount would end even sooner. She had no choice. By agreeing, she might buy time.

"Okay."

"Smart," Jo said. "Very smart." Like a military commander ordering his troops to advance, Jo gestured at Indio and Manolo, telling them to start fishing. Obviously, he was enjoying himself enormously: he was the leader who had negotiated a favorable truce that exploited his enemy's weakness, and now he would deploy his forces to reap the rewards of his wisdom.

Paloma watched as Indio and Manolo baited hooks and dropped their weighted lines overboard. She put on her mask and leaned over the side of her boat and looked down into the water.

The manta was still there, still immobile, ten feet below the surface. The fishing lines passed four or five feet in front of the manta's left wing. If the manta were to decide suddenly to leave, and if, as usual, it gained momentum by slowly raising and lowering its wings and gradually flying forward, its left wing would collide with the fishing lines. It might brush them aside and proceed unharmed. But if the wing were to strike the lines solidly, and if there were tension from above and below—preventing the slack that would be needed to permit them to buckle and slide aside—the lines might slice through the flesh. Or they might lodge in the flesh, as the fisherman's nets had, and bite deeper and deeper as the manta struggled.

The injury would be similar to the one Paloma had just treated, but more severe, for the thin monofilament line could cut through the flesh and, perhaps, even amputate part of the wing. The outcome then would be certain death.

Paloma put on her flippers and slipped the snorkel through her mask strap.

"Where're you going?" Jo asked.

Manolo called out, "Stay away from my line."

"Don't worry," Jo said to him. "We made a deal. She knows she better not fool with me."

Paloma said nothing. She rolled over the side of her boat, breathed deeply, and dived to the manta. She checked the wound and saw that the flesh she had packed in was staying firm; it had not begun to unravel and shred. Perhaps it would heal and grow. Without the constant abrasion of the ropes, probably it would not get worse.

There were no predators or parasites nearby, which told Paloma that the manta was not emitting distress signals. Its mechanisms must be gaining confidence of survival. And that made her feel good.

What the manta did not need, however, was a new injury.

So, after Paloma had examined the wound and patted it and gently stroked the flesh around it, she hovered above the furled horn on the right side and reached down and pressed on it. She wanted to guide the manta, and since it had responded once before to her touch on one of its horns, she was guessing that the horns were as sensitive as a horse's mouth, and that the manta would react to pressure on its horns by moving in a way that would relieve the pressure.

When the manta did not respond at once, Paloma pressed harder, bending the horn toward the bottom. She felt a shudder as, somewhere deep in the core of the giant, a message was received, almost as if a command had been given for the boilers to be stoked, the engine to be started, the vessel to be moved. Silently, the right wing dipped, the left wing lifted, and together they heaved once up and down. The pressure pushed Paloma away and forced an explosion of bubbles from her mouth. When the bubbles cleared, she saw the manta bank to the right and keep rolling, like an airplane in a spin, as it flew toward the bottom.

Jo had watched this through his viewing box on the surface. Now, as the others held their lines, he took up a honing stone and began to rub it in tight circles against the point of a harpoon.

"What are you going to do with that?" Manolo asked.

"The deal just said no nets."

"But what you gonna stick?"

Jo gestured at the deep water where the manta had gone. "He'll be back."

Manolo whistled. *"There's* a few pennies."

"I *told* you I'd take care of you."

"You did?"

"Sure. Remember? I said all you had to do was tell me where she'd gone, and I'd take care of the rest."

"Oh."

"You two stick with me and we're going to be fine," Jo said, smiling. "Just fine."

Below, Paloma watched the manta swim toward the bottom. It was on its back, showing its brilliant white underbelly, and as it arrived at the rocky top of the seamount it continued its slow and easy roll, spinning and descending, like a child falling down a sand pile, until the black of its back became one with the dark water of the abyss and Paloma could see it no more.

She wanted to follow it, to roll with it down the side of the seamount, to make discoveries with it and be part of the harmony of the sea.

Instead, her body sent her signals that told her she was very much a human being and that if she intended to continue to be a live human being, she had better ascend.

On her way up, she continued to look down, happy that she had been able to help the manta, hoping that it would survive, sad that in order for it to survive it would probably have to stay away from this seamount that was no longer a sanctuary, and—struck by this last realization—suddenly very angry.

At the distant limit of her vision, something was moving, thrashing violently. For a second, Paloma thought it was the manta—perhaps it had snagged a fishing line, or been attacked by something—but then the animal was drawn a bit closer, into her field of focus, and she saw that it was too small to be the manta.

Then, as it drew still closer, she could see that whatever it was was struggling to return to the bottom, fighting something that was forcing it to the surface. Because she had never seen such sights on the seamount, it was two or three seconds before she realized what she was watching: a fish caught on a hook, being dragged up to the boat.

And then the fish was only a few feet from her, struggling less and rising fast, and she saw what it was and felt a rush of bile into her throat: a triggerfish—exactly like the one, perhaps exactly the one, she had seen valiantly defending its egg cache.

Impulsively, she put out a hand, hoping to grab the line and free the fish, but she was too far away, and before she could move closer, the fish had passed her. She looked up through the last three feet of water between her and the surface and saw the fish, limp now with exhaustion, splash into the sunlight and disappear into the shadow of Jo's boat.

She reached for the side of her own boat, broke through

the surface and spat out her snorkel, and, choking, shouted, "Put it back! Quick!"

Manolo looked at her as if she were mad. "What?"

"Throw it back!" Paloma gasped. "You don't have much time."

Manolo looked at Indio, and they smiled and shook their heads at one another.

Manolo said, "I've got all the time in the world."

"But . . . you . . ." The words were a jumble in Paloma's mind. Thoughts crossed over thoughts, and they all bunched together and blocked each other out. She wanted to, *had* to tell Manolo that the triggerfish must be returned to the water immediately; that in less than a minute the sun would begin to harm its skin and cause ulcers; that in only two or three minutes, the fish would asphyxiate, for it could not draw oxygen from air, that it was probably already in some kind of shock from the struggle on the line but that it might survive if it could get back into the soothing saltwater *now*.

But in spite of all she wanted to say, nothing came out of her mouth except, ". . . you don't understand."

Again Manolo smiled, and what should have been obvious to Paloma all along now struck her like a blow to the head: it was *she* who hadn't understood. And what she hadn't understood was that Manolo had no intention whatsoever of returning the triggerfish to the water, that he regarded the triggerfish as fairly caught and rightly his, and that he would consider anyone who tried to prevent the fish from dying in the bottom of the boat to be a thief.

Now that she did understand, she could say only, "But why?"

"Why what?"

"You don't eat that fish. Nobody eats triggerfish."

"Cats do."

"*What?*"

"Grind it up, make pet food out of it. Very nourishing." Manolo held up the twitching triggerfish and whinnied, "Here, kitty . . . here, kitty." Then he dropped the fish back into the bottom of the boat.

"But . . . but . . . that beautiful thing," Paloma sputtered. "You'd waste its life for . . ."

"What waste? Get a lot of 'em, they pay for 'em." Manolo reached for another piece of bait on his hook.

Paloma knew better than to argue; it would be a waste of time—not only her time, but the fish's time. Every second she spent trying to save it, it was dying.

"Throw it *back*!" she screamed.

Manolo gazed at her, and there was no expression in his eyes. "Okay," he said. "You've convinced me."

He reached into the bottom of the boat and picked up the triggerfish by its tail. He pretended to examine it for a moment, then said, "Looks a little faint. Better wake it up." He swung the fish high and slammed it down on the gunwale of the boat. The sleek body, once purple and gold, now mustard and dull grey, shivered once and was still.

Manolo looked to Indio, who was grinning, and said, "That didn't work. I don't get it." Then he turned to Paloma. "You know so much about fish. Here. You try." And he threw the fish across the water.

It landed in front of Paloma and splashed water in her face. The flat body floated on its side. The fins did not flutter, the gills did not pulse. The eye, which in life was a black so vivid that somehow it manifested fear and fury, calm and curiosity, was now as flat and dead as a porthole into an empty room.

Paloma held the corpse, to keep it from drifting away in the tide. She said nothing, for there was nothing she could say that would make any difference—certainly nothing that could change what had already happened, and probably nothing that would change what was going to happen.

She looked at Manolo, who was baiting his hook and glancing furtively at Indio for approval, and at Jo, who had been looking at her but quickly shifted his eyes away as soon as he saw her looking at him. Now he pretended to be deeply concerned about a knot in his fishing line.

Jo is trying not to look embarrassed, Paloma thought, but he *is* embarrassed because he has no real control over these others. Even he wouldn't be stupid enough to pull a stunt like Manolo's so soon after trying to appear reasonable. But he could not stop Manolo—would not have tried to stop him, for Manolo would have told him to stick a fish hook up his nose and pull out his brains, and Jo's self-image as commander-in-chief would be exposed for what it was: basically a fraud, tolerated by the others for only two reasons—the boat (which had been Jobim's) belonged to him, and he had engineered the deception that found Paloma's seamount.

In a way, Manolo had done Paloma a favor. Like a deft surgeon with a sharp knife, he had excised from Paloma a tumor of softness, of gullibility, of desire to be liked, of willingness to trust. Like one of the ancient pirates who used to sneak up on his victims flying a friendly flag and then, at the last moment, break out his pirate banner, Manolo had shown their true colors.

Without a word, Paloma reached behind her for her knife. Swiftly, she cut the triggerfish in half, then in quarters. As soon as blood began to billow in the water, the tiny sergeant-majors materialized and searched in frenzy for the meal that must be there.

Paloma let the pieces of triggerfish fall one by one, and through her mask she watched each one as it was consumed by the swarming sergeant-majors.

She felt numb doing this, as if somehow she was compensating for the evil that Manolo had done, restoring a natural balance that had been upset by his brutality. He had killed an animal and would have let it rot in the sun until it could be ground into powder—an end that denied the animal's life any dignity. She had at least achieved a disposition that was cleaner, quicker, and more natural. Forget that the triggerfish had died at the hands of a pig. Its body was now being returned to its home, serving to nourish the other creatures of the seamount, and prolonging the life of the community.

The blood dispersed and became part of the sea; the pieces of fish descended into the mists, shrunk to nothing by the frantic nibbling of the little fish that, from here, looked like clustered bees. Only the bones would reach the bottom.

Paloma climbed into her boat and removed her mask and flippers. In the other boat, all three were now fishing, and they did not notice her as she went forward and tugged at her anchor line to shake the killick loose from the rocks below. The killick was well caught, and Paloma had to bounce the rope several times, pulling it this way and that, hauling it tight and giving it slack, to force the iron to shift position and work loose. At last, she felt an easing of the strain on the rope, and when she pulled now, it came up at a steady pace.

Free of the rocks, Paloma's boat drifted off the seamount. Moored to Paloma's boat, Jo's boat drifted with it.

Jo was the first to sense that something was wrong. The others' lines were already down; they had been hanging within a couple of feet of the bottom. When the tide carried the boat, it carried their lines as well, so they felt no difference. But Jo was just letting his line down when the boat came adrift. He waited for his hook and sinker to strike bottom, but they kept falling, for by now the boats were away from the seamount and over a bottom that was four thousand feet away. Jo's line fell and fell, and the deeper it went the faster it fell, until his entire spool of line was all but empty.

He turned and looked at Paloma's boat in time to see her pull her killick aboard and cast his boat away from hers. He shouted, "Hey!"

"I have to go home," Paloma said calmly. "Put down your own anchor." Then she knelt in the pirogue and raised her paddle.

"But where's the bottom?"

"Right there," Paloma said, pointing vaguely to a spot in the sea a couple of hundred yards away. "You can't miss it. Not a fine navigator like you."

The others were already hauling in their lines, and Jo rushed to bring his aboard. He shaded his eyes and squinted at the shore, hoping to recall landmarks barely noted when he had approached the seamount. He started the outboard motor and put it in forward gear at half throttle and aimed it against the tidal flow, reasoning that to recapture the seamount all he would have to do was reverse the direction of his drift.

"Put the bucket over," he ordered Indio. "Tell me when we're there." They had not been drifting long, so he assumed he would be directly over the seamount within a few minutes.

Indio put the glass-bottom bucket over the side, then gripped it tightly with both hands, for the movement of the boat against the strong tide tended to tear the bucket from him. All he saw below was blue.

"Well?" Jo said impatiently.

"Nothing."

"You got to be wrong."

Indio looked up from the bucket. "Kiss a goat. Look for yourself." Indio snickered and added, "Mister fine navigator."

Jo put the motor in neutral and took the bucket from Indio. The tide caught the bow of the boat and swung it wide to the left and pushed it half a circle around, then struck the stern and pushed it after the bow: slowly, the boat was drifting in circles. Jo paid no attention. He stared through the glass-bottom bucket at the endless carpet of blue beneath him.

"Impossible!" he said.

Manolo smiled. "A miracle!"

"God's will!" chimed Indio.

"Shut up!" Jo said. He brought the bucket aboard and put the motor in gear and gave it full throttle. The boat lurched forward, rose to a plane, and travelled several hundred yards before Jo got his bearings and turned the bow against the flow of the tide. He continued uptide until he judged he had compensated for his movement sideways, then stopped and told Indio to look again.

"Nothing."

Manolo said, "I think you're way off to the side."

"I can't be," Jo insisted.

"You could be above it," Indio suggested. "You travelled long enough."

"No. Did you see how far we drifted?"

Manolo said to Indio. "There's only one thing for sure: he doesn't know his butt from his bucket about where he is."

Jo said, "You could do better?"

"I couldn't do worse."

Manolo looked at Indio, who looked at Jo and shook his head and murmured, "What an ass."

Jo was confused. His command was unravelling, and he could not deal with sniping from two people at once. And so he focused on one, on Indio, and said, "Get out."

"Get out of what?"

"The boat." Standing in the stern, Jo pointed at the sea. "Get out of my boat."

"And what?" Indio said, laughing. "Walk home?"

"I don't care. It's my boat, and I say get out!"

"And I say—" Indio mocked his imperious tone "—go suck a lemon!"

Jo took a step toward Indio, Indio grabbed the bulwarks on either side of the boat, the boat yawed dramatically, Jo lost his footing and started to fall overboard. To save himself, he twisted in mid-air and fell across the motor. The motor was hot, and Jo yowled like a scorched cat and pulled his hands away from the motor and lost his balance and rolled into the water. He hit head-first and went under for a second and came up sputtering and clawing for a hand-hold.

Indio guided his hand to the side of the boat and said, feigning concern, "What'd you do that for? You always tell me you don't like swimming."

Jo gurgled and sputtered and tried to utter a threat, but all that came out was drool.

"If I were you," Manolo said, "I'd get back in the boat."

Jo struggled to haul himself aboard and then lay panting across the after thwart. He scowled at the other two, and hated them for forming an alliance against him, hated them for seeing through him, hated them for making fun of him, hated everything because there was nothing he could do about anything. Except . . .

Jo shaded his eyes and stood up and looked across the water. Far away and moving still farther, appearing from this distance no bigger than a piece of driftwood, was Paloma's pirogue.

If she hadn't cast them loose, none of this would have happened. They would not have lost the seamount, and, in trying to find it, Jo would not have suffered the collapse of his authority. All he had left to give him superiority over Indio and Manolo was his boat, and that was not enough. They could always find someone else with a boat.

What he hated most about the collapse of his façade was that he had been so careful, so meticulous in erecting it. By being extra-cautious on the sea, he had assured that his seamanship had never been tested; by staying in the same fishing spots, he had never had to try his nonexistent navigational skills; by announcing that he wanted to learn to dive, he had scored points for courage, while knowing full well that once he had stolen from Paloma the secret of her seamount she would never agree to teach him anything.

He didn't care about the respect of others except insofar as it encouraged them to help him reach his goal—the acquisition of enough money to leave this island and get away from this wretched sea and into a city, where life depended on the function of mechanical things that he could create and care for and repair.

Here he was a misfit, and he knew it, but he had survived. Until now. With a single thoughtless gesture, Paloma had destroyed his credibility with Indio and Manolo. The only way to restore that credibility was to destroy its destroyer, to prove once and for all that he was stronger, more worthy, than Paloma. And such a proof would settle more than the matter of the moment: it would avenge the humiliation he had felt when his father had replaced him with a girl.

He would bring her to her knees before him. She would acknowledge his superiority, beg for his mercy, promise to obey him, and . . . He would think of other things when the time came.

Jo turned and yanked on the motor's starter cord. The motor caught at once, which he took as a good omen, and he pushed the throttle open and spun the boat around.

"Where we going?" Manolo asked. Pounded by the thumping bow, he half stood, letting the muscles on his legs absorb the strain.

"She's gonna put us back on that seamount," Jo shouted above the noise of the engine.

Indio said, "I bet we could find it ourselves."

"If we had a week," Jo replied. He poked a finger at Indio's chest. "Every minute we're not fishing that seamount, she's costing us money. She's costing *you* money. You want to go to La Paz and fly on an airplane and see things and meet people?"

"Yeah. You know that."

"Then blame her that you're stuck here." Now he pointed at Paloma's pirogue, which was growing larger and closer every moment. "She's the one got you chained to the island; she's taking the money from your pocket."

"I never thought of that."

"Well, think of it. Because we're gonna stop it right now."

Paloma was more than halfway home when she heard the outboard bearing down on her. Immediately she sensed Jo's mood—if not his precise intention—because the engine noise broadcast an unmistakable message: only someone ignorant of boats or out of control would run an engine at full speed in the open sea. It was dangerous to the sailors and damaging to the engine. Jo knew boats. The engine pitch was at peak hysteria, and so too, Paloma sensed, was Jo.

It had probably been a mistake to cast Jo's boat loose, for she had known he would soon be lost. He had never learned how to interpret tides and currents, couldn't differentiate the subtle shades of blue and green that would tell him how deep the water was and what kind of bottom was below. What she could not have known was how vulnerable he was, and how quickly his embarrassment would change to rage.

Paloma stopped paddling and waited, for there was no point in trying to outdistance him. She wondered if there was anything she could say that would defuse him. The engine noise came closer, a shrill and painful scream. She looked up and saw the white hull rise out of the water and slam down, spewing rooster-tails of spray from both sides of the bow. The boat was aimed directly at her.

Still she waited, now shaken by a new possibility: might he actually ram her pirogue? Could he be *so* stupid? He might sink the pirogue, true, but he would certainly damage his own boat as well. She wondered if she should jump overboard and go underwater and wait for him to pass. But then he might take her boat. Besides, it was a cardinal rule that you never abandoned your boat unless it became absolutely . . .

They were upon her.

The white bow rose over her and came straight at her, and for a split second she thought she would be crushed. Then, suddenly and violently, the bow skewed off to the left and she had a flashing glimpse of Jo's face and the shrieking moment before a mount of water struck the pirogue and lifted it nearly vertical. Paloma threw herself against the far bulwark, against the lean of the boat, and it righted itself and settled into a trough. Quickly she steadied herself and stood up to see where Jo's boat had gone. She had to know where he was so she could see him if he came at her again.

The boat was thirty or forty yards away, turning in a tight circle, running over its own wake, caught in crisscross patterns of swells and chop, the motor spewing smoke and screeching as the propeller bit through pockets of air instead of water. Manolo stood in the bow, bracing himself with the anchor rope, his head thrown back, laughing. Indio sat amidships, steadied by an arm pressed against each bulwark. And Jo knelt in the stern, turning the boat and aiming it once again at Paloma.

This time he turned away a second sooner—Paloma was able to keep the pirogue from capsizing simply by shifting the weight in her knees and balancing with her hands—and then he stopped. His boat wallowed a couple of feet away.

"Get aboard," he said, indicating his boat.

"Why?"

"You're going to take us back to that seamount."

"Find it yourself."

"I'm not asking you; I'm telling you. Get aboard!"

Without thinking, Paloma raised a hand and ticked the thumbnail off her front teeth at Jo. As soon as she had done it, she knew it had been a mistake, for the rude gesture compounded the effect of her refusal: it showed not only defiance but contempt. Jo blushed, and Manolo and Indio exchanged snorts of amazement, for neither of them had ever seen a female make that gesture to a male. It was beyond insolence; it was unthinkable.

Jo put his boat in gear and turned away, and Paloma could see the veins in his neck protruding thickly. He drove the boat perhaps thirty yards, then turned again toward her.

"One last time," he called to her. "Will you take us back to the seamount?"

Silently she shook her head.

"Yes you will. I gave you a chance to do it the easy way, but if you want to go the hard way, that's okay with me."

She heard his engine yowl as he revved it in neutral, and she knew what he intended to do. He wanted to capsize her, to separate her from her pirogue so that she would have to beg him for a ride, and he would pick her out of the sea only if she would take him to the seamount.

But she would not give in, would not surrender the seamount, would not betray herself and her promise to her father just for the sake of putting money in Jo's pocket. If he wanted the seamount, he would have to find it himself and take it himself. She knew that eventually he would find it, but it would not be with her cooperation. Meanwhile, for as long as he wanted to upset her pirogue, she could keep it upright by balancing with her hands and knees. Soon enough he would get bored, or decide that he had made his point, and he would go away.

Then she saw the oar.

His boat was directly in front of hers, his bow facing hers. He always carried two oars, in case his motor died and he had to row home, and now he had fitted one into an oarlock and had directed Indio to hold it horizontal, so that most of the hardwood shaft stuck straight out from the side of the boat and the oar blade was turned so its sharp edge faced straight ahead, straight at Paloma.

Again Jo gunned his engine in neutral, the way an airplane pilot does before takeoff to make sure the engine will give maximum power at the critical moment. Together, Jo and his boat seemed to be some strange monster pawing the sea, preparing to charge.

Now, for the first time, Paloma felt genuine fear, for she knew she had badly miscalculated. She was no longer dealing with Jo, but with a mindless, violent creature who had surfaced only once before and whose single appearance had finally and irrevocably ruined Jo's relationship with his father.

THE SCARS CAUSED by Jo's panic underwater had healed. Jobim had not only forgiven him but had even come to regard the episode as his own fault for having pushed Jo too hard. Jobim had taken Jo's training back a few steps and had proceeded more slowly, more gently.

They had still been a team.

It was late summer, in a lull between the migratory cycles that mark the end of one fishing season and the beginning of another. Every year at this time, the islanders had a fiesta. It was an ancient festival that had been going on since well before Viejo's memory, must have gone on even before the time of the Spaniards, for some of the masks that some of the children wore represented old gods (their names long since forgotten) that lived here before the Christian God.

The centerpiece of the fiesta was a fishing tournament. Anyone could enter and could fish with anything he wanted—hooks, harpoons, spears—anything except nets. The winner was the fisherman who returned with the most weight of fish.

Jobim had entered the tournament every year, and every year he came in last. He had no interest in prizes, no need for public approval, no fondness for catching masses of fish. What amused him about the tournament was the challenge of trying to catch fish in ingenious ways, ways that gave the fish a more-than-even chance.

One year he fished without a boat and with barbless hooks. He swam out to the nearest shoal and fished with bent pins. He hooked several fish, most of which straightened out his homemade hooks and fled. With his last hook (a huge safety pin), he snagged a big grouper and, by playing it with infinite patience and care, brought it to the surface. Only then did it occur to him that he had no way of getting his 50-pound prize to shore. So he removed the safety pin from the lip of the grouper and turned the exhausted fish around and pushed it back down into deep water.

Another year he had used a boat but no fishing gear. He anchored his boat and surrounded it with chum—a savoury blend of tiny baitfish and guts and blood. The chum attracted schools of jacks and legions of sergeant-majors and a dozen groupers and a few sharks, all of which swarmed around his boat. Jobim's challenge that year was to catch the fish barehanded, as a bear does in a stream. His trophies at the end of the day consisted of countless puncture wounds in his palms, caused by his grabbing fish by their sharp dorsal spines, and one mangled fingertip, souvenir of a grouper who had mistaken his finger for a bit of chum.

This particular year he had entered the tournament with Jo as his partner. They were going to fish underwater, using spears Jobim had fabricated by copying a picture he had seen in a magazine. The spear was a steel rod, propelled by a rubber sling attached to a wooden sleeve.

Perhaps with long hours of practice a fisherman could learn to be accurate with one of these spears, but Jobim had finished making them the afternoon before the tournament, so he and Jo had been able to practice for only an hour or two.

The balance in the sling was precarious: usually, the spear skewed away too soon and shot up or down or off to the side. Or the spear skidded and slipped on its way out of the sleeve, and plopped listlessly and harmlessly out and down. Or Jo held the sling wrong, and it slapped so hard against his wrist that it left an angry red welt.

Though he had never dared say so to his father, Jo desperately wanted to win the tournament, for he felt he needed a badge of accomplishment to give him stature with his friends. He had hoped that by fishing underwater with his father's invention, he would have an advantage over the competition. Now that he saw that the invention wasn't so marvellous, however, he was distressed.

"I'll never hit anything with that," he had said. "We don't have a chance."

"Probably," Jobim agreed, unaware of the significance that Jo was attaching to the tournament. "But we'll have fun. Most people only *use* the sea; we *enjoy* the sea."

But Jo didn't enjoy the sea; he wanted to get out of it what he could, and be done with it.

By midday, he and Jobim had caught nothing. There were plenty of fish around, but neither of them could hit a thing. Every time Jobim missed, he would moan underwater and pretend to tear his hair and then would laugh and dive to retrieve his spear. Every time Jo missed, he cursed bitterly. Finally, he left his father alone in the water and returned to the boat.

All around them, other fishermen were hauling fish aboard their boats. Nearby were some of his friends, with their fathers, and when they saw that he had caught nothing, they taunted him for being incompetent and for obeying a father so foolish as to try to catch fish by sticking them with a steel rod.

Jo felt the blood rushing to his face and pounding in his

neck, and before he knew what he was doing he had leaped to his feet and cocked his spear and unleashed it at the nearest boat. The spear had clanged harmlessly in the bow of the boat, but it had scared the fishermen enough to drive them away—shouting angry threats at Jo.

And then Jo—frantic now beyond reason to prove that he was a winner, the best, that even if his father was strange, Jo himself knew how to get things done—pulled a small bag from a cubbyhole beneath a thwart. He had never thought he would have to use this bag, didn't know what would happen if he did, but he was glad he had brought it along, for the situation called for extreme measures.

The bag contained firecrackers—the big, canisterlike ones with the waterproof fuses—bought in La Paz for the fiesta and stolen by Jo from the common store.

Now he would show them who could catch the most fish. The firecrackers would explode underwater, so no one would hear them. Stunned fish would float to the surface. He would gather them up, pile them in his boat and later stick them with his spear to make it seem that he had caught them. It didn't occur to Jo that there was anything wrong with this stratagem: devious, yes; tricky, yes; clever, certainly. But wrong? The rules said only, no nets. Jobim might even admire his ingenuity.

Jo lit one of the firecrackers and threw it overboard, from the side of the boat away from where he had last seen Jobim's shadowy form underwater. As he watched it sink and waited for it to explode, he wondered just how much damage a little explosion like that would do to a fish.

He never thought to wonder what it would do to a man—until, after he had heard the muffled WHUMP, he saw his father thrashing, struggling toward the surface and saw the clouds of blood streaming from his ears.

When Jobim's head had broken the surface, there had been a moment before his eyes rolled back and he fainted from shock and pain. In that moment his eyes had locked on Jo's, and in his eyes were accusations of stupidity, recklessness, and cowardice.

Jo had screamed, "I'm sorry! I'm sorry!" over and over, but no one had heard him.

Now, waiting for Jo to charge at her again, Paloma knew that the same kind of switch had been tripped again in Jo's head. Whether a reservoir of restraint remained within him she could not tell, but, for the moment, she was faced with an irrational animal whose fury was being fuelled by encouragement from his unthinking mates.

With the engine in full throttle, Jo reached back and flipped the gear lever from neutral into forward. For a second or two, as the pitch of the propeller blades changed and they sought to grip the water, the boat moved not forward but down. The bow rose, then fell, and the boat was up on a plane, flat on the top of the water.

He was determined to capsize her, and so intense was his obsession that until he succeeded he was prepared to hurt her or maim her or perhaps even kill her.

She had resisted so far by counterbalancing. But if she could not use her knees and hands, if she were forced to lie on the bottom of the pirogue, a weight as immobile and unsecured as a sack of grain, when a wave struck the boat and lifted one side high out of water, her weight would roll to the other side and destroy the boat's natural balance and force the high side to keep rising until, finally, it passed the point of no return and pushed the boat upside down.

What frightened her was not the thought of capsizing, but the knowledge of how Jo intended to compel her to lie on the bottom of the pirogue. At full speed, he would sweep the pirogue with his extended oar, from bow to stern. If Paloma stayed on her knees, balancing with her hands, the oar would strike her in the stomach. If she ducked down, it would strike her on the top of her head or her back, for the pirogue was so shallow that she could escape the oar completely only by lying flat.

If she didn't duck quite far enough, or if she lifted her head in an impulse of resistance to capsizing, the oar would hit her in the neck or the face. In this last second, as her eyes focused only on the oar and saw it as a scimitar, she thought of flinging herself overboard but decided against it because she knew it would deprive Jo of the satisfaction he craved. *He* had to do something *to* her.

So she threw herself forward onto her face and covered the back of her head with the palms of her hands and braced her elbows against the sides of the pirogue.

She never saw the oar, never heard it, but she felt the puff of pressure wave that it pushed before it as it swept the pirogue, and she felt the oar's blade nick the pirogue's wooden sides and bounce and nick again.

Then the wake of the motorboat slammed into the pirogue and heaved it upward. Paloma was no longer on her face, but on her side, then over on her back, and then there was only greyness and a hollow slapping sound and she was under the boat. She stayed there, breathing the air trapped beneath the boat, trying to get control of herself and guess what, if anything, Jo planned to do next.

The engine noise told her that the motorboat was moving away and that Jo had throttled back. She heard incoherent voices, talking calmly, and then the engine noise grew louder again. The boat was returning, but slowly this time.

The engine noise dropped to the low mutter of idling speed, and she heard the wavelets lap at the motorboat's hull as it wallowed.

"Where is she?" Indio's voice filtered into the chamber where Paloma's head stuck out of water. He sounded worried.

"You've drowned her!" said Manolo.

"She's not drowned," Jo said. "I'll show you where she is."

Suddenly Paloma's ears were battered by a sharp, metallic clang that echoed from side to side of the wooden cavern. Jo had hammered something—what, she could not imagine—against the upturned bottom of the boat.

"Hey!" he called. "Ready to take us to the seamount?"

Paloma did not reply. Partly, she didn't know what to say, didn't know what another flat refusal would goad him into doing. But partly, too, she hoped that by remaining silent she might scare him—even briefly—into believing she had drowned.

"I knew it!" came Manolo's voice. "She's dead!"

"No," said Jo, but there was a lilt of uncertainty in his

voice, a hint of fear. Again the metal thing struck the bottom of the boat, but softer than before. "Paloma!" he called.

"Paloma!" Indio shouted.

"Leave it to me!" Jo snapped at him. And then Jo took a gamble: "Paloma, I know you can hear me. In my hand is a harpoon. If you don't agree to take us to the seamount, I will punch a hole in the bottom of your boat with my harpoon. Your boat might not sink, but it won't paddle, either, so you will stay here and float with it till kingdom come . . . or you will take us to the seamount in return for a ride home. Your choice."

The harpoon dart dug at the boat, and Paloma heard the steel point grind into the wood fibres. It might take him time to dig a hole through the bottom of the boat, but there was no doubt he could do it. And if the hole was big enough, the pirogue would behave exactly as he said: it would wallow awash and drift with the tide.

She had to surrender; it was the only reasonable thing to do. But why should she apply reason to a situation that had so far been completely irrational? Jo hadn't used reason in what he had done. Why should she? So she stayed beneath her overturned boat, listening to Jo's labored breath as he gouged a hole in its bottom.

First she saw a pinprick of light, and then a shaft the size of a coin, and wood splinters fell on the water before her. Then the head of the harpoon jammed through the hole and turned a couple of times and was withdrawn.

"There!" Jo's shadow crossed the hole and disappeared. "Good-bye, Paloma. You may think you're being proud, but all you are is pigheaded."

Paloma heard Jo pull on the starter cord of the motor. The motor sputtered but did not start.

"We can't leave her," she heard Indio say. "We have to make sure."

"Sure of what?" Jo said. As he talked, Paloma felt herself growing cold, not from the water but from the icy logic oozing from the mouth of this person who was her brother. "Make sure she's under the boat? Make sure she's all right? Why? Suppose she isn't. What are you going to do about it? Nothing. When we get back to shore, we say we have no idea where she is, which is the truth because we don't. You don't talk about it to anyone because you know that if you do I'll come for you. And you believe I mean what I say because I do."

Listening to Jo, Paloma realized that he had accomplished at least one of his goals: he had restored a certain stature to himself among his peers. He could not be different or special by being better or more skilful than the others, so he had set himself apart by being reckless, unpredictable, dangerous. If he could not make them respect him, the next best thing was that they should fear him.

"But believe me," Jo went on, "she is under the boat and she is all right. She will come back to shore and she won't talk about what happened because she'll be too embarrassed, and besides, no one can do anything about it and they probably wouldn't believe her anyway, and if she does talk a lot and complain to our mother I'll get her sometime, and she's like you—she knows I mean what I say and she better treat me better than she has."

Paloma heard the outboard wheeze and jump to life, and she could feel through the water that Jo had put the motor in gear and was driving away.

10

SOON SHE COULD no longer feel the faint tapping in the soles of her feet, the sensation caused by the tiny shock waves emitted by the turning of the propeller. She guessed that the boat was already about a hundred yards away.

She wondered whether she had been right or wrong, smart or foolish, principled (as she believed) or pigheaded (as Jo had said). At best, she had delayed Jo a few days. He would find the seamount eventually and do his damage, perhaps destroy it. And the delaying tactic had cost her . . . what? She couldn't even guess yet. Here she was in the middle of the sea, with the end of the day approaching and no way to get home unless she could devise some way to patch the hole in her boat.

But futile though her gesture might prove to be in the long run, it had been the right thing to do. Jobim would have approved. He would have told her that she had struck a blow for life. And she knew that to strike such a blow himself, he would have gone to almost any extreme.

Once or twice, he *had* gone to extremes. She recalled now a story he had told her about an incident he described as one of the most important, and dangerous, of his life. He was telling her, he had said, to teach her that there were times when you had to take big risks over matters of principle. And he had sworn her to secrecy because if the truth were ever to surface, it could start a war between Santa Maria and some of the other islands in the Sea of Cortez.

Late one summer, the fishermen of Santa Maria had discovered that one of their prime fishing grounds—a deep sea-mount in open water far from shore—was fast becoming bar-ren. Every day it was more difficult to get a fish on the line, and what few fish there were looked scruffy and battered.

Their first thought had been that one of their number was using nets, but it was pointed out that huge nets were imprac-tical in such deep water. None of them had a boat equipped with the powerful electric winches, the wide cockpit, and the support structures necessary to handle the nets.

Then they had concluded that some waterborne plague was killing all the fish. Every now and then, the depths of the sea would spawn and spew up clouds of poisonous micro-organisms that contaminated hundreds of thousands of fish—either making their flesh toxic to human beings, or killing the fish themselves. But again, someone pointed out that if the fish were being killed, they would float to the surface and be seen, and if the fish were being made poisonous, surely by now people would be aware of someone falling sick or dying, either here or in La Paz.

So it had to be something else, something new and strange and alarming. A few people insisted that it was God's way of punishing the fishermen for being careless over the genera-tions, for taking too much too indiscriminately.

Jobim knew that it had nothing to do with God. As usual, people were turning to God because He was a quick answer for unanswerable things. The more Jobim saw and heard, the more he smelled the scent of man.

Contributing to the fancies of the other fisherman was the fact that not one of them had ever seen the top of the sea-mount. None of them dived, none knew anything about what underwater terrain actually looked like. They assumed that fish lived somewhere down there, waiting, presumably, for the chance to bite a baited hook.

But Jobim had seen seamounts, if not precisely this one, and he knew what to look for, and so one afternoon he had paddled out to sea and anchored. Even if he hadn't already known why he had never dived on this seamount, his anchor line would have told him: the killick dropped straight down and shot past five fathoms, past ten fathoms, past fifteen and eighteen and twenty fathoms (the last marked spot on the anchor line) and stopped, at last, at twenty-two fathoms—132 feet.

Jobim could not dive that deep. No one he knew could dive that deep. In fact, as far as he knew, no normal person could breath-hold dive to 132 feet. To dive that far would be like crawling down a tower made of two dozen men standing on one another's shoulders, or like falling from the top of the tallest building in La Paz. There would be no bottom visible for more than half the way down, and when and if you got more than half the way down, from there you wouldn't be able to see the surface.

But Jobim knew enough about his own capabilities to be willing to try—not to go all the way, but to go far enough so he could see the bottom. So he hyperventilated and sped hand-over-hand down the anchor line, toward the blue-black mists, through the gloom where there was no up and no down, until he could see the top of the seamount far below.

He went farther, waiting for the body signs that would tell him to stop, and before they came he had been able to see enough to need to see no more. From 90 or 100 feet he had seen most of the top of the seamount, and the landscape told an obvious tale.

The soft corals and sea fans were lying on their sides, ripped up by their roots like a tree in a *chubasco*. Many of the hard antler corals were broken into small pieces among the rocks. The vegetation of most of the bigger rocks was covered with a layer of sand. One brain coral the size of a bathtub was split in two, and its halves lay in a sand valley like slabs of melon.

There were fish—a few small ones darting in and out of the rocks, and a good-sized *cabrío* that looked healthy until suddenly it flipped over on its back and swam in frantic circles, and one moray eel, dead and wedged into a crevice as if by a swift surge of tide.

The seamount had been devastated by a series of quick, terrible storms whose force had killed nearly every living thing and had maimed the survivors.

Had nature sent the storms, Jobim would have been sad. But he knew they were caused by men, and he was angry.

Fishermen from another island—Santu Espiritu, a few

miles away—must be coming here at night and tossing over-board sticks of dynamite with long waterproof fuses. Long fuses were for the protection of the fishermen: a fuse too short would burn down too fast, and the dynamite would explode too close to the boat, cracking open the bottom and perhaps sinking the boat. But long fuses were a disaster for the sea-mount: they burned all the way down to the bottom, so the dynamite exploded not in open water (where its concussive force would kill the fish in the immediate area) but among the rocks and sand and coral, where pressures would build and channel and spread, killing animals in their dens and destroy-ing the seamount itself.

Underwater, dynamite was a much more terrible weapon than it was on the surface. In air, a stick of dynamite—not packed in anything to contain and amplify the explosion, like rock or cement, not covered with anything to shatter and be-come shrapnel, like glass or pebbles—wouldn't do much dam-age beyond about ten yards. It was said that the detonation of a single stick of dynamite underwater could be felt more than half a mile. It could cause havoc over an area of thousands of square feet.

After the explosions, the fishermen would spread nets on the surface and scoop up the corpses of the animals as they floated up from below.

This was a quick, economical and final kind of fishing. No risk of damage to expensive lines and hooks. No need for baitfish. Everything on the seamount was killed instantly. No time-consuming wait for a fish to bite. Best of all, the fish came to the surface on their own; you didn't even have to pull them up.

It was efficient and illegal and universally condemned as immoral, sacrilegious and self-defeating, for everyone knew that it destroyed fishing grounds and could only hasten the day when whole communities would be forced by starvation to become (the ultimate nightmare of them all) beggars on the streets of Mexico City. Even the worst louts among fishermen considered dynamite fishing beneath contempt.

But Jobim knew enough about certain kinds of people, about how stupidity and brutishness and greed could com-bine to drive a person to do things that even a moment's rational thought would perceive as destructive, to self as well as others. It was the promise of great profit at little expense and no risk, of quick money in the hand right now and don't worry that there won't be any more when the fish are gone. Someone else can weep over that. I'll get mine while I can, and other people can worry about themselves.

It was the same mentality that led the company that made fertilizer in the city to pump its chemical wastes into the harbor. The company got rid of its wastes, which was economical and good. The government, however, began to think that it wasn't a good idea to keep pumping chemicals into the harbor where people swam and fished, so it told the company to stop.

The workers had rioted and tried to burn down the government building, because they said the company couldn't afford to haul its wastes elsewhere, and if it had to do so, some workers would lose their jobs and all would lose an impending raise in pay. The government backed down; the company continued to pump wastes into the harbor.

Two and a half years later, the harbor died. The chemicals had formed a poisonous sludge that coated the bottom and choked all the vegetation and shut off the oxygen in the water and killed every living thing. Guests at the luxury hotels, who swam in the harbor, began to come down with ghastly skin ulcers.

The government ordered the hotels to close and told the chemical company to stop pumping chemicals into the harbor. But the chemical company had made no plans to haul its wastes elsewhere, and so, compelled to stop using the harbor, it closed down.

Because there were no longer any hotels to stay in or restaurants to eat at or waters to swim in, the tourists and vacationers stopped coming to the city, and all the gift shops and boutiques closed and pitched their workers into the streets.

The workers at the chemical company had gotten their raise in pay, and for a few months had enjoyed the money. But because of their insistence on that new money they had lost everything. And it was not just they who were punished, but all the other workers who had lost their jobs. And eventually, "all" became everybody, for the city was deprived of a reason to exist, and slowly but inevitably it ceased to exist.

Nowadays it was a dusty cluster of empty buildings in a ring around the still-dead harbor, with the skeleton of the chemical company standing on a promontory as a reminder to passersby of the fragility of things.

But such lessons were hard to learn and easy to forget, and right then, over that seamount, Jobim had proof that some people still hadn't learned. Almost everyone in the islands had a cousin, or at least an acquaintance, who had chosen quick and easy money at one time or another. Perhaps he had sold the fishing boat his father had left him and taken the money to the city where he intended to go into business for himself, not realizing that he was already in business for himself, the business for which he had been trained and at which he was as good as any in the world. And when he got to the city he found that it was already full of businessmen who were all too eager to relieve him of his money (which was certainly not enough to start a new business anyway), so very soon his money was gone and he was begging for a job cleaning toilets in the city comfort station and smelling, instead of fish and sea air, ammonium chloride that burned the lining out of his nose.

But those people, everyone's cousin or friend, harmed only themselves and their families. These men from Santu Espiritu threatened to destroy the livelihoods of everyone on their own island, on Santa Maria, and on all the other islands as well. For they would not stop until they had cleaned out every seamount, every fishing ground they knew of, had heard of, or could find.

And Jobim knew what they would be saying to themselves, how they would be justifying behavior for which each of their mothers would have spat on them. They would say to one another, and hear one another say in reinforcing response, until they all believed it: if we don't do it, somebody else will; people are no good, and the only ones who survive are those who look out for themselves, and survival, after all, is what life is all about.

Jobim would stop them, but he would have to do it alone. If he alerted other Santa Maria fishermen and they all went out in boats and waited for the raiders from Santu Espiritu, the raiders would see their boats and would flee. There would be a chase and a fight and a lot of people would be hurt. Or, if the raiders escaped to Santu Espiritu, they would deny everything and accuse the people from Santa Maria of making up stories to cover their own misdeeds. There would be a long and bitter fight between the two islands in which everyone would be hurt except perhaps those who deserved to be. And they, meanwhile, would be out at night in new places, destroying life on new seamounts.

So Jobim made a special trip to La Paz and went to see a boyhood friend, a man whose father had received and sold the fish for Jobim's father many years ago. The friend worked in a salvage yard, where ships and boats and machines and cargoes and all sorts of other huge metal things that had been raised from under the water or saved before they could sink were brought to be restored or cut up for scrap.

Jobim and his friend had a beer, then two, and while his friend kept saying (time and again but in different words) that he envied Jobim for being able to be his own man and work at his own pace and live his life on the sea instead of in a place where the noise and the dirt were enough to drive a man crazy, Jobim kept asking questions about the newest methods and the tools of salvage—especially about new ways of separating metals under water, things like hunks of steel or parts of ships.

He said, finally, that a ferryboat had sunk near Santa Maria and was becoming a nuisance to the fishermen because it kept snagging and tearing their nets. The ferryboat was too big to move, but he thought that if he cut it into pieces, perhaps he could tow the pieces into deeper water where they would be out of the way. Would he need to hire underwater welders to do this? Would his friend's salvage company do the job for him? Of course, he couldn't pay much, but . . .

"Thing like that, you wouldn't cut it up," said his friend.

"Oh?" Jobim had known that all along, but he was trying to lead his friend into giving him more information without his friend's knowing why—in case what Jobim had planned went wrong and any part of it was ever traced back to his friend.

"You'd blow it up. The new stuff we use cuts sharper than

a knife and a hundred times quicker than a torch. You mix it, prime it, set it, fire it and POW! The job is done."

"What is this stuff?"

"They call it PLS. It's a liquid, *two* liquids. You carry it in two separate jugs till you're ready to use it, because once it's mixed it starts to generate heat and if it gets too hot it goes off by itself."

"How much would I need to blow up a ferryboat?"

"Depends how big the ferryboat is and how many pieces you want it in."

Jobim described his imaginary ferryboat. It was old and ratty and not too big, and it hadn't been carrying anything of value when it sank. He wanted to be sure there was nothing about this boat that would be of interest to a salvage company. "How much do you think your company would charge to blow it up?" he asked when he was finished.

His friend shook his head. "We wouldn't touch a small job like that."

"I didn't think so. This . . . PLS . . . you talk about, is it hard to use?"

"Easy. Anybody can do it, long as they're careful."

"Even me?" Jobim smiled.

"Someone good with his hands as you? A snap." Then his friend saw where Jobim was taking the conversation, and he said, "But there's a problem."

"Where can I get some?"

"That's the problem. You can't. Have to have a licence for it. It's what they call unstable, and they don't want just anybody to have it and leave it lying around."

"How much would I need?"

"From what you say, a couple of gallons. Say, a gallon of each of the two parts. But you might as well want a ton. You can't buy it."

"Your company . . . wouldn't have any extra . . ."

His friend shook his head. "If we did, we couldn't sell it unless you get a licence."

Jobim didn't know what to ask next. To keep the conversation moving, he said, "That ferryboat is costing a lot of people a lot of money. It's taking food from the mouths of children."

"I wish I could help you. If we were caught, we'd lose our business."

"Of course," Jobim had said. He didn't want to push too hard and put his friend in a difficult position. "You don't have any you could just . . . spill for me, do you?" He smiled again, to show his friend he was joking.

"That stuff, you don't spill," his friend said with a laugh. "There's no such thing as extra. After a job, what's left over we have to throw away."

"Where do you throw it?"

"In the sea."

"Where in the sea?"

His friend waved his hand toward the water. "Right out there. Off Cabo San Juan."

Jobim lowered his voice. "How far off?"

"Not far. Maybe a hundred yards. At the edge of the shelf."

"How deep is the shelf?"

"Fifty, sixty feet. A lot of the stuff falls over the edge, though."

"Some doesn't, I bet."

"I wouldn't know."

"You throw it away mixed?"

"No. It could go off. It's in its separate elements."

"In cans?"

"In plastic bottles."

". . . that don't rust."

His friend nodded.

Jobim looked at the height of the sun in the sky and said, "I have to get back on this tide." He stood and held out his hand to his friend. "It is good to talk with you."

Shaking hands, his friend said, "One more thing, just for your . . . interest: the plastic bottles are different colors. It takes one red and one white to make a whole . . ."

". . . a whole pink one."

Jobim stopped at a store where they sold hardware and electrical parts. Then he returned to his outboard motorboat and made sure that both his gas cans and his freshwater jug were full, because the trip home could take anywhere from six to eight hours, depending on wind and tide. He told everyone at the dock that he was heading straight for Santa Maria, and he took messages from cousins for cousins, from friends for friends.

At the mouth of the harbor he turned right, which was the way home, and waved one more time. The people on the dock waved back and as far as they were concerned he was gone, which was true, although he stopped for a few minutes for a couple of quick plunges off Cabo San Juan.

For the next two days after he got home, Jobim stayed ashore and tinkered. He scavenged things from here and there and built things from this and that and endured all the teasing from his neighbors about how the schools of *cabríos* and jacks were running thicker than ever. People wondered what he was doing, and they asked delicate questions that hinted at the basic question—"What are you doing?"—but they never asked that outright. They all knew Jobim well enough to be aware that he permitted them to know about him only those things he wanted them to know.

Usually, when he was involved in an eccentric project, he let slip information little by little, and saved the final result as a surprise—at which everyone would either marvel (if it was a success) or laugh (if it was a splendid failure). When he failed spectacularly, he laughed harder than anyone. But, in front of children, he made sure they realized that failure was just as important as success because you had to fail in order to know that failure wasn't worth fearing. If you feared failure, you would never try difficult things, and trying was more important than failure or success. (It was a lesson Jo persistently refused to learn: he loathed risks and was frightened by the unknown.)

This time, Jobim let slip no information about anything. He acknowledged only that he was working on some silly notion that was doomed to failure but that had preyed on his mind for so long that he had to play it out to its conclusion.

One night after supper, he told Miranda he was going for a walk, and he disappeared into the twilight. Much later, all anyone would remember was that they were positive they hadn't seen him again that night. He hadn't taken out his boat, that was certain, because many men were down at the dock cleaning fish and sewing nets; he hadn't been entertaining the neighborhood children, because people recalled that

that was the night they had taken turns ministering to the little girl who had been stung by a scorpion; and he hadn't been in his own house until just before dawn. As far as anyone knew, he hadn't been anywhere. (He confessed to Paloma that he had enjoyed causing the mystery; it added spice to the otherwise predictable daily routine of the island.)

In fact, he had gone to the opposite side of the island—uninhabited, wind-burned, rocky, dotted with little puffs of the hardiest vegetation—where there was no lee in which to keep a boat or build a house or even pass a moderately comfortable night.

He skidded and scrambled down the steep slope. About three quarters of the way down, he stopped at a hole in the rock face and tore away the branches he had stuffed into its mouth. Inside was a large plastic garbage bag and a wooden platform about three feet wide and six feet long, to the bottom of which had been attached, with bolts and ropes, four old automobile tire tubes.

He dropped the platform the last fifteen or twenty feet into the water and, with the plastic bag slung over his shoulder, hurried after it and climbed aboard it. He positioned himself on his knees, at the exact centre of the raft with the plastic bag tucked between his legs. Like a surfer on a board, he began to paddle away from the island.

He had picked his night carefully: it was flat calm, so paddling was easy, and there was no moon. There was just enough of a ground swell so his little raft would not be visible in the starlight: an observer's eye would be accustomed to a gently moving horizon: something as small as the raft would blend in. The timing and direction of the tide were exactly as he wanted them.

It was after ten o'clock at night when he arrived at his destination, a spot of water in the open sea, to most eyes no different from any other spot of water in the sea, but to his at the precise juncture of imaginary straight lines drawn from three landmarks faintly perceived—more sensed than seen—by the light of the stars.

From the bag he took a line and a killick. He dropped the killick overboard and waited for it to set in the rocks on the seamount. He checked his drift and the amount of anchor line left and decided that he had ample play: he could pull himself uptide, or let himself drift down-tide, over a distance of a couple of hundred feet.

From the plastic bag he took two gallon jugs, one red and one white. He poured half of each overboard, on opposite sides of the raft, which was a silly caution but one that gave him comfort. Then he poured the contents of the white jug into the half-full red jug, and screwed the cap onto the red jug. The white jug he returned to the plastic bag.

The cap of the red jug had been prepared ashore. A hole had been drilled through it, primer cord fitted through the hole and sealed. The primer cord looked like thin plastic clothesline, which was essentially what it was, except for the fact that it was filled with a substance like gunpowder that burned much hotter and many times faster.

To the other end of the primer cord Jobim had connected, by electrical contacts, a hand-powered generator. You squeezed it, and squeezing it turned some wheels that squirted power into the primer cord.

He lowered the full red jug into the water. If it had been empty and open, the plastic jug would eventually have filled and sunk. But filled now with a liquid of approximately the same density as water, and capped off with a bit of air trapped inside, it floated. Its neck bobbed, and the white primer cord waved back and forth, very visible against the black water.

Jobim didn't want the jug to float on the surface. He wanted it to have enough negative buoyancy so that it would tend to sink and yet be able to be held close to the surface by the tension of the tide working against the primer cord. The tide would try to pull the jug down and away; the primer cord would hold it up and near, and Jobim could pull in or let out more cord until he had the jug suspended where he wanted it —four feet below the surface.

So from the plastic bag he took a handful of pebbles, and he dropped them into the red jug and recapped it and tested it and put more pebbles in and tested it again until, finally, it was right.

And then he lay on his stomach on the raft, and he waited.

With nothing to do but wait, he worried. He worried first that he had thrown away too much of the PLS liquid, that the combined gallon he had saved wouldn't answer his purpose. But if his friend had said two gallons would blow a ferryboat to bits, surely one gallon would do for this job. After all, he was not trying to replicate World War II.

Then he worried that he had too much of the liquid, that it would do too much damage. Maybe he ought to . . .

Just then the light breeze brought the sound of voices. There were men approaching, and they were not being careful to keep their voices low. They had no fear of being overheard, this far out to sea. The only precaution they had taken was to paddle rather than use their motors, for they knew that the sound of a motor carries for miles in still air across still water.

Jobim lay quietly on his raft, his head down so he would make no silhouette against the night sky. He heard four distinct voices separated into two distinct pairs: two boats, travelling together but keeping a convenient distance from one another.

So far, he had guessed right: there had to be more than one boat, because to spread and gather the net from one boat would take so much time that dead fish floating on the surface would begin to drift out of range. A third boat, on the other hand, wouldn't contribute much but would add risk: the more people who knew about these expeditions, the more chance there would be that someone would talk too much. Besides, the fewer partners, the larger each partner's share.

Now, Jobim guessed, the two boats would stay close together. One would drop an anchor, and the other would moor to the stern of the first boat. They would check the drift and ready their nets, and then they would throw the dynamite— probably one stick off each side. The dynamite would explode so deep that all they would feel up here would be a weak thump of pressure on their wooden hulls. Then the anchored boat would feed out the net, and the other boat would drop back and drift with the tide, dragging the net, and paddle in a wide circle, returning finally to the anchored boat.

After a few minutes' wait, all that would remain would be to draw the net tight and haul in the fish and fill their boats and paddle home.

The voices drew closer, and still Jobim heard the sounds of paddles swirling through water, and he knew he had made a terrible error: by picking what he regarded as the ideal spot, he had picked the exact spot they were coming to. They were going to paddle into him, or at least into his anchor line.

Then what? At worst, depending on who these people were, Jobim would find himself in a fight for his life against four men, all carrying knives as an item of clothing and who had sticks of dynamite that they could lob at him from a safe distance; he didn't give himself much of a chance. If he could get close enough to them, and if he had time, he could blow everybody up, including himself, but that wasn't what he had in mind. At best, the four men would deny everything and proceed along as if they had important business elsewhere, and tomorrow night they would show up somewhere else, somewhere Jobim could not wait for them.

But the paddling stopped. Jobim heard the splash of an anchor and the rasping sound of the anchor line rubbing against wood.

They had stopped precisely where he had hoped they would—between five and ten yards down-tide from him, in the line of the drift. He heard something bang against one of the glass net-floats in the anchored boat, and a casual argument about the length of the fuse on one of the sticks of dynamite. He hoped the argument would turn bitter, even for a moment, for raised voices would cover any noise he might make.

Still lying flat on his raft, with his cheek pressed to the wood, he eased the red jug overboard and let it slip back in the tide. He could not place the jug yet—he would have to raise his head to do that—so he held the primer cord and waited for the men to busy themselves.

He heard the scrape of a match and saw the flaring light as it reflected off a stubbly chin. A hand cupped the match, and two fuses touched the flame. The fuses hissed briefly, then sparkled, and an arc of sparks flew off each side of the boat as the sticks of dynamite were thrown into the water. Immediately the men turned to the net and began carefully to prepare it for an orderly slide into the water.

Jobim raised up on his elbows and fed the primer cord behind his boat, letting it out a foot at a time, watching the white cord and hoping the men would not turn around and see it, trying all the while to see in his mind how far down the sticks of dynamite had fallen. It would be nice (not necessary, but nice) if the men could be made to believe that what had befallen them was the result of someone getting access to, and tampering with, their gear, for that would reinforce Jobim's scheme—to convince these people that they were known and marked. But for that, his explosion would have to be coordinated exactly with the detonation of the dynamite below.

He had the jug far enough back now, and he tied off the primer cord and picked up the squeeze generator and closed his eyes, envisioning the falling dynamite. His imaginary perspective was from the seamount, looking up, and he saw the two sticks falling in a slow spiral toward him, and almost on top of him, and so he squeezed the generator once, then again, then again, and he heard the wheel turn, faster and faster as power built and built . . .

There was a sound of ripping as the primer cord detonated, and then as Jobim opened his eyes the world before him erupted. The water beneath the two boats bulged and burst, and in graceful slow motion the wooden boats disintegrated. The force of the explosion directly underneath them separated their planks and dispersed them, and as the bulge of water ruptured, it blew the four men upward, in disarray, like circus clowns on a trampoline.

In a microsecond before the unleashed energy reached Jobim's raft, he thought he had miscalculated and was going to follow the men into the air. But the rubber tubes lashed to his raft absorbed enough of the first hammer blow so that when the raft was heaved clear of the water it did not come apart, and it slapped back down on the sea in one piece, rocking crazily. Even his anchor held; all he had to do was keep from being rolled overboard. He reached into the plastic bag and brought out a powerful electric torch, one of those used to illuminate the surface of the sea for night fishing over the abyss. He did not turn it on, but knelt on his raft with the light in his lap and waited.

There was new turmoil as the men hit the water and sank and came up again and screamed, their shrieks tumbling over one another, unheard, for each man listened only to himself.

"Help!"

"I can't swim!"

"I'm hurt!"

"Oh, God!"

"Mother of Jesus!"

"I'm drowning!"

"Mother of God!"

"Help me!"

"Jesus Mary and Joseph!"

"Help help help!"

Eventually each man found a piece of debris to cling to, and their panic subsided and transformed into anger and outrage and bickering and worry about drowning and drifting away and being eaten by prehistoric monsters of the deep. Floating in the sea in daylight was bad enough; at night, it was the stuff of nightmares. These men were fishermen. They knew what kinds of things lurked down there, and they knew there were things they did not know, things that had bitten off steel leaderwire and straightened giant hooks, things that came up in the night to feed.

If only they could have the security of feeling their feet touch solid bottom . . . but out here, if their feet had touched anything, they would have gone into shock.

"What was that?"

"Nothing."

"Yes it was. I felt something."

"It's in your head."

"There it is again. Oh God!"

"What? What is it?"

"It's dead!"

"What's dead?"

"It's a fish! A dead fish!"

"Where? Where?"

"There's one! Oh God!"

"I felt one! It's all puffed up!"

"There's another one! They're everywhere!"

"Jesus!"

"I'm sick!"

"I told you that fuse was too short!"

"You fool!"

"Somebody must have . . . oh God! Another one!"

"How far is it to . . . ?"

"Don't think about it."

"We're going to drown!"

"Stop it!"

"All of us! We're all going to die!"

"Shut up!"

"Holy Mary mother of God . . ."

"Shut *up*!"

"I'm drifting away!"

"Kick this way, then!"

"I am, I am . . . Oh God! Guts!"

"Forget it!"

"There it is again!"

"What is?"

"It brushed me!"

Jobim switched on the torch, and the four floating men were stunned by the cone of light. They gasped and tried to look behind the light, but the beam was too strong, and they had to close their eyes or turn away. For a moment, they must have thought they were saved, for there were weak smiles. But when Jobim said nothing and did not move toward them, they knew they were not to be rescued, at least not now.

Jobim waited until he was sure their minds had passed through befuddlement, and worry and into true fear, before he spoke. Then he spoke slowly and made his voice as low as he could, trying to sound like an oracle or a cave creature or, in any case, something mysterious and menacing that each of the men would recall in private moments and that would make them shiver and the hair rise on their arms.

"We are Los Vigilantes," Jobim said, and he paused for dramatic effect. "We have followed you and found you out, and we know you. You are evil men."

"No!" cried one. "We're just . . ."

"Quiet!" Jobim roared. He wished there were drums and thunder behind him. "You are evil men, and evil gets what evil gives. You would take the food from the mouths of babies and bring pestilence upon the land." (Words like that had to be effective, he thought. After all, that's the way they talk in the Bible.) "You will die."

"No!" the four voices howled in chorus.

"All men die. There is a time for dying, and your time will come. But perhaps not today."

Silence.

"Perhaps not tomorrow."

Silence.

"But be warned. Your faces are known to us now." He moved the light among the men, so the core of the cone, the brightest spot of light, shone briefly on each face. "One of us will always be with you, through all the days of your life. And when next you sin, know it will not be a secret sin, for the one of us who is with you will know." Jobim stopped. Something was taking shape in his mind, something mischievous. "You will not know who we are. We might be your closest friend, perhaps your brother. You can trust no one. No one. Never again."

Slowly the circle of four men was growing wider, for they had not had the wit to hold hands and so were drifting apart. In a moment, Jobim would not be able to keep all four within the beam of light. "If ever you return to this place," he said quickly, "or to any other place to do the deed you have done, bid farewell to your loved ones, for you will not see them again."

Jobim switched off the light and sat still, hoping to appear to have vanished.

There were a few moments of silence. Then the men realized several things at once: they were not, after all, going to be rescued; if they were to survive, they would have to stay afloat until either they reached land or daylight came and a passing boat could pick them up; and, finally and most alarming, like ripples from a rock dropped into calm water, they were spreading farther and farther apart.

"Where are you?" called one.

"Here!" two answered at once.

"Come this way."

Splashes, swimming.

"Not that way! This way!"

"I did!"

"What's that?"

"Another dead fish. They're everywhere!"

"We're going to drown!"

"Shut up!"

"Shark!"

"Where?"

"I guess it wasn't."

"Jesus . . ."

Jobim sat on his raft and listened. The voices faded quickly, for the tide was strong. They would be many miles away by morning, and probably miles from each other as well, for each man was an object of different density and buoyancy and resistance to water movement and would thus move at a different pace and be subject to different eddies and currents.

One or two might be picked up by boats, for there was occasionally ferry traffic between the Mexican mainland and the Baja peninsula. They would be dropped at the ferry's next port of call and would have to work their way home, begging rides from village to village to island. And when they got home, what would they say had happened? Suppose one of their comrades had arrived before them. How would they coordinate their stories?

One or two were certain to drift onto uninhabited ground, there to scratch for survival until they could attract the attention of a fisherman going by or a family out to gather wood. There were lizards to eat if you could catch them, and a rattleless rattlesnake that tasted good if you could bite it before it bit you, and birds' eggs if you could find the nests hidden in the crevices in the high rocks. There wasn't much freshwater, and what there was lay in stagnant pools that probably contained bacteria that would make you sick. But you could survive.

Jobim doubted that any of them would die, and he did not consider himself responsible if one of them should die: he had cast them into the water whole and healthy and in good weather. Anyone should make it to shore who did not do something stupid.

Furthermore, if one or more of them did die, Jobim would have considered it justice, for in his opinion what they had done to the seamount branded them as no more worth preserving than a rabid bat.

Soon the voices were gone, and there were no sounds except the soft slapping of the water against the bottom of the wooden raft. Jobim pulled his anchor. As the killick came up and he reached for it, his weight shifted to one end of the raft, and that end dipped beneath the surface of the water. A big gold *cabrío* floated onto the raft, into Jobim's lap.

The concussion of the dynamite had not only killed the fish, it had disfigured it. Its belly was swollen; its tongue had inflated like a balloon and filled the yawning mouth; its eyes bulged from their sockets and stared in blank perplexity.

The seamount was dead now. It would be many, many months before life returned in any profusion, and years before it returned to anything like normal.

No, he would not be sad if one of the men did not make it all the way home.

11

PALOMA WAITED FOR silence, and then waited some more, in case Jo had turned around and rowed back and was lurking nearby. At last she ducked her head under water and came out beside the pirogue. She was alone on the sea.

She pulled herself up onto the overturned bottom of the pirogue and examined the hole Jo had dug with his harpoon. It was about the size of her fist, easy enough to patch with wood once ashore, but big enough to keep her from getting to shore.

She tried to think through her choices. She could stay with the overturned boat until she drifted onto land—tonight or tomorrow or the next day or . . . It might be many days, and she might succumb to thirst or exposure. And suppose the weather went bad. To try to ride out a *chubasco* by straddling a hollow log was suicidal.

She could abandon the boat and swim for home. Absolutely, positively not. Not worth considering.

Or, she could try to patch the pirogue here and now.

With what? She had no wood, no canvas, no leather, no nails or tacks, no hammer. She could plug the hole with herself: she could sit on it. But then she couldn't paddle, because every time she moved the hole would open and water would rush in. She pictured everything she had brought with her, analysing its potential to be shaped into a plug. Her hat? No, the straw fibres were too loosely woven; water would pour through them. Her flippers? She could cut one up and fit the piece of rubber into the hole. But the rubber wouldn't stay; it would float free. The glass faceplace of her mask? She had no way of securing it to the wood.

Her mind evaluated every item and discarded it. And then, as she looked at the wood fibres, she saw beside them other fibres, closely woven though not as thick as the wood, and she had the answer: her dress. She could stuff her dress into the hole, and it would keep the water out. The fabric was already saturated with saltwater, so no more could penetrate it. And, packed tightly in a ball, the cloth fibres would bind and become nearly waterproof.

She peeled the sodden shift up over her head, then ducked under the pirogue and, from the inside, packed the cloth into the hole. It made a tight plug—nothing that could survive the pounding in a heavy sea, but secure enough for an easy paddle on calm water.

She ducked out again, hauled herself up onto the bottom and reached over and grabbed the far edge. Bracing herself on one knee, she pulled, and there was a liquid sucking sound and a pop as the suction broke and the pirogue jumped free of the water and righted itself. It was still full of water, though; only an inch of freeboard stuck above the surface. Since the boat was a hollow log, it would not sink, but if Paloma were to climb aboard, her weight would drive the pirogue's sides down flush with the surface. Every minuscule movement she made would tip the boat and allow more water to slosh aboard. She could not bail it out from inside.

So she clung to one side with one arm, and with the other hand began methodically to splash water overboard. She forced herself not to be impatient, for she knew that this was what she was going to be doing for the next several hours, probably well into the night. And she did not hurry, for she didn't want to tire herself and risk a cramp in an arm or leg. She could stop a cramp, but a muscle that had once gone into spasm was sure to cramp again unless it was rested for hours. Each succeeding cramp would be harder to relieve than the one before, and she did not want to be forced too early to use extreme remedies. It was said that the only way to relieve a terrible cramp was to cause worse pain elsewhere in your body, the theory being that the mind can only focus on one pain center at a time and it will concentrate on the most severe, and will thus stop sending cramp signals to the afflicted muscle.

Everyone, Paloma included, agreed that cramps could be affected dramatically by the mind. No matter what caused the cramp initially, you made it worse if you panicked, and you relieved it, to a greater or lesser degree, by detaching yourself from it and regarding it rationally as a muscle that has contracted and must be commanded to relax. Icy calm, of course, was a prescription more easily issued than filled, especially if you were swimming and the cramp knotted you up into a ball that reduced your buoyancy to a point where you could barely stay afloat, or if you were running, being chased by somebody or something, and a cramp knocked you to the ground.

As she continued to bail, the muscles in her upper arm began to stiffen and ache. To be free to massage that arm with her other hand, she had to release her grip on the boat. Immediately the tide caught her and dragged her away from the pirogue, but she was confident of her strength as a swimmer and was not worried.

She was more than fifty yards away from the pirogue when she finally felt the fibres in her arm muscles relax and soften, and she stopped massaging the tissue. Unhurriedly, she began to breaststroke against the tide.

To anything observing her from below, she appeared to be a sizeable, healthy animal going about its business, emitting no signs of vulnerability, no signals of prey. After ten or fifteen minutes, it had seemed she was not moving at all; she seemed no closer to her boat than when she had started.

But she had marked her beginning against a set of peculiarly shaped rocks on the bottom, and she knew she was making progress—very slow, probably no more than a couple of feet with each stroke, and half of that she was losing before she could take her next stroke; but she was gaining ground. She was not tiring; she could swim like this indefinitely, and eventually—it might be a couple of hours from now—the tide would ease and she would gain a little more with each stroke. Then it would go slack, and she would gain still more. Finally it would turn, and she would make it to her boat in a few strokes.

Her left leg went first. She had a split-second warning, and then she felt her toes begin to roll over one another and snarl. She reached down with her hand and tried to squeeze the lower calf muscle, but it was too late. The muscle fibres had already balled into a knot the size of an orange. She rolled onto her back and used both hands to squeeze her leg. Kneading with her fingertips, she softened the knot and felt it begin to relax. Suddenly the knot dissolved and she thought the cramp was finished and she straightened out her leg and then, before she knew what was happening, with a violent, almost audible spasm an even bigger knot lashed itself into the back of her thigh. Her heel snapped back against her buttock, like the blade of a jackknife closing.

She was drifting fast, was already much farther away from her boat. She told herself not to think about it, but to make an effort not to think about it was to think about it even harder.

She tried to use her hands to straighten out her leg, but her arms weren't long enough to give her adequate leverage. So she brought up her other foot and forced the toes between heel and buttock and pushed down.

Then the other leg went, perfect mimic of the first one. And now she felt she was like one of the beggars on the carts in La Paz, the ones whose legs had been lopped off below the knee. She had no balance, she was top-heavy, and she rolled in the water like a trussed pig.

At first she thought she would faint from the pain. She *hoped* she would faint, for she was one of those people who tend to float on their backs, and as soon as she lost consciousness the cramps would disappear and she would roll onto her back with her head out of water.

When she didn't faint, she tried to swim toward her boat, using only her arms, but that was hopeless; she lost ground and grew quickly tired. She knew she had to attack the cramps with her mind.

So she stopped swimming and said to herself: You're drifting away. What is the worst thing that can happen? You'll drift so far that you can't get back to your boat on this tide. You won't drown because you know how to float forever (unless a *chubasco* comes along, and there's no use worrying about that now). So you'll drift and drift, and sometime the tide will turn and take you back toward your boat. Even if you drift wide of your boat, all that will happen is that you'll travel until either you strike land or someone picks you up. So, really, you have nothing to worry about. (Somewhere, in the far recesses of her mind, she knew she could not float forever, or even for more than a few days. She would fall victim to thirst or hunger or the sun. But her mind did not let that knowledge intrude.)

Then she looked down through the water and saw that there was one "worst thing" she had neglected. She had drifted far off the seamount by now, and way down, in the blue shadows just before darkness, were two sharks, circling slowly. They were not the familiar hammerheads. Even from this distance she could discern the bullet shapes and the pointed snouts, and she knew they were a kind of bull shark— quick, bold, aggressive, ill-tempered, and completely unpredictable.

Each circle brought the sharks a bit closer to the surface; each circle was a bit quicker than the one before. And Paloma knew immediately what was happening: she was sending new signals, signals that said she was no longer a sizeable, healthy animal going about its business—now she was a wounded, panicked animal that could not defend itself and might make easy prey.

All right, she told herself: I've got to stop behaving like this or they'll home in on me and tear me to pieces. As she heard the words in her brain, she felt a rush of panic, and so she tried even harder to straighten out her legs; and the harder she tried the tighter they knotted.

What would it be like to be attacked by a big fish? Would it hurt, or would it be so quick it wouldn't hurt much at all? No, it would probably hurt. What kind of pain would it be? What's the worst pain you can imagine?

She bit her tongue. Holy Mary, how that hurt. She bit harder. Nothing could hurt worse than this. She bit still harder, and now she tasted blood in her mouth and saw little puffs of red seep from between her lips into the water. The blood might draw the sharks closer.

But all she could focus on was the pain in her tongue. It was a blade, a flame, a needle.

The cramps collapsed.

She didn't know it until she stopped biting her tongue. As when you ease off on the throttle of an outboard motor, she expected the pain in her mouth to fade to a background, idle-speed sensation, and the pain in her legs to accelerate and take over. The pain in her mouth did fade, but nothing replaced it. She looked down and saw that her legs had unlocked themselves and the muscles in her calves were no longer twitching.

Very tentatively, she began to swim, aiming vaguely in the direction of her boat but more to test her muscles than to accomplish much. She used her arms and shoulders and let her legs follow along in a weak scissor-kick.

There was no pain, but there was no progress either. Her arms alone were not enough to move her body against the tide. Still, she kept swimming, to exercise the muscles and restore circulation to the tissue. She maintained a smooth and easy stroke, conveying calm and control.

After a few minutes, she looked down again, and she searched the edge of the gloom for the circling sharks. She saw only one and only part of that one, a flicker of grey shadow, heading away. She was a healthy animal once more, and to the sharks' perceptions a formidable foe instead of vulnerable prey.

She swam on for more than one hour, watching the boat grow smaller and smaller against the sea. Once in a while, a small muscle would give a warning twinge, a threat of spasm, and she would stop and massage the muscle and shake it. She did not want to stop for long, though, for continual exercise kept her warm, and warmth encouraged her blood to circulate. If she allowed herself to grow cold, her circulation would drop, her muscles would be starved of oxygen and they would cramp.

She swam without thinking, focusing on each stroke as an act of its own, independent of every other stroke and of all other acts, to be begun and completed with mechanical perfection toward an overall end that did not exist. She forced all other thoughts from her mind, for they could generate emotions that could alter her body chemistry and cause trouble—a cramp, a stitch in her side, a knot of gas in her stomach, or superhyperventilation, which could make her faint.

The first sign she had that the tide was changing was a feeling of warm, still water on her skin. She had swum into a mid-sea current that had slackened with the tide and was lying on the surface like curdled milk on a cup of coffee. She stopped swimming and looked around. The sea, which had been merely calm, was now flat and slick. Such swells as there were were so slow and lazy that she could not perceive them.

She saw a piece of floating weed and swam to it and threw it as hard as she could toward her faraway boat. It landed ten feet away and lay still. It didn't move to her, away from her, or off to one side. The tide was dead slack. Now if she swam she could not lose, she could only gain, and soon the new tide would begin and would push her along. Her pirogue was anchored, so it would not move.

With every stroke she took she imagined the boat growing infinitesimally larger. She travelled about a mile in the first hour, swimming on the slack tide. The second mile took her twenty minutes, for the tide had turned and begun to run. In another fifteen minutes she was sitting in her pirogue, working her fingertips into the soft tissue of her thighs.

She had been frightened, but now she felt proud, too, for she had survived on her own. Every decision had been hers alone to make, and every decision had been correct. True, Jobim had taught her the skills and given her the knowledge that helped her survive, but putting it all into practice, actually *doing* it, felt wonderful.

She shivered. The sun had dropped so far that the pirogue cast a sharp shadow on the sea. During the hours around midday, the sun had added heat to the water, and for a few hours more the water would retain that heat. But then the cooling air would leach the heat from the water. Paloma guessed that the temperature of the water had fallen five degrees or more since her boat had capsized.

Kneeling in the bottom of the boat, she scooped with her hands and splashed with her paddle, and scooped some more and splashed some more. She saw the sun slide to the horizon, then seem to hesitate, then plunge beneath it, leaving a sky of richer blue dotted in the east by faint stars. She saw a light or a campfire wink on a distant island. Nearby, somewhere behind her in the twilight, a small ray jumped into the air and slapped back down with a stinging splash, and Paloma started at the knowledge that out here she was never alone, day or night.

The boat was dry now, as dry as it would be until the sun could get at it tomorrow and evaporate the water from the wood. She had not been on the high sea at night for a long time, so she double-checked the landmarks she could still see and stood up in the pirogue to search for the first lights of Santa Maria. Then she started to paddle toward home.

Miranda would be frantic. Paloma never stayed out this late, and her mother would *know* something had happened to her. She had drowned. Something had eaten her. She was injured and floating alone in the dark. Miranda's imagination would be working double time, and soon she would be resigned to the fact that Paloma was dead, that fate had torn another loved one from her bosom.

No, not fate. She would blame God, for it was God's will that Jobim should die, and now He had taken Paloma as well. Why? she would ask. Was He testing her? What did He want her to do? Why didn't He give her a sign? She would do anything, if only she knew what to do.

But God would keep Miranda from becoming hysterical in her grief. Once she had worked it out in her mind that Paloma's disappearance was divine will, there would be nothing she could do about it, including worry. After all, if God meant it to be, then to worry was implicitly to challenge God's will, to lament was to complain about God's will. Unthinkable.

Jo, of course, would be no help whatever. He would feign innocence and concern and would sympathize with Miranda's thought of the moment. If she was contemplating the mystery of God's will, he would shake his head in wonder. If she asked what she had done to deserve so cruel a fate, he would put an arm around her and assure her that hers was like the story of Job—she would be well rewarded in the Kingdom of Heaven. They would talk about Paloma and recall nice things about her and weep together.

The thought of the scene infuriated Paloma and made her paddle harder. But then she thought of the reception she would receive, after all this sentimental ritual, and she smiled. Miranda might even resent her return—very briefly—for she would have set her mind to martyrdom, and Paloma's arrival would be a second shock.

Jo would pretend to be delighted, but the pretence would be entirely for Miranda's benefit. He would skulk around, and in his eyes there would be a warning to Paloma to keep silent about what had happened today. Still, Paloma guessed that somewhere inside Jo there would be secret relief that she had returned, for she could not believe—despite his fits of rage—that his conscience could condone murder.

Probably Paloma would keep silent. For what would talking about today accomplish? There was no one to punish him, for even if people believed what she had to say, the offense would not seem serious. She had not been harmed. There was no way she could convey the recklessness, the willingness to hurt, that she had seen in her brother. He could not be punished for evil thoughts.

A three-quarter moon had risen in the black sky, and it cast a path of gold before the pirogue, a path that led Paloma home.

Her reception was almost exactly as she had imagined it: Miranda shrieked and clutched Paloma to her breast and thanked God for answering her prayers and proclaimed a miracle. She asked what had kept Paloma, and Paloma glanced at Jo and (unable to stop her tongue) said she had been foolish enough to let herself be delayed by nothing, really nothing, a stupid little tidal maelstrom that had carried her too far from shore. She should never have let it happen and (another glance at Jo) it wouldn't happen again.

Once more she had misjudged him. He didn't realize he was being teased. He viewed her explanation as another victory: he had warned her not to tell the truth, and she hadn't. He felt he was in control—of his mates, who had to respect him, if only for his daring; and of Paloma, who must fear him.

Jo crossed in front of Miranda and hugged Paloma—turning his head and touching her with the same affection with which he would have caressed a leper—and said he had been worried about her.

Miranda sensed something awry between her children. She could feel a current of hostility surging back and forth, and she knew that they were communicating in a kind of code that expressed nothing directly but sparked with hints of antagonism. She was apprehensive but helpless, so she covered her anxiety with a veneer of relief that everyone was home safe and sound.

And she was further diverted from worrying by the arrival of a few neighbors, who dropped in to chide Paloma for causing her mother concern and to tease Miranda about being so concerned. See? they said. We told you she'd be all right. Miranda interpreted that as a reprimand and responded to it by scolding Paloma for staying out so long. What she was really saying was: How could you cause me to make a fool of myself in front of my friends? Paloma knew that, and she apologized and said that yes, after all, she *had* been in some danger and was lucky to be back alive—thus justifying Miranda's concern and giving her a tale to tell her friends.

And through it all, Jo sat in the corner on a chair tilted back against the wall, and smiled.

12

IN THE MORNING, Paloma did not go out to the seamount. She told Miranda that her terrible experience of the day before had frightened her and that she wanted to stay ashore for a day or two and help with the wash and the house. Miranda was pleased. Paloma could tell the other women in her own words what a miracle it was that she was still alive, so the other women couldn't accuse Miranda of exaggerating and they would see that her worries had been well founded.

Miranda also chose to regard Paloma's decision as a hopeful sign: perhaps she was outgrowing this foolishness with the sea and would recognize and begin to accept a more traditional position in the community.

The reason Paloma stayed ashore was that she knew that if she went out to the seamount and watched Jo and his mates, she would not be able to keep silent, she would surely provoke another confrontation with them. And this time, someone would get hurt.

She had walked to the top of the hill above the dock and watched them and the other fishermen prepare their boats for the day. She could hear most of what was said and guess at the rest, for the conversation did not change much from day to day, and she knew that Jo was not telling other fishermen where he and Indio and Manolo were going. Jo waited for the others to leave, pretending to be furious at being delayed by tangled fishing lines.

Paloma took some small comfort in his selfishness: if Jo was smart enough to know that it was against his interests to tell anyone about the new seamount, his greed would delay, for a while at least, the mass slaughter of the animals.

But she could take no comfort from the last piece of gear she saw Jo and Indio sling aboard: a big net, with lead weights at the bottom to drag the snare down to the top of the seamount.

When he was sure he was alone, Jo started his motor and headed to sea. He did not yet know precisely where the seamount was, but, given a whole day to search for it, with no pressure from Paloma or any competitors, he was certain to find it: with one of his mates peering through the viewing box, Jo would drive the motorboat in straight lines up and down the general area until, eventually, he would have to pass over the seamount.

Depending on the tide and the bottom currents and the movement of the vast schools of baitfish and of the other, tinier creatures at the small end of the food chain, it was possible that Jo might be prevented from doing much damage right away. He might toss his net and let it sink and haul in nothing but a stray pufferfish, for the big schools of robust jacks and *cabríos* moved constantly, following their own food, and catching them as they passed over the seamount was a random chance.

But it would happen—if not this morning, then this afternoon, if not today, then tomorrow—because with so many schools of so many fish passing over the seamount so many times every day, even if Jo's ignorance led him to anchor his boat in a wrong place at an inopportune time, he was bound, sometime, to spot a big school through the viewing box.

Paloma watched until the wake from Jo's motor melted into the moving water and the white hull of the boat itself was consumed by the shining light on the sea.

The dock was empty, so she could work on her boat without bothering anyone. She found some pieces of canvas and some pieces of plywood, and she cut and shaped them into patches that would block the hole inside and outside, and she nailed them in place and sealed them with daubs of pitch.

Then she walked back to the house.

Miranda was darting around the house like an agitated bird, and Paloma knew she was feeling a bit nervous, a bit excited, a bit apprehensive—a bit of a dozen different emotions, some of which complemented others, some of which contradicted others, and the sum of which confused her.

Mainly, Miranda was happy that Paloma would be staying with her and doing woman's work, and she wanted to make sure that the day was good for Paloma because she worried that if Paloma had a bad day she would go back to the sea, immediately and for good.

She longed to recover her daughter, to claim the companion Jobim had deprived her of by taking Paloma to sea. She wanted to be able to be proud of Paloma, proud of having a daughter who would be working with her. Raising a female child to do female work was a normal thing, a healthy thing, a good thing in the community. It made Miranda a normal person, someone to be accepted and treated like everybody else. She wanted to show Paloma off to the other women, partly as a symbol of her own achievement. But in the back of her mind she worried that Paloma might say or do something that would not seem normal, and that might make things more difficult than ever.

She was worried that the other women might not like Paloma and that Paloma might not like the other women. She wanted everybody to like everybody, but that meant that the women would have to contain their ceaseless complaining about everything. Paloma had been taught by her father that complaining was a waste of time. If something was not to your liking, went Jobim's guideline, change it. If it couldn't be changed, accept it. If you could neither change nor accept it, then alter your own circumstances to cope with it. But under no circumstances whine about it, because whining accomplished nothing but aggravation.

Paloma would have to be accommodating, too. She would have to conceal her contempt for complainers. And that, after all, was fair, because Paloma was not familiar with the women's lives and problems. She could not evaluate the genuineness or seriousness of the complaints.

If all you did all your life was wash clothes and clean house and cook food, why, then, the minute details of clothes-washing and housekeeping and cooking would be the most important things in your life. It was vital that Paloma be convinced that these details were not trivial and silly, at least not to the women, and so she must not scoff at them.

As Miranda flitted about the house, dusting things that didn't need to be dusted, cleaning things that were already clean, putting away things that she never put away, she started sentence after sentence, then stopped and started again, then tried another avenue of thought, then stammered and changed the subject. She was so fearful of being too specific that she was too vague, and it took Paloma several minutes to realize what Miranda couldn't say. When finally she caught on, she said, "Don't worry, Mama. We all have hands."

"What?" Miranda stopped.

"I row with the palms of my hands. They sew with their fingertips. If they cut one of their palms, it's nothing. They laugh at it. If I cut a palm, it's a tragedy. But if I cut a fingertip, it's nothing. We all have hands."

Miranda did not completely grasp why hands were central to the expression of what she had been trying to say, or to Paloma's comprehension of it, but there was an atmosphere of compassion to Paloma's voice that gave Miranda confidence that everything would be all right.

And it was, finally.

At first, the women treated Paloma carefully, eyeing her as a curiosity. This was only natural, since they had all regarded Jobim as a curiosity, and more—as an oddity, almost a menace. He had obeyed the laws and customs he agreed with and either rejected outright those he disagreed with (if he felt that they unwisely deprived a person of a freedom) or tolerated them with silent disdain (if he felt that they were harmless vehicles to convey the insecure along a path to self-regard). Jobim's attitude could make him appear superior, and he might have become intolerable to many people had he not shown just as piercing an eye for his own failings. Even so, there were men—mostly those who used rituals to give themselves stature they could not otherwise attain—who did not like Jobim and were not particularly sorry when he was no longer on the island. And some of those men were married to the women with whom Miranda worked. The women knew how close Paloma and Jobim had been and knew that Paloma had been behaving like her father's child. They would need to be convinced that Paloma intended to act more like a woman now.

She convinced them. She kept her mouth shut except to answer direct questions, and replied respectfully, even when she judged the questions to be either provocative or inane. She listened attentively to every monologue and nodded sympathetically, though the women's words made no impression on her brain: they rattled around like marbles in an empty shell, for the occupant of the shell was elsewhere—out on the water, imagining what was going on on the seamount.

She worked hard, abusing muscles she was not accustomed to using, never stopping to rest as most of the women did, not permitting herself a grunt of weariness or a sigh of tedium—until, that is, she discovered that the women wanted her to be exhausted and to appreciate physically the hardness of their lives. She did appreciate, and so she did echo a few of their complaints. And at the end of the day, several of the women took Miranda aside and complimented her on how well Paloma seemed to be turning out.

Walking up the hill under a heavy load of wash, Miranda was silent but obviously elated. Paloma thought that if the day had accomplished nothing else, it had given her mother some happiness, which was a rare and good thing.

Paloma did not stop wondering, though, how many animals had died during Miranda's brief happy time. She flayed herself for not stopping the animals from dying, even though she knew it was foolish of her to take blame.

While she helped sweep the house and hang the wash to dry and feed the chickens for the second time and stoke the cook fire, Paloma forced her thoughts to stay ashore. But as soon as the chores were done and Miranda turned to cooking the evening meal, Paloma went outside and looked at the sky to tell the time.

The sun was very low; it was late, later than Jo and the others would normally stay out. And as she looked toward the path that led down to the dock, she saw several of the fishermen strolling home, which meant that they had already been ashore for an hour or more, for it took that long to unload fish and clean them and swab the boat and stow the gear.

Perhaps some trouble had befallen Jo and his friends . . .

nothing too serious, for Paloma was not capable of wishing real harm to anyone. But something inconvenient, time-consuming, uncomfortable, perhaps something frightening that might discourage them from returning again to the seamount.

Perhaps they had fouled their net on the bottom and had been capsized trying to retrieve it. They would have to right their boat and row home, for the saltwater-soaked motor would never start.

Or perhaps they had cast their net into a mass of king mackerel or wahoos and seen it torn to shreds as they struggled to free the thrashing, snapping animals before they could drag the boat underwater.

Perhaps now, as night approached, they were being harassed by a herd of porpoises who had smelled the fish in their boat and wanted some and were playfully bumping, jarring, slamming the boat with their noses and tails. The fishermen would toss a few fish over, and the porpoises would interpret that as encouragement to play even harder, so they would bump the boat from underneath on both sides and the boat would rock and spill more fish into the water, which would convince the porpoises that their game was a rollicking success and one to be continued with increased vigor. Jo and the others would hear the clicks and whistles and grunts as the porpoises chatted with one another, and in the thick, impenetrable blackness they would translate the conversations as the ravings of monsters. Soon they would panic and lose the balance of the boat and be tossed into the water, there to be engulfed in splashing, roiling foam filled with fish blood.

Paloma liked the last possibility best. Yes, that's what she could dream was happening to them if they weren't home soon.

But, walking toward the path to the dock, she suddenly realized there was a more likely reason for Jo's lateness—and it was a reason that made the palms of her hands go cold and wet, and then a trickle of sweat ran down her sides and a bubble of fear made bile rise in her throat.

From the top of the hill she saw that this was the true reason.

Jo's day had been successful beyond his dreams. They had netted so many fish and killed them and brought them aboard that they had had to drive the boat home at its slowest speed to keep it from swamping and sinking. The slightest wave of water would rush over the bow of the boat; the merest tipping of a railing would cause a flood.

As the boat puttered toward the dock, Paloma saw Jo and Indio and Manolo all sitting on fish, hip-deep in fish, surrounded by mounds of fish.

In a single day's netting they had caught more fish than in a month of line-fishing. But that alone was not what distressed Paloma. The great schools of jacks and *cabríos* could sustain—did sustain—heavy losses quite often, and they soon returned to full strength. There were so, so many of them, and they reproduced with such speed and in such profusion, and the sea was so vast that the few regular fishermen could not hope to catch up with them all; they could endure all but catastrophic onslaughts—dynamite, say, or a sudden invasion by the huge factory ships from the Orient, both of which were forbidden by law.

No. Worse for Paloma than the quantity of the catch was its quality, worse than the numbers were the species. Even from this distance and in the dwindling twilight she could see how Jo and his mates had fished, for they were pawing through the corpses in the boat and flinging overboard those that did not measure up to their suddenly high standards.

When they had caught little, they had taken everything and claimed to need every bit; they had to feed their families and sell the rest. There was no waste, they claimed, no disrespect. The death of anything gave life to something else. Very noble.

But now that they had plenty of fish—more than plenty—and the guarantee, as they saw it, of endless more, why should they bother to save anything that did not bring silver coins just as is, without further effort? Why bother with fish whose price was by the ton, not the pound, fish that had to be carted away and dried and ground up into meal? If those fish came up in the net and got killed, it was more economical to throw them away than to process them. And if some of them were fish that did *not* school, did *not* breed countless young so that many must naturally survive, did *not* exist in profusion on the seamount, well, to clean out these "trash fish" this way was probably efficient, probably a good idea, because it meant that each successive netting would yield a higher percentage of the more lucrative species.

As for maintaining a balance of life on the seamount, a balance that had taken nature scores of decades to establish, they would argue that it was well known how resilient nature was. Nature would always come back from anything. If this seamount was fished out, move on to another one, and by the time that one is fished out, maybe this one will be coming back. Or another one will. There is always more. You just have to be smart enough to find it.

By the time Jo and Indio and Manolo had finished culling through their catch, night had come, and they did the last of their work by the light of the rising moon. They were tired and hungry, so they did not bother to clean their boat or prepare their gear for tomorrow.

"We can do the boat in the morning," Jo said as they strode up the path. Paloma was crouching in the brush at the top, watching the three shadows approach.

"Now we know where the place is."

"And what's on it. Baby Jesus! I've never seen anything like that."

"I bet we could go late and be back by midday."

"We could go twice, do two trips a day."

"*You* go twice. One load like that's enough for me. My back's about to break."

"Maybe we ought to get another boat." This was Jo's voice, moving past Paloma and on up the hill.

"That'd mean more people."

"Why share?"

"We could double the catch."

"For the same profit, though. We'd have to go partners."

"No we wouldn't. We could make a deal: we take them there—maybe we blindfold them so they can't find the place again—then we take all our catch plus half of theirs."

"I don't know."

"Me neither."

"We meet after supper," Jo said. "To talk. We don't have to decide anything."

"Okay."

"Remember: nobody talks to anybody. Or you're out." Jo added gravely, "Finished."

"Sure, sure."

The voices stopped and footsteps faded as the three dispersed, each to his home.

Paloma waited until she could hear no sound but the breeze rolling over the island. Then, staying in the shadow of the bushes in case someone should return for a forgotten tool, she crept down to the dock.

The moon was high enough so its light penetrated the shallow water by the shore and cast a faint mantle of white on the rocky bottom.

But there was little bottom to see, for most of it was littered with the dead.

There were floating corpses and corpses that had sunk, corpses that tried to bob to the surface but were blocked by others, corpses battered and mangled and without colour, their brilliant capes faded into a sameness at death. And their eyes, all black and blank, stared glassily at nothing.

Jo and his mates must have thrown away a fourth of their catch, all but the biggest of the most valuable kinds, the ones that would bring at least a silver coin apiece. Here in the water by the dock were smaller jacks and yellowtails, a few little *cabríos*, and other groupers that should have been pulled from the net alive and put back in the sea immediately, for they were the future of their species.

Here too were those fish Jobim had called the innocents, those that had no market value, could not be sold as individuals, and were not worth gathering in the numbers, the tons, that would produce fish meal or cat food and be worth a few pennies at the factory.

They were the pufferfish, gentle and shy and gallant in their defiant instant obesity, contributors to no one's purse and no one's table, but hilarious jesters for anyone who dived into the sea.

They were the angelfish, whose chevrons changed colour in every stage from infancy to adolescence to maturity, like an army man displaying seniority, radiantly beautiful at every age, the fluttering sentinels of the seamount.

The smaller rays—stingrays and leopard rays and eagle

rays—recluses who hid beneath a veneer of sand and exploded in a puff at a stranger's approach, snared in flight from
one hiding place to another.

A turtle so young, still soft of carapace, its wrinkled throat
garrotted by a strand of netting, its flippers limp, its tail a tiny
comma flopping on the belly shell.

And others, like sergeant-majors and parrot fish, grunts
and chubs and hogfish and porgies, all killed and cast away to
wash in the shallows and rot.

The carnage was immense; this was not fishing.

Here, kneeling on the dock, leaning over the edge and gazing into the water, Paloma saw her reflection shimmer in the
moonlight, and she realized she was weeping.

She wanted to run up the hill and call out to the other
fishermen, the grown men, and lead them down and show
them this massacre, but she did not, because it was night-time
and her interruption would not be welcome. She wanted to
bring Viejo down, and point out to his dim eyes all the bodies,
all the waste. But she did not, because she knew her outrage
would not be shared. There would be some tongue-clucking,
some intentions expressed to teach the young men how better
to cull their catches. But that was all.

And by morning, what she saw before her would be no
more, for Jo was not an utter fool: they had arrived home at a
full flood tide, and for the next six hours, as the tide ebbed,
the bodies would be sucked out to deep water where some
would sink and others would be eaten and others would be
caught in passing currents and carried off somewhere, so that
when the other fishermen arrived at the dock in the morning,
all that would remain of the carnage would be a few floating
fish and a few half-eaten skeletons on the bottom—a normal
amount of flotsam and jetsam from a day's work.

Even now, the corpses on the surface were beginning
slowly to drift away from the rocks on shore, obscuring her
view of parts of the bottom but letting her see into new cran-
nies.

She saw an animal between two rocks. It looked to be
curled up, like a sleeping puppy, as if it had chosen to lie cosy
in death. She dropped to her stomach on the dock and
reached down and stretched for the bottom, wrapped her

hand around slick and solid flesh and brought it up and set it on the dock.

It was a green moray eel, young and unscarred, and more than any other of the animals it touched her. For while the other animals were simply dead, not alive any more, this moray was contorted in the agony of its death, frozen at its final moment. It was tied in a knot that made it seem to be more than merely dead: it seemed that it would be dying forever.

This was a hideous snapshot of an animal that in life had had dignity but that in death had been transformed into a gargoyle.

Paloma knew well that morays often died in this grotesque way. It was, in one strange sense, a natural death, for it reflected the morays' behavior in life.

Morays lived in holes or small caves or crevices or under rocks, and they lurked at the entrance to their lair, mouth open, gills pulsating rhythmically, hypnotically, skin color blending with their surroundings.

When prey passed by, the moray would shoot out its body —a single tube of muscle—and snatch the prey and begin to swallow it. The mean-looking fangs in the mouth were but gatekeepers: beyond, back in the throat, was another set of teeth that gripped the prey and forced it down, down in rippling spasms, down into the gullet.

If the prey was large, larger than the eel's weak eyesight had anticipated, and if it struggled and threatened to yank the eel from its hole, the eel would anchor its tail around a rock or a coral boulder and contract its central muscles until no free-swimming prey could resist.

Thus, breath-hold divers were doubly careful about poking around in holes in reefs. First, there was the fear of being bitten, because the bite was excruciating and the wound it caused was ragged and would not close and the eel's mouth was coated in a slime that contained virulent infectants. But worse than the bite was the knowledge that if the eel grabbed a hand or a foot or a shoulder and could not sense the size of the prey (for it would not actually try to eat something so much bigger than itself as a human), it would anchor its tail and sink its fangs deeper and hold on until the prey stopped thrashing and the eel could come out of its lair and see what it had caught.

Once in a while, a moray would catch itself unawares—half out of its hole or swimming in the ocean from niche to niche—would snatch a prey and have no rock on which to fasten a grip. Then it would tug against itself.

It would whip into a perfect knot, wrapping the tail around the head and back down through the loop made by neck and body, and it would pull its prey through the loop, flopping and bouncing and rolling down the reef and out into the open water—secure that it had an anchor and its prey did not.

Mostly, the eels knotted themselves this way when they encountered a force stronger than they—like a steel-barbed hook that fastened in the back of their throat and was attached to a filament that slid between the fangs and could not be bitten off and was connected, finally, to a man on a boat above who had strength and patience and the ability to tie off his line and let the moray exhaust itself.

Fishermen hated morays. They bit at any bait, large or small, so there was no way to avoid catching them. They were useless, for no customers would buy them and no islanders would eat them. They were dangerous: they were never dead by the time they reached the boat, and they were always tied in a slimy, slippery knot, and unless you were prepared to cut away and lose your leader and swivels and hook, you had to retrieve the hook from down deep around the second set of teeth in the throat. The boat was rocking, the eel was thrashing, the other fishermen were grousing because you were upsetting them and their gear and the boat itself, while you tried to bash the eel on the head and render it unconscious so you could slit its gills or get inside its mouth with a pair of pliers.

The combination was perfect for a severe, painful, perhaps incapacitating bite.

So moray eels were "bad" animals—ugly, useless, dangerous, probably offspring of the devil or, at least of some of his underlings.

One day, Jobim had hooked a moray and brought it up to the boat. It was tied in a knot, and as it struggled in the water it swung like the pendulum of a clock. Paloma had never seen a live moray before, and, looking down through the roiled water, she did not know what it was. It looked like a mess of living weed.

"Give me the pliers," Jobim had said.

She handed him the pliers and watched as he gently brought the eel to the surface.

"Hold this." He had passed her the fishing line, and she felt it twitch and thrum with the eel's desperation. He held the pliers in his right hand and, with the same hand, slid two fingers down the leader to within an inch of the eel's mouth. Then he pinched the leader and pulled the eel clear of the water and, with his left hand, grabbed the eel behind the head and squeezed.

She had never imagined a creature like this. It wasn't a fish, it was a monster. It's black pig's eyes bulged and glistened. Its mouth was agape and strung with strands of mucous slime. Its gills, what she could see of them amid the pile of bulbous green flesh, throbbed. It grunted. It hissed.

"Kill it!" she shrieked. "Kill it!"

"Why?"

"Kill it!"

"You want it dead, you kill it." Jobim had nodded at the cudgel he kept in the boat to stun sharks.

"Don't *you* want it dead?"

Jobim didn't answer. He was staring fixedly into one of the eel's eyes. The muscles in his arms and shoulders flexed and twisted as he fought to keep the eel from writhing free. Then he squeezed harder with his left hand, and the eel's mouth opened wider, and he squeezed still harder, and the two jaws separated and made a line that was almost vertical, as if the bottom jaw had unhinged completely.

Jobim opened the pliers and pushed his hand into the eel's mouth.

"He'll bite off your hand!" Paloma had cried, and she grabbed the cudgel and raised it with both fists over the eel's yawning mouth.

Jobim pushed his hand farther down the gullet, and Paloma saw the eel's flesh bulge as his knuckles passed through. His hand was gone, and his wrist, and half his forearm. Still the eel writhed and hissed, and every fibre in Jobim's left arm danced. He lowered his eyes closer to the eel's eye, and he probed with the pliers, feeling for the barb of the hook. He found it, and his hand twisted beneath the pulsing green skin, and slowly his arm and wrist began to withdraw, coated with shiny slime, and his hand came free, then the pliers and the steel hook.

Still holding the eel's head in his left hand, he lowered the entire body back into the water and slowly sloshed it back and forth to get water flowing once again over the gills. When he was sure the eel would not succumb to shock and stop breathing, he released it.

The ball of green muscle sank a foot or two, then uncoiled like a waking snake, then wriggled to stretch the tired tissues, and then—suddenly aware and awake and sensing that it was vulnerable in open water—it darted with quick, snapping thrusts toward the bottom.

Several times Paloma had asked Jobim why he hadn't killed the moray, and annoyingly, he had persisted in answering her question with a question. He was busy untangling the fishing line that had coiled around his knees as he fought to free the moray.

"Why should I kill it?"

"It could've bitten your hand off."

"It could not have bitten my hand off. It could have bitten me."

"Isn't that bad enough?"

"To make me kill it? No. I hooked the animal by accident. I hurt it. I put a hook in its throat and dragged it out of water, where it knew it couldn't breathe and was going to die—instinct told it that—and I squeezed its head so hard that its mouth had to open, and then I jammed a steel thing and a big bone down its throat and poked around and caused it pain and terror. Bitten me? I wouldn't have blamed it for biting my head off. Now, why, on top of all the things I'd already done to that animal, should I kill it?"

As Paloma opened her mouth to speak, Jobim added quickly, "And don't say, 'Why not?' 'Why not kill?' is a question you must never ask. The question must always be 'Why kill?' and the answer must be something for which there is no other answer."

Paloma had no good answer for "Why kill?" and so she said nothing.

That afternoon, when they had finished fishing, Jobim had moved the boat to the shallowest part of the seamount and told Paloma that he would take her for a dive. She was tired and didn't feel much like getting wet, but a dive with Jobim always promised fun and excitement and was a treat she would never decline.

Jobim cut a fish into small pieces and put them in a plastic bag tied to his waist, and together they pulled themselves down the anchor line. On the bottom, he motioned for her to stay at the anchor line, and he went off among the rocks, looking for something. Soon he had found whatever it was, and he waved her over to him. His face was six inches from a crevice in the rocks, and he pulled her down beside him.

In the second that it took her eyes to focus and her mind to recognize what she was gazing at, she concluded that her father had gone mad and was trying to kill her.

Guarding the crevice with its gigantic head and puffing cheeks and black eyes and gaping mouth was a moray eel so large that it made the other one seem like a garden snake. Its head filled the hole, and each time the gills rippled they scraped the coral sides. Paloma believed that if the eel should shrug, it could consume her entire skull.

She jerked backward in reflex, but Jobim caught her arm and forced her to return to his side. He took a hunk of fish from the bag at his waist and held it up to the moray's face. For a moment the eel did not move. Then it slid slightly forward, as if on a mechanical track, and Jobim dropped the morsel of fish, the eel let it fall into its mouth and closed its mouth and swallowed, and the gills rippled in unison and the eel slid backward into its hole.

Jobim fed it another piece, and another, and by then he knew that Paloma was short of oxygen so he motioned that they would go up.

As they rose, Paloma looked down and saw that the eel had slid more of its body—four or five feet—out of the hole and had turned its head and was looking up at them. Then it must have decided that they were truly gone, for it slid back and disappeared.

When, on the surface, Paloma tried to speak, Jobim waved her silent and touched his chest, signalling that he wanted to hurry and return to the bottom.

This time the eel seemed to have watched the last part of their descent, for its head was a foot outside the crevice and its eyes were tracking them.

Jobim handed Paloma the bag of bait. She shook her head, no: she wouldn't do it. But he forced the bag into her fist and put a hand on her shoulder in assurance and embrace.

She knew enough to keep the bag itself concealed, for any fish, once it knew the location of the source of the morsels you were feeding it, would ignore individual bits and would dive for the bag and rip it away from you.

The first piece she held a full two feet from the eel's mouth, until Jobim pushed her hand closer. The eel slid forward; Paloma dropped the bit of fish; the eel swallowed.

With each new piece she grew bolder, for the eel made no motion to do anything but what she intended, and the last piece from the bag she actually lay within the eel's lower jaw and pulled her hand back well in time for it to close its mouth on nothing but the fish.

Back on the surface again, she was elated and amazed. Her thoughts came so fast that her words could not keep up with them. Finally, by pointing and puffing and speaking as slowly as she could, she was able to convey to Jobim that she wanted to cut up another fish and return immediately to feed the moray.

"Not me," he said sombrely. "He could bite my hand off."

"What?"

"It's too dangerous."

"But . . ."

"I think we should kill him before he hurts somebody."

Now Paloma knew what Jobim was doing, and she screamed and splashed water at him, and he threw back his head and laughed.

While they rested, he cut up a bigger fish into bigger pieces, for the moray had been bigger than he had guessed it would be. He told Paloma that morays were like sharks, in that you never knew how big an individual might be: the hole you poked your hand into might contain an eel no longer than your arm and not as thick, or it might house a creature taller than a man and as broad as his chest. This one was probably seven or eight feet long, and its head was more than a foot wide.

They had spent many minutes away from the eel, and it was not there when they returned. But as soon as one of their shadows crossed before the crevice in the rocks, the huge green head slid forward and hung there, gills and mouth pulsing together.

Jobim was like a dog trainer, teaching the animal to beg for its food. Each morsel he held farther and farther from the hole, urging the eel to slide farther out. But he did not tease the animal: when Jobim had established where the food would be, there he left it. The eel's decision-making machinery was rudimentary and primitive, and if Jobim had pulled the food back after the eel had committed to exposing itself a certain distance, the eel might have registered signals of betrayal and danger, which might have driven it into a defensive posture, which might have expressed itself in an attack on Jobim.

The eel would not come all the way out of the hole. Apparently, it needed the security of knowing that its tail was anchored in the rocks so that if anything should go awry, it could dominate the encounter.

And as Jobim told Paloma when they were back in the boat, he saw no reason to encourage the animal beyond its own limits, especially on first meeting.

"You mean we can do it again?" It hadn't occurred to her that something so special could be repeated.

"We'll see. Some people can."

"What do you mean?"

"With most people, something like that is luck. They get there, the conditions are right, the animal doesn't feel threatened, he's hungry, they don't do anything stupid, so they succeed. But they—the people—are not in control. They're just fortunate that things went their way. Some people, very few, *make* it happen. There's something—I don't know what it is, maybe it's like the sounds we can't hear and the sights we can't see. Some people have something special with animals. It may be the same thing some animals have with each other,

that they send and receive each other's signals so they understand each other. By nature, animals in the wild don't trust
people, and they shouldn't. But these few people, the people
who have this thing, animals trust."

"You have it, then."

"I have a little of the good thing, but not a lot. I never know
from animal to animal. Maybe we were lucky with this eel
today. Maybe he was in a good mood. We'll see."

Paloma said hopefully, "Maybe I have a lot of the good
thing."

"Maybe. But don't hope too much. It's nice, the good thing,
but it can be dangerous, too."

"Why?"

"You can believe in it too much, believe you can do anything. You try to put yourself in the animal's mind and imagine yourself as the animal, and suddenly you think you can
control it. You forget that you're a human being and *it* isn't.
You try to reason with it. It can't reason. You take one step too
many. If you're lucky, you end up with scars and a good lesson. If you're unlucky, you get hurt. Or killed."

They had returned to the eel the next day after fishing. As
Jobim set the anchor, Paloma had asked if he thought the eel
would still be there.

"Why would it go away? Where would it go?"

"How would I know?"

"Animals usually have a reason for going somewhere or
staying somewhere. *They* don't know they have a reason, but
their bodies know. Their instincts tell them. Most sharks have
to move because if they don't they'll sink to the bottom and
drown. Simple. Schools of fish have to move because the little
things they feed on move, and if they're to continue to eat
they'd better keep up with their food. Reef fish stake out a
territory on the reef and patrol it all their lives unless something comes along and drives them off. Moray eels will find a
hole and make it their own as long as enough food passes by
for them to grab. When it doesn't, they'll find another hole.
This big fellow has no reason to move now: he has comfort,
safety and, best of all, since yesterday he doesn't even have to
hunt. Some fools are bringing him dinner."

The eel was there, hovering in its hole, and it had to be coaxed to take the first bite of fish.

He's sulking, Paloma thought. He's angry because we went away.

Once the feeding reflex was stimulated, the eel became ravenous. More and more of it hung out of the hole, and Paloma, her confidence blooming, backed farther away, trying to bring the eel entirely out into the open.

She did not see, and never knew, that Jobim, as he stood a foot or two to one side, had a knife clenched in the fist he held behind his back.

She fed the eel five separate pieces of fish as it hung in the water, stabilized by barely perceptible ripples of the fins that ran along the top and bottom of its body.

There were half a dozen pieces of fish left in the bag, and now Paloma took a piece of fish from the bag with her left hand and slowly, calmly drew it wide and back toward her shoulder. With a brief shudder, the eel followed the fish.

Paloma drew it back around her head, where she slipped it into her right hand and continued to lure the eel around behind her. The eel's tail was over her left shoulder, its head over her right, when she gave it the piece of fish. It swallowed the fish and stayed there, wrapped around her shoulders like a fine lady's stole.

She fed it two more pieces of fish, and there were three left. She glanced at Jobim and saw that his eyes were wide and the veins on either side of his throat were thick as anchor line. For a second she thought he was afraid for her, and perhaps he was, but then it struck her that neither of them was breathing, could breathe, and yet both had to breathe.

Paloma took the last pieces of fish in her right hand, squeezed them into a ball and held them up before the eel's open mouth. She pushed them upward so the eel would have to rise slightly to reach them, and as it did she ducked down and pushed backward with her feet and shot on a sharp angle toward the surface.

Jobim didn't chastise her; he didn't have to. Each knew what the other was thinking, and mostly their thoughts were the same: Paloma had been reckless but had succeeded, had taken a risk and had won; she had the good thing, probably a lot of it, but it was something she would have to learn how to use. And she should not try stunts like this without Jobim close by.

All the way home in the boat, they had only one exchange.

She had said, "I think I'll call him Pancho."

He had replied, "It's not a 'him.' It's an 'it.' It doesn't have a name, and don't give it one."

Still, she had permitted herself to think secretly of the eel as Pancho, and every day she was out with Jobim she had looked forward at the end of the day to visiting with Pancho.

On every visit the eel would curl around her shoulders, sometimes after only a bite or two of fish. Occasionally, it would let its weight drop onto her shoulders, and it would lie there, and she could stroke its smooth skin while she fed it.

And then one day it was gone.

Paloma thought they had come to the wrong hole, but the landmarks underwater were too familiar. They searched every hole in that section of the seamount, then swam over the rest of the seamount, hoping that if they passed close enough to the eel's new hole, it would come out. But it had gone.

"You said it wouldn't go away." Paloma felt hurt, deceived, as if either Jobim or the eel had tricked her into believing that if she fed the eel, it would stay there, for her, forever.

"No I didn't. I said it would have to have a reason to move. I guess a reason came along."

"What reason?" No matter what her father said, she would challenge it. She wanted to prove him wrong, to show him up, to make him feel guilty by being . . . by being what? She didn't care. She wanted to punish him for her disappointment.

"I don't know. Maybe a secret clock inside him said it was time to go somewhere else. Maybe a secret calendar said it was time to find a mate."

"I thought you said he wasn't a 'him.' You said he was an 'it.' "

Jobim smiled, and, seeing him smile, Paloma could not resist smiling too.

"*It*, then. Maybe it got foolish and tried to eat something too big, and that something turned around and ate it."

"What could eat it?"

"Only a big shark. No, I don't think that happened. He might have gotten old and gone wherever eels go to die."

"Do they go somewhere to die?"

"I don't know. That's what I mean: we don't know. We *can't* know. He was here yesterday and he isn't here today. There's nothing we can do about it."

"But . . . he liked us. I could tell."

"Don't do that to yourself, Paloma." Jobim had stopped smiling.

"He knew us. I know that."

"We accustomed it to us as feeders. That's all. It didn't *like* us. It won't *miss* us. It doesn't have feelings like that. It isn't that level of being."

"How do you know?"

"I . . ." Jobim stopped, and looked at Paloma, and smiled again. "I don't, not for sure."

"What about the good thing?"

"You have the good thing, as much as anyone can have it with an eel. With anyone else, it would have stayed in its hole or taken a bite out of them. It trusted you. That's what the good thing is, trust."

Now PALOMA KNELT on the dock in the moonlight and held the knotted eel in her lap. Gently, she tried to undo the knot, to reduce the hideousness of the slaughter, to erase the reminder of the eel's last agony. She pushed the slippery tail up through the loop made by the coiled body, then pulled it through the loop and lay the body on the dock. But rigor mortis had already gripped the animal, and the flesh was set in a gnarled contortion. It would not straighten out, but rocked on the wooden dock and banged its rigid snout against the planks.

She picked up the eel and dropped it off the dock. It fell on top of other corpses that were slowly being swept toward deeper water, and then it sank beneath them.

Still kneeling on the dock, Paloma let her glance travel along the path of gold cast on the water by the moon. It did not begin or end, but seemed simply to happen, magically, somewhere out there in the blackness this side of the horizon, and to disperse, spent, somewhere in the blackness behind her.

If ever she thought of trying to place her father, to locate him where he was now (and she avoided doing this often, for her mind could not cope with it and it made her uncomfortable and stretched her belief so far it seemed it must break), she located him there, between the sky and the sea, at the source of the path of the moon.

"What can I do?" she said aloud, to Jobim. "Don't say Nothing, because that's what I've been doing, and look what's happened." Paloma gestured at the water. She didn't wait for a response she knew would never come. "They're going to kill our seamount, and when they've killed ours they'll move on to another one and kill that, too, and they'll get richer and richer, and because they're blind, they won't see where it has to end. And I can't do anything about it because I'm alone and nobody will listen to me and even if they did they wouldn't do anything. Mama doesn't know anything about it, and if she did, she'd say it was God's will and that's that." Paloma paused, fearing she had given offence. "I'm sorry, but that's the truth and you know it. Viejo says anyone can do anything he wants, and if all the fish are gone one day, well, that's the way of the world."

Now she shouted into the night. "But it's *not*! I won't let it be!" Her words echoed across the water.

"All right. I'll be calm. But we can't just let it happen. It's yours, too, you know, not just mine. It's everybody's. I'll do what I can, but I don't know what to do! I can't go blow them up, like you did. I couldn't kill them. I couldn't."

She was gazing at the spot where the gold seemed to begin. She did not expect a response, and she did not receive one, not in the sense of an answer: no words rang in her head, no solution sprang into her breast. Nor was she "visited," the way people said they felt when they had a religious experience, where an angel touches your life and changes you. And certainly she did not sense the presence of a deity. There were no thunderclaps or great winds or deep voices.

But something did begin to happen inside her.

It was a warmth that started at her fingertips and seemed to creep up her arms and over her shoulders and down into her chest and through her stomach and into her legs. For a second she recognized it as the same kind of sensation she had when she was about to faint, but there was no faintness, no lightheadedness at all. It was, rather, a fullness, as if something missing had finally been put into place.

And that missing something, now that it had been found, seemed to impart an order to things, or she felt a purpose and a sense of confidence and a sure knowledge that there was an answer and that she would find it if she obeyed her natural instincts instead of bending to the whipsawing of conflicting emotions and impulses.

What those instincts would tell her to do and what the answer would be and what any of it would mean for her or for the seamount or for anything, she had no idea.

But so suffused was she with this feeling, and so positive was she that it meant *some*thing, that once again she gazed at the spot in the sky where the gold began, and she nodded.

SUPPER WAS OVER by the time Paloma returned to the house, and the plate of food Miranda had left for her on the table was cold, but the new feeling that was running through her was consuming energy, so she was hungry and she sat down to eat.

Jo was there. Normally by now he would have been in his room, but he had lingered.

"Did you have a good day?" he asked Paloma.

Paloma's mouth was full, and she did not respond right away.

Jo said, "I had a *fine* day."

Miranda said, "That's nice," to cover the fact that Paloma had not replied. She was determined that there would be civility in the house, even if she had to fabricate and maintain it herself.

"Many more days like this, I'll have enough money for school."

"So," Miranda said, "you will leave me, too."

"Too? Papa didn't leave you."

"No? Where is he, then?"

"He didn't go away on purpose."

"If he had lived a normal life," Miranda said, and Paloma was surprised at the bitterness in her voice, "like a normal person, he would be here today." She looked at Paloma, her eyes urging her to learn the lesson.

"We don't know that," said Jo. "But that's what I want to do—live a normal life."

"In some stinking garage in Mexico City?"

Jo ignored his mother's remark and said to Paloma, "I think Papa would have wanted it for me, too, don't you?"

Paloma looked at him but said nothing.

"Sometimes I think that's why I found the seamount. I think maybe he led me there." Jo smiled. "Don't you?"

Paloma clenched her teeth and kept silent.

Jo spoke this time to Miranda. "This seamount of Papa's is very rich. By the time I'm through with it, it will give me enough money to take care of all of us. You won't have to worry about money again, Mama." His eyes shifted to Paloma. "Viejo always says that the sea exists to serve men, and I know Papa would agree. Yes, this seamount is what he left us, and I will see that his will is carried out."

Now it took all Paloma's strength to keep her mouth shut. It outraged her that Jo was summoning their father's spirit to justify ravaging the seamount. But she knew Jo was trying to enrage her, to goad her into a discussion in which she had to be the loser: if she agreed with him, she would be sanctioning the destruction of the seamount in Jobim's name; if she disagreed, she would appear selfish, short-sighted, and unconcerned with Miranda's welfare.

So she busied herself with her food until Jo had yawned and stretched and left the house to go to his room.

Preparing for bed, Paloma knew that Miranda was looking at her and was worried. Miranda had felt the mute fury in Paloma's silence, and had taken more alarm in Paloma's lack of response than she would have in a fiery argument.

Miranda sensed that something was afoot, and she was right. She didn't know what, of course. But then, neither did Paloma.

13

PALOMA STOOD ON the hill and watched Jo and his mates prepare their boat for sea. Again they waited for the others to depart, for they were determined—especially now that they knew how rich the seamount was—to keep its location their secret.

Paloma guessed that the evening before they had been questioned by other fishermen about their formidable catch, and they must have mumbled or evaded or lied outright, for today they started out in the wrong direction and changed course toward the seamount only when they were confident they were being neither followed nor observed.

Paloma returned to the house and puttered around for a while. She was not upset about accomplishing nothing, for she had no intention of doing anything specific. She had no plan. She did not know why she had returned to the house, though it seemed as good a thing to do as any other.

She was coasting, riding the day, letting it take her where it would, and she felt as if she were outside herself looking in, watching with a detached interest. It was not that she felt guided by something or someone else, it was more an inner assurance—based on nothing rational at all—that whatever was going to happen would happen.

Miranda eyed Paloma nervously from time to time but made no comment. She suggested things for them to do— move this bed and sweep under it, take that mat outside and beat the dust out of it—and Paloma agreed instantly and worked diligently. But Paloma was not really there.

At midday, Paloma said she was going for a walk, and Miranda nodded. As far as Paloma knew, she *was* going for a walk; she had no fixed destination. But once she neared the top of the hill that led down to the dock, the sea summoned her so powerfully that she could not possibly resist.

She went to the dock and pulled her boat out from beneath it and noted that her fins, mask, snorkel and knife were in the pirogue and that her patch had sealed the hole in the bottom. She climbed aboard and paddled toward the seamount.

Their backs were to her as she approached. They were setting their net, letting it catch the tide and billow and sink in a wide, deep arc. When it had settled, they would pull an end of the net into each end of the boat, tightening the purse, forcing the mass of fish into a ball of panic. Their boat sat high in the water, which meant that so far they had made no good casts or, perhaps, had not yet tried, waiting instead for the big schools to come by. This cast alone, if it were good, could fill their boat.

They would go home richer but unsatisfied, knowing that if one cast could produce a catch worth so much money, two or three could double or treble their reward. So tomorrow they would probably tow a second boat, maybe a second and a third. Their secret would be harder and harder to keep, and soon the entire fleet would be there.

They did not see her or hear her, and she knelt in the pirogue up-tide, adjusting her position with little flicks of her paddle, watching. If they had turned around and asked what she was doing, she would not have had an answer. She was there; that was all she knew.

After a while, Indio did chance to turn and he nudged Jo, whose head snapped around, eyes narrowed.

They eyed each other for a long moment, until Jo turned back to his net and said casually, over his shoulder, "Come to watch?"

She did not respond, but stayed where she was, a dozen or so yards from their boat, looking at their backs. Jo made sure he was elaborately occupied with the nets, but his mates were obviously distracted and unsettled by her presence. As they paid out the net, they muttered to one another, and though Paloma could not discern who was saying what, she grasped the sense of the conversation.

"What does she want?"

"You think she'll do anything?"

"Like what?"

"She wouldn't dare."

"She better not."

"I don't like it."

"Shut up."

"What about the net? We said . . ."

"Forget it. She's beaten. She's given up."

"Then what's . . . ?"

"Forget it, I said. Watch this." Jo scooped a handful of rancid fish guts from the pool of oily water at the stern of the boat below the motor and cocked his arm and flung the mess toward Paloma. It fell several feet short of the pirogue. Instantly, a pack of sergeant-majors materialized and devoured it.

Paloma did nothing, said nothing, in no way acknowledged the gesture.

"See?" Jo said to the others. "She won't do anything. We've talked. She knows what's what. Now: look through the glass and tell me if they're still there."

Manolo put the viewing box on the surface of the sea and looked down. "Right there. They haven't moved. God! Look at them all! We won't get 'em all in this boat."

"Then we'll tow 'em home in the net. Tomorrow we better bring a barge out here. This is too good."

Though Jo did not look at Paloma as he spoke, she knew he was speaking for her ears, taunting her.

But still she said and did nothing, for she didn't know what she could say, or what she could do. If her silence annoyed any of them, that was fine; speaking could only strip away the mystery about why she was there. Perhaps if they became genuinely angry they would make a mistake and lose their net or stagger clumsily and capsize their boat . . . But these were fantasies, idle wishes, hopeless hopes.

Their net was cast and was sinking, and they were concentrating on each foot of fibre to make sure it didn't foul against anything or snarl itself into a tangle. When it was all the way out, they would let it sit for a few minutes before hauling it in

—to give ample time for masses of fish to wander into the trap.

Paloma felt a faint touch of pressure on her knees, a slight surge that lifted her pirogue an inch, no more, and let it settle again. It might have been the wake of a distant boat, but there were no boats in the distance; it might have been the wave from a breaching animal, but no animal had breached nearby; it might have been the weakening signature of a long-distance seismic wave, but that she would see travel on the surface and lift Jo's boat, too.

Only her boat had moved, which meant that whatever was happening to cause the change in the water pressure was happening directly beneath her.

She cocked her head over the side of the pirogue and backpaddled so she would have a better angle on the water below. All the water looked black, which didn't strike her as peculiar until she realized that the water farther away was its normal blue.

Then she knew immediately what had fooled her eyes, and she smiled to herself. The manta had returned. It was lying a few feet below the surface, and the black carpet of its back was so close that it seemed to extend to the horizon.

Then, silently, she reprimanded herself, for there was no reason to believe it was the same manta ray. There were many manta rays around seamounts, and she had chanced to paddle her boat into the vicinity where one was cruising, and it had probably noticed the shadow her pirogue had cast and had moved over to take cool shelter in it. Rays that came to the surface in the heat of the day often took refuge beneath a ship or a dock, for direct sunlight quickly became uncomfortable. It was a simple, instinctive, animal thing to do, and for Paloma to attribute more or different sensibilities to so primitive an animal she knew to be folly.

But she wanted to be positive nonetheless, so she pitched her anchor overboard and let the line pay free from the pirogue, then held her mask to her face and bent over and put the faceplate on the water.

It could not be the same manta. There was no wound, no sore, no shredded flesh. Yet there was *something* strange about the area around the left horn. It looked dented or nicked, as if there had been an injury some time ago. Could there be two enormous mantas on the same seamount with an injury in the same place? She could not believe it possible, so she decided to go down and look.

The fishermen still had their backs to her, were still setting their net, so they did not notice when Paloma slipped over the side and took a few deep breaths and disappeared.

When the net was set a moment later, however, one of them turned around and nudged Jo to show him the empty pirogue. All Jo said was, "Give me the glass."

As soon as Paloma was under water she knew it was the same manta, no question. But the wound looked ancient. The flesh had grown together—probably, Paloma thought with pride, because I packed it so tightly and took off the ragged pieces. All that remained were scars, and an indentation behind the horn, and a crease where the ropes had gouged deep into the flesh. There was no blood, no seepage, and as Paloma stroked the animal she saw that the abused flesh had even begun to regenerate the protective mucus that covered the rest of the body.

The manta lay perfectly quiet as Paloma's hands explored the injured horn, and against all her knowledge and all of Jobim's reasoned arguments she began to believe that the manta had returned, like a child revisiting a doctor, to show Paloma how successful her treatment had been. She knew it was stupid and impossible and not worthy of someone who respected the sea, but she believed it nevertheless.

Her body triggered the first familiar alarms to send her to the surface, and she resented them and dismissed them and pretended she was a fish, until the second set of alarms forced her to leave the manta. She looked down as she ascended, hoping the manta would remain until she could return, and because she did not look up she did not see that Jo had moved his boat. It now lay beside her pirogue, almost touching it.

She had taken a couple of breaths and cleared her mask before she felt the presence of the other boat and looked up and saw Jo standing in the bow of the motorboat, holding his harpoon.

"Bring him up," Jo said sharply.

"What?"

"Bring the devilfish up."

"What are you talking about? I can't bring him up."

"Yes you can. Do what you do and bring him up."

"I can't! But even if I could, why?"

"He has to weigh two tons. Good money."

"Money? For a *manta*?"

"A silver coin for every hundredweight. Cat food."

Paloma thought he was simply teasing her, insulting her for the amusement of his mates. "How would you get it home?"

"Tow it. You'll see."

"You're crazy."

"Bring it up!" Jo said. "Now!" He raised the harpoon over his head, threatening not Paloma so much, nor the manta ray, as in a gesture of defiance.

Paloma could feel, in her legs, movement in the water below. She looked down through her mask and saw that the manta was flexing its wings—not moving yet but about to. She felt a spasm of fear, for the manta could be about to come up on its own, and if it surfaced anywhere near Jo's boat—as sometimes they did out of playfulness or curiosity—Jo would surely plunge his harpoon into the animal and nothing she could do would help it.

The dart on the end of the harpoon was hinged: moving forward, during the throw and as it sank into flesh, it would lie flush with the shaft of the harpoon itself. But when the harpooner set it, by pulling the shaft away and tugging on the rope, the dart would spring open into a horizontal, and where it had gained a smooth entry it would find no exit at all. The harder the rope was pulled, the firmer the dart was set.

The manta would never know what had happened.

It would have come to the surface unaware of danger and would have felt sudden, searing pain and would try to flee. Jo would give it line, would let it run, holding the rope just taut enough to keep the dart set and hurt the manta and tire it as it pulled the boat after it. Gradually, Jo would increase the pressure, hoping to make the manta bleed, which would tire it further, knowing that now every time the manta sounded deep the pain would be worse and so it would tend to stay near the surface.

After a while, the manta would stop its struggle and would lie exhausted on the surface, exploding in a brief flurry of panic only when the boat drew near. Little by little, Jo would pull in the line, and let it out again if the manta struggled, and pull it in again until finally the manta had no more fight. Then Jo would draw the boat right to the manta and would either beat it on the head with a club until he found its brain and stunned it so its gills could be slit and it would bleed to death, or he would find a way to tie a rope around the animal so it could be dragged backward through the water until it drowned.

If the manta came up on its own, it would be dead before this day was done.

Quickly Paloma hyperventilated, and Jo, thinking she was obeying him, instructed Manolo to hold his legs and steady him so that when the giant rose to the surface his throw would be true.

Paloma dived to the manta. It had raised its wings, and she could see the motion begin that would sweep the wings down again and drive the animal up, for it was angled upward, its head higher than its tail. She went directly to the horn on the right side, wrapping her arms around it and pressing down hard, willing even to cause it pain if that would make it roll down and away and free from people.

The animal stopped its rise and gently bent its head down and to the right, in perfect response to Paloma's hands. Together they began a graceful roll to the bottom.

Paloma felt something quick and sudden in the water, and she turned her head and saw Jo's harpoon hanging by its rope a foot from her head. Cast in fury and frustration, powered by the arm of one enraged, it had been driven six or eight feet into the water.

The thought flashed through her mind that a stronger arm might have struck her with the harpoon, and that thought was followed by the knowledge that a truly strong man would never have flung the harpoon.

The harpoon hung for a second, then was retrieved.

Paloma released her grip on the horn. The manta eased out of its roll and levelled off at a depth of perhaps a dozen feet. Still moving away from the boats, it started to rise. Paloma would have to breathe soon, so she did not try to stop the manta's ascent. If it rose to within a couple of feet of the surface, she could drop off there and dash up and gulp air and hope to return to the manta before it began a new loop toward the deep. She wanted to guide it as far away from the boats as she could, and then she would drop off for good and know that it was safe, for with his net down Jo could not haul his anchor and start his engine and give chase.

Paloma had one hand on the manta's upper lip and one on its wing, and her legs and feet flew free as the manta banked and dipped and soared, changing direction on apparent whim but coming closer and closer to the surface. Paloma had no idea where she was, but she felt sure that the animal had changed course so many times that it must have travelled far from the boats.

Then, as the surface swept closer and changed from a blue veil to the shimmering lustre of wet glass, she saw the looming figure of Jo, standing in the bow of his boat, harpoon poised above his head.

The manta had brought Paloma back to where it had found her. It had let her guide it on a wide, eccentric circle, had changed direction at random, for in the memory of its brain there must be stored a signal that told it how to return her to where she belonged.

She lurched forward, tried to grab a horn and push it down and drive the manta under again, but it was too late. The manta broke through the surface, not in a jump but like a turtle coming up for air. And it kept flying, moving its wings just beneath the surface, carrying Paloma on its back, carrying her straight at the boats.

Looking over the hunch of the wing, along the horns, Paloma saw Jo as he for the first time saw that Paloma was riding on the back of the beast. His hands jerked and his eyes widened and he let out an involuntary shriek of surprise and took an involuntary step backward, forgetting that his legs were gripped by Manolo. He started to fall, determined to throw the harpoon, flung out his arms, let go the harpoon and sprawled on his back in the boat.

The harpoon arced up into the air, askew, and Paloma saw it strike the water butt-first and heard Jo howl in pain and rage, before the manta once more dipped its horns as Paloma took a breath and together they dived beneath the surface of the sea.

They went under the boat. Paloma did not try to guide the manta, for she wanted it to go away on its own, and she would not try to turn it unless it seemed to be heading for the boats. She thought of dropping off, but sensed that it would come back for her, wherever she was.

The manta was going deep, almost straight down. Ahead of its wings Paloma saw two streaks, and she realized that they were not shafts of sunlight but the lines that connected Jo's boat to the net. The manta passed between the lines and continued straight down, toward what Paloma could now see as a misty hump near the top of the seamount—the net itself, surrounding a clot of hundreds, thousands of frantic fish.

If the manta did not see the net and turn, it would foul in the net and wound itself again, and perhaps foul Paloma in it as well, and if she became tangled she would surely drown. She tried to turn the manta, but it would not turn. It was flying as hard and as fast as it could, directly at the net.

It was in the last fraction of a second that Paloma knew that the manta did see the net, did know where it was going, knew what it was doing. The immense ball of trapped animals loomed out of the dusty fog, and just before chaos Paloma's mind took note of how vivid were the eyes of the desperate fish.

With a last thrust of its great wings the manta plunged forward into the net.

On the surface, in the boat, the fishermen stood ready for the manta to surface again. They scanned the sea, searching for telltale bubbles or swirls. In the bow, Indio had his hand on the anchor line, prepared to pull the anchor up; in the stern, Manolo's hand was on the starter cord of the motor. They could release their net and buoy it and leave it briefly if they had to, and they would if they were to harpoon the manta.

Amidships, Jo held the harpoon high.

"Holy Mother! Where are they?"

"She can't stay down this long."

"How do you know that?"

"Nobody can."

"What d'you mean by that?"

"I don't know. I just . . ."

"If you don't know, keep your mouth shut." Jo was annoyed at the awe in their voices. "She has big lungs, that's all."

"And she rides the devilfish into the deep. That's all. A lot you know."

"I said shut up!"

The talk took no more than a second or two, and during it Indio noticed that the anchor line was drawing taut, and by the time the talk was done the others had seen that the lines connected to the deep net were stretched and throwing droplets of water as the rope fibers trembled.

"Jesus!" Jo shouted, the only coherent word he was able to utter, and from then on there were only screams and shouts and cries for help.

The manta had driven on, into the middle of the mass of fish, until Paloma was engulfed in jacks. They were under her arms, down her back, between her legs, flapping through her trailing hair. They squirmed and gulped and defecated and shivered. The water roiled and clouded, but it made no difference because she could not have seen more than two inches in front of her even in clear water: all was fish.

Somewhere in the attic of her brain, alarms began to sound, but another sentry in her head told her there was no point trying to obey the alarms: she could never make it from here to the surface in time.

The manta flew on, pumping its massive wings up and down, its horn protruding through the net, its head pressing against it. The net held, and strained, and the manta slowed for a moment.

Above, on the surface, the panicked fishermen felt their boat begin to move. The anchor had been pulled off the bottom and was dragging, and anchor and boat were being hauled through the water by the unseen creature that drove the net forward and down. And because the force was downward, the boat tipped and began to ship water; the fishermen didn't know what to do but bail, frantically.

Then the net burst. The manta had simply overpowered it. It burst first in the centre, and the fish squirted out the hole like grease from a tube. But the manta did not squirt out; it flew on and pulled the connecting lines even tighter until, one by one, the fibres popped. One line snapped first, whipped the net around free at one end, releasing the manta to start for the surface with Paloma on its back and destroying the equilibrium of pull which was the only thing that had kept the boat steady above.

The change was not felt immediately, for the lines were long and it took time for the pressure to travel. But when the change came, it struck suddenly and without prelude. The bow of the boat, from which the first line had snapped, jumped out of the water and spun. Indio, who had been kneeling on a thwart, found himself kneeling on air as the boat shot out from under him. Then he fell onto his back in the water and sunk until his violent thrashing returned him to the surface.

Seeing the bow fly up, Manolo had reached to steady himself on the motor, but the stern had sunk and the motor he reached for wasn't there. He pitched overboard and somersaulted under water and came up sputtering as the boat yawed away from him.

Jo was now alone in the boat, kneeling on knees bruised and bleeding, watching the sea with horrified eyes, wondering what next would erupt from the unknown below.

The manta flew for the surface, its wings pushing maelstroms that spun fish and blew sand and roiled water.

Paloma gripped lip and wing, but as the distant sunlight rushed toward her she knew she would not make it. All her alarms were in full cry—the pounding was thunderous in her head, the pain excruciating in her chest, her eyes seeing the light of safety as a pinpoint that expanded and contracted, expanded and contracted, as consciousness slipped from her.

The manta flew straight up, not this time to angle and glide but to fly free in the air.

Air was only a few yards away, now a few feet, a split-second in the flight time of the great animal rushing for the sun, when the switch went off and Paloma's brain shut down and she lost consciousness. All her muscles relaxed, including those in the fingers that held her grip on the manta ray, so she slid away as the broad plain of black back exploded from the water and launched itself high into the air.

It rose above the cringing Jo, higher and higher until it blocked the sun and cast a black shadow on the boat. Water flew from it all around and caught the light and shone in a corona that lit the edges of the ray, and Jo knew he was being besieged by a creature from hell. His lips moved in reflex prayer, his throat uttered guttural whimpers, and he threw his hands over his head to ward off doom.

The manta reached the height of its flight and for a moment hung in majesty against the brilliant sky. Then the heavier head and shoulders began to fall, leaving the tail where it was, and the giant embarked upon a graceful slow-motion back flip.

Jo saw it coming, and he screamed in fear of death, and fell overboard.

He splashed and sank, and even through several feet of water he could not block out the noise, the terminal, shattering crash as tons of cartilage and sinew came down upon the boat and disintegrated it.

The transom with the motor attached broke off and sank of its own weight. The rest of the hull, struck suddenly by such mighty force, splintered, and the splinters fluttered into the sky and rained down on Jo and on Paloma, who was floating on her back by her pirogue a dozen yards away.

The manta did not stop, was not stunned. It forced beneath the surface what few pieces of the boat remained and continued its roll down, backward and away, then righted itself and shuddered and cruised slowly toward the sunlight again.

What woke Paloma was the lapping sound of the waves from the manta's splash against the wood of her pirogue. For a moment she didn't know where she was, and she grabbed her pirogue for safety. Before her and to the sides the sea was empty. Behind her, down-tide to the west, she could see nothing because of the blinding reflection of the sunlight on the water. She heard sounds that could have been voices, but they meant nothing to her; perhaps they were sounds fashioned by instruments in her own addled brain.

Her feet touched bottom, a hard, slick rock ledge near the

island, and though she wasn't sure how she had got there so fast she was glad to be home.

Bottom? She shook her head and looked at the pirogue and at the horizon and at the softly rolling sea swells. She was in at least ten, maybe twenty, fathoms of water. Then what was she standing on? For there was no question that she was standing on *something*. She drained water from her mask and put her face down and saw that the manta had come beneath her and had risen, like a balloon, until it rested just at her feet.

Did it want something? Was it injured again? Paloma took a breath and knelt on the manta's back, and, very slowly, it began to move. She stood, and the manta stopped. She knelt, and it started to move again; she stood, and again it stopped.

It's behaving like a dog, she thought; it's waiting for me. But that, she knew, was impossible; the animal didn't have such "higher" instincts. And she was reluctant to impute to it "higher" qualities as motives.

And yet she was impelled to respond, even if only to the appearance of a motive. So, disregarding the contradiction of all she knew or reasonably believed, she hyperventilated and dropped to her knees on the manta's back and gripped with her hands.

This time the manta did not start slowly—it dived fast, shooting for the bottom. Within a few seconds, the top of the seamount rose before Paloma's eyes. She expected the manta to slow and level off and cruise among the canyons, but it didn't. As it neared the upper rocks, it banked, like a fighter plane beginning a rollover dive, and aimed down the sheer side of the rock wall toward the blue mists.

Paloma's ears were popping, for she had never descended this fast or this far, and though she was nowhere near a crisis of oxygen, the strange new pressures in the strangely cold water made her pulse pound. She wanted to let go, but she didn't dare: she wasn't sure she could make it to the surface, however far it was.

At the edge of the darkness, down deep where there were no more reds or yellows or greens, where the blues looked indigo and the indigos violet and the violets black, the manta suddenly levelled out, banked sharply to the left, and entered a canyon in the wall of the seamount.

It slowed and stopped and hung above the sand bottom, its wings almost touching the rock sides of the canyon. Paloma looked up and could not see the surface—no sun, no shafts of light, just a vague lightening of the grey of the water—and a tic of panic shook her chest, the same kind of panic she felt when she looked down from a very high place. She lowered her eyes and told herself not to look up again, for there was no point: she would either go up with the manta, or she would not go up at all.

What was this place? Why had the manta come here? Perhaps it was to places like this that mantas came for refuge— deep, cool, away from the sun and the surface, protected by the canyon walls from the open-sea currents.

Below was sand, above was water, on the sides were walls of rock like any other rock, except . . . Something was strange about these rocks. They seemed to be themselves studded with countless small stones.

She wanted to get closer, to see more clearly this place she could never dive to on her own. She rose away from the manta, praying that it would not now suddenly decide to abandon her, and kicked quickly to one of the walls.

She reached out to touch one of the stones, and before her fingertips had made contact she knew what these strange walls were made of: each of the stones was not a stone at all, but an oyster.

At first they had been unrecognizable to her because they were larger than any she had ever seen—out of reach of all fishermen, they had been allowed to mature completely—and because they were camouflaged—out of the sweep of the currents, they had been covered with living vegetation.

She reached immediately for her knife, but it was not there. She didn't stop to wonder why, or to search for it further, but instead she gripped an oyster with her hand and twisted and pulled until it came away from the rock face of the canyon.

Her fingertips were scratched and shredded, her palm bleeding from little cuts, but she felt no pain. Using both hands now, she grabbed and twisted and pulled the oysters free and stuffed them into her dress, dropping them down to her rope belt. When her front was full, she pushed the oysters around her sides to her back, not feeling the sharp shells slice her skin.

Finally, she fell off the wall, exhausted and aching for breath and stuffed fuller than a roasting chicken. She landed on the manta's back. Had it been a horse, she would have spurred it on, for she needed to go now, and in but one direction—up.

And the manta took her up, flying with the swift grace of a bird seeking the sky. Soon she saw sunlight and blue crystal.

At the last second, the manta slowed so it would not leap clear of the water, and like a whale it rolled through the surface and lay with its back in the air. And on its back lay Paloma, with her arms spread wide and blood running between her fingers.

The manta stayed with her until she had rested and swum to her pirogue and climbed aboard and emptied her dress of oysters. It stayed still as she knelt in the pirogue and watched it, silently, reverently.

And then, as the leading edge of the red swollen sun touched the horizon, the great ray flipped a wing and dipped its head and kicked its tail in the air, and was gone, leaving a ring of ripples that spread across the twilight water and were soon gone, too.

For a long time, until the sun had sunk and the sky had darkened and the first stars were faintly seen, Paloma continued to kneel in the pirogue, letting the tide take her.

Far away in the night, she heard the voices of Jo and Indio and Manolo, and the words she could discern across the still water were contentious and bitter and accusing, for now they were safely floating and no longer feared for their lives. Later she would get a motorboat and retrieve them. She thought they would no longer be eager to return to the seamount.

The manta would not return, either. She felt certain of that, though she could not have said why she was certain. Perhaps it was part of having some of the good thing. Perhaps it was a feeling that nature had needed to restore a balance that had been set askew, and to restore it had used the manta ray and, to an extent, had used Paloma as well. And now that the balance had been restored, the manta was released to fly free.

But what did she mean by nature? What was . . .

She stopped thinking, and she looked at the spot in the sky where soon the moon would rise and hang like an amulet and cast its golden path on the water, and she smiled and said aloud, "Thank you."

ABOUT THE AUTHOR

PETER BENCHLEY belongs to one of America's most cele-
brated literary families: his grandfather was the humorist
Robert Benchley and his father the novelist Nathaniel Benchley. His interest in the sea began at the age of nine during
summers on Nantucket and led to his research into sharks
and the writing of *Jaws*. He went on to write other bestsellers,
including *The Deep, Q Clearance,* and *Beast*.